*continued ...*

# OPENING
# ATLANTIS

# HARRY
# TURTLEDOVE

A ROC BOOK

ROC

Published by New American Library, a division of
Penguin Group (USA) Inc., 375 Hudson Street,
New York, New York 10014, USA
Penguin Group (Canada), 90 Eglinton Avenue East, Suite 700, Toronto,
Ontario M4P 2Y3, Canada (a division of Pearson Penguin Canada Inc.)
Penguin Books Ltd., 80 Strand, London WC2R 0RL, England
Penguin Ireland, 25 St. Stephen's Green, Dublin 2,
Ireland (a division of Penguin Books Ltd.)
Penguin Group (Australia), 250 Camberwell Road, Camberwell, Victoria 3124,
Australia (a division of Pearson Australia Group Pty. Ltd.)
Penguin Books India Pvt. Ltd., 11 Community Centre, Panchsheel Park,
New Delhi - 110 017, India
Penguin Group (NZ), 67 Apollo Drive, Rosedale, North Shore 0632,
New Zealand (a division of Pearson New Zealand Ltd.)
Penguin Books (South Africa) (Pty.) Ltd., 24 Sturdee Avenue,
Rosebank, Johannesburg 2196, South Africa

Penguin Books Ltd., Registered Offices:
80 Strand, London WC2R 0RL, England

Published by Roc, an imprint of New American Library, a division of Penguin
Group (USA) Inc. Previously published in a Roc hardcover edition.

First Roc Mass Market Printing, December 2008
10  9  8  7  6  5  4  3  2  1

Copyright © Harry Turtledove, 2007
All rights reserved

ROC REGISTERED TRADEMARK — MARCA REGISTRADA

Printed in the United States of America

# PART ONE

*New Hastings*

# I

Edward Radcliffe steered the *St. George* toward Le Croisic. Soon he would take the fishing boat out into the Atlantic after cod. Before he did, though, he needed salt, or his cargo would spoil before he brought it back to England. The marshes of Guérande, in southern Brittany, yielded the best salt in this part of the world. That was what he wanted. Edward Radcliffe, though far from rich, had never been one to settle for anything less than the best.

He was nearly fifty, a big bull of a man, with broad shoulders, weathered red skin, and a thick shock of hair going from yellow toward white because of the sun at least as much as because of the years. Two of his sons, Richard and Henry, were part of the little cog's crew. They showed what Edward had looked like before the years began to challenge him.

Le Croisic stood on a spit of land that stuck out three miles into the sea from the marshes. As always, ships from every land in the western part of the world crowded the waters around the port. They all had different lines and rigging. A lubber couldn't have told one from another—but then, Edward Radcliffe neither knew nor cared about the various breeds of sheep.

He was, however, no lubber. When he saw a Basque boat, he didn't think it came from Ireland. The French built different from the Dutch, and the English different from either. Endless variations on each theme ... "You know what?" he called from his place at the tiller. "Ships are no more alike than women are."

A couple of the fishermen nodded. More of the crew laughed at him. "We've got to take you into town and get you drunk, Father," Henry said. "You're thinking too much. You need to salt down your brain."

Everybody laughed at that, even Edward. "Sharper than a viper's fang to have a snot-nosed brat," he said. With a chilly wind driving them on from the northwest, everybody's nose—including his own—was dripping snot. Henry stuck out his tongue. Like Richard, he was even bigger than their father, and at the high spring of his strength rather than at the beginning of its autumn.

"We need to go into town," Richard said, more than half to himself. He would have been a lubber if he could. He didn't love the sea the way Edward and Henry did. But he was a fisherman's son, and so he sailed with them.

The *St. George* squeezed into a place at the quays just ahead of a Basque boat. The Basques, dark, blocky fellows with eyebrows that ran straight across their foreheads with no break above the nose, shouted what sounded like abuse in their peculiar language. People said the Devil himself couldn't learn it. Edward didn't know about that, but he knew he couldn't—and, besides English, he could get along in Dutch and French and, not quite so well, Breton.

"First things first," he declared. "We get the salt. We bring it back to the boat. Then we worry about everything else."

Nobody told him no, which only showed how much the crew respected him. The fishermen were *men*—they wanted to gamble and drink and whore before they sailed off into the wild wet wasteland of the Atlantic. They'd already had a rough passage around Cap Finistère—*Land's End,* the same name as the westernmost tip of Cornwall—to get here. They'd earned relief. And they would get it . . . once they did what needed doing.

Master Jean Abrgall sold the best salt in Le Croisic. *The flower of salt,* he called it—none of the gray, ordinary stuff mixed in. "Hello, you old thief," Radcliffe greeted him in Breton when the fishermen came up to him. Abrgall spoke perfect French, too, but he preferred the tongue he'd spoken since he was a baby.

*"Yer mat, gast Saoz,"* he replied in that tongue. *Cheers, whore of an Englishman,* it meant—something like that, anyhow. Radcliffe bowed, as if at a compliment. Abrgall gave him a thin smile: the equivalent of another man's guffaw. He went on, "So the sea serpents didn't bite you and the mermaids didn't drag you under, eh?"

"Not yet," Radcliffe said. "What have you got for me, and how much will you gouge me for it?"

"Not so much, and it'll cost you more than you want," the salt merchant answered. "Come have a glass of wine with me, and we'll talk about it."

"You want to get me drunk so you can cheat me easier," Edward Radcliffe said. Unperturbed, Abrgall nodded. Radcliffe went on, "Well, seems only fair to give you a chance. How's your family?"

"They are well, God be praised." Abrgall crossed himself. So did the fisherman.

They drank. They ate a little salt cod—maybe some of Radcliffe's, but more likely from a Breton fisherman. Both men knew about what the Englishman would end up paying, but how you got there was part of the game.

They swore at each other in several languages. Abrgall called Radcliffe something in what had to be Basque. "What does that mean?" Radcliffe asked.

"Beats me," Abrgall admitted. "I never could make sense of that God-cursed tongue. But it sounds good, doesn't it?"

Once the bargain was sealed with a handclasp, Radcliffe paid the salt merchant. He and his men lugged crates of shining white crystals back to the *St. George.* Dealing with Jean, you knew the quality would be there all the way to the bottom of each crate. Some dealers would put the cheap gray salt below, hiding it with a layer of the pure flowers. You learned the hard way not to spend your coin with people like that. Some fishermen never learned, and so the bastards stayed in business.

"All right," Edward said when the hauling job was done. He was hot and sweaty, as they were. Every little cut and scrape all over his body stung; if you worked around salt, that would happen to you. "Now we've done the work. Now we can have a day of fun. Go back into town and drink and wench as you please. I'll stay with the boat—she's mine, after all."

"No, you go, Father," Henry said. "You're entitled to enjoy yourself once in a while. I'll stay. I don't mind."

On such chances, worlds turn.

Edward and Richard Radcliffe walked into a dive called the Salicornes. Along with a grape vine, the place had a bunch of the stuff hanging above the door. In English, it was called samphire or glasswort; in springtime, its burgeoning growth turned the salt marshes purple. The locals ate boiled fresh samphire in season, and pickled it to eat when it wasn't fresh. As far as Edward was concerned, the locals were welcome to it.

When he and his son went in, the most ridiculous argument he'd ever heard had almost reached the knife-drawing stage. Some Breton fishermen and some

Basques were quarreling over what year it was. They were doing it in French, which neither side spoke well—but neither spoke the other side's birthspeech at all.

"It's 1451!" the Basques shouted.

"No, by the Virgin—1452!" the Bretons yelled back. "Were you at sea so long, your wits got soaked in salt and you lost a year?"

Picking his way through the chaos, Edward asked the tapman, "Can I get myself a mug of red wine? And what are you having, son?"

"Red wine will do for me, too," Richard replied.

"Here you go, friends," said the fellow behind the counter, dipping two mugs full. He wanted nothing to do with the shouting fishermen.

But the Radcliffes couldn't stay out of the quarrel so easily. "Here are strangers who care nothing for any of us," one of the Basques said. "They will tell the truth and shame the Devil. It's 1451, not so?"

Edward's hand dropped to near his gutting knife, too: not on it, but near. "Well, now, friend, I don't mean to give offense, but I do believe it's a year later than you think."

The square-jawed Basque looked as if that knife had gone into *his* guts. The Bretons whooped and cheered. "Come drink with us, truthful man!" they cried. "Come eat with us, too!"

"Bide a moment," Edward said. He set another coin on the counter and pointed to the Basque fishermen. "Give these lads a round of whatever they fancy, and as much bread and cheese and salt meat as the silver will buy besides. I have no quarrel with them, and I want none." He meant that; Basques were even worse than Frenchmen for remembering feuds forever.

His gesture satisfied this table full of them, anyway. They rose one by one and bowed, each with a hand over his heart. Edward and—after a nudge from him—

Richard bowed back. Then they could go over to the Bretons without seeming to be on their side.

"Drink up!" said the man who'd been loudest in inviting them to come. "If you bought for those Basque buggers, we'll buy for you. Do you know Breton, or just French?"

"I can have a go in your tongue," Edward answered, and Richard nodded.

"They can! They can!" the fishermen whooped in their own tongue. Also in Breton, the talky one said, "Good to meet you, by all the saints. I'm François Kersauzon. Will you be giving me your names?"

"Kersauzon, is it? I've heard of you, friend," Edward said, and introduced himself and Richard. "If anyone's done better in our backbreaking business, I don't know who he'd be."

"I've been lucky," Kersauzon said. Sun and salt had feathered his coppery hair with gold strands. He was slimmer than either Radcliffe, but had a fisherman's broad shoulders and scarred, callused hands.

"Lucky? I'll say! More cod and bigger cod than anybody else brings back," Edward said. "I'm jealous. I won't try to tell you any different."

"Plenty more where those came from, too," Kersauzon said easily. He wasn't drunk, no, but his tongue was loose in his mouth. One of his crewmen tried to shush him, but he didn't want to shush. "Don't fret over it, Jacques. Plenty more, yes. Is it the truth? Or is it even less than the truth? The Englishman gave the truth for us—we can give it for him."

"*Kor ki du,*" Jacques answered. Edward hid a smile. *Black dog shit*—Jacques wasn't convinced.

Radcliffe grabbed a stool from another table and brought it over to the one where Kersauzon and his friends were sitting. His son did the same. The famous Breton raised his mug. "Your health!"

*"Yer mat!"* Edward said, and drank with him. The crooked smiles some of the fishermen wore told him he didn't speak Breton all that well. They didn't bother him; he already knew it. But he won points for making the effort.

"Here," François Kersauzon said. "As you drink with us, so you can eat with us, too. Enjoy it!"

He cut a slice of the tavern's bread for Edward and another for Richard. Then, as Jacques squawked some more, he started sawing away at the most remarkable joint of meat the Englishman had ever seen. It looked like a smoked and salted goose's drumstick ... except that it was larger than his own calf, large enough to stretch almost from one side of the table to the other.

It was dark meat, like goose. It tasted a lot like goose—but, Edward thought, not quite the same. He knew he might be wrong. Goose he usually ate fresh, and the smoking and salting could well have changed the flavor. It was almost like eating goose ham.

"Good. Mighty good." He talked with his mouth full. Richard, busy eating, nodded. Edward went on, "So along with all your big, fat cod, you went and killed the roc out there, too?" He was only half joking. He'd always thought the roc was only a bird sailors told stories about. He'd always thought so, aye, but now he wondered. Wouldn't you need a bird the size of a roc to get a drumstick like this one?

Kersauzon and one of the other Bretons both said the same thing at the same time: "Honnnk!" They pitched their voices as deep as they could: almost deep enough to make the table vibrate. All the fishermen from Brittany, even sour Jacques, laughed like loons.

"Well, friend François, you know something I don't," Edward said.

Before he could go on, Jacques said, "Never thought I'd live to hear a Saoz admit that."

"A Gallaou is worse," François Kersauzon said, an observation that surprised Radcliffe not at all. The Bretons lived right next door to the French, so of course they disliked them more than the English. The Channel kept Edward's countrymen far enough away to seem less menacing than their nearer neighbors.

"If it is the roc, where did you find it and how did you keep it from sinking you?" Edward persisted. "And if it's not, by Our Lady, what is it?"

"Will you pay me to hear the story? Will you pay me a third of your catch this year to hear it?" Kersauzon asked. He might have drunk a good deal, but he wasn't too sloshed to be sly.

"That's outrageous!" Richard exclaimed.

The Breton shrugged. He gestured toward the enormous, inexplicable drumstick. "If you don't care to hear the story, no one will make you. But you can still eat your fill. We don't begrudge it."

"A third of my catch?" Edward said slowly, in Breton. Then he said it again, in French, to make sure he had it right. François nodded. The Englishman went on, "And in exchange for this, you promise me . . . ?"

"That you will hear my story, and that it will be true," Kersauzon answered. "Past that, I promise nothing. How can I? Ours is a chancy trade. Things may go well, or they may not. Who can know ahead of time? A third of your catch may be worth nothing, too. God forbid it, but it may be so."

Richard Radcliffe set a hand on his father's arm. "Let's get out of here," he said in English. "He's run out a line and baited a hook, and he'll haul you in and cut your guts out and dry you in salt."

"Your father would be gamy, even in salt," Kersauzon said, also in English. Richard turned red.

"Tell me your story," Edward Radcliffe said. His son exclaimed in dismay. Edward held up a hand. "I will pay your price, friend François. Maybe I am a fool. It could be. Plenty of others have said so. And I will give you one small promise in return."

"Which is?" the Breton asked politely.

"If you lie, or if you cheat, I will hunt you down and kill you."

Several of the Bretons growled. Jacques reached for his knife in a way that warned he wasn't about to cut himself more of the strange smoked flesh that tasted so much like goose. François Kersauzon didn't flinch, or even blink. "A bargain," he said, and thrust out his right hand.

Edward clasped it. Kersauzon began to talk.

*Maybe I am a fool ... Plenty of others have said so.* Radcliffe wondered whether his words would come back to haunt him. If they did, he would keep his promise. It was as simple as that.

All around him brawled the immensity of the Atlantic. He'd never been a cautious sailor, clinging to the sight of land. You couldn't be, not if you wanted to make a halfway decent living with your lines and nets. But he'd never sailed so far into the green-gray-blue of the ocean before, either.

Ahead of him, like a will-o'-the-wisp, the *Morzen* bobbed on the swells. François Kersauzon's cog—her name meant *Mermaid*—was a little smaller, a little faster, than the *St. George.* If she'd wanted to, she could have given Radcliffe the slip. But she reefed her big square sail a bit and stuck with the English vessel.

Edward Radcliffe stood at the *St. George*'s stern, holding the tiller that connected to the rudder. A few cogs still used old-fashioned twin steering oars, but he liked the new arrangement better. It let the builders square up the stern, so the cog could hold more than it would have otherwise. The *Morzen* was made the same way. Up ahead, Kersauzon was doing the steering; by now, Edward was as familiar with his distant outline against the sky as he was with those of his own sailors.

"I don't like this," Henry grumbled. "I don't like it one bit. Those damned tricksy Bretons are laughing up their sleeves at us. You wait and see if they're not, Father."

"Fine sleeves they have for laughing, too," Edward said. His son gave him a dirty look. He was joking and not joking at the same time. A Breton *kabig*, with its hood, its wooden toggles, and its sturdy oiled cloth, was one of the best foul-weather jackets around. His own wool coat didn't shed water so well, though it was probably warmer.

One of the sailors pointed into the sea off the port bow. "Something funny floating there," he called.

"Thanks, Will," Radcliffe answered, and steered towards it. "Grab a dip net and see if you can snag it."

"I'll do that," Will said, and he did. When the *St. George* came up alongside of whatever it was, he thrust the pole-handled net into the sea. Grunting with effort, he pulled it in again. Another fisherman hung on to him to keep him from going over the rail. He thrust a fist in the air in triumph. "Got it, skipper—damned if I don't."

"Good for you!" Edward said, and then, to Henry, "Take the tiller for a bit, will you, lad? I want to see what he's brought in."

"Whatever it is, it won't be worth the third part of our catch—silver doesn't float," his son said. But he took his father's place at the stern.

Edward went forward, his gait automatically compensating for the cog's roll and pitch. Had he thought about how he was doing that, he probably couldn't have done it. "Well, Will, what have you got?"

"It's a leaf, like. Off a tree or a bush?" Will didn't sound sure. When Edward Radcliffe got a good look at the thing, he decided he couldn't blame the other fish-

erman. It was undoubtedly a leaf. But it was like none
he'd ever seen before. It was bigger than a leaf had any
business being. For a couple of heartbeats, he wondered
if it was something on the order of a pine branch. That
didn't look like a pine branch, though—it looked like a
stem. And it didn't have needles growing from it. Those
couldn't be anything but leaves, even if they were frond-
like, almost feathery.

He scratched his head. "Pretty peculiar, all right. I
wonder if the Bretons know what the devil it is."

Another fisherman came up beside them. "You know
what it reminds me of?" he said.

"I don't, Ned, but I hope you'll tell me," Edward
answered.

"It reminds me of the leaves on a palm tree," Ned
said. "A real palm tree, I should say—we mostly use
yew branches on Palm Sunday, on account of real palm
trees won't grow in England. But I saw 'em once in
Cádiz, when I sailed down there on a trading run with a
Dutchman."

"A palm tree," Radcliffe echoed. Ned nodded. The
skipper rubbed his chin. His beard was coming in thick
now. Nobody shaved at sea; you were asking to cut your
own throat if you tried. "We're a mighty long way from
Cádiz—farther off than we were at Le Croisic. How in
blazes would a palm leaf drift all the way out here?"

Ned spread his hands, which were as callused and
battered as the skipper's. "I don't know. It's not just like
a palm leaf, either. More like one than anything else I
know of, though."

"Maybe it says Kersauzon wasn't—isn't—lying after
all," Radcliffe said. "We can hope so, anyway."

"We'd better hope so," Ned said, which also wasn't
wrong. He went on, "And Cádiz may be a long way off,
but that there leaf says some kind of land isn't. It's pretty
fresh—anybody can see that."

"I was thinking the same thing," Radcliffe said. "I—"

He broke off then. A bird flew up to the *St. George* out of nowhere—which is to say, he didn't notice it till it landed on the rail not a long spit from him. Its shape and size put him in mind of a good English blackbird. So did its yellow beak. And, when it opened that beak, so did its song.

But it was no blackbird, nor any other thrush he'd ever seen before. Yes, its back was dark brown, but it had a brick-red breast and belly, not quite so bright as a redbreast's but close.

It let out a few more bars of sweet music. Then, as Radcliffe took a step towards it, it sprang into the air and flew away—off to the west. It didn't land on the *Morzen;* Edward didn't think it did, anyhow. No, it kept on going. And where else would it be going but . . . ?

"Land," Ned said. "Got to be land."

"Yes. I think so, too. And I begin to think François Kersauzon was telling us nothing but the truth," Edward Radcliffe said. "I didn't believe that when I took his bargain. If half of what he claimed was so, part of our catch would have been a small price to pay. But if all of it's true . . ."

"Well, what then?" the fisherman asked.

Edward stared west, after the vanished songbird. "I don't know," he whispered, more than half to himself. "I just don't know. And I don't think anyone else does, either."

More birds—plainly land birds—perched on the *St. George*'s rail or in her rigging or atop her yard over the next few days. Edward Radcliffe would have bet that the cloudbank hanging off to the west hid the unknown land from which those birds came. He started thinking of it in his own mind as Atlantis, the fabled country set somewhere out in the ocean with which it shared a name.

For some time, though, he had no chance to sail west.

Along with everyone else on the boat—and, he was sure, everyone on the *Morzen,* too—he was too busy pulling cod from the sea. Kersauzon sure hadn't been lying about what a fine fishing ground this was. Edward had never seen anything like it in waters closer to England.

Some of the cod were almost as long as a man, and heavier than big men like Edward and his sons. The fishermen had to gaff them to bring them aboard, and even then the cod flapped and fought, desperate for life. Before long, the *St. George*'s deck was running in blood and slippery with fish guts. The crew flung offal over the side as fast as they could. That only brought sharks and other wolves of the sea alongside to feast on the unaccustomed bounty. Gulls and skuas and other sea birds fought for their share, too, and screeched in rage when they didn't get everything they wanted.

Listening to those furious, dissatisfied cries, Edward straightened for a moment and said to Henry, "They might as well be men, eh?"

His son nodded. "They're greedy enough, all right. But there's plenty here for all of them. Plenty here for the Bretons and us, too—François wasn't wrong about that. And you weren't wrong to take him up on it." Henry managed a wry grin. "There, Father. D'you see? You can say, 'I told you so,' and I just have to put up with it."

"So do I," Richard said.

Instead of coming out with the words every child—and every man and woman grown—so hated to hear, Edward Radcliffe only grunted and went back to gutting fish. The knife he used was a sturdy tool, not far removed from a falchion or shortsword, yet for some of the cod that were coming out of the sea it was barely big enough. He stropped it against leather again and again, and longed for a steel to do an even better job of keeping the edge sharp.

The *St. George*'s master salter was a lean fellow named Hugh Fenner. "Good thing we have a full load from Abrgall," he said, spreading flower of salt inside the body cavity of a fish Edward had just gutted. "We'll use every speck we got in Le Croisic."

"Well, I hoped for a good catch then—I always do," the skipper replied. "But I own I never dreamt of anything like . . . this."

"By Our Lady, who would? Who could?" Fenner said. "Some of these cod are so meaty, we need to carve 'em into thinner slabs to make sure the salt can cure 'em before they spoil."

"More work. As if we didn't have enough already," Edward said. "But do what you need to do, Hugh, and make sure the lads all jump when you tell 'em to. The catch comes first." That might not have been the Apostles' Creed, but it was the Fishermen's.

"Don't you fret, skipper. Everybody'll do what needs doing. That's what we're here for," Fenner said.

Radcliffe nodded without taking the master salter seriously. Telling him not to worry was like telling him not to breathe. Worrying was part of his job—a big part. If the captain didn't worry, who would? Nobody. And if nobody worried, what would become of the fishing boat when something that people should have been worrying about happened? Nothing good—he was only too sure of that.

"We'll fill the hold full—Devil take me if we don't," Hugh Fenner said. "We could fill it full two or three times, all the fish we're taking. Jesus and Mary, we hardly need the hooks and lines. The cod're so thick, we could dip baskets in the water and take 'em out that way."

He was likely right. No wonder François Kersauzon had led them here. This bank had more fish than any one boat could handle. Radcliffe thought it had more fish than a hundred boats could handle, or a thousand. In exchange for the secret, the canny Breton got an extra third of the catch for no extra work. It struck Radcliffe as a good bargain for both sides.

Whether it would strike Kersauzon the same way five or ten years from now, Edward wasn't so sure. The *St. George* would keep coming back, and next time around would owe nothing to the other boat. *I can sell the secret, too, if I want to or need to,* Radcliffe thought. It wouldn't last. A secret this big, this rich, couldn't last long by the nature of things.

The wind shifted. Radcliffe's eye automatically went to the rigging, though of course he knew the sail was furled. The breeze had been coming out of the west. Now it swung about so that it blew toward the clouds fixed in the mysterious distance there. Maybe it would shift them at last. He hoped so—he wanted a look at what they hid. He'd heard Kersauzon's stories about Atlantis, and he'd seen one enormous smoked leg of fowl. All that whetted his appetite, both literally and figuratively.

As soon as he was sure the swing portended no danger to the cog, he plunged back into the unending labor of gaffing and gutting and salting fish. Some time went by before he looked up again, startled, and realized he'd forgotten to do anything of the kind for much too long.

Dripping knife in his hand, he stared and stared. *Green as England in springtime* was his first thought after he finally got a glimpse of ... Atlantis. Yes, the name seemed to suit more than well enough. A longer look said his first thought wasn't quite true. This green was darker, more somber, than that of his native land. But that didn't mean he didn't want to see this new countryside up close. Oh, no. It didn't mean anything of the kind.

Oars creaked in the oarlocks as the *St. George*'s boat neared the shore. Edward waved to François

Kersauzon—the *Morzen*'s boat was going ashore, too, only a short bowshot away. The Breton skipper waved back. "Is it not as I told you?" he called, his voice thin across the waves.

"Seems that way." Edward looked over his shoulder, toward the two fishing boats anchored in eight fathoms of water. He didn't believe in taking chances; he wanted plenty of ocean under his keel. Plainly, Kersauzon felt the same way. That surprised the Englishman not at all—you didn't get to be a captain if you were reckless. Or, if you did, you didn't stay a captain long.

He and his sons and Hugh Fenner and two other fishermen had a longer pull than they would have if he'd brought the *St. George* into shallower water. So did the Bretons from the *Morzen. So what?* Edward thought. Anyone who minded work had no business going to sea in the first place.

He wondered whether Kersauzon and the Bretons would race to the shore. Sensibly, they didn't. Anyone who gave himself extra work when so much wasn't extra had to be a fool. François Kersauzon might be a lot of things, but Radcliffe would have sworn on Christ's holy relics that he was no fool.

The boat fought through the breakers and grated to a stop on a beach half sand, half mud. "You go out first, Father," Richard said. "You brought us here. I never would have—I thought the Breton was cozening us." The rest of the Englishmen in the boat nodded.

"I thank you," Edward said. His back creaked as he straightened. When he stepped ashore, his boot squelched in mud. He knew he ought to come out with something grand, something people—or at least he—would remember for a long time. But he was no traveling player or glib peddler, to find fancy words whenever he needed them. "Well, we're here," wasn't what anyone would call splendid, but it was true.

Kersauzon hopped out of the other boat and trotted toward him. The Breton took the new land for granted. It wasn't new to him, not as a whole, even if this stretch might be.

"What do you think?" he asked, as proud as if he rather than God had shaped the ground on which they stood.

"It's . . . different," Edward answered. The murmur of waves going in and out, the wind's sigh, the smell of sea in the air—all those things were familiar enough. So were the grasses and shrubs just beyond the beach. Past that, familiarity broke down. Radcliffe pointed to a strange plant. "What do you call that?"

"I don't know its right name. I don't know if it has one," Kersauzon said. "But I've been calling those barrel plants."

Radcliffe nodded. Right name or not, it fit well enough. The trunk—he supposed it was a trunk—looked like a stout, bark-covered barrel. From the top sprouted a sheaf of big, frond-filled leaves like the one Will had netted from the Atlantic.

More barrel plants, some bigger, some smaller, dotted the landscape. Their leaves were of varying sizes and shapes and of different shades of green, but they all seemed built on the same plan—a plan Edward had never seen before. Farther inland, the woods were of conifers, but not of the sort of conifers he knew. "Have you a name for the trees, too?" he asked.

"I do—I call 'em redwoods," François Kersauzon replied. "Cut down a small one and you'll see why—the lumber is the color of untarnished copper. And Mother Mary turn her back on me if I lie, Englishman, but some of them are bigger than any trees I ever set eyes on back home."

"Are there men here?" Richard Radcliffe asked. "Moors or Irishmen or other savages?"

"I've not seen any," Kersauzon said. "I don't swear I'm the only fisherman ever to find this shore. Basques or Galicians who don't get their salt at Le Croisic—or maybe even those who do, for the Basques are close-mouthed bastards—may come here, too. But I've yet to run across a native. It's a new land."

Edward spied a flash of motion—motion on two legs—behind a tall barrel plant. "Then what's that?" he demanded, wondering if the Breton was tricking his son and him.

Kersauzon only laughed. "Bide a moment, friend, and you'll see—and hear."

"Honnnk!" The note was deeper than a man could have made it. Edward gaped at the curious creature that came out from behind the barrel plant. It walked on two legs like a man, but it was some sort of enormous bird. Its neck and head were black, except for a white patch under its formidable beak. The shaggy feathers on its back were dun brown, those on its belly paler. The legs were bare and scaly, like a fowl's—but what a fowl it was!

When the honker—the name flashed into Edward's mind—spread its wings, the fishermen laughed. Those tiny appendages could never lift it off the ground. He wondered why the bird had them at all.

It reached down with its beak and pulled up a mouth-ful of grass, then another and another. "So that's where you got your great drumstick, is it?" Edward said.

"It is indeed," Kersauzon replied. "The poor, fool-ish things have no fear of man—another reason I think there are no natives here. You can walk up to one and knock it over the head, and it will let you. It will lie dead at your feet when it should be running or kicking."

"I'll do that right now, then," Hugh Fenner said. Half apologetically, the master salter turned to Radcliffe. "You get tired of even the best fish after a while. If we roast that overgrown goose, we've got a feast for the whole crew."

*When we come to a new land, do we mark it by our first kill, the way Cain did?* Edward wondered. But his stomach growled at the thought of meat, too. "Go on if you care to," he told Fenner.

The master salter advanced on the honker. Fenner's confidence grew with every step. Sure enough, the monster bird seemed curious at his approach, but not afraid. He had a stout bludgeon on his belt. One good wallop with that ought to shatter the stupid thing's skull. . . .

A flash in the air, a harsh screech, a shriek from Fenner, and then he was down and thrashing with a great hawk or eagle clinging to his back and tearing at his kidneys with a huge, hooked, slicing beak. The honker might not fear men, but the sight of that eagle sent it running back for the shelter of the—redwoods, Kersauzon called them.

Shouting and waving their arms, Englishmen and Bretons rushed to Hugh Fenner's rescue. The eagle screamed harshly but flew away, blood dripping from bill and long, curved talons. Hugh lay where he'd fallen. He didn't move. A sharp stink said his bowels had let go. Edward grabbed for his wrist, then let it fall. The master salter had no pulse.

"He's gone." Radcliffe heard the dull wonder in his voice. Man could kill—but so could Atlantis.

# II

*F*rançois Kersauzon seemed as upset about Fenner's death as Edward Radcliffe was. "As God is my witness, friend Saoz, I've seen those eagles take honkers before, but I never dreamt they would take men," he said.

"We probably look like honkers—a good name—to them," Henry said.

"Except smaller and maybe easier to kill," Edward added, staring into the trees where the eagle had flown. That was a formidable bird, bigger and fiercer than any golden eagle or sea eagle he'd ever seen. And if its prey walked on two legs . . .

As Kersauzon had said, the honkers seemed to have no fear of man. But that one had disappeared into the woods as soon as the eagle struck Hugh Fenner. Men might be an unknown quantity, but the birds that struck from the sky were enemies. Honkers had no doubt of that.

"Poor Hugh. He died unshriven." Richard crossed himself. So did the other fishermen, English and Bretons. Edward's younger son went on, "We have to bury him here. We can't very well salt him down and take him home."

"I'll say the words over him," Edward said. His sons and the other Englishmen nodded. He'd had to do that before, more than once, when someone on the *St. George* took sick and died or perished by some mischance. He was no priest, but he could hope his prayers helped a soul win through at least to purgatory. "A little piece of Atlantis will be English forevermore."

He'd spoken his own language, but Kersauzon, as he'd seen, could follow English. "Atlantis?" the other skipper echoed. "We've just been calling it the Western Land, but that's better, by God—a name to stick in the mind. Atlantis!"

Edward tried to remember if they had a shovel aboard the *St. George.* He didn't think so. He scuffed at the dirt with the toe of his boot. It was soft. Whatever they had, they could manage. "Are there wolves here, or gluttons, or anything else that might dig up a grave?" he asked.

"Haven't seen anything of the kind," Kersauzon answered. "Haven't seen any four-footed creatures at all, or heard them howling in the night."

"Some uncommon big lizards," one of his fishermen put in.

When Edward Radcliffe thought of a lizard, he thought of a scurrying thing as long as his finger. An uncommon big one might be—what? As long as his forearm? Anything larger than that was beyond his ken.

This whole land was beyond his ken—except that he was standing on it. Off to the west, beyond the trees, he saw the distant saw-toothed outline of mountains against the skyline. What lay beyond them? He snorted. He had no idea what lay on *this* side of the mountains, except for peculiar plants, even stranger birds, and eagles ferocious as demons from hell. But Richard was looking out toward those far-off peaks, too.

No other men here, not settlers, not natives. No wolves, no bears. As he rowed out in the boat to see what digging tools the *St. George* had, he remarked, "If you fished in the sea and cleared some land for a crop, you could live here. You could live here pretty well, I think."

"If you're going to live here, you'd need to bring some women over," Henry said.

Edward nodded, and that thought pulled him back to the present, or at least to the near future. "When we get home, I'll have to tell poor Hugh's Meg what chanced here," he said, and grimaced. "I don't look forward to that. Even paying her his full share, I don't look forward to it. How many children have they got?"

"Five, I think it is," Richard answered, "and Meg's likely to have another by the time we see England again." Edward nodded once more; he thought he remembered the same thing, and wished his son had told him he was wrong.

"Are you thinking of settling on these shores, Father?" Richard asked.

"Aren't you?" Edward said; Henry might be older, but Richard was the sharper of his boys, no doubt about that. "No moneylenders, no lord to bend the knee to, no king to pay taxes to. We're free when we're at sea now, but on land we might as well be slaves. Wouldn't you like to be free all the time?"

"No church," Richard murmured. Did he want to be free of the priest, too, or was he complaining of the lack? Edward couldn't tell.

Henry was more resolutely practical: "No boatwrights. No netmakers. No blacksmiths. No horses, no sheep, no cattle . . ."

"Not unless we bring 'em with us." Edward glanced over to the *Morzen*. "If we don't settle here, how long do you think these Bretons will wait? If they're on the spot, they'll have these fishing banks all to themselves, the bastards."

"They're bad enough on the other side of the Channel," Richard said. "Would you want them living a long spit down the coast from you?"

"Well, if the other choice is spending the rest of my days jealous because they're here and I'm not, maybe I do." Edward Radcliffe weighed his words and nodded yet again. "Yes, son, maybe I do."

The crews of the *St. George* and the *Morzen* spent ten days on Atlantis. The longer Edward Radcliffe stayed, the more he wanted to come back, to settle and never to leave. He kept glancing at François Kersauzon out of the corner of his eye. Was the same thought in Kersauzon's mind? How could it not be?

Henry did knock a honker over the head. It was as easy as the Breton said it would be. The enormous bird stared at the man with a kind of dull curiosity as he walked up to it. It wasn't afraid of him; it had never learned to be afraid of things that looked like him. It died without ever knowing it should have learned to fear.

More than anything else, that made Edward sure Atlantis had no natives. If even savages lived here, the local beasts would have learned to run away from them.

And Edward found himself eyeing François Kersauzon in a new way. The other skipper was properly alert, but if *he* got knocked over the head. . . . Half in regret and half in relief, Edward shelved the idea. He wasn't afraid of wearing the mark of Cain. He was afraid he would have to kill all the Bretons to make killing Kersauzon worthwhile. And he was afraid he would lose too many of his own fishermen in the fighting. Sometimes—not always, but sometimes—peace was smarter than war.

Perhaps three miles south of where he'd first come ashore, he found a river flowing strongly out into the sea. Henry was with him when they came to the mouth of the stream. The younger man pointed inland. "It's bound to come down from the mountains," he said.

"No doubt. It would have to, with so swift a current," Edward agreed. "It runs hard enough to power a great plenty of grinding mills."

"Aye, belike, if the mills have a great plenty to grind," his son said. "No grain growing here, not yet."

"No, not yet." Edward looked inland again. He was also looking into the future—through a glass, darkly, which is as much as it is given to a man to do. "But do you see any reason why grain shouldn't grow here?"

"I seen none," Henry replied, "which is not the same as saying there is none. We don't know."

"I want to find out!" Edward said. "I want to live here, where when I'm ashore I can do as I please. I can hunt deer without poaching on the lord's land—"

"I haven't seen any deer here, either," his son broke in. "No one has, that I know of."

"Fine. I can hunt these honkers, then," Edward said impatiently.

"Oh, yes—they make fine sport." Sarcasm dripped from Henry's words. "The excitement of the stalk, the thrill of the chase . . ." He mimed bringing his club down on a big, stupid bird's head.

"They make mighty good eating, though," Edward said, and his son couldn't very well argue with that—the one Henry had killed was smoking on the beach where they'd landed. Edward went on, "And if there are no deer here now, what's to keep us from bringing them across the sea like sheep or cattle or horses or—?"

Henry interrupted again: "Everything else we'd need to live."

"Well, what of it?" Edward said. "Are you telling me we can't do that? We can find this place again, or near enough—we know the latitude. And if we don't settle right here, any other stretch of the coast would do about as well. Will you tell me I'm wrong?"

"No, Father," Henry said. "But it's a big step, to uproot ourselves from England and cross the sea to try to make our homes on an unknown shore."

"It won't stay unknown long. By Our Lady, it's not unknown now—we're standing on it," Edward Radcliffe said. "And if we don't make homes here, the Bretons or the French or the Basques or the Galicians will. Then we won't even be able to fish here. They'll be in their own back fields, you might say, and we'll have to cross the Atlantic both ways. We'd never stay in business against them. Do you want that? We'd be second best forever. That's no fate for Englishmen. That's no fate for *Radcliffes*!"

Henry sighed. "Father, it sounds good when it comes from your lips. But when we get home, what's Lucy going to say to me?" He put his hands on his hips and raised his voice to sound like his wife, who'd always struck Edward as a bit of a shrew: " 'You want me to leave my kin and cross the sea? You want me to put our babies into a fishing boat? You want to sail away from my mother?' "

"By God, yes to that!" Edward said—Lucy's mother was more than a bit of a shrew.

His son went right on imitating his daughter-in-law: " 'You want me to carve a farm holding out of nothing while you fish the way you always did? You expect me to live without neighbors, without friends?' "

"We won't be the only ones going—tell her that. We'd better not be, or the venture fails," Edward said.

"True enough. What can you promise the others, except a dangerous voyage over more sea than anyone in Hastings cares to think about?"

"Besides the best place to fish they ever saw? Besides land that stretches to the horizon, there for the taking? Besides freedom from lords? How about freedom from peasant risings, too?" Edward said. Only a couple of years earlier, Jack Cade and his rebels had almost chased the King of England from his throne.

Henry nodded thoughtfully. "There is that. What do you suppose Mother will think?"

"She'll go along," Edward said, more confidently than he felt. Nell Radcliffe had a mind of her own and a tongue sharper than Lucy's. She would go along if she thought going along was a good idea. If she didn't, she wouldn't be shy about saying so.

"Well, we'll see," Henry said, which only proved he too knew his mother well.

Crossing the Atlantic from west to east was easier than sailing the other way, for they had the winds with them through most of the journey. They put in at Le Croisic, where Edward paid François Kersauzon the price to which they'd agreed. Seeing a Breton take so much salt cod from the hold of an Englishman's ship made the locals smirk.

Edward looked suitably chagrined as he piled fish in front of the *Morzen*. He didn't believe many Bretons knew of Atlantis yet. What did they think? That Kersauzon had won some enormous bet from him? He wouldn't have been surprised. Let them think what they wanted, though. He knew, and Kersauzon knew.

Two could hold a secret. Could Kersauzon keep the fishermen on the *Morzen* from blabbing? The odds were against it. The Bretons had brought back more smoked honker, and Radcliffe had a leg bone. They would have to explain where those came from. What would they say?

Whatever they said, it would make the other fishermen—and even the local lubbers—curious. They would want to sail west. That meant Edward needed to move fast if he wanted his countrymen to take their fair share of Atlantis.

He needed to move fast—and he couldn't. Contrary winds held him in Le Croisic day after day. He fumed and swore, but he couldn't do anything about it. His only consolation was that what held him in port held the Bretons, too. That wasn't quite true: they could go down the coast to the south. But he didn't think they would spill the secret to Frenchmen. They scorned the French even more than Englishmen did, which wasn't easy.

At last, the wind shifted. He took the *St. George* out of the harbor and sailed around Cap Finistère and into the Channel. The waves there, squeezed between Europe and England, grew taller and more menacing than they had been out in the open ocean. Even fishermen with strong stomachs stayed close to the leeward rail. The waves helped push the cog along, though. She made good time on the last leg of the voyage home.

Hastings was the westernmost of the Cinque Ports: in reality seven towns, though the name had room for only five. They pooled their resources against pirates. There Edward felt safe enough—corsairs were after silk and silver, not salt cod. What he brought home wasn't worth stealing, but a man could make a good living at it. What more could you want?

The old, deserted Norman castle still stood on West Hill, looking down on the town. William the Conqueror had based himself in Hastings, of course—everybody knew that. With Plantagenets still ruling England, no one said—out loud—that he wished the Saxons had won the fight not far away. What would the country be like today had Harold prevailed? *Different,* Edward thought, and he was bound to be right about that.

He brought the *St. George* into the Stade, the fishing boats' harbor. "You're back late," a dockside lounger called. "We'd almost given up looking for you."

"You're holy men, though," another man said. "With so many Masses going up for your souls, how can you be anything else? I wish I were so sure I had all my sins washed away."

"Not much room to sin in a fishing boat," Henry said with a grin. "We'll have to make up for it now that we're here."

A dealer hurried out onto the pier where the fishermen were tying up. "You'll want to sell your fish to me, won't you, Edward?" he said, his voice as greasy as cod-liver oil.

"If you give me a proper price for them, Paul," Radcliffe answered. "If you act like a Jew the way you do most of the time, I'd sooner sell them to an honest man instead."

"You wound me," Paul Finley said, but this was as much a dance with formal steps as the dicker with the Breton salt dealer had been. And when Finley saw the size of the cod and the slabs of cod that came from the *St. George*'s hold, even his air of world-weary contempt for anything that had to do with salt fish cracked. "I don't know the last time I set eyes on the like," he admitted, which meant he'd never seen fish that came close to these. "Where did you catch 'em?"

"I planted them in the dark of the moon, the way you do with crops that grow below the surface," Edward Radcliffe answered gravely. His men sniggered. Sooner or later, one of them would get drunk and spill the word. With a little luck, it would be later.

Paul Finley gave him a very strange look. "I almost believe you."

"Fair enough, for I almost told the truth," Edward said.

The dealer's eye raked the fishing boat. "I don't see Hugh. Tell me nothing happened to him, please—he's a good man."

Edward's mouth tightened. "We lost him, I'm afraid. You'll keep that to yourself, by God, for I've not yet spoken to his wife and his father." He remembered the master salter's scream and the eagle tearing at his kidneys and flying off with his blood dripping from its beak and claws.

Finley crossed himself. "Lord have mercy on him. This was at sea?" Before anyone had to lie, he answered his own question: "Well, of course it was. Where else would it be?" He forced himself back to what lay before him. "You have the hold full of fish this size and quality?"

"Two-thirds full," Edward said, his voice flat: if Paul Finley wanted to make something of that, he would have to do it himself.

He raised an eyebrow. Before he spoke, though, he seemed to think better of it. "Mm, that's your business— or your misfortune, depending. If you'd come home earlier in the season, you would have got a better price for them."

"You'll take any way you can find to knock down what we did out there, won't you?" Radcliffe spoke without heat. He knew Finley was still following the steps of the dance.

"You do your job, I do mine," the dealer said easily. "You want to make money when you sell, and so do I." He named a price.

Edward Radcliffe's bellow of rage was a permitted step, but not a common one. You needed to feel some of that fury to show it, and he did. "Even you know that's thievery, Paul. I've heard what worse cod than this is bringing." He named a price close to three times as high as Finley's.

They went back and forth, back and forth. Edward knew his quality. He also knew his hold was one-third empty, which made him hold out for every farthing on the fish he did have. Finley came up ever so slowly, like a drowning man who didn't want to break the surface.

Both of them were sweating when they finally clasped hands. "If you're going to be that tough with a full load of fish . . ." Finley shook his head. "Lord Jesu! Maybe I ought to let some other dealer see how he likes matching wits with you." He counted out silver and gave it to Edward. "That's what we said, yes?"

Radcliffe counted the money. It wasn't that he thought Finley was trying to cheat him. But checking never hurt anything. He nodded. "Yes, that's what we said." Their hands joined again.

"One of these days, you'll tell me where you really came by cod of that size," Finley said.

"Yes, one of these days I will, and it may come sooner than you think," Edward agreed. "But not yet, Paul. Not yet."

Childbearing and hard work had coarsened Nell Radcliffe's figure. The years had lined her face and streaked her red-blond hair with gray. When Edward looked at her, he still saw the beauty he'd married more than half a lifetime earlier. He made love like a sailor newly home from the sea—in the daytime, which would have scandalized the neighbors had they known, and had so many of them not been fisherfolk themselves.

Then he told her why the *St. George* was so late coming home, and of the new land he'd trodden. "Atlantis?" she echoed, the fine lines at the corners of her eyes crinkling as they narrowed. "But Atlantis is a story, a fable, a make-believe, like the drowned city of Ys and the bells you hear under the water."

"Funny you should talk of Ys, when a Breton guided me west to Atlantis," Edward said. "But it's no dream. We still have the bone from a smoked honker leg—we ate the meat on the way home, when the fishing flagged. And Hugh Fenner died on the coast of Atlantis."

"How?" Nell asked.

"Bad. Hard." Edward left it there. He didn't intend to say more to Meg Fenner, either, or even that much. "But all the same, it's a true place, a good place, a place of great promise—you should have seen Paul's eyes when he got a look at the cod. Not Paradise, or Hugh would live yet, but a good place. A fine place."

"You sound like you want to go back," his wife said.

He nodded, there beside her in the bed so much wider and softer than his bunk aboard the *St. George*—and he was lucky to have a bunk on the cog, when his sailors slung hammocks instead. "I do," he said. "It's a broader land than this one, and a man could live there free of a lord. A man could *be* a lord there, by heaven, for who would say he could not?"

Nell stirred, so the leather lashings under the mattress creaked—not the way they had a little while before, but enough to make him smile. "You don't just want to visit," she said slowly. "You want to stay."

"I do," Edward repeated.

"What about me, then? What about your children? What about—everything?" Her wave took in not just the house, not just Hastings, but all of England.

"I'd want you to come along, that's what. We'd make a new life there, a new town—we could call it New Hastings, if you like."

"I like this Hastings well enough," Nell said.

"Talk to Richard and Henry. They're as wild for Atlantis as I am," Edward said, though he wasn't quite sure that was so about Henry. "Talk to Mary and Kate and Philippa"—his daughters, all of them married to fishermen. "Do you think they'd be sorry to have gardens as wide as they could grow them, and no noble landlord and no rent to pay?"

"I think they'd be sorry to sail to the edge of the world and maybe off it," Nell answered. "I think I would be, too. I thought I'd live my whole life in Hastings. I never wanted to do anything else."

Edward Radcliffe had to remind himself not to get angry. Nell wouldn't be the only one who'd want to stay right here. Most people were like limpets, clinging to one spot. If you went farther than a day's walk from where you were born, it was the journey of a lifetime, and you'd bore your neighbors with it the rest of your days. Fishermen and traders were different; it was easy to forget how different. Edward had seen far more of the world than his wife had. He was eager to see more. She wasn't eager to see any.

"If life is better there, why not go?" he asked, doing his best to keep his voice gentle.

"Who says it would be better? We'd have to start from the beginning, with nothing at all," Nell said.

"We'd have everything we could bring with us from England," Edward said. "Livestock and seeds and saplings and cuttings and tools . . ."

"And someone would steal them from us as soon as we set foot in this place. If you men spend all your time fishing, who would drive off our enemies? We couldn't call on a lord or the king for soldiers, the way we can here if those nasty French dogs cross the Channel."

Patiently, Edward answered, "There'd be no enemies. We would have the first settlement, the only settlement, on those shores."

"Would we? What about that Breton pirate who sold you the secret—a third of the catch, Christ have mercy!" Nell said. "Is he lying with his wife right now, filling her head with wind and air about the marvelous land on the other side of the sea? Will there be a town full of those rogues around the cape from ours? They don't even talk a language a regular person can understand!"

He almost reminded her he spoke Breton, but feared it would do more harm than good. And he didn't know François Kersauzon wasn't planning to settle down in Atlantis. He feared Kersauzon was. The Breton was nobody's fool; if Radcliffe could see the advantages, so could he.

"And what about the wild men who'll live there?" Nell said. "They won't even know our Lord's name, and they'll murder us in our beds first chance they get."

"No wild men." There Edward spoke with assurance.

"How can you know that, on the tiny visit you had?" his wife demanded.

"Because the beasts in Atlantis had no fear of us," he replied. "If they knew men at all, they would know to be afraid of them." Even wolves and bears feared men. They killed men sometimes, but they feared them, and fled when they could.

"Well . . . maybe," Nell said grudgingly. "Or maybe there just weren't any savages close by."

"If there are men anywhere in Atlantis, they'd be there. That land was too fine to stay empty." Edward squeezed his wife. "Don't say no right away. Think it through. You can't imagine what you're throwing away if you turn your back on this."

"I know what I've got now," she said. "I can imagine worse a lot easier than I can imagine better."

"It will be better there," Edward said. "For us, for our children, for their children, and for all who come after them, as long as there be Radcliffes." The fervor in his voice amazed him.

"Well, maybe," Nell said again.

Before long, Hastings bubbled with the name of Atlantis. If you wanted to go and settle someplace, you couldn't very well keep where you were going a secret. Word spread fastest among fishermen and merchants, who had the ships to get to the new land. But others heard, too: the smiths and potters and carpenters who sold them the things they would need on the distant shore, and after that those in authority.

Edward Radcliffe was dickering with a farmer named George Tree over several laying hens and a rooster when a black-robed priest strode up to him. "I would have speech with you, Master Radcliffe," he said importantly.

"What do you need, Father John?" Radcliffe asked.

"Step aside, if you please." The priest made it plain he wanted no one else to overhear.

"Whatever you like, holy Father." Edward nodded to the farmer. "I'll be with you in a bit, George."

"Them birds won't fly away while you're gone," Tree said.

Father John had the smooth pink complexion and double chin of a man who'd seldom known hunger. He also had a blade of a nose and shrewd black eyes. "Do I hear rightly?" he asked after leading Edward down the muddy street till they could talk in reasonable privacy. "Do you purpose sailing off to the edge of the world and leaving the holy mother church behind?"

"I do want to sail off, yes, Father," Radcliffe said, and the priest's mouth tightened. Quickly, the fisherman went on. "But I never dreamt of leaving the church behind. If a priest would come with us, we'd count it a blessing. There should be a chapel in Atlantis—why not?"

"I . . . see," Father John said slowly. Edward hoped he hid his own tension; he didn't want every clergyman in town preaching against his venture. If anything could ruin his plans, that could. If people decided God was against them, they wouldn't go. Father John tapped a forefinger against the side of his leg. "If a priest did come with you, you would give him proper support?"

"We'd be glad to have him, as I said. We'd give him what we could. I can't say he wouldn't have to work some on his own, though," Radcliffe answered. "It's a bare shore, you understand. We'll all be working hard, at first, hard as can be. How can we have a drone among us, meaning no offense?"

"Priests are not drones. Drones toil not, nor do they

spin." Father John's voice was as stiff as his spine. Radcliffe thought priests fit the definition more than well enough, but saying so wouldn't do. Sure enough, Father John went on, "Who would intercede with God, but for priests? Who would baptize, who hear confession, who give unction at the end of life?"

"No one," Edward said, as he had to. He didn't want to go out of life without unction, the way luckless Hugh Fenner had. But he was a stubborn man in his own right. "A priest who is respected among men is better than one who is not," he insisted. "Anyone who pulls his own weight in this world will be better liked than a man who expects to be waited on hand and foot. Holy Father, you know there are priests like that. We both wish there weren't, but there are. We don't need one like that where everyone else is bending his back like a beast of burden."

Maybe his earnestness got through to Father John. "What sort of priest *do* you need then, eh, Radcliffe?"

Edward calculated for a heartbeat and part of another. As if he hadn't, he answered, "Why, one much like yourself, holy Father."

Had he read his man aright? "Me?" Father John rapped out. "Why would I want to sail to the back of beyond—beyond the back of beyond?"

"Where would you find a better chance to be your own man?" Edward asked. "You'd be . . . like a bishop, almost." He didn't wink at Father John. If the priest thought of himself the way Radcliffe hoped, he would rise to the bait on his own.

"If I am to be sent alone to a strange shore, I should become one," Father John said. "This is to enable me to ordain new priests so that the Church may continue in that far-off place."

"You will know such things better than I do, the same as I'm likely better at salting a cod," Edward said. "Do you think you can make the necessary arrangements?"

"Well, well," the priest said, and then again: "Well, well." He rubbed his smoothly shaven chin. "Do you know, sir, it is possible that I might."

"All right, then," Edward said, as if that were a complete sentence. By the way Father John smiled, it was.

Edward Radcliffe was a man of some consequence in Hastings. Any successful fishing captain was. All the same, he didn't expect a summons to the castle, and he didn't expect the summons to be delivered by four large, unsmiling men in chainmail. The largest and most somber of them growled, "You are to come with us at once, in the name of Sir Thomas and in the name of his Majesty, Henry VI, King of England!"

*Henry VI, King of as much of England as he can persuade to obey his writ at any given moment.* The thought ran through Edward's mind, but he kept it to himself. Sir Thomas Hoo, the local baron, was a loyal follower of the king's. "I am at your service, gentlemen, and at Sir Thomas', and of course at the king's," the fisherman said. If he tried telling them anything else, he had the bad feeling he would die as unpleasantly as Hugh Fenner.

Sir Thomas' men had horses waiting in the street. They even had one for Radcliffe. He took that as a good sign. If they were going to throw him in the dungeon, they would have made him walk, probably with a noose around his neck to advertise his disgrace to the town.

He was more accustomed to riding a pitching deck than even a sedate gelding. Two of Sir Thomas' retainers sniggered as he awkwardly swung up onto the horse's back. "You've got more practice at this than I do, friends," he said. "In the *St. George,* in a storm on the North Sea, you'd be the sorry ones, as I am here."

"Just ride," said the one who seemed to do their talking for them. Ride Radcliffe did, not well but well enough.

The wooden motte-and-bailey castle William the Conqueror built as soon as he landed in England and its stone successor had long since grown useless: the sea had chewed away most of the land that once stood between the old fort and the water's edge. Its replacement, a solid mass of gray stone, safely stood farther inland.

Their horses' hooves drumming on the lowered drawbridge, Edward and his escorts rode into the castle. Sir Thomas Hoo stood in the courtyard, watching some young soldiers hack at pells with swords. Sir Thomas was no youngster. He was five or ten years older than Radcliffe, and his strength, once massive, was beginning to fail. His stooped shoulders and wrinkled, jowly face warned of the storms of life's winter ahead.

He rolled his eyes at Edward's dismount, which was no more graceful than the way the fisherman had mounted. "What's this I hear about you wanting to put all of Hastings on board ship and sail off with it to some unknown shore?" he growled without preamble.

"By the holy Cross, Sir Thomas, if you heard any such thing, you heard lies!" Edward exclaimed.

"Oh, I did, did I?" Sir Thomas Hoo's eyes were red-tracked and rheumy, one of them clouded by the beginnings of a cataract. But they were very shrewd. "If it's all moonshine and hogwash, why do I hear it from so many folk? Eh? Answer me that!"

"If you believed everything you heard from a lot of people, sir, you'd be a sorry soul, sir, and that's the truth," Edward said. A couple of his escorts scowled; one of them dropped a hand to the hilt of his sword. Then Sir Thomas grunted laughter, and his retainers relaxed. Radcliffe went on, "Rumor always outruns fact. And any man who wishes me ill would work to make it outrun fact the more."

"It could be," the castellan said. "I don't say it is, but it could be. Well, then, what *do* you intend?"

"A small settlement on the new shore," Radcliffe answered. "The fishing grounds there are finer than any in the North Sea. That I saw for myself. Would we want to let the Bretons and Basques and other foreigners seize the advantage over Englishmen in using them?"

"Fish. Cod." Sir Thomas made them into words of scorn, if not into swear words. He glowered at Edward from under shaggy, gray-streaked eyebrows. "You want to get away from peasants in rebellion against their rightful lords and from French sea dogs."

*I should say I do,* Edward thought. The French had almost burnt Hastings to the ground not long before. But he couldn't admit what he wanted. Without the least hesitation, he shook his head. "How could we leave our homeland behind for good?" he said. "Where would we sell the fish we caught if we did?" That was a legitimate question; he couldn't imagine cutting all ties with England even if he and his kin spent most of their time in Atlantis and off its shores.

"How many folk would fare with you on this madcap venture?" Sir Thomas asked.

"A couple of dozen families, sir, and we'd need to bring the seed grain and livestock to let us make a go of it in the new land," Edward answered. "Does not the Good Book speak of casting your bread upon the waters? This is England's bread, and she shall find it again after many days."

"You've been talking with Father John." Sir Thomas turned that to an accusation.

"I have, sir. He will vouch for me." Edward Radcliffe hoped he would.

"He's ambitious, too." The castellan scowled once more. "Well, go, then, and I know not whether to wish you Godspeed or say be damned to you. Atlantis? Nonsense!" He hawked and spat and turned away.

# III

$\mathcal{G}$etting animals aboard the *St. George* vexed Edward, to put it mildly. "I never worried about Noah before," he growled to Nell. "Now I feel sorry for the poor devil."

"*I* feel sorry for his wife," Nell said. "Chances are he made her do all the work."

"If you think I'm going to sleep from here to Atlantis, you're bloody well out of your mind," Edward said. "The cog won't sail herself, and the fish won't catch themselves, either." The hold, which still stank of fish, was full of hay and grain instead. They had to get the sheep and hogs and chickens and ducks across the sea before they ran out of fodder and water for them. Could they do it? He thought so, but feared it might be close.

He had no cattle or horses on the *St. George*. The boats that carried the bigger beasts had fewer of the smaller ones. He hoped things would work out. He didn't know they would, but he hoped so. *What else can I do?* he thought.

Richard said something hot as a smithy's forge when he stepped in sheep shit. "Get used to it, son," Edward advised. "It won't be the last time." Richard said something even hotter. Henry laughed at him, which only proved *he* hadn't stuck his foot in it . . . yet.

On another cog not far away, Father John's tonsured head gleamed under the bright sun of early spring. Two other priests were also coming along on this leap into the unknown. Edward Radcliffe smiled to himself. The other two were pliable, tractable fellows, men without ambition for themselves. If any of them was made a bishop, when one of them was made a bishop, it would be John. So far from any other prelate, he might almost be a pope.

Edward cupped his hands to his mouth and shouted to the other boats assembled in the Stade: "Are we all ready?" Two or three skippers echoed his cry to make sure everyone heard. Nobody said no. "Then let's away!" he said.

Sailors ran to the lines and let the big square sails fall from the yards. The wind came off the land, and pushed the cogs out of the harbor and into the waters of the Channel with the greatest of ease. Women and children squealed in excitement; not many of them had put to sea before.

The water in the Channel was the way it usually was: rough. Those squeals didn't last long. Ruddy English complexions went ghost-pale. "The rail!" a fisherman shouted. "Get to the damned rail!" He was just too late—and somebody would have a mess worse than sheep shit to clean up.

"Is it . . . always like this?" Nell asked, gulping.

"No, dear," Radcliffe answered. His wife looked relieved in a wan way till he added, "Sometimes it's worse." She searched his face, hoping he was joking. When she saw he wasn't, she groaned. He said, "You'll get used to it after a while, though. Almost everyone does."

"Almost?" Nell got out through clenched teeth. She gulped again, and ran for the rail. Unlike the first victim of seasickness, she made it. She even knew which rail to run to. People who ran to the windward side only made that mistake once—trying to clean themselves afterwards ensured that.

Fishermen screamed at passengers to get out of the way as they swung the yard to catch the breeze. They screamed at the livestock, too, but the animals didn't want to listen (neither did some of the children). One irate soldier booted a hen into the English Channel.

"Don't ever do that again, Wat," Edward told him. "We'll need those birds when we get to the other side."

"If I trip over the damn thing and go into the drink myself, *I* won't make it to the other side," Wat retorted.

"You won't make it there if I toss you in the drink, either," Edward said. Wat was twenty years younger. A long look at the jut of Radcliffe's jaw and the size of his knobby fists, though, made the other man turn away, muttering to himself.

Edward was glad to be back at sea. He felt he belonged here. His time ashore he endured; he came alive on the waves. That wasn't anything he talked about with Nell, any more than he would have told her if he'd taken up with another woman. He didn't want her jealous—it would only have made things worse.

The *St. George* took much longer to shake down to routine than she usually did. The fishermen knew what routine meant. Their wives and children didn't, and had to learn. The animals didn't, either, and learned even more slowly, if at all.

People who weren't used to the rations grumbled about them—or they did when they finally got their sea legs under them and found they had appetites after all. Radcliffe thought the food was extravagant: to go with the ship's biscuit, they had much more bacon and sausage aboard than usual, and less salt cod. The fish needed to be soaked before you could eat it. They had so many more mouths aboard than usual, they couldn't afford much water for that.

"This biscuit has weevils," Nell said when they'd been at sea about a week.

"Yes, that happens," Edward agreed. "I'm sorry, but I can't do anything about it."

"But it's disgusting!" she said shrilly.

"It can happen on land, too," he pointed out. "It does."

"Not like this." Nell held the biscuit under his nose. "It's crawling with bugs!" He couldn't see them when she did that—his sight had begun to lengthen. It didn't mean he didn't believe her, because he did. She went on, "All the ship's biscuit is probably like this."

Edward nodded. "It probably is."

His wife glared at him. "Well, what are we supposed to do about it? We can't pitch it into the ocean the way we ought to, not if it's all bad. We'd starve."

"I'm afraid so." Radcliffe was also afraid Nell would grab something and try to break it over his head. He regretfully spread his hands. "I don't know what to tell you, dear. If you toast your biscuit over a candle flame, you'll drive out most of the bugs. Or if you close your eyes and don't think about it, you just . . . eat."

"I already tried that," she said bleakly. "It doesn't work—they crunch under your teeth. They taste bad, too. Maybe I'll toast it and see how many weevils come out. Maybe I don't want to know."

"I never did," Edward said. She needed to remember this happened to fishermen all the time.

She flounced off, as well as she could flounce on a pitching deck. Her long wool skirt swirled around her ankles. After a couple of strides, she turned around for a parting shot: "Do they have weevils in your precious Atlantis?" Before he could answer, she did it for him: "They would." *Then* she stormed away.

Later that day, Edward asked her, "Does the toasting help?"

"A little," she said grudgingly. More grudgingly still, she added, "You did try. I thank you for it."

"There's my Nell," he said. The scowl his Nell sent him told him all was not yet forgotten, even if it might be partway forgiven.

The fishermen went to work sooner than they would have on a regular run. Everything they caught stretched the supplies on the *St. George* further. Edward wouldn't have bothered salting most of what the lines brought in. But, as fishermen knew and few others ever had the chance to learn, fish just out of the ocean made far better, far sweeter eating than fish dried and salted or fish starting to go off at a fishmonger's stall.

The dogs didn't turn up their noses at fresh fish guts, either. That eased Radcliffe's mind; he hadn't been sure how he would keep them fed all the way across the Atlantic. Dogs would eat almost anything if they had to, but they did best with something meaty.

Fish suited the cats fine. There weren't enough rats and mice on the cog to keep them full for such a long voyage. Edward knew from experience that there were bound to be some. He also knew from experience that, no matter how many cats he had aboard, they wouldn't catch all the vermin.

He wondered whether Atlantis had rats and mice of its own. Hard to imagine a place that didn't. He laughed a little. If by some accident the new land lacked them, it wouldn't much longer. They were bound to come ashore and bound to get loose in the wilderness. It was a shame, but he didn't know what he could do about it.

Swine were bound to get loose, too. They were much closer to wild beasts than sheep and cattle and horses. Swine, at least, made good hunting and good eating.

Day followed day. Edward had a compass, to give him a notion of north. He had a cross-staff, to give him a notion of latitude—as long as he kept the date straight. As soon as he got out of sight of land, he had only a rough guess, based on how far he thought he'd sailed, about longitude. He wished someone would figure out how to keep track of it, but no one had.

"Are we almost there?"

He expected to hear that from his grandchildren, and he did. He was less happy to hear it from his sons' wives, and from his own. The more he heard it, the more it grated on him, too. "Do you see land out there?" he would ask, and point west. There was, as yet, no land to see. When whoever was grumbling admitted as much, he would say, "Then we aren't almost there, are we?"

When the fishermen started pulling cod that weighed as much as they did out of the gray-blue water, Edward smiled to himself. The lubbers aboard went right on wondering where land was. Edward knew it wasn't very far. They really were almost there—and he said not a word.

He thought they would spot land the very next day, but they didn't—fog closed in around the little fleet of cogs and held them wrapped in wet wool for the next two days. Sailors shouted to one another and blew horns to keep from drifting apart, because no one could see from stern to bow of one fishing boat, let alone farther.

Edward hadn't been worried till then; everything on the journey west had gone as well as he could have hoped, or maybe even better. But those two days made him pace and mutter and crack his knuckles and do all the other things a badly rattled man might do. He wasn't fretting only about one cog colliding with another, either. Here he was, off a shore about which he knew next to nothing. How many rocks and shoals did it have, and where did they lurk? Was a rock he couldn't see only a few feet away, waiting to rip the bottom out of the *St. George*?

To ease his mind, he cast a line into the water. It came back showing thirty fathoms and a sandy bottom. That made him feel a little better, but only a little. A rock could rise suddenly, and he knew it too well. He set one of the fishermen to casting the lead every time he turned the glass. "If we go under twenty fathoms, scream at me," he said.

No screams came, only the shouts and braying trumpets from the other fishing boats. Radcliffe didn't mind those. He would have started and sworn had a horn bellowed from right alongside the *St. George,* but that didn't happen, either.

"You're jumpy as one of the cats," Henry told him.

"It's my boat," Edward said simply. "It's my notion to start a new town in the new land. And if anything goes wrong, it's my fault."

"We're fine, Father," Henry said.

"We are now. We are now, as long as God wants us to be." Edward crossed himself. A moment later, so did his son. "If God decides He doesn't want us to be—"

"Then we can't do anything about it anyway," Henry broke in.

"We have to do everything we can do, everything we know how to do," Edward insisted. "If we don't, we've got only ourselves to blame. God put the rocks wherever He put them. If we don't look for them, though, that's our fault."

"Whose fault is it if we strike one just after we cast the lead and find naught amiss?" Henry asked.

"Ours. No. His. No." Edward's glare should have been hot enough to burn off the fog by itself. "You're trying to tie me in more knots than the lines."

His son laughed. "Well, if you're storming at me, you won't keep stalking the deck and scaring the poultry."

"I'm not scaring the—" Hearing his own voice rise to a level he usually used only in a gale, Edward started to laugh. "All right—maybe I am."

"As long as you know you might be, maybe you won't," Henry said, and then half spoiled it by adding, "so often, anyhow."

Edward made as if to cuff him. He'd done that plenty with both boys when they were younger. If he tried it in earnest now, he feared he would be the one who ended up lying on the deck. Henry and Richard had their own boys to tame these days. Henry knew he was joking here, and made as if to duck. Then he clapped Edward on the back.

"If I go down, which God prevent, I'll go down in good company," Edward said.

"Which God prevent, is right," Henry said.

A sunbeam in the face caught Edward by surprise. It caught him by surprise twice, in fact: he didn't remember falling asleep on the deck some time in the dark hours before dawn, and fog had still shrouded the *St. George* when he did. But now the sun shone, the sky was blue, and a warm breeze from the southwest carried the green smells of land with it.

He sprang to his feet. "Land ho!" he bawled—the line on the western horizon was hard to make out, but he had no doubt it was there. "Land ho! Praise the Lord! He *has* brought us safe to this new shore!"

Other cogs began shouting it, too, but he thought he was the first. If those shouts were what woke him and not the sunbeam after all, he didn't want to know about it.

Nell came over to his side. She peered west, shading her eyes with the palm of her hand. "That's it?" she said. "It doesn't look like much."

"Not yet." Edward bowed, as if he were a nobleman. "Kindly give us leave to draw closer, if you'd be so gracious."

His wife dropped him a curtsy. "Oh, very well, since 'tis you as asks." Her impression of a high-born lady's airs and accent also left something to be desired. They grinned at each other.

With the wind in that quarter, drawing closer wasn't easy. They had to slew the big square sail around on the yard again and again, tacking toward the land that almost seemed to retreat as they beat their way westward. But they did gain, even if not so fast as Radcliffe would have liked.

And they did find their first rock on the new shore. The sea boiled white just above it. "That's a bad one," Henry said. "If the tide runs a little higher, it'll hide the bastard altogether—but it won't lift a boat high enough to get over it."

"Note the landmarks," Edward said. "We'll chart these waters one day. By God, we will."

"This isn't right where Kersauzon brought us," his son said.

"I know." Edward sighed and nodded at the same time. "We did the best we could, and this is what we got. A few leagues north? A few leagues south? Who can say? Maybe we didn't have the latitude quite right when we were here last. Maybe we drifted in the fog. I don't know. But that's Atlantis ahead, the land where we're going to put down roots."

Henry muttered something under his breath. Edward couldn't make out what it was, and supposed he might be lucky. He knew Richard had more enthusiasm for the new land than Henry did. Well, Henry was here, whether he was glad to be here or not.

The fishing boats kept fighting toward the alluring coast ahead. The only way the wind could have been worse would have been for it to blow straight into their faces. No boat could make headway against a directly contrary wind; they would have had to drop anchor and wait for it to swing around. Edward might have been tempted to do that anyway, were the land not so near— the constant tacking wore out the crew. With women and children and beasts on deck, it was harder, more dangerous, more aggravating work than it usually would have been, too.

But the hard work had its reward; to Edward Radcliffe's way of thinking, hard work commonly did. The *St. George* dropped anchor in eight fathoms of water as the sun sank toward the newly notched horizon ahead. "Can we get ashore before sunset?" Richard asked.

"Only one way to find out," Edward answered. The boat went into the water. The fishermen began to row. Looking around, Edward spied other boats heading for the beach. He hadn't raced François Kersauzon, but he did now. "Pull hard, damn you!" he roared, and pulled hard enough himself to come close to jerking the thole pin out of the gunwale. "Pull hard! No one's going to beat me back to Atlantis!"

In a twinkling, all the fishermen in all the boats were rowing as hard as they could. Edward was working harder than he had on the *St. George,* but exhaustion fell away. He laughed as he worked his oar and shouted out the stroke to the others in the boat. And he heard other laughs float across the green sea. The men racing to be first ashore weren't racing because they had to but because they wanted to, and it made all the difference in the world.

Sand and mud grated under the boat's keel. Edward sprang out into ankle-deep water. "Mine!" he shouted, throwing his arms wide. "Mine!"

He thought he was the first man on the beach. If he was, though, he wasn't by much. Other skippers and fishermen stepped out onto the shores of Atlantis. Little gray and brown shorebirds skittered along at the edge of the advancing and retreating waves, pausing now and again to peck at something or other. They left their tiny hentracks behind to be washed away by the next incoming surge.

Richard set a hand on his father's shoulder. "We're here again," he said.

"We are. By God, we are," Edward Radcliffe agreed. "We're here again, and this time we're not going to leave."

"What's that?" said one of the fishermen who'd rowed the boat ashore. "We aren't going back to the *St. George*?"

Edward laughed. "We'll go back, Alf. But we'll go back to get what we need to set up a new town here. It may be a while before we go back to England." *I wonder if I'll ever go back. I wonder if I'll want to,* he thought, and then, *I suppose I'll have to, one of these days. It's not the same as wanting to.*

Alf nodded; he might not be bright, but he was willing. "Well, that's all right, then," he said. "That's what I came for, that is."

The biggest adventure was getting the horses and cattle off the cogs and onto the land ahead. Some skippers solved it with brutal simplicity by pushing the animals over the side and making them swim. Others ran their lightly laden cogs aground at low tide and lowered gangplanks so the beasts could descend. When the water rose, it lifted the fishing boats and let the skippers move them out to sea again.

"Where are these honkers you kept telling me about?" Nell demanded as soon as she came ashore. She bent to wring out the dripping hem of her skirt, giving Edward a glimpse of a still-shapely ankle.

"Well, I don't know just where they are," he admitted.

"I expect we'll see them sooner or later, though—sooner, unless I miss my guess. We saw a good many when we were here before." Remembering what else they'd seen before, he raised his voice to a carrying shout: "Watch the sky! The eagles here are huge, and they have no fear of men—they think we're prey."

Those little shorebirds had darted between—sometimes even over—men's feet, too. In England or France, they would have kept their distance. It seemed they'd never met men before, and didn't know such creatures were dangerous.

And that was only a tiny strangeness among so many larger ones. The plants were the same curious mixture of conifers, ferns, and those barrel-trunked plants with the leaves that shot up from the top of the barrel. The honkers—even if absent at the moment—were like nothing Edward or anyone else had seen before. And the red-breasted thrushes acted like blackbirds but looked more like oversized robins. And all this within an hour's walk of the shore!—for no one, yet, had dared venture farther inland.

Some of the first things the newcomers made were salt pans at the edge of the ocean, to trap the seawater and let it evaporate, leaving salt behind. What they got would not be anywhere near so fine as the pure white flower of salt bought in Le Croisic. Right this minute, though, Edward worried more about quantity than quality. He wanted to be sure he had the salt to preserve enough cod to get the settlers through their first winter on the new shore.

He didn't worry about having enough cod. The banks off the east coast of Atlantis were abundant beyond anything he'd ever imagined, and he knew the great fisheries in the North Sea as well as any man alive. "Maybe the North Sea was like this when fishermen first started going out there," he said after the *St. George*'s boat brought in load after load of huge, plump gutted fish. "No more, though. We've taken the very best out of it, and that best is still here."

"It is," Henry agreed. "The fish we don't salt down, we'll be able to use to manure the fields." He held his nose. "The smell will be bad, but the crops will be good."

"Yes." Edward Radcliffe nodded. "So much to do all at once, but this goes so well, it frightens me."

His son frowned. "Frightens you?"

Edward nodded again. "By Our Lady, it does. We work. We sweat and swink and toil. We build. And what if some sea wolves—Bretons or Basques, say—swoop down on us with swords and spears, and steal all we've made by our labor? I know what I want to buy when we see England again."

"What's that?" Henry asked.

"Some fine iron guns, by God, and powder and shot for 'em," Edward said. "A couple here ashore, and a couple on the *St. George*, too. I want to be able to fight if I have to, not to be raiders' meat."

After pursing his lips in thought, Henry also nodded. "I do like that notion. And if we're not the only ones putting down roots in this new soil . . ."

He let the words hang. "What then?" Edward prompted.

His son's grin was wide as the ocean between them and Hastings. "Why, we could turn wolf ourselves! I could stay at sea!"

"I didn't come here to go warring, asea or ashore. I came here to get away from all that," Edward said. "With the peasants up in arms, with the damned Frenchmen roaring across the Channel, with Lancaster and York glaring at each other and both ready to swoop, there's war and to spare back home if you're so hungry for it."

Henry looked down at his feet. "You shame me, Father."

*By God, I hope so,* Edward thought. But he didn't want to leave Henry with no pride, so he said, "I didn't mean to. But think on what you're talking about, that's all. War usually looks better to the fellow who brings it than it does to the poor buggers who have it brought to them."

"Mm, something to that, I shouldn't wonder," his son said, to his deep relief. But then Henry pointed a half-accusing forefinger at him. "Who was just talking about buying fine iron guns?"

"I was," Edward said. "But I didn't talk about raiding with them, only about standing off raiders. There's a difference."

"No doubt," Henry said, and Edward beamed. Too soon—Henry hadn't finished. "The difference is, after a while you want to try out the guns, no matter why you got them in the first place."

Edward Radcliffe winced; that held too much of the feel of truth. "It won't happen that way while I have anything to say about it," he insisted.

"All right, Father," Henry said. "I hope it doesn't happen for many, many years, then." Edward noticed he didn't say he hoped it never happened at all.

They did call the settlement New Hastings. The houses they made were of wood, not stone, because those went up faster. Cutting back saplings and clearing away the undergrowth were easier than they would have been back in England: no berry bushes or wild roses full of thorns and no stinging nettles. Plowing under the ferns that grew in the shade was even easier than dealing with grass on the meadows.

And, when the crops came in, they flourished even before the settlers manured them with fish. "I don't see any bugs on the plants!" Nell exclaimed. "Is it a miracle?"

"Ask Father John or one of the other priests," Edward answered. "Maybe the bugs here don't know how to eat our crops, or don't like the way they taste. Is that a miracle? Richard doesn't like the way squash tastes."

"Richard is not a bug," Nell said. Since Edward couldn't very well argue with that, he walked off shaking his head.

The weather got warm, and then warmer. It got muggier than it ever did in England, too. Edward had known the like down in the Basque country, but the people who'd spent their whole lives in Hastings wilted like lettuce three days after it was picked.

An eagle swooped down and killed a child. It tore gobbets of flesh from the small of the girl's back before flying off. She died the same way Hugh Fenner had, in other words. Even though she was already dead, Father John gave her unction while her mother screamed and screamed. They buried her next to the log hut that did duty for a church. No stonecarvers were on this new shore yet, but at Father John's direction the carpenter made a grave marker out of the red-timbered evergreens that seemed so common here. *Rose Simmons, vibas in Deo,* the inscription read: *may you live in God.*

How large would the churchyard grow? Edward dared hope his flesh would end up there, and not at sea for fish and crabs to feast on. *Thy will be done, Lord,* he thought, *but not yet, please.*

Another eagle killed a sheep. That would have been a sore loss in England—not that eagles there attacked beasts so large. It was worse here, because the newcomers could spare so little. A smaller hawk carried off a half-grown chicken. A big lizard—bigger than any Edward had imagined—ate a duckling. But there were no foxes. That alone helped the poultry thrive.

Edward chanced to be ashore one morning in early summer when a twelve-year-old told off to keep an eye on the livestock ran back into New Hastings screaming, "Things! There's *things* in the fields!"

Like everyone else, Radcliffe tumbled out of bed. He pulled on his shoes and went outside. "What do you mean, things?" he demanded.

"See for yourself!" The boy pointed to the bright green growing grain. "*I* don't know what they are! Demons from hell is what they look like."

"They aren't demons," Edward said. Those two-legged shapes might be strange to the boy, but he'd seen them before.

"They have the look of something otherworldly." Father John crossed himself, just in case.

But Edward Radcliffe shook his head. "No, no, Father. Those are the honkers I've been talking about. They think we've spread out a feast for them. They don't know they're a feast for us." He raised his voice: "We can't let them eat our grain and trample what they don't swallow. Get clubs. Get bows. We'll kill some—they're good eating, mighty good—and drive the rest away."

When he went out into the fields, he saw that these weren't quite the same kind of honkers as he'd seen the year before. They were bigger and grayer and shaggier of plumage. Their voices were deeper. But they showed no more fear of man than the other honkers had. You could walk right up to one of them and knock it over the head. Down it would fall, and another one ten feet away would go right on eating.

If you didn't kill clean, though . . . A man named Rob Drinkwater only hurt the honker he hit. It let out a loud, surprised *blatt!* of pain. Before he could strike again and finish it, one of its thick, scaly legs lashed forward. "Oof!" Drinkwater said. That was the last word—or sound—that ever passed his lips. He flew through the air, crashed down, and never moved again: he was all broken inside.

The honker lumbered off, still going *blatt!* The cry got the other enormous birds moving. Fast as a horse could trot, they headed off into the undergrowth. Every stride knocked down more young, hopeful wheat and barley.

Ann Drinkwater keened over her husband's body. The rest of the settlers stared from the dead honkers to the damaged crops and back again. "Will they come again tomorrow?" Richard Radcliffe asked. "Will they come again this afternoon? How many of them will we have to kill before the rest decide they shouldn't come?"

Those were all good questions. Edward had answers to none of them. "We'll butcher these dead ones," he said. "We can smoke some of the meat, or salt it, or dry it. We can't let it go to waste. After that—"

"They're afraid of the damned eagles, if they aren't afraid of us," Henry said. "If we screech like them, maybe we can scare off the honkers."

"We'd have a better chance if we could fly like them," his brother said, and Edward judged Richard likely right.

Numbly, the settlers got to work. Henry carried a pile of honker guts well away from the place where the creature had died. He made sure he included the kidneys, though they might have gone into a stew if he hadn't.

He waited in some nearby bushes, a hunting bow in his hand. Down from the sky to the offal spiraled . . . a vulture. Even the vultures here differed from the ones back in England. This one was almost all black, down to the skin on its head. Only the white patches near the base of the wings broke the monotony.

Henry came out and shooed it away before it landed and stole the leavings. It flew off with big, indignant wingbeats. Edward watched it go before he realized it had a healthy fear of men. He wondered what that meant, and whether it meant anything.

His son went back into cover. Henry had a hunter's

patience—or, more likely, a fisherman's patience he was for once applying to life on land. And that patience got its reward when an eagle descended on the kidneys and fat much more swiftly and ferociously than the vulture had. Edward wasn't too far away when it did: he was close enough to notice the coppery crest of feathers on top of the great bird's head as it tore at the bait Henry had left for it.

With a shout of triumph, Henry sprang up, let fly . . . and missed. He couldn't have been more than eight or ten yards away, but he missed anyhow. The eagle might not have feared men, but a sharp stick whizzing past its head startled it. It launched itself into the air with a kidney in its beak.

Henry said some things that were bound to cost him time in purgatory. He made as if to break the bow over his knee. "Don't do that!" Edward called. "We haven't got many, and we haven't the time to make more without need, either. Besides, it's a poor workman who blames his tools."

"I couldn't hit water if I fell out of a boat." Henry was still furious at himself.

"There, there," his father soothed, as if he were still a little boy. "You're a fine archer—for a fisherman."

"Ha!" Henry made a noise that sounded like a laugh but wasn't.

"Keep at it," Edward said. "It's a good idea. If we don't kill these cursed eagles, they'll go on killing us."

"And the honkers, too," Henry said. "They're as bad as deer or unfenced cattle in the crops. How much did we lose today?"

"I don't know. Some. Not more than we can afford, though, I don't think," Edward answered. "And the eagles are more dangerous than honkers ever could be."

"Tell it to poor Rob Drinkwater. Tell it to his widow and his orphaned brats."

"A horse or a mule can kick a man to death, too," Edward said. "That's all honkers are—grazers that go on two legs, not four. But when God made those eagles, He made them to kill."

Henry thought it over, then nodded. "He made them to kill honkers, I'd say. And we look enough like honkers, they think we make proper prey, too."

Edward Radcliffe started to say something, then stopped and sent his son a surprised glance. "I hadn't looked at it so. Damned if I don't think you're right."

Henry walked over, retrieved his wasted arrow, and put it back into the quiver with the rest. "We'll have enough to get through the winter with or without crops, seems like," he said. "Between the cod and the honkers, we'll do fine."

"Aye, belike," Edward said. "But I want my bread, too. And Lord knows I want my beer. If we have to fence off the fields to keep the honkers out, well, we can do that."

"It will be extra work," Henry said. "We're all working harder now than we would have on the other side of the ocean."

"*Now* we are, yes," Edward agreed. "But that's only because we have to make the things we take for granted back there. Once we have them, things will be easier here than they were in England. Why else would we have come?"

Henry laughed. "You don't need to talk me into it, Father. I'm already here." He made as if to break the bow again, but this time not in earnest. "I'd be gladder I'm here if only I were a better archer."

"Each cat his own rat," Edward said. "Plenty of fine bowmen who'd puke their guts out on a fishing cog."

"One of the girls was screeching about a rat the other day," Henry said. "It must have got ashore in a boat—I don't think this country has any rats of its own."

"I don't, either, but I was waiting for that to happen," Edward said. "No rabbits here, either, or none I've seen, which is a pity, for I like rabbit pie and jugged hare. You can't keep rats and mice out of things. We brought cats, too, so there won't be *too* many vermin."

"I saw a cat with a lizard's tail in its mouth yesterday," Henry said.

"Yes, and they hunt the blackbirds that look like robins, too," Edward said. "Never worry about cats. They don't starve."

"I wasn't worrying," Henry said. "Next time we go back to England, though, maybe we could bring some rabbits over. They're good eating and good hunting."

"Well, maybe we could," Edward said.

# IV

Rabbits. More chickens and ducks. Two more sows, with their piglets. And Tom Cawthorne, a bowyer and fletcher, and his family. They all came back to Atlantis on the *St. George*. With the good hunting in the woods back of New Hastings, Edward was glad to get a man like Cawthorne. The bow- and arrow-maker probably wouldn't have come if his oldest son hadn't just got a girl with child. Dan Cawthorne didn't want to marry her, and so....

"If you didn't want to marry her, why did you sleep with her?" Edward asked the youth—he was seventeen or so—once they got out to sea.

Dan looked at him as if he were not only crazy but ancient. "Why? Because she wanted me to," he answered. By the way he said it, only a fool could imagine any other reason. "We didn't think anything would happen. Don't you remember what it's like to—?" He broke off, not quite soon enough.

*To have a stiff yard all the time.* That was what he'd been about to say, that or something a lot like it. And Edward did remember. His yard still worked well enough, but it wasn't stiff all the time, the way it had been when he was seventeen. He sighed. One of these days, Dan would get older, too. Edward tried again: "Well, if you like lying with her so much, why wouldn't you wed her?"

The bowyer and fletcher's son sent him another *you idiot* look. "Don't you know Judy Martin at all, Master Radcliffe?" he said. "As soon as she puts her clothes back on, she starts talking, and you'd have to hit her to make her shut up. I'm not even sure that would work."

Edward paid little attention to how much sixteen-year-old girls talked—these days, anyhow. There had been a time when he could have gone into great detail on the subject, but that was thirty years gone for him. He laughed and shook his head, wondering why he was worrying about this anyhow. If anything, Dan Cawthorne had done him a favor. If Dan hadn't got Judy Martin in trouble, Tom Cawthorne wouldn't have wanted to leave Hastings for an unknown shore.

Right now, the shore was unknown to Edward, too. Anything could have happened while he made the long round trip to England. Plague might have broken out. There might have been natives in the new country after all, despite the signs to the contrary. Or Bretons or Galicians or Basques might have happened upon New Hastings. Maybe, if they had, they would have stayed friendly and traded. Then again, maybe not.

His eye went to one of the two swivel guns the *St. George* now mounted. She wasn't a warship. She was nothing like a warship, which would have had high castles fore and aft packed with archers. But she could fight a little now if she had to. Against what she was likely to meet in Atlantean waters, that would do.

The ocean was rougher this time out than it had been on the first journey to settle the new land. The wind was more contrary, too, so the fishing boat stayed at sea more than a week longer before it came to Atlantis. The Cawthornes went greener and greener. Dan's bravado evaporated. At one point, clutching the rail, he moaned, "I wish I would've stayed and listened to Judy the rest of my days!"

"You'll change your mind once we get ashore," Edward told him.

Dan Cawthorne managed a feeble glare. "Why aren't you puking your guts out, too?" he asked. Then, as if talking about it reminded him of it—which it could do for some people—he gulped and bent over and started to retch.

"This isn't a bad blow," Edward said. "You should see a real storm, if you think this is something."

Dan took his right hand off the rail just long enough to cross himself. His left kept its death grip. "God spare me that!" he choked out, and spat something disgusting into the green, boiling water.

When the fishing cog finally reached the banks off the coast of Atlantis, Edward and the rest of the crew started pulling big cod out of the sea. Dan and Tom watched in fascination. The Cawthorne women—and even Dan's little brother, who couldn't have been more than eight—seemed more horrified. "How can you do that to the poor fish?" Tom's wife cried as Radcliffe gutted a fat four-foot cod.

"Well, Mistress Louisa, we'd go hungry if I didn't." Edward kicked the offal towards one of the sows, which fed greedily. "Don't you ever kill any of your own meat?"

Louisa Cawthorne gave a reluctant nod. "I do, and I cry every time I wring a pullet's neck."

She was a tender-hearted creature, then. She was tender in other ways, too. Sailing with a woman aboard when your wife wasn't proved an unexpected strain. Edward kept his hands to himself, but his dreams were warmer than the ones he usually had at sea.

He breathed a sigh of relief when they sighted land at last. He didn't see New Hastings, or the smoke rising from its fires. That didn't surprise him; he hadn't seen any English fishing boats—or any others—bobbing in the ocean. Navigation was anything but exact; Edward wasn't even sure whether he was north or south of the new settlement.

He shot the sun with his cross-staff. Then he did it again, and then once more. If he weighed all three measurements together and gave a little something extra to the one he trusted most, he thought the *St. George* lay south of where she should have been. Most of the fishermen agreed with him. Nobody was positive, though. One of the men said, "Well, we'll go north and see what happens. If we don't like it in the end, we can bloody well turn around."

Edward nodded. That sounded about right to him. And that very afternoon, a fisherman shouted, "Sail ho!"

If she was an English cog, everything would be fine. If she wasn't . . . Edward ordered the swivel guns loaded with scrap iron. If you got ready for a fight, sometimes you could stay away from one.

The lines of that cog did look familiar. Edward Radcliffe squinted north. Where had he seen her before? He cursed. "Bugger me blind if that's not the *Morzen*!"

Sure enough, the hail that came was in Breton: "Ahoy, the *St. George*! Is that you, Moses?" Yes, that was François Kersauzon's voice, all right.

"Moses?" Edward shouted back. "What are you talking about, you blasphemous toad?"

"You mistake me for your mother," Kersauzon said sweetly. "And is it not that you have led your people to the Promised Land? I saw your new town, and all the cogs in the sea close by. You've done well, Edward, well enough to make me jealous."

They were closing fast on each other. Radcliffe looked to his guns. If he opened fire now, maybe he could cripple the *Morzen* and finish her off at his leisure. He didn't want anyone jealous of New Hastings. If François Kersauzon didn't come home to Le Croisic, wouldn't that make other Bretons less likely to sail far into the west? The temptation!

But Kersauzon hadn't done anything to him, or, from what Edward gathered, to New Hastings. He'd done Edward a favor, in fact, by leading him to Atlantis. Yes, he'd profited from it, but he'd deserved to. If Edward returned evil for that great good, wouldn't he pay in the next world, pay for all eternity? He crossed himself. He was a believing man. He didn't want to imperil his soul.

And so he waved to the west, to the waiting Atlantean shore. "It's a broad land, François," he said. "Room for Englishmen and Bretons—and Frenchmen and Basques, too, I shouldn't wonder."

"It could be that we'll end up neighbors here one day, then," Kersauzon replied. "I always thought Englishmen were better at a distance, but what can you do?" His comic shrug was very French. He would have got furious had Edward told him so.

Instead, Radcliffe made sure he really was south of the English settlement. Kersauzon didn't mock him for asking. Where dead reckoning left off at sea and prayer began was a question every sailor had to face now and then. The two cogs parted with fishermen on each calling, "Good luck!" to the other.

Henry came back to Edward as he steered the *St. George* toward New Hastings. Quietly, the young man said, "I wondered if you'd fight him."

Edward Radcliffe sighed. "I wondered the same thing. But how could I? We wouldn't be here if not for him."

His son sighed, too. "Well, Father, it's not that you're

wrong. I only pray you won't spend the rest of your life sorry for being right."

"God forbid it!" Edward said, and crossed himself again.

New Hastings thrived. How could it do anything else, set on fertile soil with the closest enemies an ocean away? Swarms of fish came out of the sea. Crops and livestock burgeoned. Hogs and rabbits got loose in the wild, but no one had imagined that they wouldn't.

Not many years went by before honkers grew scarce around the settlement. People complained that they had to walk a day or two to find the big flightless birds and kill them. The birds couldn't seem to figure out that these strange two-legged creatures were a menace to them.

Red-crested eagles grew scarcer, too, though not fast enough to suit Edward Radcliffe. The eagles killed a child and a woman, and seemed especially fond of the fat above the kidneys of sheep. Shooting them while they attacked was hopeless.

Shooting them while they perched, on the other hand . . . The great fierce birds often sat in trees on the edges of the woods so they could spot honkers grazing in the fields and meadows beyond. The eagles did see humans as prey, but didn't seem to see them as threats. Archers could get close to the trees and let fly.

After a while, the eagles around the settlement thinned out. Mothers still watched their small children more carefully than they would have back in England, for the danger from the sky was diminished, not gone.

When Edward Radcliffe sailed the *St. George* back to England again, six years after he first set eyes on Atlantis, he found the country fallen into the civil war everyone had dreaded so long. The port officials at Hastings roughly demanded whether he favored the White Rose or the Red. Finding they were loyal to the House of York, he declared for the White Rose himself, though in truth he couldn't have cared less whether the king was Yorkist or Lancastrian.

He didn't need long to find that most of the people in Hastings felt the same way he did. Who ruled hardly mattered to them. All they cared about was that someone should rule and bring the land peace. As usual, the lords who fought were profoundly indifferent to what the people wanted.

Edward wasn't. The trouble in England made people in Hastings who'd laughed at him on his last visit suddenly eager to find quiet across the ocean. "Marry, it'd be wonderful to go about my business without worrying about soldiers stealing my stock or burning down my shop," a leatherworker said.

"They wouldn't do that in New Hastings," Radcliffe said. "There are no soldiers in New Hastings."

"No soldiers!" The other man might have had a vision of a miracle. "Isn't that a fine thing!" He paused, scratching his poorly shaved chin. "D'you need a man who makes leather?"

"Well, we might," Edward replied.

"I'd pay," the artisan said. "By God, I'd pay plenty to get away from these swaggering thieves in chainmail. I have a daughter who's fifteen, and I'd pay even more to get her away from them."

"I understand that," Radcliffe said. If his womenfolk were here now, he would have wanted to get them away, too. He rubbed *his* chin. Getting money for taking new settlers across the ocean hadn't occurred to him till now. He wondered why not. "We'll see what we can do for you, friend."

"I am your friend—your friend for life—if you take me away from this," the leather maker said.

Radcliffe knew not to count on that too much. Gratitude went bad almost as fast as fish did. But it might last to the other side of the sea. "Let's talk," he said, and so they did.

The leather maker wasn't the only one who spent silver for his passage. That proved just as well, because Edward had to pay a fat bribe to take the *St. George* out of the harbor. Even then, he left under cover of darkness. But he did leave, and once he was at sea he didn't worry about anybody catching him.

Once they'd put Land's End behind them, Henry came over to him and said, "I wonder how long it will be before ships full of people we never heard of start dropping anchor right offshore."

"How would they know where to go?" Edward asked, automatically setting himself against the rolling and pitching of the cog in the Atlantic's long, tall swells.

His son laughed at him—one of the less endearing things a son can do to his father. "Word has to be all over the Cinque Ports by now—likely all up and down the coast," Henry answered. "Load what you hope is enough food into a cog, sail west and a bit south till you think you're going to fall off the edge of the world, and what do you know? You end up in Atlantis!"

"What do you know?" Edward Radcliffe echoed in distinctly hollow tones. It wasn't that Henry was wrong. No, it was that he was much too likely to be right. If you had the nerve to sail the open sea, you could come to Atlantis. And if you were sure Atlantis was there, if you were sure you wouldn't fall off the edge of the world, wouldn't that help you find the nerve to set sail? Edward clapped a hand to his forehead. "All the riffraff of the kingdom, landing in our laps!"

That wasn't fair. Riffraff wouldn't be able to sail a cog so far, or to afford passage in one. But just then, anyone he hadn't handpicked to come to New Hastings seemed like riffraff to him.

And Henry, damn him, was grinning. "Not just our riffraff, either," the younger Radcliffe said. "Somewhere between Atlantis and Le Croisic, François Kersauzon and his son are talking the same way—what do you want to bet? The land is there. More and more people know it's there. A land with no kings, a land with no soldiers . . . Why *wouldn't* half the folk in the world want to pack up and move to a place like that?"

When Edward looked at it that way, he could see no reason why lots of people wouldn't want to travel to Atlantis, either. But he said, "I'll tell you one thing, son. If Atlantis *does* start filling up, it will need soldiers soon enough, to keep some folk from taking what others have."

"No doubt," Henry said. "Then the soldiers will start taking on their own, because that's what soldiers do."

"I know," Edward said unhappily. He sighed. "And I suppose that's why we need kings—to keep soldiers from taking too much."

"Well, sometimes kings can do that," Henry said. "And sometimes . . ."

He didn't go on, or need to. The war in England they'd barely escaped did most of his talking for him. "God grant that civil war stay far from Atlantis' shores," Edward said.

"I'm sure He will—for a while," his son replied. "How many of the folk in New Hastings stand with the White Rose, how many with the Red?"

"I have no idea. I never tried to find out," Edward Radcliffe said.

"As long as you can say that, and say it truly, we're safe from civil strife," Henry said. "As soon as you know, as soon as you *need* to know . . ."

"Yes." Edward could gauge the political winds along with those of the world. "May that day stay far away, too." His son—both sons—had bumped heads with him

a great many times growing up. But Henry, having at last
attained manhood himself, only nodded now.

The War of the Roses did stay away from the western
shores. Neither Yorkists nor Lancastrians cared who
followed their emblem in the lands across the sea. Not
enough people dwelt there to matter to either side.

Yes, the war stayed away. But flotsam and jetsam
from it did mark Atlantis. As Henry had foretold, a
good many Englishmen thought a land without soldiers
and without kings sounded wonderful. They swarmed
aboard anything that would float and sailed west.

Some of them, no doubt, starved before they got
anywhere close to Atlantis. It was a long journey
across rough seas. If the winds went against you, if you
crammed too many people aboard for the food you carried, if you couldn't pull in enough fish to make up for
your dwindling store of biscuit, if your water butts went
dry or got too foul to drink before you sighted land—if
any of those things happened, you were doomed.

The fishermen who sailed out of New Hastings didn't
see the worst disasters. They saw the folk who planned
better, but not quite well enough. Every so often, a shipload of living skeletons would come ashore. Caring for
them strained what the settlers could do. The land was
rich; hunting and fishing were good. But what would
have been plenty for a small village proved a good deal
less than that with more mouths to feed.

Edward Radcliffe was almost relieved when a well-
equipped flotilla from Dover founded a new town eighty
miles down the coast from New Hastings. They called
the place Freetown, though some of the people who set
it up seemed more interested in running things than he
ever had.

But, as he said when he came back from a visit, "The
more, the merrier. The land can hold them, and once

they get in a couple of crops they'll be able to help us with the rest of the newcomers, the ones who have no notion of what they're doing."

"Will they help, or will they just turn them away?" Henry asked.

"They'd better not." Edward's hands folded into fists. "If they try to leave us with all those folk ... Well, we won't have it, that's all. But if they're proper Christian men, they'll remember the parable of the Good Samaritan."

"And if they aren't, we'll remind them of it, by God," Henry said. Edward nodded.

Richard Radcliffe seemed discontented in a different way. He hadn't gone to Freetown. He hadn't gone back to England with his father and older brother, either. When he wasn't working his farm, he spent a lot of time staring west. "How far does Atlantis run?" he asked one winter's day. "What's on the other side of the mountains we can see?"

"Plenty close to the sea to keep us busy for a while," answered the relentlessly pragmatic Edward. "One of these days, I expect we'll find out what's over yonder, but where's the hurry?"

Richard might not have heard him. "I'd like to head up the Brede," he said: they'd named the closest stream for one that ran not far from the town where they were all born. "Who knows what lies in the forests? We could float trees down to New Hastings. . . ."

"We?" Edward said.

"I'm not the only one," Richard replied. "So much land for the taking. I feel—fenced in here."

"How did you stand it aboard the *St. George*?" asked Edward, who knew his younger son hadn't always had an easy time on the fishing boat.

Richard shrugged. "What choice had I? I couldn't start a farm in England—the land was all taken. If I lived in town, I'd be cramped, too. So I tried to keep my mouth shut and do what needed doing. But here I have choices, and I aim to make the most of them."

"Well, I don't know how I can hold you back if you're bound and determined to go," Edward said. "Go on, then, and God bless you—and yes, we'll be able to use the timber, for houses and for boats."

Eight or ten families went up the Brede with Richard and his wife and children. Edward watched them lead their livestock along the riverbank with a curious mixture of pride and fear. He didn't know what could go wrong with them in the woods, but he worried all the same. If anything did, they would be too far away for the folk remaining in New Hastings to help them in a hurry.

And they hadn't been gone more than a couple of weeks when a boat came up from Freetown. The Dovermen were in high dudgeon. "Do you know what?" one of them said in portentous tones.

"Not yet," Edward answered, "but since I think you're about to tell me, I will pretty soon. What's your news?"

"There's a town full of God-cursed Frenchmen down the coast from us!" the Freetown man cried.

"Frenchmen, you say? Or is it Bretons?" Edward asked.

"By Our Lady, it only matters to them!" the man from Freetown said.

"Is that François Kersauzon's settlement?" Radcliffe persisted.

The fellow who'd been talking just shrugged. One of the other new settlers nodded. "That was their leader's name, yes," he said. "They all speak French with a funny accent, the ones who speak it at all, but I could follow that much."

"I have no quarrel with Kersauzon. No one here does," Edward said. "He was the one who showed us the way to this land. We owe him a debt, if anything." Several people standing close by him nodded.

That wasn't what the men from Freetown wanted to hear. "Atlantis should be English! Atlantis *must* be English!" howled the one who liked to hear himself talk. "We ought to chase those French scuts back across the sea with their tails between their legs!"

"Do you think they'd stay chased?" Edward inquired. "Would you?"

"I'd kill the French dog who tried to make me leave!" the Freetown man blustered. "And if I did go, I'd come back with a fighting tail and make the knaves sorry they ever troubled me to begin with."

Radcliffe sighed. Some men were impressively blind. "Why d'you think Kersauzon's one pin different? If you tell him to go, he'll spit in your eye. If you somehow make him leave, he'll come back with soldiers himself. Do you want to farm and fish here, or do you want to fight?"

The question sounded sardonic, but he meant it. Some men did fight for the sport of it. He'd never understood that himself, but he knew it was so. To him, life was hard enough without making it harder still. Others, though, used brawls to spice up their days the way cooks used cinnamon and cloves and pepper to spice meats.

"I ought to let the king know he has such spineless subjects here," the Freetown man grumbled.

"If you do, I will hunt you down and kill you," Edward said matter-of-factly, as if he'd remarked, *The sun will come up tomorrow.* "And now you have quite worn out your welcome. Get out. If you fight Kersauzon, who is my friend, you may expect to fight me, too. I tell you that now, so you cannot say I will have taken you by surprise, and I aim to tell him the same as soon as may be."

"You won't get away with this, Radcliffe," the man from the new settlement said.

With a shrug, Edward answered, "I'm not trying to get away with anything. Only a blind idiot would think any different. Since you do, you have named yourself."

Muttering, their fists clenched, the Dovermen got into their boat and went south toward Freetown. "What do we do now?" Henry asked. "They won't let it lie—they aren't the sort who could."

"I know." Edward sighed. "We always find a serpent in Paradise, even if we have to bring it with us. We'll need a watch, to see that the Freetown men don't seek to serve us and the Bretons the same way. We'll need to hold the *St. George* between here and Freetown for a while—I am glad I got those guns. And we really will need to warn François Kersauzon."

"Which may provoke the Freetown men enough to make them complain of us back in England," Henry said.

"Let them bellow and bawl like branded calves, for all I care," Edward answered. "Will King Henry send knights here to make us behave when civil war's aflame back home? Give me leave to doubt, son—give me leave to doubt."

"What would you do if he should send knights?" Henry asked.

"Well, it depends on how many," Edward said. "A few? Our longbowmen can deal with a few knights, be-shrew me if they can't. An army of 'em? An army of 'em would tell me he's gone quite mad. But if he does send so many—if he can send so many—why then going up the Brede with Richard looks better and better. We can live off the land. Can knights newly come here do the same? I would rejoice to see them try."

"Something to that, I shouldn't wonder," his son said. "I will thank the Lord, though, if we don't have to put it to the test."

"So will I." Edward nodded. "Yes, by God, so will I."

\*       \*       \*

Edward Radcliffe took an unarmed cog well out to sea before sailing south. He didn't want any of the Dovermen's fishing boats spotting him. His ploy worked: the first boat he saw was the Breton *Amzer Gaer*—the *Fairweather,* she would have been in English. When he hailed her, her skipper thought he was a Freetown man and made ready to fight.

"No, God butter you and the Devil futter you!" Edward shouted in Breton. "I'm Kersauzon's friend—can't you get that through your bloody thick head? Take me to him. I have news he must hear."

"Why should we believe a lying Saoz?" the Breton yelled back.

"If you don't know who Edward Radcliffe is, you son of a dog, I'll board your scow myself and pound some sense through your hard skull."

The Breton fisherman was bigger and younger than he was, but backed down before his fierce temper. "Why didn't you say you were Radcliffe? That's not your *St. George.* Yes, I'll listen to you—for a while, anyway."

"Thank you so much," Edward said with a mocking bow. "But I don't want to talk to you. I want to talk to Kersauzon—I know he doesn't keep his brains in his backside. Where have you hidden this new town of yours?"

"Cosquer lies south-southwest of here. You'll know it by the big rock offshore," the Breton answered.

The name made Radcliffe smile: it meant Old Village. Only the Bretons would use that kind of name for a place on a barely explored shore. "Obliged to you. God give you a good catch." He could be polite enough—after he got what he wanted.

"And you the same, Saoz *gast,*" the other man shouted. Edward laughed as he swung his cog on the new course. How many times had the Bretons called him an English whore? Not enough to make him believe he was one, anyhow.

The rock in front of Cosquer was almost big enough to make a small island. Several of the strange Atlantean almost-trees with barrel trunks and leaves sprouting from the tops of them clung to its side. As for the village itself . . . Edward laughed again when it came into sight. Here was a bit of Brittany transplanted to a far land, all right. The thatched roofs had a steeper pitch than they would have in Hastings. The windows were different, too, even if the houses were built from wood rather than stone.

Henry was thinking along with him. "Only thing missing is a circle of standing stones in a meadow by the town," he said.

"By God, you're right," Edward said. "Damned if I'd be surprised if the stubborn buggers didn't put some up to remind 'em of home." He pointed. "Isn't that the *Morzen* lying right offshore?"

"Sure looks like her." Henry eyed François Kersauzon's cog. "She didn't carry those swivel guns last time we saw her."

"You're right—she didn't." Edward frowned. Those guns were longer and would probably shoot farther than the ones aboard the *St. George*. "If Kersauzon wasn't thinking along those lines before he saw us last, maybe we gave him the idea."

Half a dozen men pushed a boat into the Atlantic and rowed out toward the cog. "Ahoy, Englishmen!" Yes, that was Kersauzon's bellow, made louder by the hands he cupped in front of his mouth. "Is it you, Radcliffe?"

"No. It's your mother-in-law, come from Brittany to nag you," Edward answered.

"Anything but that!" François Kersauzon cried in mock terror. "Come ashore if you care to, and see what you have to nag about."

"I'll do that, and gladly, but first let me say my say—the Freetown men are not your friends."

Kersauzon clapped a hand over his heart. "I am shocked to hear it," he said, which made Edward and Henry both chuckle. More seriously, the Breton continued, "And you say you are?"

"Against them? Yes, by God!" Edward said. "I told them the same, too."

"You had better come ashore, then!" the Breton fishing captain said. Even across a broad gap of ocean, Edward could see how wide his eyes got. "Yes, you had better come ashore, because we have much to talk about."

"Let's get our boat in the water," Edward called to his crew. To his son, he said, "Would you rather come and dicker with me or stay here and do whatever you have to do in case there's trouble?"

"Do you need me to help put something over on the Bretons?" Henry answered his own question: "No, of course you don't. You can diddle them slick as grease all by yourself."

"I thank you for your trust in me," Edward Radcliffe said dryly.

He didn't faze Henry a bit. "Any time," the younger man replied. "We won't have trouble at sea from Kersauzon's people, either. Right now, after what you just said, they'd pick you for Pope if they had the chance. But if the Dovermen decide to raid Cosquer today ... I'd better stay here."

"All right." The fishermen Edward chose to row him to Kersauzon's new village all spoke some Breton, or at least some French. They'd be able to make themselves understood once they made it to dry land—and maybe they would hear something the settlers didn't want them to.

Kersauzon waved when he saw the English boat

heading toward his. A little to Edward's surprise, the
Breton's rowers didn't make a race of it. They went back
to shore sedately instead. A couple of the English fishermen sent Edward questioning looks, but he shook his
head. Why push things? They'd get there soon enough
any which way. And besides . . .

"Warmer here than it is in New Hastings," he called
to Kersauzon. It was warm enough, in fact, to make the
sweat stand out on his face, and unpleasantly sticky,
too.

Unpleasantly for him, at least. François Kersauzon
made a joke of it: "You are from the north, so you settle
in the north, and you think chilblains are every man's
God-given right—is it not so?"

"We like the weather we're used to," Edward said,
and left it at that. The boat's keel grated on hard sand.
He hopped out and helped haul it farther up the beach.
Kersauzon and his men were doing the same with theirs.
Edward pointed to the land they'd cleared in back of
Cosquer. "Are those vines you've planted there?" he
asked.

"What else would they be?" the Breton replied.
"Beer is all very well—I have nothing against beer. Who
could? But I want wine, too. And I'll have it . . . soon.
Not yet, mind you, but soon. Maybe we can trade this
for that, eh?"

"Maybe we can," Edward agreed. "My other son—
not Henry, who's with me, but Richard—is starting a
new settlement deep in the woods. Before long, we may
have more lumber than we can use ourselves. And who
knows what else we'll find once we look around a bit?"

"Who indeed? You're ahead of us. I think even
Freetown"—Kersauzon pronounced the name as if it
tasted bad in his mouth—"is a year ahead of us. But do
you say the Dovermen want a war with us?"

"They're sure thinking about it. They're thinking

hard, I'd say," Edward answered. "I told them to their faces I'd sooner stand with you if they start a fight. They didn't care to hear that, but I told them anyway."

"You are a gentleman." François Kersauzon bowed, as if to a nobleman in his own country. "It could be that Cosquer and New Hastings should band together and take this Freetown pesthole off the map before more trouble comes from it."

Radcliffe had wondered whether the Breton would say that. Not without some regret, he shook his head. "No, I don't want to. There's enough fighting across the sea—why bring more here? That's the other thing you need to know: if you strike first at Freetown, New Hastings will stand with her, too."

Kersauzon scowled at him. Some of the other Bretons swore. One or two of them ostentatiously turned their backs. Their leader asked, "Who appointed you the man to say who may war and who may not?"

"I say nothing of the kind," Edward answered. "I only say what will happen if a war does start."

"And if Cosquer and Freetown move against New Hastings together?"

"Good luck," Radcliffe said. "Watch your back—you'll need to."

Kersauzon stared at him, then started to laugh. "Well, when you're right, Saoz *gast,* you're right. But how long do you think you'll be able to keep the peace all by yourself?"

"I don't know. As long as I can." Edward sighed. "Sooner or later, something will go wrong. We aren't in Eden, so it has to. We're closer to Eden here than we were back home, though. I feel that in my bones. So maybe—I hope—it will be later, not sooner."

# V

An axe on his shoulder like a soldier's spear, Richard Radcliffe strode through the woods of Atlantis. No man had ever seen what he was seeing now; the only tracks in the soft, damp earth were the big, deep three-toed ones that belonged to honkers and other, smaller, bird prints.

The air smelled spicy. It smelled *green,* Richard thought. It made you wish you could fill a bottle with the scent and take it back with you. Wherever people lived for a while, things started to stink. Smoke and manure and slops and unwashed bodies ... Getting away was a relief to the nose.

Moss and ferns grew between the curious barrel trees and the pines that rose above them and the enormous trees—redwoods, the Bretons'd named them—that towered over the pines. Some of those redwoods seemed a bowshot tall. No way to be sure just how immense they were till you felled one and measured it. Since the monsters were as thick through the base as three or four men were tall, that wouldn't happen right away.

Something stared out at Richard from behind a barrel tree. He stood still and waited. His father was right: the creatures here had no natural fear of man. After a moment, this one came out and walked along with a rolling motion that brought a smile to his face.

"Oil thrush," he murmured. Not since Adam and Eve had people needed names for so many new creatures. The birds and lizards and snakes of the new land were for the most part unlike any the settlers had seen back in England. Oh, ravens croaked from tree branches and sometimes harried hawks and eagles. Barn owls glided ghostly through the night. Fork-tailed swallows dipped and darted after flying insects. They were all familiar enough. And the red-breasted thrush that acted and sounded like a blackbird was easy to get used to. But the oil thrush . . .

It had the shape of one of those red-breasted thrushes. (Some people were calling them robins, though they were bigger and less vivid than the redbreasts back home.) It had the shape, yes, but it was the size of a chicken, or even larger. Its legs were long and strong, its wings too stunted to lift it into the air. And its beak . . .

Richard smiled. It was as if someone had made a thrush out of clay and pulled and stretched the beak till it could go no farther. It was more than half as long as the oil thrush's body. A beak like that might have made a formidable weapon, except that the bird didn't seem to realize it could use its beak so. The oil thrush stared at Richard with a beady black eye, its head cocked to one side.

When he just quietly stood there, the bird peered down at the ground instead. Suddenly, that long, strong beak stabbed into the dirt. When the oil thrush pulled its beak out, a plump earthworm wriggled between the mandibles. A twist of the bird's head, and the worm disappeared.

On waddled the oil thrush. Six or eight feet farther along the trail, it paused again. Was it listening? Sniffing? Richard had no idea. But its beak thrust down again, and came forth with another worm. This one tried to wrap itself around the bird's beak to keep from getting swallowed, but to no avail.

Richard followed the flightless thrush. It looked back at him, as if to say that was an unusual thing for anyone to do, but then kept walking. It didn't seem to take alarm when he bent down and picked up a fist-sized stone. The gray rock was cool against his palm; little bits of mud and moss clung to his fingers.

He was only a few feet from the oil thrush when he let fly. The stone knocked the bird over. A startled squawk burst from its throat as a puff of feathers floated up into the air. Richard finished it off with the axe.

As always when he hunted here, he felt a little guilty. It was like playing draughts against an idiot child—of course you were going to win. But he was hungry, and one thing the settlers had found was that the oil thrush made tasty eating.

He bled and butchered the bird, keeping the liver and heart and gizzard to toast over the fire when he buried the rest of the offal. A layer of golden fat under the skin led the settlers to give the oil thrush its name. Back at New Hastings and Bredestown, they rendered the fat over a slow fire and used it in lamps and in cooking and for grease. Richard didn't have time for that. As he cooked the bird, some of the fat melted and dripped down into the flames. The rest he ate with the dark, flavorsome flesh. The taste reminded him of woodcock, perhaps because both birds lived mostly on worms.

Several different kinds of mushrooms grew close by the fire. They looked good. He knew a couple of kinds were safe, so he ate of them. The ones he wasn't sure of, he left alone. He didn't need to take chances on them, not when the hunting was so good.

And he could roll himself in a blanket and sleep by

the fire with very little fear. No wolves and no bears here to harry a lone man. He did get a surprise the next morning, when he found a snake curled up not far from him. It slithered in amongst the ferns and disappeared before he could grab a rock or a stick to smash it.

Some snakes here, the settlers had found, were more deadly than any vipers back in England. English poisonous snakes were the size of a man's arm. The ones here could be as long as a man was tall. They had bigger fangs and delivered more venom.

He ate the rest of the oil thrush and pressed on. Every so often, he paused to blaze one of the smaller trees. The marks would help him find his way home again. Meanwhile ... Meanwhile, he had Atlantis all around him, and it was wonderful.

When he sailed on the *St. George,* he would sometimes stand at the bow and look out over the sea. The broad sky and the endless, ever-changing wavescape let him almost forget for a while that he was cooped up aboard a fishing boat. When he smelled stale cod, the illusion of aloneness in immensity wavered. When he had to clamber into his hammock of an evening, it vanished altogether.

Here in Atlantis, it was no illusion. Fern and shrub and moss, pine and redwood and barrel tree, honker and oil thrush and red-crested eagle: he was alone among them, and no thinking being save God Himself had ever set eyes on them before.

The same held true for the serpents and the peculiar frogs and the big snails and the even bigger bugs. Well, almost the same: Richard was willing to believe the Devil had looked at them along with God.

He picked his way around a marsh. Dragonflies and darning needles of astonishing size and variety buzzed above the reeds and the stagnant water. A bird snatched one out of the air and flew over to a stump with it.

The bird bashed the dragonfly against the stump till it stopped struggling, then wiggled it around till it was in a good position to be swallowed. The dragonfly vanished. The bird's tail bobbed up and down. "*Phee-bee!*" it sang in a self-satisfied voice.

Turtles stared at Richard from the water. They didn't have domed shells like the pond turtles he was used to in England. They were flat as flapjacks, and as big around as the pan in which a woman might cook flapjacks. They had cold yellow eyes and jaws big enough and strong enough to bite off a finger. You could catch them with a hook like trout. They made good enough eating.

Near the edge of the marsh, a honker plucked up water plants with single-minded determination. It was of a variety different from the ones that raided the fields in New Hastings. It was a good deal smaller; Richard doubted its head would have come up much past his shoulder even if the bird raised it instead of leaning forward as it was doing. The ones near the coast could tower over a man if they did that. This one was a dull brown all over, darker on the back, lighter on the belly; it didn't have the black neck and white chin patch of the coastal honkers. And its feet had more web between the toes than the coastal birds' feet did.

When it honked, its voice was higher and lighter than those of the honkers by the coast. But it had one important similarity to them: it also didn't know it was supposed to be afraid of men. It kept right on feeding as Richard walked up to it.

He carried a stout bludgeon on his belt. The honker glanced at him, but it didn't even try to dodge when he clouted it. Down it went, kicking with the random thrashes any creature from fish to man might make when suddenly killed. Richard jumped back to make sure those flailing feet didn't catch him. They weren't aimed his way, which didn't mean they couldn't hurt him.

After the honker stopped twitching, he butchered it. Its heart was almost as big as his fist: big enough, with a chunk of liver, to make a meal. He cut off a big chunk of thigh meat to take with him when he traveled on. The rest of the carcass he left where it lay. Hawks and vultures and snakes and lizards were welcome to it. He could always find another honker or oil thrush to kill a little farther west.

As evening fell, frogs began to sing. They came in all sizes, from little peepers no longer than the last joint of his thumb up to baritone croakers large enough to make a cat think twice. Like so much in Atlantis, they were at the same time familiar and strange. Frogs in England sang with small inflated sacs on either side of their throats. Atlantean frogs, by contrast, had a single, larger throat sac under the chin.

The frogs' croaking couldn't mask another swamp sound: the buzz of mosquitoes. Atlantis had more of them than England did, and fiercer ones, too. Summer here got hotter and stickier than it did over there; maybe that had something to do with it. Richard put more wood on the fire, hoping the smoke would hold them at bay. No matter what he hoped, it didn't.

The bigger fire did let him see farther out into the night, though. Eyes glowed back at him. He wasn't frightened, as he would have been back in England. These eyes were all low to the ground and set close together. They belonged to frogs or lizards or snakes. No four-legged killers prowled Atlantis' wilds.

Darkness deepened. The chorus of frogs grew louder and more various. A pair of big frogs hopped straight at each other, both of them croaking as loud as they could. They were only a couple of feet apart when one broke and ran, vanishing into the night beyond the campfire's bright circle.

An owl hooted. The note was different from the ones

English owls used, but unmistakable all the same. Then Richard saw a moving light that wasn't paired. "Glow-worm!" he said in delight. Some people called them fire-flies. England had only a few. In summer, they made the air itself here seem to dance.

Something else also scooted through the night air, from left to right. It was bigger than a mosquito, bigger than a glow-worm, and it didn't dance in the air the way bugs did. The motion was straight and not too swift. Richard scratched his head. That straight track also meant it was no bat or nightjar come to feed on the in-sects drawn to his campfire.

He scratched his head again. In that case, what was it? Had he seen only one such strange scoot, he would have shrugged and gone back to eating toasted honker liver. He even had coarse sea salt to scatter on his sup-per. After he finished, he intended to swaddle himself in his blanket so that, if the mosquitoes wanted him, they would have to find the tip of his nose.

Then he spotted another of those curious fliers, and then another. They all came from the left and vanished to the right. "What the—?" he said, climbing to his feet. Atlantis was full of surprises. He seemed to have run into another one, one that made his curiosity itch.

He walked out about as far from the fire as he thought the things were flying. *As like as not,* he thought, *I'll scare them away.* He shrugged. If he did, he would go back to the honker liver, that was all.

But he didn't. One of them, whatever it was, scooted right past in front of his face. Startled, he grabbed for it, but he missed. Another one went by. He missed that one, too, and swore. The trouble was, he could see them only when they came close to the fire. That didn't give him much time to catch them.

It would have to be luck, then. If they kept coming, he was bound to snag one sooner or later . . . wasn't he?

After five or six fruitless lunges, he started to wonder. Then he did catch one. The cool, moist smack against the palm of his hand made him wonder whether he was glad to have it even as his fingers closed.

"What have I got?" he said out loud. He turned so that firelight would help him, and opened his hand.

A little frog, green with streaks of yellow, stared up at him out of big black eyes. It looked like any other tree frog he'd ever seen—except for its hands and feet. The fingers and toes were ridiculously long, with webbing stretched between them. The frog had to use those webs to glide through the air the way a ship used sails to push it along.

Richard started to laugh. He set the frog down on the ground. It hopped off into the darkness the way any other little frog might have. He wiped his hand against his trousers. "Atlantis!" he said. "You won't find another place where the birds don't fly and the frogs damn well do."

Laughing still, he went back to his supper.

These days, Edward Radcliffe's bones creaked when he got out of bed in the morning. Sometimes sitting by the fire for a while or going out into the warm sun would get him moving again, almost as freely as he had when he was younger. Sometimes he creaked and ached from dawn to dusk, and woke up aching if he had to ease himself in the night.

Hard to believe fifteen years had gone by since François Kersauzon talked him out of a third of his catch in exchange for a secret—hard to believe till he looked around, anyway. New Hastings was more than a village at the edge of unknown wilderness nowadays. It was well on the way to becoming a town. Farms and mills went up the river all the way to Bredestown, and beyond. Whenever Richard came back from a journey into the woods, he kept muttering that he would have to pull up stakes and move west again. Things were getting too crowded where he was.

Edward didn't think that would change, either. The War of the Roses went on and on in England. Once people had had their homes plundered and burnt, once men had been robbed and killed and women violated, the idea of getting on a ship and heading for a strange land across the sea no longer seemed so frightful. And so New Hastings swelled, as did Freetown; settlers founded other towns up and down the northern part of the east coast of Atlantis.

François Kersauzon's Cosquer also flourished. Two or three other Breton villages grew not far away from it. Edward had heard that there were Basque and Galician settlements in the southern regions of the new land, but he didn't know for a fact whether that was so. The Bretons came up to New Hastings to trade; most of them still wanted nothing to do with Freetown. No folk from the Spanish kingdoms had turned up here yet. Still, it had to be only a matter of time.

When Radcliffe looked west toward the mountains no man had yet visited—not so far as he knew, anyhow— what struck him was how much things had changed since he founded New Hastings. The dark forests of pine and redwood had been driven back for miles, replaced by farmlands and meadows and groves of apples and pears and plums that were still young but now starting to yield fruit.

"It's not so bad here now, is it, Nell?" he asked his wife.

"Not so bad as it was when we first came here, that's sure enough," she said. "And you got to go back to England, too. Me, I was stuck here all that time."

He frowned. "If you think all that sea voyaging was easy or fun . . . Well, you should have tried it yourself, is all I have to say."

Nell didn't back away from an argument—she never did. "We had to make do here when there wasn't enough to make do with. Before we had a blacksmith, breaking a tool was as bad as it could be, because we couldn't get another one, whatever it was. And the first houses were sorry affairs. Everyone who was here made a better shipwright than a proper carpenter."

"No danger of going hungry, though," Edward said, and Nell couldn't very well argue with that. Between the cod the fishermen pulled from the offshore banks and the big, foolish honkers, there was always plenty to keep a man's—or a woman's—belly full.

His wife did say, "I missed bread till the crops started coming in the way they should."

Edward only shrugged. When a fishing boat ran out of biscuit, men lived on what they could catch. He didn't much care what he ate, as long as he had plenty of it.

"You hardly see honkers any more, not here by the seaside," Nell remarked.

"Still plenty of them inland. They still make good eating. And as long as they come down into the fields to steal what we plant, what else are we going to do but kill them?" Edward said.

"Oh, I know. But the landscape seems so—so ordinary without them."

"I was thinking the same thing, or close enough." Edward smiled at his wife. If they didn't think the same way a lot of the time, they wouldn't have stayed as happily married as they had. "One of these days, it will be hard to tell Atlantis from England."

"No, it won't," Nell said at once. "In England, the nobles and the king's men can tell ordinary people what to do. They can take our money and use it to hire soldiers who steal from us. None of that foolishness here, by Our Lady."

"Not yet, anyhow," Edward said. "I wonder how long

it will be before some duke or earl fits out a ship with guns and comes across the ocean to try to tell us what to do."

"To try to squeeze money out of us, you mean," Nell said. "That's what it comes down to in the end."

"Well, so it is," Edward agreed. "I just thank heaven we haven't had a fight with Freetown and we haven't got into a brawl with the Bretons yet, either. Tell me that's not coming, too. Make me believe it."

"I wish I could," his wife said. "We didn't leave all our troubles behind when we came over here, did we?"

Radcliffe shook his head. "I wish we would have, but it's too much to ask for. We have more room here, so not all of them show up the way they did back home, but they aren't gone."

As if to prove his point, a lookout on the beach winded a horn. That meant a strange ship was nearing New Hastings. Edward hurried into his house and came out with an axe. He wasn't young and he wasn't spry, but he didn't need to be either to defend the home he'd built from nothing. He hurried down toward the muddy strand.

But it wasn't a strange ship approaching—it was Henry's cog, the *Rose*. She wasn't the *White Rose* or the *Red Rose*: simply the *Rose*. No one here saw any point to angering whichever side eventually won the civil war. She was made from Atlantean lumber; her sails were made from Atlantean wool. Danes and Norwegians used woolen sails. They were heavier and baggier than linen, but the flax crop here was just beginning to come in.

Unlike Richard, Henry didn't mind putting to sea in anything at all. Edward thought his older son had traveled farther up and down the coast of Atlantis than any other man alive.

This run, the *Rose* was coming up from the south. Henry proved that. When he came ashore, he had a strange bird on his shoulder: it was bright green, with a yellow head, a red face, and a large, hooked beak. It squawked shrilly, then said something in a language Edward recognized.

"That's Basque, by God!" he said. "What does it mean?"

"I don't know, but it'll start a fight in any tavern full of those one-eyebrowed buggers," Henry answered.

"Is the Devil teaching birds Basque now?" Edward asked. "Is he trying to make liars out of the people who say he can't learn it himself? Or did you find the settlement people have been talking about?"

"I found it. Gernika, they're calling it, after a place in their country," Henry said. "They picked a good spot for it, most ways. A river bigger than the Brede flows into the ocean there, and an island offshore makes the harbor as well shielded from bad weather as any I've ever known—it puts New Hastings and Cosquer to shame. But by Our Lady, Father, it's hot down there! The worst of summer here seems like nothing beside it. And sticky! Your clothes melt to your skin. You stink all the time if you don't bathe, or even if you do, and you come down with rashes and ringworms and I don't know what all else."

"Well, then, they're welcome to it," Edward said. "How can they make a living in country like that? Why would they want to settle there?"

"The land is rich—no way around that," his son replied. "You stick a seed in the ground and you have to jump back in a hurry or the growing plant will poke you in the eye. And the hunting is good, they said."

Edward Radcliffe raised an eyebrow. "They said that? Where did you learn Basque? From your bird?"

"Clarence here speaks more of it than I do, and that's the Lord's truth," Henry said. "But some of the Basques down there know enough French to get by, and I do, too. You speak better, but I can get along."

"All right. Gernika, is it?" Edward clucked to himself. "We do need to start mapping this coast. Too many different folk settling along it to manage without knowing who lives where. Building a new village too close to somebody else's holding is the easiest way I can think of to start a fight."

"I'm doing it as best I know how," Henry said. "I'm not the best chartmaker in the world, but anything here is better than nothing. We can know latitudes, anyway, and curves of the coast."

"Better than nothing, as you say." Edward paused, remembering what Henry had said a moment before. "What do you mean, the hunting is good there? What have they got that we don't?"

"Well, for one thing, they have snakes big enough to swallow a honker—plenty big enough to swallow a man," Henry answered. "And they've got these river lizards. . . . I don't know what else you'd call them. But they aren't lizards the way we have lizards in England, or even like the ones here—big as your arm. These are *lizards*—fifteen or twenty feet long, with big mouths full of big teeth. They eat turtles and honkers—and people, too, if you aren't careful down by the riverbank. Their hides make good leather. The Basques showed me some."

"They sound like . . . what's the name for the creatures in the Good Book?" Edward Radcliffe snapped his fingers in annoyance. "Dammit, I can't recall."

"Bishop John would know," Henry suggested.

"He would, yes." Edward didn't sound thrilled. "He knows almost everything. If you don't believe me, just ask him." Henry laughed, for all the world as if his father were joking.

But finding a name for those big river lizards kept bothering Edward. He and Henry went to the church at the center of New Hastings. It was only whitewashed redwood, but it was, as far as he knew, the finest in Atlantis. And Bishop John, paunchier and grayer than he had been when he set out from England all those years before, looked the very model of a prelate. The Radcliffes spelled out their problem for him.

"Those sound like crocodiles," John said gravely.

"Crocodiles!" Edward nodded. "That's what you call the things. I couldn't hook the name to save my life."

"You ever see one, Father, you'll remember what they are from then on," Henry said. "The Basques have their own word for them, too, but to me it sounds half like sneezing and half like spitting."

"Basques?" Bishop John asked. "I know you took the *Rose* south, Henry, but I don't know what you found—besides crocodiles, I mean." Henry told him, in less detail than he'd given his father: plenty of time for that later. The prelate heard him out, then said, "More and more folk flock to this shore. I thank God that we haven't yet brought our wars across the sea with us."

"I think *yet* is the word," Edward Radcliffe said. "I fear it's only a matter of time, though."

John crossed himself. "I shall pray you are mistaken."

"Oh, I pray for the same thing, your Grace," Radcliffe said. "But I want to be ready all the same, in case God doesn't feel like listening."

Henry's wife was a slim redhead named Bess. She clung to him outside the New Hastings church as if the *Rose* were another woman and not a ship at all. "Must you go away so soon?" she asked. "It seems you only just got home."

He kissed her, sensing that was some of what she wanted. It only made her cling tighter, though, and start to cry. "We have to learn what sort of land we have here," he said. "We have to know how big it is, how wide—"

"Do we have to find out right this minute?" Bess flared. "Do you have to do all the finding yourself?"

"It's not like that," Henry said. "Richard goes off into the woods for weeks at a time, and—"

"And it drives his wife wild." Bess seemed bound and determined not to let him finish a sentence. "Do you think Bertha and I don't talk about it? We have to talk to each other. Lord knows we don't get much chance to talk to the two of you."

"We need to explore," Henry said. "If we didn't—"

"If *you* didn't" —his wife poked him in the chest with a blunt-nailed forefinger, to make sure he understood that *you* was a singular—"you could settle down and farm and spend more time with me and your children. Would that be so dreadful?"

"You didn't fuss this much when I left Hastings on fishing runs," Henry said. "Sometimes I'd be gone longer then than I am on the trips I take these days."

His wife eyed him with a curious mix of exasperation and affection. "In those days, you had no choice. If you didn't help your father bring in the cod, we wouldn't eat. But now you don't *have* to go wandering. Neither does Richard. You do it anyway. Both of you do it anyway. It's not right. It's not fair." Her voice broke. More tears swam in her sea-green eyes.

Henry had never talked things over with his brother. He didn't know how they stood with Richard. He only knew for himself. "If I stayed on a farm all the time . . . It wouldn't be you, love." He wanted to make sure he said that, because it was the truth. "But if I stayed in the same place all the time, if I saw the same things around me all the time . . ." He shook his head. "Something inside of me would die. I'd be living in a cage."

"And the *Rose* isn't?" Bess crossed herself. "Mary, pity women!"

Richard thought a ship was a cage. But Richard also

had to think a farm was a cage. He'd proved that, again and again. So instead of putting to sea, he'd thrust deeper into the Atlantean wilderness than any man alive. Didn't it add up to, if not the same thing, then something not so very different?

Deeper into the wilderness than any man alive? Henry suddenly realized he couldn't be sure of that. Bound to be restless Bretons, restless Basques, even restless Dovermen ... Deeper into the wilderness than anyone who'd started from New Hastings, anyhow. That would do.

Bess shook her head. She said, "The *Rose*," under her breath in a tone not far from hatred. But then she went on, "What's the use? If I burnt that cursed scow to the waterline, you'd only go and build another one. And you'd enjoy doing it, too." By the way she said it, that was the worst crime of all.

And she wasn't even wrong. Henry had enjoyed building the *Rose*. If he had to craft another cog, he thought he could do a better job the next time. He kissed Bess again, not sure whether that would make things better or worse. He wasn't sure after he'd done it, either. He was sure of one thing, though: "I've got to go. I'll be back before too long."

"It will only seem like forever," Bess said bitterly.

He kissed her one more time. Some men who went to sea for weeks and months at a stretch worried about their wives being unfaithful while they were away. Some men who went to sea for weeks and months at a stretch had children that looked like their neighbors who stayed home. People mostly didn't talk about such things, which didn't mean they didn't happen.

Henry didn't worry about Bess. He knew he could count on her. And he didn't reward her for her fidelity by going into strange women when he came into a strange port ... not very often, anyhow. If he'd brought home the gleets and passed them on to her, she would have been even less happy with him than she was now.

"Come back to me, do you hear?" Bess said.

"I always have," Henry answered. "I always will." *I pray I always will.*

He walked out onto the beach, right up to the edge of the Atlantic, and waved out to the *Rose*. The mate waved back; the cog's boat went into the water. A couple of fishermen rowed it toward shore.

One of these days, the settlers would have to build jetties out into the ocean so cogs could tie up more conveniently. Either that or they would have to find a proper sheltered harbor instead of this bare stretch of coast open to wind and sky. If they did, New Hastings might wither away. Henry shrugged. Bess wouldn't like that, but to him one place on land wasn't much different from another. Like his father, he only felt at home with a rolling, pitching deck under his feet.

The boat's keel scraped sand and mud. "Hop in, skipper," one of the fishermen said.

"Bide a moment." Henry turned back to wave to Bess and blow her a kiss. She waved back. Both rowers snickered. They were bachelors. They didn't understand how a woman could get under a man's skin and into his heart. He hoped they would find wives for themselves one of these days. More men than women came to Atlantis, so it wasn't a sure bet.

He wondered whether that was so for the Bretons and the Basques. If they had more girls than men . . . well, wouldn't that make a strange sort of commerce among the new settlements? But, from what he'd seen farther south, it seemed more likely to be the same with them as it was here.

"Ready to fare north this time?" the other fisherman asked as they started back to the *Rose*.

"Damned if I'm not, Sam," Henry answered. "We

won't stew in our own juices sailing that way, anyhow. Only a couple of little settlements that anyone knows about north of New Hastings, too. Most of what we find will be new."

"That anyone knows about, yes," Sam said. "But who can guess whether there's a pirates' nest up there?"

"Not likely," Henry said. "We'd know if there were pirates, because they'd prey on us. We've lost a couple of boats since we came here, but nobody thinks it was on account of anything but bad weather and uncharted rocks. Plenty of both to go around, Lord knows."

"You're not wrong there," Sam admitted. "Still and all, though, what do we know about those other settlers? Maybe they fish part of the time and farm part of the time—aye, and steal part of the time, too, whenever they see the chance."

"Maybe they do," Henry said. Sam had a notion of what he was talking about. Henry couldn't swear he'd never turn pirate himself. If the chance for a big haul appeared out of nowhere, if he was sure he could get away with it and not start a feud that would hurt him and his for generations yet to come . . . Well, who could say what he'd do if something like that came along? The *Rose* carried swivel guns to ward off raiders, which didn't mean she couldn't turn raider herself.

He clambered up the nets stretched along her port side. Sam and Geoff—the other rower—came right behind him. The fishermen in the cog grabbed hold of their hands as they scrambled up over the gunwale and pulled them aboard. Then they brought in the boat, stowing it abaft the mast.

The mate was a broad-shouldered fellow named Bartholomew Smith. "Are we ready?" Henry asked him.

"Ready as we'll ever be," he answered. "Weighing anchor is all that wants doing—and then we find out what happens when we get colder instead of hotter."

"You're not old enough to remember fishing runs in the North Sea," Henry said. "Count your blessings that you're not. This could be something like that."

"Then why are we doing it?" Smith asked.

"If we don't, someone else will." For Henry, that was reason enough and more.

# VI

*O*cean. When you looked west from the *Rose*'s bow, there was nothing but ocean. *How far?* Henry Radcliffe wondered. All the way to Cathay? All the way to the edge of the world, where it spilled off in God's waterfall? All the way to some land as unimaginable as Atlantis had been when Henry was a young man?

He didn't know. How could he? He wanted to, hungered to, find out. But that was a voyage for another time, with another ship. The *Rose* was a fine coasting vessel, and the best job a gang of amateur shipwrights could have done when they hacked her out of timber. For striking out across the broad, stormy Atlantic to shores unknown? Well, no.

"Where now, skipper?" Bartholomew Smith asked.

Whenever Henry heard that, he started to look around to see where his father was. But Edward Radcliffe stayed behind in New Hastings. He still put to sea, to fish or to go down the coast to one of the other settlements. Heading off to nowhere for the fun of it, though, was beyond his old bones and creaking muscles.

Or maybe he just thought the *Rose* didn't have much

of a chance of coming back from nowhere. And maybe he was right. But if he was, he judged with an old man's sour wisdom. Henry hoped that kind of judgment passed him by. Yet if enough years piled onto him, it probably wouldn't.

"Where now?" he echoed. "West along the coast for a while, and we'll see what it does. If it goes straight, we do the same. If it tends south, we follow. If it tends north . . . well, we still follow, but I won't like it so well."

"Who would?" the mate replied. "Can't run all the way up to Iceland, though, or the squareheads would have found this country a long time ago."

Henry grunted. He hadn't thought of that, and he should have. "We won't go hungry, anyhow," he said. "Plenty of little fish to net out, and plenty of birds getting fat feeding on them."

Even as he spoke, a bright-billed puffin plunged into the sea and came out holding three or four sardines. Murres and auks and guillemots also preyed on the abundant fish. So did bigger birds that looked like auks but seemed unable to fly. They swam like small porpoises instead.

Smith must have been thinking of them, for he said, "Shame we can't render some of these birds down to oil, like the thrushes ashore. They'd yield tun after tun, Devil take me if they wouldn't."

"We ought to think about setting up a trying works here," Henry said. "Not just for the birds, but for the whales, too." He'd seen several of the big beasts blowing and breaching not far from the *Rose*. If one of them had risen right under her . . . There were all kinds of reasons why ships didn't come home.

"Far as the whales go, I'm surprised we didn't find the damned Basques up here ahead of us." Bartholomew Smith made some gabbling noises that were supposed to be Basque.

Henry laughed, even if the mate's imitation didn't sound much like the real thing. "They're whaling men, all right," he agreed. There were no more intrepid whalers than the Basques. They had their reasons, too. Like any other fish, whale meat was allowed during Lent and on Fridays. Henry himself was mighty fond of salted whale—*craspoix,* the French called it—and peas.

The big auklike birds were easy to catch. Like so many of Atlantis' creatures, they were ignorant of men. Some of the flying sea birds behaved the same way, but others were warier. Henry wondered what that meant. Did some of them stay in Atlantean waters all the time, while others flew to lands where men were liable to hunt them? Or were some simply stupider than others? A nice question, but one he had no idea how to answer.

Before the *Rose* got very far west at all, her progress slowed even though the wind remained favorable. The water through which she sailed changed color, too, turning lighter and bluer than it had been before. It was also noticeably warmer than the stretch of ocean from which they'd just come.

"Strong current," Henry remarked.

"Right strong," Smith agreed. "Seems to scoot along the shore here."

"It does. Might almost have been put here to make sure we don't get anywhere in a hurry," Henry said.

"You don't suppose—?" The mate sounded alarmed. Even by the standards of his age and trade, he was a superstitious man.

By the standards of his age and trade, Henry wasn't. "No, I don't think anything of the kind," he answered. "Old Scratch has better things to do than worry about the likes of us. Or I hope he does, anyhow." He crossed himself, on the off chance.

Bartholomew Smith did the same thing. "I hope so, too." His voice quavered a little.

Satan did seem busy elsewhere. Just as Henry hoped, the coast soon started tending southward. Strong breezes blew down from the north to push the *Rose* on her way. She didn't travel as fast as she might have, for the current coming up from the south fought against her, but she did travel.

And the warm current seemed to bring balmy weather with it as it came. They still lay far to the north of New Hastings, but the climate here in the west was far milder than it had been on Atlantis' eastern shore.

"I wonder what it's like here come winter," Henry said.

"Foggy, I warrant," Smith replied. "All this warm water striking cold air . . . Might make London look to its laurels."

"Have you ever seen London?" Henry asked.

The mate shook his head. "Why on earth would a Hastings fisherman want to go and see London? Have you, skipper?"

"No, never once," Henry admitted.

"Well, there you are," Bartholomew Smith said. "And I've been a *New* Hastings fisherman as long as you have, and I don't much want to go back across the sea any more, either. By God, I like it here."

"So do I. Any land where no lord can tell you what to do and you don't owe taxes to anybody . . . I like that fine," Henry said.

When they found a good-sized stream flowing into the ocean, they rowed the water butts ashore to refill them. A gaggle of honkers stared at them in mild curiosity, as if to say, *You're the strangest-looking birds we've ever seen.* They were the strangest-looking honkers Henry had ever seen. They were a pale gray, with orange feet and beaks. Their wings were bigger than those of any variety near New Hastings, though still utterly useless as far as getting them off the ground was concerned.

One of the honkers puffed up its chest and flapped its silly wings at another. "Honnnk!" it screeched. The other bird skittered away, as well as something as tall as a man and considerably heavier could skitter.

Getting the water butts back onto the boat once they were filled was slow, careful work. If you made a mistake, you could put one right through the bottom. Henry was calling out instructions when the rambunctious honker ambled up to him. Perhaps because he was making noise, it seemed to think him some kind of rival. It went through the same sort of display it had with the other honker, puffing itself up, flapping its wings, and making a noise like a badly played horn full of spit.

Henry straightened up. He was, he noted with satisfaction, a couple of inches taller than the orange-legged honker. He jumped up and down. He waved his arms. "Yaaah!" he yelled at the top of his lungs.

The honker started at him in bird-brained disbelief. Then, with a piglike grunt of dismay, it backpedaled, turned, and hastily retreated. The fishermen cheered Henry to the skies. "Well done, skipper!" Sam cried. "I didn't know you spoke its language!"

Laughing, Henry answered, "Hell, it's got to be easier to learn than Basque. And if it decided to give me more trouble, I could always clout it over the head."

"That works pretty well with the damned Basques, too," Sam said.

"It does," Henry agreed. "But they've got harder heads than honkers, and they're liable to try and clout first."

"You're right about that. Can't trust any of those foreign folk," Bartholomew Smith said. It never occurred to him, or to Henry, or to Sam, or to any of the other Englishmen, that foreigners might feel the same way about them. In fact, the mate added, "Bugger me blind if we can trust those bloody Dover bastards, either. Freetown? Free, my arse!" He spat to show what he thought of the neighboring settlement.

Sam nodded. "The Bretons are a better bargain than the Dovermen, even if Kersauzon's getting old. Your father's right about that, skipper."

"Yes." Henry tried not to sound too glum. Thinking that François Kersauzon was getting old reminded him that his father was, too. The graveyard back of the church already had its share of headstones and more. He didn't want to think about its having one more in particular. And thinking about death and dying reminded him of something else. "Keep an eye out for eagles," he called. "Wherever we find honkers, chances are we'll find them, too."

They'd grown scarcer around New Hastings—and, from everything he could see, along the rest of the eastern coast as well. But men were new in these parts. The red-crested eagles would think they were nothing but strange honkers—nothing but food.

To his relief, the work party got the water butts loaded and back to the *Rose* without trouble. Honkers watched without understanding as the cog weighed anchor and sailed south.

Fishing in the warm current that ran up the west coast of Atlantis wasn't anywhere near so fine as it had been farther east. There were fewer sea birds to nab, too; their numbers depended on those of the fish they ate. Every so often, then, the *Rose* would come in close to shore. Honkers were never hard to find, and never hard to kill. Their smoked and salted meat fed the fishermen on the journey south.

"Don't know what we'd do without them," Henry Radcliffe said, cutting a slab of meat from an enormous thigh.

"We'd go hungry, that's what," Sam said. Grease ran down the fisherman's chin.

"I'm glad they're so stupid," Henry said. "It makes hunting them so easy, you almost feel ashamed."

Sam shook his head. "Not me. I'd be ashamed of starving when you can just knock them over the head."

The men who went ashore to kill the honkers also came back with pine cones, which had tasty seeds. Other than that, though . . . "No berry bushes," one sailor grumbled. "You'd think there'd be swarms of them, too, in weather like this. Nice and damp, but not too cold—feels like spring every day."

Henry nodded; that was nothing but the truth. "I wonder why there aren't," he said. "None by New Hastings, either—only the ones we brought from England."

"Not many proper trees, either," the sailor said. "No oaks, no elms, no chestnuts, no willows, no apples or pears or plums . . . Bloody pines and these redwood things. And ferns, like there should be fairies flitting through them."

"Haven't seen any, God be praised," Sam said. "No more wee folk in Atlantis when we got here than men."

"Don't let Bishop John hear you talking of fairies and wee folk, or he'll give you a penance you won't fancy," Henry warned them. They both nodded. You might believe in such things, but you didn't talk about them where churchmen could overhear. They'd make you sorry if you did.

Up in the crow's nest, the lookout sang out: "There's an inlet ahead!"

Before long, Henry could see it from the deck, too: an opening a couple of miles across, with the sea entering to some considerable distance. He nodded to Bartholomew Smith. "We'd better go in and see what we have there."

"Aye, skipper." The mate nodded. "Could be a prime harbor." He laughed. "Could be, I mean, if there were any people here, and if there was anything to ship from here, and if there was any place you'd want to ship it to from here."

"Damn it, Bart, if you're going to grumble about every little thing . . ." Henry said. The mate and the rest of the fishermen laughed.

A few minutes later, a breeze from out of the northwest wafted the *Rose* through the inlet and into the calm waters of the bay. Everyone looked around, trying to see every which way at once. "Oh, my," Sam said softly, and that summed things up as well as anything.

The bay widened out to north and south beyond the inlet, leaving the best and biggest natural harbor Henry had ever seen. He nodded to Bartholomew Smith. "Well, you were right," he said.

"I couldn't have been much righter," the mate replied. "Almost makes me want to settle here, just to make sure nobody else does."

"Right again," Henry said. "By Our Lady, what an anchorage! You could put a navy here."

"Or a flock of pirates," Smith said.

"You named the trouble there," Henry pointed out. "What would they have to steal? This is a bare shore." He paused thoughtfully. "Well, it's a bare shore now. Maybe it won't be one of these days, but not yet."

Gulls and terns wheeled overhead, white wings flashing in the sun. Ducks and geese bobbed in the green-blue water of the bay. A shag plunged from on high, emerging with a fish in its beak. Ashore, redwoods taller than a spire speared the sky. The more Henry looked around, the more he too wanted to stay.

Now, all at once, he understood what had pushed his brother ever deeper into the forests of Atlantis. You wanted to find something like this, to be the first one ever to set eyes on it, to think it was all yours, if only for a little while. He looked east toward the shore there, half expecting to see Richard coming out from the trees—

not that he could have seen a man at such a distance. But Richard hadn't even crossed the mountains yet . . . or, if he had, he hadn't admitted it.

"Somewhere here, there'll be a river coming in," Henry said. "We can fill the butts at its mouth. And after that, after we clear the inlet again, I think it's time to head home. We won't find anything finer than this."

"What'll we call this place?" Sam asked.

"Paradise Bay," Bartholomew Smith suggested.

"I'm not sure God would like that," Henry said.

The mate went on plumping for his favorite, but Henry's point carried the day. "Well, what *do* we call it, then?" Smith grumped, scowling at his shipmates.

Henry had a name on the tip of his tongue, but it didn't want to come off. "What's the name of the land that was supposed to lie off the coast of England, the one where Morgan Le Fay took Arthur?"

"Avalon!" three fishermen called out at the same time.

"Avalon! Thank you." Henry nodded. "That was supposed to be a wonderful country. It should do for this place, eh?"

Nobody said no. Even Bartholomew Smith unbent enough to allow, "Well, you could have done worse, and I thought you were going to."

"Avalon it is, then. We'll get water and meat before we sail out again," Henry said. "We won't find a finer place to do it, that's sure."

A river did run into the bay. They named it the Arthur. They filled the water butts there, then spent some time skylarking in the pure, cool water. Henry Radcliffe fought shy of that; the water was *too* cool for him. Avalon Bay seemed locked in an eternal April. Farther south along this coast, perhaps some other anchorage basked in an eternal July. That would suit him better for splashing and snorting and ducking.

Skylarking ... His smile went wistful. His grandchildren wouldn't know what a skylark was. He hadn't seen one, or heard its explosion of song from on high, since coming to Atlantis. Horned larks hunted bugs here, but their more musical cousins hadn't crossed the ocean.

Honkers came down to the river to drink. Knocking them over the head was as easy as it usually was. You had to be careful to do the job right, that was all; if you didn't, a wounded bird would kick your guts out through your back. But as long as you killed clean, you could go through a whole flock and knock one bird after another over the head. The honkers would stare in surprise, but what was going on didn't register as danger to them.

When they saw the wide-winged shape of a red-crested eagle in the sky, though, they would scramble for the closest trees, honking and gabbling in alarm. They knew the eagles meant to kill them. And fleeing, gabbling honkers meant the fishermen had to beware. Maybe the eagles thought they were honkers, too. Maybe the fierce-beaked birds didn't care. But they would strike at men without hesitating—like the honkers, they didn't know enough to be afraid.

To Henry's way of thinking, the eagles were only thorns on the rose. (Nostalgia again. No wild roses here—only the few brought from England, and the ones sprung from their seed.) "If we had our women with us, I'd start a town here today," he told the mate. "As is, next summer will have to do."

"It will likely do well enough, too," Smith replied. "We're the only ones who've ever seen this place."

"And I praise God for that, too. Anyone who did see it would want it," Henry said.

"Well, skipper, I won't quarrel about that," Smith said.

Getting out of Avalon Bay wasn't quite so easy as getting in had been—another thorn on the rose. The *Rose*

herself had to wait till a warm breeze blew off the land
and wafted her out through the opening and into the
rougher waters of the Atlantic once more.

A few of the fishermen needed to run for the lee rail
when the cog started behaving like a restive horse once
more. "Damned if I didn't lose my sea legs there," one
of them said sheepishly, spitting into the drink to get the
last of the puke out of his mouth.

"You'll have plenty of chances to get them back,"
Henry said. He steered the *Rose* straight west, out into
the ocean. If the wind suddenly shifted, he wanted to
put some distance between the cog and the land behind
her; clawing off a lee shore in a storm was every sailor's
blackest nightmare.

And then he got his biggest surprise since he watched
his father agree to pay François Kersauzon a third of
his catch for the secret of the Breton's fine new fishing
ground. "Sail ho!" the man in the crow's nest cried. "Sail
ho off the starboard bow!"

Henry's first thought when the shout went up was
outrage pure and simple. How *dared* anyone but he
come into these waters? Then fresh wonder filled him.
The other ship was coming out of the northwest? *Did*
legendary Cathay lie beyond Atlantis? Was the Great
Khan's fleet stumbling onto this new land at the same
time as he was? Wouldn't *that* be a marvel wild beyond
belief?

Before long, he could see the other ship from the *Rose*'s
deck. A wry smile spread across his face. How likely was
it that the Great Khan built his ships to look just like the
cogs the men of Western Europe had known for generations? Not very, not unless Henry missed his guess.

Then he made out the oak-tree flag, and a slow smile
spread across his face. Whatever else that ship held, it
wasn't fearsome warriors from Cathay. Bartholomew
Smith realized the same thing at the same time. "Bugger

me blind if they aren't a bunch of bloody Basques!" he said.

And the men on the other cog would be able to see England's red St. George's cross on white. Would they be wondering about the *Rose* the same way Henry was wondering about them? Better not to take chances. "Load the guns," Henry said quietly. "Don't make a fancy show of it, but do it. You never can tell what foreigners have in mind."

To the Basques, Englishmen were foreigners. Henry squinted across the narrowing gap of sea. Yes, they carried guns, too. Yes, they were also loading them. Henry swore under his breath. He didn't want to fight, dammit. But he didn't want that other cog to be able to rake the *Rose* with impunity, either.

One of the Basques pointed toward Henry's ship. Like most of the men from that corner of the world, he was dark-haired and heavy-bearded. He wore linen and wool, not quite in the same cuts as an Englishman would have, but not so very different, either.

All the Basques on the other cog were dressed that way. All the Basques were, yes, but not all the people were. Beside Henry, the mate pointed. "Who are those funny-looking bastards up near the bow?"

"I don't know. I've never seen folk like them." Henry stared. Like the Basques, the strangers had black hair. But their chins were smooth and their skins weren't just tanned—they were coppery. Their clothes were in shades of buff and brown. *Made from hides?* Henry wondered. He cupped his hands in front of his mouth. "Ahoy, the Basque ship! *Parlez-vous français?*" Surely somebody over there would know a language you didn't have to be born a Basque to speak.

And somebody did. "Hello, Englishmen!" one of the men on the Basque cog yelled back. "Yes, we understand you."

"Who are your friends? Are they from Cathay?"
Henry asked.

All the Basques who spoke French thought that
was the funniest thing they'd ever heard. "No, by
God," their spokesman answered. "They say they are
Pattawatomi."

"They say they're what?" Henry wondered if the last
was a word in Basque.

But evidently not, for the man in the other cog repeated it: "Pattawatomi. It's the name of their clan or
tribe."

"Where did you find them?" Henry asked. "I didn't
think Atlantis had any people of its own."

Before answering, the Basque talked with some of his
countrymen. Then, a little reluctantly, he said, "No, they
aren't from Atlantis."

"Well, then?" Henry said.

More confabulating on the other ship. At last, and
even more reluctantly, the Basque spokesman pointed
west. "There is another land, a new land, about ten days'
sail that way. We thought we were the only ones who
came to this side of Atlantis."

"A new land? With people in it? How can it have
people in it when Atlantis has none?"

With a shrug, the Basque replied, "If you want to
know how, ask God. I cannot tell you that. But I can tell
you it is the truth, and here are these Pattawatomis to
prove it."

The men in skins eyed him impassively. They had
broad faces with high cheekbones and strong noses. One
of them held a wooden club with a ball of polished stone
in the head.

"I will tell you another thing. This new land is large—
maybe even as large as Atlantis—so why not?" the
Basque said. "If it had no folk of its own, it would be
better to settle than Atlantis is."

"Why, when it is so much farther from everything?" Henry asked.

"Because the trees and the animals are more like the ones we know. There are oaks, with acorns growing on them. And there are squirrels in the oaks, too. Not red squirrels like ours, but gray ones. Still—they are squirrels. Where will you find oaks or squirrels in Atlantis?"

"Did you see honkers? Or red-crested eagles?"

"We saw eagles, but smaller than the ones in Atlantis. They have white heads and eat fish like our sea eagles. We saw no honkers, only ordinary geese—but they have black heads and white chins like some honkers. We heard wolves howling in the night."

Wolves were almost hunted out of England. "Your new land is welcome to them," Henry said.

"We have them at home. I used to hear them howling outside my village in the wintertime," the Basque said. "They would kill sheep. Once in a while, if they got hungry enough, they would kill men."

"What will you do with the Patta-whoever-they-ares?" Henry asked.

"I don't know yet," the Basque replied. "Maybe we'll trade with them and take them back to the new land one of these days. Maybe we'll just keep them and put them to work. They look strong, don't they?"

The two cogs had come close enough to give Henry a good look at the copperskinned men from the unknown country. They *did* look strong; they were taller than most of the Basques. Even so . . . "They look like warriors to me."

"They shoot bows, and they have those clubs, but we saw no iron among them," the Basque said. "No helms, no swords—they have knives, but they're made of chipped stone. We can beat them if we have to."

"Yes, but can you make them work if you keep them in Atlantis?"

"Like I said, it could be we'll find out. Where are you bound now?" The Basque changed the subject—not very smoothly.

"Back to New Hastings." Henry gave him the truth. He didn't have ten days' worth of supplies aboard the *Rose*—not this trip. "God keep you safe on your voyage back to Gernika." *God keep you headed south of west. You won't spy Avalon Bay then—not if He's kind, you won't.*

Again, the spokesman talked things over with other men before replying. Not too obtrusively, English gunners stood near their swivels. If the Basques wanted trouble, they could have it.

"And you—you go with God as well," the Basque said after a long, long pause. The two cogs passed each other. Men on the other vessel looked ready to shoot, too. The range lengthened, lengthened some more . . . and pretty soon it was too long for the guns the *Rose* carried. Only as the tension slid out of his spine did Henry realize how tight he'd been strung.

"More new lands," he murmured. "New lands beyond Atlantis. I wouldn't have looked for that. It seemed big enough by itself."

"There's land west of Iceland," Bartholomew Smith said. "You talk with some of the squareheads and you'll hear about it. But it's as cold as Iceland is, or maybe worse. They don't go there very often."

"I've heard some of those stories, too." Henry laughed. "I always had trouble believing them. And here we are in a new land of our own, and now with news of more new lands beyond. I ought to do penance for doubting."

"Well, skipper, if everybody did that who ought to, you'd have plenty of company," the mate said. "Me, I'm just glad we didn't have a sea fight on our hands."

"So am I. They were thinking about sinking us to keep their secret. If they thought they could get away with it, they would have done it, too."

Smith nodded. "Can't keep a new land secret forever, though. We're likely lucky those copperskinned fellows never sailed east and found Atlantis ahead of us. I think you're right—they looked like men who could fight."

"They did," Henry Radcliffe agreed. "But if they can't work iron ... Even the Irish bog-trotters can do that. Turn your back on one, and he'll take a knife and let the air out of you like a boy poking a pig's bladder with a stick."

"No doubt about it," Smith said. "Well, between Avalon Bay and the miserable Basques, we'll have a deal of news when we get home."

Henry looked over his shoulder. The Basque cog was still sailing southwest, away from the *Rose*. That gave him a better chance of seeing New Hastings again— and it gave the Pattawatomis a better chance of seeing Gernika. He wondered what they would make of the Basque town. He wondered if he'd ever find out.

The pier didn't push out as far into the sea as Henry would have liked. But it was there, and it hadn't been when he sailed north from New Hastings. He was glad to be able to tie up at it instead of anchoring offshore and then rowing in, as he'd done more times than he could count.

A gull strutted along the planking. Plainly, it thought the pier had gone up for its benefit alone. It fixed him with a yellow stare and skrawked at him as he walked past. How dared he, a mere man, profane the timbers where its webbed feet had gloriously preceded him?

As soon as he was walking on solid ground and not on those gull-honored planks, his wife almost flattened him with a hug. After he untangled himself from her— which took a while, because he didn't want to—his father spoke dryly: "I'm glad to see you, too, Henry."

"And I'm glad to be seen." Not having seen Edward

Radcliffe for some months, Henry wondered if he'd been that stooped for a while now or if it had happened all at once while he was gone. He didn't know.

"What's it like on the other side?" His father laughed. "Never thought I'd say that to somebody who hadn't died."

"If you want to talk to ghosts, that's your business," Henry retorted. "If you want to ask me ... Well, the weather's better there, by God. Seemed like spring all the time."

"It *was* spring all the time you were there—or a lot of the time, anyhow," Edward reminded him.

"We stayed into summer, and it didn't get hot and muggy the way it does here," Henry said. "And there is a bay with the best harbor I've ever seen anywhere. Avalon Bay, we called it. If King Arthur had seen it, he never would have wanted to leave."

"Yes, but a harbor on a coast with no people on it is like a tree falling in the forest with no one to hear," his father said. "It may be there, but so what?"

"There will be people on that coast," Henry said. "And there are people beyond that coast. I know, because we saw them." He told his father and his wife and the rest of the people who were listening about the Basques and the strange Pattawatomis.

"A new land? Another new land? With people in it, this time?" Edward said.

"Funny-looking people, but people just the same," Henry answered. "And the Basques say the trees and beasts are more like England or their country than Atlantis. They talked about squirrels in oak trees and howling wolves."

"I haven't seen a squirrel in years," Edward said, at the same time as Bess was going, "I miss squirrels." His father added, "They're welcome to the wolves, though."

"I said the same thing, or near enough," Henry answered.

"And who are the strangers?" his father asked. "Did the Basques find the court of the Great Khan of Cathay?"

"I asked them the same thing, and they thought it was funny. It didn't seem that way to me, and it didn't sound that way from what they said."

Edward Radcliffe chuckled grimly. "Believing what Basques say is a fool's game. By Our Lady, sometimes understanding Basques is a fool's game."

"The one who talked to me spoke pretty good French," Henry said. "He said the strangers didn't know the use of iron. One of them carried a club with a stone ball for a head—that argues the Basque was telling the truth. They wore hides. They had no gold or silver ornaments. If they come from the Great Khan's court, ruling Cathay isn't what it used to be. Easier to think this new land lies between us and Cathay, wherever Cathay may be."

"Your children may go to the new land—I expect they will," Edward said. "I might like to see it before I die. But I think my bones will end up here in Atlantis—and that won't be so bad."

*He sounds like Moses, wanting a look at the Promised Land,* Henry thought, and then, *No—for him,* this *is the Promised Land. He really has got old.*

But after a moment, he realized Atlantis was the Promised Land for him, too. He was curious about what lay to the west. He wanted to see it, and more than once. But, having pulled up stakes in England to settle here, he wasn't eager to do it again. As his father said, maybe one of his boys would be, if they didn't find Atlantis roomy enough. Or maybe his brother would. . . .

"Where *is* Richard?" he asked.

"Out in the woods," Bess said. "As usual."

"He was talking about going over the mountains,"

Edward added. "I half wondered if you would see him when you came ashore on the west coast."

"So did I. That would have been funny," Henry said. "I wonder which of us would have been more surprised."

More people were coming off the *Rose* and telling loved ones and friends what they'd done and what they'd seen on the journey around the northern coast of Atlantis. Henry heard several sailors trying to pronounce *Pattawatomi*. Every man said it differently. Henry couldn't very well complain—he wasn't sure he was saying it right himself. He wasn't sure the Basque had pronounced it very well. Any people that gave itself such an outlandish name probably spoke a language as bad as Basque, too. Henry hadn't thought there was any such creature, but maybe he was wrong.

Then Bess put her arm around his waist and gave him an inviting smile. He suddenly and acutely remembered how long he'd been at sea. "I'm going to have a look at the house, Father," he said. "We'll talk more later."

"Send the children out to play before you look too hard," Edward answered. "Lord knows I had to chase you and your brother and sisters out the door after a few fishing runs—yes, just a few."

Henry remembered that. He'd been puzzled when he was small, puzzled and hurt. Why wasn't Father gladder to see him? Well, Father was, but he was glad to see Mother, too. And Henry was very glad to see Bess. They walked off side by side. In a little while, he thought, he would be gladder still.

# VII

*P*retty soon, Richard Radcliffe would reach the down-hill slope. That was what he was waiting for—proof he'd made it into the western part of Atlantis, proof he'd got through the mountains at last.

*If only I'd done it last year!* He'd been exploring in the Green Ridge then. He hadn't got to the crest and over. And so his brother, sailing around, got to the far side of the new land ahead of him. Richard muttered under his breath. In a way, you hardly mattered at all if you weren't first.

But only in a way. The Radcliffes hadn't got to Atlantis first. By all accounts, though, New Hastings and Bredestown and the other settlements that sprang from their first visit were growing far faster than Cosquer. Richard didn't know for a fact whether that was true; he'd never gone down to the Breton town. The more he traveled through the heartland of Atlantis, the less patience he had for his fellow human beings, even the ones who happened to be Englishmen and -women.

Oh, he was glad to see, glad to touch, his wife when he came back from one of these jaunts. But even rut-

ting palled sooner and sooner nowadays. Before long, he
itched to be gone again. Other people were a stench in
his nostrils, and the more of them there were, the worse
the stench got. They lived with it all the time, so they
didn't even know it was there. Richard hadn't himself,
not till he was able to go away into the woods here for
days at a time.

"How did I stand the stinks on a fishing boat?" he
wondered aloud. He often talked to himself when he was
out alone. Why not? And the answer was easy enough
to find: he'd stood it because he'd known no better, the
same way he'd stood getting jammed together with the
other fishermen on the *St. George,* jammed almost as
tight as the gutted slabs of salt cod they made.

Here in the wilderness, his words seemed to take on
an importance they wouldn't have back in New Hastings, or even Bredestown. They echoed back from the
boles of the trees that leapt skywards the way cathedral
spires dreamt of doing. Some of the trees he'd seen rose
higher than any cathedral spire—he was sure of that.

Only birdcalls—honkers' loud, nasal notes and the
more melodious songs of smaller birds—had ever dis-
turbed the stillness in these mountain passes before.
Richard smiled. No, that wasn't quite true. There was
also the chirping of the big green katydids that scurried
and hopped through the undergrowth. They were as
long as his thumb, and twice as fat. They couldn't fly; like
the honkers, they had useless little stubs of wings. They
didn't even hop particularly well. But, like mice back in
England, they came out at night to nibble at whatever
they could find.

And sometimes, here in the mountains, they came out
by day, too, or what passed for day. Fog lingered long in
the valleys here. Sometimes, as it thinned, Richard could
see the green slopes above and to either side of the pass
he was trying to get through. That was when he came

out into the open; under the trees, mist might linger all through the day.

He knew he'd gone astray a few times, just because of the mist. Few trails wound through these forests. There were no deer or wild boar here to make them. Nor had men tamed these woods, as they had England's. Honkers made some paths, but honkers didn't care to go deep into the woods. Most of them were by choice creatures of the meadow and the forest edges. They sheltered under the trees to save themselves from the savage beaks and tearing talons of red-crested eagles. Without the birds that slashed down from the sky to slay them, they would have spent their time in the open.

The constant moisture made the air seem thick and textured in Richard's lungs. It also made the spicy scents of sap and needles even stronger and sweeter than they would have been were the weather drier. Of course, in drier weather the redwoods that gave the forest its upper story could never have grown.

Somewhere not far ahead, a stream gurgled. Richard came up to it, dipped up a cup, and drank. The clear, cold water that ran down his throat seemed as sweet and almost as strong as wine. It wasn't the greenish, nasty stuff that came out of the butts when you'd stayed at sea too long. It wasn't the vile stuff that came down to Hastings, either, already foul with inlanders' shit and piss and the leavings from tanneries and breweries. This was *water,* the way God intended it to be.

A frog stared at Richard out of golden eyes. That single singing sac under its throat still seemed strange to him. But so much of Atlantis was strange by English standards; why should that one small thing stand out? He couldn't have said why, but it did.

The frog didn't hop off the rock, as a sensible English frog would have. It didn't recognize him as a threat, which could have made him all the more dangerous to it. Luckily for it, he wasn't hungry right now. He plucked a leaf from a fern and dropped it in the stream.

It floated off . . . toward the east. "Damnation!" Richard muttered. He was still on this side of the watershed. One of these days, if that leaf didn't sink, it would wash out to sea somewhere not far from New Hastings. He wanted leaves to float west, and to follow them to Atlantis' farther shore. Thanks to Henry, he knew it was there.

More than half of him wished his brother hadn't found Avalon Bay, or anything else that had to do with Atlantis' western coast. What he already knew made his own explorations seem less weighty. Going off towards a land you already knew something about was like listening to a story where you already knew the ending. What lay in the middle might still be interesting, but it wasn't the same.

A flapjack turtle stuck its pointy-nosed head out of the water and eyed him with reptilian suspicion. He was suspicious of it, too. The creature had formidable jaws. He didn't want it taking off a finger joint if he tried to catch it. Flapjacks made good eating, but plenty of other prey was easier to hunt.

He pressed on. Light filtered through the mist, through the redwood canopy, and through the lower story of pines in sudden, startling shafts, almost as if it came through a stained-glass window in a cathedral. The tall columns of the tree trunks only strengthened the resemblance.

Richard thought God more likely to live in this pristine outdoor chapel than in any building men threw together. You could see the Creation here. The birds and the wind in the branches played a sweeter melody than any that burst from the throats of a choir. And the conifers' smell that filled the air in the woods made his nose happier than all the frankincense and myrrh brought in from distant shores.

Bishop John would not have been glad to hear his opinions. But Bishop John never would. Richard Radcliffe had no desire to fall foul of the Church. He hadn't even told his wife of his notions about the woods. She wouldn't understand them anyhow; she hadn't traveled far enough under the trees.

Maybe someone from Freetown had as little use for his neighbors and as much for the new world in which he found himself as Richard. Maybe one of François Kersauzon's Bretons, or a Basque from Gernika, also made a habit of plunging deep into the heartland of Atlantis for no better reason than to see what he could find. Maybe, but Richard had found no signs of other wanderings in the course of his own.

"What would I do if I did?" he wondered. He shrugged. He had no idea. It was like wondering what you would do if the mast suddenly toppled. The idea seemed far-fetched enough to be silly.

And yet, once it lodged, it didn't want to leave. He kept looking around. Every small forest sound made him wonder if he should draw his bow. He knew that was foolish, but he couldn't help it.

He'd been blazing trees to mark his path. He kept on doing it, but made his blazes point in the other direction, as if he were coming from the west. That might confuse a stranger who found them. Or it might do nothing but make him feel better. He did it anyhow.

Some of the snails that crawled up trees and foraged on ferns here in the mountains were almost the size of his fist. His first thought when he saw one was that a Frenchman would have thought he'd died and gone to heaven. His next thought was that the Frenchman might not be so foolish after all. A snail that size had a lot of meat, even if it came with eyestalks.

And, roasted over a small fire, giant snail didn't prove bad at all. It was bland enough to make him wish he'd brought more salt along, but he couldn't do anything about that now. He noted that a clean empty shell might do duty for a cup if he ever broke his.

Some of the slugs in the woods were even bigger than the snails. He needed longer to notice them, though: they were a dark green that made them look like patches of moss. But patches of moss didn't usually leave behind a trail of slime as wide as two fingers side by side when they glided along. And the slugs, of course, had eyestalks, too. They reminded Richard of slowly moving cucumbers.

They also had a lot of meat. He decided he wasn't hungry enough to find out what it tasted like. If he was missing a treat . . . then he was, that was all. One of these days, some other traveler, more intrepid or more desperate than he was, might find out.

He wondered how long he'd been walking downhill before he realized he was. Excitement flowered in him. Was he past the watershed at last, or was this nothing but a trick of the ground? He didn't see it rising up ahead of him, but he couldn't see very far ahead.

"A stream. I have to find a stream," he said. Finding one didn't take long, not in that moist country.

Did the water taste different, or was he imagining things? He couldn't say, not for sure. He scrabbled around in the dirt till he found a few pine needles, and he dropped them in. He felt like shouting when they slid off toward the west.

He went another half-mile or so, then repeated the test in a different rivulet. When a leaf also floated westward there, he let out a whoop that came back from the redwood trunks: "I'm on the other side!" He pressed on.

When a ship came out of the east in the middle of November, Edward Radcliffe was surprised. The Atlantic turned blustery by then; he wouldn't have wanted to put to sea at this season. Sometimes you had to, but he wouldn't have wanted to. This was a fancy trading cog, too: not a beat-up fishing boat like most of the ones that crossed the sea to Atlantis.

He walked out along the pier to meet her and see what her crew wanted. Cold, nasty drizzle blew into his face. Yes, it was November, all right, even if few of the trees here in the new land lost their leaves.

Edward stared at the fellow looking down at him from the forecastle. Under a sleeveless leather jerkin, the stranger wore a tunic of crimson silk. Edward couldn't remember the last time he'd seen silk. He didn't think any of the settlers had brought any hither. Oh, maybe a hair ribbon; maybe even a scarf. Surely no more than that.

He hadn't seen a look like the one on the stranger's face for a long time, either. He needed a moment to recognize it for what it was. The newcomer was looking down at him, all right. That was a man of high birth surveying a social inferior. It wasn't a look Edward was glad to see: he thought he'd left such fripperies behind for good.

When he didn't speak, the stranger glowered more. As far as Edward was concerned, he could glower all he pleased. And he could freeze, too, for all Edward cared, and he was probably doing just that; silk might be pretty, but it wasn't warm. Edward's dun-colored woolen cloak was homely, yes, but it shed cold and rain.

At last, grudgingly, the newcomer said, "God give you good day, old man."

"And you," Edward Radcliffe replied, more grudgingly still. True, he was old, but he didn't care to be reminded of it.

"Tell me, old man" —the stranger didn't just remind him of it, but rubbed it in on top of that—"do you know, do you have any idea, whom you will have the honor of meeting when he steps off this God-cursed scow?"

If he thought that ship was a scow, he knew nothing about the sea. Well, likely he didn't. As for the alleged honor . . . "No," Edward said. "Don't much care, either." He turned and started to walk away.

"Hold, varlet, or you die before your feet touch solid ground!" barked the man in silk. As if by magic, three archers had appeared behind him. Each aimed a clothyard shaft at Edward's short ribs. The rain would play merry hell with their bowstrings soon, but not soon enough.

The archers had the look of hired muscle. If the stranger told them to shoot, shoot they would. They would worry about it later, if they worried at all. Radcliffe stopped and came back. "Well, you talked me into it," he said.

"I thought I might." Yes, the bastard up there was used to giving orders, used to having them obeyed, and used to enjoying having them obeyed. His self-satisfied smirk said so even more clearly than his snotty tone of voice. "I ask you once again, old man—and better than you deserve, too—do you know whom you'll have the honor of meeting when he disembarks? Think carefully on your answer this time, if you want to meet him on your feet and not lying at his."

"No, I don't know. Please tell me," Edward said—carefully.

Anyone who knew him would know he was seething. Anyone who knew him would know, too, that only a fool angered him and thought to come off unscathed. This fellow didn't know him, or care to, and didn't worry about angering him: all of which only proved the man a fool. But he was a fool with important news, for he answered, "Why, none other than his grand and glorious Lordship, the Earl of Warwick."

"We have no Lordships here," Edward blurted.

"You do now, by Christ, and you'd bloody well better get used to it, for he's here to stay," said the man in the red silk tunic.

"Warwick? Here? To stay? What happened?" Like everyone else in Atlantis, Edward got news of the civil war in England in bits and fragments, as new shiploads of settlers came in to New Hastings. The Earl of Warwick was King Edward IV's cousin. His help had let Richard of York briefly claim the throne a few years earlier. Without him, Edward wouldn't have sat on it. There had been talk he'd fallen out with the King over Edward's French policy, but this. . . . *This is exile,* Edward realized. *He must have risen, risen and lost.*

"He had . . . a disagreement with his Majesty." Now the man in silk chose *his* words with care. "This being so, he was . . . encouraged to travel across the sea, to seek his fortune in these new lands the fisherfolk stumbled upon."

Did he have the faintest idea he was talking to the leader of those fisherfolk, to the first Englishman who'd done the stumbling? Obviously not. Would he have cared had he known? That seemed just as unlikely.

"And so," the fellow up on the forecastle went on, "he has sailed here to Freetown, that he may—"

Edward Radcliffe threw back his head and laughed like a loon. Loons swam in the ponds and rivers here, as they did in England. Their wild cries were almost as characteristic of this wilderness as those of the honkers.

The man in the silk tunic went almost as red as it was. "Silence, wretch!" he roared. "Give me one good reason I should not order these my men to shoot you down on the instant like the dog you are."

"Why, you sorry blockhead, you don't even know where the devil you arc," Edward said, laughing still. He pointed south. "Freetown lies down the coast. Go there and be welcome." *If you and Warwick are wel-*

*come anywhere in Atlantis, which I doubt.* "This is New Hastings."

"New ... Hastings?" The stranger spat the words out as if they were bad fish. "You lie! Surely you lie! That cur of a captain swore ..."

"By the Cross, by Our Lady, by God, sir, this is New Hastings and no other place in all the world." Edward knew a certain fleeting sympathy for the man who'd captained this cog. On a choppy sea, of the kind you were almost bound to have this time of year, gauging even your latitude was no easy feat. If he'd had clouds for several days, as he easily might have done, he wouldn't have been able to take a sun sight. He would be going by God and by guess, and they would have let him down.

"New ... Hastings." The stranger turned away and started screaming at the top of his lungs. Phenomenal lungs they were, too; he could have made himself heard from stern to bow on a bigger ship than this in the middle of a savage blow.

One of the men who came running was plainly the skipper. The other, just as plainly, was Richard Neville, the Earl of Warwick. He couldn't have been far past forty, but his hair and beard had gone very gray. He had a strong prow of a nose and clever dark eyes set too close together. His man bellowed abuse at the captain. The poor man did his best to defend himself. His best was none too good. How could it be, when he found himself in the wrong?

Warwick listened for a while, then walked over to the rail and peered down at Edward. With his man still berating the skipper in the background, he said, "So this is New Hastings, is it?" The noble's voice was surprisingly soft and gentle. Unlike the fellow in the red silk, he didn't need to bluster to get what he wanted.

"I'm afraid it is ... your Lordship." Edward hoped

the nobleman didn't notice the pause he needed before he brought out the title of respect.

But Warwick did notice; Edward could tell. Warwick was one who would notice everything and forget nothing. The whole world and its mistakes would be grist for his mill. He'd gone wrong at last, though, or he wouldn't be here. For a great noble, for a man who aspired to the kingship, Atlantis would not be the earthly Paradise or anything like it. It would be the nearest thing to hell. How could you be a great man, a mighty man, when everyone was putting forth all his might merely to wrest a living from the vast wilderness the settlements bordered?

And where in the wilderness was Richard these days? Had he found Avalon Bay yet, or some other point on the western coast of Atlantis? When would he find his way home again? Edward had the sudden bad feeling he might need every pillar he could find.

"New Hastings," the Earl of Warwick repeated, as his retainer had not long before. But he spoke in musing tones, as if he were hefting a new tool and wondering whether it would serve him well enough to use.

"Yes, your Lordship." This time, Edward didn't hesitate.

Something glinted in the noble's eyes. *Oh, yes, you say the words, but you don't mean them, and you can't fool me into thinking you do.* Maybe Edward was reading too much into a single glance. Maybe, but he didn't think so.

"Well, I daresay I can do as well for myself here as I could at Freetown," Richard Neville said, perhaps as much to himself as to Edward. He went back to speak to his lackey and to the captain.

A moment later, the captain bawled an order. A gangplank thudded down from the waist of the ship. Soldiers strutted out onto the pier. "Move aside, old man," one of them told Edward. "This place is ours now."

\*      \*      \*

Richard Radcliffe smiled in the November sunshine. In England, it would have been cold and cloudy and likely rainy. In New Hastings, it probably would have been colder yet. Maybe it would have rained. It might even have snowed; it had done that more than once this time of year since he settled in Atlantis.

Now he was on the other side of the mountains. Now, as far as he was concerned, he was on the right side of the mountains. Henry had said Avalon Bay had weather like an unending April. Richard saw that his brother was right. He was somewhere not far from the famous bay—if a bay could be famous when only one shipload of men had ever seen it—and here it was: April, or as near as made no difference.

November in truth, but birds still sang in the trees. Leaves stayed green—a dark green, as most greens were in Atlantis, but green nonetheless. The grass under his feet as he stood out in the meadow was as lush as if it were the height of spring. It hadn't died and gone all yellow, the way it would have in England or New Hastings.

He knew what that meant. This grass hadn't seen a freeze. Maybe it would when winter advanced further … if winter did advance further here. Richard wouldn't have bet on that. As far as he could tell, it really was springtime the whole year around.

Back behind him lay the mountains he'd crossed with such labor, a ridge of green now against the eastern horizon instead of the western, where he'd grown used to seeing it. He'd come into one new world when he first set foot on Atlantis. Now he was in another one—in his view, a better one.

The sea called him. He could smell it again, a smell he'd known all his life but one that had gone out of his nostrils as he crossed Atlantis' fog-filled spine. He couldn't see it yet—the ground rose ahead of him. But it was there.

And beyond that sea lay more land, with strange people living in it. He'd heard that from Henry, too, and from the fishermen on the *Rose.* He shrugged. Seeing that new land meant getting into a cog again. He supposed he could if he had to. If he didn't have to, he didn't want to. Atlantis was plenty big enough to satisfy him.

A crow cawed from the edge of the woods. It wasn't just like an English carrion crow—the call was different, and it didn't have such a heavy beak. It wasn't just like a rook, either: it lacked the pale patch on its face. But it couldn't be anything but some kind of crow.

Ravens in Atlantis, as far as he could tell, were just like the ravens back in England. Crows here were similar, but not identical. Jays were quite different: they were blue and white and crested, not pinkish brown. But they were plainly jays. Their feisty habits and raucous calls proclaimed that to anyone with eyes to see and ears to hear.

Richard wondered why it should be so. Why did birds that acted like English blackbirds have robinlike red breasts here? Why were there so many Atlantean birds that couldn't fly? Honkers, several kinds of duck, oil thrushes . . . He scratched his head. The question was easy to ask, but he had no idea what the answer was.

He trudged on. Before long, he was sweating—in November! That made him smile. He knew the kind of work he would have to do back in New Hastings to sweat there. Just walking along wouldn't do it, not at this time of year.

Thinking of oil thrushes made him hungry. He would have to hunt before long. Well, at least hunting was easy here, when the quarry didn't know enough to run away. Going after rabbits in England hadn't been like that. Deer and boar knew enough to flee, too, not that the likes of a fisherman could go after them.

He didn't miss working hard on a hunt. He did miss apples and pears and plums and all the juicy berries he'd known back in England. Nothing like those here. The settlers had planted orchards, but they weren't bearing abundantly yet. The trees in those orchards were the only fruit trees in Atlantis.

One of the native barrel trees had a sweet sap that could be boiled down into a honeylike syrup or fermented into something halfway between beer and wine. It was pleasant, but it wasn't the same as wandering through the woods and finding fruit. He couldn't do that here.

No matter how much he craved the sun, he didn't stay out in the meadow longer than he had to. Around New Hastings and Bredestown, red-crested eagles—and their attacks on settlers—had grown scarce. Here in the west, though, no one had hunted them. No one had gone after their nests. The birds were still common, and still deadly dangerous. A lone man had scant hope of fighting one off if it took him for a honker.

Under the trees, Richard breathed easier. The birds went right on singing as he walked along. The big katydids fell silent at his approaching footfalls. They feared men. They feared everything, because so many things ate them.

Richard had eaten them two or three times, when he couldn't catch anything bigger. If you peeled off their legs and feelers before you roasted them, and if you ate them in a couple of bites, without much thinking about what you were doing . . . If you did all that, they tasted a little like shrimp. But they tasted more the way he thought bugs would taste—sort of greenish—and so he wasn't anxious to repeat the experiment.

A salamander on a tree trunk eyed him. It didn't scurry away or show any sign of alarm. Nor did it try to look like something else, the way so many crawling things did. Even in the gloom under the trees, it stood out: its background color was blood red, while the spots that measled it were a brilliant yellow.

He left it alone. There were brightly colored salamanders back near New Hastings, too. They weren't identical to this one, but they had to be close cousins. He'd seen what happened when a dog ate one: it took a few steps, then fell over dead. A few years earlier, they'd found a two-year-old girl who'd gone missing also dead, with half a colorful salamander in her mouth.

"You can do as you please for all of me, deathworm," Richard told the creature, and gave it a wide berth. For all he knew, just touching it could kill. He didn't care to find out the hard way.

High overhead, a red-crested eagle screeched. Richard flattened himself against a tree—*not* the one where the salamander insolently rested. He didn't think the eagle was hunting him—he didn't know the eagle was hunting anything. Why take chances, though?

It screeched again, from the same place. He peered up, up, up. Peer as he would, he couldn't see the bird. It was high up in a redwood, and anything high up in a redwood was higher than it could be anywhere else. Countless branches all shaggy with needles hid the eagle from the ground. No doubt it could see a long, long way from there. If a honker anywhere within its range of vision walked out onto a meadow to forage, the red-crested eagle could take wing and strike.

Even though he couldn't see it, Richard didn't feel altogether safe from the eagle, for he feared it might be able to see him. One thing the settlers had learned: the eagles had better eyes than they did. A bird would appear out of nowhere to strike at a honker or a man, or to carry off a lamb or a dog or, once or twice, a toddler. A fishing-boat skipper with eyes like that could name his own price, but the birds outdid mere men.

This one called again. Now it was in the air. As its

screeches receded into the distance, Richard breathed easy again. Whatever it was after, it wasn't after him. That meant he could press on.

Faint in the distance, he heard honker alarm cries. The bird must have struck. Whether it had killed ... If it hadn't, chances were it would soon find some other perch. He needed to be careful, but you always needed to be careful when you were the only man in strange country.

Something slithered away through the ferns. Atlantis had far more serpents than England did, and more of them were venomous. You had to watch where you put your feet. Well, you didn't have to, but you were liable to be sorry if you didn't. Some of the vipers twitched their tails, perhaps in anger, just before they struck. If they happened to lie coiled among dry leaves, that twitching might make enough noise to warn a wary man. Or, of course, it might not.

He hadn't got a good look at this snake. He didn't know if it was one of the poisonous kind. He wasn't inclined to go after it and find out, either.

The ground sloped up under his feet. Then he topped the low rise and headed down instead. The afternoon sun flashed off water ahead.

At first, Richard could make out no more through the screening of trees and ferns ahead. A pond? A lake? He hadn't gone much farther before he realized that, if it was a lake, it was a big one. He pushed harder. Now he wanted to get out into open country, at least long enough to take a good look at what he'd found.

Sunshine meant he'd come to the edge of the woods. "Oh," he said softly as he got the look he wanted. After a moment's wonder, he added, "If that's not Avalon Bay, then this coast has two of them."

He could see the quiet water of the bay, the lips of land that almost closed around it, and the opening that gave access to the wide ocean beyond. Henry hadn't lied—this was a harbor in a million. It hardly mattered that there was nowhere to go from here. This was the sort of place where you wanted to build a town just because you could.

And there might be somewhere to go, after all. There were those copperskinned men the Basques had found, the ones with the name Henry and his crewmen pronounced differently every time they tried it. Did they have anything worth trading?

Another land across the sea, one you could reach from Atlantis . . . That was a surprise. But then, Atlantis itself was a surprise—one surprise after another, in fact. Richard wondered whether François Kersauzon rued the day when he sold the secret to his father. A third of a hold of salt cod? It didn't seem enough, not when the Englishmen had done so much more with the new land than Kersauzon's Bretons had.

Even the Basques had done more with Atlantis than the Bretons had, and the Basques had got off to a late start here. Richard paused, peering out into the bay. He thought the Basques had got a late start here. No matter what he thought, though, could he prove it? Like the Bretons, like the Englishmen, Basques and Galicians sailed deep into the Atlantic after cod. Just because his own father heard of Atlantis from the Bretons, that didn't mean the Basques and Galicians must have. Maybe they'd stumbled over the new land on their own.

*Have to ask them, next time I see one—whenever that is,* Richard thought. He had no idea when it would be. He'd never traveled south. Basques came up to New Hastings every now and again, but he couldn't remember the last time one went inland to Bredestown. Richard was curious about the copperskinned unpronounceables. How had they made out after they got to Gernika?

He looked out at the ocean again, or what he could

see of it through the mouth of the bay. It wasn't impossible, he supposed, that he would see a sail out there on the Atlantic. Henry hadn't taken the *Rose* out around the northern cape this year, but maybe the Basques had gone around to the south and then sailed west toward their new land, their inhabited land.

Henry hadn't wanted them to find Avalon Bay. That had made sense even before Richard saw this marvelous harbor with his own eyes. Now that he had, he was as sure as his brother that nobody but Englishmen had any business exploring or making a home here.

A river ran into the northern part of the bay. Henry had said so. Henry and his crew hadn't taken a boat up the river, so nobody knew whether the stream ran west from the green ridge of mountains Richard had penetrated or came down from the north.

If it did rise in the mountains, it would make a wonderful highway across the western half of Atlantis. You could build a raft or a boat up in the mountain country and then ride the rest of the way. You could if there weren't too many rocks or mudflats, anyway.

That would be worth knowing. Richard went on blazing his trail as he headed north toward the river. If it didn't suit his purposes, he could always go back the way he'd come out. He didn't want to: he'd already been over that ground once. But he could, which was comforting in its way.

Shorebirds flew up in shrieking clouds when they caught sight of him. They wouldn't have done that on the eastern shore, or not to the same degree. A lot of the birds in the east were as naive about people as honkers were. What did that say? Was it close enough from here to the new land with the copperskinned people that more western shorebirds made the journey and grew familiar with hunters? Richard couldn't see what else it was likely to mean.

He swore under his breath. He'd seen snipe in those clouds of birds, and snipe made uncommonly fine eating. The ones back near New Hastings were tame enough to catch by hand. Not these. If he wanted them, he'd have to get them the hard way.

Even without snipe roasted in clay, he went on. Over along the eastern edge of the bay, what was water, what marsh, and what land seemed as much a matter of opinion as anything else. Although it was bright daylight, mosquitoes buzzed. Henry had made it plain the water was deeper out by the insweeping arms of land. One of those would be the place to build, then.

Birds swooped here and there after the swarms of insects. Some of the swallows were achingly like the ones he'd left behind in England. Others were larger, with a purple cast to their feathers. Instead of flitting all the time, some birds perched on branches and stumps and made forays against the mosquitoes. "*Pee*-bee!" they called gaily. "*Pee*-bee!"

Richard found the river a little before sunset. It meandered through low country, so he had trouble being sure, but he thought it came down from the east. "I'll find out tomorrow," he said.

With a bone hook, some worms he dug out of the boggy soil, and a length of line, he had no trouble pulling a couple of trout from the stream. They wouldn't make as good a supper as snipe would have, but they were a lot better than nothing.

He wondered how things were back in New Hastings. Cold and wet and boring, unless he missed his guess. Not much happened there, not these days. When he got back, he'd give people something to talk about for a while.

# VIII

Three of the Earl of Warwick's troopers tramped down the middle of New Hastings' widest street, pulling their boots out of the mud at every step. Rain pattered down, which would make the mud even thicker and gluier before long. The troopers' mailshirts jingled as they walked. To keep the rain off of their byrnies and helms, they wore hooded wool cloaks they'd taken from the settlers.

Edward Radcliffe wore a cloak himself, and a broad-brimmed hat in lieu of a hood. He made sure he steered well clear of Warwick's men. The less reason they had to get angry at him, the smaller the chance they would do something he'd regret. He watched them trudge by. They paid him no attention at all.

The soldiers seldom went about in groups smaller than three, not any more. Two of them had suffered unfortunate accidents while walking around by themselves. Nobody could prove anything. Even Warwick admitted as much. But the exiled noble had called Edward in to the house he'd appropriated and laid down the law like Moses coming down from Mount Sinai.

"This will stop," Warwick said bluntly. "It will, or I shall turn loose my wolves, and New Hastings will not be the happier for that."

"Your Lordship, I had nothing to do with it," Edward said.

"I believe you. If I didn't believe you, you would be dead, and I would be talking to someone else." Richard Neville didn't waste sweet words on his social inferiors— which meant he wasted them on no one in Atlantis. "Still, these people listen to you. And they had better, if they don't want to see what slaughter looks like. They will not play me for a fool. D'you understand me?"

"Oh, yes. You always make yourself very plain, sir," Edward Radcliffe answered. "But may I ask you one question?"

"Go ahead." By Warwick's tone, he was granting a favor to a man who didn't deserve it.

"Even if your soldiers hold New Hastings down, what good will it do you? What will you get from it?"

Richard Neville stared at him. They might both use English, but they didn't speak the same language. "If I cannot be a lord in England, Radcliffe, I shall be a lord—no, a king—here. This may be a miserable puddle of a realm, but it is *my* miserable puddle of a realm. Do you understand me now?"

"I certainly do, your Lordship," Edward said.

"Good. Then get out."

Get out Edward Radcliffe did, thanking heaven the noble let him leave. And he spread the word, as Warwick wanted him to do. But he spread it for his own reasons, not for the earl's.

"We don't want a king here, do we?" he said when he visited his son after getting away from Warwick, and answered his own question: "No, by God, of course we don't, not if he uses his soldiers to steal from us and to hold us down."

"Why shouldn't we knock 'em over the head as we find the chance, then?" Henry said—and he was only the first of many. "If we get rid of a few now, the rest will be easier to dispose of later."

Reluctantly, Edward shook his head. "If Warwick keeps them all together, think what they can do to us. Do you want England's worthless war coming to the shores of Atlantis?"

"Sooner or later, we'll have to kill them all." Again, Henry was only the first who said that. The Earl of Warwick's soldiers had not endeared themselves in New Hastings.

"How can we, without raising the whole settlement?" Edward asked. "They have training. They have discipline. They have armor. One of them is worth more in the field than one of us."

His son smiled a most unpleasant smile. "We have longbows."

He was right. A clothyard shaft from a longbow would pierce any mailshirt ever made. A shot at close range would pierce plate. But he seemed to think being right was enough. Edward Radcliffe feared he knew better.

"Unless we kill them all at once, the rest take their revenge," he said. "The whole settlement is hostage to them. Trying and failing is worse than not trying at all."

Henry shook his head. "Nothing is worse than not trying at all. If we don't try at all, what are we but their dogs?"

"Patience," Edward told him. "Patience. What we have to do is, we have to make sure we don't fail when we try. And we have to make sure Warwick and his wolves—his name for them, not mine—think we *are* their dogs till we try. If they're ready for us, if they're waiting for us, our work gets that much harder. Am I right or am I wrong?"

"I am a man, not a dog," Henry said, but then, shaking his head, "I'll be a quiet man, I suppose—for a while."

"That's what we need." Edward didn't try to hide the relief in his voice.

He had to play the dog, too, no matter how it galled him. And acting subservient wounded him all the more because he knew he wouldn't be worth much if it came to a fight. For a man his age, he was healthy enough. He could still see well—at a distance. He hadn't gone deaf. He still had most of his teeth. All the same, he was nearer seventy than sixty. He wasn't very strong, and he wasn't very fast. His wind wasn't what it had been, either.

When he grumbled about it, Henry set a hand on his shoulder. "Don't fret, Father. You've still got more brains than any three men in Atlantis, and that includes Warwick. When we move against him, we'll move because of you."

"You flatter me," Edward said. "I think you're wrong, though. When New Hastings rises against Warwick, chances are it will be because a soldier does something so horrible, he'll make everyone hate him—and his lord. These things work out that way."

"If you say so." Henry winked at him. "What I say is, you show you've got all those brains by knowing such things."

"What *I* say is, you're a miserable pup," Edward said with rough affection.

Henry winked again. "And where do I get that? From you or from Mother?"

"Don't let her hear you ask, or you'll get it, all right," Edward said. They both laughed, as if he were kidding.

Snow on the ground and sleet in the air told Richard Radcliffe he was back on the east side of the mountains again. His breath smoked, as if he were a dragon. He had a dragonish temper right now. Just a few miles back, the weather had been tolerable—not warm, but tolerable. No more.

"We're living in the wrong place. We all ought to pack up and head for Avalon Bay," he grumbled. Fog spurted from his mouth and nose with every word. And if that didn't prove his point, he couldn't imagine what would.

He also couldn't imagine getting everyone in New Hastings and Bredestown to pack up and travel across Atlantis or sail around it to get to the land where it was always April. Most people were like plants; they found a spot, and they put down roots. He didn't even intend to try to talk the whole English settlement into leaving. A few men, a few families, might. More likely, nobody would.

"Bloody fools," Richard said, scuffing through the snow. He kept his head down, partly to ward against the nasty wind and partly to spot any tracks there might be. If he could follow a trail straight to a honker or an oil thrush . . .

When the weather got cold, you needed to eat more. The fire inside you needed more fuel to keep going. And, before long, he found some. This country was extravagantly rich in extravagantly stupid game. The oil thrush he came upon eyed him in mild confusion as he approached. Maybe, like the red-crested eagles, it thought he was some strange kind of honker. It probably wondered what he was doing right up to the moment when he knocked it over the head.

He found shelter behind a fallen pine. Dried-out needles made good tinder: he dug around under the trunk till he found some the snow hadn't reached. Once he got the fire going, he fed it with twigs and branches. The warmth felt good—felt wonderful, in fact. He butchered the oil thrush and started cooking a leg. He hadn't done the best job of plucking it; the stink of singeing feathers filled his nose. Grease dripped down onto the flames and made them sputter and pop.

He carved chunks of meat off the bones with his knife. He didn't admire his own cookery. Part of the bird was nearly burnt, the rest nearly raw. He didn't care. After tossing the gnawed leg bones aside, he cooked the liver and the heart and the gizzard, and then the other thigh. The breast and the wings had less meat on them.

A couple of soft, slow, almost sleepy chirps startled him. Then he started to laugh. He wasn't the only one who thought the fire felt good. One of those mouse-sized katydids had taken shelter against the cold under the downed pine. With the fire close by to heat it up, it revived. Maybe it thought spring had come early.

"Sorry, bug," Richard said. "Pretty soon, I'm going to push on, and then you'll go back to sleep." In England, dormice snoozed away the winter. No dormice here. No mice of any kind, except the ones that had sneaked aboard the cogs that brought the settlers from England. No native rats, either. Richard didn't miss them. Who but a cat would?

After he built up the fire to burn for a while, he rolled himself in his blanket and went to sleep. It wasn't a soft bed, but it would do. Now he hoped the weather wouldn't warm up. If it started to rain, it would soak through even his thick, greasy woolen blanket. Then weariness claimed him, and he stopped worrying about the weather or anything else.

He was shivering when he woke up. That meant he woke sooner than he might have. It was still dark, with only the faintest hint of twilight in the east. New Hastings lay farther south than its namesake in England, so its wintertime days were longer and its nights shorter than the ones he'd grown up with. All the same, its winters seemed harsher than the ones in the land he'd left behind. He wondered why that should be so, but had no doubt it was.

"Father should have settled farther south yet," he muttered as he poked the embers to red life, fed more tinder onto them, and got the fire going again. From everything he'd heard, the cold season was milder down in Cosquer and much milder down in Gernika. The Bretons and Basques had it easier than their English counterparts did.

Of course, that coin was two-sided. New Hastings' summers were hotter and stickier than the ones back in England. The farther south you went down Atlantis' east coast, the more pronounced that got. By the time you reached Gernika, wouldn't you turn into a puddle of sweat?

There had to be a better way—and there was, on the far side of the mountains. From what he'd seen and from what Henry had reported, the weather near Avalon Bay came close to perfection the whole year round. Again, he wondered why there should be such a difference, and, again, he didn't know. That the difference was there and that it was real, he couldn't help believing. He'd seen it. He'd felt it.

His stomach growled. He roasted the oil thrush's other drumstick and broke his fast with it. He left the rest of the carcass behind when he went east once more. In England, he wouldn't have, for he wouldn't have been confident of catching anything else. Even a halfway decent hunter, though, had a hard time going hungry in Atlantis. He'd left a lot of big birds behind him, dead, in his travels. He could always kill another one when he needed to.

Downhill again. Downhill all the way to New Hastings. All he needed to do was find the trail he'd blazed and follow it, and it would take him home again. What could be easier?

"Yes? And then what?" he asked himself aloud. When he got back, how many people would care where he'd gone? How many would care what he'd done? Oh, some would, but most of the settlers just wanted to get on with the lives they'd made here. They thought him strange for plunging into the wilderness every chance he got. He wondered why they'd bothered leaving England.

Even his wife thought him strange for plunging into the wilderness—and for leaving her alone. He hoped she hadn't done anything to make a scandal while he was gone. Fishermen who went to sea for weeks and months at a time ran that risk. Richard had no reason to think Bertha was unfaithful, but he knew it was one of the things that could happen to a traveling man.

Of course, it was also one of the things that could happen to a man who lived over his shop. If a woman was going to, she was going to. The same held true for men, but women had a harder time doing anything about it.

He was perhaps halfway down from the mountains to the sea when he got a surprise—he saw a hog drinking at a swift-running stream. A heartbeat later, the hog saw him or smelled him or heard him. It snorted and trotted away. Unlike honkers and oil thrushes, it knew what a man would want from it.

"By Our Lady, they've come a long way!" Richard exclaimed. If he'd seen this one here, some were bound to have traveled even farther west. He wondered if any swine had reached the mountains or gone over them. He laughed. They would give the local beasts a lively time.

Halfway up the towering spire of a redwood, a parrot screeched. Others started to call, too, till the woods echoed with their cries. That made Richard laugh again. Back in England, he'd heard of parrots, but never seen them. From everything he'd heard, they lived in hot countries. Not in Atlantis. Here they were, screaming their heads off in the middle of winter. You never could tell.

At last, near the headwaters of a small stream running east, he came to a pine marked not with one of his usual blazes but with a *B*. He smiled. That blaze marked the Brede. All he had to do was follow the river, and it would take him home.

But when he neared Bredestown, he got another surprise, and one not nearly so welcome as the hog. More game out in the woods was always welcome. Strange men tramping the edges of the cleared ground wearing helmets and chainmail were anything but.

"Who the devil are you?" one of the strangers said when Richard stepped out from the shelter of the trees.

"*What* the devil are you?" the other one added.

He looked down at himself. His clothes were filthy and tattered, his beard long and unkempt. When he was alone in the forest, what difference did it make? It made one now.

"My name is Richard Radcliffe." Talking to other people, especially to strangers, felt odd after so long in his own company. "I've been to the other side of Atlantis, and now I'm back. Who are *you*?"

"Why, the Earl of Warwick's men." By the way the soldier said it, even someone just back from the other side of Atlantis—or the other side of the moon—should have known that. In case Richard didn't know that, the man added, "Warwick's in charge here now."

"Is he?" Richard said tonelessly. Both soldiers nodded. Both of them kept hand on swordhilt. Richard got the idea they would make him sorry if he said that didn't suit him. That being so, he didn't. "When I set out, the earl was on the far side of the sea. So were you two, I expect," seemed safer.

Both men at arms nodded. "But we're bloody well

here now, so we have to make the best of it," the bigger one said. He had a scar on his upper lip and two missing front teeth. He also had bushy eyebrows, which came down and together as he frowned. "Radcliffe, is it? You'll be the old grumbler's other son?"

No one had ever talked about Richard's father that way before. Richard had brawled—who hadn't?—but he was no warrior. He wouldn't have cared to take on one of these bruisers, let alone both of them, even if they weren't armored. Another soft answer seemed best, so he gave one: "Henry is my brother, yes."

They put their heads together and muttered to each other. Richard wondered whether he ought to bolt back into the woods. But the soldier with the missing front teeth said, "Well, now that you're back, you'd damned well better keep your nose clean—that's all I've got to tell you."

"You'd damned well better keep all of you clean." The other soldier held his nose. "You stink like a dung heap, *friend.*"

Richard had no doubt the Earl of Warwick's man was right. "It's been cold," he said with such dignity as he could muster. "Not much chance to wash." It hadn't been all that cold on the other side of the mountains, but the soldiers didn't need to know that. When you were all by yourself, though, what point to washing? Most people didn't bother very often even when they weren't by themselves: Warwick's men stank of sour sweat, too. But Richard had no doubt he was riper. He looked forward to a bath.

After a last couple of growls, Warwick's men let him go on. A sigh of relief gusted from him as soon as they got far enough away not to hear it. Cows and sheep and a few horses grazed on the meadows and gleaned what they could from the fallow fields, manuring them with their dung. Dogs barked and growled. A brindled cat sneaked around the corner of a barn. It might almost have been England.

It might, that is, till Richard looked past the plowed and settled ground. Those somber woods had no counterpart in the lands across the sea. Here and there in the settlement, a pine or a barrel tree still stood. The redwoods were gone. Not only was their timber useful, but living under their shadow would have made the English feel like mice living under a church steeple.

Prince, the family dog, snarled at Richard as he came up. Then the beast took his scent and stared like a player doing a comedy turn in a mummers' show. *Is that really you?* his line would have been.

"Yes, you miserable hound, it is me," Richard said.

Whining, the dog came up and licked his hand. He wondered what would happen if he stayed away long enough for Prince to forget him. He would get bitten, that was what.

Bertha was down on her knees in the garden plot by the farmhouse. You could keep things alive through these winters if you looked after them. Up to a certain point, carrots and parsnips got sweeter if you left them in the ground. And far fewer pests plagued them here than would have been so back in England.

Richard's wife glanced up from her work. Her mouth dropped open. The way he looked didn't faze her—she'd seen him come home from the woods before. She scrambled to her feet and ran to his arms.

"Hello, dear," he said. She felt good pressed against him; her solid warmth reminded him how long he'd been away.

"So good to see you." Bertha tilted her face up for a kiss. "I was beginning to worry—not a lot, but some."

"Just a long trip, not a hard one," Richard said. "But who are those damned brigands in chainmail? Where did they come from?"

He didn't hold his voice down. His wife looked alarmed. "You've met them, have you? Be careful how you talk about them. If anyone makes them angry, he pays."

"Somebody ought to make them pay, by God," Richard said. "Those byrnies won't hold out arrows."

Bertha crossed herself. "Sweet suffering Jesus, you sound like your father. He's wild to do them in, but they don't give many chances."

"What's this Warwick doing here, anyway?" Richard asked.

"He was sent here for our sins—and for his own," his wife answered. "He made the king angry, so Henry sent him off to Freetown, to do his worst there. But his captain landed here instead, and now we're stuck with him."

They went inside. She poured water from a bucket into a kettle and set it on the fire to heat. Richard smiled. He'd be able to bathe soon. But the smile didn't last. "We're going to have to do something about him," he said.

"You *do* sound like your father," Bertha said. "He goes on and on about how he didn't come to Atlantis to bend the knee to any nobleman. One day he'll say it too loud, or to the wrong man, and it will get back to Warwick. And then the trouble will start."

"To the wrong man?" Richard frowned. He'd been away from human company too long; he needed a moment to realize what that had to mean. "Some of the settlers would betray him to this robber chief?"

"Watch what you say!" Bertha repeated. But she nodded, unhappily. "Some would. They want to get along any way they can. They don't want trouble. If I've heard that once, I've heard it a hundred times. 'I don't want trouble,' they say, and pull their heads into their shells like turtles."

"They'll have more trouble if they bend the knee to this dog of a Warwick than they will if they give him a good kick in the teeth," Richard said. His wife started to speak again, then closed her mouth instead. He suspected he'd just sounded like his father one more time. Well, his father knew a hawk from a heron when the wind was southerly, all right.

Bertha took the kettle off the fire. She mixed the hot water with a little cold—not too much, because it would cool fast enough on its own. Richard stripped off his filthy clothes and scrubbed at himself with a rag and some of the harsh, homemade soap she gave him. By the time he was done, his skin had gone from assorted shades of brown to pink. She trimmed his hair and beard with a pair of shears she'd brought from England.

"You look like the man I married again," she said when she finished, "and not the Old Man of the Woods any more."

"I feel like the man you married, too." He reached for her. They kissed. Laughing, he picked her up and carried her over to the bed.

Edward, these days, stayed close to home. He knew he had trouble keeping his mouth shut. If he hadn't known, Nell would have made a point of reminding him. He hadn't had to worry about saying what was on his mind, not for years. No one in Atlantis had. People needed to worry now. If you didn't watch your words, Richard Neville's bully boys would make you sorry.

The Earl of Warwick acted like a king, or at least like a prince. His bravos held New Hastings hostage. They lived off the fat of the land, taking what they wanted. One of the things Warwick took was Lucy Fenner, the late master salter's daughter. She was nineteen now, or maybe twenty. People said she was the fairest on this side of the Atlantic: a red-haired beauty with a figure to make a priest forget his vows. She could heat up a cold night—Edward had no doubt of that. He was getting old (no, Devil take it, he'd got old), but he wasn't dead.

He also wasn't a bandit chief, to take a woman whether she was willing or not. Warwick . . . was. Lucy, these days, went around with red-rimmed eyes and an expression beyond sorrowful. She'd never imagined beauty could be dangerous to her. Whether she'd imagined it or not, she was finding out the hard way.

"Mary, pity women," Nell said when Edward remarked on that.

"It's not Mary's doing that Lucy got snatched from her family," Edward said. "It's that dog of a Warwick."

"He's a dog with teeth," Nell warned.

"I know," Edward said grimly. Fear of what Warwick's troopers would do was the only thing that had kept New Hastings from rising against its new and unwelcome overlord. "Someone needs to give him a boot in the ribs, to remind him he's not supposed to do that kind of thing here."

His wife wagged a finger in his face. "Not you. You're not going to throw your life away over a chit of a girl."

"I wouldn't do that," Edward said with dignity. Nell only snorted. Still with dignity, he went on, "If I rise against Warwick, I won't throw my life away. I'll make him throw away his."

"Can you?" Nell asked—the right question, sure enough.

"If I don't think I can, I won't move," Edward said. "He has his bully boys, and he has the men he's scared into thinking he's a sure winner, and he has the handful of curs—I won't call them men, because they don't deserve the name—who lick the boots of anybody they think is strong. We have the rest of New Hastings."

"Is that enough?" Nell asked anxiously. "Against trained men with armor . . . I don't think there was a mailshirt in Atlantis before Warwick came, let alone that suit of plate he wears."

"You only need armor if you intend to kill your fellow man and you don't intend to let him kill you," Edward said. "Why would we have wanted it till now? But we have shields, and we have our bows, and"—his voice dropped to a whisper—"in Bredestown, where Warwick's hounds don't go so much, the smith is making swords."

"Warwick's hounds almost took Richard when he came out of the woods by the Brede," his wife reminded him.

"I didn't say they never went to Bredestown. I said they didn't go there so often, and they don't," Edward Radcliffe answered. "And Adam Higgins is no fool—there's always something else on the anvil, so no stinking bravo's likely to see him forging a blade."

"I'm not worried about soldiers seeing him so much as I am about some Judas selling him to Warwick," Nell said.

Edward put an arm around her. "Speaking of being no fool, my dear . . ."

"Oh, pooh!" Nell shook him off. "I'm an old gossip, is what I am. And one gossip knows how much trouble another one can cause. Is there anyone in Bredestown who doesn't like the smith? If there is, that's someone we have to watch."

"By Our Lady!" Edward said, and laughed at his own choice of oath. "By Our Lady, indeed! I wonder how men ever get anything done, with women keeping an eye on their every move before they make it." He paused, looking thoughtful. "I wonder *whether* men ever get anything done—anything their women don't want, I mean."

"I have no idea what you're talking about—none." Nell's voice was so demure and innocent, Edward started to nod. Then he caught himself and gave her a sharp look. Her face was demure and innocent, too—so very demure and innocent that he started laughing again. She poked him in the ribs. "You believed me. For a heartbeat or two, you believed me."

"You'll never prove it," he said.

"I don't need to prove it. I know you too well to doubt it." Now Nell sounded supremely confident. And with reason: "I'd better after all these years, don't you think? Who else would have put up with you for so long?"

"No one in her right mind—that's sure enough," Edward said. Nell made a face at him. He made one back. They both laughed this time. Edward wondered if he was slipping into his second childhood. If he was, he was having a good time doing it—or he would have been, if not for the Earl of Warwick.

Henry Radcliffe paced the *Rose*'s deck. She lay not far offshore: far enough to keep a bad winter storm from flinging her up onto the beach and breaking her all to flinders. No storm now. The day was cold, but almost bitterly clear—a good match for the state of his mind at the moment.

Not quite by chance, one of his mittened hands came to rest on the wrought-iron barrel of a swivel gun. "I wonder if we could hit New Hastings from here," he said in musing tones. "I wonder if we could hit a particular house in New Hastings from here."

"Hit the town? I think the piece'd reach that far," Bartholomew Smith said. Henry nodded; he gauged the range, and the gun's power, about the same. The mate went on, "Hit one house in particular? That'd take the Devil's own luck, don't you think?"

Regretfully, Henry nodded again. "Afraid I do."

Smith eyed him. "Which house have you got in mind?"

"Oh, let's just say I was thinking of putting a ball through my father's door, to wake him up if he was sleeping."

"You can say that if you want to." Smith looked around to make sure no one besides Henry was in earshot. "Me, I'd sooner put one through Warwick's door—or through Warwick, though from here that'd take more than the Devil's luck."

"It would, wouldn't it?" Henry said sadly. He sent the mate a hooded glance. "So you're not fond of his Lordship?"

"Lucy Fenner's mother is my first cousin," Smith said.

"I should have remembered that." Henry thumped his forehead with the heel of his hand. "Well, no, then you have good reason not to be."

The mate scowled. "Lucy's a good girl, a sweet girl, damn him. Not her fault she was born pretty, and she shouldn't have to pay for it like that."

"Women have been paying for their looks that way since the days of Adam and Eve," Henry said. Seeing the mutinous expression on the mate's face, he quickly added, "Not that that makes it right."

"I should say not," Bartholomew Smith spat. "The day is coming when Warwick'll push all of us too far, like he's already pushed me. I think it's coming soon, and when it does . . ." His strong, scarred hands folded into fists.

"My father feels the same way. I do believe he's felt that way since he first set eyes on Warwick, before the earl even set foot on our soil." Henry looked around again. No one was paying him or Smith any special heed. In a low voice, he continued, "When the day does come, he aims to fight."

"Skipper, I always knew your father was a good man," Smith said. "I always knew he was a smart man, too. Only question is, can we kick those bastards when we have to?"

"That's what's held him back this long. And, he says,

even winning you can pay too high a price. If the battle tears New Hastings and Bredestown to pieces, if half the people die and half the houses and shops burn down, we'll all be years getting over it," Henry said. "When he was a lad, he says, his old grandfather would tell him stories about what England was like just after the Black Death passed over the countryside."

The mate shuddered and made the sign of the cross. "God keep the plague on the other side of the sea. That bloody Warwick's plague enough for these lands."

"Plague enough and to spare," Henry agreed. "But that's just Father's point. A war here could be as bad as the plague. It could set us back the way the Black Death set England back. That's why he doesn't want to fight unless we can beat the soldiers in a hurry without ruining ourselves in the doing."

"That's sensible, no doubt about it," Bartholomew Smith said. "How long do you think poor Lucy will want us to go on being sensible?" Henry grunted; that shot hit the target in the bull's-eye. Smith asked another question: "Isn't it better to die on our feet than to live on our knees?"

Henry grunted again—he hadn't dreamt the other man had so much fire in his belly. Slowly, he answered, "It is, yes. My father would not say otherwise. But he *would* say it's better still to live on our feet. He's looking for a way to do that, which is why he waits."

"God grant he find one," Smith said. "How long can he—how long can we—keep waiting, though? If we get used to saying, 'Yes, Lord,' to whatever Warwick demands of us—well, we'll be living on our knees then, and I fear me we'll forget how to climb up on our feet again."

"I don't think it will go that far," Henry said. "Back in England, even the king has trouble telling his people what to do. That's why the wars go on and on. If the

king can't make Englishmen obey, Lord have mercy on
a poor earl who tries, eh?"

Smith's smile touched his lips, but not his eyes. "Don't
they call Warwick the Kingmaker, though?"

"That was his nickname, all right. But the king he
made unmade him. And if a mere king can cast him
down"—Henry winked—"don't you suppose a settlement full of Englishmen can do the same when the time
comes?"

"Belike you're right." Despite his words, Smith still
didn't smile with his whole face. "It had better come
soon, I tell you, for Lucy's sake. A woman's not like a
man, you know—she keeps her honor between her
legs."

"Warwick has dishonored her, but he hasn't taken her
honor away. It's not the same thing," Henry said. "Everyone knows what he would have done to her kin if she
didn't yield herself to him. That would have touched off
the fight, I expect, but it wouldn't have done the Fenners
any good."

"No, it wouldn't. . . . Touched off . . ." Smith set his own
gloved hand on the wrought-iron barrel of the swivel
gun. He swung it toward the house the Earl of Warwick
had taken for his own, as he'd taken Lucy Fenner for
his own.

*As he aims to take New Hastings for his own,* Henry
thought. When you got down to it, wasn't it that simple?
Warwick didn't want to be a kingmaker here: he wanted
to be a king himself. It would be a small kingdom. Maybe
that would suffice him, or maybe he dreamt of taking
England in King Edward's despite, using Atlantis as his
base. If he did, Henry judged him a madman, but wasn't
a madman all the more dangerous for being mad?

"We'll settle him," he declared. "What does Atlantis
need with kings?"

"King Warwick?" Smith followed his thoughts without trouble. "King Neville? King Richard? Whatever he'd style himself, let him carve it on his tombstone instead."

"My brother would make a better King Richard than Warwick would," Henry said. "He's better suited to the job, too, by God."

"How's that?"

"He doesn't want it."

# IX

$\mathcal{E}$dward Radcliffe was coming to dread a knock on the door. He never had before, not in all the years since coming to Atlantis. In that stretch of time, a knock on the door meant a friend had come to call. Now a knock was much too likely to be trouble calling.

This particular knock on the door came just before supper. Chicken and turnips and parsnips and cabbage bubbled in a pot, filling the house with savory fragrance and making Edward's stomach rumble. He said something unchristian when a fist thudded against the planks of the door.

"Tell whoever it is to go away," Nell said.

"Nothing I'd like better." But when Edward went to the door, he found that his visitors were not likely to take no for an answer. They were five of Richard Neville's biggest, roughest bravos, all of them armored, all of them with drawn swords except for one who carried a crossbow instead. "Well, well!" Edward said. "What's all this about?"

The soldiers with the swords hefted them. The fellow with the crossbow aimed it at Radcliffe's chest. The biggest ruffian growled, "His Lordship wants to see you. And I mean right away."

"Does he?" Edward said mildly. All the soldiers nodded. Edward asked, "Suppose I don't care to see him right away?"

"That would be too bad—for you," the trooper answered. "And he would still see what was left of you."

There was a line between bravery and stupidity. Edward Radcliffe knew which side of the line defying five young, tough, armored men lay on. "Well, supper will just have to wait in that case, won't it?" he said.

"Smartest notion you've had in a long time, Granddad," the big soldier agreed. "Now get moving, before he gets sick of waiting."

"I'm coming." Edward raised his voice to call out to Nell: "His Lordship has something to talk about with me." She squawked in dismay. He was dismayed, too, but he didn't think squawking would do any good. He nodded to Warwick's men. "Lead on. I'm honored to have such a fine escort."

They snorted, almost in unison. "We aren't doing it for your honor, old man," the big soldier said. "We're doing it for his."

"Really?" Edward said, as if that hadn't occurred to him. He didn't think pushing them any further was a good idea. He stepped over the threshold and into the street.

He remembered when New Hastings literally hadn't been there. Now it could have been any other English seaside town—if you didn't notice the redwood timber, and if you didn't raise your eyes past the fields to the dark woods that didn't lie far away.

Guards stood in front of the house Neville had appropriated: the biggest one in town. They carried spears taller than they were. The sharp edges of the spearpoints glittered blood-red in the fading light. "So he came, did he?" one of the guards said. "How about that?"

"He came, all right," the crossbowman answered. "See? He's not so dumb as he looks."

"Couldn't prove it by me," the guard said. "Take him on in, then. His Lordship'll let him know what's what."

"Right." The crossbowman gave Edward a little shove. "You heard Peter. Go on in."

"Thank you so much," Edward said. The fellow with the crossbow smirked. Plainly, he didn't recognize irony when he heard it. Too late, Edward realized that might be good luck; had the archer recognized it, he might have made him sorry.

Inside, the Earl of Warwick sat in a chair with a back. That emphasized his noble blood; like most people, Radcliffe had only stools in his house. "Lucy!" Warwick called. "Fetch my guest something to drink!"

"Yes, your Lordship." Lucy Fenner hurried in from the kitchen. The silk gown she wore must have come from England with the exiled earl. It bared too much of her, and clung too tightly to what it didn't display. She lowered her eyes to the ground, and scurried away as soon as she'd set a mug in Edward's hand.

He raised an eyebrow even before he tasted it. The rich bouquet told him what it was. "Did the wine come from England, Lord?" he asked.

Warwick shook his head. "I took it in trade from the Bretons," he replied. "It's horsepiss alongside what a proper vintner could do, mind, but any wine is better than none."

Edward hadn't known the settlers François Kersauzon had brought to Atlantis were finally turning out enough wine to turn some loose. "I thank you for your kindness," he said, and surprised himself by more or less meaning it. "Been a good many years since I've drunk anything but beer and ale and barrel-tree sap."

"I deserve better," Warwick said simply. "The one trouble is, getting what I want isn't always cheap."

"Sorry to hear that, your Lordship." As long as the earl was giving him wine, Edward would sound sympathetic.

He thought so, anyhow, till Warwick continued, "Since it isn't, I am going to have to take . . . certain measures, I suppose you would say."

Maybe the exiled noble hoped the wine would fuzz Edward's wits so he'd blithely accept anything he heard. If that was what Warwick had in mind, he was doomed to disappointment. "What kind of measures, sir?" Radcliffe asked. He still sounded polite, but he was sure he also sounded wary. And with reason, for he was.

Warwick sent him a sour stare. Yes, the noble had wanted him fuddled, all right. Well, no matter what Warwick wanted, he had what he had. He needed only a handful of heartbeats to see as much. "I shall have to start levying a tax on the settlers here," he said regretfully, as if it were Edward's fault that he'd been reduced to such measures.

"A tax?" Edward blurted. He could have sounded no more appalled if Richard Neville had denied that the Son and Holy Ghost were proper Persons of the Trinity. "You can't do that!"

One of the bully boys who'd fetched him hither growled like a dog on a chain. The Earl of Warwick raised a languid-seeming hand, and the soldier fell silent. He still glared in Edward's direction, though, and his knuckles whitened as his hand clutched the hilt of his sword.

"You are a bold man, Radcliffe—a bold man or a fool," Warwick said. "How dare you tell me what I may and may not do? I suggest you think carefully before you answer. Think very carefully, in fact."

"Lord, I could think from now till doomsday and not think you had the right to tax me," Edward said. "I am sorry if my being so plain offends you, but that's the truth. Why, in England the king himself has to ask leave of Parliament before he taxes his people."

Richard Neville's mouth tightened. "I will thank you not to speak of the king in my presence. If you value your neck, Radcliffe, you will honor my—request."

"I don't know if I can, sir, not while we're talking about taxes," Edward said. "How do you claim a power here that he doesn't claim in England?"

"How? Simple." The Earl of Warwick drew from his belt a dagger whose hilt was ornamented with gold wire and began cleaning his nails with the point. "This miserable, godforsaken place isn't England. It's bloody Atlantis, and you people here never tire of telling me so."

"But we are Englishmen, Lord. We have the rights of Englishmen." Till that moment, Edward's main concern had been making sure that England paid no attention to Atlantis. Parliament might have decided to levy taxes here, too, and to whom could he have appealed if it did? To no one at all, as he knew too well.

Warwick eyed him like a cat watching a mouse it was playing with but hadn't yet decided to kill. "You claim those rights when you feel like it. Otherwise, you're glad England lies across the sundering sea."

That arrow quivered in the center of the target. Edward couldn't, and wouldn't, admit as much. He took a deep breath. "You are not our king, Lord. You have not got the right to do this."

Warwick went on cleaning his fingernails. The dagger was slim, pointed, and sharp—quite a bit like him. "I have the might to do it, sirrah, as you will learn to your sorrow if you prove lunatic enough to challenge me."

"We are Englishmen, Lord," Edward Radcliffe repeated stubbornly. "You have no right to steal from us this way—and that is what it is, stealing. If you try to take what is ours, we will appeal to his Majesty."

Even as he said the words, he wondered whether that was a good idea. The Earl of Warwick, with a small force of soldiers behind him, was an annoyance, and no small one. But the King of England could call on the whole strength of the island if he chose—and if he wasn't caught up in the coils of civil war. He might prove a more dangerous master than any local lord.

Or he might not, if the local lord made as much trouble as this one was doing.

The threat didn't seem to worry Warwick. He neither flinched nor paled. Nor did he raise his voice as he said, "I will kill every one of you if you try." He was just stating a fact; he might as well have said, *Red-crested eagles will kill honkers if they can.*

*If I am a honker, by God, I can honk all the way across the ocean,* Edward thought. "Meaning no disrespect, Lord, but that is a silly thing to say," he replied.

"Silly, is it?" *That* roused the noble's ire. "Explain yourself, and quickly—you are talking for your life."

"We're fishermen, for heaven's sake," Edward answered. "Cod are what brought us to Atlantis in the first place. We have lots of boats, and they can sail across the Atlantic. How do you propose to stop them all?"

Richard Neville's jaw dropped. Edward almost laughed in his face. The only thing that stopped him was the fear that he would never leave this room alive if he did. The Earl of Warwick plainly was a calculating man; you didn't get the name Kingmaker if you couldn't see past the end of your nose. But Warwick hadn't seen something here—his astonishment and dismay showed as much.

"You!" he said thickly. "I'll hold you to blame if boats go out and don't come back."

"Then bring Bishop John here now so he can shrive me," Edward said. "Boats go out all the damned time. They stay away a long time, too. They have to—otherwise, we'd go hungry. How will you know if one's gone to England and not just to the fishing banks? You won't, not till it's too late for you."

By the way Warwick's jaw worked, he might have been gnawing on a piece of meat that proved tougher than he'd expected. "Get out," he told Edward. "Just— get out. But if you think you can stop me from levying taxes when I have a mind to, you'd best think again."

"You will do what you think best, your Lordship," Radcliffe said. *And so will we.* He didn't say that out loud. Maybe Warwick would figure it out for himself. Or maybe it too would come as a surprise to him. If it did—too bad.

"Taxes?" Richard Radcliffe said when his brother came out to Bredestown to give him the news. To his embarrassment, surprise made his voice break like a youth's.

"That's right," Henry said grimly. "He thinks he's strong enough to squeeze them out of us."

"I almost hope he's right," Richard said.

Henry dug a finger into one ear. "Did I hear that?"

"Damned if you didn't. If Warwick thinks he can have soldiers prowling all over the settlement, and if he thinks he can take away what he didn't earn, well, plenty of people will want to go somewhere else, and I'll be glad to take 'em there."

"Wouldn't you rather fight him, so we make sure something like this can never happen again?" Henry asked.

"I'll do that if I have to," Richard answered. "But packing up and leaving is even easier. Atlantis is a big place. If we settle somewhere else, nobody'll come after us for years."

"No doubt," Henry said. "And if Warwick wins here in the meantime, the tax collector will be the one who does."

Richard winced. That, unfortunately, was all too likely to be so. "Well, what do you want me to do?" he asked.

"Stand with the rest of us. Stand, I say. Don't run,"

Henry told him. "I know you'd sooner go off into the wilderness all alone and look at the birds and the frogs and the snakes. We've got our own snake here, and we need to slay him."

"A bowman who knows his business could do that for us," Richard said. "I will if you want me to. Warwick can't hide in his house the whole day through."

But Henry shook his head. "He doesn't come out without bodyguards. Too likely they'd run down whoever shot him. And even if they didn't, no one knows what the soldiers would do if he got killed. They might try slaughtering everyone in sight to avenge him."

"They'd seal their own fate if they did," Richard pointed out.

"Which is true. And which might not have anything to do with anything—chances are it doesn't. Father says Warwick is a man who thinks past the moment. Not many folk bother. From what I know of soldiers, they mostly don't. Or will you tell me different?"

"Well, no," Richard said, much as he would have liked to say yes. "Are we going to fight Warwick, then?"

"Unless he pulls in his horns, we are," his brother said.

"Slim odds of that."

"Mighty slim."

A longbow hung on the wall next to the fireplace. Richard had brought the bow from England. Nothing the bowyers had found here measured up to yew. They made good enough bows. He'd brought a fine one. A longbow had almost the range of a crossbow, and could shoot many times faster. The only problem was, a longbow needed constant practice and a crossbow didn't.

"I wish we had hand cannon, not just the swivels on the *Rose*," Richard said. "Warwick's bully boys would think twice before they bothered us if we did."

"They'd better think twice anyway," Henry said.

"I'm sure we can beat them if we gather our strength together," Richard said. "But will we really do that?"

"If Warwick is fool enough to keep trying to tax us, we will," Henry answered.

"Do you know something? I think you may be right," Richard said.

Henry beamed at him. "We never agree about anything," he said. "If we both feel the same way about this—"

Richard cut him off. "It isn't a sign that we're bound to be right. It only means Warwick is bound to be wrong."

"That will do well enough," Henry said. "Better than well enough, in fact."

Edward Radcliffe didn't suppose he should have been surprised when the Earl of Warwick's men pounded on his door again early one chilly morning. Whether he should have been or not, he was. He said something that made Nell cluck reproachfully. Then he said something stronger than that.

The pounding didn't stop. "Open up, you old fool!" one of Warwick's bully boys bawled. "We know you're in there—where the devil else would you be?"

"Time to pay what you owe," another soldier added.

What Edward said then made Nell frown, not for the blasphemy but from fear of the soldiers outside. "Don't make them angry," she told him. "Say what you will, this isn't worth getting killed over."

He looked at her. "I'm afraid you're wrong," he said. "If Warwick thinks he can rob New Hastings, he'd best think again. The folk here *will* stand up to him. Maybe it should start with me. I've lived a full life. What have I got to look forward to? Slowness and sickness—not much more."

Nell grabbed his arm. "Don't talk like a fool. Slaying yourself is a mortal sin, and what else would you be doing if you tried to fight those—those. . . ." She stopped. Whatever she wanted to say, it had to be hotter than the endearments that had burst from Edward's lips a moment before.

*Bang! Bang! Bang!* "You'd bloody well better open up in there, or somebody'll close your cursed coffin for you!" Warwick's bravo yelled. "This is your last chance, and you ought to thank us for it."

With a sigh, Edward walked to the door and unbarred it. One of the soldiers out there held a torch. He hadn't been kidding. But he dropped it in the mud of the walkway. It hissed and sizzled and went out. "You want something of me?" Edward inquired, his voice deceptively mild.

"Too bloody right we do," a soldier said. Radcliffe recognized him as one of the earl's sergeants. He had a list of what his overlord required. "You are assessed at two pounds, seven shillings, ninepence ha'penny. Give us the coin and we'll be on our way."

This was robbery even more naked and raw than Edward had looked for. "You must know I have not got it," he said. Oh, he'd buried some money in a safe place, but not that much. He didn't think anyone in New Hastings had that much ready cash. Trade on this side of the Atlantic was mostly barter. Nobody here needed much in the way of actual silver.

He wondered whether Warwick's men *would* kill him on the spot for refusing. But the sergeant seemed unfazed. Referring to his list again, he said, "His Lordship declares the following valuations for taxes collected in kind. One horse is to be reckoned at one pound. One cow is to be reckoned at fifteen shillings. One sheep or goat is to be reckoned at ten. One pig is to be reckoned at eight. One salted honker carcass is to be reckoned at four. One goose is to be reckoned at two. One duck is to be reckoned at one and sixpence. One hen is to be reckoned at one shilling. Salt cod is to be reckoned at a shilling for five pounds' weight."

"His Lordship has it all ciphered out, doesn't he?" Edward said. The values Warwick set on beasts weren't even unfair—or they wouldn't have been back in England, where there were so many more animals to take. That was clever of the nobleman—people couldn't say he was cheating them by cheapening their goods.

He was cheating them by taxing them at all, but that was a different story.

The sergeant nodded seriously. "Too right he does, friend. We'll take what we need to take to pay your tax bill, and not a bit more. You can watch whilst we do it."

"Honest thieves, you are," Edward said, only a little irony in his voice.

"That's us." The sergeant nodded once more. "Anybody who doesn't fancy his tax bill or the way we collect it, he's welcome to complain to the earl."

"Oh, that will do a lot of good," Edward said.

"Aye, belike." Warwick's sergeant chuckled—he knew how much good it was likely to do. He turned to the common soldiers. "Paul! Matt! John! Go to the barn and take what's due his Lordship."

"Right, Sergeant!" they chorused. It was nowhere close to right, but they neither knew nor cared about that. Off to the barn they went. They emerged with enough livestock to square Edward's scot . . . by their reckoning, anyhow.

"You're nothing but thieves!" Edward called to them from the path that led to the street. Nell called them something much less complimentary than that. They just laughed.

They laughed, that is, till someone hiding behind a squat barrel tree fifty yards away also shouted, "Thieves!" and let fly with a longbow. The arrow thrummed through the air and buried itself with a meaty *chunk!* in the middle of the sergeant's chest. He stood there staring at it for what seemed a very long time. When he opened his mouth to say something, only blood burst from between his lips. His knees buckled. He fell to the ground, where he kicked a few times and lay still.

The three common soldiers gaped, as astonished as the sergeant had been. Another arrow hissed toward them. It missed by the breadth of a hair, and slammed into a sheep's rump. The animal bawled in pain and bolted, more blood dripping in the dirt.

That seemed to snap the soldiers from their stunned spell. Two of them rushed toward the barrel tree. That was brave. If the archer kept his head, he could slaughter them before they got close enough to hurt him. They'd just seen that their byrnies weren't proof against his shafts, not at close range.

But he must have been as caught up in the madness of the moment as everyone else, for his next shot flew between the two of them. He had no time for another one—all he could do was run away. Run he did, with the armored men pounding after him but losing ground at every stride.

"Is that Richard?" Nell hissed to Edward. "If God is kind, you'll tell me that isn't Richard."

Edward could tell her nothing of the sort, for he also feared it was their younger son. If Warwick's troopers recognized him, too, that would bring trouble down on all the Radcliffes' heads.

But trouble was coming faster than recognizing Richard would bring it. The third soldier, the one who hadn't gone after the archer, stalked back towards Edward and Nell. He swung his sword up to slash with it. Rage twisting his face, he shouted, "You knew that murdering bugger lay in wait for us!"

"No," Edward said.

"Liar!" the man cried, and broke into a heavy trot.

"Run!" Edward told Nell. When she didn't, he shoved her toward the farmhouse. He looked around for a weapon then, or for anything that would let him defend himself. He snatched up an axe handle—no axehead attached, worse luck. "You've got me wrong," he told the soldier, who was now very close.

"Save your lies for the devils in hell—that's where you're going, all right," the soldier said, and aimed a cut at Edward that should have taken his head off.

Somehow, he turned it with the axe handle. Nell screamed like a scalded cat. Warwick's man swore. Absurdly, Edward wasted a moment wondering what good telling lies to devils would do. Wouldn't they know them when they heard them?

The soldier slashed again. Edward got the axe handle between himself and the blade once more, but it flew from his fingers. He stared at his hands as if they'd betrayed him—and so they had. That never would have happened twenty years earlier, or even ten.

But it had happened now, and he would have to live with it—though not for very long. "So long, old man!" the trooper shouted. He slashed once more. This time, the sword bit. Edward howled.

Next thing he knew, he was on the ground, with Warwick's soldier hacking at him as if he were a badly butchered sow. Nell grabbed the man's arm, but he knocked her aside. He swung up the sword again. It fell—right on Edward's neck.

So died the first Englishman to set foot on Atlantis, the founder of the first English settlement in the new land, not far from where the settlement began. It was in the year 1470, the sixty-ninth year of Edward Radcliffe's age, the tenth year of the reign of King Edward IV in England, and around New Hastings still the first year of the reign of Richard Neville, the Earl of Warwick. And the manner of his passing helped determine the Englishmen in those parts that Warwick's reign should reach no further.

"Like a dog!" Henry Radcliffe raged. "They cut him down like a dog on his own farm! I'll garter myself with Warwick's guts, the Devil damn me black if I don't."

"I never thought they would go after him," his brother said. "My idea was, I'd either kill them all or lead them a merry chase." His mouth twisted. "I didn't do either, not well enough."

"No, you didn't," Henry agreed. "And now we're all paying the price for it."

He and Richard crouched in the woods, somewhere west of Bredestown. They'd got their families away before Warwick's men could swoop down on them. Richard seemed utterly at home under the redwoods. He made little shelters of branches and twigs and bark, and by all appearances was as content in one of them as he would have been in front of his own hearth. He was as happy to eat honkers and fiddlehead ferns as he would have been with white bread and butter and fat mutton.

"We shouldn't pay the price. Warwick and his men should," Richard said.

"Well, yes. They should," Henry said. "The trouble is, they aren't. We're out here with the honkers and the oil thrushes and the cucumber slugs."

"Nothing wrong with them," Richard said.

"Nothing wrong with them, no," Henry replied. "But the bloody Earl of bloody Warwick, the man who bloody murdered our father, he's sleeping in a bloody soft bed back in New Hastings, and swiving Lucy Fenner in it whenever that strikes his fancy. And there's something bloody wrong with that."

"Oh, yes. There is," Richard said quietly. "And I aim to do something about it."

"You? By yourself?" Henry had trouble hiding his disbelief. "If not for you—" He broke off.

"If not for me, Father would still be alive. That's what you were going to say, isn't it?" Richard demanded. Henry might not have wanted to say it, but he nodded. Richard scowled at him. "Maybe you're right and maybe you're wrong, and maybe I'll have somewhat to say to you about that when this mess with Warwick is over. But that can wait—that has to wait. For now, I'll just ask you this: do you think Father would have wanted to live in a place where a noble could steal his beasts because the bastard called it taking taxes?"

"Well, no, but   "

"But me no buts," Richard broke in. "As soon as bloody Warwick tries to lift anyone else's chattels, he'll have a bigger rising on his hands—this is tinder in dry grass, whether he knows it or not. And if you think I can't do anything about him by myself—well, watch me, big brother. Just bloody watch me."

He slipped east, toward the seashore, toward the settlements, as the sun set that night. Henry couldn't watch him after that, because he moved with a swift, silent assurance the sailor had no hope of matching. Richard knew Henry scorned his trips through the woods. Henry was a seaman to his marrow, as their father had been. For him, dry land was a necessary nuisance.

Richard was different. Richard could slip through the woods so quietly, even the mouse-sized katydids went on chirping. Killing honkers was easy, but killing them before they knew you were there was anything but. Richard could do that. He thought he could also kill men before they knew he was there. He looked forward to it, in fact.

A nearly full moon gave him all the light he needed. Before long, he came to the camp Warwick's troopers had made just inside the forest. Several loudly unhappy men sat around a fire. "How are we supposed to catch those buggers?" one of them grumbled. "They could be anywhere by now."

"Too right they could," another soldier agreed. "Damn trees go on forever."

"We'll beat the bushes for a while, and then we'll go and tell his Lordship we had no luck," a third man said. "What else can we do?"

They all nodded. They were luckier than they dreamt. Richard Radcliffe could have potted a couple of them as easily as made no difference. But he had his heart set on harder game, more dangerous game. He went on. The foul-mouthed soldiers never knew he passed them over.

Things got harder when he came into settled country, but not much. Few people were out and about at night. Dogs barked, but never for long—he carried gobbets of honker meat to make them lose interest in him. One farmer swore at his hound for raising a ruckus. Otherwise, the night stayed still. Richard slid past Bredestown and down along the riverbank toward New Hastings.

Torches blazed on poles thrust into the ground around the house Warwick had taken for his own. Richard Radcliffe smiled a predatory smile. Warwick's men would have done better to leave it dark. That would have made it a tougher target. The light the torches threw didn't reach anywhere close to the edge of bowshot. And standing in that light blinded the sentries to whatever might be going on beyond its reach.

One of those sentries yawned. He said something to the man standing beside him. They both laughed. Richard took his place behind a pear tree whose trunk had grown man-thick in the fifteen years or so since it was planted. He strung the bow and fitted the leather wristguard to his left hand. Then, in one smooth motion, he fitted a shaft to the bowstring, drew, and let fly.

The arrow caught the soldier who'd yawned a few inches above his navel—the bright torchlight made aiming easier, too. The trooper did what any suddenly wounded man would do: he screamed and clutched at himself. As he crumpled, his friend stooped to give what help he could. Richard's second arrow punched through the man's neck. He let out a gurgling wail and fell beside the other guard.

Richard had a third shaft nocked and waiting. If the cries outside didn't bring Warwick out, what would? And when the noble showed himself . . .

But he didn't. Another soldier opened the door to see what had happened. Richard let fly at him, too. He must have had uncommonly quick reactions, for he jerked the door shut an instant before the arrow slammed into it. The shaft stood thrilling in the redwood planks.

If Richard had had some tow and a source of flame, he could have burnt the house with fire arrows. *I should have thought of that,* flashed through his mind. Remembering after the fact, sadly, was easier than getting the idea ahead of time.

He heard the back door open and shut. He couldn't see back there from where he crouched. Men spoke to one another in low voices. He couldn't catch what they were saying, but he didn't need to be Alexander the Great to figure it out.

Before long, he could hear boots thumping on the ground. He'd lost some of his night vision staring toward the torches. He couldn't see what Warwick's men—or maybe Warwick and his men—were doing. Again, though, he didn't need to be much of a general to know. They would work toward him, wait till he did something to show himself, and then close with him and finish him with swords and spears.

It was as good a plan as they could make under the circumstances. But it would work only if he waited around and let them get that close. That didn't look like the best thing he could do. The best thing he could do looked like disappearing now. So he did.

He had practice moving quietly. Maybe he wasn't quite quiet enough, or maybe one of them made a better woodsman than the rest. "There he goes, dammit!" somebody behind him called. "After him! He's heading west."

"No need to chase him," another voice said. This one was cold and calculating and deadly as a pitfall trap with a bottom full of upthrusting spears. If it wasn't the Earl of Warwick's voice, Richard would have been mightily surprised. It went on, "Make for the western edge of the cleared land beyond Bredestown, quick as you can. If you hurry, you can get there before him and keep him from sneaking into the woods."

Richard nodded to himself. Yes, that almost had to be Warwick. He thought fast, and he thought straight. They might be trouble if they interposed themselves between him and safety. They would be more trouble if he couldn't get back into the woods before daybreak, but he thought he could. Bredestown didn't lie *that* far upriver from New Hastings. Even after all these years, not much of Atlantis was settled.

He had to get away now. He took advantage of every bush and every copse of trees. Before long, his eyes adapted to the moonlight again, and he could see farther and more plainly. But Warwick's men would have the same edge, worse luck.

Barking dogs told where they were, or where they might be. No dog barked around Richard for long. He still had plenty of his meaty bribes left. Those convinced the hounds of New Hastings he was a splendid fellow.

Would Warwick have the wit to send someone *into* the woods to alert the unhappy men who'd gone after the younger Radcliffes? Richard's lips skinned back from his teeth in a savage grin. If one of the noble's men didn't warn them he was around, he'd let them know himself.

He didn't go up the Brede, as he'd come down it. That was the shortest way back to the wild country, which also made it the way Warwick's men were likeliest to take. All right—they were welcome to it. As long as he got into the trees before the sun rose, he was fine. He could lie up in a fern thicket and stay safe while they tramped by not ten feet from him.

He had to cross a meadow to get to the wild wood. Cows turned their heads to stare at him: people didn't belong out here at this time of night. *Too right they don't,* he thought. But he made it back among the pines and redwoods and ferns, back to the cool dampness of the forest, back to the spicy scents that seemed as good to him as the odor of baking bread and better by far than the smells of the livestock brought here from England.

The smell of burning wood led him to the fire Warwick's troopers had set to warm themselves. It had died into embers now. They lay rolled in blankets, all but one who yawned and nodded and hit himself in the thigh with his fist to stay awake. Warwick hadn't thought to warn them after all. He might be a good general, but he didn't remember everything.

Richard strung his bow. He shot the sentry first. He'd hoped for a clean, quiet kill, but the man let out a dreadful shriek when the arrow tore into his belly. The other soldiers sprang awake, grabbing for their weapons. Richard shot two of them, too, then slipped away.

He'd hurt Warwick tonight. He'd hurt him badly, but he hadn't killed him. Warwick was a man who would take a deal of killing.

# X

*H*enry Radcliffe couldn't believe Warwick would keep on gathering taxes after what happened with his father. Had the nobleman contented himself with going after the surviving Radcliffes, most of the settlers might have decided it was none of their affair and tried to get on with their lives. But Warwick acted as if there were no feud. And he soon brewed up a bigger one.

More and more people fled into the woods. Richard began to worry. "We can't feed them all," he said. "Not enough game here to keep 'em eating."

"Then we have to fight Warwick straight up," Henry said.

"If it were just Warwick and his bully boys, we could do it. But he has settlers on his side, too," his brother said. "I don't want a war of settler against settler. It will leave bad blood for years."

"Bad blood's already here," Henry said. "Warwick's started burning some of the farms and houses that belong to people on our side. And he's giving others to his friends. Chances are that will make him more friends, too."

"Not everyone got away with a bow," Richard complained.

"Fine," Henry said. "Do you want to give up?" Richard only glared at him.

The next day, Bartholomew Smith came up from New Hastings with only the clothes on his back. "There's a skeleton crew on the *Rose*," the mate said. "They're for us. They've gone out to sea, far enough to keep Warwick's wolves from surprising them."

"That would be better if we could work together with them," Henry said.

"Why can't we?" Richard said. "Easy enough to go up and down the coast, out farther than the soldiers are likely to. But what comes after that?"

"What comes after that?" Henry saw the answer as clearly as if God had whispered it in his ear. For all he knew, maybe God had. Words spilled out of him, a flood of them. His brother and the mate listened. The longer Henry talked, the wider their eyes got.

At last, the fit left Henry. He slumped forward, exhausted. Richard leaned forward and set a hand on his shoulder. "We can do this. We *will* do this." Then he said, "Father would be proud of you." That was when Henry was sure he hadn't been spouting nonsense.

Bartholomew Smith said, "You sounded like a great captain, skipper—like somebody who's won battles in the War of the Roses."

"I don't want to sound like a captain. I don't want to have to sound like one," Henry said. "And I don't care about roses, except I wish more of them grew here. If not for Warwick, I never would have worried about any of this."

"Well, then, he's got a lot to answer for, by Our Lady," Richard said. "Only thing is, he doesn't know it yet."

\* \* \*

Like his father, Henry Radcliffe was a leader of men. Richard had never much wanted to tell anyone what to do. He'd never wanted anyone else telling him what to do, either. No wonder wandering alone through lands no other man had ever seen suited him so well.

Hurrying through the Atlantean woods with a dozen grim, angry, determined men at his back felt very different. Bartholomew Smith would have made a better leader, but everyone looked to Richard. He was Edward's son. The magic had to be in him. They thought it did, anyhow.

Maybe their thinking so would help make it true. He could hope so. He had to hope so. If it didn't, he was only leading them into disaster.

Farms above Bredestown were thin on the ground. Only men with some of the same hermit streak that ran so wide in Richard built on the edge of the wilderness. But Richard and his followers had no trouble coming out of the forest wherever they pleased. Warwick's soldiers weren't about to go in among the trees again. They defended a perimeter closer to the sea.

"Go away!" shouted the first man whose house the raiders approached. "I don't want anything to do with the quarrel. I just want to be left in peace."

"Will Warwick heed you if you say that?" Richard asked angrily.

"No. All the more reason you should."

Richard felt the force of the embittered argument. He might have made it himself. But he couldn't listen to it now, not unless he wanted to let his father down. "We have to fight him," he said. "Otherwise, he'll be king in truth over us. Do you want that?"

"No. Don't want you doing it, neither."

"Not me, by God!" Richard said, and said not a word about his brother. "If we want to live our own lives, we have to free the land of the Earl of Warwick. We have to, dammit! Then I can go back to the woods and make my wife wonder whether I'm ever coming home again. And that's all I want to do. Don't you understand? *Warwick won't leave you alone.*"

"He hasn't done anything to me yet," the man said. "When he does, that's the time for me to worry about it."

"No." Richard shook his head. "That's when it's too late to worry about it." He turned to the men at his back. "Come on. We'll find men who aren't puling babes somewhere else." *We'd better, or we're ruined,* he thought.

And they did. Some men could see the writing on the wall, unlike the blockhead at the first farm where they stopped. Some had kin whom Warwick's hounds had already despoiled. And some, like Richard himself, didn't want anybody telling them what to do. "I don't much like you," one of those told Richard as he grabbed his bow and slung a full quiver over his shoulder, "but you're the ague, and that Warwick, he's the plague."

"Too bloody right he is," Richard said. "I don't care if you like me or not. Put up with me till we dig the God-cursed badger out of his sett. Then you can go back to thinking I'm a fool, and I'll go off into the woods and forget all about you. Is it a bargain?"

"It is," the farmer answered. "Not the best one, maybe, but the best I'm likely to get."

Richard wondered whether they would have to fight before they got to New Hastings. They did. Maybe one of the men who didn't want to fight on his side slipped away and carried word to Warwick's soldiers. Maybe they just happened to be in the wrong place at the wrong time. However that was, a clump of them spotted Richard's ragtag force as it came out from behind some trees. The troopers wasted no time figuring out who was who. They strung their bows with frantic haste and started shooting.

"Back into the wood!" Richard cried. "The trunks

will give us cover!" They would need it, too; a man screamed as he was hit. The soldiers had mailshirts and helmets and swords. Only a few of Richard's men had swords; most made do with belt knives or axes. None of them wore armor. If Warwick's troopers came to close quarters, they would slaughter their foes. They knew it, too. Some of them lumbered forward while others kept shooting to disrupt the Atlanteans' archery.

How fast could a man in a byrnie cover a couple of hundred yards? Not fast enough to keep the settlers from shooting before they got to the edge of the copse. Rings of iron kept glancing hits out, but an arrow that struck square would punch through any armor made.

Another Atlantean shrieked. He fell, clawing at the arrow in his throat. His blood rivered out, hideously red. Still another farmer took a clothyard shaft an inch above the nose and died before he knew it.

One of Richard's arrows caught a soldier in the left shoulder. Though it got through, it did less harm than the bowman would have liked. The soldier yelled, but he broke off the shaft and kept coming.

"Away!" Richard shouted. "This isn't the place for a big fight!" He didn't want the men to empty their quivers here. Archery was the one skill they had that let them confront Warwick's fighters. Without arrows, they could only run when armored men came after them. *We'll, we've got arrows, and we're running anyhow,* Richard thought glumly. He misliked the omen.

They had to leave their wounded behind. That was no good. Lord only knew what the angry troopers would do to them. But Richard didn't see what else he could do. Trying to drag them along would have slowed the whole band. If the soldiers caught up with them, the rising would die before it ever came to life.

"You should have planned this better," one of his men panted as they trotted north and east.

Richard looked at him. "What makes you think I planned it at all? Those bastards were there, so we fought them. We hurt them, too."

"And they hurt us," the settler answered. "Worse, I daresay."

"That's what fighting's all about, Peter," Richard agreed. "When we get the battle we want, we'll hurt them worse."

"How do you know?" Peter asked. Richard told him how he knew—or how he hoped, rather. The man trotted on for a couple of paces, then nodded. So did Richard, thoughtfully. *If anything happens to him before the big fight, I have to knock him over the head. Can't give him the chance to spill his guts to Warwick's men.*

One thing: men without mailshirts could run faster than men with mailshirts could chase them. After Richard's followers pulled away, he relaxed—a little. He still had a decent-sized force behind him, and he was still moving in the direction he wanted to go. It could have been worse. But it would have been better if they'd reached the seaside unbloodied.

Black midnight, blacker than the Earl of Warwick's heart. Henry Radcliffe and Bartholomew Smith crouched on the beach, a couple of miles south of New Hastings. "You're sure they know the signal?" Henry said.

"They'd better," the mate answered, which wasn't what he wanted to hear.

Henry set dry pine needles and other tinder on the sand. He clashed flint and steel above them again and again till they caught. No matter how many times you did it, starting a fire was rarely quick or easy. He breathed on the flames when he finally got them going, coaxing them to brighter life. Smith fed them more fuel. At last, the two men had a fire that gave some warmth against the chilly breeze.

They'd picked this spot not least because it was as close as they could come to New Hastings without being seen from the settlement. All the same, Bartholomew Smith sounded worried when he said, "What if they spy it?"

"Then we run," Henry answered. "In the darkness, we'll lose them." They would probably lose each other, too, but they could find each other after they'd shaken off Warwick's men: after daylight, if need be. He went on, "But Warwick's eyes should be on the north—that's where Richard is." He hoped that was where his brother was. That was where Richard was supposed to be.

Smith peered out to sea. "Where's the bloody boat? The longer we have to wait here—"

"Don't worry," Henry said. "They have to see the fire. They have to put men into the boat. They have to row ashore. They—"

Sand grated under a keel. "Come on," someone called. "What are you waiting for?" Bartholomew Smith and Henry both laughed, in relief as much as for any other reason. They hurried to the boat and scrambled in.

As soon as Henry had a shifting deck under his feet again instead of the dull, unmoving dirt, he felt like himself. Richard was welcome to the woods and the oil thrushes and the mountains. Henry came alive on the ocean. Clambering up from the boat and over the *Rose*'s gunwale made him feel ten years younger.

"Where now, skipper?" a sailor asked.

"North," Henry answered at once. "North past the lights of New Hastings." He could see them from the *Rose,* where a swell of land had blocked his view from shore. "Then we anchor till we see just where we have to go."

"Better we sail a little too far now, while the wind will let us," Bartholomew Smith said. "If it swings around and blows out of the north—and it's likely to do that, this season of the year—we don't want it to leave us stuck where we can't do anything."

"You're right, and we'll do it," Henry said at once. He set his hand on a swivel gun. The iron was cold, almost cold enough to make his flesh stick to it. He raised his voice to a shout: "Are we ready, lads?"

"Ready!" the fishermen shouted—the ones, that is, who didn't shout, "Yes!"

"Then let's do what we can do," Henry said. "Let's do what free Englishmen can do."

Their cheers put heart into him, the way sweet French wine would have. His father had been the same way: more truly himself when magnified in the eyes of others. Richard didn't have that—didn't want it. Henry wondered why not. He also hoped his brother could find some of it in the days ahead. If he couldn't, whatever the *Rose* did might not matter at all.


Richard Radcliffe didn't know how many times he'd eaten honker half burnt, half raw. Here he was, doing it again. Grease from someone else's oil thrush made the fire sizzle and sputter.

"We can beat them," he said. "We can, and by God we will!"

Most of the men sitting by the fire nodded. They wouldn't have been there if they didn't think they could beat Warwick's soldiers. All the same, one of them said, "Wish I had me a byrnie."

"Sure need one on a fishing boat, don't you, Carl?" another one said. "You fall in, you go straight to the bottom."

"Wouldn't make much difference to me," Carl replied. "I can't swim anyway."

Surprisingly few sailors knew how. Richard was no great shakes in the water himself, though he could keep his head above water for a while—long enough to be rescued, if he was lucky. *One more reason to be glad I don't put to sea any more,* he thought.

"Throw more wood on the fire," he called to his men. "We want Warwick's buggers to know we're here."

If Warwick's men didn't know their foes were encamped north of New Hastings, they were blind as well as stupid. Richard's rebels had fed the fire on the beach all night long. They wanted the soldiers to come out against them. Richard thought they would get what they wanted, too. And when they did, they would find out whether they'd been wise to want it in the first place.

Richard looked out to sea. The *Rose* lay about where she ought to. How much difference she'd make ... again, they would find out. When the plan spilled out of Henry, it sounded brilliant. But all sorts of things that seemed brilliant turned out not to be. You didn't know till you tried them, which was liable to be too late.

Carl, sensibly, was looking toward New Hastings. He crossed himself. "They're coming out," he said.

Warwick's forces advanced slowly and deliberately. Since the soldiers who'd come from England with him wore mailshirts, they couldn't advance any other way. The earl himself had a fine suit of plate. He rode a horse big enough to bear him and the heavy armor. The rising sun struck fire from his lancehead.

Accompanying his troopers were men as bare of mail as Richard's followers. Radcliffe ground his teeth. Those were settlers, men like the ones he led—except they'd chosen the other side.

"They have more men than we do," Carl said quietly.

"I know," Richard answered.

"They have armor, and we don't," the other man went on.

"I know," Richard repeated.

"If they beat us, they'll kill most of us—maybe all of us."

"I know," Richard said one more time.

"If it doesn't work, I won't forgive you."

"If it doesn't work, you'll be too dead to forgive me, or I'll be too dead to need forgiving, or else we'll both be dead and things will even out."

Carl gravely considered that. To Richard's surprise, he chuckled under his breath. Richard clasped his hand. They took their places and waited.

One of Warwick's men came up the beach toward them. He had no flag of truce, but held both hands out before him so Richard and his men could see they were empty. When he got within hailing distance, Richard shouted, "That's close enough. Say your say." The brisk northerly breeze flung his words toward the trooper. It would aid his side's arrows, too—not a great deal, but some.

The trooper cupped his hands to his mouth. "Give it up!" he bawled. "You can't hope to win."

"Be damned to you," Richard answered. His men raised a defiant cheer.

"My lord says, if you yield now, he will let you go into exile: go where you will, so long as it's far from here, with your families, with whatever you can carry, and with one beast and one fowl for each person. Think on what you do. After this fight is won, you won't find him so generous, those of you who don't burn in hell."

"Be damned to your lord, too." Richard spat on the sand. All things considered, the offer *was* generous—so generous that Richard didn't trust the Earl of Warwick to honor it once he'd got his way bloodlessly. He looked at his men. None of them seemed inclined to give in. That heartened him.

Warwick's trooper shrugged mailed shoulders. "On your heads be it—and on your heads it will be." He turned and walked down the strand. Richard was tempted to put an arrow through his kidneys. One more man he wouldn't have to kill later. But no. The advantage wasn't worth the risk. If he broke a truce, the enemy would show no mercy if they won. They might—not to him, surely, but to his comrades—if he stayed within the rules. The soldier reached his own line unpunctured.

Richard watched him shake his head and spread his hands. A moment later, Warwick's lance swung down so that it pointed straight at the men who dared defy him. He didn't charge, though, not yet. Richard's men would have pincushioned him and his horse if he had. Longbowmen could stand against knights. They'd proved that time and again on the fields of France. Against a lone knight, they could have proved it with ease here in Atlantis.

Slowly, Warwick's men advanced almost to the edge of archery range. His bowmen formed a line behind his troopers. What he had in mind was easy enough to see. The archers would keep Richard's men busy while the troopers—and, presumably, Warwick himself—advanced against them. If Richard's men fought the archers, the regular soldiers would close and slaughter them. If they aimed at the troopers, the bowmen would cut them down from long range.

"A plague!" Carl exclaimed. "My brother's over there, the cursed, mangy hound."

"And? Do you want us to try to spare him or try to shoot him down like the dog he is?" Richard asked.

Before Carl could answer, the troopers shouted, "Warwick!" and trudged forward, swords drawn, shields raised against the storm that would soon fall on them. Warwick's archers began to shoot.

At first, their arrows hardly seemed to move in the sky. But then, terrifyingly fast, they were on Richard and his comrades. You could dodge one, but if you did you were likely to step into the path of another. Richard had never had so many men trying to kill him all at once.

"Shoot!" he shouted. "Pick your own targets!" A

better general, or a more certain one, might have concentrated on the troopers or the archers. He hoped split-
ting the difference would serve well enough. If he was
wrong . . . then he was wrong, that was all.

He let fly at a trooper, and missed. Swearing, he
looked over his left shoulder. Where was the *Rose*? If
she didn't do what she was supposed to do pretty soon,
he and his men would have to run. They couldn't face
armored soldiers with swords at close quarters. And if
they started running, where would they stop? Wouldn't
they be doomed to outlawry and skulking through the
woods the rest of their days?

She looked close enough to Richard, dammit. One
of his men fell with a groan. He let fly again. His shaft
pierced a shield, but evidently not the trooper behind it,
because the soldier kept coming.

Richard's quiver would run dry soon. His men
couldn't have many more arrows than he did. He'd also
have to run when he couldn't shoot any more. Henry
had wanted to cut this close. But what was the difference
between close and *too* close?

*Simple,* Richard thought, nocking another shaft as an
enemy arrow hummed venomously past his head. *If it's
too close, we lose.*

The leadsman in the *Rose*'s bow cast the line again and
again, calling out how much water lay under her keel.
He'd already called out less water than she drew more
than once. Why she hadn't run aground Henry Radcliffe
didn't know. Maybe God loved her and hated the Earl
of Warwick. Maybe she was just lucky. Either way, she
was at last just about where she needed to be—and just
in time, too. Or he hoped she was just in time, anyway.

He stood at the bow starboard swivel gun. Bartholomew Smith stood by the stern gun at the same side.
"Ready?" Henry called.

"At your order, skipper," the mate replied.

Henry sighted down the wrought-iron tube. It was loaded with stones and scrap metal and whatever else they could stuff into its maw. "Fire!" he shouted, and lowered a tallow-stinking torch to the touch-hole.

*Boom!* The thunderous noise terrified and exalted him at the same time. You could never be sure a gun would go off when you fired it. You could never be sure the barrel wouldn't blow up, either. He whooped when Smith's gun *boom!*ed a heartbeat after his. Then he peered through the choking, stinking smoke to see what the two shots had done.

He whooped again, pumping a fist in the air. They'd caught Warwick's men from the flank, and torn them to bits. More than half the armored soldiers were down and kicking or down and suddenly still forever. And almost all the rest were running for their lives. They were battle-hardened, battle-ready men, but disaster striking out of nowhere stole the courage from anybody.

"Reload the starboard guns!" Henry shouted. The sailors leapt to obey, swabbing out each barrel, pouring in fresh powder, and then loading more junk to fire. Henry pointed his piece a little to the south, toward the Earl of Warwick. What did *he* think at the unexpected overthrow of his hopes? "Port bow gun—*fire!*" Henry yelled.

*Boom!* That one was aimed at the earl, too. Warwick was farther from the *Rose*—probably a quarter of a mile. Maybe God really was on the settlers' side. Or maybe a horse made a bigger target than a man, for the noble's mount staggered, then fell, pinning him beneath its weight.

Another chunk of iron or stone knocked over an archer behind Warwick. Together, the two downfalls made the rest of the settlers who'd taken the nobleman's side realize they might not have decided wisely.

"Drop anchor!" Henry cried. It splashed into the sea. He didn't want the wind to sweep them past the enemy's archers. The *Rose*'s timbers groaned as she slowed. *Boom!* That was Bartholomew Smith's gun, ready before Henry's. More of the archers who'd backed Warwick fell. The rest ran faster than the armored soldiers. None of them would ever have faced gunfire before. A lot of them would never even have heard it. It was frightening enough when the gun wasn't aimed at you. When it was . . .

Henry didn't aim his piece at the fleeing settlers. Once Warwick was dealt with, they'd be good neighbors again. They would want to pretend they'd never been here, and he was willing to let them, though he wasn't so sure Richard would be. The soldiers, on the other hand . . . If you wanted to keep your flock safe, you had to get rid of the wolves.

He lowered the torch to the touch-hole. *Boom!* The powder stank of brimstone, and Warwick's men had to think hell was visiting them there by the strand. More of them toppled, writhing on the sand and mud.

"Reload!" Henry yelled again. His ears rang. The rest of the sailors' must have, too. "We'll give it to them one more time!"

Richard Radcliffe stood over the Earl of Warwick. Even with his dead horse dragged off him, he wasn't going anywhere; he'd broken a leg in his fall. Pain twisted his face as he glared up at Richard. "Well?" he said through bloody lips. "You've won, villein. Make an end to it, if you'd be so kind. Damned saltpeter!"

"I ought to let you suffer first," Richard said. "You killed my father."

"Not in my own person. And you, in your own person, did murder my men and spur them to avenge in blood."

"They were robbing him of what wasn't theirs to

take." Richard didn't need to argue any more—didn't need to and didn't intend to. He drew his bow and shot Warwick in the face. The nobleman kicked for a few minutes, then lay still. Richard let out a long sigh. The worst was over.

His men were finishing Warwick's wounded troopers: cutting their throats or shooting them or knocking them over the head. A few troopers still slogged back toward New Hastings. If they surrendered, he supposed he would let them live. If they wanted to go on fighting, they wouldn't last long, not with their liege lord dead.

One of the settlers who'd sided with Warwick lay on the sand, an arrow through his calf. He eyed Radcliffe apprehensively. "What are you going to do to me?" he asked as Richard approached.

"I was going to take out the arrow and bandage you up," Richard said. "You were a bloody fool, Tim, but you won't be that kind of bloody fool again."

The wounded man started to cry. "God bless you," he grizzled. "Oh, bless you."

"Shut up, or you'll make me sorry I don't do something worse," Richard said roughly. He'd never known what to do with praise. He knelt by Tim and cut away his breeches so he could see how the arrow had gone through. "I'm going to break off the head and then pull the shaft back through. It will hurt some, and you'll bleed some—not too much, with luck."

He cut through the shaft with his knife till he could snap off the head without moving the rest of the arrow very much. Tim groaned anyway. Richard didn't suppose he could blame the other man for that.

"Ready?" he said. Then, before Tim could answer, he pulled the shaft out the way it had gone in. The other man howled and twisted. Blood poured from both ends of the wound, but it didn't spurt, so Richard hoped the arrow hadn't cut any major blood vessels. He bandaged Tim with the length of breeches leg he'd cut off. "If I get you a stick, can you walk?" he asked.

"Not yet," the other man replied. "Better to wait till the bleeding's stopped for a while." Richard grunted; Tim made sense.

"We did it!" someone called from the sea. Richard looked up. His brother was coming ashore in the *Rose*'s boat.

"We did, by Our Lady," Richard agreed. Henry jumped out of the boat and looked down at Warwick's corpse. He stirred it with his foot, then stepped away. Richard said, "This sort of thing mustn't happen again. Not ever." He looked at his hands, which were red with Tim's blood. Shaking his head, he washed them in the ocean. "We shouldn't fight ourselves. There's room here for all of us."

"Well, when word of this gets back to England, the king will know better than to foist worthless nobles off on us," Henry said. "He didn't even mean to give us Warwick—that bloody skipper couldn't find Freetown."

Richard shrugged. "Freetown, New Hastings—what difference does it make? He would have plagued them the same way he plagued us. Atlantis shouldn't be England's dumping ground, dammit."

"No, eh?" His brother's grin was crooked. "Then what are we doing here?"

"Making our own lives, with nobody to tell us what to do or how to do it," Richard said. "I like that fine, thank you kindly. Once we get all this nonsense settled, I'll go back into the woods—it'll be good to get away."

"You're welcome to them. A few nights under the trees were plenty to last me a lifetime." Henry looked down at dead Warwick again, and then over at Tim. "I'm surprised you didn't do for him, too."

"Part of me wanted to," Richard answered. "But with

Warwick gone, he won't be any trouble. It's done. Better to let it go."

"I thought so," Henry said. "I wasn't sure you would."

"Well, I do," Richard said. "Enough is enough, or it had better be. If we don't let it go, Tim's great-grandson will be stealing my great-grandson's sheep and burning his barn. We'll have feuds here like a pack of damned Frenchmen. That's not what Father wanted."

"Father was no meek, mild man," Henry said. "He stood up to Warwick when he could have bowed down before him. He was ready to fight if he had to."

"If he had to." Richard bore down hard on the words. "But he wouldn't have troubled Warwick if Warwick didn't trouble him. He never told anybody here what to do, not unless someone asked him for advice. That's how I want things to go from here on out. Nobody should be able to order anyone else about."

"When Adam delved and Eve span, who was then a gentleman?" Henry quoted the peasants' cry in Wat Tyler's rebellion ninety years before.

"Sounds fair to me," Richard said. "Warwick didn't want to work. He wanted to take what other people worked for. Well, he could get by with that in England till he made the king angry at him, but why should we put up with it here? He didn't deserve what he stole. He deserved what he got."

"I'm not quarreling with you, Richard," his brother said.

"Good," Richard Radcliffe replied. "You'd better not, not about this."

The only building in New Hastings large enough to hold most of the crowd that gathered was the church. Bishop John had built big on purpose, as if planning a church for a town the size of the old Hastings from which they'd sailed.

But Bishop John (how had he got so gray and stooped?) wasn't in the pulpit on this bright Wednesday morning. Henry Radcliffe was. Richard hadn't wanted the job, and wouldn't have done it well had he wanted it. Speaking to lots of people made him shy. Henry tried to imagine a shy man skippering a fishing boat. The picture wouldn't form. He had his flaws, but that wasn't one of them.

"We are one folk again," he said, and his voice, which was big enough to reach from bow to stern through a gale, was big enough to fill the church, too. "One folk," he repeated. "We fell out for a while, but that's over. My father is dead. Warwick is dead, too. Men who backed both of them have died. Isn't that enough? Isn't the Battle of the Strand enough? Do we need to go on hating each other, go on killing each other, any more?"

He looked out to the people of New Hastings. He wasn't altogether sure what they would say to that. Some of the men on his side had wanted to see everyone who'd chosen the Earl of Warwick dead. They were shaking their heads with everybody else, though. Maybe it was harder to stay bloodthirsty in a house of God. He could hope so.

"Let's remember what we did here these past few weeks," he went on. That got everyone's notice. People must have thought he would say, *Let's forget.* "Let's not remember to keep old feuds alive. Let's remember to make sure new feuds don't start. The one we had cost us too much. We need no more like it."

Standing beside him, Bishop John smiled and nodded. "This is the voice of Christianity speaking," he said. "This is the voice of God speaking. Let it be so." He made the sign of the cross.

Henry crossed himself, too. He didn't know whether God was speaking through him. He only knew he never wanted to have to try to kill his neighbors again. He didn't want them trying to kill him, either.

He nodded to his brother. One by one, Richard carried up the mailshirts of Warwick's last soldiers, the
ones who'd yielded themselves after the Battle of the
Strand. They stood in the church, too. Henry could see a
couple of them, and could see their apprehensive faces.
The ironmongery next to the pulpit made quite a pile. A
couple of other men brought up helmets and swords and
laid them by the stack.

"We don't need these things," Henry said earnestly.
"By God and all the saints, we don't, not among ourselves. Oh, we ought to have them so we can make a better fight if more robbers from across the sea try to take
away what isn't theirs to take, but we should never use
them to lord it over each other. Never!" He slammed his
fist down on the pulpit.

He thought Richard first began to clap. That didn't
surprise Henry Radcliffe; his brother had never wanted
anyone lording it over *him*. What did surprise Henry
was the way everyone else in the church joined Richard,
till the applause came back in waves from the vaulted
ceiling and till a bat, sleeping up there in the rafters, was
frightened awake and fled squeaking out into the unaccustomed day.

Slowly, like a storm at sea, the clapping ebbed. Hearing it let Henry feel more confident continuing, "The
men who gave up their armor and weapons have taken
oath that they will not trouble us again. As long as they
hold to their promise, let them be treated like any other
men of New Hastings. They loyally served their master,
the Earl of Warwick. Now that he is gone, they will loyally serve the settlement."

He got more applause—not so much as he had before, but enough to show that the settlers agreed with
him . . . and enough to show the surviving soldiers that
they wouldn't be killed out of hand. Relief wreathed
their features when they realized that. Henry thought

they were safe enough, as long as they didn't stir up trouble. That would have to do.

"Times will change," he said. "We saw that when Warwick came. We'll see it again—we will, and our children, and our children's children, and down through the generations to the end of days. As long as we try, though, and as long as God helps, we can ride out all the storms the way we rode out this one."

This time, Bishop John led the clapping. As applause filled the church once more, the bishop spoke to Henry in a low voice: "A good thing you're a secular man, or you'd steal my see from me."

"I don't want it, your Grace," Henry answered. "I just want to be able to get on with my life." *I sound like Richard,* he thought.

"For now, you have that. You could have Atlantis, I think, if you wanted it," John said.

"I don't," Henry said again. "Atlantis can go on however it pleases, and that will suit me fine. I wonder what sort of town New Hastings will be in a couple of hundred years." He looked to the west. "I wonder what sort of town Avalon will be by then. . . ."

# PART TWO

*Avalon*

# XI

There was a day when Avalon was the wildest, wickedest, wantonest city in all of Atlantis and all of Terranova, too. It wasn't a long day, not even so long as the prime of a man's life, but there was never another one like it, not before or since, not anywhere. And when it ended, it ended in a way worthy of what had gone before.

Red Rodney Radcliffe brought the *Black Hand* into Avalon Bay after a profitable summer raiding the towns and shipping of the Terranovan coast. The Dutchmen and the Spaniards beyond the broad Hesperian Gulf cursed his name. The Spaniards called him a heretic. The Dutchmen, who were Protestants themselves, called him worse than that. Rodney Radcliffe only laughed. They could call him whatever they pleased, as long as they couldn't catch him—and they couldn't.

Nothing could catch the *Black Hand*—so Red Rodney swore. He wasn't far wrong, either. The brigantine, made of fine Atlantean redwood and pine, scudded over the waves. With the wind astern, she could make twelve knots. She'd come from Terranova to Atlantis in just over three and a half days, and left whatever might be chasing her far behind.

"Land ho!" came the cry from the crow's nest atop the mainmast, and then, a moment later, "Damned if that's not the Gateway, dead ahead!"

The mate, a one-eyed bruiser named Ben Jackson, lifted a three-cornered hat from his head: the closest to a salute Red Rodney was likely to get. "Nicely steered, skipper," he said.

"I thank you." If Radcliffe sounded smug, who could blame him? He'd brought his ship across a thousand miles of open ocean and put her exactly where she needed to go.

"Better than Moses, by God," Jackson said with a gap-toothed grin.

"I should hope so!" Red Rodney grinned back. He took blasphemy for granted—as who on the *Black Hand* did not? "Moses wandered forty years before he led his people to the Promised Land, and he died before he got in. We're here again—not for the first time, nor even for the twenty-first. And I'm not ready to turn up my toes just yet."

"Better not be. Think how many pretty ladies'd be sorry if you did." The mate tipped him a wink. "Or even the ones who aren't so bloody pretty, if you've been at sea long enough."

"If you want to waste your time with ugly women, that's your affair," Radcliffe said. "Nothing but the best for me. The best ship, the best crew, the best loot—"

"We've got plenty of that," Jackson broke in.

"We do," Red Rodney agreed. Furs and prime pipe-weed lay in the holds, along with a mayor's silver plate and a governor's gold. He'd seized two fat merchants to ransom, and upwards of a dozen copperskinned Ter-ranovan natives. The men would be hewers of wood and drawers of water; one brothelkeeper or another in Avalon would be glad to buy the wenches.

The copperskins' moans floated up from below. The Dutch merchants kept their big mouths shut. They would be fine even if they had to say farewell to some of their fortunes. They would, that is, unless their kinsfolk preferred the loot to the merchants, in which case they would cook over a slow fire. But the natives knew a short life, and not a merry one, awaited them. Why not mourn?

A pinnace and two light galleys patrolled the Gateway. The freebooters of Avalon might have to fight to hold what was theirs. Forts on the northern and southern spits that closed Avalon Bay so well mounted heavier guns than any ship of the line would carry.

"Run up our flag," Red Rodney called. The black hand on white flew from bowsprit and stern, and from atop the mainmast. The brigantine carried a fine set of flags in her locker. She could show England's St. George's cross, either alone or differenced with the red-crested eagle of the eastern Atlantean settlements. She could show the red and white stripes of a Portuguese merchantman, Sweden's gold cross on blue, Spain's red and white and gold, Holland's red and white and blue, the crown and fleurs-de-lys of France, or even the Corsican Moor's head.

Or she could show her true colors, as she was doing now.

One of the galleys rowed out to meet her. It stayed off her bow, where its gun could strike without fear of reply. Galleys were nimble, galleys were quick—but galleys weren't seaworthy enough for long cruises, and carried too many men and not enough supplies to go far. They did make first-rate guard dogs, though.

Thin across the water, a challenge came: "Show yourself, Red Rodney!"

"I'll do it!" Radcliffe shouted back as he strode to the bow. "Is that you, Stephen? How are Meg and the brats?"

"Good enough, good enough," the captain of the galley answered. "And how was the hunting out west?"

Rodney struck a pose. "Better than good enough, by Christ!"

"Then pass in!" Stephen said. The galley slipped out of the brigantine's way. Graceful as a dancer, the *Black Hand* glided into Avalon Bay.

There were days when William Radcliff wished his name were Jones or Bostwick or even Kersauzon. By all the signs, this was going to be one of them. No matter that the trading firm he ran from the growing town of Stuart—a trading firm whose ships sent salt fish and timber and other goods from Terranova all the way to Arkhangelsk—was as honest and reliable as the phases of the moon. No, much too often no matter at all.

The gentleman come to do business with Radcliff today was a stout Londoner named Elijah Walton. He wore a fancy powdered wig and badly wrinkled velvet that must have stayed folded in its trunk all the way across the Atlantic. "A pleasure to meet you, Mr. Radcliff," he said, extending his right hand.

"And you, Mr. Walton." When William took the master merchant's hand, he was surprised at the strength of his grip. More to Walton than met the eye, then.

He surely had all the fashionable vices. He took from his pocket a small enamelware box, took out a pinch of the powdered Terranovan herb it contained, and then inhaled it. After an explosive sneeze, he held out the box. "Care for some snuff yourself, sir?"

"No, thanks. I don't use pipeweed in any form, I fear. I trade in it, but it's not to my personal taste." In wool and linen, the only hair on his head that which he was born with, Radcliff knew he seemed a crude settler to the sophisticate from the mother country. *Well, so what?* he told himself. *He is what he is, and I am what I am.*

With a shrug, Elijah Walton made the enameled snuff-box disappear. "May I ask you a question, Mr. Radcliff, without fear of offending?"

More to him than met the eye . . . and also less. William was as sure he knew what the question would be as he was of, well, the phases of the moon. "Go ahead," he said, no doubt sounding as resigned as he felt.

"Ah, you will have heard it before, then." Nothing wrong with Walton's ear. "I shall ask it nonetheless. The similarity of the surname, but for one character, the prominence of men of that surname, however spelled, in Atlantis these past two centuries . . . Have you a family connection with Red Rodney Radcliffe of Avalon?"

"To my shame, Mr. Walton, I do. We both descend from Edward Radcliffe through Henry. Rodney's grandfather and mine were brothers, so we are second cousins. Knowing this does not delight me—nor, I daresay, him. But I would not dissemble."

"That no doubt speaks well for your integrity, which I have already heard highly praised," Elijah Walton said.

William shrugged. "You are too kind, sir. I might also remark that my lying here would serve little purpose, since you can inquire of almost anyone in Stuart and learn the truth in short order, did I try to conceal it."

Something in the way the master merchant's rather protuberant gray eyes glinted told Radcliff that he had already made those inquiries, and knew the answer before asking the question. *A test, then. Well, I passed it, by Christ,* William thought. Walton did not admit to any such thing aloud, however. Instead, he asked, "Why the curtailed spelling on your branch of the tree?"

"That happened in my grandfather's day, or so I am told," William Radcliff replied. "He hated waste in any form, and so lopped off the final *e.*"

"I marvel that he did not leave you but a single *f*," Walton observed.

"The story is that he thought hard on that, but decided not to for fear men might pronounce the name *Radclif.*" William lengthened the *i* in the last syllable. "I cannot say of my own knowledge whether this be true—he died when I was a boy."

"One more impertinent question?" the Londoner asked, a small smile playing across his full, red lips.

"Ask, sir, ask," William said. "If it be impertinent enough, I will put you out on the street once more, and be damned to your business."

To his surprise, Walton's smile got wider. "And if it be impertinent *enough,* you will put me out on the street without bothering to open the door before you pitch me through it. Well, I hope to avoid that, at any rate. All I wish to know is, what is your opinion of your . . . notorious cousin?"

"Again, this is something you could learn from others besides me," William Radcliff said. "In a word, I despise him. Not only does he dip the family name in the chamber pot, not only does he revel in befouling it, but he also preys on my ships whenever he finds the chance. If I could kill him with my own hands, it would be a pleasure—and a privilege."

Walton took another pinch of snuff. This time, he had to slap the lid back onto the box lest his sneeze blow its expensive contents all over Radcliff's office. "Potent stuff!" he said, dabbing at his streaming eyes with a blue silk handkerchief. "Well, sir . . . Very well indeed, in fact. How would you like to win that privilege and take that pleasure?"

William Radcliff leaned toward Walton so intently that the older, paunchier man gave back a pace. "Tell me more," Radcliff said.

*     *     *

Avalon despised law, scoffed at law, reviled law . . . and lived by law. What the pirate town would never have accepted if imposed from outside, its freebooters took upon themselves without a qualm. A virgin carrying a sack of gold could go from one end of Avalon to the other without let or hindrance—so long as she was, and was known to be, under the protection of one pirate lord or another.

Flags fluttered from the hilltop forts of Avalon: Red Rodney's black hand on white, Christopher Moody's swordarm and skull on red, Cutpurse Charlie Condent's three skulls and crossbones on a long black pennant, Goldbeard Walter Kennedy's naked headsman holding an hourglass, Stede Bonnet's skull and heart and dagger, and more besides. Some of the chieftains hated others, and would attack them on sight anywhere else in the Hesperian Gulf, the Atlantic, or the Bay of Mexico. In Avalon, though, a truce and the rule behind it had held for most of a lifetime.

*You don't shit where you eat.*

Red Rodney Radcliffe sometimes dreamt of uniting all the pirates of western Avalon under the black hand. He dreamt not of harrying the Terranovan towns but of seizing them and ruling them—of going from pirate to king. Only one thing kept him from trying it: the certain knowledge that all the other chieftains would combine against him the instant he tried to change them from equals to subjects.

He knew he wasn't, he knew he couldn't be, the only captain with dreams like that. He also knew he would cut the ballocks off any man who tried to make him bend the knee. Knowing that kept him from trying to impose himself on the others.

With his loot and his hostages and his slaves safe inside Black Hand Fort—one of the best, since it lay close to the harbor and had a reliable well even though it was on high ground—he could relax. Fields of indigo and sugar cane were beginning to stretch across southern Atlantis. With sugar naturally came rum.

At sea, Rodney doled out a glass of grog to his men each day. He took no more for himself, lest they think he thought he was better than they were. Ashore? Ashore, he could drink to his heart's content, and so could they. When he couldn't steal rum, he traded for it like an honest man, and he wasn't the only freebooter who did.

"This is the life!" he told his daughter. The rum sang in him, but he hadn't drunk himself sleepy yet. He hadn't drunk himself mean yet, either.

"Well, of course it is." Ethel Radcliffe was eleven, and knew no other. None of the women Rodney had taken into his bed since her mother had dared mistreat her in any way—or not for long. One wench who roused his ire in that regard left Black Hand Fort most suddenly, naked and with stripes on her back. Ethel drank rum, too, and swore and scratched as she pleased. She was a dead shot with a pistol.

Red Rodney laughed and tousled her buttery-yellow hair. "One of these days soon, by God, I'll bring you along with me when I set sail. Blast my mizzen if you wouldn't make a better raider than most of the dogs I could scrape up here."

"Do it!" the pirate's daughter said eagerly. "I want to shoot a Dutchman, or even a copperskin. Can I shoot one of the copperskins you brought back?"

"Sorry, love. Not this lot," Rodney answered.

Ethel pouted. "Why not?" Her voice took on a sugared whine that could coax almost anything out of her father.

Almost—but not quite. "Because they're worth good silver to me, that's why not," Rodney Radcliffe said. "And they cost blood to take. That makes 'em too dear to kill for sport." Whether killing them for sport was wrong didn't worry him. Silver did. Silver was one more measure of a man's rank among men.

"But I want to," Ethel persisted. She didn't care to come up short at anything—which only proved she was her father's daughter.

"No," Red Rodney said, and the flush that mounted to his cheeks came from choler as well as rum. "My men listen to me. You'd bloody well better, too. If they don't listen, I make 'em sorry. You think I can't make you sorry?"

He didn't put his foot down very often. When he did, he was likely to crush whatever lay beneath it. That could include Ethel, as she had painful reason to remember. The whine didn't go away, but it did change course: "Well, what can I shoot, then?"

"If you have to shoot something, go up on the stockade and shoot the first stray dog you see. Nobody'll miss that," her father answered. "And after you do, get one of the slaveys to chuck the carcass into the bay. Don't leave it lying there to rot and stink. Does that suit you, you little rakehell?"

"I'd still rather shoot a copperskin," Ethel said. Red Rodney's face must have sent up storm warnings, for she backtracked in a hurry: "A stray dog will do, I suppose. Better than nothing." She hurried away.

A few minutes later, a pistol banged. Rodney was tearing into roasted honker then, and couldn't hear the dog howl. He guessed it did, though, because Ethel didn't come back unhappy. A smile spread over his face. He'd done what a father should do: he'd pleased his little girl—and he'd got her out of his hair for a while.

He didn't smile so much about the honker. "What have we got here?" he demanded. "This sorry bastard's no bigger than a rooster's drumstick." He exaggerated, and by no small amount, but he'd seen plenty of bigger honker legs.

"Begging your pardon, sir, but it's the best the hunters brought back," the cook replied.

"Likely tell, likely tell," Rodney said. "When I was Ethel's age, by Christ, the honkers were three times the size of this miserable bird."

"Hunters say, sir, that the big ones are all gone—at least from close enough to Avalon to bring them back before they spoil," the cook told him. "They have to shoot the smaller, scrubbier kinds instead. Even those are harder to find than they were once upon a time."

"Sweet suffering Jesus!" Rodney poured himself more rum. "Will we have to start raising sheep and goats and cows? Are we farmers or are we men?"

The cook maintained a prudent silence. He was no pirate himself. He'd cooked for the governor of Nieuw Haarlem in Terranova till Red Rodney captured him and carried him back to Avalon. After eating some of his food, Rodney refused a ransom for him. The cook hadn't done badly here—or rather, he might have done much worse, and he was smart enough to know it. If he said too much, his lot might change in a hurry.

"Running out of honkers!" Rodney said. "Bloody hell! What's Atlantis coming to if we're running out of honkers?"

Meinheer Piet Kieft had impressive waxed mustaches and an even more impressive pot belly. The governor of Nieuw Haarlem nodded to William Radcliff. "I do not love your cousin," he said in gutturally accented English.

"Well, your Excellency, I must say that I'd wager I've not loved him for longer than you have," William replied. "He has robbed me, plundered my ships, done all he could to hurt me."

Piet Kieft snapped his fingers and poured more rum into his pewter cup. "Did he ever make you jump out a window naked when you were about to futter a serving girl with the best tits in the world?" He paused meditatively. "It was a second-story window."

"Oh, dear," Elijah Walton said before William could respond to that. "I'd heard you were somewhat discommoded in that raid, your Excellency, but I confess I did not realize the full extent of your, ah, difficulties. Please accept my sympathies."

"And mine," William added. He hoped, for the serving girl's sake, she'd been about to get on top.

"This is not even the worst of it," Kieft continued. "That son of a sow of a Red Rodney Radcliffe, that black-handed bastard, he stole from me my prime cook, and would not sell him back to me. It is war to the knife between me and him."

*Yes, you look as if you've spent all the time since starving,* William thought. Piet Kieft hadn't come to Stuart to be mocked, though. "Well, your Excellency, now is the time to see whether we can pay him back."

"Pay him back for sacking my town—*ja,*" Kieft said. "I sack his. Pay him back for stealing Cornelius and making Katrina giggle when she sees me instead of opening her legs? ... Even if I cut his heart out, it is not enough." His piggy little eyes flashed. He wasn't pretty, but William Radcliff wouldn't have wanted him for an enemy.

"You have ships," Walton said. "Mr. Radcliff here, our kindly host, has ships. I also have ships at my beck and call. If we gather together our separate contingents and sail against Avalon with overwhelming force—"

"It will be the greatest miracle since the Resurrection of our Lord and Savior Jesus Christ," Radcliff finished for him.

"Your lack of spirit is distressing," Walton said.

"I don't lack spirit—no such thing," William replied. "But who will bell the cat, and when, and how? I admire you, sir, for persuading Meinheer Kieft to confer with us.

Nevertheless, people have been mooting the fall of Avalon since the pirates first seized it. That is many years ago now, but they hold it still."

"They go on holding it, too, if we don't work against them," Piet Kieft said. "I aim to work against them—and most against Red Rodney—no matter what you do. But Master Walton is right. We have a better chance if we work together. I will do this. I do not even claim command."

That made William Radcliff blink. That a Dutchman would take orders from an Englishman at sea . . . was no small miracle itself. The Dutch reckoned themselves the best sailors in the world, and the English would have been hard pressed to prove them wrong. England and Holland had fought two naval wars in the past generation, and the Dutch had got the better of it both times.

"Well, well." William Radcliff turned to Elijah Walton. "If our comrade is so generous, can we fail to match him?"

Walton frowned. "My instructions are that an Englishman should lead the fleet against the corsairs."

"And what am I if not an Englishman—and the man on the spot?" Radcliff asked angrily. "If you call me a damned honker, sir, as if I were a New Hastings man, I will wish you joy of our enterprise—and much luck in taking it anywhere without the aid of Radcliff of Stuart."

"Be not overhasty, Mr. Radcliff, I pray you," Walton said. "All these insults come from your own mouth, and none from mine."

"You say this. Can you prove it? Will you prove it?" William pressed. "Or, by saying I am but an Atlantean, will you make me out to be a worthless settler, not deserving to associate with, let alone lead, his betters from the mother country?"

Coughing, Elijah Walton answered, "You cannot

deny, sir, that your roots have been transplanted away from English soil these two centuries past."

"Bugger my roots. My heart is English," Radcliff said.

Piet Kieft stirred. "You started this, Walton. You set the pot on the fire. Will you now take it off and let it go cold because you cannot get all of your way? Or did you come here for just that purpose, so you could go back to London and say, 'I tried, but we could reach no agreement against these corsairs'?"

"Before God, Meinheer Kieft, I did not!" Walton exclaimed.

Kieft looked around William Radcliff's baroque jewel box of a study: the bookshelves, with volumes in English and Latin and French; the polished brass astrolabe on the wall, part decoration, part tool; the ready-cut quills and the jars of ink; the coffee simmering over a low fire; the calico cat curled up asleep on a cushion. "This place seems English enough to suit me. Does it not seem to you the same?"

Perhaps Walton flushed, or perhaps it was a trick of the light streaming in through the south-facing octagonal window. The veritable Englishman's gaze fixed on a honker skull, cleaned and polished, that held down one of the piles of paper on Radcliff's desk. The honker seemed to stare back from empty eye sockets.

"Oh, come now, sir!" William said. "Come now! You might see the same, the very same, in a merchant's residence in London, or a scholar's, as a curiosity of natural philosophy. Deny it if you can."

Instead of denying it, Elijah Walton grunted. "Oh, very well," he said—most grudgingly, but say it he did. "Shall we style you Grand High Admiral of the Hesperian Gulf, then?" He gave a mocking seated bow.

"I care little what you call me," William Radcliff answered. "If I do what I set out to do, everyone who comes along will try his damnedest to filch the credit from me. And if I fail, I'll be that stupid honker from Atlantis, and all the blame will come down on my head. You win either way, Mr. Walton."

Piet Kieft chuckled and nodded. He too knew what being a settler meant. As for Walton . . . he did not seem entirely displeased at the prospect.

A pigeon fluttered into the roost at Black Hand Fort. Pigeons had spread with men in Atlantis. Several native varieties of dove lived here, including a couple with wings too stunted to let them fly, but there had been no pigeons till people brought them hither.

This particular pigeon had a piece of parchment tied to its left leg. The handler who spied the parchment gently removed it, read the note on the inner surface, and hot-footed it to Red Rodney's chamber.

His knock didn't quite interrupt the pirate captain at play, which was lucky for him. Rodney's companion squeaked and yanked a silk coverlet—loot from one of the small, Spanish-held islands south of Atlantis—up to her chin. "Don't fret yourself, Jenny. He wouldn't dare bother me if it weren't important," Radcliffe said. As he pulled up his breeches, he also raised his voice: "What's toward?"

"A pigeon from Stuart," came the voice from the other side of the door.

"Ha!" Red Rodney threw on his shirt, too. He was still barefoot, but he didn't care. He went without shoes aboard ship more often than not, the better to feel the deck under his soles. "I knew it had to be something that mattered."

"And I don't?" Jenny said sulkily, but he was already striding toward the door.

His mind moved perhaps even faster than his feet. Of course he had spies on the east coast. Who in his right mind wouldn't? He assumed his foes had spies in Avalon, too. They had reason not to love him and reason to try to find out what he was up to. With luck, he could feed them full of lies.

And maybe they were trying to do the same to him. Well, he'd find out. His thumb came down on the latch. He scowled at the man in the hallway. "What's going on, Mick?" *It had better be interesting,* his voice warned.

"Pigeon just in from Stuart, skipper," Mick repeated, and held out the message the bird had carried.

Red Rodney needed to squint to read it; the handwriting was precise but tiny, to cram as much as possible into a small space. As he read, he started to swear. "You've seen this?" he demanded.

"I have indeed," the Irishman answered.

"Well, keep your mouth shut about it till I decide what to do. Can you manage that?"

"Sure and I can."

"You'd better, by Christ. Dutchmen and Englishmen and my own cold-hearted cousin. If that's not a mix cooked up in hell, I don't know what would be. They aim to gut us, Mick, gut us like a honker after you knock it over the head. Are we going to let them get away with it?"

The pigeonkeeper muttered something in Erse. Rodney Radcliffe didn't know what it meant, but it didn't sound as if the man favored giving their enemies an easy time. No one in Avalon would. What the English did to pirates they caught could make the hardest man shiver of nights. And what the English did was a mercy next to what happened when the Spaniards got hold of you. The Spaniards liked whips, and they liked fire. . . .

He read the scrap of parchment again. The Spaniards didn't seem to be part of the gang William Radcliff was putting together. Rodney assumed his cousin crouched at the center of the plot. Where else would a spider go?

Returning to English, Mick asked, "How do you aim to stop the spalpeens, now?"

"We'll have to fight 'em. We can't very well run away, now can we?" Red Rodney said. The other pirate shook his head. Rodney muttered under his breath. *Could* freebooters fight as a fleet? They would have to, wouldn't they? He could see the need. Would his fellow great captains be able to? How many of them were in Avalon right now? How many would get back soon?

"You'll need a grand parley, won't you?" Mick said.

"I was thinking that very thing," Rodney answered. "A grand parley. Been a while since we had one." The pirate chieftains of Avalon were independent princes. They parleyed to keep from fighting among themselves: rarely for any other reason. Would they hearken when Rodney summoned them?

*They'd better hearken, by God,* he thought. *Otherwise, the first we'll know of the enemy is when he starts cannonading us.*

Even figuring out where to hold a grand parley took more in the way of diplomacy than most corsairs had in them. He couldn't invite his fellow captains to Black Hand Fort. Oh, he *could,* if he aimed to start the squabble he wanted to head off. They would think he was trying to lure them all to one place at the same time so he could get rid of them at once. If he got an invitation like that, he would think the same thing himself. He had to find neutral ground.

Some unkind or possibly jealous soul had called Avalon the Sodom of Atlantis. A visitor from the other coast, the somber coast, had marveled that so many pirates were sick. Then he saw how the freebooters drank, and marveled even more that they weren't all dead.

Mary's Paradise would do if no other place sufficed. It was the biggest, bawdiest, grandest brothel and tavern in Avalon. Red Rodney knew he would have to pay

Mary Carleton a goodly sum to take her establishment out of circulation long enough for the chieftains to meet there. No one in Avalon did things from the goodness of his—or her—heart. Maybe he could get some money back from his fellow captains. Or maybe not.

Jenny squawked when she heard that Red Rodney purposed talking with Mary Carleton. "You want some poxy trollop!" she shrilled. "You'll swive her, and then you'll fetch the foulness back to me!"

"I'd be poxed if I tried buggering Goldbeard or Cutpurse Charlie, that's certain sure," Red Rodney replied with a laugh, "but I want 'em there to do them a favor, not to try to take their favors."

"Oh, yes." Jenny didn't want to believe him. "And you won't even look at the doxies falling out of their dresses. They're as common as a barber's chair, they are—one's out and the next one's in. And who was the man who paid five hundred pieces of eight just to see some strumpet naked?"

"I've heard the story, but I don't know the sorry bastard's name," Radcliffe answered. "It wasn't me—I'll tell you that. If I'd laid down so much silver, I'd've got more than a look for it."

"Sure enough—likely you would have got the gleets," his lady love said.

However snide Jenny was, Rodney sent a man he trusted to dicker a price from Mary Carleton. She proved more reasonable than he'd expected. "I know which side my bread's buttered on," she told Radcliffe's emissary. "We'll get enough of the ordinary business now that the *Black Hand*'s back in port."

That being settled, Red Rodney sent messages to the other chieftains of Avalon, to the men who would have to lead the fight against the Dutch and the English and the eastern settlers if there was going to be one. Some of them were, or had been, his foes. He sent to them anyhow, under flag of truce. He hoped curiosity would bring them to Mary's Paradise if nothing else did, for he was not in the habit of doing that. A captain of an earlier generation, when a priest asked him on his deathbed to forgive his enemies, answered, "I have none—I killed them all." Red Rodney wasn't quite so deadly, but not from lack of effort.

Some of the other pirate lords promised to come. Others said no at first. Patiently, Rodney sent to them again. *You hurt only yourselves if you stay away,* he wrote. *If you want to go on doing what you're doing, you need to hear me.*

When he went down to Mary's Paradise, he wore a ruffled shirt—not quite clean—and a jacket of velvet shot through with gold threads that was splendid even if it didn't fit him quite so well as the Spaniard for whom it was made. He carried a cutlass, a dagger, two pistols in his belt, and a tiny one in his boot. His guards dressed more plainly but carried just as many weapons.

"You can futter the wenches if you find any you fancy," he told them. "But God help your scurvied souls if you get drunk. You're here to fight if you have to, and not to fight if you don't need to. No brawling for the fun of it, not today."

And maybe that would do some good, and maybe it wouldn't. His crew was better ordered than most, but men who'd put up with Royal Navy discipline didn't turn pirate to begin with. And even Royal Navy sailors roistered ashore. Besides, if one of the other chieftains' men started trouble, or if his own followers could claim they did . . .

Well, he would worry about that if he had to, the same way he would worry about Jenny slipping hemlock into his beer. He tried not to think about how black her scowl was as he left Black Hand Fort.

He had a standard-bearer carrying his banner, and

another carrying a white flag to show he didn't intend to fight unless he had to. Similar processions wound down from the other fortresses. No one pulled out a pistol or fired a matchlock. It wasn't quite a miracle, but Red Rodney took it for a good sign.

Mary Carleton greeted him under a red lantern. "Welcome," she said. "The room is waiting."

"Thank you, Mistress Mary," he said, more respectfully than he'd thought he would. She had to be at least thirty-five, but she was still a fine-looking woman.

Rum and roast meats sat on the table. A couple of captains had got there before him. They were already eating and drinking. One of them nodded to him, saying, "This is a good spread. What kind of nonsense are you going to spout?"

"I wouldn't throw away this kind of money to spout nonsense," Red Rodney answered. He poured himself some rum and waited to see who would come and who wouldn't.

To his surprise, all the captains he'd invited showed up. Some of them scowled at him. Some scowled at one another. But nobody grabbed for a sword or a gun. "Let's hear your lies, Radcliffe," said Bertrand Caradeuc in buzzing Breton accents. A gold hoop glittered in his right ear.

"You want lies, go home to your mistress," Red Rodney answered. Most of the chieftains laughed. A few glowered: the ones, he guessed, who feared their mistresses *were* filling their ears with lies. He swigged from his mug of rum and went on, "The sheep are starting to think they're wolves. The honkers are trying to grow eagles' wings. The bastards in Stuart aim to kill us all."

"And you know this because . . . ?" Goldbeard Walter Kennedy inquired. He was an enormous man, several inches taller than Rodney, who was no stripling himself, and wider through the shoulders. The beard that gave him his sobriquet spilled halfway down his chest.

Radcliffe told exactly how he knew it, though he didn't name his spy in Stuart. "We can let them pick us off a ship at a time, the way they're bound to want to," he said. "Or we can stand together and show 'em we're not to be trifled with. Which would you rather?"

"How do we know you're not lying so you get to tell us what to do?" Caradeuc inquired.

"Because I won't lead us even if you bloody well ask me to," Red Rodney replied. The renunciation hurt, but he knew he had to make it. "Pick somebody else. In this fight, I'll follow him, whoever he is. If I have a quarrel with him, it can wait till later. Everything else can wait till later."

He impressed them with that. He'd thought he would. They weren't used to backing away from power. They were used to grabbing with both hands. They wrangled and shouted and swore, and finally chose Michel de Grammont to command. Fewer of them hated him than anyone else. That seemed a good enough reason to them. What kind of high captain he would make . . . They'd find out.

# XII

*W*illiam Radcliff was furious, in a cold-blooded Stu-
artish way. When he got command of a fleet to wipe the
pirates of Avalon off the map, he rashly assumed the fleet
would assemble some time before Judgment Day. Now
he was wondering if he hadn't been unduly optimistic.

It wasn't as if Stuart lacked a fine harbor in which
to assemble. Avalon boasted one as good, but assuredly
no other anchorage in Atlantis came close. Two rivers
and several islands met there, and Stuart lay at the heart
of them all. No matter how the wind blew, ships could
get in and out and find secure places to put up. William
was hard pressed to think of a harbor in Europe or Terranova that could say the same.

He wondered why his several-times-great-grandfather
hadn't settled here rather than down at New Hastings.
The only thing he could think of was that Edward Radcliffe must have been content to put down roots wherever the wind happened to blow him ashore. That only
proved the Founder wasn't so sly as people made him
out to be.

*And am I?* William Radcliff wondered. He had authority to bind and to loose a whole fleet. The only difficulty was that, despite promises from both Elijah Walton and Piet Kieft, the fleet at the moment consisted of his own merchantmen and not one vessel more.

Merchantmen, by the nature of things, weren't warships. They weren't particularly fast: they were built to haul, not to sprint. And, most of the time, they weren't heavily armed. He'd done what he could to correct that, but guns heavier than twelve-pounders were impossible to lay hold of in a peaceful settlement. Walton had promised heavier cannon to turn merchantmen into reasonable facsimiles of ships of the line, but so far the promised guns were as chimerical as the promised ships.

"You will drive trade away and make your friends repent of their friendship if you curse everyone who comes near you," his wife remarked one afternoon, when his sarcasm curdled into blasphemy.

"I beg your humble pardon, Tamsin," William answered. "Still and all, I would take oath—"

"You have sworn too many profane oaths already," Tamsin Radcliff broke in.

"I would take oath," William repeated stubbornly, "that the Devil has in hell a special firepit he stokes extra hot, for the purpose of properly tormenting souls who make promises they do not purpose keeping."

"I am certain all will be as you wish in due course." Tamsin had a sunny nature. She needed it, or the master merchant's frequent glooms would have oppressed her more.

"If the promise be fulfilled in due course, that will not be as I wish," Radcliff said. "Do you suppose they are sitting idly by in Avalon?"

"By no means," his wife replied. "More likely than not, they are drinking and wenching and dicing and brawling. Why would they turn pirate, if not to do such things?"

She wasn't wrong. All the same, William said, "Also, without the tiniest bit of doubt, they are readying themselves for our onslaught against them. They will surely have learned of it by now. Had we moved against them sooner, we might have taken them unawares."

"You cannot move alone," Tamsin said.

William nodded heavily. "If I could have, I would have long since. No, for a sea war on such a scale, I needs must have confederates. And a man who must rely on others to see that certain things are done is a man who must resign himself to knowing they may never be done."

"And are the freebooters of Avalon better off in this regard?" Tamsin asked. "Can one man among 'em snap his fingers and have the others follow his whim like so many trained mastiffs? Or do they wait upon developments and quarrel over them the same way you and your friends do?"

He stared at her. Then he kissed her. She let out a startled squawk; that wasn't something he commonly did in the middle of the day. "You are a wonder," he said. "A wonder—do you hear me?"

"I hear you. I am glad to hear you," Tamsin Radcliff said primly. "But why do you say it?"

"Because you remind me of something I almost forgot," William answered. "I see all my own troubles, but none of my foes'. Yet they must have 'em, for are they not flesh and blood, even as am I?" He scowled. "Red Rodney, the mangy hound, is flesh of my flesh, blood of my blood, as that fat toad of a Walton tires not of reminding me."

"You are not to be blamed for it." Tamsin was loyal to his branch of the family.

"Not by you, perhaps. In London and in Nieuw Haarlem, too many can't tell the difference between a Radcliffe and a Radcliff." He pronounced Red Rodney's version of the family name with three syllables, as no

Radcliffe ever born had done. His wife nodded, so she saw his point. He went on, "If half of them blame me for what he does—"

"All the more reason to be rid of him for good," she said.

"All the more reason, yes—and all the less chance." William drummed his fingers on his thigh. "I want to be at sea, not tied here waiting."

"If the Dutchman and the Londoner fail you, you should put to sea by yourself," Tamsin said. "All our ships put together can beat Red Rodney Radcliffe." She pronounced the name with three syllables, too.

"We can beat Red Rodney, yes," William said. "We cannot beat all of Avalon banded together. And the freebooters will fight like cornered rats, for they know what awaits them if they lose. Without marines to stiffen them, I doubt my men would fight so well. Why should they? They put to sea to trade, not to war. They will fight if forced to it, yes, but not for the sport of it."

"They will fight for money—or some of them will," Tamsin said shrewdly. "A big enough price on the heads of the pirate captains—"

"They've had prices on their heads for years." William sounded as gloomy as he felt. "They're out there yet, robbing and stealing and murdering. They make us all look like jackasses." His hands balled into fists. "By God, Tammy, they trifle with us. I am no man to be trifled with, and anyone who thinks otherwise will to his sorrow discover himself mistaken."

"Have you any way to hurry Kieft or Walton?" his wife asked.

He shook his head. "They trifle with me, too, and they think I shall forget it because we are on the same side. You know me. Do I ever forget anyone who does me a bad turn?"

"No. But, contrariwise, you never forget anyone who

does you a good turn, either. Had you not the one quality to go with the other, I could not love you—and I do."

"A good thing, too. I'd go on the rocks without you. But unless we lance this abscess on our western coast" —William's mind kept coming back to what lay uppermost within it—"all of Atlantis will go on the rocks. And, regardless of what Piet Kieft and the sainted Elijah Walton may say, I do not intend to let that happen."

Black Hand Fort had a crow's nest. That was a funny name for it, but served well enough. It was a big wooden bucket mounted high atop a redwood trunk thicker than a mainmast. Red Rodney Radcliffe and his lookouts could go there, clambering up the lines nimble as monkeys, and see for miles in every direction.

Ethel could, too, and she loved to do it. Red Rodney wished she wouldn't. He told her she mustn't. He paddled her behind when she did—and he still found her in the crow's nest when he went up one morning to look around.

She flinched when he scrambled over the edge and into the bucket. "I'm sorry, Father," she said, and then, her spirit reviving, "I'm sorry you caught me."

"Not as sorry as you will be soon," he said, but his heart wasn't in the threat. He had too many other things on his mind.

When he looked down at Avalon's harbor, he didn't like what he saw. Too many brigs and brigantines. Too many sloops. Too many shallops. A few race-built galleons, but only a few. Most of the pirates' ships were small and swift, able to put up a great spread of sail and run after their prey or run away from danger. They could fight when they had to, but only when they had to.

How would the fleet of pirate ships stand up against a new English or Dutch ship of the line? Pirate ships rarely mounted anything bigger than twelve-pounders.

They were made to take merchantmen and to flee from naval vessels. What if they couldn't flee? What if they had to defend their home port?

He muttered under his breath. Even in the twenty-odd years he'd roamed the seas, ships of the line had grown larger and more deadly. A first-rate man-of-war could mount thirty forty-two-pounders, thirty twenty-four-pounders, twenty twelve-pounders, and twenty more smaller guns. A broadside from a ship like that would turn a brigantine to kindling and splinters in the blink of an eye.

In a fight out on the open sea, it wouldn't matter, because brigantines and sloops and shallops could run away from any ship of the line ever built. But if the men-of-war were bearing down on Avalon . . . If they were doing that, the corsairs couldn't very well run, not unless they wanted to run away from their town and their harbor and start fresh somewhere else.

Red Rodney didn't want to do that. Neither did the other chieftains, or they wouldn't have agreed to fight. But agreeing to fight wasn't the same as knowing how to go about it. Another long look at the ships that lay at anchor inside Avalon Bay said as much.

"Pa?" That was Ethel. By the way she called to him, she'd been trying to get his attention for some little while. "Why aren't you thumping me, Pa? You always do when you catch me up here." Getting a thumping seemed better to her than seeing the regular order of things overturned. Some people were like that.

He gave her a straight answer, thinking her due one: "I'm trying to figure out how our little ships can beat the big ones our enemies are going to throw at us."

"Well, that's not so hard," Ethel said with a child's boundless confidence. "If they're bigger, we've got to be faster and smarter, so we hit them and they can't hit back."

"Easier to say than to do," Rodney warned.

"You say that? *You?*" Ethel sent him a reproachful look. "Don't they call you the Horror of the Hesperian Gulf?" Pride at being a Horror's daughter rang in her voice.

"They do," Rodney agreed. "And I am what they call me." He had pride of his own, plenty of it. He also had worries of his own, plenty of them. "If it were just the sea fight, I'd not worry. But those buggers back in Stuart want to close our shop down. They want Avalon, is what they want. The town can't put on topgallants and spankers and sail away from their bloody fleet." He could be more open about his fears with his daughter than with his henchmen or his fellow corsair captains. Come what might, Ethel wouldn't call him coward.

She did point north, to the fort warding Avalon's northern tip, to the galleys guarding the Gateway, and to the other fort on the northern spit that helped form the bay. "We can keep them out," she said, confident still. "Red-hot rounds and chainshot will make the bally blighters sorry they ever tried to poke their noses in."

Radcliffe grinned. His daughter not only thought like a pirate, she talked like one, too. He tousled her hair. "Well, chick, maybe you're right," he said. *I hope to Christ you are,* he thought, but that didn't pass his lips.

Marcus Radcliffe was a lean, dark, weather-beaten man who wore a honkerskin rain cloak, feathered side out, above his shirt and breeches. He seemed out of place in settled Stuart, and especially out of place in William Radcliff's elegant study.

Radcliff poured Radcliffe a glass of sherry. "Your health, cousin," he said, smiling.

"And yours, coz," Radcliffe said to Radcliff. They both drank. Marcus Radcliffe thoughtfully smacked his lips. "Not bad, not bad. I'm more used to ale and beer myself."

"Well, you're not the only one. I drink them a lot of the time myself," William allowed. "But I try to serve my guests something finer."

"Kind of you." Marcus Radcliffe sipped again, and then again. By the way the level of the wine in his glass sank, he thought it fine enough.

William poured the glass full again. "Though the name is the same, or near enough, we are not close cousins, are we?"

"Not hardly." Marcus had a harsher accent than William. "You come down through Henry, and I through Richard. My father would always say your line wanted money, and got it. My line wanted freedom, and we're still looking for it. The more Atlantis fills up, the harder it is to come by."

"Money buys freedom," William Radcliff said. "Freedom from want, freedom from trouble . . ."

"You haven't got troubles?" Marcus Radcliffe laughed. "Why'd you ask me here, then?"

"Because I have a question, and you seem the man best suited to answer it," William replied.

"Long way from New Grinstead to Stuart, just for the sake of a question," Marcus said.

To William's way of thinking, it was a long way from New Grinstead to anywhere. The little town sat far back in the woods west of New Hastings, more than half-way to the Green Ridge Mountains. As far as William knew, no towns lay farther from the coast. From New Grinstead, Marcus Radcliffe and others like him could plunge into the Atlantean wilderness, with no one to tell them where to wander or when to come home.

And that was what made William's distant cousin valuable to him. "Here is that question, and make of it what you will," he said. "Do you believe you could lead an army of a thousand men, with all the necessities they would need for fighting upon their arrival, across Atlantis to Avalon by a date to be agreed upon?"

"Ha!" Marcus said, and then, "You really have it in for Red Rodney, don't you? And he's closer kin to you than I am."

"In a word, yes," William said tightly. "Well?"

"It's not like Terranova." Marcus Radcliffe seemed as thoughtful now as he had tasting the sherry. "We wouldn't have to fight our way through tribes of copperskins. There'll be a few in the woods, and a few runaway niggers from down in the south, but not many. And they'd run from an army that size. They wouldn't try to fight. So *that* would be all right, anyhow, or I think it would."

"Then you can do it?" William heard the eager hunger in his own voice.

"I didn't say so. I'm still working it through. That's a long march, that is—upwards of three hundred miles, even if you're talking about starting from New Grinstead. Subsisting your soldiers . . . wouldn't be easy, and it might not be possible."

"Why?" William demanded. "Does not every man who goes into the woods acclaim the marvelous abundance and splendid hunting they afford?"

"That's a fact," Marcus said. "You want me to go to Avalon and be there on such-and-such a day ready to fight, I'll do it. You want me and ten of my friends to go, I think we could do it. After that, it gets harder. No maize to eat, the way there would be amongst the Terranovans. No roads, so no supply wagons. Even horses have a hard time—sometimes the meadows are few and far between. And you'd have to have horses, for men can't carry close to a month's worth of food on their backs. They'd shoot some on the way, but a thousand men couldn't shoot enough to stay fed. I don't believe the woods hold enough to feed a compact mass of a thousand men." He spread his hands. "I'm sorry, coz. The more I think on it, the worse the chances look. You start with a thousand soldiers, you might have a couple of hundred starving souls make it all the way to Avalon."

William would have been angrier at his kinsman had he not feared the same thing. He did ask, "Are you sure?"

"Sure? Who can be sure of anything before it happens except the Lord?" Marcus answered. "But I do think it likely, and, in case your next question is whether I'd care to chance it, I have to tell you no. I'm not sure that's your next question, mind, but I do think it likely."

"Do you indeed?" William gave him a crooked grin. "Well, I wouldn't have an easy time making a liar out of you."

"Sorry not to be more help, coz, but I don't care to shit my life into the chamber pot, either," Marcus Radcliffe said.

"You have a pungent turn of phrase," William observed. "You ought to write for the gossip sheet they started here. You would make everyone despise you, than which nothing, I am sure, would delight the publisher more."

"No, thanks," Marcus said. "Now that I've answered your question for you, I'm for New Grinstead again, and for wherever else I please."

"As long as you came so far, will you tolerate two questions rather than one?" William asked.

"Well, I might," his backwoods cousin drawled, "long as you pour me out another glass of that wine. Those grapes died happy for sure."

"I think I might oblige you there." William filled Marcus' glass again, then his own. "Let me try this: if we ever see the promised Dutch and English ships, could I persuade you—and you persuade some of your backwoods fellows—to serve aboard my merchantmen, as marksmen at sea and as a landing force when we reach Avalon?"

"I know some people who don't shy away from a fight, and that's a fact," Marcus said. "Don't know whether they'd fancy one on the ocean. Don't know whether I would myself, either. I have to cipher that out."

"Chances are you'll have all the time you require," William Radcliffe said dolefully. "The next ship we see of those promised will be the first."

"If my friends treated me that way, I'd make 'em sorry for it—to hell with me if I wouldn't," Marcus said.

"If my friends treated me so, I should make them sorry for it, too," William replied. "The gentlemen who promised, however, are not my friends: merely associates with whom I share certain interests. I love them not, nor they me."

Marcus drained the last of his wine. "Why put in with 'em, then?"

"Nothing simpler," William said. "Because one of the interests we share is seeing Red Rodney Radcliffe, damn his black soul to hell, hanged in chains."


"Signal flags!" Red Rodney Radcliffe exclaimed in high glee as he stood at the wheel of the *Black Hand*. "Do you ever reckon a bunch of bally freebooters'd fly signal flags like the bleeding Royal Navy?"

"Not me," Ben Jackson answered. "We have enough trouble getting our own bastards to do like we say most of the time, let alone the buggers who fight for somebody else."

"It's a corsair fleet. It's a corsair navy, by God!" Red Rodney raised his voice to call to the sailor who was raising the flags aloft: "Signal *form line of battle*, Quint!"

"I'll do it, skipper," Quint said, and he did. He'd served in the Royal Navy himself till he jumped ship at

Stuart and made his way to Avalon. Piracy suited him better than shouts and curses and kicks from petty officers, with the lash or the yardarm waiting if he got too far out of line.

Almost every shallop and brigantine that sailed out of Avalon carried at least one man who'd been part of the Royal Navy and knew something about signal flags. Quite a few men who couldn't write their own names or read them if they saw them were intimately familiar with dozens of flags.

In the Royal Navy, the admiral could and would punish any captain who refused his orders. Radcliffe wished he could do that. But he would have a war on his hands if he tried, and not the one he wanted. Besides, he wasn't the admiral, not in the formal sense—he'd turned the job down.

The other pirate captains had done just what he hoped they would when they chose Michel de Grammont to lead them. De Grammont wasn't even important enough to come to the meeting when he was named. The majority of the pirates of Avalon were English, which made it hard for them to take a Frenchman seriously. His ship wasn't a big or a strong one. In other words, he made an ideal figurehead.

Red Rodney wished his own ship were built for him from the keel up, not sailed out of a Dutch port on the Terranovan coast in a hail of musket bullets. Then she could look the way she did in his mind's eye, with the figurehead of a big black hand below the bowsprit. Everyone would know her from a mile off, and fear her—and fear him, too. That would be very fine.

Not everybody was falling into line. The other pirates didn't want to follow his orders—or anyone else's. Not for nothing were they called freebooters. Even if obeying someone else would do them good, they weren't interested. If obeying someone else would save their necks? They were up against that now. It didn't seem to matter.

The mate saw the same thing. "Maybe we ought to fight Dutch-style and not like Englishmen," Jackson said. "Then it'd be every man for himself, like, and all the ships could do what they do best."

"And they could get blasted out of the water one at a bloody time," Rodney said.

Ben Jackson scowled. Like any other corsair, he liked his own conceits best. "It works for the Dutchmen," he said stubbornly. "They make England bleed every time they tangle."

"Of course they do," Radcliffe replied. "They have ships to match the English men-of-war, so they can tangle with 'em one on one. Can we do that? Can any ship in Avalon take on a three-masted ship of the line by her lonesome?"

Jackson went on scowling. But he shook his bullet head. "Reckon not." He didn't want to admit it, but he didn't have much choice.

"I reckon not, too," Red Rodney said. "So we have to find some other way to beat those scuts. If it's not fighting in a line, what is it?"

He meant the question to make the mate agree there was no other way. Instead, Jackson proposed one. That surprised Radcliffe. What surprised him more was that, the longer the mate talked, the better he liked the idea.

When Jackson finished, Red Rodney threw back his head and laughed out loud. He pounded the mate on the back. Jackson was bigger and probably stronger than he was, but Rodney staggered him all the same. "By God, we *will* do that!" he exclaimed. "We will, and we'll see how the honest gentlemen of Stuart like it!" He laughed some more.

\*     \*     \*

William Radcliff went down to the harbor almost every day. It wasn't so much that he hoped to see warships gathered there. He did hope to see them—but, after so much disappointment, those hopes weren't high. He went anyway. Merchantmen came into Stuart; others sailed out. Some were his; others belonged to his rivals. He kept an eye on as many of them as he could. If the man who ran a trading firm didn't know what was going on, how could he tell the people who worked for him what to do?

"Sail ho!" The cry came from the east, from the lookouts who watched for incoming ships. Pirates had raided Stuart a generation earlier, and caught the town by surprise. That would never happen again.

Stuart had better walls and bigger guns on those walls than was true a generation earlier, too. It also had more men who could snatch up a musket and fight. A generation before, Stuart had been new and raw, a town on the edge of settlement. Now it was part of the hinterland. New, raw towns were springing up to the north and to the west.

"Sail ho! Sail ho!" The cry rang out again and again. Somebody added, "It's a bloody forest of masts out there!"

William couldn't see them yet. And then, all at once, he did. For a moment, alarm swept through him: that was no fleet of merchantmen. He'd planned to go after Avalon. Were the pirates aiming to beat him to the punch in spite of Stuart's improved fortifications?

Then he breathed easier. Pirates didn't sail three-masted ships. They didn't have the crews to man them. Maybe a big fleet from Terranova was coming in. Or maybe, just maybe . . .

"By God!" William breathed, seeing the Union Jack flying from the mastheads of each ship. "They took their own sweet time, but they finally went and did it."

Six ships of the line and six smaller vessels tied up at the quays. Sailors swarmed ashore to do what they would in Stuart's taverns and brothels. And, in due course, Elijah Walton waddled off the largest man-of-war, the *Royal Sovereign*. Its figurehead, King Charles in a flowing, curly wig, was almost frighteningly realistic.

He gave William Radcliff a bow well flavored—perhaps overflavored—with irony. "Your fleet, Admiral—as much of it as the Dutchmen aren't doling out," Walton said. "I do not see them here. Have you any notion when they intend to make an appearance—or, indeed, if they do?"

"No, sir. I do not," William replied evenly. "But then, up until your sails were sighted, I would have said the same of the Royal Navy."

"Do you insult me?" Walton's voice went silky with danger. "If you do, we can continue this discussion through our friends. After that, the fleet may find itself with a new admiral."

"If you are a man insulted by plain facts, sir, I shall discuss the matter with whomever you please," William said. "Had you let me finish, you would have heard me counsel a bit more patience, so much already having been required."

He watched Walton chew on that. At last, grudgingly, the Englishman replied, "Well, perhaps it were best to save our bullets for the blighters on the other side. Perhaps, I say. If you feel otherwise, I assure you I shall endeavor to give satisfaction."

*I'll kill you if I can,* he meant. The language of ceremony was a strange and wonderful thing. William Radcliff bowed. "If at the end we find each other incongenial, we can pursue it then. In the meanwhile, as you say, there are others we should oppose in arms. One thing at a time, sir."

"One thing at a time," Walton agreed. "Not the worst

motto I've ever heard. Would you care to come aboard and view your flagship?"

"I should be pleased to do so, and thank you for the courtesy," Radcliff said.

The *Royal Sovereign* differed from a merchantman not in essence but in scale. Elijah Walton rattled off the numbers as the two men strode the main deck and the quarterdeck. The ship was 234 feet long, had a beam of 49 feet, and displaced around 1,500 tons. She carried 780 sailors, most of them men who could find no easier way to earn a living or whose families had gone to sea for generations.

Walton didn't say that, but William Radcliff knew it full well even so. He sprang from such a family, though not all the Radcliffes and Radcliffs were tied to the sea as they had been in the days of Edward the Founder. Marcus and many others had sunk deep roots in the soil of Atlantis.

"And you will want to see the guns," Walton said.

"Indeed. They and the sails are the point of the whole affair, eh?" Radcliff said.

He ended up admiring them more than he'd thought he would. His merchantmen went armed, too, to beat back pirates if they could. He was intimately familiar with twelve-pounders and smaller pieces. That made him think the forty-two-pounders on the lower gun deck would have nothing new to show him. But he turned out to be wrong. The sheer brutal mass of those big iron monsters took his breath away.

When he remarked on it, Walton smiled. "A man who knows tabby cats may think he knows lions, too—he may, that is, until he hears a lion roar."

"That have I never done," William said.

"I have. It is the most astounding thing," Walton said. "When you hear that sound, you are afraid. You may be the boldest warrior since Hercules, but *you are afraid,* at some level below conscious thought. It is as though the knowledge that this beast eats men were somehow stamped upon your soul."

"Interesting. I should like the experience one day. Did you hear a lion in the wilds of Africa or at a London zoological garden?"

"The latter, I fear," Elijah Walton replied. "I have been off the African coast—a place full of sickness, of no value to anyone but for the trade in slaves it affords— but I did not hear the creatures there. In London, yes. Strange, is it not?"

"It truly is." Radcliff looked back toward the houses and shops of Stuart: a few built of stone, but more from the abundant Atlantean redwoods and pines. "This is a growing town. One day soon, we ought to have a zoological garden of our own, that our folk might see the marvels of other lands."

"And of your own," Walton said. "So much of what dwells in Atlantis is unique to it."

William Radcliff shrugged. "Our folk are used to honkers and red-crested eagles and cucumber slugs and the like. Well, the explorers and settlers are. In regions inhabited for some little while, you understand, these creatures grow scarce and die out, to be replaced by productions more familiar to your common Englishman. Believe it or not, sir, much of Atlantis is a civilized land."

"Let it be as you say." That was also the language of courtesy, and meant Walton didn't believe it for a minute.

One deck higher, the long twenty-four-pounders threw lighter balls than the carronades below, but threw them farther. "Let a couple of these tear through a lightly built pirate's scantlings and watch the water pour in," William Radcliff said with a certain gloating anticipation.

"How can they propose to stand against us?" Walton asked. "Our ships so greatly outweigh theirs, the fight scarcely seems fair."

"I cannot imagine their opposing us on the sea," William answered. "More likely, they will seek to keep us from entering Avalon Bay and from sacking their hellhole of a town. What other sensible thing could they do?"

"None I can see," the Englishman said.

He was a sensible man. So was William Radcliff. They were too sensible to see that, when fighting sensible opponents, acting sensible himself might be the least sensible thing Red Rodney Radcliffe could do.

Aldo Cucari wasn't even a pirate. He was a fisherman who put to sea from Avalon. He didn't have enough to make stealing his small substance worth the corsairs' while. They laughed at him for working so hard, but they bought his fish.

He spoke French with a funny accent, and English with a funnier one. But when he came to Black Hand Fort and asked to talk to Red Rodney, the ruffians at the gate let him through. He didn't quite interrupt a tender moment between the pirate chief and Jenny, but he came close enough to leave her miffed. "Will we never be free of gabbling little nuisances?" she grumbled as Rodney dressed.

He only laughed. "Just goes to show you never raised a child, sweetheart." And away he went, a pistol on his belt. He knew Aldo, but you never could tell.

Someone had given the fisherman a cup of wine. He had no pistol, nor even an eating knife. When Rodney strode into the room where he waited, he jumped up, set down the wine, and bowed almost double. "Ah, *buon giorno, Signore* Rodney *Rosso, Signore* Radcliffe!" he cried. "I is just in from out of the north."

Red Rodney nodded. "That's what they told me, by God." Finding out what was going on up in the north was worth getting out of bed, even if Jenny didn't think so. "What did you see up there?"

"Dutchmens," Aldo Cucari said solemnly. "Three big Dutchmens, ships of the line. Six smaller Dutchmens, like to the ships that sail out of Avalon. They go east."

"Bloody hell. Of course they do." Three men-of-war, half a dozen brigantines or the equivalent. Six more men-of-war from London, with a like number of smaller supporters. However many merchantmen William clipped-*e* Radcliff could scrape together at Stuart, plus their auxiliaries. The merchantmen wouldn't have the speed or the firepower of a first-rate ship of the line, but they'd be bad enough. Red Rodney glowered down at the small, swarthy Italian. "You swear this is the truth?"

"By the cross, *signore.*" Aldo Cucari crossed himself. You could be a Papist in Avalon, or a Protestant, or a Mahometan, or even a Jew. No one cared enough to kill you for it, which wasn't true all over Atlantis. Aldo went on, "By my mother's honor, *signore.*"

People laughed at Aldo for working hard, but no one had ever called him a coward. And if you challenged his mother's honor—if you challenged the honor of any man's mother—he was bound to kill you if he could. "All right, then," Radcliffe said. "You've told me what I need to know, and I'm grateful."

The fisherman bowed again. "It is my honor, too, *Signore* Rodney."

"Honor's all very well, but you can't eat it. See what you can buy with these." Red Rodney pressed two gleaming gold sovereigns into Aldo's callused hand.

One more bow. "You is a man of great heart, *signore,* and a man of open hands as well. I hoped for one sovereign—I thought my news is worth one. But two? Two! Only a man of great heart would give two."

He stepped forward, embraced the pirate captain, and bussed him first on the right cheek, then on the left.

Frenchmen and Spaniards would do the same thing sometimes. Red Rodney clapped Aldo on the back and made a joke of it: "You aren't pretty enough for that."

"Ah, well." The fisherman grinned and fired back: "If I is doing it for looks, you isn't pretty enough, neither."

He came very close to dying then, even with Rodney's gold coins in his hand. Only blood washed away insults in Avalon—if you decided they were insults. If you laughed them off, though ... Rodney did. "I may be ugly, but I have fun. How about you?"

"Every so often I find a girl who—how you say?—she no see so good. Or maybe is too dark to see good. Who knows? Who cares? I has fun, too."

Rodney shouted for more wine. The servant who brought it was a copperskinned Terranovan native. Everybody called him Old Abe; he'd been in Avalon almost as long as Rodney had been alive. Smallpox scars slagged his face, but he'd lived through the disease and never needed to worry about it again. A lot of copperskins turned up their toes in a hurry after they met Europeans or Atlanteans. That was one reason white settlement was spreading on the western mainland, though not so fast as it was in previously uninhabited Atlantis.

"Here's to fun!" Rodney said, and Aldo Cucari drank with him. But even as the rough red wine slid down his throat, he was weighing the odds. Nine ships of the line? People farther east had hated Avalon for a long time. They'd always said they had, anyhow. Never till now, though, had they seemed serious. It was hard to get much more serious than nine ships of the line and assorted auxiliaries.

Well, they might be—they were bound to be—gathering at Stuart. But from Stuart to Avalon was a long way: long in terms of sailing, even longer in terms of the spirit that animated each town. Aldo, anyone might think, would have fit better in Stuart. But he'd lived there for a little while, and didn't care for the dull, stolid burghers who ran the place. Whatever else Avalon was, dull and stolid it wasn't.

The pirate captain poured wine with the same lavish hand he'd used to pass out money. Raising his cup, he shouted, "Here's to frying my God-cursed cousin!" Aldo drank with him—why not? And Rodney Radcliffe laughed and laughed. "Yes, here's to frying him, in his own damned pan!"

# XIII

*W*illiam Radcliff's secretary was a plump, nearsighted man named Shadrach Spencer. William was making a complicated calculation about just how much to charge for Terranovan pipeweed in London when Spencer stuck his head into the office and said, "I beg your pardon, sir, but there is a . . . gentleman here whom I think you should see."

He didn't casually say such things: one reason he'd worked for William for more than fifteen years. "Well, send him in, then," William said, setting down his quill. "Let's find out what he has to say."

As Radcliff expected from his secretary's tone, the individual in question was no gentleman, but a backwoods ruffian who put him in mind of his distant cousin, Marcus. The man carried a parcel wrapped in cloth. He wore a wool shirt and suede breeches with fringes; no razor had sullied his cheek for several days. All the more reason to receive him as if he were the heir to a duchy. "Good day, sir. I am William Radcliff," William said, bowing. "I fear you have the advantage of me."

"My name is Dill, Hiram Dill." The backwoodsman shook hands politely enough, then remarked, "Thirsty work, riding in from past the edge of town."

"Shadrach, tend to that, would you?" Radcliff said.

"Certainly, sir." His secretary bustled off, returning a moment later with a flagon of fine—or at least strong—gin from Nieuw Haarlem and two glasses. He poured for William and his guest.

"Your health, sir," William said to Hiram Dill, raising his glass.

Dill drank. His eyes got wide. "I'm bound to be healthy if I pour this stuff down," he said. "It'd poison anything that tried to sicken me, and that's the Lord's truth."

Courteously, Radcliff poured him a refill. As Dill drank it down with as much alacrity as he'd shown for the first sample, William asked, "And what was it impelled you to ride in to Stuart from, as you say, past the edge of town?"

"Well, I was hunting for the pot last night, and I let fly with my shotgun at a pigeon flying by, and I bagged me . . . this here." Hiram Dill had a sense of the dramatic, whatever his other shortcomings might have been. He undid the cloth around his loosely wrapped parcel.

It was a pigeon, as ordinary a pigeon as ever hatched. Atlantis boasted several varieties of *extra*ordinary pigeons. One was cream-colored, with bright red eyes. One, too big and heavy to fly, had a feathery crest that looked like curly hair. One was a dark green bird that disappeared completely against the needle-filled branches of redwoods and pines.

But this was a plain English pigeon, like the ones that cooed and strutted in the streets of Stuart hoping for handouts. Its head was green, its body shades of gray and white. The only unusual thing about it was a bit of parchment tied around its right leg.

"A message?" William asked. Hiram Dill nodded. William asked another question: "You've read it?"

"Well, sure," Dill answered. "Couldn't very well know you needed to see it if I hadn't, now could I?"

"No, indeed," Radcliff said gravely. "And what does it say?"

"See for yourself," the backwoodsman replied. His scarred and calloused fingers surprisingly deft, he undid the message from the bird's leg and handed it to William.

The fine, tiny, spidery hand defeated William's sight, which was beginning to lengthen. He called in Shadrach Spencer. "Read this out for me, if you would be so kind."

"Of course, sir." His secretary held the parchment so close to his eyes, it all but bumped his nose. "It says, 'In Stuart harbor nine ships of the line, twelve armed merchantmen, fifteen lesser ships. Sailing soon against Avalon.' "

"I am not surprised to learn we have a spy amongst us, but neither am I heartened to learn it. The iniquity some men will embrace . . ." William shook his head. Then he brightened. "As for you, Mr. Dill, I freely own myself to be in your debt."

Hiram Dill didn't say anything. His face, however, bore an expression remarkable for its cupidity. He had brought the pigeon to William for no other reason than to hear those words from his lips. William spoke to his secretary in a low voice. Spencer nodded and hurried off, as he had when Radcliff asked him to fetch the gin.

This time, he needed longer to return. When he did, he pressed a small velvet sack into William Radcliff's hand. Radcliff, in turn, presented the sack to Hiram Dill. "With my compliments, sir."

Judas could no more have kept from counting the wealth he'd got from the Romans than Dill could have stopped himself from opening the sack and seeing what lay inside. "Five pounds!" he exclaimed. "God bless you, Mr. Radcliff! I didn't look for so much, and that's the Lord's truth, too."

"You have earned it. I would say, earned it and more, did I not fear that would make you importunate," William said with a smile. "I have known for long and long that the pirates of Avalon spied upon Stuart. How they spied upon us, no one here knew—till now."

Hiram Dill grinned back. "I expect there'll be a deal of pigeon hunting in town the next little while."

"I expect you are right, Mr. Dill," Radcliff replied. "I expect you are just exactly right. And I expect someone will be very unhappy when we uncover him for a pole-cat, for a lying, tricking snake in the grass."

"What will you do to him? Something worth watching, I hope," Dill said.

"Oh, yes." Radcliff nodded. "I don't know yet what it will be, sir, but I promise you that anyone who sees it will remember it to the end of his days."

Red Rodney Radcliffe was not a happy man. When he was unhappy, he thought himself duty-bound to make everyone around him unhappy, too. "Damn it to hell, why haven't we heard from Stuart?" he growled. "Somebody over there has his thumb up his bum. How are we supposed to know when the God-cursed fleet is sailing if they don't send pigeons?"

"Maybe something's gone wrong with the birds," Ethel suggested.

"No doubt. They've come down poxed, on account of wasting their silver at the bird brothels. They need a better class of pigeon pimps." Red Rodney laughed. He thought he was funny, and that was all that mattered to him.

His daughter was harder to amuse. "Maybe the fat fools back there have finally twigged to your using pigeons, and they're shooting all the birds they see going out."

"Good luck to 'em!" Rodney said. "They'd do better to shoot the bugger who sets the birds free."

He meant that as a sardonic retort to put Ethel in her place. But the words seemed to hang in the air. The more he mulled them over, the likelier they felt. Ethel must have felt the same way, for she asked, "What can you do about it if they have shot him?"

"Damn all, I fear," Red Rodney said morosely. "I'd have to get somebody else with pigeons to Stuart. That might not be easy, not if the bastards there are waiting for me to try it."

"You could put pigeons on a scout ship up near North Cape," Ethel said. "They wouldn't give as much warning as birds from Stuart would, but they fly faster than any ship can sail."

Radcliffe started to trot out all the reasons why that was a foolish notion, but stopped with his mouth hanging open. Try as he would, he couldn't find any. Instead, he gave Ethel a big, smacking kiss. "The Devil fry me black if you won't command the *Black Hand* after I'm gone. You've got the natural wit for it."

"And the charm, too." Ethel simpered. She wasn't old enough yet to have the kind of charms she wanted. But she also wanted to take a pirate crew into battle. Even now, she would likely do a good job of it.

He tousled her hair. "Your day will come, sweetling, but not quite yet." Ethel pouted. He took no notice of her, which was her good luck; had his temper flared, he would have made her sorry.

Instead, he called for Mick. The master of the dovecote nodded and knuckled his forehead when Red Rodney told him what he had in mind. "Aye, skipper, we can do that—damned if we can't," he said. "You were in a sneaky mood when you thought of it, eh?"

"I'm not to blame," Radcliffe said, not without pride. "It's my daughter's notion."

"Well, good on Ethel, then," said Mick, who knew which side his bread was buttered on.

That very afternoon, a pinnace slipped out of Avalon harbor. Armed with only a handful of four-pounders, the little ship couldn't hope to outfight even the lighter vessels that would be sailing from Stuart. But she boasted a broad spread of sail, so she had a chance of getting away. And she carried several pigeons in wicker cages, so even if the enemy did run her down she could warn Avalon that danger neared.

Ethel was wild with rage when she found out the pinnace had sailed without her. "Why didn't you let me go?" she shouted at her father. "You said I could've done it!"

"I said your day was coming. I didn't say it was here," Rodney replied.

"*I* say it is!" Ethel screeched.

"You can say all sorts of things," he said. "That doesn't mean you can back them up."

"Who says I can't?" She drew her pistol with startling speed and aimed it at his chest.

The bore of any firearm pointed straight at you seemed six or eight times as wide as it really was. Red Rodney made no sudden moves. Furious as she was, Ethel might have squeezed the trigger first and thought about it only afterwards—which would have been rather too late for him. "Put that thing away," he said. "She's already sailed, and she's miles from here by now. I can't call her back."

"Not fair!" Ethel wailed. The pistol swung away from Red Rodney. He darted forward and grabbed her wrist. The gun went off. Something smashed. He didn't see what, and he didn't much care. As long as that heavy lead ball didn't thump into *him* . . .

Ethel was tough and brave and strong—and not

nearly big enough for any of that to do her the least bit of good. Rodney got her over his knee and smacked her behind. Her wails—or maybe the pistol shot—brought people on the run. "Only a mistake," Red Rodney told them. "She's finding out better now."

"Oh, no, I'm not!" Ethel yelled.

"Oh, yes, you are, by God!" Her father continued to apply himself to her seat of learning. "You don't aim a damned gun at somebody unless you aim to kill him. And you'd damned well better not aim to kill the bastard who spawned you. Have you got that, you little hellcat?" He did his best to make sure she'd got it.

By her tears, by her red, blotchy face, and by his own hot, red palm, his best was plenty good. He didn't stop, though, until she sobbed, "Enough, Father! Enough!"

That took longer than he'd thought it would. He admired her strength to hold out—but he would have gone to the rack before he said so. "Mind from now on. Do you hear me?" he growled.

"Yes, Father." She stared down at the floor. She didn't try to sit down after he let her go; he suspected she would sleep on her stomach when night came.

"This isn't a game, dammit," Rodney Radcliffe said roughly. "This is a war. If the buggers in Stuart win it, they'll knock Avalon flat and they'll hang everybody they can catch. You had a notion that gives us a better chance. I'm going to use that notion the best way I know how, with you or without you. I don't have room to do anything else. Have you got *that*?"

"Yes, Father." Ethel kept her eyes downcast.

"All right, then. Remember it."

"Oh, I'll remember, Father." She looked him in the face then. "You don't need to worry about that." She turned and walked away. Red Rodney felt as if a goose—or, by the weight of the strides, a honker—had just walked over his grave. No, Ethel wouldn't forget till she was dead or he was. And her expression told only too clearly which one of those she wanted.

Royal Navy ships carried Royal Marines: bullocks, sailors called them with affectionate scorn. They were tough, stolid men in red uniforms who fired from the fighting tops and led boarding parties and raiding parties. The ships of the line from Nieuw Haarlem had similar contingents aboard. The Dutch marines might have been stamped from the same molds as their English counterparts, save only that they wore different clothes.

William Radcliff's merchantmen normally took no marines with them. Traders fought only in emergencies, not as a matter of course, and couldn't afford so many mostly idle hands aboard. Everything that happened between Stuart and Avalon, though, would be in the nature of an emergency. William recruited hunters from all over English-speaking Atlantis. They would not be so well disciplined as their counterparts in the men-of-war, but he thought they would serve.

His distant cousin Marcus Radcliffe came to Stuart at the head of a company of sixty backwoodsmen. They had no uniforms. Each wore what suited him and carried the kind of musket he liked best. If they came from a mold, it was not from the one that had produced the English and Dutch marines.

Marcus gave William a salute that would have provoked an apoplexy in a sergeant of Royal Marines. "Well, coz, here we are," he said. "Hope we can give those pirates a bad time one way or another."

"One way *and* another, I suspect," William said. Yes, the backwoodsmen were sadly short on spit and polish. He thought they could fight anyway, and wished the rest of his recruits left him as confident. "From now till the fighting's over, you're a captain, with a captain's pay."

"Good," Marcus said matter-of-factly. "I don't chase

silver as hard as you do, but I don't scare it off when it ambles into my sights, either."

"Fine. I'll put you and your men into the *Pride of Atlantis.*" William pointed to the ship. "And do you recollect what we spoke of when last you visited Stuart?" He didn't go into detail, not when he hadn't yet tracked down the pigeon fanciers who kept Avalon informed of what went on here.

Marcus nodded. "I'm not likely to forget. Come the time, you won't find us behindhand. You may count on that."

"Good. I didn't think I would find you so, and I intend to count on it." William sketched a salute, then made his way down to the *Royal Sovereign.*

"The admiral!" the boatswain cried, and piped him aboard. All the men on deck saluted as he came up the gangplank. The naval salute was knuckles-out, so the person honored couldn't see a sailor's pitch-dirtied palm.

Among the men saluting on deck was Elijah Walton. "We await your orders, Admiral," he said with no irony William could hear.

Standing by him was the *Royal Sovereign*'s captain, a red-faced veteran mariner named Adam Barber. He was the man with whom and through whom Radcliff would have to work. "Take us out of the harbor, Mr. Barber," William said, wincing at his accidental rhyme. "Once we're on the open sea, we'll have the leisure to shake ourselves out into a proper line."

"Aye aye, sir," Barber replied. He shouted the necessary orders. Signal flags fluttered up the lines to let the other ships know what they were supposed to do. Were pigeons flying out of Stuart even now, letting the corsairs of Atlantis know their doom was on the way? Men with shotguns waited southwest of the city, but the odds of stopping the birds were slim, and William knew it.

Sweating, swearing sailors hauled up the anchor and

the heavy rope that attached it to the ship. Slowly, slowly, they made the capstan turn. The noise it made was half rumble, half squeak. Their chanty, rising over that noise, was loudly and jauntily obscene.

Sails unshrouded. The masts and spars filled with canvas like a tree—an imported tree in Atlantis, where most of the natives were evergreens—coming into new leaf in springtime, but a thousand times faster. The *Royal Sovereign* slid away from the pier, slowly at first but then with more speed and more confidence.

"Nothing like getting under weigh, is there?" William said.

"Well, sir, I don't think so, and that's a fact," Captain Barber replied. "I suppose other folks can have other notions." He turned to the pilot, a Stuart native who knew the waters of the harbor as intimately as he knew the contours of his wife's body. "I place myself in your capable hands, Mr. McCormick."

"And I'll try not to make you sorry for it, sir," David McCormick answered. As the *Royal Sovereign* slid past a clump of barrel trees, he swung the wheel a couple of spokes' worth to port. "The deeper channel here lies this way. We'd likely not go aground anyhow, not unless the tide were lower, but all the same—why take the chance, eh?"

"If I have to take a chance in battle, that's one thing," Barber said. "It comes with my station, you might say. Taking a chance on the way to battle ... is something I don't care to do, thank you very much. Choose the deeper channel every time, sir."

"That is well said," William Radcliff put in. "Enough danger we can't steer clear of. What we can avoid, best we do."

Captain Barber eyed him in some surprise. "Meaning no offense, sir, but you have better sense than I was led to believe." Elijah Walton tried to hide in plain sight.

"Well, perhaps I do and perhaps I don't," William said. "Either way, though, we'd do best to save our fighting for the pirates. Quarreling among ourselves won't get us anywhere but into trouble."

Red Rodney Radcliffe waited for a pigeon from Stuart letting him know the enemy fleet had sailed. He waited and waited, but no bird came. Something was wrong. He didn't know what, but something was. William Radcliff wouldn't wait, not with all his ships assembled.

"They must have caught your bird fancier," Jenny said when the pirate chief grumbled about it.

"Too bloody right they have," Rodney said gloomily.

And if they had, what did that mean? It meant he was waiting and waiting for a message he wouldn't get. It also meant he was damn lucky he'd sent that pinnace north. *God bless Ethel,* he thought. Without the little ship and the birds aboard it, his unloving and unloved cousin's ships might have come up to Avalon unannounced and undiscovered.

A surprise would have meant disaster, nothing less. The whole point of fighting the enemy men-of-war was keeping them far away from the corsairs' base. If they took Avalon . . . If they did, individual pirates and pirate ships might go on here and there. But the present order of things, where the freebooters were almost a nation and where their vessels ruled the Hesperian Gulf, would die.

He took a fat gold ring out of a strongbox and pressed it onto one of Jenny's fingers. It was too big for anything but her thumb. Red Rodney didn't care. "Keep it, sweetheart," he said.

She kissed him. He was generous cnough, but not usually so generous as this. "What did I do? What did I say?" she asked.

"Never mind," he said. "You're you. That's plenty."

Jenny stared at the thick gold circlet. "But I want more!"

"You always do," Red Rodney said, not without affection. "You make a good pirate, Jenny."

"Huh!" That didn't suit her the way it would have suited Ethel. He might have known. She wanted to be a fine lady. What she was doing in Avalon with a dream like that . . . Well, people didn't always end up where they wanted to. You had to do what you could with what life gave you—either that or you had to give it a good swift kick and make it do what you wanted. Women had a harder time there than men did.

No sooner had that thought crossed his mind than someone knocked on the bedroom door. He and Jenny were decorously clad this time; she didn't have to duck under the covers. He opened the door. There stood Mick. "Ha!" Rodney said. "Is it word from Stuart at bloody last?" Maybe he'd worried over nothing.

"No, skipper—from the pinnace." The Irishman held out an unfolded scrap of parchment.

"Give me that!" Radcliffe snatched it out of his hands. *We are not far from North Cape,* he read. *Enemy now coming into sight. Fleet is about the size you guessed it would be. Will get away if we can.* The message was dated the fourteenth. "What's today's date?" Red Rodney demanded.

"The fifteenth, isn't it?" Jenny said from behind him. Mick nodded.

Rodney Radcliffe calculated how fast the enemy fleet could sail. With reasonable winds, they would get to Atlantis in three or four more days. They would, that is, unless they were stopped. He had the chance to do just that.

"We move!" he shouted, so that both his mistress and the pigeon man jumped. He went on shouting, too, so that first his own crew and then the rest of the corsairs of Avalon would pay attention to him. And they did. The ragged, mismatched fleet sailed the next morning. Aboard the *Black Hand*, Red Rodney wore a smile that stretched from ear to ear. If William Radcliff wanted the pirates wrecked, he would have to do it the hard way.

William Radcliff looked discontentedly toward the Atlantean coast. Here in the west, with the warm current bathing the shore, the weather stayed mild much farther north than it did on the other side of the Green Ridge Mountains. "I wish we'd been able to sink that pinnace," he grumbled.

"Don't worry, Admiral," Elijah Walton said. William thought the Englishman used the title to pacify him, the way a mother might give a baby her breast. Walton went on, "We made the bastards aboard it beach themselves so they wouldn't be caught. They won't pass word on to the freebooters that we bear down on Avalon—we'll get there long before they can."

"You are a clever man, sir—but, perhaps, not so clever as you might be," William said. "How have the pirates been spying out our every move in Stuart?"

"By pigeon. But you seem to have put a stop to that."

"Well, I can hope I did." William Radcliff shrugged broad shoulders. "Whether I did or not, though, I couldn't very well stop the men aboard that little ship from loosing whatever birds they had. And I think it very likely they had some. Why was that ship there, if not to spy out our coming? No other reason makes sense. And they would pass word on to Avalon as quickly as ever they could. They would know we'd have swift ships aplenty, and that they might be overtaken themselves. Only pigeons make sense, then."

Walton chewed on that with even less enthusiasm than he used for eating at sea. He was not a good sailor, not when the ocean turned rough, as it had in the voyage up from Stuart to North Cape. "Well, you are right," he said at last. "You are right, and I wish to heaven you weren't."

"Oh, so do I," Radcliff replied, "but what difference does that make? If we fail against the freebooters, the ones who ran off the beach before we burnt their pinnace will come down to Avalon sooner or later and find their fellows carrying on just as they were before."

A regiment might be unable to sustain itself traversing a long swath of Atlantean terrain. Marcus Radcliffe had made that all too plain to William. But a smaller group, as long as they kept their heads, would not have much trouble finding enough to eat.

"Maybe a band of copperskinned renegadoes or escaped blackamoors will fall on them before they reach their promised land," Walton said.

"Maybe, but not likely, not in this quadrant of Atlantis," William Radcliff said. "Far more Negro slaves in the French and Spanish holdings in the southeast, and the same holds true in lesser measure for the Terranovan natives. This is the least settled part of the land."

"A pity, for it seems no less fruitful than any other, and rather more so than some farther east," Elijah Walton said. "The only thing holding it back is its remoteness—well, that and the dampening effect a bloody nest of pirates is apt to have on the settlements of honest men."

"Its time will come." Radcliff spoke with sublime confidence. "One day—and sooner than many believe, especially back in England—this land will be as well settled as the home islands, and far more populous and prosperous."

Walton looked shoreward himself. No axe had ever touched these redwoods. No farmhouses stood out in the meadow. No cattle or sheep or horses grazed upon them. No smoke betrayed human habitation anywhere close by. A honker, symbol of all that was old and wild about Atlantis, stared incuriously out to sea. The Englishman neither said anything nor needed to.

Stubbornly, William Radcliff said, "That time *will* come, sir. Not in my lifetime or yours, perhaps, but it will. You may rely upon it. We shall also continue with the deposition of the Terranovan savages from their long-time haunts until they cease to encumber the western continent."

"There I can scarcely disagree with you, not when some of the savages have gold," Walton said. "A great pity the Spaniards jumped on them first, but we have not got poor on Spain's leavings, indeed we haven't. If the corsairs plundered only Spain's ships, I should not mind them a bit."

"Nor I," William said. "But, since they plunder me and mine, I will end them if I can. And with a fleet like this under my command, I believe I can do nothing else."

The fleet was a grand sight, spread out across the sea, the great ships of the line bunched together in the center, with faster, more nimble vessels on either wing. Nothing matched the splendor of a big sailing ship's stately passage over the sea. It put Radcliff in mind of a dowager gliding across the dance floor in skirts that swept out and concealed all the motion of her lower body. But for the thrum of the breeze in the rigging and the laundry-line sound of a sail filling with wind now and then, the journey was almost silent, which only added to its grandeur.

However grand and splendid it might be, it wasn't fast enough to suit the admiral. He didn't know what he could do about that. Well, actually, he did know: he could do nothing. Even with a breeze from the north, the fleet had to make headway against the warm current that came up from the other direction. Farther out in the Hesperian Gulf, the current did not flow, but the added distance and the unending uncertainty about longitude made evading the current anything but a sure time-saver.

"We may still come upon Avalon unawares," Walton said.

"We may, yes, but I doubt we shall," William replied.

"Oh, ye of little faith." The Englishman's smile took most of the sting from the words.

"I have faith," Radcliff said. "I have faith that the freebooters are less foolish than you make them out to be."

And his faith, such as it was, was vindicated when shouts from the fleet's crow's nests came down to the decks: "Sail ho! Sail ho! *Sail ho!*"

"Sail ho!" the lookout shouted from high in the *Black Hand*'s rigging. "Sail ho! *Sail ho!*" The third repetition seemed to carry an almost desperate urgency.

Red Rodney Radcliffe peered north. He couldn't see anything from the brigantine's deck. He would soon enough, though—all too soon. Sailors had known the world was round long before landlubber scholars realized as much. The way things came up over the sea's long, smooth horizon showed it plain as plain.

"Send *form line of battle abreast!*" he shouted to the Royal Navy renegade who made signals for him.

"Aye aye, skipper!" Quint answered with a grin, and ran up the flags.

Not far away, the nominal admiral's ship would hoist the same signal, and hardly anyone would know Red Rodney had ordered the move first. He only hoped the freedom-loving captains who commanded the other ships would take the order seriously.

The bastards on the other side would do what their admiral told them to. Rodney Radcliffe was only too sure of that. He usually despised the men of Stuart and England and Nieuw Haarlem for their slavish obedience. In battle, though, he knew how much it mattered.

He was too busy looking to port and starboard to see what his colleagues and comrades were doing to pay much attention to what lay ahead for some little while. When he did turn his eyes to the north again, his stomach lurched as if he were prone to seasickness. He had never seen such large ships so close before. A pirate with an ounce of sense sheered off when he spied a first-rate ship of the line. He wasn't likely to last long against one in a straight-up fight.

They were in line of battle, the men-of-war and their accompanying scavengers. All their ships sailed as if animated by a single will. So Rodney thought, anyhow, till he spied the gaggle of Dutchmen keeping station on one another rather than with their English comrades. But they didn't do much harm to the enemy line, and conformed to the movements of the rest of the fleet.

His own ships, on the other hand . . .

If he hadn't known they'd practiced staying together and fighting as a group, he never would have believed it. They straggled all over the sea. If they formed a line, it was a line drawn by a drunk.

At least they sailed toward the enemy fleet. The wind blew from a little north of west, which gave the enemy the weather gauge and the choice of fighting or declining battle. The big ships sailed forward, their masts blooming with sails. They weren't here to pull back.

Neither was Red Rodney Radcliffe. He glanced toward those men-of-war. Then he looked west, out toward the edge of his own ragged line—and beyond. Looking that way meant looking into the westering sun. Red Rodney smiled to himself. In some ways, this couldn't have worked out better if he'd planned it for months. He had planned to fight, but knowing when the fleets would meet.... That was luck, nothing else. And luck favored him now.

Luck favored him as long as he *could* make a fight of it, anyhow. A bow chaser on one of the enemy ships fired. He saw the puff of smoke and the belch of fire before he heard the cannon go off. Bow and stern chasers were long guns, which gave them more range than the pieces on the gun decks.

The iron ball splashed into the sea several hundred yards short of the closest pirate ship. By the size of the splash, it was a twelve-pounder. Rodney muttered to himself. Twelve-pounders were broadside guns on the *Black Hand.* Would a ball from one of them even pierce a ship of the line's thick iron planking?

He'd find out before long. William Radcliff and the men who sailed with him would want to slug it out at close range. Of course they would—they had all the advantage that way. A broadside from one of those monster ships could smash a brigantine to ruins. The corsairs' fight was slash and dart and run away.

But Avalon couldn't run. Red Rodney hated his cousin with a loathing all the more profound because William Radcliff understood that too well. Individual freebooters could survive even if the worst befell their town. Their reign over the Hesperian Gulf? That would be over, over forever.

"Shall we answer them, skipper?" called a pirate at the *Black Hand*'s bow gun.

It was a pipsqueak four-pounder, good for nothing more than frightening ships that couldn't fight back. Red Rodney nodded all the same. "Yes, by God!" he shouted. "Let 'em know we're here to give 'em what for!"

A moment later, the little popgun roared defiance at the approaching fleet. Its ball also fell short, but by less than the first gun's had. The pirates manhandled it back into position, swabbed out the bore, thrust in the worm to dispose of any bits of smoldering wadding, and then rammed home powder and ball and fired again.

Several other bow chasers on both sides went off. One ball struck home with a crash that echoed across the water. Red Rodney eyed the enemy fleet with wary apprehension. When William Radcliff or whoever was in command judged the time ripe . . .

As smoothly as if they'd practiced together for years, all the ships of the line and the smaller vessels with them swung to port. "Hard to starboard!" Red Rodney shouted to his own helmsman, and then, to Quint, "Signal *hard to starboard*!"

His own fleet's broadside would be puny next to the one that came at it, but he had to stand the gaff at least once. Yes, the corsairs would take punishment, but they would also dish some out. And they would hold the enemy in position for a little while. Rodney Radcliffe glanced west again. They needed to do that if they were to have any chance of discomfiting the dogs out of Stuart.

Then the enemy broadside spoke, and Red Rodney thought he'd fallen into the end of the world. The flame, the smoke, the thunder . . . A heavy cannon ball smashed into the *Black Hand*'s rail and decking. The brigantine staggered; Radcliffe felt the shudder through his feet. Whistling, whining splinters flew everywhere. A man not six feet from him went down with a gurgling scream, clutching at the jagged length of timber that speared his throat. Blood poured from the wound, and from his mouth. He was a dead man, one who wasn't quite finished dying yet.

The corsairs' broadside answered the one from the enemy. Even to Radcliffe's ear, it sounded thin and ragged. It didn't have the crushing weight of metal the English and Dutch and eastern Atlanteans enjoyed, and it was disrupted by taking hits from those big guns. Even so, a mast on one of the men-of-war toppled. On deck, sailors on that ship ran like ants when a foot comes down. Red Rodney whooped.

He wasn't so happy when he turned his eye toward his own side. One pirate ship was on fire, another slewing helplessly out of line with rudder shot away, yet another with both masts down. The men-of-war fired again, this time ship by ship. They were happy enough pounding pirates to pieces.

Red Rodney looked west once more. He could only hope the enemy admiral wasn't doing the same.

# XIV

*W*illiam Radcliff watched in somber satisfaction as pirate ships crumpled under the thunderous barrage from his fleet. Aboard the *Royal Sovereign*, sweating, swearing, bare-chested sailors reloaded and ran guns forward to fire again. Petty officers urged them on with shouts and with strokes from rattan sticks.

"They are fools, to try conclusions with us," Elijah Walton said. A little to the east, a pirate brig caught fire. Men scurried like mice, trying to douse the flames. William didn't think they'd be able to.

"They are fools, to turn corsair to begin with," he said. "Sometimes you have to beat a fool's folly out of him."

A roundshot slammed into the *Royal Sovereign*'s oaken flank. Screams following the crash said the cannon ball or its splinters did their vicious work. The pirates were brave enough. They were almost madly brave, to challenge ships so much larger and stronger than their own.

As if echoing that thought, Walton said, "This unequal combat makes me wonder what possible hope of victory the brigands had."

"Sir!" A midshipman still too young to shave dashed up to Radcliff. "Sir! There's signals from out of the west! Fireships, sir!"

"Fireships!" William Radcliff said, and then something much more pungent than that. Fireships were every honest sailor's nightmare. You had to get away from them, regardless of what that did to your line. Let fire get hold of a ship full of men and it became an oven on the instant.

Fireships could do worse than that. He still remembered the Hellburner of Antwerp from the century before—as who did not? It had been loaded with tons of gunpowder and more tons of metal junk and stones—and it blew hundreds, maybe thousands, of Spaniards halfway to the moon. If Red Rodney Radcliffe remembered the Hellburner, too . . .

"Tell the signalman to raise *each ship to act independently,*" William said.

"*Each ship to act independently.* Aye aye, sir!" The midshipman darted away.

Walton peered west, shading his eyes with the palm of his hand. "Damned setting sun makes them bloody hard to spy," he said.

"Yes." William nodded. And had his unloved and unloving cousin counted on that, too? William didn't know exactly how smart Red Rodney was. Tough and hard? Yes, no doubt. Smart? It wasn't so obvious. Or it hadn't been so obvious, not till now. The pirate chief knew what he was doing, all right.

Again, Elijah Walton thought along with him: "This must be why the bugger accepted battle with us to begin with. He wanted to hold us in place whilst launching his incendiaries at us."

"That seems much too likely," William said unhappily. He too peered west. Now the plumes of smoke from the burning vessels were plain to see, befouling a sky that should have been pristine. Also plain to see was his fleet's disorder. His ships steered every which way, trying to escape those flaming harbingers of doom.

The pirates had nerve. They hadn't just launched their fireships and then abandoned them to wind and wave. The weapons would have been much less dangerous if they had. Instead, men stayed on the burning vessels as long as they could, steering them toward ships in William's fleet. Only at the last possible moment did the skeleton crews dive into the Hesperian Gulf and swim toward boats the fireships towed.

And it worked, damn them. One of the Dutch ships of the line burst into flame, and a horrible beauty was born. The sails caught first, the sails and the rigging and then the yards and the mast. Flaming canvas and tarred rope fell to the upper deck, starting fresh fire there. The Dutchmen forgot their gunnery in the frantic quest to save themselves.

They might forget, but their foes didn't. Pirate ships, tenacious as terriers, went right on shooting at them. Before long, despairing sailors started jumping into the sea. Some struck out for the closest friendly ships. Others simply sank. Not all men who went to sea could swim— far from it. The ones who couldn't decided drowning made an easier, faster death than roasting. If that choice came to him, William Radcliff decided he would make it the same way.

*Crash!* Another cannon ball thudded into and through the *Royal Sovereign*'s planking. The man-of-war's gunnery had fallen off, while the pirates fought harder than ever. And, with the ship of the line doing all she could to escape the freebooters' fireships, the enemy vessels could position themselves as they pleased and give her broadsides she couldn't answer.

"What do we do, Admiral?" Elijah Walton asked hoarsely. "What *can* we do?"

Before, he'd always sounded sardonic when he used William's title. No longer. Radcliff was the man who had the authority to save the fleet ... if he could.

He opened his mouth to speak. Before he could, a thunderous blast staggered him. Sure as hell, one of the fireships had blown up alongside a British man-of-war. William was amazed the explosion didn't take the British ship straight to the bottom. It did take down two of the man-of-war's three masts, set her afire, and leave her helpless in the water. Maybe some men would get off her, but she was ruined.

"What do we do?" Walton asked again, desperation in his voice.

William Radcliff looked at the fight. He looked at the sun, which almost kissed the smoke-stained horizon. Whatever they did, they would have to do it soon. "We pull back," he said, and shouted for a midshipman to relay the message to the signal officer.

"Sail for Stuart?" Walton sounded as if that was exactly what he hoped to hear.

But William shook his head. "No, by God. They've slowed us up. They did something we didn't look for, and they caught us flatfooted. They hurt us. But we aren't beaten unless we own ourselves beaten. We'll fix ourselves up as best we can and get on with the fight."

"Upon my soul," Elijah Walton said.


Bodies wrapped in sailcloth slid into the sea, a round shot or two at the feet making sure they would sink. Fresh blood stained the *Black Hand*'s deck and splashed the masts and rigging. Soon enough, it would go dark. The stains would seem inoffensive enough then ... unless you knew the story behind them.

The corsairs aboard—those who lived—were in a festive mood. After the fireships did their fearsome work, the men had watched the fleet that seemed invincible turn away and say it had done all the fighting it cared to do. Some of the pirates even wanted to go after their retreating foes.

Red Rodney Radcliffe said, "No." Something in the way he said it persuaded even his crew of cutthroats not to press him any further. He wasn't sure whether he would have reached for his cutlass or for his pistol if the pirates had pushed, but he was ready to kill to keep from fighting any more today.

With a creak and a groan, the pumps started up again. A stream of water poured over the side. As far as he knew, the *Black Hand* had taken only one hit at the waterline, and that one was patched now ... after a fashion. All the same, the leak continued. It didn't seem to be getting any worse. He was no praying man, but he thanked God for that.

"Well, we beat 'em back," Ben Jackson said. The mate had a new bandage on his left calf, and walked with a limp.

"Damned if we didn't." Red Rodney wished he didn't sound so surprised. He tried to hide it with gruff kindness: "How are you doing, Ben?"

"It's a fucking scratch, that's all. Nothing but a fucking scratch." Jackson spat scornfully. "I got tickled by a flying toothpick. Higgins cut it out of me. I would've taken care of it myself, but it always hurts worse when you do your own."

Rodney Radcliffe nodded; he'd seen that, too. Wounds were accidents. You were always startled when you got hurt. Repairing them sometimes required deliberate damage to your own precious flesh. He'd known many otherwise ferocious men who couldn't face that.

"What do we do now?" the mate asked.

"I think all the great captains had better hash that out." Red Rodney shouted to the signalman: "Send up *repair aboard the admiral's ship* while there's still light enough for the rest to read it."

*"Repair aboard the admiral's ship,"* the Royal Navy renegade echoed. "Aye aye, skipper."

How many of the great captains still lived? As far as Radcliffe knew, all their ships but one still floated. But the number of dead and wounded on the battered *Black Hand* warned that not all of them would have dodged bad luck.

*Splash!* Another body swathed in bloody canvas went into the drink. Red Rodney scowled. "If we win another fight like this, we're bloody well ruined."

Ben Jackson shrugged broad shoulders. "Well, skipper, we're bloody well buggered if we lose, too. So where does that leave us?"

*In trouble,* Radcliffe thought. You didn't want to believe what a man-of-war's broadside could do to a ship. And the *Black Hand* was lucky. That leak wasn't . . . too bad. She still had both masts and most of her yards and rigging. Men were aloft, patching the sails. She could go where she needed to go. She could fight again . . . if she had to.

The boat ride over to Michel de Grammont's ship was a relief. While his men rowed him from one brigantine to the other, Radcliffe didn't have to think about anything. The *Aigle d'Argent* had taken less damage than the *Black Hand.* Rodney Radcliffe supposed that was because de Grammont hadn't wanted to close with the enemy, and so fewer cannon balls had come her way. At another time, he would have something to say to the Frenchman. For now, it could wait.

He clambered up over the side. "Is it that we are victorious?" de Grammont asked in accented English.

"For now, anyway," Red Rodney said. "Let's go back to your cabin. What have you got to drink?"

"Wine," the admiral answered. Rodney Radcliffe hid a sigh. He wanted whiskey or rum. But wine would do if he drank enough of it.

It was red and sweet and strong—strong for wine, anyhow. A couple of mugs began to build a wall between him and what had happened earlier in the afternoon. One by one, the other leading captains came aboard. Bertrand Caradeuc's earring was missing. So was his right ear; a marksman on one of William Radcliff's armed merchantmen had shot it off. Had the ball flown a couple of inches to the left, Caradeuc wouldn't have been there. Goldbeard Walter Kennedy wasn't. He'd lost a leg above the knee, and probably wouldn't live out the night. His younger brother, a massive man who carried the nickname Brickyard, came in his place.

"We beat 'em," Brickyard said. He'd brought his own jug of something strong, and swigged from it now.

"We did." Red Rodney sounded so gloomy about it, he made everyone else stare at him. And he had reason for sounding gloomy, too: "What do we do if they come after us again tomorrow morning? We're out of fireships, and we'd never surprise 'em twice anyhow."

Cutpurse Charlie Condent stared at him in horror. "They wouldn't do that ... would they?" He shook his head, answering his own question: "Nah. 'Course they wouldn't. I lay they're bound for Stuart now, tails between their legs."

"How much?" Radcliffe asked. "A gold sovereign? I'll take your money. I'll take it, all right ... if my damned cousin and his dogs don't take your life."

"You're on, by God!" Condent said. "You'll pay me when I see you in Avalon. Or if you turn out to be right, I'll pay you when I see you there ... or I'll pay you when I see you in hell."

Red Rodney spat when he heard that, to turn aside

the evil omen. So did Brickyard Kennedy. "Watch your mouth, Charlie," Radcliffe said.

"I didn't mean anything by it," the other captain said.

"Watch your mouth anyway," Red Rodney told him. Cutpurse Charlie Condent glared back. At another time, they might have gone for swords or pistols. Radcliffe thought about it anyway. By the way that glare lingered, so did Cutpurse Charlie. But, until they knew what the enemy ships were doing, they had more important foes than each other.

"We sank some of their ships of the line, and wrecked some others," Bertrand Caradeuc said. "They may have decided they've had enough."

"If they have, we sail home and we fill up our forces again," Red Rodney Radcliffe said. "I know I'm not the only one who lost more than he wished he did."

The other captains all nodded. He'd been sure they would. He'd never known—he'd never imagined—a cannonading like that. He counted the corsairs lucky that Goldbeard Kennedy was the only major skipper missing here. To Radcliffe's surprise, de Grammont spoke up: "*Can* we fight them again on the sea?"

"Is anybody aiming to try, if they come south again?" Red Rodney asked.

No one said anything for a long time. At last, Brickyard Kennedy said, "We beat 'em. Cutpurse Charlie's right about that. They won't dare try to hit us again. They sailed away, after all. We didn't." He sounded like a man trying to convince himself as well as his comrades.

"If they sail south in the morning, and we fly before 'em, we didn't really win a damned thing today," Condent added.

"You're right," Red Rodney said. "And so?"

Cutpurse Charlie glowered some more. "And so you led us up here to beat them and drive them away. And if we didn't, why were we such a pack of damn fools as to follow you, eh? Answer me that, you sorry son of a dog!"

Rodney Radcliffe resolved that he *would* kill the other captain first chance he got. But that chance was not now. He sighed. "We had a chance of doing it. We may have done it even yet. What other choice did we have? Let them land by Avalon? Let them into Avalon Bay?"

"What are the forts for, if not to hold those bastards out?" Condent returned.

"If we don't do everything we want out here on the open sea, we can try something else later," Radcliffe said. "If we don't try anything out here and if the forts fail us, it's over. We've lost. And even if they do come forward now and have at the forts, they're weaker than they would have been if we didn't fight 'em here."

Cutpurse Charlie Condent didn't glare any more. He only rolled his eyes. "So are we," he said, and Radcliffe found no quick comeback for that.

William Radcliff did not order his captains—or even Piet Kieft, who had to rate as a commodore—to repair aboard the *Royal Sovereign*. He used signal lamps to order the fleet to stop, and arranged the smaller, faster ships in a circle around the surviving men-of-war and merchantmen. If the pirates came forward, the heart of the fleet would have warning.

"Will you not discuss our next move with the officers who needs must make it?" Elijah Walton asked him.

"I will not, or why am I admiral?" Radcliff returned. "Tomorrow, we fight again."

"And if the captains should refuse your order?" Walton persisted.

"I shall construe that as making a mutiny, and fire upon any ships failing in obedience," William said.

"Dear God in heaven," Walton said. "You are a man who will eat fire even if you must kindle it yourself."

"I am a man who *will* see the Hesperian Gulf cleared of pirates, Mr. Walton," William said. "I am a man who *will* see Avalon razed, its present populace captured or scattered to the winds, and the place settled with men of civil disposition. It could be a jewel in the British crown of Atlantis rather than a boil on his Majesty's arse."

"You show yourself a settler. No good Englishman would speak of his Majesty so."

"I *am* a settler," Radcliff said proudly. "I am loyal to London across the sea . . . in however dilatory a fashion London may show its loyalty to me. But I am also loyal to Atlantis, and I believe I have earned the right to hold that loyalty as well. My forefathers settled here two centuries ago. When two more centuries have passed, I expect Radcliffs to dwell here yet. And in two centuries London had better look to its laurels, for Stuart will grow up to rival it."

Elijah Walton laughed. William angrily clapped a hand to his pistol. The laughter cut off, and the admiral's hand fell away. "I do beg pardon for my show of mirth, but surely you must see the absurdity of your statement," Walton said. "London is . . . well, London. Stuart makes a very tolerable town for a settlement on distant shores, but . . . my dear fellow! Have you ever *seen* London? Do you know how greatly it outshines your home?"

"I took my baccalaureate at Cambridge—my father thought that would aid me, though we have colleges of our own on this side of the sea," Radcliff said. "So yes, I have seen London, and I do not say Stuart compares now: not in size, not in riches, not in wickedness. But Stuart grows faster. Time is on our side."

But for moonlight and distant lamplight, Walton's plump face was all shadows. "Even if you should prove right, I thank heaven I'll not live to see the sorry day."

"Nor shall I," William Radcliff said. "I work towards it nonetheless. Cleansing Avalon of its human wolves will move all Atlantis some distance in the desired direction."

"Amazing," Walton murmured. "Truly amazing."

William didn't know if that was compliment or objurgation. Nor did he care. He had other, more immediate worries. He called for a midshipman. One appeared like a genie from a bottle. "Tell the men at the lanterns to signal the *Pride of Atlantis* that I desire to speak to Marcus Radcliffe as soon as he may come to this ship."

"Marcus Radcliffe on the *Pride of Atlantis*. Aye aye, sir." The youngster trotted off.

William's distant cousin came aboard about half an hour later, clambering up on the starboard side. William waited near the rail. "Is that you, coz?" Marcus asked. "Almost as dark as a copperskin's heart here."

"It's me," William answered. "How are you and your men? Did you suffer badly in the fighting? Are you ready for more?"

"We had one dead and three wounded," Marcus answered. "One of the wounded can still fight. The other two are laid up, and we'll see how they do. So you aim to go on with it, do you?"

"I do," William Radcliff said without the least hesitation. "What do you think of that?"

"I think the pirates are praying you give it up and go home," Marcus replied. "How are they supposed to beat a fleet like this two days running? *They'll* be the ones running if you hit them again."

"You're a Radcliffe, by God, even if our lines aren't close," William said, laughing. "My only worry is, the bastard leading the other side—he's a Radcliffe, too."

Red Rodney Radcliffe was up before morning twilight grew very bright. He stood on the *Black Hand*'s deck in the wan dawn light and peered north. For the time being, he didn't see anything. The longer he didn't see anything, the happier he got. Maybe the fleet from Stuart really had had enough. Cutpurse Charlie could take his sovereign and be welcome to it, even if he gloated later.

"Any sails?" Ben Jackson showed up on deck only a few minutes after his skipper.

"Not yet." Rodney sounded as hopeful as he could.

The mate grunted. "Good."

But just as the sun slid up over the eastern horizon, a shout came from the crow's nest: "Sails ho!"

Jackson and Red Rodney swore together, a scatological counterpoint. Radcliffe was dismayed enough to turn loose a question he knew to be foolish: "Are you sure?"

"No doubt, skipper." The answer floated down. "Sails in the north, heading this way. You'll see 'em yourself soon enough. Who else would they be but the buggers we fought yesterday?"

"What do we do now?" Jackson asked.

"We signal the other ships, in case they haven't seen 'em yet," Rodney answered, evading the mate's real meaning. "After that . . . Well, we have a little while to think." He still couldn't see the sails himself, though he knew he'd be able to before long.

Quint sent signal flags fluttering up the lines. Most of the other freebooters would already know the enemy was coming. Well, so what? You did what you could for everyone on your side. To Red Rodney the idea was new, and worth exploring further. That his cousin took it for granted never crossed his mind.

Some of the pirate ships returned acknowledgments. Others went on with what they were doing. They wouldn't be able to ignore him and the enemy much longer. Maybe they realized that. If they didn't, it wasn't his fault. He'd done what he could.

"There they are, skipper." Ben Jackson pointed to the northern horizon.

"I see 'em," Radcliffe said grimly. "One thing, anyway—we can always outsail 'em."

"The big ones, yes," the mate said. "But if they send their brigs and suchlike after us, maybe they can bring us to battle and delay us till the bloody, stinking, shit-eating men-of-war catch up."

Red Rodney swore. That hadn't occurred to him. Jackson was right—no doubt about it. No doubt they couldn't take another day's hard fighting, either. That meant their best hope—maybe their only hope—was making a stand at Avalon. If they drove the enemy fleet back from their base, they were still in business.

"South!" Radcliffe shouted, his mind made up. "Our course is south down the coast till we're home again. Send up the flags, Quint! We'll still make the foe sorry he ever came against us."

At his bellowed orders, men swarmed aloft to swing the yards and set the sails to help the abrupt change of course the *Black Hand* was making. She could turn tightly—could and did. One of the enemy ships of the line fired a couple of bow chasers at her, but the balls fell far short. Then she was around, and picking up speed on her new course. The man-of-war fired again. Again, the shot fell short. Before long, the *Black Hand* showed the foe her heels.

Occasional cannon fire boomed behind her. Maybe some of the enemy's lighter vessels were catching up to pirates and engaging them, as Ben Jackson had suggested. Or maybe some of the pirates didn't have the sense to pull back when the enemy came at them. If they didn't, they didn't have the sense God gave a honker. So Radcliffe thought, anyhow. His fellow captains were not in a good position to argue with him.

Looking north, he saw plumes of smoke rising into

the sky. Those came from burning ships—they couldn't very well spring from anything else, not on the sea. Red Rodney swore every time he spotted one. Some of his friends wouldn't make it back to Avalon. They were also his rivals, but he didn't dwell on that, not now.

Ethel would scorn him for turning tail. That was funny, if you looked at it the right—or maybe the wrong—way. He'd laid towns waste. He'd captured merchantmen past counting, and killed and tortured to make sure he wrung every copper's worth of loot from them. The wenching he'd done . . . His full lips parted in a reminiscent smile. Jenny and her predecessors in Avalon—Ethel's mother among them—were only a tiny part of it. He'd shown fear nowhere and never. You were ruined if you did.

But he feared facing his own daughter when he got home. Ethel didn't understand how things worked in the real world. Her head was full of stories. Most of them had him as the hero, which didn't make him feel any better now.

The *Black Hand* sailed close enough to the west coast of Atlantis to let him watch it slide past. He knew the look of the coastline as well as he knew the look of the skin on the back of his right hand. If one of the great redwoods that marked it fell, it was as if he'd scratched himself.

A challenge gun boomed from the fort on the north spit shielding Avalon Bay. He answered with one gun of his own. A galley came out to look over his ship. A couple of others from Avalon's fleet were also in sight. "What happened?" a man with leather lungs shouted from the galley.

"We lost. They're after us," Red Rodney shouted back. The men on the closest galley swore. Red Rodney had already done his swearing. Now he needed to fight the enemy . . . if he could. He cupped his hands in front of his mouth again: "Let me through! Let all of us through—all of us who make it here. We've got to get ready to hold our town!"

"What happens if we don't?" asked the man on the galley.

Radcliffe didn't answer, not with words. He let his head flop onto one shoulder and jerked up with the other fist, pantomiming a hanging. The men on the galley cursed some more. So did some of his own sailors. He wondered why. Hanging, he was sure, was the best the pirates could hope for if Avalon fell and they got caught. Drawing and quartering, the stake . . . He shuddered. So many nasty possibilities.

"Go on in," the strong-lunged sailor said. "We'll whip those bastards yet."

"Damned right!" Rodney pumped his fist in the air again, this time in defiance of the rest of the world. His men cheered. So did the other corsairs. He waved to them. Keeping their spirits high wasn't the least important part of the role he played here. They *would* have to fight, and soon.

If they were to make a go of it, somebody had to give them orders. They all had to work together. They couldn't fight crew by crew, as ships did. Red Rodney didn't intend to have anyone tell him what to do. He aimed to do the telling.

He got into Avalon first. The *Black Hand* had taken a beating, but most of the crew survived. After his ship tied up at the pier, the men swarmed into Avalon. They grabbed anyone who looked as if he could carry a musket or a pike or a sword.

Radcliffe harangued his new recruits from just outside of Black Hand Fort. "The Stuart swine and Dutch dogs and English idiots think they can take our town away from us!" he roared. "Are we going to let 'em?"

"No!" the new soldiers shouted. He suspected not all of them meant it. A barber cared more about cut-

ting whiskers than cutting throats. But, if he got them
into the line, he expected they would do well enough.
Once somebody started shooting at you, you damn well
*would* shoot back. Otherwise, the bugger on the other
side would kill you. No one was keen on that.

"We can fight. We can win," Red Rodney insisted.
"Plenty of forts inside Avalon. There's the one across
the mouth of the bay, too. Put those together with the
galley, and the bastards can't get in. So what'll they do?
They'll hang around for a while, and then they'll give it
up and go home, that's what!"

His own crewmen cheered. So did the new fish, if less
enthusiastically. He went on telling them what a slaughter they'd visit on the enemy. He also warned them what
the invaders would do if they won. He wasn't subtle, and
he was graphic. He believed what he was saying, too.
By the time he got done, he had them believing it with
him. They streamed along the muddy, crooked streets
of Avalon, ready to give their all for the right to go on
freebooting.

"Good speech, skipper," Ben Jackson said. "I
wouldn't've believed anything this side of rum could
make those wharf rats hot to fight."

"Put a cannon ball through my mizzen if that's not
a bloody good notion," Radcliffe said. If Avalon had
plenty of any one thing, it was rum. He arranged to serve
it out to the defenders. Maybe Dutch courage would
help them fight Dutchmen.

After he'd done all he could outside, he went into
Black Hand Fort. Jenny was half glad to see him, half
afraid Avalon would fall in the next fifteen minutes—
about what he'd expected. Half an hour alone with her
in the bedroom and she was all glad to see him . . . or she
pretended to be, which served well enough for now.

But that half hour, and the rest of the time since he
and his crewmen came off the *Black Hand*, gave Ethel

the chance to find out what was going on. By the time
Red Rodney spoke with his daughter, she knew as much
as he did—maybe more. "You lost," she said, nothing
but scorn in her voice. "Even with the fireships, you lost.
How *could* you?"

"Not all my fault." Only later did Rodney wonder
why he had to justify himself to an eleven-year-old. "I
was hoping we could make them turn around, but they
wouldn't do it, damn their black souls to hell. They've
got a Radcliff in charge of them, too, even if he clips his
name."

"He'll clip your neck if he gets the chance," Ethel
said. "I knew you should have taken me with you."

"And what could you have done that I didn't, your
Worship?" Red Rodney demanded.

"Made sure I killed Will Radcliff, that's what," his
daughter replied.

"How, pray tell?"

"Chainshot, barshot, red-hot shot—whatever it took
to sink his ship." Ethel had all the Radcliffe stubbornness. Sense? Maybe not. Red-hot shot was almost as
dangerous to the ship firing it as it was to the one on the
receiving end. You had to be desperate even to think
about using it . . . unless you were eleven. Red Rodney
hadn't been desperate enough. All things considered,
maybe he should have been.


"So that's Avalon Bay." William Radcliff raised a spyglass to his eye for a closer look. The image was upside
down, which didn't bother him, and fringed in red and
purple, which did. It seemed much closer than it had to
the naked eye, and that was what he really wanted.

Elijah Walton had a spyglass, too. "Not a bad harbor,"
he said grudgingly.

"No, not a bad one," Radcliff agreed dryly. It was the
best harbor he'd ever seen, and he'd seen harbors from

Valparaiso to Stamboul. "It's the people holding it now who are bad."

Those people had long guns in the fortress north of the town, guns that outranged anything the fleet carried. And a fortress didn't have to worry about firing red-hot shot the way a ship did. They wouldn't set a fortress of earth and brick on fire the way they would a ship's seasoned timbers.

The northern approach, then, looked bad. So did forcing the channel. His spyglass showed him the galleys patrolling it. Upside down, they looked as if they were about to fall into the sky and spill out all their rowers. He only wished looks didn't deceive here.

Another fortress at the northern edge of Avalon proper also guarded the channel into the bay. The town itself had a sea wall to keep invaders from swarming straight ashore. William didn't think the guns on the sea wall were anywhere close to being as formidable as the ones in the fortresses.

Inside Avalon, forts topped half a dozen hills. He didn't think they mounted big guns, either. Why would they? Little guns throwing canister would be all they needed to hold off attackers.

"What is your plan, Admiral?" Walton asked. Radcliff understood what the Englishman wasn't saying, too. *If this goes wrong, it's all your fault*—that was what he really meant.

Instead of answering directly, William turned to the signal officer. "Run up *marine commanders repair aboard,*" he said.

"*Marine commanders repair aboard,*" the lieutenant repeated. He waited for Radcliff's confirming nod before adding, "Aye aye, sir."

"Do you think you can get marines over the sea wall?" Walton asked. "Most of it is just a palisade, but even so. . . ."

"I aim to discuss the possibilities with the men who needs must do the actual fighting," William replied. The Englishman fumed, but William didn't worry about that. Walton wasn't going anywhere, not now.

Every ship in the fleet carried marines. They were the marksmen in the fighting tops, and they went ashore when there was need of that. Radcliff wasn't sure how many Dutch marines spoke English, but he didn't worry about that, either. Some of them would, and they could translate for their comrades.

Marcus Radcliffe came up over the *Royal Sovereign*'s rail after most of the other marine officers. As usual, he wore nothing resembling a uniform: only homespun wool trousers and a linen shirt. His sole ornament was a tail plume from an oil thrush thrust under the band on his colorless, floppy hat. But none of the true marines, with their fancy uniforms and accoutrements, seemed inclined to mock the leathery backwoodsman.

"If we land your combined forces south of the town, can you march up, march in, and take it?" William asked.

His distant cousin gave back a question of his own before anyone else could speak: "What'll you be doing in the meantime?"

"Cannonading," William replied.

Marcus Radcliffe considered that, then nodded. "Well, fair enough. If you knock down some of the sea wall, will you send in sailors to give us a hand?"

It was William's turn to hesitate. He was a seaman, first, last, and always. Sending in landing parties of sailors would mean coming very close—dangerously close—to shore-based defenders. In the end, though, he also found himself nodding. "If we possibly can. I understand that the distraction may help you."

Another marine officer said, "We ought to take a couple of four-pounders off one of our brigs and see if we can drag them up to their palisade down there. They'll give us the kind of door-knocker we need."

"Good," William Radcliff said. "Do it."

The marine blinked. "Just like that?"

"Just like that," Radcliff told him. "It sounds like a good idea. The worst that can happen is, the guns get left behind. If they do, you're no worse off than if you hadn't brought them. So give it a try."

"By God, sir, I wish every captain were like you," the marine said. "Too many of those buggers can't make up their minds, or else they haven't got any minds to make up."

"You don't know my coz." Marcus Radcliffe sounded sly. "He's always sure. He's not always right, but he's always sure." He got the laugh he must have hoped for, then went on, "If not for him, we wouldn't be here now, and the pirates wouldn't be in the mess they're in."

"For which I thank you. But, by the same token, we also wouldn't be in the mess *we're* in," William said dryly. "We have to beat them. We have to take Avalon away from them. If we do that, we redeem ourselves. If they hold us, they redeem themselves. How can it get any simpler?"

Nobody said anything. Maybe he'd made it as clear as he hoped. Maybe the men were even simpler than the situation. They were marines, after all, and the bullocks did not have a reputation for wit. They were human roundshot: you pointed them at a target, and you used them to smash it flat.

"Looting should be good," one of them remarked. "The corsairs have stashed their booty in Avalon for years now."

That might have inspired them more than anything William said. He didn't mind. As long as something did, he was content.

# XV

*R*ed Rodney Radcliffe woke with a warm, bare thigh draped over his and with the sound of thunder in his ears. He was used to the one or the other; both together were something new. He needed a moment to remember he wasn't at sea and another to remember he wasn't in a brothel in some distant port. This was Avalon. This was Jenny.

And this was a fine, clear morning, with sunbeams sliding between the slats of the shutters on his bedchamber window. Which meant that wasn't thunder. Which meant . . .

Full memory returned. Red Rodney spilled Jenny off him and sprang out of bed, swearing horribly. His lady love let out a most unladylike squawk. He was pulling up his breeches when somebody pounded on the door. Jenny squawked again. "They're bombarding us!" Ben Jackson shouted through the planks.

"I know. I hcar. I'm coming, dammit." Radcliffe needed only two strides to get to the door. That gave Jenny just time enough—or maybe almost time enough;

Red Rodney didn't look back—to cover herself before he threw it open.

He rushed to Black Hand Fort's palisade. No, that wasn't thunder. That was his cousin's fleet hammering at the sea wall and the closer forts with all the guns the ships carried. Black Hand Fort was safe enough; lying near the bayside, it was beyond the reach of even bow chasers. But the closer forts were taking a pounding, and so were all the shops and dives and houses between them.

And so was the wall. It had been built to hold invaders out, but no one had imagined an onslaught like this when it went up. Even the hard-bitten Jackson sounded uncertain when he asked, "Can we keep 'em from breaking in?"

"We'd better," Red Rodney answered, which was nothing less than the truth. He looked around. Someone he would have expected to watch the fireworks with him wasn't here. Not Jenny—she'd still be cowering under the coverlets. But . . . "Where's Ethel?"

His first mate hesitated again, which was most unlike him. "Well . . ." he began.

"Well, what? Out with it, damn you." Rodney's voice took on a rumble more ominous than the cannonading— or so he intended, anyhow.

"Well, skipper, when the shooting started, she ran down toward the sea wall, to lend a hand where she could." Ben Jackson got it out in an unhappy rush.

"She—?" Radcliffe clapped a hand to his forehead. "Why the devil didn't you stop her?"

"On account of she was gone before I could," Jackson answered. "Christ, don't you think I would have?"

"Well, yes," Radcliffe admitted. A roundshot hit something made of stone, flew high in the air, and then crashed down again. A plume of smoke rose inside

Avalon. The bombardment had started at least one fire, anyhow. "God damn William Radcliff to hell and gone!" Red Rodney shouted.

"Yes, skipper." Jackson hesitated again, then asked, "What do we do?"

Rodney Radcliffe didn't hesitate. That was one of the reasons he was the captain and Ben Jackson the mate. "I'll take most of the men down by the sea wall. If they send boats against us, we'll make 'em sorry—see if we don't. You hold here with the rest, just in case some of our so-called friends think to get gay while everything's topsy-turvy."

The mate nodded. "I'll do it." As long as he had his orders, or as long as the task in front of him was too obvious to require them, Jackson was as good as any man unhanged. Red Rodney laughed harshly. What happened over the next few hours would tell if they stayed that way.

Armed with muskets and cutlasses and pistols and pikes and hatchets and anything else they could lay their hands on, the corsairs from Black Hand Fort rushed west through Avalon's crowded, chaos-filled streets. They had to fight their way through every now and again. Most of the people under bombardment were sensibly fleeing east, out of range. Some of them were armed, too. If they lacked the mother wit to step aside, they paid the price for stupidity.

What had to be a forty-two-pound ball smashed into a grogshop not fifty feet from Red Rodney. The dive was there—and then it wasn't. It turned to rubble before his eyes. A spinning roof-tile caught one of his men in the belly. The pirate went down, and he didn't get up again.

They had to brave more roundshot of all sizes as they neared the sea wall. One ball plowed a bloody track through the freebooters, killing three men and maiming two more before mere flesh could halt its progress.

Radcliffe left the shrieking, wounded men where they lay and hurried on.

Another fire had started by the time he got close to the wall—started and showed every sign of spreading. It might wreck Avalon even if the attackers didn't get into the town. Rodney swore some more. At the moment, that was all he could do. He hoped he would be able to go on doing it. A cannon ball tore the head off a man only a couple of paces behind him. The spouting corpse ran on for several strides before crumpling in a muddy puddle.

Up to the wall at last. Where was Ethel? Anywhere close by? Radcliffe looked this way and that. He didn't see her anywhere. A big roundshot—it had to be another forty-two-pounder—flew only a few feet over his head and crashed down somewhere behind him in Avalon. Were it lower . . . He shuddered. It wouldn't have had to hit him to kill. Sometimes the wind of a cannon ball's passage was enough.

"Give it back to 'em!" That high, shrill voice could only belong to Ethel.

Rodney hurried south along the sea wall. *There* she was, and damned if she wasn't commanding a six-pounder's crew as if she'd been doing it for years. The cutthroats obeyed her, too. Maybe they knew whose daughter she was. Maybe they just knew they needed someone to keep them firing fast.

*Smack!* That was the sound of Red Rodney's open palm landing on Ethel's backside. She squalled like a cat with its tail caught in a door and leapt into the air. Murder blazed in her eyes. "Who—?" she shouted. Then she saw her father, and the fury faded. "Oh. You. I might have known."

"Yes. You might have, by Jesus. You might have known to stay in the castle, where you'd be safe."

"If they get over the walls, no one is safe," Ethel

answered, and shouted for her crew—and it *was* her crew—to run out the gun and fire it. Red Rodney muttered under his breath. The worst of it was, he couldn't even tell her she was wrong.

Marcus Radcliffe came back to William Radcliff and asked, "Are you all right, coz?"

"Yes, dammit. This is the third time you've asked me," William said in some irritation. "I am neither woman nor child. I can keep up."

"You're neither backwoodsman nor marine, either," Marcus pointed out. "You know how to tell other people what to do. I don't know how you are at doing things on your own hook."

"I cope," William said. His foot skidded in a patch of mud. He flailed his arms for balance, but he didn't fall. Several marines were already muddy. So were a couple of Marcus Radcliffe's rustics. William hadn't fallen ... yet.

Swearing, sweating marines dragged a four-pounder through the woods south of Avalon. The gun's carriage, made for the deck of a ship, was less than ideal for rough, muddy ground. Somehow, though, the bullocks hauling it had managed to keep up with the rest of the landing party. They would take out their anger on the palisade—and on the men atop it.

William hoped not many men would be atop it. With luck, the cannonading from the fleet would draw all the corsairs to the sea wall. Then the marines could just walk into Avalon. That would be wonderful—if it worked.

Marcus Radcliffe plainly thought William odd if not daft for joining the landing party. But the decision would come here. One way or the other, it would. William wanted to be in place to see it. The fleet could go on without him for a while. He was sure Elijah Walton and Piet Kieft would be just as happy to go on without him.

Had he been in charge of Avalon, he would have cleared the woods farther from the palisade. The landing party could approach almost to within musket shot of the works without being noticed. Were they all backwoodsmen like Marcus' recruits, they might have got closer yet, but even the red-coated marines could hide behind tree trunks and in the midst of fern thickets.

And hide most of them did, while the gun crew aimed the four-pounder at the long wall ahead. The gun was of brightly polished brass; William could only marvel that no one in the town noticed it till it was almost ready to fire. The diversion from the sea must have done all he wanted and more.

A startled shout rose from the palisade just as the marine lieutenant in charge of the piece said, "You may fire now, Sergeant."

*Boom!* The ball wasn't even as big as William's fist. But it was plenty big enough to smash one of the upright trunks ahead when it thudded home. The marines in the gun crew got to work reloading. "Give them a volley!" Marcus Radcliffe bellowed. Muskets and rifles thundered. A couple of men on the palisade went down.

"Charge!" yelled a captain in a red coat. Marines and backwoodsmen   and William Radcliff—rushed the palisade. They all screamed like wild Terranovans. Maybe that would scare the freebooters. Maybe it would lift their own spirits. William could hope so.

He knew how to shoot and load a musket. He had a rapier on his hip, not a cutlass. He also carried a loaded pistol in his boot. He hadn't done a lot of fighting, but he thought—he hoped—he knew how.

Some of the marines hauled scaling ladders forward. They'd blasphemously lugged those through the woods along with the cannon. *Boom! ... Crash!* The cannon smote the palisade again. One way or another, the landing party was determined to break into Avalon.

Only a couple of shots came from the enemy. Not many corsairs stood on the palisade, and some of the ones who did promptly fled when they saw marines bearing down on them. Radcliff might have done the same thing. They had a chance to save themselves. If they stayed on the palisade, they were bound to be butchered—they didn't have enough men to keep the bullocks and backwoodsmen from getting up there with them.

"Ladders high!" an officer shouted. There wasn't even a ditch outside the palisade to make things harder for the attackers. No one in Avalon really seemed to have believed attack could come from this quarter.

Believe or not, here it was. A pirate shot down at a climbing marine. The ball hit the red-coated Englishman in the face. As he fell, he brought down two other men below him. But others took their places. Marines were as stolid as men could be in the face of death or maiming.

William didn't mind letting a good many of them precede him up onto the palisade. They were younger and stronger and better trained than he was. But he swarmed up a ladder himself. He hadn't come this far only to watch. He aimed to fight, too.

He almost didn't get the chance. A bullet cracked past his head as he hurried toward the closest stairway down into Avalon. Marcus Radcliffe was a few feet behind him. The backwoodsman chuckled. "Nothing like it when they shoot at you and miss, is there?"

"Better that than their shooting and hitting," William agreed.

Marines formed lines and advanced through the streets. Some people fled before them, screaming in fear. Others charged at them with whatever weapons came to hand. Marcus' backwoodsmen shot down several of those before they got close. The leathery, nondescript Atlanteans carried rifles accurate to a much greater distance than the usual smoothbore musket. The marines took little damage from the pirates who closed. The pirates fought as individuals, the marines as a team. They killed methodically, without much malice and without much waste motion.

Following their lethal line, William Radcliff didn't think he'd have to do much himself. But a man with a cutlass lurched out of a grogshop, stared blearily, and rushed him. William fired his pistol at point-blank range—and missed. He threw the pistol at the corsair's head. It struck the man a glancing blow, and gave Radcliff the chance to draw his own rapier.

The first stroke from the cutlass almost broke his blade and almost knocked the long, thin, straight sword from his hand. His own first thrust almost spitted the pirate, who sprang back just in time. But the freebooter's foot went out from under him in the mud. As the fellow staggered, William skewered him.

The pirate howled like a hound. He didn't crumple, though, the way William hoped he would. He kept right on fighting.

"Stick him again!" Marcus shouted. "People aren't as easy to kill as you'd think."

*How do you know?* William wondered. But that was a question for another time. His next thrust caught the corsair in the throat. Blood rivered out. The man gobbled something and finally fell.

"That's the way, coz!" Marcus said. "Let's go on and finish the job."

William brandished the blood-dripping rapier. "Yes, by God! Let's!"

"You see?" Red Rodney shouted. "They haven't the stomach for landing!" With all the freebooters on the sea wall, he wouldn't have wanted to land there, either.

Whether the enemy wanted to land or not, though, they went right on cannonading Avalon. Every so often, a roundshot would tear a bloody slice out of the corsairs or knock over some of the palisade, which caused more casualties.

Casualties or not, the English and the Dutch and the men from Stuart could pound away from now till forever, and they wouldn't break in. Radcliffe cursed them and shook his fist and cheered whenever the gun Ethel went on commanding shot at the ships offshore. So much powder smoke drifted in from their guns and the ones fired at them that he coughed between cheers. His eyes streamed. His face was probably black as an indigo-growing slave's down in southeastern Atlantis.

A man tugged at his arm. "Red Rodney!" the fellow cried.

Even through the roar of the guns, Rodney heard the fear in his voice. "What is it?" he asked, an ominous rumble in his own.

"They're in the city! They're over the palisade and in the city!"

"What? Are you daft? We're holding 'em out!"

"No. I wish I was." The pirate pointed south. "They're over the palisade down there. Swarms of 'em—great bloody bullocks in red coats, killing anything that moves."

"Oh, Christ Jesus! Bugger me with a worm!" Rodney Radcliffe said. And the enemy *had* buggered him—buggered him and Avalon. They'd drawn all the defenders here to the sea wall, and then come right up the town's arse.

"What do we do?" wailed the man with the bad news.

"What *can* we do? We've got to fight 'em," Radcliffe said grimly.

He started pulling men out of the struggle on the sea wall and pointing them back into Avalon. He shouted. He punched. He cajoled. He swore. Little by little, he started getting the corsairs to pay attention to him.

They didn't escape the hell of battle even after descending from the wall. Roundshot from the enemy fleet crashed down at random. Sometimes they would come down on a man, or on a clump of men. When that happened, it wasn't pretty.

All the same, Red Rodney shouted, "Keep on, damn you! Keep on! The bloody marines will murder us if you don't!"

Other pirates with loud voices also urged freebooters into the fight. Maybe they were captains, too. Maybe they were just men with eyes to see where trouble lay. It didn't matter. As long as they could see that much, nothing else mattered.

Avalon was not a big city. The pirate from the sea wall didn't need long to bump up against the bullocks. When they saw the men in the red coats, they roared in rage and charged with whatever weapons they happened to hold. Stinging volleys of musketry drove them back, and bayonets outreached swords. The marines were ferociously well disciplined. Red Rodney had always thought sheer fury could overpower anything that stood in its way. Discovering he was wrong was bitter as gall.

It was also almost fatal. A musket ball tugged at his left sleeve. When he looked down, he discovered his arm was bleeding. It was only a scratch, which didn't mean he wanted it. Had the ball flown a few inches to the right . . . He didn't even want to think about that.

"Musketeers! Pistoleros!" he bawled. "Into the houses! Shoot from cover! Don't make it easy for those poxy whoresons!" He'd always been proud of the pirates' independence. When every man was as good as every other man, no man could tell any man what to do. If the freebooters wanted to listen to him, they would. If they didn't . . .

If they didn't, they would die. The marines surged forward. The ones with bayonets plugged into the muzzles of their muskets used the weapons as spears, impaling corsairs who couldn't get at them to reply. Other marines kept a deadly hail of bullets in the air. So did some enemy fighters in plain clothes. They could hit a man at two hundred yards, sometimes farther. There weren't that many of them, and they didn't fire fast, but they caused trouble all out of proportion to their numbers.

Red Rodney sprang like a wolf. He beat a bayoneted musket aside with his sword, then struck the marine holding the piece. His stroke clove the bullock from crown to chin. The man toppled, dead before he hit the ground.

But another marine lunged at Rodney Radcliffe, forcing him to jump back or be spitted. The pirate chief managed to escape. The marine in the second rank stepped up to the first, and the line rolled ahead as it had before. One dead marine? So what?

Radcliffe had always scorned such regimentation. A man, he thought, should fight for himself, for his hope of glory or gold or women, willing or otherwise. To fight because it was your job, as if you were a chandler or a cordwainer? Where was the glory in that?

Nowhere at all, which didn't mean it didn't work. The marines, job or no job, advanced. The corsairs, glory or no glory, fell back—or else they just fell, and did not rise again. The marines systematically finished them off, one after another. For all Red Rodney's cries and exhortations, he couldn't stop the foe. Fear began fighting fury in his heart.

William Radcliff stood with a pair of marines on the roof of a three-story building in southern Avalon. "Hoist the red flag," he told them.

"Right you are, sir," they chorused. They probably would have said the same thing if he'd told them to jump off the roof. (The building was a house of ill fame. To the bullocks' undisguised disappointment, the girls had fled.)

One of the marines had a big square of red cloth. The other carried a long pole that would do for a flagstaff. William had some tacks with which to fasten the cloth to the pole. Once that was done, they waved the makeshift flag. You could see it a long way. With luck, even the sailors in the fleet would be able to spy it.

Radcliff hoped they could. They were supposed to be looking for the signal. It ordered them to put sailors into boats and attack the sea wall. The marines had drawn a lot of defenders from it. The cannonading had killed more—and should have breached the wall as well. If the sailors could gain lodgements ... If they could do that, then Avalon, assailed from flank and rear at the same time, was bound to fall.

Wasn't it?

*Thwock!* A bullet tore through the red cloth. The corsairs might not know what the signal flag meant, but they knew they didn't like it. *As if I care,* William thought.

He walked to the edge of the roof for a crow's-nest view of the fighting. Another bullet snapped past his head. He ducked. That wasn't cowardice—even the nerveless marines did it. But then he stepped back—no point giving the freebooters an easy shot at him.

Besides, he had a pretty good idea of how things were going. His ears could tell him almost as much as his eyes. The pirates hadn't given up. All the same, the marines were steadily driving them back. If the sailors could break into Avalon by way of the sea wall, he wouldn't have wanted to wear his cousin's shoes.

"You men keep on," he told the bullocks with the signal flag. "I'm going down to fight some more."

As he started down the stairs, he heard one marine tell the other, "I didn't think the old bugger had so much fire in his belly."

*I'm not old,* Radcliff thought indignantly. Next to the marines, he was. He hurried down. He almost tripped on the stairs and broke his neck; that would have been a humiliating way to show he really was the antiquity the bullocks thought him. But he caught himself and went outside without further damage.

Smoke filled the air. A lot of it was brimstone-stinking gunpowder smoke—a lot, but not all. Several fires blazed in Avalon now. Fire was always the great fear, ashore and at sea; once it caught hold, it was hard, terribly hard, to fight. Even if the pirates somehow threw back the forces that harried them, their haven would never be the same.

*Their haven will never be their haven again,* William thought, determination filling him. He didn't think he could end all piracy in the Hesperian Gulf by seizing Avalon. He did hope he could break its back. That would be enough to satisfy him. It might even be enough to make him go down in history. He laughed at himself when that occurred to him. As long as his ships could get where they were going without let or hindrance, history didn't count.

Two marines came out of a grogshop. Blood dripped from one man's bayonet; blood and brains fouled the stock of the other's musket. They both nodded respectfully. "Couple of bastards in there who won't bother their betters any more, sir," said the man with the nasty musket.

"Good riddance to them," William said. "May we comb out the rest of the lice in Avalon the same way."

Nodding, the marines hurried forward, toward the struggle. Radcliff followed more sedately. *As befits my years,* he thought with a wry grin.

He didn't want only pirates picked at random dead. He wanted to know their chieftains were gone—Goldbeard and Cutpurse Charlie and the other flamboyant leaders who could gather a good-sized fighting tail behind them with a snap of the fingers. And, most of all, he wanted Red Rodney Radcliffe swept from the face of the earth. Even if they spelled the name differently, Red Rodney blackened it with every breath he took. Only fitting, then, that he shouldn't take many more.

William's hand tightened on the basket hilt of his sword. If he could dispose of his cousin himself . . . it would be something out of a romance. William shrugged. He was willing to forgo the glory—and the risk of getting killed instead of killing—if he knew *someone* had put paid to Rodney Radcliffe.

A great clamor of musketry broke out to the northwest. William almost forgot his cousin. The landing from the sea was starting. If the sailors could break in . . . "Avalon is ours," he muttered.

When Red Rodney Radcliffe heard the commotion behind him and to his right—the commotion from the sea wall—he stopped dead in the middle of a narrow, unpaved street. Had a marine with a charged musket or a bayonet stood close by, he would have died in truth, his guts spilling over the mud and slops. His hopes had been low. They sank further now.

Ben Jackson knew that clamor for what it was, too. "Are they in?" the mate asked hoarsely. "Can they get in there?"

"I . . . don't know," Radcliffe answered. Under the circumstances, it was about the worst thing he could have said.

"What do we do?" Jackson demanded. "Go back to Black Hand Fort and stand siege?"

Red Rodney only grunted. It wasn't a hopeful grunt. The great captains' forts weren't provisioned for long sieges. They were strongholds where crews lived, from which they sallied, and to which they retreated in time of crisis. They were made to hold out other pirate bands, not determined soldiers. No one who built them had imagined soldiers could break into Avalon.

All that flashed through Radcliffe's mind in a heart-beat. He shook his head. "Not unless we have to. We've got to drive them out, not let them drive us in."

Jackson nodded; he could see that, too. But he listened to what was going on at the sea wall. "I think they *are* in, damn them," he said.

"I think so, too," Radcliffe said. "That doesn't mean we can't drive them out again, though ... does it?" He wished, too late, he hadn't added the last couple of words.

Ben Jackson shook his head like a hunted animal—which, at the moment, he was. Red Rodney was another one, and he knew it. Well, some hunted animals had teeth and fangs of their own, and could turn the tables on their pursuers. Not many beasts in Atlantis did, but that wasn't true through most of the world. The pirate chief aimed to fight back as long as he could.

A bullet cracked past him. He saw a marine down at the end of the street. He pulled a holdout pistol from his boot top and fired at the bullock. The marine let out a horrible howl and clutched at his shoulder. Rodney stared at the pistol in delighted surprise. He'd hoped to scare the man in the red coat. Hitting him was an unexpected bonus.

He wanted to recharge both his guns. He wanted to, but he had no chance. Jackson was shouting for freeboo-ters to come up and join them. The wounded marine's roar of pain brought his comrades at the double. They did look after one another, no doubt about it.

Marincs and pirates smashed together in bloody collision. Red Rodney hacked and slashed. He threw one pistol in a bullock's face. The marine went down, clutching at his nose. Radcliffe kicked him. Not far away, beset by three men at once, Ben Jackson fell, blood spurting from a belly wound and from his throat. Rodney feared he would never get up again.

Pirates and marines fell, clawing and biting at one another till they could fight no more. Red Rodney's band had more men in it than did his foes' party, but one marine was worth more than one corsair in this kind of brawl.

A bayonet had pinked Radcliffe's leg. A sword had scored a bleeding line down his right arm. He wasn't quite the last man standing, but the marines who still lived were hurt worse than he was, and drew back out of range of his cutlass.

Backed by three hale marines, a middle-aged man with a rapier came around the corner. When he said, "You are Rodney Radcliffe," each individual word might have been chiseled from stone.

"Damn right I am," Red Rodney snarled. "Who the bloody hell are you?"

The stranger bowed. "I have the honor—if that be the proper term—of being your cousin, William Radcliff, at your service." He bobbed up and down again.

Rage ripped through Rodney. "You filthy bugger! You've ruined me!"

"Good," William said coolly, "for that was my purpose. If you yield now, I promise you a quick end. I regret—though not very much—I have nothing better to offer."

"I'll give you something to regret!" Red Rodney shouted. "You'll regret coming up against me face-to-face, by God! You won't gloat over my carcass, that's for sure." He swung up his sword for a limping charge.

William Radcliff appeared unwounded. He also knew how to handle that long, thin, straight sword—a stop thrust almost skewered Rodney. Well, there were ways. Red Rodney smashed at the rapier. If he could break the blade, the other man was his meat.

But William proved a better man of his hands than the pirate had dreamt he could be. He took the slashes and turned them without batting an eye. He ran the point of his blade into Rodney's left shoulder. And Rodney could not reach him, no matter how he tried.

Then one of the marines fired at point-blank range. The bullet slammed into Red Rodney's chest. Blood filled his mouth. He knew it was a bad wound. Then he took another one, this time in the belly. He slumped to his knees.

"You don't fight fair," he choked out.

Through growing darkness, he saw William Radcliff nod. "Indeed not," the merchant admiral replied. "I fight to win. Nothing less is worth fighting for." A third musket bellowed, and Rodney knew no more.

William Radcliff eyed Ethel Radcliffe like a man eyeing a beautiful but poisonous snake. She'd already tried to knife him once. Now she was—he devoutly hoped—disarmed. "What am I to do with you?" he asked.

"You'd better kill me," she answered matter-of-factly. "Christ knows I'll kill you first chance I get."

"I have no stomach for slaying children," he said, "and we are kin, of sorts."

"My shame, not yours," Ethel said.

"If I send you to Stuart—"

"I will hunt you down," the pirate's daughter broke in.

She meant it. Whether she would mean it a few years from now was a different question. For the time being, though, she was as dangerous as a hogshead of gunpowder in a fire. "I have no quarrel with you," William said. "Mine was with your father."

"Well, I have one with you, for my father's sake," Ethel said. "Look to your life—more warning than a scorpion like you would give, Radcliff." She somehow contrived to make him hear the missing *e* that separated his name, and his kind, from hers.

William thought he would laugh at a death threat from a child. At such a threat from most children, he would have. From Red Rodney Radcliffe's daughter? No. She'd called him a scorpion. To him, she seemed to have all her father's venom in a small, innocent-looking exterior. *A strawberry-blond coral snake,* he thought uneasily.

Trying to calm her, he said, "We've been merciful where we could. Ordinary pirates, men of no rank, who yielded to us may go free. Many of them will make good enough honest sailors. Nothing will happen to you, nor to. . . . Is that your mother?"

"Who? Jenny?" Ethel Radcliffe laughed in his face. "Jesus, no! Just one of my father's doxies. He had enough of 'em." She sounded as proud of Red Rodney as one of his men might have.

"Indeed," William said stiffly. Where Ethel spat defiance, Jenny had offered anything she had to give to keep from meeting the gibbet. And she had a lot, as he'd found out to his pleasure and perhaps even to hers. He'd never intended hanging her, but she didn't need to know that. What Tamsin, back in Stuart, didn't know wouldn't hurt her a bit. William made himself return to the business at hand. "What *shall* I do with you?" he asked Ethel again.

"I told you once what I aim to do. If you don't care to listen, it's your funeral." She punned with vicious relish. She would probably kill the same way. It had to run in the blood.

He made up his mind. "I will send you to New Hastings," he said. The old town was far enough from Stuart to leave him feeling safe. "You may learn a trade there, or pursue such education as fits your pleasure and abilities. And I will dower you, richly enough to let you marry and enjoy the blessings of domestic felicity." *Or as many of them as a hellcat can enjoy, at any rate.*

Ethel Radcliffe looked him in the eye. She didn't spit in his face, but he thought she wanted to. "Salve your conscience all you please, old man. I'll kill you anyhow."

He had her taken away then. She went peaceably enough. He wasn't going to worry about her any more. He told himself he wasn't, anyhow.

It wasn't as if he didn't have other things to worry about. Elijah Walton wanted to place all of Avalon—indeed, the whole west coast of Atlantis from Avalon northwards—under the direct rule of the King of England. "He provided the wherewithal by which it was won," he said.

"Piet Kieft will be surprised to hear it," William remarked. "So will the House of Orange. And so am I. Did my armed merchantmen do nothing here? Did my backwoodsmen not take this town with the Royal Marines?"

"They made their contributions," Walton said with a grace both easy and, Radcliff reckoned, false. "But truly, what difference does it make unless you are a damned Dutchman? His Majesty already rules the Atlantean settlements. This would but extend that rule."

"It would not, for we have our longstanding rights and privileges to guard against tyranny and misrule," William said. "Land ruled straight from London would not."

"Say you that his Majesty is a tyrant?" Walton no doubt thought he sounded dangerous, but he'd had little to do with Ethel Radcliffe.

"I said nothing of the sort, sir, and will style you liar and knave should you publish it abroad that I did," William replied. "But king follows king as autumn follows summer. Who knows what the next reign may bring, or the one after that?"

Elijah Walton waved his words away. "You quarrel over the shadow of an ass."

"I think not," William Radcliff said. "Nor will the English settlements here. As for the French and the Spaniards here in this western land . . ."

"One more reason for the Crown to rule here: to protect you from them," Walton said.

William laughed in the Englishman's face, as Ethel had laughed in his. "As the Crown warded off the corsairs?" he inquired.

Walton reddened. "You mistrust the spirit in which this proposal is offered."

"By God, sir, I do indeed," Radcliff said. "And I tell you again, I am not the only one who will. If you wish to see insurrection against the Crown flare all through English Atlantis, you have but to persist in your mad policy."

"You jest," Walton said. "You bluff."

"I am willing—I am even glad—to have the king rule me . . . from a safe distance, both in travel and in law," William said. "Were his rule more intimate, it would prove less congenial. I am not alone in this sentiment, nor anywhere close to it. Heed me or not, as you like. I have told you the truth." His warning was at least as determined as Ethel's had been.

"His Majesty will not be pleased," Elijah Walton warned. Radcliff only shrugged. And he carried the day. *No one can stop the Radcliffs when they set their mind to something,* he thought, and then, remembering Red Rodney's daughter, he rather wished he hadn't.

# PART THREE

*Nouveau Redon*

# XVI

*V*ictor Radcliff squelched through muck. Englishmen weren't supposed to come this far south in Atlantis. Radcliff thought he must have passed the French
settlements and entered Spanish territory. At the coast,
it would be. There, telling who lorded it over a piece of
ground was easy enough. Everyone's settlements faded
toward nothingness the farther into the interior a man
went.

New Hastings had been settled three hundred years
before, but that was almost as true up there as it was
anywhere else in Atlantis. People who liked exploring
for its own sake were thinner on the ground here than
they might have been. A lot of them went on to Terranova, beyond the Hesperian Gulf. A broader land, it
offered that kind of man more scope.

But you could find something new here if you worked
at it. Plenty of Englishmen crossed the Green Ridge
Mountains to travel from New Hastings and Hanover
(formerly Stuart) to Avalon, following a route pioneered
by Richard Radcliffe when Atlantis was a strange new
world. Some of them turned away from that route and

founded little villages in the hinterland. No one knew
how many such villages there were. A lot of the people
who lived in them wanted nothing to do with the outside
world, and kept to themselves.

Or you could range farther afield, as Victor was doing.
So many things here in the south seemed strange to an
Atlantean who'd grown up near New Hastings. The
weather was a good place to start; it reminded him of a
steam bath. New Hastings could get weather like that.
So could Hanover. Down here, the news came when it
wasn't beastly hot and beastly muggy.

With the different weather went different plants. The
theme was the same as it was all over Atlantis: conifers
and what the Atlanteans called barrel trees and ferns.
But instead of the pines and towering redwoods near
New Hastings, instead of the firs and spruces north of
Hanover that made such splendid masts, here most of the
conifers were cypresses growing on knees half lifted out
of the swamps. The rest, on higher ground, were scrubby
pines different from the ones farther north. There were
more varieties of barrel tree, too; both Frenchmen and
Spaniards cooked up a formidable spirit from the sap
inside some of them. And the ferns grew in riotous
profusion wherever there was shadow and moisture—
which is to say, almost everywhere. Victor had seen them
sprouting from between the bricks of country homes. In
every shade of green, in every size from smaller than his
hand to twice as tall as he was, they formed the forest's
understory.

Something almost under Victor's boot said, *"Freep!"*
and jumped into the water with a splash. He froze for
a moment: he hadn't seen it till it moved and croaked.
*Only a frog,* he thought. Down here, though, *only* wasn't
necessarily so. Some of the frogs here had bodies twice
the size of a man's fist. They ate anything that wasn't big
enough to eat them.

Others were of more ordinary size, but colored black streaked with vivid scarlet or gold or turquoise. Nothing ate them—not more than once, anyhow. They were poisonous. It was almost as if their colorful hides warned the world to leave them alone.

A flapjack turtle peered at Victor from the swamp. All he could see of it were its pointy-nosed head and snaky neck. Flapjack turtles made better eating than the frogs. But they could fight back. One that size could bite off a man's finger with no trouble at all.

A lizard skittered away into some ferns. Another one, larger, eyed Victor from a cypress branch well out of his reach. Both of them were harmless. Some of the lizards down here, though, grew longer than a man was tall—and those were the ones that lived on land. It said nothing about the sawbacked monsters that haunted streams. The Spaniards called them all dragons even if they didn't breathe fire. The name seemed fair enough to Victor. They were formidable beasts, with formidable teeth and claws. They couldn't flourish up in the English regions of Atlantis; the winters were too cold. Victor didn't miss them a bit.

When up in New Hastings, he also didn't miss the snakes big enough to coil round these lizards, suffocate them, and swallow them. He kept a wary eye on the fern thickets through which he pushed. A snake big enough to kill and eat a dragon was big enough to kill and eat him, too.

They also had flying snakes down here, and you didn't have to get into the barrel-tree juice to see them. Victor supposed they didn't really fly, but the name had stuck. They spread themselves flat and glided from one branch to another or from a branch down to the ground either to escape from becoming something else's dinner or to catch their own. Three or four different kinds had learned the trick; one was venomous, but the rest weren't.

Victor's nostrils suddenly twitched. He stopped in his tracks. His right hand fell to the stock of one of the flint-lock pistols he carried on his belt. He smelled smoke. Smoke meant men, and men, even more than dragons or flying snakes, meant trouble.

Men could be doing any number of unsavory things. They could be backwoodsmen from English-speaking Atlantis like him, down to see what the Breton- and Basque- and French- and Spanish-speaking settlers were up to. They might come from any of the groups that didn't speak English, and they might be spying on any of the others—or even on their own. They might be settlers who'd moved deep into the swamps because they wanted nothing to do with their own lords. They might be French or Spanish soldiers, coming after set-tlers who'd moved deep into the swamps.

Or they might be runaway slaves: Negroes or cop-perskinned Terranovan natives. New Hastings had a few slaves, and big, rich Hanover more than a few. Most of the blacks and Terranovans up there were domestics— cooks and maids, coachmen and body servants. Rich merchants owned them for the sake of swank, and treated them as they would have treated servants of a lighter hue. Most blacks and copperskins in English At-lantis were freemen and -women.

Things were different here in the south. Down here, slaves worked in the fields, and they worked hard. The plantations that raised indigo and cotton, rice and sugar cane, pipeweed and peanuts, couldn't have functioned without them. Getting the most labor from slaves and giving them as little as was necessary to keep them working and to keep them from rising up was an art in these settlements.

It wasn't an art the Terranovans and Africans ap-preciated. They took off whenever they saw the chance. Better to scratch out a free living in the swamps, they thought, than to live on their masters' dubious bounty. And if they could get up to the English-speaking settlements, they would probably stay free. Litigation between settlements from one kingdom and those from another could go on for years—or it could move a little slower than that.

Plantation owners and overseers hunted slaves with hounds and with guns and sometimes even with fist-trained eagles. Runaways fought back with mantraps and anything else their ingenuity could devise. Some of them—the Terranovans especially—were good bowmen. Victor Radcliff knew the first English settlers in Atlantis had been formidable archers. That was three centuries gone by, though. These days, any white who wanted to shoot something did it with a gun.

Victor thought about giving the campfire or whatever it was a wide berth and going on his way. Regretfully, he shook his head. He couldn't be sure he'd be able just to go on his way. If he knew those strangers were out there in the swamp, one of them was liable to know he was here, too. All the undergrowth was made for snipers and bushwhackers. Maybe somebody was drawing a bead on him right now. . . .

When you had a thought like that, your first instinct was to duck. If you had any brains, you followed that instinct, too. It might save you. Victor pulled in his head like one of those flapjack turtles. He ducked down so the ferns all around did a better job of hiding him. Then he crawled away.

Maybe he was crawling away from nothing. He didn't know for sure. He didn't mind making a fool of himself in front of turtles and frogs and oil thrushes and parrots. In fact, he ended up making a fool of himself in front of a mouse. It twitched its whiskers and vanished under a drooping frond a couple of inches above the ground.

"Damned things are everywhere," Victor muttered to

himself. There hadn't been a mouse or a rat or a dog or a cat in Atlantis before settlers started coming. Now you found them even in the wilderness.

By contrast, honkers had grown scarce, especially in long-settled districts. Before long, they might all be gone. Victor shrugged. That wasn't his worry.

He sniffed again, then crawled toward the fire. *Follow your nose,* he thought. Well, what else could he do when he couldn't see the campfire or hear the people who gathered around it?

And then he could hear them. He froze, then moved forward even more slowly and carefully. Yes, the bad French and Spanish said they were runaway slaves. One Negro and two copperskins, he thought; they had distinctively different accents. His own French was nothing special, though he could make himself understood.

Another sniff brought him the scent of roasting meat. His stomach growled. He winced—a noise like that could betray him, and it was nothing he could do anything about.

There they were, dimly seen through the screen of multiply lobed little leaves. Victor stayed very still. He saw a Negro and one copperskin. They were cooking a turtle and a couple of big frogs over their fire. One of them said something and held up his supper. The other laughed.

*Runaways, all right*, Victor Radcliff thought. They wouldn't go out hunting him unless they thought he was hunting them. Since he wasn't . . . Best just to slide away after all.

He was about to do exactly that when someone jumped him from behind. While he'd scouted the camp, someone had sneaked up on him. A large, strong, muscular someone, too. And as silently deadly as a crawling snake—Victor had had no idea anybody was there till the instant before he found himself fighting for his life.

The fight didn't last long. When the sharp edge of a knife kissed Victor's throat, he went limp. His assailant laughed, low and hoarse. "Figured that'd make you get smart," the man said in copperskin-accented French. The knife dug a little deeper. "Now, you come along with me."

Numbly, Victor came.

Roland Kersauzon peered out from the walls of Nouveau Redon. He was not quite the lord of all he surveyed, but he was the lord of a good deal of it. And he was named for one famously stubborn man, and descended from another. Roland the warrior might have saved everything but his pride if he'd blown his horn sooner and summoned Charlemagne back against the Spanish Mussulmen. And François Kersauzon remained a legend in these parts even if he was three centuries dead and gone.

François had never set eyes on Nouveau Redon, not in all the years he'd dwelt in Atlantis. It lay only fifty miles inland from Cosquer on the Blavet. He'd never gone fifty miles inland or, probably, even twenty miles inland. That would have meant turning his back on the sea. François Kersauzon was too mulish a fisherman to want to do any such thing.

Slowly, Roland made a fist and brought it down on the gray stone of the battlement. Nouveau Redon, everyone said, was the strongest fortress in all of Atlantis, French, English, or Spanish. And it needed to be. Roland muttered something a quarter Breton, three-quarters French, and all irate.

If only François hadn't sold the God-cursed Englishmen the secret of Atlantis for a load of salt cod! (Or, even more humiliating, for *part* of a load of salt cod. Some of the stories put it that way.) Then the Bretons would be happy over here, the English would be happy over there, and . . .

*"Merde,"* Roland said. That kind of thinking was bound to be foolish. Sooner or later, the English would have found these shores on their own. But it would have been later than it was, which would have been better—certainly as far as a Breton was concerned.

Nouveau Redon sat atop a knob overlooking the Blavet. The river approach was difficult. The landward approach, except for a narrow road hacked out of rock, was harder yet. Roland didn't see how anyone could storm Nouveau Redon as long as it had a few soldiers inside the walls.

He did see a horseman urging his mount up that narrow road. Even though the rider was alone and unable to move fast, muskets and cannon loaded with grapeshot covered his approach. Nouveau Redon was ready for anything.

By the time the rider reached the narrow plain in front of the town, he was sweating and fanning himself with his hat. His horse was lathered and blowing. He seemed glad to rein in before the main gate. After yelling back and forth with the guards at the gate, he rode into Nouveau Redon.

Before long, more shouts rang out: "Lord Roland!" "Come down, Lord Roland!" "Lord Roland, this man's here to see you!"

Roland Kersauzon said, *"Merde!"* again, louder this time. This was the moment he'd been waiting for. Not to put too fine a point on it, this was the moment he'd been dreading. He hurried down the stairs—hurried with what the lawyers called deliberate speed. The stairway attached to the wall was narrow and steep; if a man on it fell, he might break a leg—or his neck.

Reaching the ground without mishap, Roland rushed to the gate. A man could break an ankle—or his neck—if he tripped on the cobbles, too. Old men grumbled and wished the streets were still unpaved. Roland didn't miss the stinking mud one bit. Cobbles made his city as modern as any in Europe.

"Lord Kersauzon," said the horseman when Roland came up. "I bring news just here from France." He held out a paper folded and sealed with ribbon and wax.

"News." Kersauzon's mouth tightened as he took the letter. "Do you know what it says?"

"Formally, no," the rider replied. "Informally . . . Well, the word's all over Cosquer. Gossip flies faster than the wind."

"All right." It wasn't, but Roland couldn't do anything about it. He scraped off the seal and cut through the ribbon with a small, sharp knife he pulled from his belt. Then he unfolded the paper and read it. His sight was beginning to lengthen, but he didn't need spectacles for reading yet. Sadly, he nodded to himself, as if learning that an aged and long-infirm uncle had finally died.

"Is it—?" One of the gate guards couldn't hold in the question.

With a sigh, Roland nodded again. "War," he said. "War against England."

"But why?" The gate guard checked himself. He sketched a salute. "Forgive me, sir. I know the English— they are dogs and sons of dogs. I know most of them are godless Protestant heretics, bound for hell."

"Everybody knows that," another guard put in.

"But of course. Everybody does," the first soldier agreed. "Still, the English have always been dogs and sons of dogs. They've been godless Protestants for a very long time, anyhow. So why do we have to go to war with them now?"

"It's the fighting in Europe," said the courier who'd brought the message to Nouveau Redon.

Roland Kersauzon nodded. "It is indeed. We have joined with Austria and Russia to give Frederick of Prussia the thumping he deserves. The English—dogs and sons of dogs that they are—have sided with Frederick. And so we shall punish him and England as they deserve."

The courier and the guards clapped their hands. One of the soldiers tossed his hat in the air. Then he made a frantic grab to keep it from landing on a lump of horse manure. With an embarrassed grin, he set the tricorn back on his head. Another gate guard said, "We'll whip them." Everyone cheered again. Nobody threw a hat this time, though. The guard pointed to the paper Roland Kersauzon still held. "Does that just tell you the war is here, sir, or has it got orders for us, too?"

"Orders," Kersauzon answered. "First, we are to make sure Nouveau Redon is in the proper condition to defend itself, should it have to."

"Won't be hard." Two or three men spoke together, with almost identical words. One of them added, "You'd have to be a crazy fool to try and take this place."

"I think so, too, but who's to say the English aren't crazy fools?" Roland answered. The guards nodded— they also seemed to think the English were likely to be crazy fools. Kersauzon went on, "And you're right: it won't be hard to ready the town. It's strong to begin with, and we've kept the works and the garrison in good order, thank God." He glanced down at the sheet. "But there's more than that."

"What is it?" Again, several men asked the question in chorus—he knew how to tell a story and spin it out.

"We are to gather together an army from all the settlements under the rule of the King of France, and to march against the English and take away what has been theirs for too long," he replied grandly. "So it is commanded of us, and so shall it be."

When the guards huzzahed this time, several hats went flying. A couple of them landed on the ground, but none, luckily, in the horse dung. Townsfolk came out of shops and taverns to see what the commotion was about. When the guards shouted out the news, fresh commotion spread.

One of the men asked, "The Spaniards are on our side, is it not so?"

He sounded anxious, and with some reason. Men who followed the King of France were almost as likely to reckon Spaniards dogs and sons of dogs as they were Englishmen. True, no one could accuse the Spaniards of being godless Protestant heretics. But if Spain allied itself with the godless Protestant heretics of England, that could prove unfortunate in Atlantis, where English and Spanish settlements lay to the north and south of France's.

Kersauzon slew the soldier's worry with a smile. "They are on our side, yes. Their ships will join with ours. Their soldiers will slay Englishmen wherever they find them. We have but to stretch forth our hand, and the English settlements here will fall into it like a ripe apple."

How the men cheered then! They danced in a circle, spinning now widdershins, now sunwise. Had an English army been anywhere close by, it could have marched into Nouveau Redon without firing a shot. But the English were far away. Roland Kersauzon danced as enthusiastically as any gate guard. Why not? His orders were to ready an army and advance. Oh, he was also ordered to ready defenses at need, but he took that as a formality. After all, if he was advancing, he wouldn't need to defend, would he?

Of course not. That was so obvious, even an Englishman could see it.

Victor Radcliff's bad French saved his life. The three runaways who'd grabbed him feared he was a slave-catcher. Once they realized he was nothing of the sort, and especially once they discovered he was an Englishman, they treated him like a long-lost brother.

One of them, as he'd thought, was black, the other two, copperskins. They fed him turtle and frog and fish and snails. Having convinced them he wasn't French, he wondered if he ought to eat the snails. But the runaways did, with every sign of enjoyment, and so he did, too. Each snail gave him a couple of bites of tasty meat; the shells were the size of a man's clenched fist. You wouldn't have found snails like those chewing up the lettuces in a garden outside Paris.

You might not have found them up by New Hastings, either, and you wouldn't have up near Hanover. Big snakes and lizards stayed in the south, where the weather never got worse than mild. Snails spread farther, but not too much. The hot, sticky southern climate suited the Negro fine. In his vile French and worse bits of Spanish, he said it reminded him of Africa.

As far as the two copperskins were concerned, he was welcome to it. They knew more Spanish than French, and even a few words of Basque—as much as any foreigner was ever likely to learn. They spoke to each other in Spanish, too. After a while, Victor realized they were from different clans or maybe different countries. The language of one made no more sense to the other than Hungarian did to an Irishman.

The Negro called himself Blaise. The Terranovans went by Francisco and Juan. Those weren't the names any of them had been born with. They gave Victor their real names, and laughed at him when he mangled them. "You white men, so many things you can't say," Blaise told him.

Victor Radcliff smiled and shrugged. He could say one thing: *I am a free man.* Neither Negroes nor copperskins raided white men's lands for slaves. They didn't know how to build the ships or the guns that would have made such a thing possible. Their people did have a yen for the trinkets white slavers used to buy chattels and save themselves the trouble of fighting for them.

Blaise and Francisco and Juan had a yen for freedom. At first, as they started traveling north, they seemed to think Victor had been wandering through the swamp for his own amusement. They didn't expect him to know what he was doing there. "White men, they are without hope away from their towns," Blaise said.

Instead of arguing, Victor vanished. One second, he was walking along beside his new companions. The next, they went one way and he another. He didn't warn them he would do it. He just ducked off behind a barrel tree and headed off on his own.

He listened to them exclaim. Francisco swore. Juan started to laugh. "Maybe this *blanco,* maybe he knows something," he said.

"Maybe. Or maybe he just got lost." Blaise was as reluctant to think a white knew what he was doing as many whites would have been to give him the same credit.

Then Victor reappeared and tapped him on the shoulder. "Am I lost? Or are you?" he asked politely.

Blaise almost jumped out of his skin. "How you do that?" he demanded.

"Magic," Victor said, deadpan.

That won him more attention than he wanted. The Terranovans and the African took him literally. He wasn't sure whether they wanted to use his sorcerous talents to help them escape bondage or to kill him so he couldn't bewitch them.

"His ghost will haunt us even if we do kill him," Blaise muttered when he thought Victor was out of earshot.

Victor smiled his most enigmatic smile. That set the black and the two copperskins muttering once more. They stopped bothering him. And he soon proved he could stay with them. He also showed he knew how to hunt—and he had a flintlock rifle and a pair of pistols. He could have had all that and eyes in the back of his head without their doing him any good. Even the fiercest, most deadly warrior had to sleep sometimes.

He solved the problem by pretending it wasn't one. If he took sleeping around them for granted, they wouldn't think he was afraid to. That would give them one less reason to knock him over the head.

He hoped.

When he woke up the next morning . . . Well, he did wake up the next morning. Nothing else mattered.

Off in the distance, a hound bayed, and then another and another. "They're after me!" Juan blurted, his blunt-featured face going as pale as it could.

"After all of us," Francisco said sensibly.

Although Victor suspected they were after him in particular, he didn't say so. It might alarm his new companions, or they might decide he was lying. They were runaway slaves, after all. People trying to hold on to an expensive investment had good reason to hunt them with dogs. Why would anyone do such a thing to a white man, though?

The French had their reasons. Victor knew that too well. Mentioning those reasons struck him as unwise. Francisco, Juan, and Blaise might decide they could sell him to the French for their liberty. They might prove right, too.

Amazing how many people couldn't keep their mouths shut, even when their lives depended on it. Victor had never had that trouble, anyhow. "Well, we have to get away, no matter whom they're chasing," he said.

"Easy to say," Blaise replied. "Not so easy to do." As if to back him up, the hounds bayed again, on a different, more excited note. "They have our scent."

"Best thing to do, then, is to make sure they don't keep it," Victor said.

"Here there is water," Juan said. "This makes it harder for them. But harder is only harder, *sí?*" He sounded worried.

"Let them come," Victor said. The runaway slaves stared at him. He pulled a small leather pouch and an even smaller bottle from a larger pouch on his belt. Sprinkling fine black powder from the small pouch, he explained, "This is ground pepper." He also dabbed a few drops from the bottle on the ground and the nearby leaves.

"And that?" Francisco asked.

"That is the gall from the snake called the lancehead," Victor said. "Dogs do not like it." He'd committed a serious understatement.

Francisco and Juan might not have understood how large the understatement was. Blaise did. The Negro burst out laughing. Then he took Victor Radcliff's face in his two large hands and kissed him first on the right cheek, then on the left. Sure enough, he'd had a French master.

"And now," he said, "we should get out of here. We will know when the hounds are . . . confused."

"We'd better," Juan said.

They hurried off to the north. The dogs' howls grew louder no matter how they hurried—four legs moved faster than two. Before too long, though, the hunting howls changed without warning to sudden, frantic yips. All the runaways laughed then. Blaise kissed Victor again. Victor could have done without the familiarity, but found he couldn't blame the black man for it.


Roland Kersauzon rode down to the coast to see how the muster was going. Cosquer might have belonged to a different world. Roland hadn't seen the sea for years, or missed it. He was, and was proud to be, a man of Atlantis, not one who looked back to Europe. He'd never been to Europe, nor did he care to go there.

When he got to the coastal settlement, he found a new reason to be unhappy. At the quays, along with ships from France and Spain and Portugal and their settlements in Atlantis and on the Terranovan mainland farther west, lay others from England and from her Atlantean colonies. War declared? No one in Cosquer worried about that, not when there was money to be made.

In high dudgeon, Roland repaired to the harbormaster's office. "War? Yes, indeed. A great pity," that worthy declared. "Would you care for a cigar, *Monsieur*?"

"No, thank you," Roland said icily. He had his vices, but pipeweed wasn't one of them. "I would care to know, however, why we tolerate ships of the enemy. For all you know, they are full of spies."

"Oh, I doubt it, *mon vieux*," the harbormaster replied. He lit his own cigar at a candle, then puffed out a cloud of aromatic smoke. "What would they need to learn of our city that they do not already know?"

"How many troops we have in it, how many ships of war, the state of our shore batteries ... I could go on." Roland Kersauzon scowled at the lackadaisical official. "I am charged with defending the settlements and with carrying the war to the enemy in the north. How can I do that, pray tell, if he learns everything we aim to do before we do it?"

The harbormaster let fly with more cigar smoke. "Forgive me, but I think you are getting excited over nothing—it could be over less than nothing. If they want to fight in Europe, they are welcome to. But why should that foolishness trouble us, eh? Bad for trade, leaves hard feelings, and doesn't really settle anything anyhow. They'll just fight another stupid war in twenty years' time to fix up what they didn't get right this go-round."

Roland had the uneasy feeling that that might be so. Nevertheless, he said, "I am charged with doing as well as I can this time. That means seizing enemy ships in the harbor and preventing them from sailing to enemy ports."

"But it will cause such a disruption!" the harbormaster protested. "And the English will only do the same to our ships, so what do we gain?"

"It is a necessary military measure," Roland said. "See to it at once."

"And if I refuse?" the harbormaster asked.

"I have the authority to demand your obedience," Roland Kersauzon said softly. Perhaps because he didn't shout and carry on, the harbormaster looked stubborn and shook his head. With a sigh, Kersauzon drew one of the flintlock pistols he wore on his belt. The click when he cocked it filled the harbormaster's office. The man's eyes crossed fearfully as he stared down the bore of the weapon, which could not miss from a range of less than a yard. Still in a low voice, Roland continued, "And I will blow your stupid head off if you give me any more back talk. Is *that* plain enough for you?"

"You are a madman!" the harbormaster gasped, sweat starting out on his face.

"Very much at your service, sir," Roland said with a polite nod. "I am also a patriot. Can you say the same?"

"But of course!" With that pistol aimed an inch above the bridge of his nose, the harbormaster would as readily have confessed to being a Chinaman. "In the name of God, put up your gun!"

"And will I see action if I do?" Roland amended his words: "Action of the proper sort, I should say? Not foolishness. If you summon someone and try to have me arrested, he will be sorry and you will be sorrier. Do you understand? And, even more to the point, do you believe me?"

"*Oui, Monsieur,*" the harbormaster choked out. "The pistol is most persuasive."

"I thought it might be. That is one of the reasons I carry it," Roland said complacently. He swung the flintlock aside and eased the hammer down. "Very well. No duress. Let's see how you do now."

The harbormaster didn't disappoint him. The functionary exploded into motion, shouting and waving his arms. Roland Kersauzon followed him to make sure all the shouting was to the point. It was. People stared at the harbormaster—he probably hadn't moved so fast in years. But, once they stopped staring, they did what he said. They did it with more enthusiasm than he seemed to expect, too. They swarmed aboard one ship from England or English Atlantis after another.

If they did some private pillaging while they were aboard, Roland intended to lose no sleep over it. This was war. And if he had to remind people what that meant, well, he would.

Victor Radcliff stared in dismay through the screening of ferns to the ford ahead. The French soldiers at the ford had no idea he and the three runaways were there. But the soldiers' presence was what dismayed him.

"You said no *soldados* this time." Francisco didn't sound happy with him.

"I didn't think there would be," Victor answered.

"You say no *soldats* last time, too." Blaise used bad French instead of bad Spanish.

"I didn't think they'd be there, either, dammit," Radcliff said. "They never are. Except now. Something's happened."

"*Sí.* We happen," Juan said.

"No, no, no." Victor shook his head. "We aren't important enough to cause all this. We shook the ones on our trail a while ago now. These buggers shouldn't have any idea we're around, but they're here anyway. I'm as surprised as my great-grandfather."

"Is that a saying in your language?" Blaise asked. "What does it mean?"

"Not a saying in my language. A saying in my family," Victor replied. "My great-grandfather was the man who took Avalon away from the pirates a long time ago."

"Ah. Avalon. I know of Avalon," Juan said. Blaise nodded. Francisco didn't, but it didn't matter for the sake of the story.

"One of the pirate chiefs was my great-grandfather's cousin," Victor went on. "My ancestor killed him, but brought his daughter back to New Hastings. She was only a child, so why not? She grew up. She married. She had children of her own. And one day, more than twenty years later, she went up to Hanover—it was still called Stuart back then—and she called on my great-grandfather. He was old and rich by then, and glad to see her . . . till she pulled out a pistol and shot him dead."

He spoke a mixture of Spanish and French, to give them all a chance to follow. And they did, well enough. They laughed—not too loud, because the soldiers weren't far away. "As surprised as your great-grandfather," Blaise agreed. "What did they do to the pirate's daughter?"

"To the pirate's daughter? They hanged her. Ethel's last words were, 'I told him I would pay him back, and I did.' We're pigheaded, we Radcliffs." Victor spoke not without pride.

Juan had a more practical question: "Are you stubborn enough to know another ford? Or do we build a raft to get across?"

Victor pointed toward the Green Ridge Mountains. "There is another one, about half a day's travel west. It means more doubling back to get you to settled country and properly set up as freemen, but . . ." He spread his hands.

"We go," Blaise said. The black plainly led the runaways. Neither copperskin argued with him.

Not many men knew about the more distant ford—fewer on the French side than on the English, Victor judged. What he and his companions would do if it was garrisoned, too ... he would worry about then. He'd never been one to borrow trouble. He found enough as things were. Most people did.

The sun was sinking in the west when they found the ford. They scouted it with unusual care, but no French troops seemed anywhere close by. Victor crossed first, his firearms above his head to keep them dry. The runaways followed through the waist-deep water.

They'd all come out dripping onto the north bank when an English voice shouted, "Hold it right there, or we'll ventilate you!" Several men with bayoneted muskets emerged from the undergrowth.

"I've never seen soldiers here before!" Victor exclaimed, also in English.

"You bloody clot! Don't you know there's a war on?" a sergeant demanded. He sounded tough but not unfriendly: Victor's accent disarmed him.

A war! Victor blinked. "Now that you mention it," he said, "no."

# XVII

At Roland Kersauzon's order, French soldiers had seized a bridge over the Erdre, the river that formed the border between the French and English settlements (the English called it the Stour). They had to fight a brisk little skirmish to do it. Had they moved a couple of days later, enough enemy soldiers might have come south to forestall them.

"Do you see?" Roland said to anyone who would listen. "There is a lesson here. Speed counts. Even a small delay, and the English would hold a bridgehead on our soil, not the other way round."

Because he commanded the army, the other officers—and the sergeants, and the cooks, and the grooms, and anybody else who chanced to be within earshot—couldn't simply walk away from him. They had to listen to his words of wisdom. Some of them had to listen several times. He repeated himself without shame: most of the time, without noticing he was doing it.

Supply wagons rolled up from Cosquer and from Nouveau Redon. In days gone by, hunting could have kept a good part of the army fed. So old men insisted their fathers had told them, anyhow. But no one had seen a honker near the coast for many years. Oil thrushes hadn't vanished, but they were getting scarce, too. Even more ordinary ducks and geese had been heavily hunted.

And so Roland and his soldiers ate sausages and smoked pork and onions and hard cheese and biscuits baked almost hard enough to keep weevils out of them. They washed down the unappetizing food with *vin très ordinaire,* and with beer that wasn't much better. Some of them drank from the Erdre instead. Roland discouraged that; it was more likely to lead to a flux of the bowels.

"There are towns upstream," he reminded the men— and reminded them, and reminded them. "Where do you think they empty their chamber pots? Into the river, *naturellement.* We ought to call it the Merdre, not the Erdre."

He was inordinately fond of the pun. Others who heard it smiled widely the first time, smiled politely the second time, and stopped smiling after that. Roland, who didn't keep track of who'd heard it and who hadn't, found his subordinates sadly lacking in a sense of humor.

Two drummer boys beat out a brisk tattoo as the main French force followed the skirmishers across the Erdre and into English territory. Roland Kersauzon rode across on a white horse. If a man was going to lead an army, he needed to be seen leading it. So thought Roland, along with every other European commander of the eighteenth century.

He paid a price. The gold braid and epaulets on his blue velvet jacket weighed almost as much as a back-and-breast of days gone by. More gold braid ornamented and weighed down his tricorn. The hat did shield his eyes from the sun, but it was heavy enough to make his neck sore. He sighed with relief every time he took it off.

He could have doffed it any time he chose. No one would have doubted who led the French settlers. He could have, but he didn't. He was as stern with himself as he was with the men in his charge.

They marched on, leaving a garrison at the bridge to make sure the English didn't nip in behind them and take it away. Roland felt very grand and martial. His soldiers seized livestock and supplies from the farms they passed. The army would eat better because of it.

Scouts rode in front of the main force. Kersauzon didn't want to get taken by surprise. He'd known for years that Englishmen weren't to be trusted. He didn't care to have them prove it against his army.

And so, when a sharp racket of musketry rang out up ahead, he called to the buglers: "Blow *form line of battle*. Then blow *advance on the foe*."

The horn calls rang out. The gap between the first and the second stretched longer than Roland would have liked. The French force was less thoroughly drilled than it might have been. Garrisons from several towns had been melded together to make an attacking force. They were brave enough—Kersauzon had no doubts about that—but they hadn't marched side by side for years. They'd be veterans by the time this campaign ended, but they weren't yet.

Roland rode forward with the advancing infantry to see what the trouble was. He didn't need long. The English had picked a spot where trees came close to the road on both sides and run up a barricade of logs and boulders there. They were shooting from behind it, which let a handful of men thwart a much larger number. Roland didn't think that was sporting, but the English settlers doubtless didn't care.

"We will give them a few volleys from the front," he said. "While we keep them busy, we will send men into the woods to either side. Once they flank the enemy out of his position, we will tear down the barricade and re-sume our advance."

He'd never commanded troops in battle before. Every-thing seemed bright and clear and obvious. He gave his orders with confidence. The soldiers eagerly obeyed. Con-fidence in a leader brought out confidence in his men.

His men approached the barricade. A couple of En-glish settlers popped up and fired at them. One bullet missed. The other grazed a soldier in the leg. He had to fall out, but called to his comrades as they marched past: "Go on! Go get them! Don't worry—I'll be with you again soon!"

They moved to within sixty yards or so: close enough for a decisive volley. Then two blunt, ugly little cannon muzzles poked through cunningly concealed openings among the logs. They were three-pounders: light field guns that could keep up with cavalry on any reasonable ground.

A man cried out in English. Both guns belched fire and smoke at the same time. They also belched canister. At that range, they couldn't have missed if they tried. Men from the first three or four rows of French settlers fell as if scythed. The ones still standing looked around in surprise, as if wondering where their friends had gone. Some of them shot at the enemy. Most were too startled or too appalled.

Roland Kersauzon was appalled, too. A man who stopped canister at close range wasn't picturesquely wounded, as the man pinked by a musket ball had been. He was blown to rags, to bloody fragments a butcher's shop would have been ashamed to sell. And, no matter how mutilated he was, he didn't always die right away. The shrieks from maimed soldiers chilled the blood.

"Where are our cannon, *Monsieur*?" a lieutenant asked.

"They're coming up," Roland said unhappily. The

line of march had got longer than it should have. He hadn't tightened up, for he hadn't expected to do any serious fighting for a while. There was another lesson: if you didn't act as if a battle might break out any second, you were making a mistake.

And that one had a corollary. Mistakes in wartime could be fatal. This one had been, for too many of his men. Only luck none of those lead balls tore into his own belly or smashed his skull.

"What do we do now, *Monsieur*?" the lieutenant asked. "Shall we charge the barricade while they reload?"

Too late, Roland learned caution. He shook his head. "No. If they have another gun waiting, they'll murder us." He turned to the bugler. "Blow *fall back.*"

Although that horn call wasn't particularly mournful in and of itself, it seemed so to Kersauzon because of what it ordered. Fall back the French settlers did, dragging their wounded with them. Dead men and pieces of men lay where they'd fallen. The hot iron stink of blood fouled the air.

Would the English come out to attack? Would their cannon start firing roundshot, which could kill from much farther than canister? Whatever they did, they wouldn't enjoy it for long. Once the outflankers got behind them, they would have a thin time of it.

The lieutenant pointed at the barricade. "*Monsieur*, I believe they're pulling out!"

Roland raised a spyglass to his eyes. Like a ship captain's glass, or an astronomer's, it inverted the image while magnifying it. Sure enough, the glimpses of enemy soldiers the barrier gave him showed they were withdrawing. Either they were cowards or (more likely, he decided with regret) they'd figured out his plan and wouldn't wait around to be trapped.

"So they are," Roland said heavily. "Well, we can let them go—this time. Then we'll tear down the barrier

and advance again. We'll be more careful from now on."
*I'll be more careful from now on,* he meant. The young
lieutenant politely nodded.

Once in English Atlantis, Juan and Francisco went their
own way. Francisco talked of traveling overland to Avalon and then crossing the Hesperian Gulf and going
back to Terranova. How he would find his own clan
again, Victor Radcliff had no idea. He was welcome to
try, though.

Juan simply wandered off. Maybe he went looking
for his own folk, too. Maybe he just went looking for
work or a woman or whiskey or whatever else he might
want. He was a free man here.

So was Blaise, but he seemed inclined to stick with
Victor. "You do interesting things, *Monsieur,*" he said in
his oddly accented French. "I think I do more interesting things myself with you than without you."

Victor had never had—and never wanted—a body
servant. He couldn't very well tell the Negro that staying with him was pointless, because he'd be spending so
much time in the woods. Blaise could take care of himself there, at least as well as Victor and maybe better.
And so . . . Victor found himself stuck.

His fiancée thought it was funny. Margaret Dan-
dridge was a level-headed girl from a New Hastings
trading family. "He's very sweet," she told Victor. "And
he's sharp—he's already starting to pick up English."

"I know," Victor answered. "He's learning to shoot,
too. They wouldn't let him do that while he was a slave.
He's good at it. I think he'd be good at anything he
turned his hand to."

"You're lucky to have him, then," Meg said.

"I suppose so." Victor didn't sound so sure. After a
moment's hesitation, he explained why: "Do I have him,
or does he have me?"

He had plenty of other things to worry about. No one in the English settlements had looked for the French settlers to move so aggressively after war broke out. An English army was supposed to be on the way across the sea. Everyone had thought the French would do the same, so forces from the two mother countries fought it out.

But Roland Kersauzon had other ideas. English Atlantis had to dance to his tune, one way or another. Either the settlers had to recruit forces of their own, or they had to yield to Kersauzon without fighting and hope the professionals from the home island could rescue them.

They recruited, of course. Every farmer with a shotgun for bagging ducks and driving off wild dogs, every backwoodsman with a rifle, made a likely soldier. The men who joined on their own or were dragooned into the service of crown and settlements got green coats of several different shades, some of cotton, more of linen—cotton came from the French and Spanish south.

Because he was an experienced backwoodsman—and because he was a Radcliff—Victor acquired a major's commission, with gilt epaulets on the shoulders of his green coat. He didn't particularly like the emblems of his rank; they made him a better target. No one wanted to listen to him, so he wore the epaulets in camp. When he got to the field, he could take them off.

Somehow, Blaise acquired a sergeant's stripes. He wore them proudly. Victor hadn't asked for any rank for him. Maybe he got it by magic. Maybe he knew which palms to grease, though he had precious little money for greasing.

Victor thought the Negro's new status would cause trouble, and it did. A hulking young man named Aeneas Hand told him, "I'll be damned if I let a lousy nigger order me around."

Blaise was there to hear that. He tapped Hand on the shoulder. "You no like?" he asked in English flavored by both French and his African birthspeech—he *was* a quick study.

"No, I don't." The white man—who had perhaps four inches and forty pounds on Blaise—set himself. His hard hands balled into fists. "What are you going to do about it, you turd-colored monkey?"

Flat-footed, without changing expression or even seeming very interested, Blaise kicked him in the crotch. Aeneas Hand let out a startled grunt and folded up like a clasp knife. Blaise kicked him again, this time in the pit of the stomach. Hand couldn't have fought back after the first disaster. The second left him on the ground, desperately struggling to breathe. Blaise kicked him one more time, in the side of the head. Hand went limp.

"Did you kill him?" Victor asked.

"Nah." The Negro shook his head. He hadn't even broken a sweat. He continued in French: "Throw water on him. He wake up. Head hurt two, three days, same with balls and belly." He looked down at Aeneas Hand. "What he call me? I don't understand it."

"Never mind," Victor said in the same language. "If you knew, you would have killed him."

A couple of other recruits came over to stare at their fallen comrade. "Godalmighty!" one of them said. "What happened to him?"

"He offended the sergeant here." Victor pointed to Blaise. "And he found out that wasn't such a good idea, didn't he?"

"Sure did." The man looked from Aeneas Hand to Blaise and back again. "Offended him, did he? If he really went and got him mad, I reckon he'd be in pieces."

"Wouldn't be surprised," Victor Radcliff agreed. "Fetch a pail of water and souse Aeneas with it. He's learned a lesson. I hope nobody else in this company has to."

Hand had begun to stir by the time the water cascaded over him. Sure enough, it revived him. Blearily, he looked up at Blaise. "You don't fight fair," he said.

"Fight fair? Fight fair?" That startled the black man out of English and into profane French: *"Sacre merde!"* Blaise thought for a moment before going on, in English again, "You right. I no fight fair. I fight, I win. Only way to fight. I sergeant." He tapped his stripes. "You mess me again, I kill you. Understand?"

Aeneas Hand nodded, then winced and looked as if he wished he hadn't. Water dripped off his chin and from the end of his pointed nose. "Reckon I do."

"Reckon I do, what?" Blaise touched the chevrons again.

"Reckon I do, Sergeant," the big recruit allowed.

"Good." Blaise allowed himself a smile. He reached down and hauled Hand upright. "We get on now."

And they did. Having been so thoroughly beaten, Aeneas Hand spread the word that Blaise was sudden death on two legs. A couple of smaller incidents with other recruits did nothing to show he was wrong. Victor Radcliff began to wonder whether he or his man would have worn the epaulets had Blaise been born with a white skin.

Gravediggers' spades tore into the soft brown earth. Dirt thudding on dirt had an ominously final sound. Roland Kersauzon watched as a priest gabbled quick Latin over the shrouded corpse, then jumped away. A sickly-sweet stench rose from the body. It wasn't because the young soldier had stayed unburied too long; he'd died that night, only a few hours before this dawn. But smallpox had its own fetor.

Roland muttered to himself. Too many soldiers were dying of smallpox and measles. Men who grew up on farms out in the countryside and spent their lives alone in the woods missed the diseases in childhood, when they were most often milder. Catch them then and you were immune forever after. Catch them as an adult . . .

He rubbed his arm. He had smallpox scars there, but nowhere else. He'd missed the sickness as a boy himself. He'd been inoculated with it at Nouveau Redon and taken a light case. Now he was as immune as if he'd been through a harsh bout caught by accident.

Inoculation had come to the French settlements from the English, to Atlantis from England, and to England, he'd heard, from Turkey. He wondered how widely it was practiced in English territory here. Were the English settlements' recruits less likely than his own men to come down sick? He hoped not—that could decide who won the war.

The gravediggers tipped the corpse into the hole they'd made. Both of them had smallpox-slagged faces; they feared no contagion. The priest was unmarked. No wonder he didn't want to stay by the body a moment longer than he had to. But a dying man, or a dead one, needed a hope of heaven. If a priest wouldn't shrive him, he'd surely go to hell instead.

If a priest died after shriving a few men, what then?

*Then you find another priest,* Roland thought, *with luck a man who carries the scars on his own face.* That would be more . . . economical. Till this moment, Kersauzon had never thought of priests as expendable munitions of war, but they were. That they were also other things didn't mean they weren't.

A veteran sergeant—one who bore the marks on his face—came up to Roland and saluted. Voice as mechanical as an artisan's automaton, he said, "*Monsieur,* I'm sorry to have to report to you that in my company alone we have another half a dozen sick. Two of them, I fear, aren't at all well."

If a veteran sergeant said something like that, the

priest would perform his office again before long. *"Nom d'un nom!"* Roland burst out. "So many, and just from your company?"

*"Oui, Monsieur."* Who would have imagined the underofficer's voice could become even more colorless than it was already?

"And other companies will be reporting similar calamities?" Kersauzon persisted.

"If they are honest, I think they will."

"How are we to go forward with so much sickness?"

The sergeant didn't answer that, not in words. His eyebrows said, *You're the commander. Why are you troubling me with that? It's your worry.* And it was. Kersauzon sighed. "Thank you for letting me know. You're dismissed." He received another precisely machined salute, and the underofficer made his exit.

Other sergeants and lieutenants did report sickness in their men. One lieutenant reported himself unwell. The hectic flush on his face and a bright glitter in his eye said he'd be worse before long. Roland said nothing of that past telling him to lie down and take it easy.

"But we're in English territory, *Monsieur*," the young officer protested. "We should move forward."

"We will—in a while," Roland said. "But we need to have a healthy army if we are to fight with any hope of victory, *n'est-ce pas?"*

*"Oui,"* the lieutenant said, and argued no more.

More and more reports came in. "This is a disaster!" Kersauzon cried. He'd expected the bloody flux among his men. But so many casualties from smallpox and measles took him by surprise.

The corporal who'd brought the latest word of men down with smallpox—and of others afraid to get anywhere near them—shrugged then. The marks on his face said he'd been through the disease and come out the other side. "It's war, *Monsieur,"* he replied.

"But if I attack now, it will be like trying to strike with a broken hand," Roland said.

Another shrug from the corporal. "Then don't attack, *Monsieur*. Wait for the English to come to you. Chances are their army will have as much sickness as ours."

Fifty years earlier, that assuredly would have been true. But, if the English inoculated more than his own side did, smallpox would trouble them less. And he knew they did inoculate more. The procedure had its risks; every once in a while, someone came down with a bad case of smallpox instead of the mild dose that gave immunity. Most of the time, though, a wild case was far more dangerous.

He consoled himself by remembering that the English couldn't inoculate for measles or fluxes of the bowels. And not all of their soldiers would have had pus from a smallpox sore rubbed into a cut on the arm. Some would still catch the disease on their own. Some, yes, but how many?

Fewer than were catching it among his own troops. Roland Kersauzon was glumly sure of that. He dismissed the corporal with more respect than he usually gave underofficers. The man had helped him make up his mind, which was more than that miserable lieutenant had done.

He stood on English territory. He decided he *would* stand for a while, till the sickness burned through his army and burned itself out. Freetown could wait.

Victor Radcliff rode into New Hastings from the north. Blaise rode with him. The Negro had never ridden a horse till he escaped from bondage. No one would ever mistake him for a polished equestrian now, but he stayed on the gelding and didn't complain about being saddlesore . . . though he did walk with the bowlegged gait of a man with rickets.

New Hastings' narrow, winding streets and half-timbered houses made Victor wonder if the Tudor age really had passed away. He laughed at himself as that went through his mind. The town was older than the Tudors; its founding lay in Plantagenet times. Plantagenets, Tudors, Stuarts—all gone. New Hastings went on.

"English ships, they come?" Blaise asked.

"That's what the semaphore said," Victor answered. "Word passed from fishing boats still out to sea."

"It is clever, the semaphore." Blaise lapsed into French to say that, and went on in the same language: "In Africa, we have fires that go from hill to hill to pass messages."

"Beacon fires," Victor said in English.

"Beacon fires." Blaise repeated the phrase. "I remember." And he would, too. "But the semaphore, it is better than the beacon fires. It can say more of things."

"Just *more things,*" Victor told him.

"More things." Blaise also said that again. He shrugged. "It is a peculiar language, English."

Victor found French and Spanish peculiar when they differed from the tongue he'd grown up speaking. To what strange African language was Blaise comparing English? Radcliff wondered how much trouble he would have learning it.

He had more important things to worry about. Those ships would carry English regulars to stiffen the ranks of the raw Atlantean troops. Victor assumed the redcoats wouldn't have to worry about the sicknesses that had weakened the colonial force. The regulars would already have lived through them by now.

He and Blaise rode past the big all-planked warehouses that stood near the harbor, and then out toward the quays. Their timing couldn't have been better if they were on the stage in Hanover. A first-rate man-of-war was just tying up, with several smaller, beamier transports right behind.

"Ahoy!" Victor called to the men on the ship of the line. He descended from fishermen, but the nautical word felt strange and unnatural in his mouth. "May I come aboard?"

"Who are you?" a mate asked. He pointed at Blaise. "And who's the monkey?"

A low growl from Blaise's throat said he understood that. Radcliff had hoped he wouldn't. The Atlantean officer answered, "I am Major Victor Radcliff, of the local militia. With me is my man, Blaise." He stressed *man* more than he might have otherwise.

The mate stayed unimpressed. "And why should the general want to see the likes of you, eh?"

"Because his men and ours will be fighting the French?" Victor suggested.

"Well, 'is will," the mate said. But then, just before Victor might have drawn his pistol, the fellow grudgingly nodded. "All right. I suppose you can see 'im. Won't do too much 'arm."

He shouted orders. A gangplank thudded down. Victor came aboard, Blaise at his heels. Everything aboard the man-of-war spoke of order, discipline, restraint, confinement. At home in the wide woods of Atlantis, Victor immediately mistrusted the atmosphere.

Behind him, Blaise muttered in his incomprehensible native tongue. He would have crossed from Africa to Atlantis in the hold of a slave ship. Mistrust, Radcliff realized, was bound to be the least of what he felt here. But for those mutters and a hooded glance toward the mate, though, Blaise held his feelings in check.

"Ahh . . . Where do I find the general?" Victor asked.

"Lubber," the mate muttered. Radcliff felt as offended, and as ready to punch him, as Blaise would have if the man had said *nigger* in the same tone of voice. With a resigned sigh—what could one do about the ignorant?—the mate pointed and said, " 'Is cabin's on the poop deck, back at the stern."

"Thank you," Victor replied, meaning anything but.

Then the mate pointed again. " 'Ere 'e comes now, so you don't 'ave to go back there. Wouldn't want you getting lost, would we?" Before Victor could rise to that sarcasm, the mate raised his voice: "Your Excellency! General, sir! This officer from the settlements"—his tone, and the way he jerked his thumb at Victor, showed he was giving him the benefit of the doubt—"would like to 'ave the honor of speaking to your Excellency for a moment."

"Yes, yes." The general commanding the English expeditionary force was refulgent in scarlet and gold. If the uniform made the man, he was a made man indeed. Personally, he was less prepossessing: about sixty, jowly, with a pinched mouth that said he'd lost most of his teeth. When he nodded to Victor, the wattles under his chin wobbled. "I am Major General Edward Braddock. And you, sir . . . ?"

Victor saluted. "Major Victor Radcliff, your Excellency. I am pleased to welcome you to Atlantis."

"More pleased than I am to be here, I shouldn't wonder," Braddock replied. "I hoped they would give me a command on the Continent, but . . ." He shrugged, and that loose flesh swung back and forth again. "A man goes where he is ordered, not where he would. Tell me something of the French dispositions."

"Sir, they are halted in our territory, about thirty miles below Freetown," Victor said. No light of intelligence kindled in the general's eye, from which Victor concluded he did not know exactly where Freetown lay. With a mental sigh, the Atlantean added a gloss: "About a hundred ten miles south of where we are now."

"I see." Edward Braddock nodded, perhaps in wisdom.

His next questions were cogent enough: "Why are they halted? Why didn't they go on to assail this place?"

"Deserters say there's sickness among them, your Excellency," Victor answered.

"Ah." Braddock nodded again. "That would come of using raw troops, wouldn't it? You needn't worry about my lads coming down sick, by God! If they didn't catch the great pox—let alone the small—years ago, they weren't half trying." His chuckle held a curious mix of contempt and affection.

"Your Excellency, I had that very thought as I was riding down here. It should help us."

"Indeed. We'll come ashore, march down to wherever it is that the froggies got stuck in the mud, drive them out of our settlements, and then go on into theirs," Braddock said. "Should be a straightforward enough job of work. You'll be able to keep us victualed, I expect?"

"I think so, sir." Radcliff paused. "If I may say . . ." He paused again.

"Yes? Well? Out with it, man. I don't bite," the English officer said gruffly.

"The only thing I wanted to say, sir, is that it may not prove quite so easy as you make it sound," Victor told him. "Atlantis is a different place from Europe."

"Don't I know it!" Braddock had said he would rather have fought on European soil. Now Radcliff saw how true that was. Scowling, Braddock went on, "Still and all, soldiering is soldiering. What works in France works in Prussia and Russia and India. We've seen that. I daresay it will work here, too."

"I hope so, your Excellency," Victor replied.

A horseman rode into the French encampment from the north. He shouted Roland Kersauzon's name. Roland ducked out of his tent. "I am here," he said. "What have you learned?"

The rider dismounted. A young groom led the horse away. "English soldiers have landed at New Hastings, sir," the rider said.

"How many? Do you know?"

"No, sir. But the rumor is that they have a general in command, so they are not a small force." The scout spoke fluent English, one reason Roland had chosen him. He continued, "And the rumor is, they are marching this way."

"Is it?" Kersauzon said tonelessly. It was a rumor he would rather not have heard. "English regulars, under a general?"

"Major General Edward Braddock." The scout pronounced the name with a certain somber satisfaction. Emboldened by Roland's silence, he pressed on: "Is it that we shall also have soldiers coming from the mother country?"

"If it is, I have heard nothing of it," Roland replied. "I am what we have. We are what we have." At least the man hadn't asked whether a general was coming from France, which bespoke a certain basic courtesy. Kersauzon realized he'd answered the question regardless of whether it was asked.

"What shall we do?" the scout asked. "The English regulars, they are said to be men of extraordinary discipline. Of extraordinary ferocity, as well. How can we hope to stand against such soldiers?"

That only angered Kersauzon—angered him more, perhaps, because similar doubts flitted through his own mind. "Do you piddle down your leg when you hear 'An Englishman is coming!'?" he demanded.

"*Monsieur,* I should hope that I do not," the scout replied with dignity. "But when many Englishmen come, with an English major general commanding them, I confess I am not altogether easy in my mind."

"Very well," Roland said. It wasn't, but it also wasn't

anything he could do anything about. He gestured sharply. "You may go." It wasn't quite *You've brought me bad news—get out of here,* but it wasn't so far removed from that, either.

Rather to his surprise, the scout did remember to salute before leaving. That left Roland there by himself: also an uncomfortable place to be. He had nothing to do but brood about what lay ahead.

His army had shown it could stand against whatever the English settlers of Atlantis threw at it. Against regulars from across the sea? He wasn't nearly so sure. Those men were trained to stand in line, to load and fire, to step forward and take their wounded or slain comrades' places, and then to charge home with the bayonet, all without regard for their own safety. Unlike them, his troops were not such fools. They wanted to fight, yes, but they also wanted to live.

Kersauzon scratched his chin. Whiskers rasped under his nails—a man could not stay properly shaved in the field. He frowned. If he fought this Braddock's fight, line against line, what could he do but lose? But what other kind of fight was there?

The kind where his men's fighting style had the advantage and that of the English regulars did not, of course. Put so, it seemed obvious. But how to turn an obvious abstraction into reality?

He called the scout back.

The man came with ill grace. He was gnawing on some meat stuffed between two slices of bread: an English fashion that seemed to be spreading. And why not? It was fast and convenient and filling. Mouth full, the scout mumbled, *"Monsieur?"*

"I wish you to tell me of the land ahead," Roland said. "I am seeking a particular kind of terrain."

After a heroic swallow and another equally heroic bite, the scout mumbled again: "And that would be?"

"Something on this order." Roland described it as minutely as he could. "Have you seen anything like that?"

Another swallow. Another bite. More muffled talk—the man suddenly seemed capable of speech only with his mouth full: "Well, now, *Monsieur,* I think I just may have." He swallowed again, and—miracle of miracles!—emitted several clear words: "When I was coming back here, you understand?"

"Yes." Roland Kersauzon quivered with eagerness. "How far distant?"

"Not too," the scout replied. Or so Roland thought, at any rate; the fellow was eating again. Had he fasted all through his mission? Would he starve to death unless he stuffed his face with meat and bread *now*?

"Not too," Roland repeated hopefully. The scout nodded; that let him eat and communicate at the same time, and lessened his risk of choking to death. Roland tried to get more out of him: "Could we establish ourselves there—wherever this place is—before the English come across it?"

He'd timed things as well as he could. He finished the question just as the scout swallowed. That didn't stop the man from taking another bite before answering. Roland supposed nothing short of a lightning stroke from God could have. He looked up toward the heavens. Nothing. God might have been Baal in the Old Testament: He was talking, or pursuing, or on a journey, or maybe He was sleeping, and needed to be awakened.

At last—and as indistinctly as ever—the scout said, "*Oui, Monsieur.* I think we can do it without much trouble."

"Good," Roland said: and it was good. "Then we shall."

# XVIII

*M*ajor General Braddock didn't lack for confidence. "Once we drive the French rabble out of English territory, we shall go on to the capture of Nouveau Redon, and then march down into the Spanish settlements, thus completing the conquest of Atlantis for the Crown," he declared at supper the evening after his army began moving south from New Hastings.

The officers who'd accompanied him from England nodded. Victor Radcliff wondered whether the distinguished major general had bothered checking a map. He was talking about marching hundreds of miles. Presumably, he would need to leave garrisons along the way. How many men did he think he would have left by the time he came to the southern tip of Atlantis?

Victor saw that the rest of the Atlantcan officers were as appalled as he was. They knew how big Atlantis was, whether Braddock did or not. None of them said anything, though. Radcliff thought the march down to the border would be plenty to show the general from across the sea he'd underestimated the size of his new command.

Or maybe Braddock had overestimated what his regulars could do. By Atlantean standards, they weren't big
men. One picked regiment had soldiers all over five feet
seven, which was not a great height on this side of the
Atlantic. The rest of the English troops ran smaller still.

They were tough, though; no doubt about that.
Their legs might not be long, but they could outmarch
the bigger Atlantean recruits. They seemed as immune
to fatigue as they were to fear and to smallpox. They
traded filthy jokes in half-comprehensible dialects as
they trudged along. They took their trade as much for
granted as fishermen or wheelwrights or glassmakers.

Braddock raised his goblet, which held a fine Ma-
deira that had crossed the ocean with him. "To the King,
to victory, and to glory!" he said.

"To the King, to victory, and to glory!" the assembled
officers chorused. Victor Radcliff drank the toast with
everyone else. Nothing wrong with it as long as everything went smoothly. Even Victor thought the rugged
foot soldiers from England ought to be able to bundle
the French back over the border. A handsome victory
here might let them assail Nouveau Redon. The French
stronghold was said to be very strong. If the defenders
were battered and demoralized, though . . . Well, who
could say what might happen then?

By now, not having Blaise at his side felt odd. The
Negro had made himself indispensable in a hurry. He
was off eating and drinking with other officers' servants,
and with the cooks who'd served up these succulent
beefsteaks and rib roasts. Victor wouldn't have been
surprised if the servants were eating better yet.

"Major Radcliff!" Braddock called.

"Yes, your Excellency?" Victor replied, surprised at
being singled out.

"I looked to be dining on honkers and other native
fowl," the Englishman said. "That would have been

something out of the ordinary, at any rate—something I haven't done before. Instead, we have ... beef. Nothing *wrong* with beef, mind you, but I did not cross the sea to eat of it."

"Sir, we've long since hunted the honkers out of these coastal districts," Victor said. "Here, we are nearly as settled as you are back on the home island, and our crops and livestock reflect it. We do, I believe, have more Terranovan turkeys here than you raise in England, and we make more use of maize as well. But honkers? Honkers, these days, are rare anywhere east of the Green Ridge Mountains, and less common west of the mountains than they were."

"How disappointing," Braddock said. "If I had to come here, I looked for a thoroughly exotic clime, to reward me with its novelty. But I find England has got here ahead of me."

"It has, sir," Victor agreed. "Perhaps, after the war is won, you might be interested in journeying into the interior with me. There, I promise, you will find things you would not within sight of St. Paul's."

"Perhaps I might indeed, Major, and I thank you for the generous offer," Braddock said. "One more good reason to clean things up as quickly as ever we may."

The march resumed at first light the next morning: one more sign Braddock wanted to get things over with in a hurry. Yawning and grumbling profanely, the redcoats from England made up the core of the army. Green-coated Atlanteans were good enough for scouts and vanguard and rear guard. If there was a battle, their place would be on the wings. Again, the English regulars would take center stage.

Farmers waved as the soldiers marched by. They had, however, universally taken the precaution of driving their horses and cattle and sheep and pigs and chickens—yes, and turkeys, too—away from the army's

line of progress. Victor wondered how they knew soldiers plundered as naturally as they breathed. Eastern
Atlantis had been peaceful for many, many years.

However they knew, they were right. Chattels whose
owners were rash enough to leave them on display disappeared: a chicken here, a hatchet there. And the English
regulars weren't the only ones who stole. The Atlanteans
lifted things as if they'd been soldiering and plundering
for years. Victor Radcliff didn't know whether they were
admirable or awful.

"Some of them could have had farms along this road,"
he said. "Then they'd be hiding, not stealing."

"That's so, *M'sieu,*" Blaise agreed. "But they don't, so
they aren't."

"Right," Victor said. Sometimes Blaise's English was
as compressed as a semaphore signal. Victor wasn't sure
whether that was a defect or the sign of a profound
mind.

Blaise didn't worry about it. As far as Victor Radcliff could tell, Blaise didn't worry about anything. Most
of what that proved was how little Victor really knew
the retainer who doubled as an underofficer. A man
snatched from his native land and sold into slavery
among strange-looking people who spoke not a word of
his language . . . Such a man might find a thing or two to
worry about. Or maybe even three.

A farmer on horseback came up from the south to
report that the French army was moving again. Major
General Braddock took that as good news. "We shan't
have to storm their field fortifications, then," he said.
"That might possibly have proved tricky. If we meet
them in the open, though, God hath delivered them
into our hands." He used the old-fashioned verb form to
show his confidence.

"If they had fieldworks, your Excellency, why would
they move out of them?" Victor asked.

"If they spent so long in one place, why would they not have built fieldworks?" Braddock returned, and the Atlantean had no good answer for him.

Radcliff asked the same question of Blaise a few minutes later. "Maybe we find out," the black man said. That struck Victor as much too likely.

"Positions! Positions!" Roland Kersauzon felt like a director putting on a play. Unlike a director, he had a cast of thousands. And, unlike a director in a crowded little theater, he would have an audience of thousands, too. He had to keep that audience interested and intrigued just long enough.

The English regulars and their settler allies were coming. They'd be here soon. His own cavalry was skirmishing with the enemy's Atlantean horse, holding the scouts away so they couldn't divine what was going on here. No one was trying to hold back the main English force. On the contrary.

"Dress your lines!" Roland shouted to the ranks of musketeers who took their places athwart the road. They would stand and volley against Braddock's fearsome regulars for a while. And they would pay for it, too. He stood with them. He lacked the gall to order others to do what he dared not do himself. He would have been safer if he'd had it. He also would have been a stranger to himself.

When he looked north, he saw a cloud of dust against the sky. The redcoats and the English settlers were getting close, then. Well, good. Roland didn't want to stand out here in the meadow under the hot sun all day. He would have been cooler as well as safer in the trees behind his horribly exposed soldiers, or in the woods to either side of the meadow.

He wondered why European generals insisted on fighting battles in the open. They could control their armies better if they could see everything that was going on, true. It hardly seemed reason enough. But if Braddock was looking for a stand-up fight, the French settlers would give him one ... for a while.

Pistols banged, not very far in the distance. His horsemen were falling back against the English Atlanteans, as they had orders to do. He didn't want to stop the enemy advance: only to channel it a little. As long as they kept the other side's cavalry away from the woods, they were doing their job.

Horses trotted toward him across the meadow. Those were his riders. They waved to the musketeers as they approached and then rode past to either side. Some of the musketeers were incautious enough to wave back. Their sergeants screamed at them. They wouldn't make that mistake again.

A few horsemen reined in and looked at his force from well out of musket range, then wheeled their mounts and rode back to the north. Those were the English Atlanteans' scouts getting a look at his dispositions. Roland knew what he wanted to look like. But in war as in the theater, you could never be quite sure that what the audience saw was what you wanted it to see.

Well, he'd know soon.

Here came the redcoats, already deployed in line of battle, advancing to the bleat of the horn and the tap of the drum. They wore tall hats to make themselves seem bigger and more fearsome than they really were. As they drew close, though, Roland realized most of them were shorter and skinnier than the green-clad Atlanteans who flanked them.

As long as they were shooting, that wouldn't matter. Everybody who aimed a loaded musket was the same size. But it might count against the English in the bayonet charge. Or, on the other hand, it might not. The redcoats approached the field with the professional arrogance of men who knew exactly what they were doing and had done it plenty of times before. Their matter-of-factness was daunting.

"Can we beat them, *Monsieur*?" a young lieutenant asked, so Roland wasn't the only one whose knees wanted to knock.

"They think we are going to play their game," the French commander said, more calmly than he felt. "If we do that, they ... present certain difficulties." *They'll slaughter us,* he meant, and hoped the lieutenant didn't realize it. "This is the best arrangement for doing something else, *n'est-ce pas?*"

*"Certainement,"* the youngster replied. He kept his eyes on the steadily advancing regulars. His thoughts were still on them, too, for he continued, "So long as they give us the chance to do something else ..."

"Yes. So long as," Kersauzon agreed. "Nothing in war is certain. I would be the last to claim anything different. But I believe that fighting where we are, as we are, gives us the best chance of victory."

The redcoats marched right into musket range. Their sergeants went on dressing their lines even then. They could have started shooting. So could the French settlers. When the pause held, a heavyset, elderly Englishman—he was close enough to see clearly—rode out in front of his force and tipped his hat in the direction of Roland Kersauzon's army. Kersauzon gravely returned the courtesy. The Englishman rode off to one side of the line, so as not to get in the way of his side's musketry.

Bugle calls rang out: English and French. The front rank of soldiers in both armies dropped to one knee. The second rank stooped to shoot over their heads. The third rank stood straight to fire above the heads of the second.

*"Now!"* Roland Kersauzon shouted, at the same in-

stant as his English opposite number yelled what had to
be the same thing.

Fire rippled across both battle lines. Smoke clouded
the air. Bullets flew. Oh, how they flew! One of them
tugged at Roland's sleeve. Another knocked the hat off
his head. He caught it before it fell. He needed a moment to be sure, but no, neither of those musket balls
touched his tender flesh.

Not all his men were so lucky. Some fell and lay still.
More staggered away in pain and disbelief. The stink of
blood and that of shit from bowels pierced by bullets or
loosened by fear filled the air along with gunpowder's
choking reek.

Having fired, the first three ranks of Frenchmen re-
tired to reload. The next three stepped forward to take
their places. Their muskets were loaded and ready to
fire. Roland knew succeeding volleys would by the nature of things grow more ragged than the first two.

That was certainly true for his half-trained troops.
But the redcoats fired and reloaded, fired and reloaded,
faster than mere mortals had any business doing. They
got off three volleys for every two from the French settlers, sometimes two for one. If the settlers tried to hold
their ground much longer, the Englishmen would either
charge home with the bayonets that glittered at the ends
of their guns or simply slaughter them with that deadly
massed musketry.

"Retreat!" Roland shouted. "Retreat!" Enough buglers still stood to amplify the command. The Frenchmen
streamed back in among the trees—those who still could.

"By Jove, we've got them now," Major General Braddock said in more than a little satisfaction. The crash of
volley after volley made his horse skittish, but he himself
stayed as calm as if he were in his drawing room. Almost
in spite of himself, Victor Radcliff was impressed.

And he was impressed at what the redcoats were doing to the French settlers in front of them. The settlers were brave; if they weren't, they couldn't have stood the gaff as long as they had. But they were getting chewed to pieces. The training that made an English regular would have been reckoned cruel if inflicted on a hound. On a man . . . But, cruel or not, it worked. The regulars delivered their fire with a speed and volume Victor wouldn't have believed if he weren't seeing it with his own eyes.

Blaise saw the same thing. "These men ugly. These men bad. But these men, they fighters," he said.

Whoops and cheers from officers and sergeants announced the French debacle. "They're running, the cowardly dogs!" an underofficer shouted gleefully.

"Order the pursuit!" Braddock commanded in a great voice. Horns and human voices carried out his bidding.

"Hurrah!" the soldiers shouted as they tramped forward, still in neatly aligned ranks.

And all hell broke loose.

When volleys tore into the redcoats from both flanks, they left Victor confused for a moment. The enemy was in front of them. The enemy was broken, was fleeing. . . . The enemy was, he realized, leading them straight into a trap. No. Had led them.

Smoke rose from the left. Smoke rose from the right. More musketry tore into the redcoats from either side. Cannon boomed, their roar deeper than that from the flintlocks. The roundshot, enfilading the English, tore great holes in their lines.

And the French settlers who'd volleyed with Braddock's regulars hadn't fled incontinently, as Victor thought they had. Once they reached the cover that trees and ferns gave, they turned around and started shooting again. Each man blazed away as he saw fit. It wasn't the deadly hail of bullets a good volley produced, which didn't mean it wasn't galling.

The French settlers also proved to have field guns hidden in the woods to the rear of their lines. They fired roundshot and canister. The range was long for canister, but not too long. Regulars fell in clusters when the showers of lead balls struck home.

"My God! We are undone!" Major General Edward Braddock sounded astonished, disbelieving. "They tricked us, the dirty scuts!" By the way he said it, the French settlers had no right to do any such wicked thing.

"Can we break them?" Victor asked, more from duty than from hope. The veriest child could see that the English regulars, under fire from the front and both flanks, were the ones being broken.

So could Braddock. "No, this day is not ours, I fear me. Best we withdraw to save what we can, while—" He stopped, wincing, and set a hand on his prominent belly.

"You're wounded, your Excellency!" Victor said. Sure enough, blood stained the gray vest Braddock wore under his long red coat.

He still had spirit. "Nothing serious, my dear boy, I assure you. I—" He winced again. This ball struck the right side of his chest. "I say! Blighters are using me for a pincushion today." He coughed and grimaced and flinched. Red foam burst from his nostrils. He would die, then. No surgeon could cure a wound like that, even if fever didn't take him after the bullet in the belly.

A musket ball gashed Victor's horse. The animal screamed and bucked. He fought it back under control. Another ball drew a bloody line across the back of his hand. The redcoats' lines, neat no more, were bloodied, too. They stolidly tried to fight back. In an impossible position, bedeviled by foes they couldn't see—foes who didn't fight the way they were used to—the undertaking was hopeless.

"Blow *retreat*!" Victor shouted to the buglers. He looked around for Blaise. The Negro hadn't fled. He hadn't got shot down. "Go to the other wing. Tell the buglers there to sound *retreat,* too. On my orders and General Braddock's."

"Sound *retreat.* On your orders. Yes, sir." If Blaise had any nerves, he kept them in a place where they didn't show. Off he rode.

"I'll get you out of here, your Excellency," Radcliff told the English general.

"Kind of you to say so, young fellow, but I fear me I'm done for." The red foam was on Braddock's lips now, too. "I know somewhat of wounds. I'll not go anywhere far, not with what I've caught."

"Your courage does you credit, sir." Victor could say that and mean it. Braddock faced death with as much equanimity as any man he'd ever seen.

He waved the praise away. "I've done good fighting in my day—and some not so good, I fear, here at the end. I've loved a lot of pretty women, too, and more than a few of them loved me back. I hoped to be shot at a more advanced age by an outraged husband, but no man gets everything he wants."

"Come away, please. Maybe the doctors can do you some good." Even as Victor spoke, he knew they couldn't.

So did Edward Braddock. "Quacks might kill me faster, you mean. But I die fast enough without them. Save yourself, Radcliff. Pay these backwoods Frenchmen back, if you see the chance. Go on. Your luck won't last if you stay here. Mine's already run dry." He sagged in the saddle. He wouldn't be able to sit his horse much longer.

Tears stung Radcliff's eyes. "You'll be avenged, your Excellency. England will be avenged."

"Yes, yes," Braddock said impatiently. He coughed again. This time, a steady stream of blood came from his nose and dribbled out the corner of his mouth. His face was going gray.

Biting his lip, Victor turned his horse and rode back to the north. By ones and twos and in small groups, redcoats were stumbling out of the fight. Every so often, a man would turn and fire at what might have been pursuers. Most of the regulars wanted nothing more than to get away.

One of them nodded at Victor in a friendly enough fashion. "Cor, them Frenchies buggered us with a bleedin' pine cone this time, didn't they?"

"Well . . ." Victor admitted what he couldn't deny. "Yes."

"Did the general make it out?" the redcoat asked.

"Afraid not. He's got two wounds—bad ones. Belly and chest. I don't think he'll live much longer," Radcliff replied.

"Blimey!" the Englishman said. "So who's in charge, then? You?"

Victor looked around. He didn't see any officers who outranked him anywhere close by. "I think I may be, for now, anyhow."

"Well, Mr. Atlantean, sir, wot the 'ell do we do next?" the soldier said.

"Let's get away from the enemy first," Radcliff said. "Then we'll look around and see what we've got left. And after that, we'll try to decide how we can go on fighting. Or do you have a better idea? If you do, speak up. I'd love to hear it."

"If you want ideas from the likes of me, things *are* buggered up," the soldier said.

"Aren't they?" Victor asked, again in all seriousness.

The redcoat laughed. "They are indeed, sir, for fair. No, what you said sounds good enough—for starters, anyway."

"Yes. For starters," Victor agreed. "And that's about where we are now, isn't it? Starting from the beginning, I mean."

"Oh, no, sir," the Englishman said. "After wot 'appened to us, we'd better start before *that,* eh?"

Victor only wished he could say the man was wrong.

Ravens and vultures spiraled down out of the sky to feast on the dead. The ravens didn't mind pecking at the dying, either, though the vultures shunned anything that still moved. Roland Kersauzon had seen plenty of dead and dying men before, but never so many all in one place. Quantity, he discovered, had a quality all its own.

Then a red-crested eagle struck at one of his men walking over the battlefield and badly wounded him. Roland had thought the enormous birds of prey were gone from eastern Atlantis, but evidently not. He wondered what they ate with honkers hunted nearly to extinction hereabouts. This one, plainly, wanted to eat man's flesh. It fought with wings and beak and talons and furious screeches when his soldiers tried to drive it from its screaming victim. One of them finally knocked it over the head.

Stretcher bearers carried the injured man back to the surgeons. His shrieks would go unnoticed there among so many others. Roland had to make himself go watch the medicos at work and comfort men as they endured bullet probings and amputations with nothing to dull the pain but a leather strap to bite on or, if they were lucky, a slug of rum.

"Why did you come at all, *Monsieur*?" one of the surgeons asked. The man's leather apron was all bloody. So were his arms, to the elbows. He sounded genuinely puzzled as he continued, "The rest of us are here because we have no choice."

"Yes, I understand." Roland fought not to wrinkle his nose against the butcher's reek of blood. His wave took in the charnel house and the rest of the field. "But all this is my responsibility. I'm glad to accept the victory, but how can I without seeing what it costs?"

"Believe me, *Monsieur,* most commanders have no trouble whatever," the surgeon said. Along with two burly aides, he went on to the next wounded man. "Hold him tight, boys," he told them. "Can't let him run away while we ply our trade, eh?"

The soldier screamed. How could he help it, when an iron probe penetrated his pierced flesh? Roland turned away, working hard to control his face and his stomach.

He was relieved when a junior officer came up to him. That gave him something to think about besides suffering. "Excuse me, sir," the lieutenant said, "but the English prisoners wish to know what is to be done with them."

"I will talk to them," Kersauzon said. "My English is not of the best, but it will serve. And some of them, it may be, will know a little French."

"Yes, that is so," the lieutenant replied. He took Roland to the prisoners, who looked as apprehensive as the French commander would have in their boots. Since those boots were finer than the ones a lot of his soldiers had, the redcoats probably counted themselves lucky to be wearing them still. Some of the Englishmen stood in their stocking feet, so they'd already met plunderers.

"You are safe," Roland told them in his rusty English. "Your lives are safe. You will not be armed ... uh, harmed."

"Will you parole us, sir?" asked a man whose chevrons proclaimed him a sergeant.

"You will agree not to fight again until exchanged?" Kersauzon asked, first in his language and then in theirs. Sure enough, a few English soldiers did speak French. They translated for the others. Inside of half a minute, all the prisoners were nodding eagerly.

"We will, sir," the sergeant said, "and thank you for the handsome offer."

Roland wondered whether he ought to hold some of them as hostages, to make sure the rest kept their word. He decided that would give the redcoats ideas they didn't need. They were professionals; they had honor.

"You will give your paroles to my men in charge of receiving them." Roland resolved to appoint such men as soon as he left the prisoners. "Then you may go north, if that is what you desire." He knew his English was stilted, but it served.

"Can we get back what your men stole from us when we surrendered?" That sergeant, like any good underofficer, was always looking to turn an inch into a mile.

But Kersauzon shook his head. "Be joyous—uh, be thankful—they did not hit you on the head. Did you never plunder a foe?"

"Who, me, your Excellency? Oh, I might have done that a time or two." The sergeant didn't waste breath denying it. Roland Kersauzon would have called him a liar if he had. With a grin, the saucy fellow went on, "Couldn't hurt to ask."

"Nor help." Roland turned away.

Before long, the redcoats were giving their names to the French settlers Roland chose to take them. The military clerks wrote the names on paper borrowed from the bookkeeper over his protests. The few Englishmen who could write signed their names beside the transcriptions. The rest made their marks. Then, still showing the formidable discipline they'd displayed in battle, they marched away, heads high, backs straight. By their pride, they might have won.

"What will you do now, *Monsieur*?" one of the clerks asked. "Will you go into Freetown? With their army shattered, the English can hardly stand against us."

Part of Roland thought he ought to do exactly that.

The enemy would be dismayed and disorganized. But he was dismayed and disorganized himself. The sight of a real battlefield would do that to anyone. And his own force, if not dismayed, was also disorganized. The men who'd volleyed with the redcoats had fallen in windrows. The English might be good at only one kind of warfare, but they were monstrously good at that.

And so Roland temporized. "First we shall bury the dead—ours and theirs. When that is done, I shall decide where to go next."

*"Oui, Monsieur."* The clerk didn't argue. He even explained why: "You beat them. You showed you know what you are doing."

Bodies thudded into long trenches, some for the French settlers, others for the redcoats and English settlers. Priests read prayers above them. Maybe even the enemy heretics, or some of them, would reach purgatory and not burn forever in hell. Kersauzon hoped so, anyhow.

He ordered Major General Braddock buried in a grave of his own, and had a wooden marker with Braddock's name set over it. Even when caught in a trap, the English commander had fought gallantly. His wounds were at the front, as befit a brave man.

After that . . . After that, Roland ordered the army to camp for rest and recuperation. He still stood in English-settled territory. His own settlers had smashed English professionals. He was satisfied for the time being.

One of his lieutenants was not. *"Monsieur,* do you know what Hannibal's aide told him when he did not march on Rome as soon as he beat the legions at Cannae?"

"No," Roland replied, "but I suspect you are about to tell me."

Ignoring the sarcasm, the junior officer nodded. "He said, 'You know how to win a victory, but not what to do with it.' "

Roland only laughed. "I will take the chance. And I will say to you that Freetown is hardly Rome. We do not win the war by taking it, and we do not lose the war if we leave it in English hands for a while."

"We cannot go farther while the English hold it," the lieutenant said stubbornly. "New Hastings, Hanover . . ."

"They are far away. One thing at a time," Roland said. The lieutenant sighed, but he didn't argue any more.

Victor Radcliff found having the paroled redcoats back in Hanover caused more trouble than it solved. They knew they wouldn't be fighting any more for a while, and jeered at their comrades who'd escaped without getting captured. Several fistfights followed in short order.

Sending the paroled men north solved some of the problem, but only some. The Englishmen who remained under arms still seethed with resentment. As long as they all shared the same risks, no one thought anything of it. When some did while others didn't, the less lucky ones naturally disliked the idea of marching into battle while their friends stayed away.

The mere idea of parole bewildered Blaise. "No one has to feed prisoners this way," Victor explained. "When we capture French soldiers, we'll send them back under parole and put a like number of our men into the army again."

"Why not put them in now?" Blaise asked. "The French, they don't know."

"If they recapture a paroled man who isn't properly exchanged, they can shoot him," Victor replied. "It's a question of honor, too."

"What is honor?" Blaise asked.

Victor thought of Falstaff in *Henry IV,* Part 1. *What is honor? a word. What is that word, honor? Air. A trim reckoning! Who hath it? he that died o' Wednesday. Doth*

*he feel it? No. Doth he hear it? No. It is insensible then?*
*Yea, to the dead. But will it not live with the living? No.*
*Why? Detraction will not suffer it. Therefore I'll none of*
*it: honor is a mere scutcheon; and so ends my catechism.*

That would be more than Blaise needed to know, and
in the wrong spirit, too. Victor tried a different approach:
"Honor is keeping promises, even if keeping them isn't
to your advantage. If both sides in a fight have honor,
they can trust each other to follow the rules of war. It
means we treat prisoners and enemy civilians well,
knowing the enemy will do the same."

Blaise scratched the tightly curling hair on top of his
head. "You and the French do this?" he asked.

"We do," Victor said, not without pride.

"You are both mad, then," Blaise declared.

"It could be that you are right." Radcliff fell into
French, in which tongue the Negro was still more fluent.
"But if we are both mad the same way, it makes fighting the war easier for the helpless without changing who
wins or loses."

"Honh," Blaise said, a sound wordless but eloquent
in its skepticism. "Prisoners the French take, prisoners
you take, you should sell for slaves."

That shocked Victor. "We don't enslave whites!" he
exclaimed.

"I know. You should. Then you would know more
about slavery than you do," Blaise replied, still in French.
"The man holding the whip, he thinks one thing. The
man tasting the whip, he thinks maybe something else."

"You are a free man here," Victor said in English, reminding the Negro he'd come out of French-held territory. If slavery paid more up here in the land of wheat
and maize and lumber, it might have caught on better in
English Atlantis, too. Radcliff didn't mention that.

"Plenty black men, plenty copper men, not free down
south," Blaise replied, also in English. "You say to them,

'Help us and you free,' you get big army fast. French, Spaniards, they much unhappy."

He was probably right. Whether he was or wasn't mattered only so much to Victor Radcliff. The white man touched his left epaulet with his right forefinger. "You see this, Blaise? I am a major of Atlantean volunteers. I do not decide things here."

*"C'est dommage,"* Blaise said, and then the same thing in English: "Pity."

"I suppose so," said Victor, who had never tasted the lash. He wondered whether spreading a promise to free slaves where they were now would be honorable. Reluctantly, he decided it wouldn't. It would involve the French in a guerrilla war against their own servitors, with all the horrors that entailed. War as it was fought these days was a business of army against army, and impinged on civilians as little as possible. A slave uprising couldn't help doing just that.

"You want to win this war, eh?" Blaise said.

"Well, yes. We wouldn't be fighting it if we didn't," Radcliff said.

"Give blacks and copperskins guns. Best way." The Negro seemed ruthlessly matter-of-fact. "Make French sorry at home, they no fight up here no more."

"You may be right," Victor said. That was polite, and committed him to nothing.

To his surprise, Blaise realized as much. "You waste a chance," he said. "You not get many better ones. You have to do all your fighting yourself. War is harder. Maybe you lose. What then?"

Victor hadn't seriously imagined losing. He wondered why not. The French settlers had just devastated some of the best infantry in the world. Why wouldn't they do the same to the redcoats' remnants and to the settlers' odds and sods who were all that was left between them and New Hastings and Hanover?

Maybe they would.

"I think I would pack up and go somewhere else. Avalon, perhaps, or the Terranovan mainland," Victor said. "I'm not too old to make a new start. But we aren't whipped yet, either. Not even close."

"No, eh?" Blaise let the question hang there.

"No, by God," Victor Radcliff insisted. "If Kersauzon had pushed us hard, we might have fallen to pieces. But he didn't, and we won't. We're getting stronger by the day, with more Atlantean recruits coming in."

"Honh," Blaise said again. He didn't believe it. He saw the English soldiers and paroled prisoners quarreling among themselves, and he thought that meant the whole army was weak.

He might have been right, too. Victor didn't want to believe it, which didn't mean it wasn't true. *We won't win if we give up,* Victor thought. As long as he remembered that . . . he wasn't giving up. So what? He might lose anyhow.

# XIX

"Forward!" Roland Kersauzon shouted. He gestured to the buglers and drummers. Their martial music underscored and amplified the order.

Several thousand men moved at his command, as if he were a puppet master manipulating marionettes. And so he was, though he used obedience, not actual strings. Still, it was a heady feeling, like a slug of barrel-tree rum sliding hot down his throat into an empty stomach.

A courier rode up from the south and handed Roland a letter. Roland examined both the man and the seal with care. He would not have put it past the perfidious English to sneak in a false but French-speaking courier with a forged message to confuse him and his troops. But both the courier and the impression stamped into the wax seemed authentic. Kersauzon broke the seal with a clasp knife, unrolled the letter, and read.

"What does it say, *Monsieur*?" a lieutenant asked. "Have we been reinforced, the way the English-speaking Atlanteans were?"

"As a matter of fact, we have," Roland said. "If this is

true, two thousand of King Louis' men have landed at Cosquer and are on their way north to us." He turned to the courier again. "How far behind you are they, do you think?"

"They're foot soldiers, sir," the fellow replied, with a horseman's natural scorn. "I left them in my dust as soon as I set out."

"Well, yes. Of course," Kersauzon said. "And you were riding relays of horses, so that made you all the faster. We can't expect them for some time, then."

"I would think not, sir," the courier agreed.

*"Nom d'un nom,"* Roland muttered unhappily. "I don't want to wait for them—we've already waited long enough. But I don't want to go into battle without them, either. What to do? What to do?"

"It's your decision, sir," the lieutenant said.

Roland Kersauzon could have done without the reminder. He'd been the soul of decisiveness marching up into English territory. He'd got his backwoodsmen and half-trained militiamen a victory even he thought improbable against Braddock's professionals. Now he wanted to rest on his laurels. He wanted to, yes, but he feared that if he tried he soon would have no laurels to rest on. Maybe he'd even made a mistake pausing after the battle. If he'd pressed on right away . . .

Well, he hadn't. But he would now. He turned back to the courier. "Go tell the soldiers from the mother country I am advancing," he said. "I look for their support as soon as they are able to give it."

*"Oui, Monsieur."* The courier repeated back the message. Roland nodded—he had it right. Neither the man nor his horse seemed thrilled at hurrying back in the direction from which they'd come. But the rider sketched a salute and rode off.

"In the meanwhile . . ." the lieutenant said.

"In the meanwhile, we go on," Kersauzon said firmly.

"We would go on even if the King of France left all his men across the sea."

"What will you do, sir, if the French from France"—the younger officer smiled at his circumlocution—"have an officer with them who wants to take command, the way General Braddock took command for England?"

*Spit in his eye,* Roland thought. But he couldn't say that. If there was such an officer, it would surely get back to him. And so Roland was circumspect for once in his life: "I will point out to him that I am more familiar with local conditions than he is likely to be. I will also point out that General Braddock's misfortunes demonstrate how important familiarity with those conditions may prove."

"What if he chooses not to listen?" the nosy lieutenant persisted. "What will you do then?"

*Hope he has an unfortunate accident.* Roland Kersauzon couldn't say that, either. The theoretical officer slogging up the coast behind him would surely believe he aimed to arrange such an accident ... and the usurping dog wouldn't be entirely wrong. "I will do the best I can," Roland said. "I will do the best he permits me to do."

"Surely he will value your experience," the lieutenant said.

"But of course," Roland murmured. He didn't believe it, even for a moment. A French officer sent to Atlantis would feel the same way prisoners said the English officer sent to Atlantis had felt: as if he were exiled from civilization. And it might be true; an officer who'd disgraced himself at the court might well suddenly find himself carried across the sundering sea to do what he could for a country that didn't care to look him in the eye any more.

Now Roland had to do things quickly and do them right, before the hypothetical officer could take charge and make a mess of whatever he touched. He swore at himself for all the delays he'd tolerated.

Well, he'd tolerate them no more. "Can't you move faster, you lazy lugs?" he shouted. "What are you waiting for? Are your feet stuck in the mud? They'd better not be, by God!"

One of the soldiers grumbled that Roland had some part of himself stuck somewhere else. He was not talking about feet or mud. Roland listened without rancor. Soldiers *were* going to grumble; it was part of what made them soldiers. As long as they grumbled while they marched, Kersauzon didn't mind a bit.

"If you want us to hurry so much now, why didn't you start us sooner?" A sergeant had the nerve to ask that to his face. Atlanteans who spoke English always bragged about how frank they were and how they spoke their mind to anyone, no matter who and no matter when. The French settlers here didn't waste their time bragging about such things. They just did them.

And the sergeant expected an answer. Sighing, Roland gave him the straightest one he could: "Because I didn't know my own mind till now."

"Ah." The underofficer weighed that, then nodded. "It happens, sir. I kind of wish it didn't happen here, though."

Roland Kersauzon sighed again. "I wish it didn't happen here, too, Sergeant. I hope to correct my error. I'm sorry if that means wearing out your boots."

"So am I," the sergeant said. "I hope we can fix things, that's all."

"Me, too," Roland said, and sighed one more time.


"The Frenchmen are coming! The Frenchmen are coming!" The frightened cry echoed through the encampment the English settlers and redcoats had made south of Freetown.

It also echoed through the streets of Freetown itself. Some of the townsfolk showed the confidence in the men defending them by packing whatever they could into wagons and carriages, or onto the backs of horses and mules, or onto their own backs, and heading north at the best turn of speed they could manage.

Blaise delivered a one-word judgment on that: "Yellow." Then he asked, "Why is a coward yellow in English? Not in French. Not in my old tongue, either."

Victor Radcliff only shrugged. "I don't know why. You might as well ask why we call a cow a cow and not a sheep. Because we do, that's all."

"It doesn't help," the Negro said reproachfully.

"I know it doesn't," Victor replied. "I'm sorry. And I'm sorry that so many of the people in Freetown are sheep. They don't think we can hold the enemy. When one runs, the rest follow. And they all go, 'Baa. Baa. Baa.'" He mimicked a sheep's bleat. "Well, what I have to say to them is 'Bah!'"

He waited to see whether Blaise would notice the difference between a bleat and a sound of contempt. The Negro's broad smile—which seemed all the broader because his teeth showed up so well against his dark skin—said he did. No flies on Blaise, by God. That wasn't a saying in French, either, and probably also wasn't in the African's native tongue.

"'Bah!' is right, sir," Blaise said. "They is silly fools."

"'They are,'" Radcliff corrected. His body-servant-turned-sergeant nodded. He made fewer and fewer mistakes. Victor suddenly wondered if he threw one in every so often just to keep from making people suspicious. That wasn't the most reassuring thought he'd ever had. Instead of pursuing it, he went on, "Despite our losses, we have more men than they do, even now, and still more coming in all the time."

"Yes, sir." Blaise didn't sound impressed.

"It's true, dammit," Victor said in some annoyance. There had always been more Englishmen than French—and Bretons, before they finally amalgamated here—in Atlantis. The English came to carve out farms, or to fish, or to take advantage of the marvelous lumber here. Some of the Bretons fished, too; that seemed to be in their blood. But more looked for the same kind of work most French settlers sought: as overseers on the broad, slave-filled estates that raised sugar and indigo and cotton and, lately, Terranovan pipeweed. That left them—and the Spaniards farther south still—thinner on the ground than the English were.

All the same, Blaise had good enough reason not to sound impressed. Numbers mattered only so much. The surviving redcoats had had their confidence jolted by marching into a trap. Seeing their captured comrades freed on parole hadn't helped their morale, either. And the militiamen from the local settlements weren't so eager as they had been before their first taste of battle.

Victor hoped they wouldn't run if they had to fight again. He hoped so, yes, but he couldn't be sure.

Blaise found a new and unpleasant question: "Is true, sir, they have real Frenchmen from France now, like Braddock, he real Englishman from England?"

"I hear it's true," Radcliff said. "I don't know it is for a fact, but I hear it is. And if it is, someone in the Royal Navy needs a talking-to, by God."

"Talking-to?" Blaise rolled his eyes. "Need to kick somebody in a boat, kick him . . ." He mimed clutching at his crotch.

"That would be good." After a moment, Victor shook his head. "That would have been good. But it's too late to fret about such things now. The Frenchmen are here, and we have to stop them. If we can."

"We do it." Blaise sounded confident—but then, he generally did. Looking around to make sure no officers from England were in earshot, he added, "How you like command, sir?"

"Don't be silly," Victor said. "I'm not in command here. That English lieutenant-colonel, the earl's son . . ."

Blaise laughed. "He don't—doesn't—know anything. But he not *so* dumb. He know he . . . doesn't know anything. Some men, they don't know anything, and they don't know they don't know anything, you know?"

"Er—right." That bemused Victor Radcliff for a couple of reasons. The Negro's syntax, he was convinced, would have bemused anybody. And Blaise, all unknowingly—which fit his discourse well enough—was reproducing part of the argument from Plato's recounting of the *Apology* of Socrates.

Sure enough, the English officer approached Victor later that afternoon. "I hear the French settlers are on the march," he remarked. He was a few years younger than Victor—in his early twenties, probably—and, with fresh features and baby-fine skin, looked younger still.

"Yes, your Excellency. I hear the same," Victor said.

"If at all possible, we should stop their taking Freetown. Losing it would be a black eye," the young Englishman said.

"Yes, sir. I quite agree," Radcliff said.

"How do we go about doing that?" the lieutenant-colonel asked. "All too likely that they'll outnumber us. The result of another stand-up fight would be worrisome, to say the least."

Victor nodded. "So it would, sir. I'm not sure about the numbers"—he wouldn't call the English officer wrong, not to his face—"but they're bound to have the advantage of morale."

"What, what are we going to do, then? What *can* we do, then?" Raised in the traditions of continental European warfare, the young lieutenant-colonel thought standup battles were the only possible way two armies could meet. Seeing as much, Victor understood better how General Braddock had come to grief.

"Your Excellency, if I might make a suggestion . . ." No, Victor wasn't in command. He couldn't start throwing orders around. But if he could gently steer this over-bred but willing youngster in the right direction . . . He talked for a while, hoping the Englishman would see reason.

"Well, well," the young man said at last. "You wouldn't see such an approach taken in France or the Low Countries or the Germanies. Of that I am quite certain. Still and all, though, the so-called *klephts* in the Balkans might attempt an undertaking of this sort. . . ."

Victor Radcliff would have had a better notion of whether the lieutenant-colonel approved or not had he ever heard of *klephts* before. Since he hadn't, he made do with the question directly: "Shall we go ahead and try it, then, your Excellency?"

The Englishman looked quite humanly surprised. "I thought I said so, Major."

Maybe he had, but not in any language Victor understood. No matter, though. Saluting, Victor said, "Now it's so very plain, sir, that even a settler can understand it." The lieutenant-colonel nodded. Victor had bet himself a shilling that the man wouldn't notice irony, and sure enough . . . Now he had to collect. *I'll take it out of the Frenchmen's hides,* he thought.

Muskets banged from bushes by the side of the road. Roland Kersauzon's horse snorted and sidestepped. He brought it back under control without even noticing what he was doing. Keeping the horse in line was no problem. Keeping his army in line was proving a much harder job.

A couple of his soldiers were down from this latest bushwhacking. One clutched his leg and swore a blue streak. The other, shot through the head, lay still. The poor fellow wouldn't rise again till Judgment Day.

A troop of French settlers plunged into the bushes after the assassins. The whole army stopped, which was undoubtedly what the English skulkers had in mind. This wasn't the first time they'd disrupted his march, or the fifth. They were doing it every chance they got. And why not? It worked. It worked much too well.

Half an hour later, the pursuers—who'd gone after the bushwhackers without orders: indeed, against orders—returned, proudly carrying the corpse of one green-jacketed raider. The wretch or his friends had managed to wound two more of them before they caught him. Roland wondered whether he'd been dead when they did. If he hadn't been, they'd taken care of it immediately afterwards. It did not behoove an officer to inquire too closely into some questions. The only thing Roland said was, "Let's go on now."

On they went. An hour later, they came to another likely spot for an ambush. Roland Kersauzon ordered troops into the trees that came down too close to the road. Before the Frenchmen could get into the woods, they were fired upon. Two of them went down. Neither wound seemed serious, but even so . . . They lashed the trees with musketry. Then, satisfied they'd done what they could, they approached again—and were fired upon again.

"These miserable English wretches are like mosquitoes!" a lieutenant exclaimed in exasperation. "Their bites are almost harmless, but they can drive a man mad."

"And sometimes you can sicken from the bite, too," Roland said sadly. Learned doctors would have laughed at him. When they talked of malaria, they spoke of miasmas and fetid exhalations. To him, that only meant they didn't know what caused the sickness.

Well, neither did he, or not exactly. But he did know

there had been no malaria in Atlantis when his multiply
great-grandfather founded Cosquer three hundred years
before. It came here about the same time as African
slaves did, and soon spread from them to whites. How
did it spread? Through the air? Or, perhaps, through
mosquito bites?

Some illnesses—syphilis, gonorrhea—needed contact to spread from one person to another. Some—
unfortunately including measles and smallpox—didn't.
Maybe malaria fell into an in-between category.

*Or maybe you don't know what the devil you're nat-
tering about,* Roland thought. It wouldn't have been the
first time.

He had other, more urgent things to worry about.
That lieutenant was worrying right along with him, too.
"How are we going to stop the English from harassing
us like this, *Monsieur*?" he asked.

It was an uncomfortably good question. Since Kersauzon had no good answer for it, he picked nits instead:
"Those aren't redcoats, Lieutenant. English regulars
don't know how to fight like this. They're Atlanteans:
settlers doing the work in place of men from overseas."

"Very well, sir," the junior officer said. "How do
we stop the English Atlantean settlers from harassing
us, then?" He spoke with admirable—truly French—
precision.

Roland Kersauzon wished he didn't. Now the commander had no excuse not to answer the question—no
excuse except for his utter lack of a good response. "We
cannot keep dancing to their measure," he said at last.

*Well, how do we keep from doing that?* He could see
the question in the junior officer's eyes. It would have
been in his eyes, too, if someone had tried to palm that
reply off on him. But the lieutenant was more polite
than he likely would have been, and didn't ask the question out loud.

Eventually—after much too long—the French settlers did manage to drive away the bushwhackers. Roland hoped they did, anyhow. By then, it was about time to encamp for the night. Roland ordered an early halt, hoping to fortify the position well enough to make sure no one could assail it during the hours of darkness.

Things got no better the next morning. A couple of batteries of horse artillery came out of the woods to the west, unlimbered, and fired one quick roundshot per gun at the French settlers' line of march before tearing away again. Some of the iron balls flew high. Others tore holes in the settlers' files. One luckless fellow tried to stop a rolling cannon ball with his foot. That sent him off to the surgeons, who had to cut off the shattered appendage. His shrieks, and those of the other wounded men, set Roland Kersauzon's teeth on edge.

Then the French settlers came to a veritable fortress made from logs and mud. Cannon inside the fieldwork fired on them. Musketeers defended the artillerymen. When Roland's own field guns returned fire, the mud and dirt smothered the balls' impacts.

"Are we going to have to put on a regular siege, with saps and parallels, the way we would in Europe?" a sergeant asked.

"By God, I hope not," Roland answered. It wasn't even a proper siege, because they hadn't surrounded the enemy's work. The English had no trouble supplying and reinforcing the fort.

Somewhere south of here, the regulars from France were slogging forward. Roland had hoped to win glory without them. Now he wished they would get here to lend a hand. Cosquer had never seemed farther away.

He refused to send a messenger south to ask where the regulars were. If they wanted to hurry, that was their business. His . . . His had stalled. He didn't care to admit it, even to himself. But it seemed pretty plain that he couldn't drive the English-speaking Atlanteans out of their fort. He couldn't go on and leave it in his rear, either.

All of which left him some unpalatable choices. He could swing far inland, the drawback being that most of what was worth having lay close by the coast. Or he could turn around and retreat. He didn't want to do that; it would only give the regulars from France the chance to mock him and take over from him.

The best thing he could think of was staying where he was till the regulars caught up with him. He hadn't cared to do that before—he'd thought he could just walk into Freetown and present them with a *fait accompli.* Well, it wouldn't happen now, no matter how much he wished it would.

"If you will forgive me, *Monsieur,* you run a curious campaign," a sergeant told him. "Part of the time, you are more cautious than you need to be. The rest, you attack like a madman."

"If I think I can win, I will fight," Roland replied. "If I don't, I won't. What is so curious about that?"

"It could be that you push too hard when you push. It could also be that you don't push too hard when you don't push, if you take my meaning." The sergeant was not too young and not too skinny. Roland couldn't blight his military career; outside of this expedition, he had none. He was bound to be a baker or a miller or a carpenter or something else respectable: a solid tradesman who knew how to lead because he did it every day. And if he felt like speaking his mind, he would go ahead and do it.

Roland did him the courtesy of taking him seriously. "Maybe you're right. I can't prove you're not. But even if you are, wouldn't you rather have a commander like me than one who doesn't push when he should?"

"Hmm." The sergeant considered that as carefully as

he would have considered an offer for an upholstered chair. "Well, you've got something there, sir—no doubt about it. How much you've got . . . we'll just have to see."

"They aren't coming, sir," the scout reported.

"Damnation!" Victor Radcliff said feelingly.

"Sorry, sir," the rider said. "They pulled back out of range of our earthworks, and they're strengthening a position of their own."

"Oh, too bad," Victor said. He'd hoped to lead the invaders into temptation and then trap them the way they'd trapped Braddock and the redcoats. The French settlers' commander had seemed so intrepid. Why wasn't he intrepid enough to stick his head in the noose?

"I thought we'd poked and prodded them enough so they'd do something stupid, too," the scout said. "Guess I was wrong, though."

That the scout was wrong was one thing. That Victor Radcliff turned out to be wrong was something else again. It had much more important consequences. He drummed his fingers on his thigh. "He must be waiting for the French regulars to come up. Then he'll burst out of his fieldworks like an abscess and infect the whole damned countryside."

The scout pulled a face. "You've got a gift for the revolting phrase, don't you—uh, sir?" The polite addition was plainly an afterthought. "May the Frenchies do him as much good as Braddock did us."

"Naughty, naughty." Victor's reproof was also insincere. "King George did everything he knew how to do for us."

"Did everything he knew how to do to us, don't you mean?" the scout said. When Major Radcliff declined to rise to the bait (what went through his mind was *Amazing how I think like a fisherman, even though my line hasn't gone to sea for a while*), the man sighed and tried a new tack (*and again!*): "Well, if the froggy buggers won't come out and play, what do we do then?"

"Have to think about that," Victor answered. "Have to talk with the senior English officer, too."

"Oh, yes, sir. Charlie. A lot *he'll* know." By his accent, the scout was a New Hastings man, and so especially likely to look down his nose at officials from the mother country. By his sarcastic tone, and by his casual use of the lieutenant-colonel's given name, he lived up to—or down to—all the things people said about New Hastings men.

Grinning, Radcliff made as if to push him away. "Go on, be off with you," he said, for all the world as if he were an Irishman himself.

Blaise had been quietly standing not far away. Sometimes people called him "Major Radcliff's shadow." He wasn't quite black enough to fill that role, but he came close. The scout hadn't hesitated to speak in his presence. Nobody did, not any more. "What will you do?" he asked Victor.

"What I said I'd do," Victor replied. "I'll talk to the lieutenant-colonel, and we'll decide together."

"And if you don't like his ideas?"

Victor shrugged. "He's senior to me—but I may be able to get around that."

"I hope so, sir," Blaise said.

"Oh, there are ways." Victor didn't go into detail. He didn't know what the details were, not yet. But he knew there would be ways. If you were determined enough, you could always find them.

When he approached the young English lieutenant-colonel (*Don't think of him as Charlie, or else you'll call him that, and then the sky will fall,* Victor told himself), that worthy said, "As I see things, Major, we have two choices. We can wait for the French regulars to join the settlers and then receive them on ground of our choosing.

Or we can try to defeat the settlers before the regulars arrive, the disadvantage being that we should have to move against their fortified position. Does that seem to you an accurate summation?"

"Those are two things we can do, certainly, sir," Radcliff replied. "I can think of others that might serve us better."

"Can you indeed?" The English officer raised an elegant eyebrow. He'd have a title of nobility one day, if he didn't already. "Would you be so good as to expatiate on them?"

*As to what?* Victor wondered. He was damned if he'd inquire, though. And he thought he knew what the Englishman had to mean. "We could send a raiding party into French territory by land through the backwoods," he said. "That way, we'd make the enemy dance to our tune instead of dancing to theirs."

"And who would command such a party?" the lieutenant-colonel asked. "You?"

"If you like, sir," Victor said. "I have done a lot of exploring in the interior. I know I could find plenty of men who wouldn't starve in the woods."

"Very well. That's one thing," the Englishman said. "You told me there were others, so I presume you have at least one more in mind."

"I do, sir," Victor Radcliff agreed. "We could take boats and land down the coast in French territory, do our raiding, and then either come back the way we went or go into the interior, depending on which seemed best."

The English officer studied him. "Again, I presume you would command this mission?"

"I'm suited for it. I don't know anyone who has a better chance of making it work," Victor said.

"Which would you do if you had the choice?"

"I believe I'd go in by land, sir," Victor said. "That way, we start giving the enemy a hard time all the sooner."

"You wouldn't take so large a party as to hurt our chances of defending against the French here?"

"Oh, heavens, no, sir! We couldn't victual that kind of party, anyhow," Victor said. "A relative handful of men, moving swiftly and raising havoc—that's what I've got in mind."

"I see." The lieutenant-colonel nodded. "Well, why don't you recruit such a party and set it in motion? I think you will do the French some harm with it, and I also suspect you won't be sorry to have me out of your hair." He gave the Atlantean a crooked grin.

Victor Radcliff grinned back. "That cuts both ways, unless I'm sadly mistaken. You won't be sorry I'm not nagging you any more."

"Who, me?" The English officer gave back a look of exaggerated innocence. "Ah, if only we were on the same side!" They both laughed. Radcliff stuck out his hand. The lieutenant-colonel took it. What began as a clasp ended up a trial of strength. They were still laughing when they broke it off, neither sure who had won or if anybody had.

Whatever Roland Kersauzon had been expecting in a French general, Louis-Joseph, Marquis de Montcalm-Gozon, wasn't it. He had fair, curly hair, blue eyes, a cupid's-bow mouth, and the beginnings of a double chin. He also had an illustrious pedigree on both sides of his family. With shortcomings like those, Roland should have hated him on sight.

He should have, but he didn't. Despite the marquis' failings of appearance and birth, two things were plain. He was an honest man: if he weren't, he wouldn't have been a soldier, and he wouldn't have let himself get sent to Atlantis. And he *was* a soldier, all the way down to the tips of his elegantly manicured fingers.

"You did well to beat them once," he told Roland.

"Pitting raw troops against regulars is a dangerous business, but you got by with it. Now there are regulars on your side as well. We should take advantage of it."

"*Oui, Monsieur,*" was all Roland could manage, as if he were a raw recruit himself. A general from the mother country who actually wanted to fight! No, Roland hadn't expected that. Oh, Braddock had wanted to fight, but he'd made a hash of it. Kersauzon didn't think this much younger Frenchman would.

"We'd better win soon," Montcalm-Gozon added. "If we don't, I doubt we shall win later. The trouble we had getting men across the sea once . . . I doubt we'll try it again. If we do, I doubt we'll succeed. The English are alert now. They have more ships than we do, and better sailors. They can bring more soldiers to Atlantis any time they choose. We are not so lucky."

"They have more settlers, too," Roland said. "It seems strange, and most unfair. France is a larger country than England. But England has more ships and more folk who want to live here. Where is the justice in that, I ask you?"

"France is more sufficient unto herself than England," said the general from the mother country. "England needs to draw more things from the sea, and from across the sea. And her poor peasants come here or go to Terranova to find something better than they have at home. Try to convince a French peasant that there is anything better than what he has at home. He will laugh in your face for your trouble."

"It is a pity," Roland said.

"Many things are," Montcalm-Gozon agreed. "Now—I understand a fieldwork ahead troubles your line of advance. I should like to go forward with you and reconnoiter, if you don't mind."

"But of course, *Monsieur.*" To say anything else would have left Kersauzon open to an imputation of cowardice. "May I offer one suggestion first?"

"I would be delighted to hear it."

"Put on the habiliments of a common soldier. Drawing attention to yourself without reason is the height of foolishness, and some of the riflemen in this fort can hit a target at a startling range."

The marquis frowned. "I mislike doing such a thing. After all, I am who I am. Do you intend to do the same?"

"I do. It is not lack of courage that provokes me, *Monsieur.* But I do not care to entrust the campaign to my second-in-command. If you feel otherwise . . . Well, in that case you will do as you please."

They approached the makeshift earthwork in ordinary clothes. Louis-Joseph proved a fine horseman. Roland might have known he would. The nobleman eyed the countryside with keen interest. "Such curious plants! My botanical friends in Paris would be most intrigued."

"I believe it, your Excellency," Roland replied. "I have heard that the natural productions of Terranova are more like Europe's than are those of Atlantis."

"I have heard the same," Montcalm-Gozon said. "I believed it before I came here. Now I am convinced of it."

"I wonder why it should be so. Terranova is farther from Europe than Atlantis is," Roland said.

The marquis shrugged. "You ask the wrong man. Perhaps the savants I mentioned might find an explanation for you. Me myself, however? No, I regret to say. I am but a simple soldier."

A soldier he was, indubitably. Simple? Roland Kersauzon smiled to himself. He'd heard men mock themselves before. He knew the peril of taking one of them seriously when he did.

Montcalm-Gozon would have ridden right up to the fort if a musketeer inside hadn't fired a warning shot in his direction. That was only a smoothbore piece, and didn't come particularly close. It did say the green-coated men inside would pay more attention if the French officers didn't desist.

"Well sited, well made," Montcalm-Gozon murmured, more than half to himself. "Yes, I can see that it would be an obstacle."

"How do we get around—or get through?" Roland asked.

"They seem light on artillery," the French general replied. "If we cannonade them, it could be that soldiers might break in under cover of the bombardment. It seems to me worth a try, in any case. My own artillery train is considerably more extensive than yours."

"Let's prepare, then." Roland Kersauzon was glad French regulars would share the butcher's bill with his men. It would be high if things went wrong. He caught motion from the corner of his eye. "A messenger! I wonder what he wants."

He didn't wonder long. The man delivered his news in a staccato burst: "The damned English have sent a raiding party—or maybe an army—over the border to the west. They are stealing and burning and committing God only knows what other outrages besides."

Roland swore. So did Montcalm-Gozon. Expecting the English to sit around waiting for trouble would not do. They wanted to go out and cause it instead. Now locals and regulars had to figure out what to do about that.

# XX

War was wicked and evil and woeful. So the Good Book insisted. War brought pain and misery and suffering. So anyone with an eye to see could tell. War ruined hopes and buried young men and sent years of patient toil up in smoke.

And when everything that went up in smoke belonged to the enemy, when he hurt and was miserable and suffered, war could be a devil of a lot of fun. So Victor Radcliff discovered as his band of brigands swooped down on one plantation after another.

No border guards tried to keep them out of the French settlements in Atlantis. Maybe there were guards farther east, but not where he broke in. It wasn't far from the place where he and Blaise and the two copperskins from Terranova had escaped the untender welcome of the French settlers. Victor wondered what had happened to the Frenchmen who'd been here then. They were probably with the army south of Freetown.

"Your old master anywhere around here?" he asked Blaise.

The Negro shook his head. "No, sir. Farther south."

"We're far enough south already. Too far, by God," a raider said, wiping sweat from his face with his sleeve. By his accent, he came from Croydon or one of the other towns north of Hanover. No, he wouldn't be used to weather like this, especially not in November. Ferns here sprouted from the sides of stone fences—sometimes from the sides of stone buildings. Barrel trees grew in abundant profusion. Lizards as long as a man's leg scurried through the undergrowth. Some of the snakes were big enough to eat men.

And Victor asked, "Are there crocodiles in the rivers down where you were?"

"Oh, yes." Blaise nodded matter-of-factly. "But crocodiles in Africa, too. Be careful, mostly no trouble."

"Mostly?" The man who came from somewhere near Croydon didn't sound reassured.

"Life is life," Blaise said with a shrug. "Mostly no trouble as good as it gets. The French now, they has mostly got trouble."

His grammar stumbled—on purpose?—but he wasn't wrong. Barns and plantation houses went up in flames. The raiders hadn't come to set black and copperskinned slaves free, but they didn't stop them from plundering and taking off for the north.

"Why do you do this?" an old woman asked Victor as a stately home where her family might have lived for generations burned to the ground. "Have I ever done anything to you, *Monsieur*?"

He bowed. "By no means. But an army of French settlers—and, by now, I daresay, French regulars as well—has invaded lands that belong to my king and my countrymen. Shall we let them get by with that without repaying it where and as we can?"

"Go fight these other soldiers, then. They have wronged you, it could be. I have done you no harm." The old woman started to cry. "Ruins! Everything ruins!"

Victor didn't know whether the redcoats and English settlers below Freetown were strong enough to fight the French straight up. He knew the force he commanded wasn't strong enough to do anything of the sort. But he knew some other things, too. "If we make your settlements howl," he said, "your generals will have to leave the land they invaded and come back to defend their own."

"What good does that do me?" the woman howled as the roof on the house collapsed in a shower of sparks.

It did her no good at all, as Victor knew. But that wasn't his worry. He aimed to make all the French settlements howl the way she did. With the small force at his disposal, that might have been more than he could reasonably expect to do. If you thought small, though, you wouldn't end up with much.

"March on!" he shouted to his men, and march they did.

Some of the plantations had young women on them, as well as or instead of old ones. Some unfortunate things happened—the young women would surely have agreed. Victor tried a couple of soldiers at drumhead courts-martial, and hanged them when they were convicted. Afterwards, those kinds of outrages stopped . . . or, if they didn't, the offenders got more careful. As Blaise said, mostly no trouble was about as much as you could hope for.

"Why you slay them?" the Negro asked. "They hurt enemy, too."

"Rape is a crime even when a soldier does it," Radcliff said.

"You think the French, they don't fuck English women?" With a limited vocabulary, Blaise could be very blunt.

"They probably do," Victor answered with a sigh. "But if they get caught, French officers will punish them. They use the same laws of war we do."

"Laws of war." As before when he heard that phrase,

Blaise was bemused. "You white people plenty smart, but sometimes I think you crazy, too."

"Maybe we are. But if we're all crazy the same way, it evens out," Victor Radcliff said.

Some of the French were crazy in a different way: crazy enough to try to fight back against half a regiment's worth of men. They paid for their folly. Victor made a point of ensuring that they wound up dead. He also made a point—though a quieter one—of looking the other way when his men took their women in among the trees.

"Maybe you not so crazy after all," Blaise remarked.

"Maybe not," Victor said with a sigh. "Or maybe the extent to which I am a beast marks the extent to which I am a sane man."

The Negro frowned. "Don't understand that."

"Don't trouble your head about it." Radcliff set a hand on his shoulder. "I'm not sure I understand it, either. I'm not sure I want to understand it."

His raiders pushed east and south, in the direction of the ocean. He didn't expect to wash his hands in the Atlantic. Pretty soon, the French would scrape together enough militiamen to bar his way. The farther east the English went, the more towns and villages they ran into. And towns and villages had lots of men in them. Men with muskets hastily pressed into service didn't make the best soldiers. But Victor was uneasily aware his own men had been amateurs not long before. If you lived through a couple of skirmishes, you got an idea of what needed doing.

Again, Blaise had his own idea of what needed doing. "Should say all niggers here free, *M'sieu* Victor. Copperskins, too. You get more fighters. And the French settlers, they can't do a thing without those people."

He was bound to be right about that. Slowly, Victor said, "I have no orders to do any such thing."

"Why you need orders?" Blaise demanded.

"If we win this war, I think England will take away the French settlements in Atlantis," Victor said. "Maybe the Spanish settlements, too."

"And so?" Blaise cared nothing for that. "Most niggers and copperskins are free in English lands now."

"Slavery makes no money up in the north. The crops won't support it," Victor replied. "Things are different here. How can you raise cotton or indigo or rice or even pipeweed without plantations? How can you have plantations without slaves?"

Blaise looked at him—looked through him, really. "We don't use money in Africa. Maybe we lucky. You put money ahead of free?"

"If all the slaves down here are suddenly freed, everyone in these parts is liable to starve, Negroes and Terranovans and whites alike," Victor said.

"Pay people to work the farms," Blaise said. "They do it, I bet."

"It could be," Victor admitted. "Say it is."

"Then everybody free!" Blaise exclaimed.

"Maybe. Or maybe everyone is free to starve. Paying workers costs more than keeping slaves. If there is no profit, the plantations go to ruin," Victor said.

Blaise was a shrewd man, no two ways about it. "Make people who buy from them pay more," he said.

"And all the plantations in Terranova will undersell us, so we go to the dogs just the same. They grow cotton and rice and indigo in India, too, and I hear they will grow pipeweed there soon," Radcliff said.

"I hear about Terranova," Blaise said. "Where is this India place?"

"Beyond Terranova and an ocean—on the far side of the world."

"More world than ever I think," the Negro said. "Terranova, yes, I hear some about it—copperskins' talk, you know. They use slaves in this India place?"

"I have no idea." Victor Radcliff had never worried about it. All he knew about India was that it was supposed to be rich, and it had tigers and elephants. He'd seen a tiger once, in a zoological garden some high-minded cousin had set up in Hanover. It looked hungry. It looked angry, too, prowling its too-small cage and lashing its tail.

But Blaise persisted: "If they don't use slaves, how you say we need slaves?"

"All I said was, I don't have the authority to free slaves," Victor answered. "Politicians have to do that sort of thing; soldiers can't. I can tell slaves to run off—that's a measure of war. Freeing them is more than I can do."

"I have reason the first time," Blaise said, which showed he still knew more French than English. "White people *are* crazy."

Despite cold rain and mud, French regulars marched in perfectly dressed ranks and columns, just like English redcoats. And, as the French settlers had maneuvered the redcoats into a trap, so the English settlers tried to return the disfavor. Their fort had fallen, but they sniped at the French from whatever cover they could find. And they refused to fight fixed battles.

"What ridiculous excuse for warfare is this?" Montcalm-Gozon demanded indignantly.

"It is what I warned you to expect," Roland Kersauzon replied. "They fear your men would win in any stand-up fight—"

"As we would," the commander from the mother country broke in.

"Oh, no doubt, *Monsieur,*" Roland said politely. He didn't want to argue with the nobleman. That didn't necessarily mean he thought Montcalm-Gozon was right. His settlers had shocked the English redcoats. Maybe the English settlers could do the same to French regulars.

"As I said before, this is curious country," Montcalm-Gozon remarked. "Where it is settled, it seems European enough. Where people do not dwell, though, the plants and animals are quite different. Now and then you will see a familiar tree or bush or animal living amongst the native oddities, but only now and then."

"In my grandfather's day, I am told, you would never have seen such a thing. Settlements then were smaller and stuck closer to the coast," Roland said. "Since those days, we have brought in more plants and animals that suit us. Deer and foxes roam the forests now. Rats and mice infest our homes and barns. Cats hunt them—and whatever else they can find. Dogs run wild, too. So do chickens and our ducks and Terranovan turkeys."

"So you believe the native productions will vanish?" Montcalm-Gozon asked. "A pity to see sameness imposed on the world."

"I am, I hope, a modern man, your Excellency," Kersauzon said. "If that which comes from Europe or from Terranova serves our needs better than Atlantis' native productions, why should we not have it? In the early days here, men feared to go outdoors, because red-crested eagles might slam into them from behind and chew at their kidneys as the vulture chewed at Prometheus' liver. Now those flying monsters are few and far between, and I confess I miss them not a pin." He remembered how horrified he'd been when an eagle attacked one of his settlers.

"Once, lions hunted in Greece. Not so long ago, wolves prowled everywhere in France," Montcalm-Gozon said. "Now the lions are gone, the wolves grown scarce. I agree: this is better. But will the innocuous go by the wayside along with the dangerous? That, I believe, would be unfortunate."

"It could be so," Roland said. "Will you eat beef or mutton at supper tonight?"

"Either will do," the Frenchman replied. "Why do you ask?"

"The cattle and sheep are imports, too. So are the horses we ride," Roland said.

"As you observed, they are useful." Before Montcalm-Gozon could go on, several muskets barked from the—mostly native—woods. A French regular yelled. A profane lieutenant ordered a troop of men to go after the ambushers, and not to come back without the degenerates' tripes on their bayonets. The soldiers charged in amongst the trees.

"They won't catch them," Roland predicted mournfully.

"And why are you so sure? They are excellent men," the marquis said.

"They are excellent men standing in a battle line and beating down another battle line," Roland Kersauzon answered. "Unless some of them were poachers or robbers before they put on the uniform, what do they know about chasing woodsmen through the forest?"

Montcalm-Gozon only shrugged. "What do these Atlantean rats know about getting chased by Frenchmen?"

They knew enough to get away. The regulars came out of the woods without any enemy soldiers, alive or dead, in their grasp and with hangdog expressions on their faces. Their worst casualty was a sprained ankle. Two of them supported the man, who proved to have tripped over a root. The injured soldier went into a casualty wagon, along with the regulars the English settlers had shot. The interrupted march resumed.

"Not a good business," Montcalm-Gozon grumbled.

"Certainly not, *Monsieur.*" Roland could hardly disagree with that. Adding *I told you so* would have been rude. A slightly superior manner conveyed the message just as well: they were both French, after all.

Another rider came up with more news of devastation from the south. Montcalm-Gozon heard him out, stony-faced. Roland tried to match the noble's dispassion, but it wasn't easy. To the man from across the sea, the plantations destroyed and the people killed or dispossessed were only pieces on the board. To Roland, the estates belonged to kinsmen and friends and acquaintances. The losses were personal.

"It could be, your Excellency, that I might have to detach my native soldiers to pursue this marauding *salaud* of a Radcliff," he said.

"That would disturb the primary goal of this campaign, which is to seize Freetown," Montcalm-Gozon said with a frown.

"Ensuring that the French settlements in Atlantis are not destroyed is also an important goal, *n'est-ce pas?*" Kersauzon returned.

"Feh." The French general raised a hand. "The English attempt a nuisance raid, nothing more. If we weaken our striking force to contain them, we play into their hands."

He had a point, and Roland knew it. Nevertheless, he quoted Matthew: " 'For what is a man profited, if he shall gain the whole world, and lose his own soul?' "

Montcalm-Gozon aimed an unfriendly look his way. "I have to think of this struggle as part of one that goes on all over the world. We fight England in Europe, and in India, and in Terranova, as well as on these shores."

"France fights England all over the world," Roland Kersauzon said. "*I* fight England here. I have to think of what is best and what is worst for the French settlements in Atlantis."

"What is best for them is what is best for France," the marquis insisted.

"Not necessarily," Roland replied. Now they aimed glares at each other. Montcalm-Gozon looked ready to aim a pistol at Roland as well. The Atlantean did not want to fight the French commander, and not only because he had no idea what would happen in a duel. Even if he won a duel against Montcalm-Gozon, he lost. So it seemed to him, at any rate.

In icy tones, Montcalm-Gozon said, "You had better explain yourself."

"If we take Freetown, you win a grand and glorious victory for France," Kersauzon said. "Then, very likely, you and your regulars sail away. If the English destroy everything we've built up farther south, what good does your grand and glorious victory do us?"

"They cannot," the French nobleman said, but with an uncertain edge to his voice.

"If my soldiers accompany yours, marching away from the enemy invasion, what the devil will stop them?" Roland asked.

"You are a difficult man."

"Only to my enemies . . . *Monsieur*." Roland bowed in the saddle.

"Will half your men suffice to deal with these raiders?" Montcalm-Gozon inquired after a sour sigh.

They spent the next twenty minutes haggling, as if Roland were trying to squeeze a few extra sous from the nobleman at the fish market. Montcalm-Gozon finally consented to let Roland have two-thirds of the soldiers he thought his by right anyway. Kersauzon wanted more—he wanted all of them. But he took as many men as he could without pistols at dawn. As you got older, you learned that sometimes you had to be satisfied with less than everything you wanted from life.

Roland's men burst into cheers when he told them that most of them would be heading south. They knew as much as he did about what was going on down there—rumors spread like wildfire. He wondered how long it would have been before they started deserting.

Not very, unless he didn't know them. He said nothing to Montcalm-Gozon about the cheers. The young marquis wasn't deaf. He could hear them, and draw his own conclusions.

What those conclusions were, he didn't discuss with Roland. And Kersauzon didn't ask him, either.

Messages took their own sweet time traveling from the English and local forces in front of Freetown and Victor Radcliff's raiders. He was on his own down in the French settlements. By the time he got news and reacted to it, it was badly out of date. And so he didn't worry—too much—when he heard that the locals and redcoats had fallen back into Freetown. What good did worry do?

The English lieutenant-colonel in charge of the defense had energy. Remembering another of Victor's suggestions, he sent a schooner full of men—mostly Atlanteans—down the coast to land behind the French force and waylay the supply wagons coming up to it. For a little while, his letters boasted of the havoc that little band was wreaking. *A fine piratical band,* he called them, perhaps not knowing that Victor's branch of the broad and spreading Radcliff(e) tree found nothing fine in piracy.

Then the English officer's tone changed. *I have not heard from the men sent south for some little while,* he wrote, *and fear they may have suffered a misfortune. God grant I be wrong.*

Further despatches showed only too clearly that he wasn't wrong. Something final had happened to the raiders. Victor *did* worry about them, though he led far more men than the English officer had committed to the secondary raid.

"They shouldn't have been snuffed out like that," he told Blaise. "They were too large a band to be extinguished like a candle with a brass lid over it."

"Maybe they run into more men," the Negro said. "Maybe more men run into they."

" 'Them,' " Radcliff corrected absently. "But with all the French fighting men up near Freetown . . ." His voice trailed off.

"What you thinking?" Blaise asked.

Victor didn't like any of what he was thinking. He heard what the French were doing up in English territory. Of course the enemy would hear what he was doing farther south in Atlantis. And this was their native land, just as the English settlements had spawned his raiders. If Roland Kersauzon decided not to sit back and let Victor's men ravage plantations down here . . . If, marching south, he'd brushed aside that schooner's worth of harassers . . .

"I'm thinking we may have more difficulties ahead of us than I looked for a little while ago," Victor answered.

Blaise frowned. "What you say?"

From a man who'd made his first acquaintance with the English language not long before, the question was reasonable. "French soldiers may be moving against us." Forced to simplify his own thoughts, Victor got a lot into a few words.

"Ah." Blaise understood him this time. "What we do?"

"Good question," Radcliff replied. He wished he had a good answer, simple or complex. He gave the truth, as best he could see it: "I don't know yet. Have to find out how many Frenchmen are moving. Can we fight them? Do we have to run? What then?"

"War here harder than war in Africa," Blaise said. "More things to think on."

*Of course. We're civilized,* was Victor Radcliff's first smug thought. But how civilized was war, no matter how you fought it? Not very, not so far as he could see. "We'll do the best we can, that's all," he said.

They went on. At the first plantation where the locals didn't flee fast enough, he stole horses to add to the
handful he already had. He sent riders out ahead of his
main body, to make sure no suddenly returning French
settlers surprised him. All the scouts he chose spoke fluent French. They could—and would—claim they were
refugees if anybody wondered what they were doing
riding around the countryside.

One of them winked at him before setting out. "If I
find me a tavernkeeper's pretty little daughter, I may
settle down right where I do," the man said. "In that
case, you'll never see me again."

A military commander of the official—and officious—
sort would have thrown a fit. Victor only laughed and
said, "Do as you please, Herbert. But if we find the tavern, you'd best believe we'll burn it down."

"God curse you English dogs to the most fiery pits of
hell," Herbert said hotly—his French was fluent indeed.
Victor Radcliff laughed again, slapped him on the back,
and sent him on his way.

In the back country, roads had been narrow, rutted
tracks through the trees. Some of them probably started
as honker trails. Victor knew that was so here and there
in the English settlements. As his men pushed into more
settled terrain, the roads got wider. The trees were cut
back from either side. The ruts remained. If anything,
they got deeper and muddier from greater use.

Parrots with yellow and orange faces squawked at the
advancing settlers. Blaise said, "Parrots in Africa, too.
These not just like, but close. Make me think of home
across sea."

"More of them here than farther north, though they
come up there, too," Victor said.

"*C'est curieux,*" Blaise remarked, and then, remembering his English, "Strange. Yes, strange. So many
things here, there not same. But parrots in this place and

in that place." He smiled, coming up with the right word: "In *both* places. Why?"

"Well, there are parrots in Terranova, too," Victor Radcliff said, "especially in the hot southern parts. Maybe that has something to do with it." *And maybe it doesn't,* he thought. Europe and northern Terranova shared many plants and animals or had similar forms where nothing remotely like them existed in Atlantis. Natural philosophers had spilled barrels of ink trying to explain why. As far as Victor knew, none of them had come close to a satisfactory solution. If they couldn't agree about why so much of Atlantis' flora and fauna was so peculiar, he wasn't likely to find the answer on his own.

He wasn't even likely to worry about it very long. A couple of muskets boomed up ahead. A high, shrill shout rose: *"Les Anglais!"*

The farm the French settlers fought to hold wouldn't have been worth burning if they hadn't defended it. But the families and friends who did their best to drive away the marauders couldn't have understood that. They battled with grim determination from farmhouses and outbuildings, and would neither retreat nor give up.

*"Cochons!"* one of them yelled from a barn. "This is our patrimony! You will not take it from us!"

No matter how fierce and stubborn they were, they had about as much chance of beating Radcliff's men as a five-year-old sent into the ring against a champion prize-fighter. A rifleman picked off the French farmers one after another from a furlong away. Less accurate musket fire made them keep their heads down. Raiders worked their way forward and torched building after building.

Fire drove out some of the French settlers. Others grimly died in the flames. The defenders wounded a handful of men. They delayed the English advance by less than an hour. Smelling the stink of charred flesh,

Victor shook his head. "Not worth it," he said. "Brave, but not worth it."

"Run is better," Blaise agreed. "Things just . . . things." He gestured. "Run. Get more things when more time go."

"Later." Victor gave him another new word. He also sent him a quizzical look. "So running is better, eh? You're not a brave man, eh? You could have fooled me."

"Brave when I have to. Brave if I have to," the Negro replied. "If I no have to, I run. Brave again later, maybe." His sly smile said he was showing off the new vocabulary on purpose.

"A redcoat or one of the French regulars would call you a coward for talk like that," Victor Radcliff said.

Blaise only shrugged. "Don't care. Live coward fix things. Dead brave fool . . ." He pointed toward the burning houses and outbuildings.

"Indeed," Victor said. Blaise raised a questioning eyebrow. "I should say so!" Victor exclaimed. Blaise nodded—he got that. Victor fought to hide a grin. The Negro sergeant was too dark and too lean to make a proper Falstaff himself, but he would have enjoyed drinking with him. They were both a particular kind of practical man.

Victor hadn't tried talking with Blaise about Falstaff, and not just because of the clown's views about honor. He would have had to quote Shakespeare to have it make sense to Blaise, and even then it wouldn't have made sense to him. Shakespeare had written only two lifetimes earlier, but English wasn't the same now as it had been then.

"In Africa," Victor said suddenly, "when old men talk about how their grandfathers talked and about how their grandsons talk, do they notice any difference?"

After some thought, Blaise answered, "They say

young boys have not enough—" He frowned, looking for a word. "Like slave for master," he offered.

"Respect," Radcliff suggested.

"Thank you, sir. Respect. Yes. They say young boys have not respect for old, like in their day."

Old men had been saying things like that since Adam started complaining about Cain and Abel. It wasn't what Victor meant. "Do they say the words now are different from the way they were in the old days?"

"I no hear that. I never hear that." Blaise shook his head.

"Oh, well." Victor shrugged. He wondered how much French had changed since Shakespeare's day. That might be an interesting question to ask Roland Kersauzon . . . if the two of them weren't otherwise occupied trying to blow each other's heads off.

Right now, that seemed unlikely.

Roland swept out his right arm. "There is another band of the accursed English brigands. Hunt them down!"

Baying like wolves, his soldiers swarmed after the flee-ing men from the English settlements. (The phrase oc-curred to Roland even though he'd never seen or heard a wolf. So many of the stories that came from France featured them. He could picture them plainly: bigger than dogs, shaped like foxes, but gray and ferocious.)

A few of the men who'd come south to disrupt the French army's supply lines still showed fight. Most of them, though, wanted no more than to get away with their lives. They'd had a high old time shooting team-sters and plundering wagons. They hadn't come down here to fight when the numbers weren't all in their favor. But when Kersauzon detached his settlers from Montcalm-Gozon's regulars, they had no trouble over-whelming the company or so of men kicking up trouble along the coast.

Muskets bellowed. Puffs of gray smoke marked where shooters stood. That familiar, sulfurous smell made Roland smile. But he wished gunpowder didn't so clearly point out every man who fired. If anyone ever devised a powder that didn't smoke, he would win a great advantage in war.

In the meantime, his men and the enemy used what they had. The English settlers fought from cover instead of standing in a neat line till they got shot down. That didn't change the result, but did make things take longer. Roland's men were settlers, too. They advanced by little skittering rushes. Some of them fired to keep the English busy while the others moved up.

At close quarters, it came to bayonets and swords and hatchets and knives and fists and teeth. Only a handful of English settlers surrendered. Cursed raiders they might be, but they had courage.

"You aren't supposed to be here, you damned nuisance," a wounded prisoner told Kersauzon.

"That is the best place to be, where you are not supposed to," the French commander replied. "Your friends thought so, *oui*?"

"Well, what if we did?" the prisoner said. "Jesus, this leg hurts. Nobody ever went and shot me before."

"*Quelle dommage,*" Roland said, as if he meant it.

"What will you do now?" the captive asked.

"Go on and give your other band of raiders, the larger one, the same kind of surprise we just gave you, if God grants that that be possible," Roland answered frankly. Why not? The prisoner wasn't going to escape, steal a horse, and gallop off to tell Victor Radcliff an army was coming after him. Such things happened in romances, but not in life.

"What will you do with *me*?" the man inquired. Maybe he'd meant that all along.

"Give you to the surgeons, of course," Kersauzon said.

"We are not barbarians, to torment you for the sport of it. We are French. You are English. We are all civilized men, is it not so?"

"Boy, I hope it is," the enemy muttered. Apprehensively, he went on. "What do you think the surgeons will do?"

"Remove the musket ball, unless they decide it is better left alone. This happens sometimes, but not often."

"Remove it? Easy for you to say. It's not your leg. Will they give me whiskey to drink and a bullet to bite on?"

"We use rum and a leather strap," Roland said.

"Rum will do," the English settler said eagerly. He didn't compare the effectiveness of the bullet and the strap.

"Rum you shall have," Kersauzon promised. He gestured to the prisoner's guards. "Take him away."

Away the man went. Wounded French settlers were already howling under the surgeons' ministrations. Roland couldn't distinguish the prisoner's cries of torment from those of his own troops. Wounded men all made the same noises.

Roland wished he wouldn't have had to waste time dealing with the seaborne raiders. They were only a nuisance . . . though Montcalm-Gozon, whose supply of victuals they'd interrupted, probably would have expressed a different view. Roland didn't care about the fancy French nobleman's opinions here. Neither did the men who followed him. They knew too well what Victor Radcliff's bandits were doing to the property and persons of people who mattered to them. They aimed to stop the bandits as soon as they could.

He wondered whether, had he loosed his men as raiders, they could have wreaked as much havoc on the English settlements as the enemy was doing down here. Regretfully, he decided it was unlikely. Up in English-held territory, farms were smaller, villages were more common, and people lived closer to one another. The English had a better chance of mustering a scratch force that could slow up raiders—and raiders who had to slow up were raiders in trouble.

None of the anguished messages coming out of the southwest made him think the English settlers had had to slow down much. If they wanted to, they could probably go all the way down into the subtropical settlements that belonged to the King of Spain.

Kersauzon blinked. If the English did invade the Spanish settlements, what should he do about it? Spain and France were allied against England in the European war. They were allies here, too—in theory. But Roland would have been most affronted—which was putting it mildly—had Spanish soldiers entered the French settlements. No doubt the Spanish authorities (assuming they woke up from their long, long siestas) would be just as unhappy about French settlers fighting on their steaming soil.

And yet the Spaniards were probably even thinner on the ground than the French. Victor Radcliff brigands could do a lot of damage down there. Who would stop them? Anybody?

"A messenger!" Roland shouted. He had paper and ink and a quill with him at all times: the responsibility that went with command. He was already writing when a young horseman came up and waited expectantly.

"What do you need, *Monsieur*?" the rider asked.

"Take a letter to his Excellency, *Don* José Valverde, the governor-general of Spanish Atlantis, in Gernika. You also need to know what it says, in case it should be damaged. I am asking *Don* José for permission to follow the English raiders into his territory if they go that way. I have no designs against Spanish Atlantis: I aim only to destroy the raiders. Give me that back, if you would be so kind."

After several tries, the messenger had it straight. Roland sealed the letter (sealing wax being another essential for a man of his position) and handed it to him. Sketching a salute, the youngster rode off to the south.

*Gernika,* Roland thought. He'd never been there himself. He didn't want to deal with the Spaniards under these circumstances. What you wanted, though, and what you got . . .

# XXI

*E*ven the trees down here were strange. Some barrel trees dwarfed barrels—and men. Others had round trunks full of sweet sap. Victor Radcliff had already enjoyed the rumlike drink the French and especially the Spaniards brewed from it.

Conifers were different, too. In floral wreaths, cypress meant mourning. Here in southern Atlantis, cypresses just grew. Locals used the timber in their buildings, even if it wasn't as good as pine or redwood. The farther south Victor and his men went, the more mossy beards hung from cypress branches.

And the more snakes lurked in the trees and in the undergrowth. One of the raiders was bitten; he died in short order despite having the wound cauterized and being given all the rum he could drink to keep his heart strong.

Some of the snakes had rattles at the ends of their tails, like many of the venomous serpents Victor knew farther north. Again like those farther north, some shook their tails before striking but had no rattles to warn their victims. And some simply skulked and struck. Some were probably harmless, but after the death Victor's followers weren't inclined to take chances. If it slithered and they saw it, it died.

"Do they have poisonous snakes in Africa, too?" Radcliff asked Blaise.

"Oh, yes. Here, you don't have—" The Negro used a word in his own language. He drew a picture of the kind of snake he had in mind in the dirt. He used a twig with a confidence a lot of sketch artists might have envied. That broad flare behind the head . . .

"That must be a cobra," Victor said. "They also have them in India, I believe. People there tame them and teach them to dance to music."

"You see this? You know it is so?" Blaise asked.

"Well . . . no," Victor admitted.

"Then it is a lie, I bet." Blaise sounded very sure of himself. He was willing—no, eager—to explain why, too: "Mess with these, uh, cobras, you have to be mad. Crazy. Cray-zee." He liked the sound of that word.

"I won't tell you you're wrong," Victor Radcliff said. "It seems crazy to me, too. But people do crazy things sometimes."

"You cray-zee with cobra snakes, you are not cray-zee long." Blaise spoke with great conviction. Radcliff suspected he knew what he was talking about. Anybody who spent too much time fooling around with venomous serpents of any kind was taking his life in his own hands—and its fangs.

His scouts reported that the French settlers were moving against his men from the northeast, as he'd suspected they might. They had more men than he did: he was sure of that. Since he didn't think he could meet them on even terms, he saw only two choices. He could try to ambush them, or he could avoid meeting them at all.

Had they been the regulars from France, he would

have tried an ambush. One had worked against Braddock's redcoats; another might well work here. But not
against other settlers. They knew the tricks of the trade
as well as Victor's men. Since this was their country, they
probably knew them better.

Avoid, then. Down the tracks that led south toward
the Spanish settlements he went. Those tracks were truly
wretched. Most of the real roads in the French settlements ran from east to west, from the seacoast to the interior. The same was also true in the English settlements,
but to a smaller degree. With far more people starting
to crowd a similar amount of land, the northern settlements needed and had a real road network.

Now the English settlers plundered more thoroughly
and didn't burn till after they'd robbed. They'd eaten up
the supplies they'd brought with them, and were living
off the countryside. Radcliff had known that would happen. It worried him all the same.

"What do we do if they burn in front of us?" Blaise
asked one hot, sweaty afternoon. It was early spring, but
it felt like what would have been high summer in New
Hastings or Hanover.

Blaise had unerringly put his finger on Victor's greatest fear. "We starve," the commander answered.

"Ah." Maybe Blaise hadn't expected anything that
blunt. On the other hand, maybe he had. He showed
only what he wanted to show.

The French settlers didn't burn their own homes and
plantations to keep Victor's force from moving forward.
Maybe they didn't think of it. Or maybe they were simply less ruthless than Radcliff and his colored sergeant.
If they were, he wanted to make them pay for it.

He discovered he'd left French Atlantis and entered
Spanish Atlantis when the lordlet whose house he'd just
burned cursed him in most impure Castilian—actually,
in the hissing Andalusian dialect more commonly used

here and in Terranova. Victor surprised the hidalgo by returning the uncompliments in the same language.

"Why do you do these things to me?" the Spaniard cried, looking disconsolately from the English settlers running off his livestock to his house going up in flames.

"Our kings are at war," Victor answered with a shrug.

"You are one of the settlers from the north," the Spaniard said. "I thought you had no king."

"England has a king, just as Spain has a king," Victor replied. "If the King of England wars against the King of Spain, that makes the two of us enemies." The English settlements in Atlantis, Victor reflected, remembered their loyalty to King George only when England warred against France or Spain. The rest of the time, the settlers were more inclined to complain about how England didn't want them making things on their own or trading with other realms instead of buying from the mother country.

None of that mattered a farthing to the Spaniard. He saw his property burning and being stolen. "You offered no resistance," Radcliff told him. "We spare your life because you didn't. You can rebuild. You can start over."

The Spaniard bowed, which didn't hide the hatred smoldering in his eyes. "I hope you do not put yourself out too much, *Señor,* with this generous favor you grant me," he said. "If ever we meet again, maybe I will do the same for you—but it would not be wise to count on such a thing."

"Then I won't." Victor touched a finger to the brim of his hat. "*Hasta la vista, Señor,* and we shall see who does what to whom if we should run across each other again."

"Whoever sees the other man first will do it," the Spaniard said, which struck Victor Radcliff as all too likely.

\*          \*          \*

Roland Kersauzon had heard that Englishmen complained Frenchmen moved too slowly to suit them. He thought the English settlers were jittery fools; Frenchmen moved at just the proper pace, as anyone but a fool could see. But, to him, the Spaniards seemed to have inbred with the fist-sized snails that gnawed on ferns and barrel trees down here in the south. The snails were excellent with garlic butter. Their speed, however—and that of his Excellency, *Don* José Valverde, of Spanish Atlantis—left something to be desired.

"Why does he not answer?" Kersauzon grumbled to anyone who would listen—and to people who got sick of listening.

God only knew what horrors the English settlers were wreaking on Spanish Atlantis. Well, actually, that wasn't quite true. Roland had a pretty good notion: the same kinds of horrors they'd inflicted on French Atlantis. And yet the Spaniards promised that, if he presumed to enter their territory without *Don* José's leave, they would fight him as hard as they fought the English, or even harder.

He believed them. Such idiocy perfectly suited Spanish notions of honor. Were they doing what was advantageous to them? Such a thought never entered their heads. They were doing what a hidalgo ought to do, as they saw it. Past that, as best he could tell, they didn't think at all.

He wished the Devil would bread *Don* José Valverde and fry him for a cutlet over the hottest fire in hell. Satan had to keep a special chamber or firepit in which to torment people who wouldn't answer their mail.

Roland knew too well that he couldn't linger too much longer hard by the border of Spanish Atlantis. Keeping his army fed wouldn't be easy. And, pretty soon, malaria and bloody fluxes and maybe even the dreaded yellow jack would break out. A force the size of his needed to keep moving if it was to stay healthy, especially in this miserable climate.

But if he went away, who won? Victor Radcliff did, damn his black heart. *He* had no compunction about roving through Spanish Atlantis. He wandered as he pleased, destroying whatever got in his way. And he didn't need to wait for permission from *Don* José blasted Valverde!

"We ought to boot these Spanish guards out of the way and do what we need to do," one of Roland's lieutenants said.

"And then we would be fighting the English and the Spaniards for the rest of the war," Kersauzon answered gloomily. "And the Spaniards *would* fight us, too. Never doubt it for a minute. They understand spite. They don't understand much else, God knows, but they understand spite."

After what seemed forever and was really a week later than he'd hoped, a horseman finally came up from Gernika. Roland almost dragged him out of the saddle. The rider presented him with a letter gorgeous with multicolored ribbons and seals. When the Spaniards made something official, they made it *official.*

All of which mattered not two pins to Roland. "What does the miserable thing say?" he demanded.

"*Monsieur,* I have no idea," the fellow replied. "Another fellow gave it to me and said, 'Here. Take it on to the French commander.' "

"Oh," was all Roland said to that. It sounded more deadly than an hour's worth of inspired profanity.

He got a little satisfaction from tearing off the ribbons and cracking all the seals. Then he unfolded the letter. Some secretary must have written it; the handwriting was improbably perfect. The French in which it was written was also perfect—even a governor on a distant shore needed a decent command of the language of diplomacy.

And the letter was perfectly infuriating. *With all due respect to the French commander,* the governor of Spanish Atlantis wrote, *I am confident we shall be able to treat these English marauders as they deserve without requiring assistance from him or his men. Therefore, while appreciating his generous offer, I must decline it. I of course remain his most obedient servant....* The fancy squiggle under the body of the letter probably came from *Don* José's own hand.

"What *does* it say, *Monsieur*?" the horseman asked.

"It says that the governor of Spanish Atlantis is a God-cursed fool, that's what," Roland answered. "If he hadn't used such rough paper, I would wipe my backside with it, and better than it deserves, too. As is ..." He tore the letter in two and let it fall to the ground with the bits of ribbon and wax. Then he ground the pieces under his heel and stalked away.

His officers exclaimed in amazement and fury when he gave them the news. "The Spaniards couldn't catch the pox in a brothel!" one of them exclaimed. "How do they think they'll catch the English settlers? And why do they think they'll beat them even if they do catch them?"

"I have no answers for this," Roland said. "Sometimes, observing another man's stupidity, you find yourself compelled to admire it. You want to watch and see exactly how it leads him to disaster. This seems to me to be one of those times."

"What do we do now?" the captain asked.

Kersauzon made hand-washing motions, as if he were Pontius Pilate. "If *Don* José doesn't want our aid, he won't get it. I intend to leave some of our men here near the border. If the English settlers come back—no, *when* they come back—our soldiers can slow them down till we bring more troops to bear. With the rest, I aim to go north again. Montcalm-Gozon, at least, has the sense to know we men of French Atlantis are worth something."

"The Spaniard will find out," the captain said. "He'll also find out his own men have not the value of a counterfeit sou."

"Yes, I do believe he will." Roland Kersauzon spoke with the anticipation any man might show while contemplating the discomfiture of someone he despised. A slow smile spread across his face. "And soon, too."

A company of Spanish settlers formed a line of battle, ready to stop the English invaders if they could. Victor Radcliff didn't want to show all of his men at once, for fear of making the Spaniards run away. He brought them forward out of the woods a few at a time. After exchanging a volley or two with the enemy with roughly even numbers, he could show more of his hand.

"Will you look at those old-fashioned buggers!" he said, staring at the swarthy soldiers a couple of hundred yards away.

"How do you mean?" Blaise asked—a handy question that fit almost any situation.

"Why, their officers are wearing helmets," Victor answered. "A couple of them even have corselets—back-and-breasts. Armor."

"Good idea, no?" Blaise said.

"Good idea, yes—if you're fighting savages without guns," Victor said. The Spanish *conquistadores* had gone through the copperskinned natives of Terranova like a dose of salts. But that was a long time ago now. No European armies used armor any more—armor stout enough to turn bullets was also heavy enough to slow a man down and make him uncomfortable.

And in this weather ... If those Spaniards weren't stewing inside their fancy ironmongery, he couldn't imagine why not. He wore linen and wool, and felt stuck in a pot waiting for a housewife to throw in the onions. The Spaniards really did encase themselves in metal.

His men started banging away at them without waiting to form a neat line. He doubted the enemy would find that sporting, but it wasn't his worry. And the gunpowder smoke screened the reinforcements he ordered out of the woods.

The Spaniards were brave. They tried to advance against his musketry, and didn't seem to understand why it kept getting heavier. More and more of them fell. They didn't break, though, till he sent horsemen around their flanks. That did it. Like a lot of inexperienced troops, they were as wary as so many virgins about flank attacks.

His men didn't pursue very far. They plundered the enemy dead and did what they could for the living. Victor was relieved to find the English hadn't lost more than a handful of soldiers. He couldn't afford heavy losses, because he couldn't imagine how the English settlements would reinforce him way the devil down here.

Way the devil down here . . . When the phrase first crossed his mind, it was more one of annoyance than anything else. But Old Scratch would have felt right at home in this part of Atlantis. If hell wasn't like this hot, steamy, swampy, snake-infested place, Satan was missing a trick.

Blaise had a furrow on his left arm where a bullet had grazed him. He hissed when a surgeon poured rum on the wound. "Stings, don't it?" the surgeon said cheerfully—*his* arm was fine.

"Yes," Blaise ground out through clenched teeth.

"Got to get it clean if I can," the white man said. "Down here, a wound'll fester easy as you please."

Victor hadn't thought of that. One more reason for Satan to set up shop in Spanish Atlantis. He went over to a prisoner. "You can't beat us, you know," he said in his bad Spanish.

The captive only shrugged. "God was against us," he said. A bloody bandage covered one ear, or more likely where the ear had been.

"You can go home if you want to," Radcliff told him. The Spaniard went from dejected to suspicious in one fell swoop. Victor went on, "You can. Tell people not to fight us any more, that's all. If they don't fight, we take what we want but we don't hurt people. If they do fight, we make them sorry."

"Even if I tell them, they won't listen to me," the Spaniard predicted with the gloom so common in his folk.

"They listen to our muskets. They listen to our bayonets," Victor said. A dead Spaniard lay on the ground not far away. He'd been gutted like a trout. A bayonet was the last thing he'd ever heard.

"If you are crazy enough to let me go, I will say what you want me to say," the prisoner said. He was eyeing the dead Spaniard, too. "But I promise nothing. If the fighting keeps on, *no tengo la culpa*."

"Yes, I know it won't be your fault," Victor said. "Go on, though. You won't be the only one we turn loose to spread the word."

Something shrewd glinted in the captive's dark, liquid eyes. "If we go, you don't have to feed us. You don't have to doctor us. You don't have to bring us along . . . or kill us if we get in the way or make trouble."

He was right on every count. Victor Radcliff smiled. "Yes? And so?" he said blandly.

"You are an Englishman. But you are not a stupid Englishman, are you?" the Spaniard said.

"I hope not," Victor replied. With a thoughtful nod, the prisoner got to his feet and left the field. An English settler looked back toward Victor, who nodded and waved for him to let the Spaniard go. With a shrug that might have matched the prisoner's earlier one for fatalism, the sentry did.

Radcliff preached the doctrine of nonresistance to other Spaniards and sent them off to the east, too. That done, he went back to see how Blaise fared. The Negro stood there opening and closing his fist, making sure all the tendons still worked the way they were supposed to.

"Not too bad," Radcliff ventured.

"No, not too. But nobody ever shooted me before." Blaise's grammar still sometimes left a bit to be desired. He looked down at the bandage the surgeon had given him. "It will make a brave scar, though." Was that more of his eccentric English, or did he mean exactly what he'd said? Victor wasn't sure.

"Did you pay back the man who did it?" Victor asked.

The Negro nodded. "Oh, yes, sir. That him there." He pointed to the gutted Spaniard. "I am a blooded warrior again."

"*He* won't argue with you—that's certain sure," Victor agreed. So Blaise won his warrior stripes whenever he killed somebody? Victor knew of white men—English, French, and Spanish— who shared the same attitude.

His little army couldn't stay in one place very long. It soon started eating the countryside bare. It moved on, plundering small farms and plantations the way it had all through French and Spanish Atlantis. Some of the hidalgos tried to fight back, others didn't. Maybe the released prisoners hadn't spread the word. Maybe the men defending their property just didn't want to listen. Spaniards could be as stubborn as Englishmen.

Two days later, Radcliff got a new surprise. His vanguard ran into Spaniards coming their way. The new arrivals weren't soldiers, but men, women, and children with no more than the clothes on their backs and whatever they could carry. "Save us!" they shouted when they saw the English soldiers.

They spoke Spanish, of course. "Hold fire!" Victor yelled, for the benefit of his men who didn't understand the language. "They're friendly!"

"Devil you say!" an unconvinced settler declared.

Ignoring him, Victor asked the nearest Spaniards, "Why do you need us to save you?"

"Because the slaves have risen up!" one of them cried. "The copperskins and the blacks, they want to kill us all!"

"What's that bugger going on about?" At least half a dozen men who spoke only English asked the same question in almost identical words. Instead of answering them right away, Victor Radcliff glanced over toward Blaise. The Negro knew some Spanish. By the predatory smile on his face, he knew plenty to understand that.

Heading up through French Atlantis toward the northern border and the war against the English settlements, Roland Kersauzon was not a happy man. He would gladly have sent *Don* José to hell or to London, whichever was worse. He'd known about Spanish arrogance before, but the refusal to let him enter Spanish Atlantis proved he hadn't known all about it.

He was more than halfway back to the war he'd left behind when a courier coming up from the south caught him from behind. The man looked to have ridden hard for a long time. He thrust a letter into Roland's hand. Roland stared at the fancy seals and ribbons bedizening it. "Don't tell me this is from—?"

*"Oui, Monsieur,"* the courier replied. "From his Excellency, the governor of Spanish Atlantis. I don't know what he says."

"I don't care what he says," Kersauzon growled. "I

might like to meet him with seconds, but any other way?
I think not."

"Do you want that, then?" The other horseman
pointed to the letter at the same time as he used his
other hand to pat his blowing mount's neck.

"Want it? Dear God, no!" Roland said. "But I
suppose—I suppose—I'd better read it anyway." He
took a certain satisfaction in ripping off the ribbons and
breaking the seals. If he tore the paper a little, too—well,
so what?

The first thing he saw when he opened the letter was
that the secretary hadn't written it. It was in *Don* José's
own cramped script, and began, *General Kersauzon,
please believe that I abase myself before you. With all my
heart, I beg you to return to the land that previously re-
jected the helping hand you put forward.*

"Well, well!" Roland said, and then again: "Well, well!
Here we do have something out of the ordinary!"

"What is it?" The courier was no less eager for news
than any other mortal.

But Roland waved him to silence. He was still reading.
*Not only do the English afflict us yet, Don* José wrote, *but
we are also tormented by a servile insurrection their invasion has touched off. We are in danger of being murdered
in our beds by those who should aid and comfort us. And
you must know this is a sickness which, if not nipped in
the bud, may soon infect French Atlantis as well.*

"*Nom d'un nom!*" Kersauzon muttered, and then a
couple of Breton obscenities he only half understood.

"What's going on, *Monsieur*?" the courier asked once
more.

"The slaves in Spanish Atlantis have risen up," Roland replied, which made the other man swear in turn.
Roland went on, "Now the Spaniards want us to pull
their fat from the fire."

"Are we going to do it?" the courier demanded, and

did his best to answer his own question: "Lord knows they don't deserve it."

"No, they don't." Roland Kersauzon sighed. "Which doesn't mean they won't get it anyhow. *Don* José is right about one thing, damn him: an uprising could easily spread from his land to ours."

"If we kill enough slaves, the rest will remember their manners pretty quick," said the man who'd brought the letter. "Or if they don't, we can bloody well kill them all."

They couldn't. Roland knew that perfectly well, even if the courier didn't. Without slaves, French Atlantis—and Spanish Atlantis, too—would grind to a halt. But they would also grind to a halt from an uprising. You couldn't let slaves get away with rebellion, or with thinking they were as good as their masters. The whole system would fall apart if you did, even once.

And so, reluctantly, Kersauzon called to a bugler and said, "Blow *halt.*"

Obedient but puzzled—the French settlers had been pushing hard toward the northeast—the man obeyed. The soldiers weren't sorry to stop. Soldiers were never sorry to stop, from everything Roland had seen. Some went off to take a leak. Others lit up pipes or cigars.

Roland rode out in front of them. "My friends, I am sorry to have to tell you that we must reverse our course again," he said.

The men muttered among themselves. "Who spilled the chamber pot into the soup this time?" one of them asked.

In spite of his own fury, Roland smiled. "That sums it up only too well, *mon vieux,*" he said. "I learn that the slaves in Spanish Atlantis have risen." He held up the letter to show how he'd learned it. "The governor wants our help against them—and, I suppose, against the English settlers who inspired the revolt. And if we would rather not see an uprising in our own settlements, we would do well to give him what help we can."

They weighed that with grave attention. Not many of them came from plantation families, but even ordinary farmers who were doing well for themselves had a couple of Negroes or copperskins to give them a hand. Like plantation owners, they had to worry about their property absconding with itself.

One by one, they started to nod. Somebody said, "It's a damned nuisance, but we'd better do it."

"Once we get down there again, we ought to kick that damned Spaniard around the block," another soldier added, which brought more nods.

"Damned slaves are jumping on the Spaniards when they're down," yet another man said. "We need to teach 'em they can't get away with that kind of crap with us." That too produced a growing chorus of agreement.

"You are gentlemen—and it hasn't turned you into blockheads, the way it has with the Spaniards," Roland said. His soldiers grinned and nudged one another— they liked that. Roland wasn't lying, either. He pointed back the way they'd come. "About turn, *mes amis*. We have two jobs of work to do, and with luck we can do both of them at the same time."

Had Montcalm-Gozon or the French regulars watched the settlers reverse their course, they probably would have laughed. Kersauzon's army wasn't long on spit and polish. It didn't drill constantly, the way a European army did. But it could fight when it had to. It had already proved that. As far as Roland was concerned, an army that could fight didn't have to look pretty . . . and an army that looked pretty was worthless anyhow if it couldn't fight.

He rode past the marching men to take his place at the head of the army once more. The soldiers seemed profanely determined to punish the slaves, the English settlers, and the Spaniards for making them march and countermarch. Roland smiled to himself. If that wasn't the right attitude for an army to have, he couldn't imagine what would be.

Victor Radcliff knew less about copperskins than he wished he did. Far fewer had been brought to the English settlements in Atlantis than to those of the French and Spanish farther south. Meeting with the leaders of the slave revolt in Spanish Atlantis taught him how proud the copperskins were.

"Why shouldn't we kill all the whites?" one of them demanded. His Spanish name was Martín. He had another one, the one he'd used in the broader lands of Terranova, but Victor couldn't begin to pronounce it. Martín would have to do. Black eyes blazing, he went on, "They don't care if they kill us."

"He is right. Even if he is a Blackfoot, he is right," another copperskin said. Not all of them came from the same tribe. They were as different as Portuguese and Germans and Poles . . . if you were a Terranovan yourself. Europeans tended to lump them all together, just as the Terranovans spoke of whites without separating Spaniards from Frenchmen from Englishmen. The fellow who wasn't a Blackfoot went by the name of Ramón. He continued, "Give us weapons, and we will make the masters howl."

"We have not many weapons to spare." Victor's Spanish was imperfect. So was the Spanish the copperskins spoke—and they were imperfect in different ways. Everybody had to back and fill and try again every so often.

Martín scowled at him. "You don't want to give them to us, you mean," he growled. His right hand folded into a fist. "How are you any better than these Spanish *putos*?"

"*¿Como?*" Victor returned his blandest smile. "Simple—we're on your side. What would happen if you asked the Spaniards for arms?"

Reluctantly, Martín nodded. He didn't like the point, but he saw it. But Ramón said, "We don't ask no Spaniards for nothing. What he want from the Spaniards, we take, *por Dios.*"

"*Bueno,*" Victor said. "But you make them all join together against you."

"Why do you care?" Martín's grammar was better than Ramón's. "Then they don't fight you so hard."

"They still fight us." Victor wondered what his superiors would want him to do here. His orders were to start no slave insurrections—not directly. And he hadn't—not directly. But the enemy of England's enemy ... was a handy fellow to have around. "We can help you some—just not so much as you probably want."

"Anything is better than nothing," Martín said.

"But more are better—am better—than less," Ramón said.

"Well, the ones who do fight us don't fight you," Victor pointed out. "And, meaning you no disrespect, we are better fighters than you are."

"You think so, do you?" Martín was as affronted as Victor would have been if—no, as Victor had been when—General Braddock told him the redcoats made better soldiers than his settlers.

"I do think so." Victor Radcliff gave back the same kind of answer Braddock might have: "We have better discipline and more experience." He didn't talk about weapons, not when they were a sore spot.

And he didn't impress the copperskins. "We has something you will never has," Ramón said, again without much grammar but with great sincerity.

"What's that?" Radcliff stayed polite, almost disinterested.

"Hate." Ramón needed no grammar to get his point across.

"Hate sends you into battle," Victor agreed. "Hate without experience and discipline sends you into battle . . . and gets you killed."

That also didn't have the effect he wanted. "So what?" Martín said. "Do you know what we do, *Señor*? Do you know what they make us do? With what we do, dying in battle is a relief, an easier ending than most of us would find any other way."

*It is if you lose, that's certain sure,* Victor thought. Spanish vengeance was proverbial up and down Atlantis. Before he could say anything along those lines, Ramón added, "We may die, but we kill, too." He got things right there.

"Help us kill," Martín said urgently. "That's all we want."

"Let's see what we can do," Victor said.

He gave the slaves a few muskets. He gave them some bar lead and some bullet molds. He got his men to cough up some of the swords and bayonets and dirks they'd taken from Frenchmen and Spaniards. And he found that the copperskins were easily pleased. What didn't look like much help to him seemed a great deal more to them. They were so used to getting nothing, anything at all might have been a miracle.

"Now we make the Spaniards to pay," Ramón exulted, brandishing a rapier he plainly had no idea how to use.

Victor stepped away from him. "Have a care with that. You can hurt your friends with it, not just your foes."

Ramón's gaze was measuring. "And which is you?"

"I don't want to be your enemy," Victor answered evenly. "If you make me your enemy, you won't want that, either. Do you understand me?"

"Understand." The copperskin's voice was grudging,

but he did nod. He might not like what he heard. Victor didn't care about that. But Ramón and Martín needed to see that they would be fools to antagonize the Englishmen who were their only friends in this sweltering land.

Blaise had a different question for them: "Do you lead blacks as well as Terranovans? Or do the blacks have their own leaders?"

Ramón and Martín looked at each other. "We have blacks in our bands," Martín said slowly. "Bands with black leaders have Terranovans in them, too. We both hate the Spaniards worse than we hate each other."

Blaise grunted. Victor might have done the same thing if the Negro hadn't beaten him to it. That was an . . . interesting response. Blacks and copperskins *could* work together. Blaise had escaped with a couple of Terranovans, after all. But they knew they were different from each other as well as from the whites who exploited them.

Guiding pack horses loaded down with weapons and lead, the Terranovans headed back to their own folk. Blaise muttered something in his native language. Victor looked a question at him. The Negro seemed faintly embarrassed. "Means something like, *damned hardhead copperskins,*" he said.

This time, Victor did grunt. "What do they say about you?"

"Damned lazy *mallates,*" Blaise answered without hesitation. "*Mallate* is like you say *nigger.*"

"I've heard it before," Radcliff replied. "I wasn't sure you had."

"Oh, yes. I hear *mallate.* I hear *nigger,*" Blaise said. "Can't help it if I black. Doesn't wash off." He made as if to scrub at one arm with the palm of the other hand. "Good when I run away—I am hard to see in woods. Other times?" He shrugged. "I all right where I from.

You all right where you from. Terranovans all right where they from. Nobody from Atlantis, right? Everybody should be all right here."

That sounded good. Atlantis might have been a place where everyone could come together in equality. It might have been . . . but it wasn't. Not yet, anyhow. Victor Radcliff wondered if it ever would be. *Let's smash up the Spaniards first,* he thought. *We can worry about everything else later.*

# XXII

*E*veryone in French Atlantis called the stuff that hung from the branches of cypresses and from the round trunks and outswept leaves of barrel trees Spanish moss. Roland Kersauzon had always taken the name for granted. Now, approaching the frontier with Spanish Atlantis for the second time in a fortnight, he really noticed how Spanish moss grew more common the farther south he went.

He also noticed how deferential the Spanish frontier guards were when he returned to the border. They bowed. They scraped. As *Don* José had said, they abased themselves before him.

"If you had let me cross when I came here last time, things would be better now," Roland pointed out in his deliberate Spanish.

"Oh, but, *Señor*, things were different then," said the *teniente* in charge of the frontier post. "We had orders to prevent you from entering Spanish Atlantis, and we were honor-bound to obey them."

"No matter how idiotic they were," Roland said acidly.

"Yes. I mean, no." The young *teniente* frowned. "You are doing your best to confuse things, *Señor*." He sent Kersauzon a reproachful stare. He had a long, thin Spanish face, a drooping mouth, dark eyes, and heavy black eyebrows: a face God might have made expressly for reproachful stares, in other words.

Roland gave back a bland, polite smile. "I always do my best," he said, which left the Spaniard scratching his head.

But neither the *teniente* nor his tiny garrison did anything to hinder the French settlers who followed Roland into Spanish Atlantis. That was the point. Given the inefficiency with which the Spaniards ran their settlements, Kersauzon had feared that the frontier guards wouldn't know their governor had begged him for help. Spaniards were indeed the kind of people who would open fire for the sake of honor, regardless of whether honor and sense lay within screaming distance of each other.

The first copperskin the French settlers saw in Spanish Atlantis took one look at them, then spun around and ran like a rabbit. (In the early days of settling Atlantis, there had been no rabbits, any more than there'd been sheep or cattle or horses. There were plenty of them now: maybe more than in France, for they had fewer natural enemies here. Of course, like a lot of Frenchmen, Kersauzon was fond of *lapin aux pruneaux*—or *lapin* prepared any number of other ways, too.)

"Should we shoot him, *Monsieur*?" asked a practical—but not quite practical enough—sergeant.

"I daresay we should have shot him," Roland replied. He hadn't been practical enough, either. "Too late now." Too late it was, without a doubt. The Terranovan had vanished into the undergrowth. He knew where he was going. Pursuers wouldn't. Roland could hope he would tread on a viper in his headlong flight; there were enough, or rather too many, of them down here in the south. But, that unlikelihood aside, the copperskin had got away.

Which meant—what? The fellow was bound to be a slave. He was also obviously a slave not tending to his master's affairs. Was he a slave who was part of a band of rebels? That was less obvious, but it matched the way he acted.

Would his band of rebels want to tangle with Roland's French settlers? Unless that band was a lot bigger than Kersauzon thought likely, they would have to be crazy to try it. Then again, plenty of white men were crazy. Why not copperskins and Negroes as well?

"Where do we go now, *Monsieur*?" the sergeant asked.

Roland realized he should have inquired of the snooty Spanish *teniente*. He was damned if he would turn around again, even if it was only half a mile or so this time. He hadn't seen any white men—let alone white women—on the road since entering Spanish Atlantis. That had to mean the uprising was a serious business . . . or that the whites thought it was, anyhow, which might not be the same thing.

The sergeant deserved—needed—an answer. Kersauzon scanned the southern horizon. He knew just what he was looking for: the thickest smoke. When he found it in the southwest, he pointed. "We go there."

It turned out to be farther away than he'd expected, which meant the fires down there were bigger than he'd thought. No one seemed to be fleeing toward his army. Several Negroes and copperskins fled from it. The French settlers caught a Negro. The man tried to deny everything.

"If you are as innocent as our Lord, why did you run from us?" Roland asked.

In reasonable—almost French—tones, the black replied, "If you saw lots of men with guns, *Señor*, wouldn't you run, too?"

"Not if I thought they were friends," Kersauzon said.

"I thought you were *ingleses*," the Negro replied. "*Los ingleses* are the friends of no one but themselves."

"You're right about that, by God," Roland said. "They will use you against the Spaniards, and the Spaniards against you. They will try to get the Spaniards to fight you instead of them. They don't care what happens to you, as long as it helps them."

"No doubt you are right, *Señor*," the Negro said. "But how much does it matter? If you are a drowning man, you grab for whatever you can get your hands on. If it turns out to be a log—*bueno*. You are saved. If it turns out to be a crocodile—at least you don't drown."

Crocodiles and the other toothy horrors usually called by the Spanish name for lizards—*lagartos*—were even more common in streams down here than they were in French Atlantis. There were hardly any near the English settlements; those lay too far north for the big reptiles to stay comfortable through the winter. All things considered, Roland would rather have drowned if a crocodile or *lagarto* was his other choice.

He also needed to ask, "Why did you have to run from *los ingleses*? After all, they gain if you rise up against the Spaniards."

"You said it yourself, *Señor*," the Negro replied with dignity. "I am a man. I am not a tool to be taken down from a shelf, used, and then put back. Slaves are nothing but tools to *los ingleses*. If these English"—he pronounced the name properly, and about as badly as Kersauzon would have—"said, 'Rise up, and we will help you become free men' . . . if they said that, I would be their man forever. But they do not. They care nothing for freeing us. All they say is, 'Rise up, and make *los españoles* some trouble.' This does not inspire me, for some reason."

Roland Kersauzon swept off his hat and bowed to

the black man, who stared at him in astonishment. "It would not inspire me, either, *Monsieur,*" Roland said. "I assure you of that." He gestured. "You may go. You are free—of me, anyhow."

"But you and your men are still fighting for the damned Spaniards and against the slaves," the Negro said.

"It is our duty," Roland said simply.

"If you turn me loose, it is *my* duty to kill you if you get in my way and if I have the chance," the Negro said. "I need to go after the Spaniards first, but you are their ally."

"Tell the other slaves to wait until *los ingleses* are gone from this land. If they do, we will not raise a finger against them," Roland said. "My quarrel is with the English, not with you."

"This is a good bad bargain, but it is still a bad bargain," the black man said. "If *los ingleses* are not here, the Spaniards will have nothing to distract them from us. They will put us down, and they will make us pay for rising against them. But if we fight them now, while they also have to worry about the English, we have a chance to beat them. Maybe not a good chance, but a chance."

He wasn't even wrong, not as long as he was talking about Spaniards. If the slaves did beat their Spanish masters, the French would invade and try to suppress them. Even the English would probably do the same thing. They might not have many slaves in their own settlements, but they didn't mind making money from other people's bondsmen.

And Roland was sure the English aimed to seize French and Spanish Atlantis for themselves if they won this war. They wouldn't want Negroes and copperskins running around burning things and killing people. No, not when those same Negroes and copperskins could be harvesting crops and putting black ink, not red, in the ledgers.

Kersauzon made as if to push the slave away. "You had better leave now, before I come to my senses and decide to hold you instead."

The Negro bowed politely. "You may try, *Señor*. I don't think you will have much luck." Then he disappeared, so quickly and so effectively that he might have been part of a conjurer's trick. A leafy fern stirred for a moment. Deeper in the undergrowth, a bird let out a startled chirp.

"He's a nuisance," a sergeant said. "You should have got rid of him while you had the chance."

"It could be," Roland said. "But even if I would have, how many more just like him are there?" The sergeant had no answer for that. Neither did Roland, not in numbers. But he knew there were swarms of them.

Victor Radcliff found himself and his little band of English marauders in an odd predicament. They helped protect Spanish fugitives from the wrath of their uprisen slaves. And they gave aid and comfort to the Africans and Terranovans against the men who were convinced they had a right to own them.

Blaise didn't mind that. On the contrary—one day he hurried up to Victor almost jumping in excitement. "A woman here, she speak my language!" he exclaimed.

"Well, good," Victor said. "That must be nice. What's her name?"

"They call her Maria," Blaise answered. "She has a name in our language, too. It means in English 'little star.' "

"Pretty," Radcliff remarked.

"I can talk with she—with her." Blaise made a face. "Don't always have to think through different kinds funny words. Just . . . talk!" He really did jump into the air then, but the leap put Radcliff in mind of a dance step.

He got to see Maria a little later. He didn't think her especially pretty, but then Blaise didn't seem to find white women especially pretty, either. The black man and woman could talk together, all right. Their language seemed full of clucking and mooing noises to Victor. But he knew how delighted he would have been to find an English-speaking woman if he were stranded in West Africa.

Voice dry, he said, "You might want to tell her we still have some fighting to do. You can't marry her till that's taken care of."

Blaise's skin was already dark, but it got darker as he blushed. "Good thing she doesn't talk English. She think you making promises for me."

"I can tell her myself in Spanish, or in French if she knows it," Victor said helpfully.

"Never mind," Blaise said—in English. "Maybe I marry she—her. Maybe I don't. Don't got to decide now, though."

"What are you two talking about in that funny language?" Maria asked in fluent Spanish. "You better not be talking about me when I can't understand what you're saying."

"We're talking about the fighting, *Señorita,*" Victor Radcliff replied in the same language. "We still have to beat the Spaniards."

"And you will fight to the last slave's last drop of blood to do it." Maria had a tart wit.

"We are here, in Spanish Atlantis," Victor said. "We fought our way through French Atlantis to get here. We would fight the Spaniards even if the slaves did not rise up against them."

She weighed that. Blaise plainly hung on her decision. Victor was surprised to discover he cared, too. You had to take Maria seriously. Some people had that gift. At last, she nodded. "*Bueno.* The Spaniards have plenty to answer for. And so do you *ingleses,* for selling them so many slaves from Africa."

She didn't know—Radcliff hoped she didn't, anyhow—how deeply involved in the slave trade his family was. You could make a lot of money off Negroes. Plenty of people had. If you didn't sail to Africa yourself, your hands stayed clean while you did it, too. Radcliffs and Radcliffes were welcome in all the best places in English Atlantis. *We'd better be,* he thought. *We founded a lot of those places.*

But that was an argument for another day. "Let's get moving," he said. "We don't do anyone any good sitting around like snails on a leaf."

They left more mansions in flames as they moved south. The Spaniards who took refuge with them cursed them because they didn't do more to put down the rebellious slaves. The slaves cursed them because they didn't do more to help the uprising. Getting sworn at by both sides at once suited Victor Radcliff fine. To him, it meant he was following about the right course.

He heard rumors the governor of Spanish Atlantis had let soldiers from French Atlantis come south to deal with the English settlers. He disbelieved those rumors as long as he could: if they proved true, they would make his life harder. But he sent scouts out to the north as well as to the south. The only thing worse than having the French settlers there would be having them there and getting taken by surprise.

A scout rode up from the south shouting, "The sea! The sea!"

"Why you smile?" Blaise asked Victor. "What so funny 'bout the sea?"

Blaise had never heard of Xenophon. Victor would have bet the scout never had, either. But more than

2,100 years earlier, the Greeks escaping the Persian Empire had raised that same cry—*"Thalassa! Thalassa!"*—when they finally came to the Black Sea.

For Xenophon's Greeks, coming to the sea meant finding the broad highway home. Things weren't so simple here. Who could say what kind of ships lay off the coast? Any at all? British? Spanish? French? All of them at once, banging away at one another as if these were the bad old days of the pirates of Avalon?

Victor again remembered Ethel Radcliffe, who'd shot his great-grandfather. Mule-headed stubbornness seemed to run through every branch of the Radcliff(e) line. He needed some of his own here, and some luck, if this venture wouldn't be remembered as another piece of Radcliff(e) damnfoolishness.

"Let's go down to the sea," he said. "We've come all this way—we shouldn't leave the last few miles undone."

The ocean here was nothing like the cold, green-gray one off Hanover's muddy beaches. The water here was turquoise. It looked warm enough to bathe in. The sand leading down to it was golden as a pretty girl's hair. An enormous black bird glided past overhead; it had a leathery red sac under its throat.

Several crocodiles unhurriedly ambled off the beach and into the ocean. *Too bad*, Victor Radcliff thought. With so much firepower at hand, they would have been easy to kill. And, even though crocodiles were ugly, they made better than tolerable eating.

Victor focused on the crocodiles and the frigate bird. Blaise was the one who pointed farther out to sea and said, "What ships are those?"

"Damnation!" Victor exclaimed. Several frigates cruised along on that lovely blue sea. His first horrified thought was that some French or Spanish admiral had got much too clever for comfort. It could cause him all kinds of trouble. If he didn't move his men off the beach, those ships could bombard them, and damn all he could do about it. Or they could land raiding parties, strike at him, and then get away before he could respond. Just by being there, they denied him the seacoast. He felt trapped between their anvil and the hammer of Roland Kersauzon's French settlers.

"What to do, *Monsieur*?" Blaise asked.

"Good question," Radcliff answered dully. He raised a spyglass to his right eye for a closer look at the ships. If they were French frigates, he might persuade their skippers he and his men were Spaniards. Conversely, if the ships were Spanish, maybe he could fool the captains into thinking he was Kersauzon. It might work for a little while, anyhow, though what good it would do he wasn't quite sure. He was looking for something—anything—to try, that was all.

He slid the shiny brass tube out a little farther to bring the frigates into sharper focus. Then he started to laugh. And, once he started, he had a hard time stopping. He wanted to keep on braying idiot mirth up to the sky that was only a couple of shades lighter than the sea.

Somebody not far away said, "He's gone clean round the bend, he has."

"What you see?" someone else asked. That was Blaise, his accent distinctive.

Reluctantly, Victor lowered the telescope. "Those ships out there . . ." He couldn't go on. He started laughing again instead.

"You better tell us." Now Blaise sounded almost threatening. Several of the white men around Victor looked the same way.

He took a deep breath and held it as long as he could. Then he let it all out and did the same thing again, trying to flush the laughter from his system. Only after that did he try to speak once more: "Those ships out there . . .

They're English." That got him a load of profanity and obscenity covering as much relief as he felt himself.

As usual, Blaise was a man of direct action. He snatched the spyglass from Radcliff's hand and raised it to his own eye. He didn't understand how the lenses bent light—he thought it was magic. (Well, Victor didn't understand why the telescope worked, either. He did doubt whether witchcraft had anything to do with it.) Lack of understanding didn't mean he couldn't focus. Like Victor, he accepted the color-fringed, upside-down images as the price of magnification.

And, like Victor, he started to laugh, even if not so loud or so long. "Fuck me," he said reverently. "They are English shipses."

"What are they doing here?" someone asked, which had also crossed Victor Radcliff's mind. "Are they waiting for us?"

"Maybe they are, by God," Victor said. "But whether they are or not, they can give us a ride home." The phrase *deus ex machina* ran through his mind. If those ships weren't the visible hand of Providence stretched out on the waters ... If they weren't, then they were Somebody's idea of a cruel joke. Victor refused to believe that. He called out an order: "Show all the Union Jacks we have—the bigger, the better."

The flags had grown tattered in their journey through French and Spanish Atlantis. Victor didn't care. They wouldn't be mistaken for the emblem of either enemy kingdom. They wouldn't be—and they weren't. The nearest frigate sailed closer yet. Victor imagined its captain peering shoreward through a spyglass just like his own. Before long, the ship lowered a boat.

It stopped just out of musket range of the beach. "Ahoy!" shouted someone aboard, his voice coming thin over the water. "Who are you? What are you doing here?"

Victor explained. Then he asked the same question of the bosun or lieutenant or whoever he was in the boat.

"We were ordered down here to find you," the man replied. "Looks like we've gone and done it, too."

"What will you do now that you have?"

"Bring you back, of course."

"Good God!" Victor said. "Not that we aren't glad to see you, but who sent you down here? How did you know where we were?"

"I hear it was that army bastard, Lieutenant-Colonel What's-His-Name. Charlie," the sailor answered, showing his scorn for anything in a red coat. "He got your despatches, looked at a map, and said, 'Go *there*. You'll just about find him.' And we just about did, didn't we?"

"Bless my soul," Victor murmured. Thinking an Englishman stodgy just because he was an Englishman wouldn't do. The officer had used his imagination, and used it well. His scheme wouldn't have worked unless England ruled the seas, but England did, and he took advantage of it. And, with Roland Kersauzon's French settlers nipping at his heels, Radcliff was glad he did.

"What do we do?" Blaise asked.

"We go back to Freetown, that's what," Victor answered. "And we don't have to fight our way through Spanish and French Atlantis or plunge into the western wilderness to do it."

Blaise considered, but not for long. "Good," he said.

Leading the raiders onto the ships was a long, tedious job. Victor formed a rear-guard perimeter, and kept it in place as long as he could. After a while, it wouldn't have done much good. There weren't enough soldiers manning it. Had Kersauzon's troops descended on them then, it would have been embarrassing, to say the least. But luck had been with Radcliff all through the filibustering expedition, and it stayed with him now.

He and Blaise were the last two men from the raiding party to step into a boat. Blaise grimaced. "Last time I went in ship, they took me from Africa," he said.

Victor knew what hellholes slave ships—blackbirds, they called them—were. He knew, but Blaise *knew.* "This won't be that bad," Victor told the Negro.

"Better not," Blaise said. Grunting sailors pushed the boat into the sea. Their mates pulled them aboard. They plied the oars like clockwork automata. The land receded. The frigate drew nearer. Victor was delighted. If Blaise was, too, his face didn't know about it.

Roland Kersauzon stood on the golden beach, cursing *Don* José. He cursed the governor of Spanish Atlantis in his rising and setting, his waking and sleeping, his eating and shitting. He wished the governor's wife would take the pox from him, and he wished *Don* José would take the pox from his wife.

"If he'd made up his mind . . . !" Roland howled. "If only he had a mind to make up!"

The Englishmen were gone. They'd flown the coop. No, actually they hadn't—they could no more fly than honkers could. Roland had hoped to shoot them down the way settlers shot honkers, too. And he might have done it—he might well have done it, since he was sure he had more men than they did—if only *Don* José hadn't sent him away before urging him back. Had the governor of Spanish Atlantis been a woman toying with her lover, that would have been one thing. But he was a man of responsibility, toying with the fate of his settlements.

Yes, the English raiders were gone. Kersauzon had brought the French settlers through the madness of the slave uprising. They'd done their share—more than their share, probably, since the Spanish settlers seemed notably reluctant to fight—to quell it. They'd got on Victor

Radcliff's trail. Thanks to the wreckage Radcliff's raiders left behind, a blind man could have followed it. But it ended here.

And the Englishmen were gone. They hadn't sprouted wings. They hadn't dug into the ground like blind snakes, though Roland would gladly have consigned them to hell. And he didn't suppose they'd grown fins and scales, either. Which didn't mean they hadn't left by sea. The Royal Navy was the strongest one in these waters. Roland didn't know how the enemy's ships got to the right place at the right time, but manifestly they did. Nothing else was possible.

"What do we do now, *Monsieur*?" a lieutenant asked. Like Kersauzon, he was looking out at the lovely, deep blue, treacherous sea.

A tern dove into the water. It came out with a wriggling fish in its beak. A big black frigate bird, the sac at its throat like a scarlet pig's bladder, harried the tern till it dropped the fish. The frigate bird snatched it out of the air and flew off with it. Radcliff's English settlers might have been frigate birds, too. Like this one, they were getting away with their robbery.

"What do we do?" Roland echoed. "What *can* we do? We go back and help Montcalm-Gozon. He is the man facing the enemy right now."

The lieutenant sighed. "It's a long march. And it will seem even longer because we've done so much of it before."

"Don't I know it!" Roland started swearing at *Don* José again. When he ran down—which took a while—he said, "What other choice have we got, though? Would you rather stay here? Do you like running after the Spaniards' Negroes and copperskins?"

"Good God, no!" the junior officer exclaimed.

"Well, all right. I would have chased you into the ocean if you'd said yes," Kersauzon told him. "We go north. If the slaves harry us, we make them sorry for it. If they don't, we leave them alone. Any objections?"

"No, sir," the lieutenant said.

"Then let's go." Roland raised his voice and gave the men their new orders. They liked the idea of leaving Spanish Atlantis. So did he. He suspected the Spaniards made a lot of money from their settlements here. But they made even more from the gold and silver of Terranova. The ones who lived here were the ones who couldn't make a go of it there. They acted like secondraters, and came down hard on their slaves because they lacked confidence in themselves.

"We need shoes, *Monsieur*," a soldier called. "We've done a devil of a lot of marching, you know."

"Yes." Roland nodded. "It could be that some will come down in the supply wagons." Everyone laughed, knowing how unlikely that was. Even victuals had been in short supply lately. He went on, "Or it could be that you will find some lying around with no one using them."

The men pondered that, but not for long. They grinned and nudged one another. They'd foraged to keep themselves fed. Now they had official leave—or what amounted to it—to forage to keep themselves clothed. Roland suspected the Spanish settlers would soon regret that. He also suspected *Don* José would soon bawl like a branded calf. He suspected he himself would grow remarkably deaf to the governor's protestations.

"Where are the Englishmen?" asked a Spanish cavalry officer, encountering the French settlers tramping north. "What have you done with them?" He spoke French with a trilling Spanish accent.

"Why, they are in our rucksacks, of course," Roland replied. "We will keep them there until we quit Spanish Atlantis. And I promise you by God and all the saints that they will trouble you no more."

"In your rucksacks?" The Spaniard frowned. Since his eyebrows grew together above the top of his nose, he looked fearsome—but since he had only a handful of men behind him, not nearly fearsome enough to intimidate Roland. "If I ride south and find them marauding—"

"If you do, you may track me down and do as you please to me," Roland broke in. "But for now, *Monsieur,* you may get out of our way, for we are on the march." He raised his voice: *"Forward!"*

His men rolled down on the Spaniards. The luckless officer and his squadron could get out of the way or get trampled. The Spaniards got out of the way. The road was muddy. The meadows to either side were muddier. The horses had to keep moving lest they start to sink. The officer looked daggers at Roland, who wondered if the fellow would draw his pistol and start a fight even if he was supposed to be an ally and even if he was hopelessly outnumbered. He seemed angry enough not to care.

But, no matter what he thought, he didn't do anything. Once the French settlers passed him by, would he get back on the road? Would he ride south and discover that the English really had vanished from Spanish Atlantis? And would he conclude from that that Kersauzon really did have them in their rucksacks?

When you were dealing with Spaniards, you never could tell.

When you were dealing with Englishmen, you never could tell, either. The French were the only sensible people in the world: Roland was convinced of it. And even among the French there were unfortunate gradations. Marquis Montcalm-Gozon, for example, though surely a good fellow, did not seem nearly so sensible as a man from French Atlantis. *They're going to seed over there in Europe,* Roland thought sadly.

The sound of gunfire ahead snapped him out of his musing. "Scouts forward!" he called. "We'll find out what that is. Then we'll put a stop to it one way or another. Fix bayonets and load your muskets!"

Before long, the scouts came back. It was a brawl—almost a battle—between slaves and Spanish settlers in what was no doubt usually a sleepy little town: about what Kersauzon had expected.

"Let's go!" he said. "If the blacks and copperskins run from us, well and good. If not, it's their funeral."

They ran. He'd thought they would. They were brave enough, but had little in the way of organization. They could fight settlers who also didn't know what they were doing. Real soldiers advancing in neat ranks with bayonets gleaming under the subtropical sun? No. The slaves melted into the woods.

Cheers from the Spaniards failed to warm the cockles of the French settlers' hearts. The town was big enough for two cobbler's shops. The French settlers looted both of them. They cleaned out the taverns, too. Some unfortunate things probably happened to a few of the local women. Roland thought that was too bad, but he didn't intend to do anything about it as long as the soldiers followed orders when it came time to leave.

They did. Fewer cheers came to them when they left than when they'd arrived. Somebody fired an old fowling piece at them as they marched away. None of the junk in the gun barrel hit anybody. If some had, the French settlers probably would have turned around and done a proper job of wrecking the town. As things were, they just kept going.

"You know, *Monsieur,* the copperskins and blacks will come back as soon as we've gone a couple of miles," a sergeant said.

"But of course," Kersauzon replied. "What do you want me to do about it?"

"Well, sir, the Spaniards said we could come in if we helped them with the slave uprising," the underofficer pointed out.

Roland told him what the Spaniards could do about it. In the telling, he violated as many commandments as he could without having either a sculptor's tools or someone else's wife handy. The sergeant, a man as accustomed to harsh language as anyone of his rank, stared in goggle-eyed admiration. Having slowed down a little, Roland said, "I came down here to fight the damned English settlers. If I can't do that here, I'll go where I can do it, by God. Any questions?"

*"Mais non. Certainement pas,"* the sergeant said hastily, and went off to find somewhere to bathe his bleeding ears.

If the slaves got in the French settlers' way, Roland's men went through them. If the slaves didn't, the settlers ignored them. They took what they needed from the surrounding countryside, as if in hostile country. The locals took to running from them, and occasionally, as in that one village, shooting at them. The French made them sorry when they tried it.

A courier from *Don* José rode up to Roland when he and his men were once more nearing the border with French Atlantis. In accented French, the man cried, "His Excellency the governor demands to know why you have not performed the function he required of you, and why he has received reports that you are plundering the countryside."

"We are plundering the countryside because we have to eat, and he never arranged to feed us," Roland replied. "And we are now returning to the more important fight, the one against England."

"But the slaves still torment us!" the Spaniard cried.

"If you can't put them down by yourselves, then it could be that they deserve to be the masters," Roland said.

The courier's jaw dropped. He sputtered and fumed. Finally, after some effort, he got out, "This is intolerable!"

"If you do not care to tolerate it, you are welcome to attack my army," Roland said. "So is his Excellency. I do not promise you the most hospitable of receptions, however."

"You will pay for this—this insolence," the courier said.

"We've already paid for Spanish insolence," Kersauzon replied. "Without it, we would have been able to come to grips with the English settlers a long time ago. Instead, they got away. Should I thank you for that?"

"If you weren't already running away from our country, we would drive you out like the dogs you are," the Spaniard said.

Roland looked at him. "Consider, *Monsieur:* you are, perhaps, not in the best position to throw insults about."

How many muskets could point at a man on horseback at a shouted order, or even without one? The courier seemed to make the calculation, and not to like the answer he found. His hand slipped toward the dragoon pistol he wore on his right hip, then jerked away as if the pistol butt had become red-hot.

"You'll be sorry," he warned.

"I'm sorry already," Roland said: "sorry *Don* José doesn't know his own mind, sorry your slaves hate you so much—"

"What of yours?" the courier retorted.

"Not like that." *I hope,* Roland added, but only to himself. "Most of all, I'm sorry this has been a chase after a wild goose, a wild goose that has flown. Since I can't follow by sea, I must go by land as best I can. And so I say farewell to Spanish Atlantis, and you had better pray your own folk here do not do the same."

"God will punish you for this desertion," the Spaniard said.

"He has—He sent me you, did He not?" Roland replied. His men laughed. The Spaniard glowered. The French settlers began to march, and the courier had to move aside or get trampled into the mud. "Onward!" Roland cried.

# XXIII

When Victor Radcliff strode down the *Inflexible*'s gangplank and onto the quays at Freetown, the clever English lieutenant-colonel who'd sent the flotilla into southern waters stood waiting for him. Victor threw the Englishman the snappiest salute he knew how to give. "Much obliged to your Excellency," he said.

"I thought you might need a hand, or at least find one, er, handy, so I did what I could," the officer replied.

"Now that we're back here, what did you have in mind doing with us?" Victor wiped his sweaty forehead with the back of his sleeve—he had no kerchief. It was high summer, and as hot here as it had been in Spanish Atlantis.

"Montcalm-Gozon presses us hard," the lieutenant-colonel said. "He has proved himself an able and aggressive soldier, and of course he has a solid body of French regulars. He has, however, few settlers or other irregulars with him, not until Roland Kersauzon catches him up. This being so . . ."

Radcliff saluted again. He also grinned. "This being so, you want us to drive him as crazy as a honker in mating season."

"Whilst I should not have put it quite that way—yes." The English officer smiled, too.

"Well, I expect we can do that. I expect the boys will look forward to it, as a matter of fact, if I can get them out of town fast enough," Victor said.

"I'm sorry?" The officer's smile melted away. "I don't follow that."

"If we stay here long, some of them will get drunk, some will get poxed, and the more enterprising lads will manage both," Victor Radcliff told him.

"Oh. I see." The smile returned. "Why, they might almost be regulars."

"They're men, your Excellency." Victor wondered how much experience with soldiers the Englishman had had before King George—or, more likely, King George's ministers—ordered him across the sea. Less than he might have had: Victor was pretty sure of that.

Blaise and the other sergeants lined the green-jacketed settlers up in neat ranks. No one would escape to the fleshpots of Freetown, such as those were, if the underofficers had anything to say about it—and they did. "We got here ahead of the buggers from French Atlantis," one of the sergeants rasped. "The Frenchies who are up here'll be sorry we did, too."

As Victor walked out in front of the assembled irregulars, he reflected that the tough, pockmarked man with three chevrons sewn to his left sleeve had just given his speech for him. "Philip is right," he said, and watched the underofficer's chest expand and his shoulders rise and straighten. "Now we make the French regulars as sorry as Kersauzon's men made General Braddock. We owe 'em that much, don't we?"

Agreement came, loud and profane. The settlers had got caught along with Braddock and his redcoats. They would have if the English general wanted to listen. And if honkers could fly . . .

"Forward—march!" Blaise shouted. Bugles blared. Drums thumped. The men paraded through Freetown. Tavern owners came out of their establishments and stared wistfully at the stream of men who wouldn't be customers. Sergeants and lieutenants made sure the men didn't sneak off to taverns or to bawdy houses. A couple of plump, extremely well-dressed women who looked as disappointed as the publicans probably presided over those establishments.

More settlers and the surviving redcoats who hadn't got captured and paroled held Freetown against Montcalm-Gozon and his men. The French commander wasn't carrying on a formal siege with saps and parallels, but his campaign wasn't far removed from it. He'd been pushing the English lieutenant-colonel's forces back on the town. Had he had more artillery, he could have made things even worse. They were bad enough as it was.

The French marquis didn't have enough men to surround the town and keep his lines tight at the same time. The English lieutenant-colonel said, "Well, Major Radcliff, from here on I leave you to your own no doubt fertile devices. They seem to have met all requirements in French and Spanish Atlantis."

"Thank you, sir," Victor said in glad surprise. "I don't know if I can handle that much responsibility."

For a moment, the Englishman was nonplused. Then he realized Radcliff might not be altogether serious. He smiled thinly. "I dare hope you'll manage."

"So do I." Victor realized he was liable to find himself in the middle of warm work. He shrugged. He'd done that before. One more time couldn't be too much worse . . . could it?

*Of course it could, you stupid fool,* a voice inside him screeched. *If you stop a musket ball with your chest, or with your face, you'll see how much worse it could be, too.* Would Meg want anything to do with him if he came home with a patch over one eye or missing half his jaw? If she did, would it be from love or from pity?

At the English lieutenant-colonel's orders, the redcoats started a brisk dusk skirmish with Marquis Montcalm-Gozon's Frenchmen. They stirred up enough trouble to draw French reinforcements—and to let Victor and a large band of settlers break out through a weakly held stretch not far away.

"Who goes there?" a Frenchman asked. Victor shot him in the head with a pistol. Down went the enemy soldier, dead as a stone, a look of absurd surprise on his face. With the larger racket of musketry close by, no more Frenchmen came running to see what had happened to Pierre or Louis or Jean or whatever his name was.

Out. Away. Into the countryside. That was what Victor had in mind. "South!" he called to his men. "Quick! Quick! I want to get on their supply lines the way you bastards wanted to get on the whores back in Freetown."

Coarse, baying male laughter answered him. The settlers bumped into a few more Frenchmen as they hurried away from the lines around the town, but only a few. The French soldiers regretted it—but not for long, never for long. The settlers, urged on by sergeants and officers, put as much space as they could between themselves and the main body of their foes.

The French were foreigners here. Several of the settlers knew the roads and woods and streams the way they knew the hair and tendons and veins on the backs of their hands—and from equally long acquaintance. "Oh, sure, Major," one of them said. "I'd bet anything they'll bring their victuals and such up the Graveyard Road. It's a devil of a lot wider and straighter than the Honker's Beak."

"Cheerful name, Ned," Victor remarked. "They call it that because . . . ?"

"It's the road that goes past the graveyard," Ned answered matter-of-factly. "Nice spot for an ambush not far from there."

"Now you're talking," Victor said.

It *was* a good spot for an ambush, too. Pine woods grew close to the road on both sides. One day before too long, Victor supposed, settlers would cut them down for fuel or timber, but it hadn't happened yet. Lush ferns growing under the trees would further screen the green-jacketed English settlers. At dawn the next day, Radcliff sent a spry youngster up a tree to keep an eye out for approaching wagons.

Inside of an hour, the lookout hallooed. Victor wasn't astonished. An army needed a lot of supplies to keep going . . . and the French officers farther south wouldn't know he'd broken out of Freetown. "Shoot the horses and oxen first," Victor told his men. "We want to make sure the wagons don't get through."

On came the wagons, oblivious to danger. Hooves thumped in the dirt of the roadway. Axles squeaked. Wheels rumbled. As the wagons got closer, Victor could make out the jingle of harness and the drivers laughing and talking to one another.

"Fire!" he shouted. The woods exploded in flame and smoke.

Down went most of the draft animals. Others, wounded but not slain, screamed and reared and tried to bolt. Some of the men in the wagons screamed, too. A handful had the presence of mind to grab for pistols and muskets and fire back. They even hit a couple of settlers as Victor's men swarmed out of the woods and over the wagon train.

"Don't let any of them get away to the south!" Victor shouted. "We don't want the enemy to know what we're doing."

This time, with surprise so complete, obeying his order

was easy. The settlers rounded up the luckless drivers and guards. They put wounded animals out of their misery. Some of them started butchering dead ones. Roast ox would be tough, and horse steak would be gluey, but Victor had eaten plenty worse. So had many of his men.

They also plundered the wagons, and came away with everything from wine and brandy to pigs of lead. "Burn what we can't use," Victor said. "Don't leave anything Montcalm-Gozon's men would want."

Maybe the fires would draw French regulars. If they did, the French would find that the settlers had got loose. The enemy settlers wouldn't find the settlers themselves, though. Victor had them marching down the Graveyard Road less than an hour after horror descended on the wagon train.

And they rounded a bend that afternoon and almost ran into another northbound wagon train. "Get 'em!" Victor commanded: not the most precise order ever issued, maybe, but one that told what he wanted done.

He got it, too. The Frenchmen, outnumbered twenty to one, never had a chance. They couldn't turn around, and they couldn't fight back. He feared one or two of them did manage to escape from the rear of the train. If someone there jumped on a horse and galloped south as fast as the beast would take him, he could get out of musket range before any settlers came close to him.

"It won't be so easy next time," Radcliff told Blaise as the wagon train's funeral pyre rose into the sky.

The Negro only shrugged. "We can still do it."

Victor nodded. "Yes, I think we can, too."

They came across no more wagons before they camped for the night. Victor sent a company led by locals cross-country to the road called the Honker's Beak. If the French aimed to use the poorer road to sneak past him, they'd be doomed to disappointment.

He also told off some men to bury the lead they'd

taken. His force had plenty for its needs. More important now was denying it to Montcalm-Gozon. The settlers to whom he gave the order grumbled, but he'd expected nothing else. Somebody had to do it.

"A good day's work," he said just before rolling himself in a blanket. "A mighty good day's work."

"Can't you go any faster?" Roland Kersauzon called to his men. "The marquis will need us. I only hope he doesn't need us already."

"Begging your pardon, *Monsieur,* but you're up there on a horse," one of the French Atlanteans replied. "Easier to go from here to there on a fine gelding than it is on shank's mare." He was gaunt and poorly shaven. He'd done about as much marching as a man could do. All he had with him were a musket and a bullet pouch and a powder horn. When he got the chance, he could fight. What more did you want from a soldier?

Roland sketched a salute. "You shame me. Would you rather ride for a while? I can walk."

The settler shook his head. "No. What difference does it make now? And I suppose you need to be up there so you can give orders and make people pay attention to you."

No doubt he was right. All the same, for the rest of the day Roland felt guilty about riding.

He also fumed, as he'd fumed ever since he reached the southern shore of Spanish Atlantis just too late and found the English fled. No, he'd been fuming longer than that: ever since *Don* José refused to let him enter Spanish Atlantis. Well, *Don* José had paid for his stupidity. But the French cause was paying, too.

What was Montcalm-Gozon doing now? What were the English regulars—and the English Atlanteans, damn them—doing against him? What were they doing to him? Messengers had told Roland all was well with the

French regulars up in English Atlantis . . . but he hadn't had any messengers from Montcalm-Gozon the past couple of days.

Maybe that didn't mean anything. Maybe the marquis had nothing new to report. Or maybe he was too busy attacking Freetown to have time to deal with anything less important. Maybe. Kersauzon had a hard time believing it. The other *maybe* was that maybe something up north had gone wrong.

"Keep moving!" Roland called again the next morning. "Pretty soon we'll be over the border. Then we'll be living off the enemy, not our own countryside."

Before they got to the border between French and Spanish Atlantis, they found out some of what had happened up toward Freetown. A man riding what was obviously a cart horse reined in in front of them and shouted, "It's all buggered up!"

"What's all buggered up?" Roland demanded.

"Everything!" The teamster seemed bound and determined to give as little information as he could.

"What happened to you? What happened to your friends?" Roland asked.

Little by little, he teased the story from the man. The English were waylaying supply trains. How long could Montcalm-Gozon go without food and munitions? How had the English broken out of Freetown? When the teamster said the attackers wore green jackets, Roland got his answer to that. Those were Victor Radcliff's men, the men he hadn't caught in Spanish Atlantis. Like quicksilver—like his own troops—they could slip through any tiny opening. He wasted a few seconds swearing at them again, and at *Don* José.

"Well, it's up to us, then," he said. "If we can break through and open the supply lines, the regulars will take care of the English." *As long as the army holed up in Freetown doesn't get more reinforcements by sea,* he thought uneasily. The Royal Navy was stronger than the French sea forces, just as the English Atlanteans had more ships than their French and Spanish counterparts.

But he couldn't do anything about that. He could only fight on land. And if the English settlers lay athwart his path, he was ready—no, eager—to bull them out of the way. The sooner he did it, the better, too. He could see that all too plainly.

"How much trouble is the French general in?" he asked.

"*Monsieur,* I have no idea," the teamster said. "We never got close enough to find out."

"*Nom d'un nom,*" Roland muttered. He wanted to order double time. No matter what he wanted, he didn't do it. Even if he'd ridden more than he'd marched, he had a good idea of how much his men had left. If he exhausted them before they ran into the English settlers, his fight was lost before it started.

How much did the enemy have left? They'd done a lot of marching and fighting, too. Yes, they'd sailed back from Spanish Atlantis, but ocean voyages didn't build a man's strength. Considering the horrible food aboard ship, even a forced march cross-country might be easier.

Or it might not. Pretty soon, he wouldn't have to wonder any more. One way or the other, he would know. So would Victor Radcliff.

*If my ancestor hadn't sold your ancestor the secret of Atlantis for a mess of salt cod . . .* Kersauzon shook his head. Three hundred years too late to fret about that now. The first Kersauzon, the one from Brittany, made the mistake. Everyone else had been paying for it ever since.

"What will you do, *Monsieur*?" The teamster sounded uncommonly worried. Roland blamed him not a bit. Uncommon worry just proved the man understood the situation. Roland was uncommonly worried himself.

He gave the only answer he could: "Go forward. Find the foe, wherever he is. Fight him. Beat him. What else is there?"

"Nothing." The teamster hesitated. "I only hope the stinking greenjackets don't pop up out of nowhere on you, the way they did with us. If I hadn't been on one of the last wagons in the train, I never would have got away."

"You didn't know what you were running into. Thanks to you, we do," Roland said. "They won't surprise us. If they beat us, they will have to beat us when we know where they are. By God, my friend, I don't believe any Englishmen ever born, on this side of the sea or the other, can do that."

"I hope you're right," the man said. *Me, too,* Roland thought. But he would never share that with anyone else. Had he had his way, he wouldn't even have shared it with himself.

Victor Radcliff tried to be thorough. He tried to be cautious. So many things could go wrong in war even when you knew as much as you could about what the low, sneaky scoundrels on the other side were up to. Major General Braddock and too many of his men had discovered, to their cost, the difference between *as much as you could* and *enough*.

He and his settlers were moving south, away from Marquis Montcalm-Gozon's men. If they were going to run into trouble, or if trouble was going to run into them, it was most likely to come up from the south toward them.

But likely chances weren't the only ones. Along with stationing scouts ahead of the band of settlers and out to either side, Radcliff also put some men well behind his main body. He perplexed Blaise. "That Frenchman, he wants Freetown," the Negro said. "He not going to come after us."

"Just in case," Victor replied. "I want to be like a hedgehog, so no one can bugger me by surprise."

Then he had to explain what a hedgehog was, because Atlantis had none. Blaise got it in a hurry. "Oh! A—" He said something unpronounceable, at least by a white man. "We have them in my country. I not know you know them."

"Well, I do. They have them in England and France and Spain, too." Again, Victor wondered why Atlantis was missing so many creatures common in Europe. A lot of those beasts, or ones much like them, were also common in Terranova to the west. So far as he knew, though, Terranova had no hedgehogs.

And he had more urgent things to worry about than hedgehogs and honkers. One of the scouts he'd left behind in the north rode into camp that evening on a lathered horse. "They're on the move!" the man exclaimed. "They're heading this way!"

"Who? The French?" Radcliff was astonished. "Why? We might have made them hungry, but not *that* hungry, not this fast."

"Don't know why," the scout said stolidly. "Ain't my station to cipher out *why*. You set me there to tell you *what*. I done did that."

"Yes. You did." Victor nodded. *Why* was his job, and he understood what Montcalm-Gozon was up to no better than he understood the Atlantean dearth of viviparous quadrupeds. "Are a lot of French regulars moving, or only a few?"

"Looked like a bunch," the scout replied.

"Something's gone wrong for them up at Freetown, then. Has to be so," Victor said. The scout only shrugged. "What can we do about it now?" Victor wondered aloud. He dreamt of catching Montcalm-Gozon in an ambush to repay the French for what they'd done to Braddock. To his own regret, he knew he didn't have the men for it. "Were English soldiers chasing them?" he asked hopefully.

"How the devil do I know?" the scout said. "I saw those bastards in blue a-coming. When I did, I stuck around long enough to see it was a good mob of 'em, and then I got out o' there."

"You did right," Victor said. He muttered to himself. Now he knew more than he would have without those carefully placed scouts. But however much he knew, it wasn't as much as he needed to know. He would have to decide—and to act—with incomplete knowledge. All generals had to do that. How many of them got their noses rubbed in it like this, though?

"Done with me?" the scout asked. "My backbone's trying to saw clear through my stomach."

"Go eat. They're roasting a couple of beeves over there." Victor pointed. The beeves were actually oxen from the French supply wagons, but if you complained about every little thing. . . . "Tell them I said to give you a mug of wine, too—and they'd better not have drunk it all up."

"Now you're talking!" The scout hurried away.

Victor was gnawing on roast—well, half-charred, half-raw—beef himself when another scout rode in, this one out of the south. "There's a bunch of damned Frenchmen camped down there, Major," he reported.

"French regulars? Or French settlers?" Victor asked. The answer to that might tell him something about which side was winning the naval war in the Atlantic.

"Settlers," the scout answered, eyeing the toasted meat on a stick with a longing that said he'd had no supper. "Same buggers who've been dogging us all along."

"Kersauzon marched the legs off them to get them up here so fast," Victor said. The scout only shrugged. He didn't care. "Go get yourself something to eat," Victor commanded. "I'll worry about the rest of this."

The scout seemed only too glad to obey. And Victor *did* worry. He'd wondered if he could catch Montcalm-Gozon's troops between his anvil and a hammer of redcoats. Now he wondered if he'd got caught between hammer and anvil himself. As far as he could tell, neither group of French soldiers knew the other was close by— and neither knew his settlers lay between them. As long as he could keep them ignorant like that, he was fine. If they started acting together, he was a long way from fine. He was in more trouble than he knew what to do with.

*Have to keep them from finding out, then. But how?* He could wait for Montcalm-Gozon. Or he could wait for Kersauzon. He couldn't wait for both of them at once. If he tried, they would smash him between them.

All at once, he started to laugh. Then he summoned his officers—and several sergeants who had their wits about them. He didn't name Blaise, but no one said anything when the black man joined the council. Radcliff found he was glad to have him there. No one could say Blaise couldn't take care of himself, and help others do the same. No one tried to do any such thing, either, which Victor found interesting.

He spent a couple of minutes summing up the evening's news. "Bread on both sides of us, and we're the meat in the middle," he finished. That kind of quick meal struck him as a damned good idea.

"How do we make sure we aren't *dead* meat in the middle?" asked the sergeant named Philip, puffing on his pipe. The English settlers had lifted plenty of pipeweed on their raid through French and Spanish Atlantis.

"Well, that's why I called you together. Here's what I've got in mind." Victor spoke for another couple of minutes, then asked, "What do you think?"

Philip puffed again. The pipe jerked up and down against his teeth as he said, "We will be dead meat if you're wrong . . . sir."

"Now tell me something I didn't know," Victor answered dryly, which drew a chuckle of sorts from the veteran underofficer. Victor went on, "But we can't stay where we are and let them grind us to powder. Does anyone think I'm wrong?" No one admitted it. Thus encouraged, Victor went on, "And we can't slide off to the west and let the two French groups get together again. That would cost us more trouble than we want, now and later." He waited again. Again, nobody contradicted him. He spread his hands. "This looks to me to be the best we can do."

Off to one side, Blaise nodded. In the fading firelight, his dark skin should have left him next to invisible. Somehow, it didn't. People *noticed* Blaise. Were he an actor, he would have upstaged the others in the company at every turn. And it wouldn't have been because he was a ham; it was because he was who he was.

A lieutenant said, "Well, if it doesn't work out the way you think it will, chances are we can get away from regulars."

Blaise nodded again. So did several other sergeants. So did the officers at the council. With that lukewarm approval, Victor's plan went forward.

A rifle banged. The report was distinctly sharper and louder than a smoothbore musket's. Something seemed to tug at Roland Kersauzon's hat. He took it off. It had two neat holes through the crown, perhaps an inch—perhaps less than an inch—above the top of his head.

Another rifle spoke. A lieutenant riding a few feet away from him swore and clutched at his left thigh.

"Skirmishers forward!" Only on the second word did Roland's voice break like a boy's. He'd needed a moment to realize just how close a brush with death he'd had.

French settlers trotted north. More gunfire greeted

them. A little more slowly than he should have, Roland realized those weren't mere snipers harrying his force. Somebody didn't want his men going forward. Somebody, here, could only be the English.

*Redcoats or settlers?* he wondered. By the way the foe fought, he guessed he faced settlers. They didn't come out into the open in neat lines. No—they fought from under cover of ferns and from behind trees. They fought like his men, in other words. Now . . . How many of them barred the way?

Only one way to find out. He'd had more men than Victor Radcliff when he was chasing the English leader. He thought he still did. He sent soldiers forward on the open ground and through the woods. If the enemy wanted to stop them, he was welcome to try.

Here and there, French settlers going forward fell. But not very many of them went down, and they didn't fall across a broad front. Roland smiled to himself. Bluff, as he'd thought. They couldn't stop him. They were just trying to slow him down.

He sent more settlers up against Radcliff's men. He also sent orders for runners to come back and keep him informed about what was going on. They told him the English weren't standing and fighting. In his mind, that confirmed that they were nothing but a harassing band.

"Press them!" Roland shouted. "Break them! Close in behind them and wipe them out!" He rode forward himself, though he stayed in the open so runners could find him at need. He fired a pistol at a man in a green jacket. The English settler stayed on his feet. Roland swore and pulled his other pistol from his belt. By then, the enemy soldier had vanished among the pines.

Roland's men couldn't quite break the English settlers. They forced them into headlong retreat—but only so much of it. Wherever the woods grew thicker, the foe fought harder. There turned out to be more of them than Roland had thought at first, too. They weren't just a thin skirmishing line to be thrust back and then broken or shoved aside. They had reserves cunningly placed to make life difficult for an advancing opponent.

Another bullet snapped past Roland's head. He ducked without even thinking. People did when someone shot at them. You couldn't help it, no matter how much you wished you could. Only a handful of men seemed immune to the reflex.

Darkness came down at last. The French settlers had pushed the enemy back several miles. Roland was pleased with himself. All the French settlers seemed pleased with themselves—all but the wounded. Surgeons worked on them by firelight. Their cries split the night.

But those heartbreaking shrieks weren't what killed Roland Kersauzon's pleasure. He suddenly wondered how and why so many English settlers stood between him and Montcalm-Gozon's army. How had Victor Radcliff got past or got through the French regulars? Whatever he'd done, it couldn't be good news for the Frenchmen from across the sea.

Which immediately brought up the next question: what to do about it? His first impulse was to order his men forward right away. Regulars barely even thought about night advances. Too many things could go wrong with carefully dressed lines. Roland's men, though, could play bushwhacker as well as their foes.

In the end, he waited for dawn. As he rolled himself in his blanket, he wondered whether he'd regret it later.

Victor Radcliff wished for artillery. He might as well have wished for the moon while he was at it. His men couldn't very well have carried cannon as they sneaked through the French lines.

But now Montcalm-Gozon's men were trying to blast

his force out of the way. The Frenchmen had plenty of fieldpieces. And, listening to the roar of guns from behind them, so did the redcoats who'd pushed them out of their lines and were driving them south.

If the English settlers could hold, the French regulars were trapped. If Victor's men had to retreat ... well, he didn't want to do that, not with the French settlers coming up from the south. One of these days, historians would understand exactly how this campaign worked. They would walk the fields and forests. They would read accounts from survivors on both sides and in all four groups of combatants. They would issue learned, dispassionate judgments. For anyone actually going through the fight, confusion and fear reigned.

Regulars without guns of their own could never have withstood the cannonading the French were giving to Victor's men. Regulars would have stood out in the open in neat ranks and let themselves get butchered. Victor had watched it happen to the redcoats.

His own men knew better—or fought differently, anyhow. They sprawled on the ground and hid in back of whatever cover they could find. Some of them had even dug scrapes with bayonets and belt knives, piling up dirt in front of the shallow holes to stop or deflect bullets. Here and there, cannon balls killed. More often than not, they harmlessly shot past Victor's settlers, who weren't packed together anywhere near so tightly as regulars would have been.

As long as the Frenchmen kept cannonading his soldiers, he couldn't do much to reply. They stayed out of musket range. Even his few riflemen had trouble reaching them. He shouted encouragement to the English settlers. As long as they didn't break, they made Montcalm-Gozon sweat.

The French commander had worries of his own—or Radcliff devoutly hoped he did. He was harried from behind, as the distant racket of gunfire in Victor's ears proved. With any luck at all, he would have to turn around and face the troops pursuing him. If he did, he wouldn't be able to deal with Victor's men. That would be very good, which was putting it mildly.

Victor was thinking just how good it would be when a rider on a lathered horse galloped up from the south. "Major, the French settlers are attacking us down there," the man said, and pointed back over his shoulder.

"Damnation," Victor said, and then something more pungent in French, and then something still more pungent in Spanish. Another cannon ball thundered past them, but that was the least of his worries. "How hard are they pressing you?" he asked.

"As hard as they can," the courier replied.

"Damnation," Radcliff repeated. That wasn't what he wanted to hear. He didn't doubt it, though. If Roland Kersauzon's men had got this far north, they *would* try to bull through his blocking force. (If they'd got this far north this fast, they'd done some fancy marching, but that was a different story altogether.) "For God's sake, hold them back. We can't have them pitching into our rear right now, not when we've got warm work in front of us like this."

French cannon bellowed again. Victor knew he made a good target. He stayed out in the open, while most of his men had taken cover. The courier flinched a little as the ball flew by, but held his ground. He gave Victor a thin smile. "Really, Major? I never would have noticed."

"Heh." Victor touched the brim of his hat in a half-salute, acknowledging the man's coolness. "Go on. Get back out of range before they ventilate your kidneys. Let the men know they need to hang on no matter what the settlers do to them."

"I'll tell 'em." The horseman's grimace was as understated as his smile. "Don't know if they'll be glad to hear it." With a shrug, he wheeled his mount and rode back toward the south.

He hadn't been gone more than a couple of minutes before the French cannonading suddenly stopped. Montcalm-Gozon's lines re-formed in the sudden near-silence (the French nobleman was bound to have a rear guard of his own trying to hold off whatever trouble lay behind *him*). A horn call rang out over the field. The sun glittered off bayonets being fixed as all the French soldiers made the same motion at the same time. The horn rang out again—a different call this time. Those bayonets flashed fire once more as the Frenchmen lowered them. One more call, and, with a fierce shout, as much of Montcalm-Gozon's army as he could spare advanced against the English settlers.

It was glorious. It was grandiose. It was, frankly, terrifying. "Hold your fire till they're well within range!" Victor called. He knew a certain amount of pride that his voice didn't wobble. Here and there, riflemen opened up on the French. They could hit at ranges well beyond those a man with a smoothbore musket could use. A few blue-coated enemy soldiers stumbled and fell, but only a few. The rest stepped over them and came on.

A hundred yards away from Victor, the Frenchmen halted. The first rank of soldiers dropped to one knee. The second rank bent low above them. The third stood straight. They all fired together.

Bullets snapped past him. One hit his horse with a meaty *thunk*. The beast squealed and staggered. He jumped off before it foundered. He had his two pistols and a rapier. They didn't seem enough to repel the French.

"Get down, Major!" somebody behind him yelled. "Better shooting over you than through you."

That struck Victor as excellent advice. He flattened

out as the Frenchmen dressed their lines. A moment later, with more cheers, they charged. His men greeted them with the best volley they could. This wasn't just fire to annoy the enemy and gall him. The charge staggered when it met that wall of flying lead. French soldiers clutched at themselves and screamed as they fell. But the ones who weren't hit came on.

Victor fired first one pistol, then the other. He thought he hit one enemy soldier. From one knee, he threw a pistol in a startled Frenchman's face. He might have broken the man's nose. Then he sprang up and skewered a bluecoat who was too slow to protect himself with his bayoneted musket.

And then he ran for his life, back toward the trees. No one spitted him from behind. No one shot him in the back. None of his own men shot him in the chest or belly, though musket balls whipped past him in both directions.

A dead settler with a fully loaded rifle lay behind the first pine he came to. The man looked absurdly surprised at catching a bullet just above the bridge of the nose. He must have been about to fire when he got hit. Victor snatched up the rifle. There came a man in a fancy uniform—plainly an officer. The Frenchman's sword had blood on it. Victor fired. The officer spun, then slowly crumpled.

"Holy God!" someone bawled in French. "The general's down!"

*I got Montcalm-Gozon?* Radcliff thought dazedly. "We take surrenders!" he shouted, also in French. The enemy soldiers started throwing down their muskets and throwing up their hands.

# XXIV

*They* were breaking. Finally, after a running fight that had gone on all through the day, the English settlers in front of Roland Kersauzon's men had had as much as they could take. They'd managed to get across a creek running east to the ocean, and were still defending the fords, but Roland was sure his army could force a crossing.

He looked west, toward the Green Ridge Mountains. They were barely a smudge on the horizon, but, as usual, clouds piled high above them. The sun was setting in blood as it sank into those clouds. "Can we get over this miserable stream once night falls?" Roland asked his lieutenants.

They looked at one another. Nobody spoke right away. At last, one of the junior officers said, "I'm afraid I don't know where the shallow stretches are." Several other men nodded, as if he'd said what they were thinking.

*"Nom d'un nom,"* Roland muttered. He dismissed the lieutenants and summoned sergeants and corporals. They made an older, more raffish group than the one he'd sent away. He put the same question to them.

"I can find a ford," a weathered sergeant said confidently. "I used to run traps up here. I know what's what."

He'd poached, in other words, since this was English territory. Roland grinned. "Good. That's what I wanted to hear. As soon as it's nice and dark, we'll get moving. . . ."

But the English Atlanteans knew where the fords were, too. They started bonfires on their side of the creek at each one of them, to make sure Roland's men couldn't catch them unawares. Roland took the sergeant aside. "I know what you're going to ask me," the trapper said: "Did they miss any?"

"You're right—that's what I'm going to ask you," Roland agreed. "Did they?"

"No, damn them," the sergeant said. "Well, if you want to go five miles west, there's sort of a ford they may not have covered. I can't tell about that one from where we are now."

Reluctantly, Kersauzon shook his head. "We'd get scattered all over the landscape if we tried it. And there's no promise Radcliff's men don't have a fire burning at that ford, too, is there?"

"*Monsieur,* the only promise is, we're going to die sooner or later," the sergeant answered. "I want it to be later, in the arms of a beautiful woman. If her husband shoots me, even that's not so bad. But I know you don't always get what you want, not in this life you don't."

"Isn't that the sad and sorry truth? Her husband, eh?" Kersauzon shook his head. The sergeant grinned and winked and nudged him. In spite of himself, Roland laughed—for a moment. But the smile slid from his lips as he went on, "We'll have to pay more to cross that creek come morning."

The uncouth, backwoodsy French Atlantean shrugged a shrug a Paris *boulevardier* might have envied. "Every business has its costs," he said. "Since we aren't going to go tonight, shouldn't we grab what rest we can?"

"An excellent idea," Roland said briskly.

Even when he wrapped himself in his blanket, sleep didn't want to come. He knew he was keyed up. That accounted for some of his trouble—some, but not all. The English Atlanteans on the north side of the stream were godawful noisy. Raucous snatches of marching songs floated through the air. So did the sounds of tramping feet, as if large numbers of soldiers were on the march.

For a little while, Roland worried, there under that ratty, tattered blanket. Then he chuckled. Trying to bluff him, were they? Did they think he would believe they'd been reinforced, and hold off on account of that? If they did, they were making a bad mistake. Some of them were making their very last mistake. Chuckling once more, he slid headlong into sleep.

That veteran sergeant shook him awake. The earliest traces of morning twilight grayed the eastern horizon. "Time for the dance already?" Roland asked around a yawn.

"I think so." The sergeant jerked a thumb toward the north, across the creek. "But those noisy baboons keep tripping over their own clodhoppers."

"They want us to think every Englishman in Atlantis is hiding among those trees," Kersauzon said scornfully. "Well, I don't care what they want. I am not a four-year-old, to be fooled by such tricks. We'll get our men fed, we'll get them across the stream, and we'll get back together with Marquis Montcalm-Gozon."

Breakfast was less than he wished it were: stale hard-tack and gamy sausage. But a little ballast in the belly was better than none. He took no more than any of his soldiers. As soon as the men were fed, he formed them in long columns, one in front of each ford. The troops at the head of each column would suffer. Not all of them would fall, though, as they charged through the waist-deep water. And they would drive the English Atlante-ans before them once they got across.

Ferns rustled and quivered in the woods on the far side of the creek. Drums began to pound. Hearing those drums made the hair at the nape of Roland's neck quiver. "No," he whispered hoarsely. "It's not possible."

But it was. It was not only possible, it was true. Green-coats emerged from the greenery and formed up op-posite his own men. There were more of them than he would have expected to find in a rear-guard detachment. That made one nasty surprise. Things got worse. As the drums continued to bray, redcoats broke cover and took their places beside the English Atlanteans. Their sergeants bellowed and swore till their alignment was perfect.

"What are those *salauds* doing here?" a soldier said. Maybe the question was meant for Roland, maybe for an uncaring God.

Roland feared he knew the answer. Only one seemed likely: somehow, Montcalm-Gozon's French regulars had come to grief. The English had broken the siege of Freetown, and now they intended to break the French settlers, too.

"*Monsieur,* should we not withdraw?" a lieutenant asked urgently. "There are a devil of a lot of Englishmen on the other side of the stream."

"Yes, there are." Roland heard the bleakness in his own voice. "And they know where the fords are as well as we do. If we pull back, what will they do next, eh?"

The junior officer's mouth twisted. He didn't have to be Elijah the prophet to foretell the future here. "They'll come after us."

"Too right they will." Kersauzon couldn't even tell his men to give the foe a volley. Oh, he could, but it wouldn't do much good. In his infinite wisdom, he'd ordered his force into an assault formation. Only the few soldiers at the head of each column could open fire. Whereas the English ...

No sooner had Roland realized the English could open fire when and as they pleased than they did. The green-coated settlers simply started shooting as they saw fit. The English regulars delivered a volley under the direction of their officers and sergeants, then methodically reloaded for another one.

And Roland's men lurched back. Not only could they not reply effectively, but they were so bunched up that not even smoothbore muskets could miss. Some of them fell. Others—the ones who could—reeled away from the southern bank of the stream.

*Crash!* That second volley tore through the French settlers. They broke, running for any cover they could find. Roland was surprised to find himself still imperforate. He yelled himself hoarse, trying to stem the rout. He might as well have saved his breath, because none of that yelling did any good at all.

Victor Radcliff rode across Stamford Creek. Bodies lay on the far bank. Other French settlers, wounded but not dead, stretched imploring hands out toward him. He went on past them. Somebody on his side would take care of them sooner or later. He wasn't sure just how— maybe drag them off to the surgeons, maybe knock them over the head. If none of the wounded enemies pulled a pistol or tried anything else foolish, odds were most of them would survive.

The English lieutenant-colonel rode beside him. The young officer's face radiated enthusiasm. "By God, Major, I do believe we've really done it this time! We've broken them!" He waved happily. "And it's mostly because your men held the French regulars in place until we could come down on them from behind. Well done!"

"Much obliged, sir," Victor replied. "And much obliged to you for coming down on them when you did. We couldn't have held much longer. They would have broken through us in another hour."

"It was a bit of a near-run thing, wasn't it?" the lieutenant-colonel said. "No one knew who'd be the heroes and who the goats till it all played out, eh?" Just for a moment, his grin slipped. "Pity about Brigadier Endicott, though."

"Yes, sir," Victor agreed politely. Brigadier Daniel Endicott had commanded the English regulars who'd landed in Freetown and given the force there strength enough to break the French siege. He'd had the bad luck—certainly for him—to put his face in front of a musket ball a few days earlier. Not ten minutes afterwards, his second-in-command got shot in the leg. That left the young lieutenant-colonel the senior English officer able to serve in the field.

None of which broke Victor's heart. Endicott had looked to be even more of a book soldier than the late Major General Braddock, and Colonel Harcourt was no improvement. The lieutenant-colonel, by contrast, had begun to understand that war in Atlantis wasn't the same as war on the manicured fields of Europe. Coming right out and saying so seemed the opposite of useful.

Musketeers fired from the woods ahead. Sudden puffs of smoke marked their positions—or where they'd fired from, anyhow. Anybody with a grain of sense would go somewhere else to reload and shoot again.

Not far from Victor, an English Atlantean swore, clutched his calf, and sat down in the dirt. He drew a knife and cut at his hose to get cloth for a bandage. "I'm out of the fight for a while," he said matter-of-factly.

"You'll do fine. The surgeons will fix you up in nothing flat." Victor wondered how big a liar he was.

The English lieutenant-colonel shouted orders. Redcoats advanced on the wood. A few more shots came from it. One or two English regulars fell. The rest went on in among the trees. No doubt some French Atlanteans escaped from the southern edge of the forest. But when the redcoats emerged, several of them held up their bayonets to show the blood on them.

"Good show," the lieutenant-colonel said. "We've dealt with the one bunch—now all we have to do is finish rounding up the other, and the war here is as good as over. Then we see where it all ends up at the peace table."

That brought Victor Radcliff up short. To him, Atlantis was the world. But the English officer reminded him things didn't work that way. England and France and their allies were also fighting in Europe, on the Terranovan mainland, and in India. A stroke of the pen, a swap of this settlement for that, could annul everything won here with blood and bullets.

"They wouldn't trade away everything we've done . . . would they?" Those last two hesitant words showed that Victor knew they might.

"It's not up to me, Major. Nor is it up to you," the lieutenant-colonel replied. "The diplomats make those choices. Our task here is to ensure that they can bargain from a position of strength."

More redcoats came out of the pine woods. They'd taken a couple of prisoners. They prodded the disgruntled French settlers along with their bayoneted muskets. One of the captives had a hole in his breeches and was bleeding, but not too badly. Victor guessed his prodding had been more forceful than he would have liked. The English Atlantean wondered what the prisoner had done to deserve it. Then he wondered if the man had done anything. The fellow likely counted himself lucky to be alive, even if he was injured. Victorious troops were supposed to take prisoners, yes. But in battle all kinds of things that were supposed to happen didn't, and just as many things that weren't supposed to did.

"We've smashed up Montcalm-Gozon's regulars," Victor said. "If we can do the same to Kersauzon's settlers, we'll be in about the strongest position we can—in Atlantis, anyhow. I hear the rest of the war is going pretty well."

"I hear the same," the lieutenant-colonel said. "By what the regulars newly come to Freetown tell me, we've smashed the French and their native nabobs in India."

"That's good news," Victor said.

"It is indeed. They put up a better fight than we thought they could: I know that for a fact," the English officer said. "And as for the remnants of the French forces here . . . Well, we should be able to settle them without too much trouble, I expect." He might have been the picture of confidence.

"Sir," Victor Radcliff said gently, "I do want to remind you that the late General Braddock said the same thing."

"Oh, yes. Of course." The Englishman's tone was indulgent. "But, whilst I don't care to speak ill of the dead, General Braddock committed some serious tactical blunders. I hope we can avoid those."

"Yes, sir." Major Radcliff nodded. "So do I."

Had the English pressed their pursuit harder, they might have bagged all the retreating French settlers. Roland Kersauzon was only too bitterly aware of that. Even as things were, he had to fight a couple of sharp rear-guard actions. He sacrificed men he couldn't afford to lose to keep from losing everybody. There were bad bargains, and then there were worse ones.

"We'll have a better chance inside French Atlantis," he said again and again, trying to hearten the men he had left and trying to keep retreat from turning to rout.

"If we have to, we can stand siege at Nouveau Redon. I'd like to see the damned Englishmen try to take it."

"I wouldn't," someone behind him said. Roland's head whipped around. He wanted to know who sounded so hopeless. But all the men close by tramped along with their heads down. None of them seemed ready to single out the fellow who'd spoken what probably lurked in all their minds.

It lurked in Roland's mind, too, however much he wished it didn't. No matter how he tried to cheer up his troops, his own spirits were at low ebb. How could it be otherwise? Discovering that the English settlers had escaped him in Atlantis was bad. Discovering that the settlers and redcoats together had put paid to Montcalm-Gozon's proud regulars wasn't just bad. It was catastrophic. He'd beaten redcoats once, when they obligingly marched into his trap. Trying to cross the creek to attack Victor Radcliff's men, he'd stumbled into theirs.

*Maybe we should see what kind of terms we can get.* Had anyone else suggested that, Roland Kersauzon would have been furious. But he could make the suggestion to himself: he knew he wouldn't follow through on it.

"They're going to try to take away everything we've got left," a sergeant said with weary cynicism.

Roland nodded. "That's right—they will. That's how greedy they are, the English *cochons.* So we won't let them, eh? If you bother a turtle, what does it do? It pulls back into its shell. And good luck making it come out again."

"You aim to pull us back into our shell, *Monsieur*?" the underofficer asked.

"If you have a better idea, I'd love to hear it," Kersauzon replied. A lot of commanders might have said that for form's sake. He meant it. But the sergeant only shook his head. Roland went on. "The longer we hold out, the better the chance something good will happen somewhere else. If it does . . ."

"We're saved," the sergeant said when he paused.

He nodded again, though what went through his mind was, *Well, we may be saved, anyhow.* If the English seized all of French Atlantis but for Nouveau Redon, things were unlikely to go back to the *status quo ante bellum* no matter how long a siege the town withstood. And the enemy might do just that—there wasn't much resistance except for his settler army.

That raised another question: how long could the fortress hold out? Roland didn't know the exact answer, not in days. But he knew the form the answer would take. Nouveau Redon would stay free as long as the food held out and as long as there was no treachery. Munitions were not an issue; the fortress had plenty. A spring near the center of town ensured the fortress wouldn't run short of water.

The food could last a very long time, especially if his army expelled civilians so it fed no useless mouths. Roland had overseen the victualing of Nouveau Redon himself. Hardtack and sauerkraut and smoked meat and dried fruit were uninspiring; anyone who said anything else was a damned liar. They could keep body and soul together a long time, though.

Treachery . . . Roland gnawed on the inside of his lower lip. The longer the siege went on, the more he'd have to worry about it. If someone decided relief was hopeless but thought he might cut a deal with the army investing the fortress . . . If that happened, Nouveau Redon was in danger.

As Roland rode south—back toward the border between English and French Atlantis—one other possibility occurred to him. If the plague broke out inside the fortress, he might have to surrender whether he wanted to or not. Disease was a roll of the dice. If the pestilence or dysentery or typhus struck the invaders, they would have to give up the siege.

"They deserve a pestilence, don't they, God?" He aimed what was half a prayer, half a suggestion toward the sky. Maybe God would listen; maybe He wouldn't. Any which way, Roland figured he'd made the effort.

Had the bridges over the Erdre been down, he probably wouldn't have been able to get back to Nouveau Redon to stand siege. But they still stood. Roland and his men had come north over them . . . come north over them more than once, in fact. After crossing back into French Atlantis, he ordered the spans fired. He didn't like that, but saw no other choice. Right now, slowing the enemy down was almost as good as beating him.

Almost. Roland and his survivors kept on retreating.

Victor Radcliff watched smoke rise up over the Stour. "They're burning their bridges behind them," he said: for once, literal truth and no cliché.

"They'll have men defending the line of the river, then, if they be not utter fools." The English lieutenant-colonel sighed wearily. "And utter fools they are not. They could not have caused us so much trouble if they were."

"We'll get over the river," Victor said. "Kersauzon's on the run. He won't leave enough soldiers behind to seriously hinder us."

The English officer's eyebrow rose. For a moment, Victor wondered why. Then he realized he'd committed a solecism. He smiled. If the lieutenant-colonel could worry about his grammar as well as the campaign . . . more power to him. And, after a moment, the Englishman unbent enough to admit, "I think you make a good prophet."

Although the French settlers had burnt what they

could, the stone towers supporting the bridges' wooden superstructure still stood. And the redcoats had with them the usual contingent of military engineers, Victor hadn't expected to need their services until and unless the English army besieged the French, but they proved valuable here at the border.

One thing Atlantis had was an exuberant profusion of lumber. Axe blows rang out along the side of the river. The engineers did not try to re-create what the fleeing French settlers had destroyed. The redcoats cared only about making a way across. That they did. The Romans who'd bridged the Rhine for Julius Caesar would have approved.

"Well, well," the lieutenant-colonel said after riding across one of those improvised bridges. "So this is French Atlantis." He looked around. "Doesn't seem much different from English Atlantis, does it?"

"No, sir—except it's full of Frenchmen," Victor replied. What had the English officer expected? Something that looked like France? In the towns, English Atlantis looked like England. Farms there grew European—and sometimes Terranovan—crops. But the countryside remained stubbornly Atlantean.

If anything, French Atlantis seemed more Atlantean than the country farther north. Far fewer people actually lived here. That meant the landscape had changed less than it had where Englishmen settled. Pines and barrel trees stayed common right up to the very edges of towns. Victor's soldiers had no trouble catching oil thrushes in the woods. They ate better than the redcoats, who relied on rations and viewed local foodstuffs with suspicion.

"I ain't gonna eat one of them funny-looking things," an English sergeant declared. "Maybe if I was starving—but I ain't."

Victor didn't think oil thrushes were funny-looking. He'd grown up with them, as he had with the good-sized thrushes with dull red breasts that English Atlanteans called robins. To him, the small, bright robin redbreasts of the home island would have looked strange—had he ever seen one.

Only men from Roland Kersauzon's rear guard and occasional free-lance bushwhackers slowed the English army's advance. When the redcoats caught a *franc-tireur,* they hanged him from the closest suitable tree as a warning to other locals. "If they want to fight us, let them put on uniforms and join an army," the lieutenant-colonel said. "I would respect them then, and treat them as soldiers deserve to be treated. But this contemptible skulking must cease, and we shall make it cease by whatever means prove necessary."

Here and there, English Atlanteans had picked up guns and attacked the invading French forces. No doubt Montcalm-Gozon's men had hanged the irregulars they caught. Did that stop the English Atlanteans from harrying them? Victor Radcliff doubted it, but he didn't quarrel with the English officer. That worthy had tradition on his side, and didn't seem inclined to listen to anyone who disagreed.

Besides, what was wrong with hanging Frenchmen? After all the trouble they'd caused, Victor wouldn't have shed a tear to see the lot of them strung up. Neither would Blaise. "Ought to hang everyone who buys and sells slaves," he said.

That would touch off a revolt in French Atlantis. Victor was sure of it. The locals might understand and forgive the execution of guerrillas. Anyone who went off and did something like that took his chances. But the French Atlanteans—and the Spanish Atlanteans farther south—were convinced they had the right to own human chattels. And . . .

"Didn't Africans sell you to the white slave traders?" Victor asked.

Blaise nodded. "Hang them, too," he said. "They serve it." He made a face. "Deserve it." His English got better by the day. It still had a long way to go, though.

Before long, the direction in which Roland Kersauzon's men were retreating grew obvious. "He's going to stand siege in Nouveau Redon," Victor told the English lieutenant-colonel.

"Well, we'll just have to winkle him out of there, in that case." The English officer certainly didn't lack for aggressiveness.

Whether he lacked for brains might be a different question. "It's a formidable place," Victor warned. "It won't be easy to take."

"He's never come up against proper engineers, either," the lieutenant-colonel said.

"How much can engineers do against solid rock?" Victor asked.

The English lieutenant-colonel's smile was indulgent, almost sweet. "I believe you've got the question backwards, Major. You should ask, how much can solid rock do against engineers?"

Back where he started. Roland Kersauzon hadn't expected to return to Nouveau Redon except in triumph. He hadn't imagined the English Atlanteans stood a chance against brave French soldiers. He'd thought he could beat them with settlers. By God, he *had* beaten the redcoats with settlers! That should have decided things.

It should have, but it didn't. He failed to count on English tenacity. The enemy kept fighting. Their raiding band made Roland separate from Montcalm-Gozon—but he never did catch up with Victor Radcliff. He damned *Don* José all over again. He could deal with his enemies, but God protect him from people who claimed to be his friends.

And English tenacity also meant sending more red-

coats across the ocean. No more French regulars came
to Atlantis. Maybe the English wouldn't let them. But
maybe King Louis and his ministers simply couldn't be
bothered with sending reinforcements. Roland wouldn't
have been surprised either way.

Ordinary people streamed out of Nouveau Redon.
Roland wanted no one there who couldn't carry a musket. The fewer mouths he fed, the better. As long as he
had soldiers on the walls and supplies in the storerooms,
he was ready to defy the world—or, at least, those parts
of it that spoke English.

One good thing sprang from the wreckage of his
hopes: he worried a little less about disease than he had
before. You couldn't catch smallpox or measles more
than once. So the learned doctors promised him, and
for once he was pretty sure they were right. The ones
who could catch them already had, and had got better
or died.

He posted a strong garrison of reliable soldiers
around the storehouses. That didn't seem so important
now, which was why he hastened to take care of it. If
the garrison was in place before people started fretting
about hunger, it would stand a better chance of stopping
trouble—or making sure trouble didn't start—than if he
put it in place after soldiers started tightening their belts.
He hoped it would, anyhow.

For now, his men's fighting spirit was strong. "We'll
whip those English *cochons* right out of their boots,
won't we, sir?" said a youngster on the wall. He shook
his fist at the north. "Just let them come!"

"But of course we'll beat them." Roland wouldn't
have weakened such enthusiasm for the world. As for
letting the English settlers and redcoats come ... He
and the force he had left couldn't very well stop them.
He knew that too painfully well. If he could have, he
would have.

He made a point of checking the artillery. "We will dismay them with our range," a grizzled gunnery sergeant said. "We're up much higher than they are, you comprehend. It gives us the advantage."

"Yes, I comprehend perfectly," Roland said. "They will be sorry that they have tried to rob us of the jewel in the crown of French Atlantis."

The gunner's face lit up. "That is well said, *Monsieur*!"

"I'm glad you think so." Roland Kersauzon had never particularly believed he had a knack for the telling phrase. If he came up with one now, it was bound to be as much by luck as for any other reason.

And how much would it matter one way or the other? If the enemy seized the rest of the crown, of course he would start prying at the jewel. Someone would have to come to its rescue. Someone would have to—but would anyone do it?

No one from French Atlantis was likely to come to his aid. Such force as these lands could provide, he had. Oh, there would still be armed men among the settlers, but there was no other army of settlers. And there would be none, not to relieve him. If any army formed, it would be to quell servile uprisings. He was bitterly sure of that. What would the enslaved Negroes and Terranovan natives here be doing now? What they'd done in Spanish Atlantis? It seemed much too likely.

What hope from across the sea, then? Would the mother country send another force of regulars to help its Atlantean settlements? Even if King Louis wanted to do just that—something of which Roland had no assurance—what connection lay between desire and ability?

King George had reinforced his redcoats. That argued England was winning the war at sea. So did Victor Radcliff's mortifying escape. The best will in the world might not let France ship soldiers across the Atlantic. If it didn't . . .

*In that case, why am I still fighting? Why not surrender now?* Roland wondered. He would save his own skin, and he would save the lives of so many settlers who had already suffered so much for French Atlantis and for France.

But he could not make himself yield while still able to fight. *If they want me so much, let them come and get me,* he thought. He didn't know what was going on in the wider world; he could only guess. And even if his guesses were right now, fortune might reverse itself while he held out.

He could hope so. And he was too damned stubborn to quit. "Here I stand," he murmured. If a German Protestant had said the same thing once upon a time . . . Roland knew little of Protestants, and even less of Germans.

"Oh," the English lieutenant-colonel said when he got his first good look at Nouveau Redon.

"Yes, sir," Victor Radcliff replied, in lieu of *I told you so.* "The nut won't be easy to crack, I'm afraid."

"So it would seem," the English officer said. After a moment, though, his chin came up. "The meat inside will be all the sweeter, then."

"Once we get at it, it will." Victor didn't want to say, *If we can get at it.* The lieutenant-colonel might think he lacked confidence. He also might think the same thing himself.

"First things first," the Englishman said. "We'll surround them, cut them off. We'll offer battle. If they come out to engage us, so much the better."

"Roland Kersauzon's not that foolish," Victor said. "I wish he were."

"Well, we can hope he will be," the lieutenant-colonel said. Radcliff only shrugged. You could always hope. But hoping for something and counting on it were very different. He hoped the Englishman understood that.

Up on the walls of Nouveau Redon, a cannon boomed. The ball fell far short of the settlers and redcoats. The gunners must have known it would. Victor recognized the shot for what it was: defiance. A breeze from the Green Ridge Mountains blew the black-powder smoke toward the ocean.

"They won't act so bold when we cut them off from the river," the English lieutenant-colonel said.

Victor stared at him. Didn't he know anything about this place he aimed to besiege? "They don't depend on the Blavet for water, sir," the Atlantean said carefully.

"No, eh? Well, cisterns go dry, even if it takes longer."

"They don't depend on cisterns, either," Victor said. No, the Englishman really didn't know anything about Nouveau Redon. "They have a spring, and it's never been known to fail. We may be able to starve them out. We may be able to take the town with saps and parallels—"

"Won't be easy," the lieutenant-colonel said. Victor nodded. The ground rose sharply toward the citadel, and grew stonier the higher it got: not promising terrain for digging trenches.

"I'm afraid we'll be here quite a while," Victor said. "We just have to pray we can keep our own men supplied—and that sickness doesn't break out. If it does . . ." He spread his hands, as if to say, *What can you do?*

"We are going to take that fortress." The English lieutenant-colonel might have been an Old Testament prophet. He sounded utterly sure he was telling the truth. Radcliff envied him his certainty. The Old Testament prophets had had God on their side. Victor hoped his army did, too. He hoped so, yes, but he was less sure of it than people like Elijah had been.

The lieutenant-colonel shouted orders. Horns blared. Drums thumped. Soldiers moved out to encircle Nouveau Redon. The opening steps in a siege were as formal as those in a gavotte.

Then the Englishman gave his attention back to Victor. "Tell me, Major—have you read Caesar's *Gallic War*?"

"Yes, sir." Victor wondered why on earth the other officer chose this moment to ask that question. A bit touchily, the Atlantean added, "We aren't all barbarians on this side of the ocean. I can give you *All Gaul is divided into three parts* or talk about the aurochs and the other curious animals of the German forest. If you happen to have a copy with you, I can even make a stab at construing sentences, though I confess my Latin isn't what it was fifteen years ago."

"Don't fret. Don't fret," the lieutenant-colonel said, which only left Victor more fretful than ever. The English officer continued, "Upon my honor, Major, I meant no slight by the question. Please accept my assurances on that score."

"Very well, sir." Victor's voice stayed stiff.

The English officer pointed toward Nouveau Redon. France's fleurs-de-lys flag still fluttered defiantly up there. "Can you give me precise bearings on where inside the town that spring rises?"

"I can't—no, sir. But I'm sure you can find out if you inquire among my greencoats. Some of them will have spent more time inside than I have." Radcliff's curiosity roused. "Why, if I may ask?"

"Perhaps we can match the famous fate of Uxellodunum," the Englishman replied.

Whatever Uxellodunum's fate had been, it wasn't famous to Victor. He presumed it was set forth in the *Gal-*

*lic War.* If it was, he didn't remember it. Suppressing a sigh, he said, "I fear you must enlighten me, sir."

Enlighten him the English officer did, finishing, "No guarantees, of course—there never are in warfare. But it strikes me that this is our best—and quickest—chance of securing a victory at reasonable cost."

Victor Radcliff did something he'd thought he would never do: he doffed his hat to the lieutenant-colonel. "If we can bring that off . . . If we can, I'd give twenty pounds to be a fly on the wall and see the look on Roland Kersauzon's face."

"He is a difficult man," the lieutenant-colonel said.

"I'm sure he thinks the same of you—and of me," Victor replied. "And chances are he's right—and so are you. All things considered, I would sooner lay siege out here than stand siege in there."

"As would I," the Englishman agreed. "Montcalm-Gozon had me mured up in Freetown, which was . . . less than pleasant. But my position was still open to the sea. Your settlers returned, and then we were reinforced from England. Only the angels could reinforce Kersauzon now."

"He won't ask for them, even if God would give them. He's a proud man," Victor said. "If you don't know that, you don't know him at all."

# XXV

Roland Kersauzon hadn't thought a lot about what being besieged might be like. He'd never imagined it could bore him. But it did. One day seemed the same as another. He'd started losing track of how long he'd been shut up here. How much longer could he stay?

Till the storehouses emptied, and then a little while after that. But when they would had no simple answer. If he kept his men on full rations as long as the food held out ... he was an idiot, or a man who expected to be relieved soon, assuming those two weren't one and the same.

Three-quarters rations? Half-rations? When to swing from one to the other? Those were the worries that weighed on his mind. But what difference did it make if he decided tomorrow, not today? Not much, and he knew it.

Had he worried about water ... He didn't, though. The spring was what it had always been, what it always would be. God had loved Nouveau Redon when He sent the cold, pure water bubbling up through the rock. He'd also loved the settler who first realized what that spring meant: an impregnable fortress for French Atlantis.

The English weren't even trying to take it, or not trying very hard. Oh, they were advancing their saps and parallels little by little. They had yet to bring cannon within range of the walls, though. Roland doubted whether they could. The ground rose steeply and grew rocky in a hurry. Every new move forward would get harder and go slower.

Once in a while, guns on the wall would fire. A cannon ball killed a team of oxen hauling something toward the closest trenches. The gunners whooped and capered, proud of their shooting.

*"Magnifique,"* Roland said dryly when he learned what the celebration was about. "Now the damned Englishmen will have themselves a supper of beef."

That made the cannoneers' faces fall. They hadn't had a supper of beef for a while now. Oh, some beef went into the sausages they gnawed on, but no one in his right mind inquired too closely about what all went into sausages. Better not to know; better just to eat . . . as long as the sausages held out.

And Roland proved right. The redcoats and greencoats butchered the murdered oxen and roasted the carcasses. Mother Nature was in a cruel mood; the wind carried the savory smell of the cooking meat straight into Nouveau Redon. Roland's supper was a hard cracker, some barley mush, and a chunk of tough, stale sausage not quite so long as his thumb. His stomach growled enormously at the wonderful aroma wafting over the walls.

Also once in a while, riflemen—commonly settlers in green coats, which made them harder to spot—would sneak forward from the enemy lines and snipe at the defenders. A rifleman had a chance of hitting a man from more than a furlong. The surgeons got reminded they were there for a reason.

And the whole garrison got reminded they were in the middle of a war. "I'm almost grateful to the English," Roland remarked to a sergeant after a man took a flesh wound. "They make sure we don't go slack."

*"Oui, Monsieur."* The underofficer nodded. Then he pointed out toward the river. "They stay busy themselves, too. See how much dirt and filth they dump into the clean water."

Sure enough, the Blavet had been clear enough to reflect the sky's blue till it came alongside the English works encircling Nouveau Redon. But it ran brown and turbid as it flowed on toward the Atlantic.

"They are a filthy people themselves, and it shows in everything they do," Roland said. The sergeant nodded again. But Roland's eyes narrowed as he surveyed that muddy stain in the river. "I wouldn't have thought they were digging enough to put that much muck into the water."

"It doesn't come from nowhere," the sergeant said.

"True enough. And the river was clean—well, pretty clean—east of here before they came." Roland shrugged. No river that ran past a town could stay perfectly clear. But the Blavet hadn't looked like *that* before.

The redcoats and the English settlers were still working at their saps. Could they be working enough to make the river so muddy? Roland's shoulders went up and down once more. As the sergeant said, the dirt didn't come from nowhere. So the enemy had to be digging that much.

Scornfully, the sergeant said, "I'll bet they don't have the sense to draw their water upstream and piss downstream."

Roland Kersauzon laughed. "I'll bet you're right."

Once, this little thicket of redwoods had shaded a house outside Nouveau Redon's walls against the sun. Now it kept the French settlers shut up inside the town from seeing the opening to the mine under their mountain. Victor Radcliff wondered whether the English engineers were wasting time and backbreaking effort.

"How long do you suppose all this will take, sir?" he asked the English lieutenant-colonel.

"As long as it takes," the officer replied. "Time is one thing we have plenty of." He checked himself. "As long as the men stay healthy, anyhow."

"There's always that," Victor agreed. "And as long as the French don't manage to bring any more regulars to Atlantis."

"They were lucky to do it once, by God." The Englishman spoke with the unconscious arrogance of a man whose kingdom had got used to ruling the seas. "They'd be more than doubly lucky to do it twice."

"Here's hoping you're right." Victor left it there, returning to his earlier question: "Can your miners even begin to guess how long they'll need. Have you talked with them about it?"

"I have," the lieutenant-colonel replied. "But *as long as it takes* still seems to be the best answer I can give you. They will need some uncertain amount of time to dig their way under Nouveau Redon, and then some other uncertain amount of time to cast about for the root of the spring, so to speak. Adding one uncertainty to another can but yield a larger uncertainty, I fear. And, of course, there is no assurance that, even seeking, they will find what they seek. The siege, naturally, continues notwithstanding their success or failure."

"Naturally," Victor echoed. He looked up at the fortress. As long as it held out, English rule over Atlantis remaincd uncertain. Once it fell, if it fell ... Then the only way the French and Spaniards could regain power and influence was at the negotiating table—about which, Victor knew too well, he could do exactly nothing. If one of King George's so-called diplomats cared nothing for land to which he couldn't ride in a day or two ... Well, in that case, so much of this fighting would have been for nothing.

Victor made himself shrug. If his greencoats and the English regulars failed, those so-called diplomats would have less to work with. All he could do was all he could do. He aimed to do it.

A miner, stripped to the waist and muddied all over, carried another basket of spoil on his back out of the tunnel opening. The dirt wouldn't go into the river till after nightfall, to keep the defenders from realizing how much of it came from this one spot. The miner looked up at sky and sunshine as if he hadn't seen them for years. "Bloody good to breathe fresh air," he remarked to no one in particular.

Victor believed that. He wouldn't have wanted to scrape away far underground, in Stygian darkness illuminated only by candles and feeble lamps, never knowing if all the countless tons of earth and rock above him were about to cave in and crush him to jelly. Timber shored up the passage into the earth, but all the same ...

The man sighed. "Ah, well. Back to it." He grabbed the empty basket and vanished once more into the bowels of the earth.

"Brave fellow," the English lieutenant-colonel said. He'd been watching the miner, too, then.

"He is," Victor agreed. "Can they really dig a straight line under the ground? Or will they lose their bearing?"

"They check it by compass, inside and out," the English officer replied. "So the chief engineer assures me. They have had a deal of practice at this sort of thing grubbing out coal on the other side of the ocean, you know."

"They're beginning to do that here, too, up in the

north," Radcliff said. "Fewer trees close by where they're needed than there were when settlers first found Atlantis. And coal burns better, which also has its uses. But I don't think anyone could pay me enough to make my living underground."

"Nor me." The lieutenant-colonel shuddered. He seemed glad to point upward toward the town at the top of the hill. "Could your riflemen snipe a bit more than they have been lately? We don't want the foe to think we've given up on taking the fort by ordinary means."

"I'll take care of it, sir," Victor promised. "We don't even have to hit them, so long as they know we're shooting at them."

"Just so." The English officer smiled. "A peaceable sort of war, is it not?"

"It sure is," Victor said. If this scheme worked, if the French gave up . . .

A few days later, one of his riflemen came back swearing. "I had him in my sights—the French commander, old damned what's-his-name," the man said. "Had him in my sights, and I fired . . . and I missed. Bugger me with a redwood cone, but I missed."

"What kind of range?" Victor asked.

"Not too long—a furlong and a half."

"Bad luck," Victor said. "Shooting uphill like that— it's hard, and you don't practice it much."

"I should have got him." The rifleman refused to be consoled.

"Well, maybe you'll get another chance," Victor said.

"Not one that good, dammit." Still disgruntled, the other settler stomped away.

He turned out to be right, too. At least, he didn't come running back to Victor claiming he'd plugged Roland Kersauzon. Neither did anyone else. The commander of the French settlers went right on directing the citadel's defense. Victor began to wonder whether Nouveau Redon would ever fall.

Then, one day, the engineers digging far below the fortress ran out of the tunnel they'd labored on for so long. "Water's starting to drip through the wall!" exclaimed a muddy man with a pickaxe clenched in his right fist. "We can hear it flowing by, too."

"By God!" Victor said. He solemnly clasped hands with the English lieutenant-colonel.

"What do you do now?" the English officer asked his men. "How do you ruin the spring without drowning yourselves?"

Three of them went back into the shaft they'd evacuated. Each man rolled a hogshead of black powder ahead of himself and trailed fuse out behind. After what seemed a very long time, the engineers emerged from the tunnel once more. One of them bowed to the lieutenant-colonel and said, "If you'd care to do the honors, your Excellency ..."

"I should be delighted." The Englishman lit a twig at a small fire that crackled nearby. He touched it to each of the three fuses in turn. One by one, they hissed to life. *With three,* Victor thought, *one of them will surely reach the powder.*

And at least one did. *Boom!* The ground shook under Victor's feet. He shook hands with the English lieutenant-colonel again. "How long before we know whether we did what we wanted to do?" he asked.

"Shouldn't be long, Major," one of the engineers replied.

A few minutes later, water started flowing out of the tunnel mouth. Victor and the English officer and the engineers joined hands and danced around in a circle. What they could do, they'd done. Now they had to see what it did to Nouveau Redon.

\* \* \*

*Boom!* Roland Kersauzon was on the wall when the ground shuddered under his feet. A lot of gunpowder had gone off all at once ... somewhere. But where? He looked back at his town. No great cloud of smoke rising there. His men hadn't done their best to blow themselves up, then.

The English? Not anywhere Roland could see. The bulk of Nouveau Redon hid some of their line from him, but he would have thought any explosion big enough to make things jump like that would have produced a sizable cloud of smoke. Maybe he was crazy. Maybe being up on the wall made the explosion seem bigger than it really was. A crew of cannoneers were also looking around, wondering what had happened. When their eyes met his, they shrugged, almost in unison. Laughing, he returned the gesture.

Half an hour or so later, people started shouting his name. "Here I am!" he called. "What is it?"

"The spring!" somebody called from the narrow, winding streets. "The spring's gone dry!"

"What?" Roland yelped. "That's impossible!"

"It may be impossible," the man down there replied. "But it's true."

*"Merde!"* Roland said. *"Nom d'un nom d'un nom!"* He hurried down off the wall. Going down stairs shouldn't have made his heart pound like that. In fact, going down stairs didn't make his heart pound like that. Fear did.

Sure enough, no water gurgled from the mouth of the gargoyle who capped the spring. "It just—stopped," a still-plump cook said. "A few minutes after the ground shook, it ... stopped."

Roland cursed again, this time even more vilely than before. The cook gaped at him. Roland hardly noticed. He was seeing men far belowground, men working with spades and adzes and picks. He'd never dreamt they could penetrate to the living heart of his mountain. Underestimating what the English could do did not pay.

"What now, *Monsieur*?" the cook asked. "Nouveau Redon has no cisterns. Who would have imagined we needed them?"

"Who indeed?" Roland said dully. He looked up to the sky. A few white clouds lazily drifted across the blue. He wanted gray sweeping away the sun. He wanted rain, downpour, deluge. No matter what he wanted, God wasn't going to give it to him.

Men could live on half-rations for months, maybe even years. They could go with no food at all for a month. Take away their water and they were helpless inside a week.

Not all the water inside Nouveau Redon had vanished, of course. But if no more came in, if the weather stayed fair, the way it looked like doing . . . What *could* the defenders do then?

He saw only one answer. It wasn't a good answer, but it wasn't an impossible answer, either. Drawing himself very straight, he said, "We fight, by God!"

Having decided to do that, he wasted no time. He sent runners hot-footing it all over Nouveau Redon. The sooner his men went out and assailed the English, the less they would suffer from thirst in the meantime. Rain might buy him a few more days, but—another glance toward the sunny heavens—no, no rain in sight.

As his men gathered near the northern gate, he rose till he stood in the saddle and told them what they needed to know: "I am sorry to say it, my ducks, but the English have pulled the rug out from under our feet. They have murdered our spring—we have no more water coming into the town. But we are not without hope. Plenty of water flows down there, right below our feet. All we have to do is go take it. We've fought Englishmen before—and we've beaten them before, too. One more win, and the war is over. We can do it!"

A great cheer rose. The French settlers certainly thought they could do it. Believing a thing possible went a long way toward making it so. Roland had a pistol on his belt, a pistol in each boot, and a slashing sword loose in the scabbard.

"You will follow me," he said. "You will not turn back till I give the order. And I will never give that order!"

Another cheer rang out. "Forward!" a sergeant shouted in a great voice. In an instant, the whole army was crying out the word: "Forward! *Forward! FORWARD!*"

The gates opened. The men streamed out of them and formed a line of battle. Enemy rifles began firing as soon as the French settlers came into sight. Here and there, a man fell. The settlers were veterans by now, and acted as stolid about losses as regulars could have.

Roland pointed down toward the river. "Let's go!" he cried. Cheering, the army went.

Cannons roared. Fire licked at the French settlers from the trenches ahead. Neither English Atlanteans nor redcoats emerged to fight on open ground. The enemy fired from his earthworks. If he could shoot down the whole garrison from Nouveau Redon without exposing himself to much danger, he would do it without a qualm of conscience.

A coward's way to fight, or else a tradesman's: so Roland saw it. Which didn't make it ineffective. Oh, no. More soldiers came running through the spiderweb of trenches to take their places in front of the French settlers. Roland realized his men would have to break through before the English got enough fighters in place to stop them. Well, they were close to the first trench line now.

A musket ball caught his horse in the neck. Blood fountained, impossibly red in the sunshine. The horse let out a bubbling shriek and staggered. Roland sprang clear before it went down. He brandished one of his pistols—the sword would have been more dramatic, but he could do more with the pistol—and shouted, "I'm still fine! Let's go on and give them what they deserve!"

His good sense proved itself a moment later. A redcoat swung a musket toward him. But Roland fired first. He missed, but he made the Englishman duck. The enemy's shot went wild. Roland threw the pistol at the next closest redcoat, then drew his sword and jumped down into the trench.

The sword got blood on it in short order. Roland got blood on himself, too, but it wasn't his. An English regular almost spitted him with a bayonet, but got shot in the side before he could thrust again. The redcoat sank with a groan. Roland's blade flickered like a viper's tongue. It was quicker than any bayoneted musket, but the bayonets had more reach.

French settlers swarmed over the English defenders. The French outnumbered them here, and also had desperation on their side. As soon as Roland was sure they'd killed or driven back enough enemies, he scrambled up onto the northern edge of the trench and ran on toward the next line. "Follow me!" he yelled again.

Some of his men did. Others went through the trenches connecting the inner ring of works to that outside it. Had the English settlers and regulars had their wits about them, they could have plugged those connecting trenches with a few men. But the attack's mad fury unnerved them, and the French settlers rushed into the next ring.

*How many of these battles will we have to win?* Roland wondered, unchivalrously stabbing a greencoat in the kidney from behind. The man shrieked and dropped his musket, whereupon the French settler he was facing gutted him with his bayonet. But more and more greencoats and redcoats rushed to the fray. The English settlers and regulars might be too unnerved to fight with proper tactics, but they weren't too unnerved to fight.

Not all the Frenchmen who got into the second ring of trenches came out of it. And still more English soldiers poured into the brawl from the works all around Nouveau Redon. The longer clearing the trench took, the harder it got. "We have to move on, down toward the river!" Roland called. But what they had to do and what they could do might be two different things.

Roland fired both his remaining pistols. He hit a redcoat with one ball; he wasn't sure about the other. In the mad mêlée all around him, he wasn't sure of much. He hung on to one pistol, carrying it reversed in his left hand. Some swordsmen used a left-hand dagger to beat aside their foes' weapons and to do damage when they could. The pistol worked about as well. Roland clouted a settler over the head with it when the man got too close for him to use his blade.

"Come on!" Kersauzon shouted again and again. "We have to keep moving!"

But their progress got slower and slower. The English Atlanteans and regulars were continually reinforced. No more French settlers came forth from Nouveau Redon. Roland had put all his weight into the one blow. He'd had to hope it would prove enough. Now he wasn't so sure.

There was the Blavet, with only one more ring of trenches in the French settlers' way. "Come on!" Roland shouted once more. "By God, my friends, we can do it!"

He looked around. His men—his friends, as so many of them were—had melted away like snow in springtime. Most of the ones who came forward with him bled from one wound, or from more than one. He discovered to his surprise that he'd taken several wounds himself.

He didn't remember getting any of them. The heat of battle could be like that.

Now that he knew he was hurt, all the little wounds started to pain him. He ignored them as best he could. If the French settlers could get past the last enemy trench, past the redwoods just beyond it . . .

But the greencoats and redcoats knew what the French had to do. Gunfire spat serpents' tongues of flame at the oncoming French settlers. The corporal next to Roland groaned as he took a bullet in the belly. He folded up like a concertina.

A fieldpiece thundered, and then another one. How had the English manhandled guns to where they were needed most? But how they'd done it didn't really matter. That they'd done it did. Canister tore through the oncoming French settlers. It blew one man right out of his shoes.

Roland sat down, hard. He looked at his right leg in absurd surprise. It wasn't bleeding . . . too much. He tried to stand again. He managed to do it, which proved the leg wasn't broken. It could take . . . some weight. He hobbled forward, brandishing his sword. "Hurrah!" the French settlers shouted as they threw themselves toward the last English defenses.

The English, settlers and regulars, still wouldn't come forth to fight the French man-to-man. They stayed in those earthworks and behind those trees and poured lead into soldiers who were in a desperately poor position to shoot back.

Another man near Roland dropped. Roland grabbed his musket and used it as a stick to help himself hobble forward. He was almost to the trench when a black man wearing sergeant's stripes took dead aim at him. He knew it was all over, at least as far as he was concerned.

Then the white man next to the Negro knocked the gun barrel to one side. "Surrender!" the white called in fair French. "You fought bravely. What more can you do?"

"I may die, but I won't surrender," Roland answered. "Come out here, *Monsieur,* and we will see which of us is the better man."

"What difference does that make?" the greencoat said. "I have the stronger kingdom, and that *does* make a difference. It makes all the difference in the world."

"If you want to fight like a coward, it does." Roland would have laughed at himself if things weren't too grim for laughter. He could barely stand up, and he challenged the English settler to single combat. If that wasn't suicide, what was?

This was, this whole charge into the teeth of the English position. He'd feared as much when he ordered it. But he still didn't see what else he could have done. Without water, Nouveau Redon would have had to give up soon. The attack had had some chance.

Some. But not enough.

"Last chance, *Monsieur,*" the English settler warned.

"Be damned to you, *Monsieur,*" Roland replied.

"I'm sorry," the greencoat said. "You're a brave devil, but that won't do you any good, either." He turned to the Negro beside him. "Go ahead, Blaise."

Roland tried to spring forward. It wouldn't have worked on two good legs. The musket ball caught him square in the chest. He fell on his face in the dirt. Blood filled his mouth. As his vision dimmed, a katydid the size of a mouse scuttled past his face and burrowed under a clod of dirt. He coughed. He choked. Blackness enfolded him.

"I never dreamt they'd come this far," the English lieutenant-colonel said.

"A few of them got through and got away," Victor

Radcliff said. "I never thought they could do that. They were formidable."

"Were," the English officer echoed. "That's a lovely word, by God."

"Isn't it, though?" Victor looked around for his Negro sergeant-cum-body-servant, and saw that he was going through a dead enemy soldier's pockets. *The victors take the spoils,* he thought. Aloud, he continued, "If Blaise hadn't shot their leader there at the end, we might still be fighting."

He exaggerated, but not by much. When Roland Kersauzon fell, it took the heart out of most of the French settlers still on their feet. They threw down their muskets and rifles and swords and put up their hands. By then, the redcoats and English settlers were glad enough to accept their surrender.

Surgeons worked on wounded all the way from the riverbank up to the gates of Nouveau Redon. Where the fighting was sharpest, dead men in red and green, in French blue and colonial homespun, lay piled together in death, each one quiet now where he had fallen. The twin stinks of pierced bowels and blood—so much blood!—filled Victor's nostrils.

"Only one thing worse than a fight like this," he murmured, rubbing at a cut on his left arm. He was one of the lucky ones. But for that, he'd come away unscathed.

"What could be worse?" The lieutenant-colonel still seemed stunned at the struggle the French had put up.

"Losing," Victor said bluntly.

"Well, yes," the English officer admitted after a moment's surprise. "There is that."

So there was. Redcoats and greencoats robbed disconsolate enemy survivors of anything they happened to carry. Kersauzon's men were in no position to complain. Anyone who presumed to resent the thefts wouldn't live long. Had the French settlers triumphed, they would have done the same to their foes. Everyone on both sides knew as much.

"What *are* we to do with them?" The English lieutenant-colonel seemed to be talking more to himself than to Victor.

Victor answered anyhow: "The ones who are left, we may as well send home." His wave took in the windrows of corpses—far more French than English, because Kersauzon's men had pushed the attack, and pushed it in large measure out in the open. "Even after they get there, French Atlantis will have a great swarm of widows."

"And a great swarm of English settlers coming south to console them?" The lieutenant-colonel might be stolid and earnest, but he had a certain basic shrewdness.

"I shouldn't wonder," Victor said. "French Atlantis is ours now. There's no army left that can slow us down, much less stop us. Plenty of plantations, plenty of ordinary farms, plenty of shops in the towns that will need men to run them. There won't be enough Frenchmen to do it, not after we've killed off so many of them. And our settlements have always been more populous than theirs. Look at the way we're spilling across the Green Ridge Mountains. They have New Marseille over on the west coast, but that's just another little seacoast town."

Now the Englishman glanced up to make sure Blaise was busy plundering. In a low voice, he said, "How do you suppose your bonny English settlers will like turning into slaveholders?"

Victor Radcliff shrugged. "It's a way of life down here. How else are you going to run a plantation?"

"I don't care for it," the lieutenant-colonel said. "Slavery's against the law in England, you know."

"I don't, either, but it's not here. Not in our Terranovan settlements, either," Victor said. "Where slaves and money go together, who complains about slaves? Does that surprise you, sir?"

"Well, when you put it so, perhaps not," the English officer replied. "I shouldn't care to buy and sell other men myself, though."

"Neither would I ... sir," Victor said slowly. "But I wear cotton when I don't wear wool or linen. Much of what I wear is dyed with indigo. I enjoy pipeweed. Sometimes I eat rice when I don't eat maize or wheat. Isn't it the same for you?"

"Yes, of course it is," the lieutenant-colonel said. "But—"

"No, sir. No buts, not in that case," Radcliff broke in. "If you use what slaves make but don't care to own them yourself, aren't you like a man who eats pork but doesn't care to butcher hogs?"

The Englishman opened his mouth, then closed it again. After a moment, he tried again: "You are a bloody difficult man, Major."

"Thanks. I do my best," Victor said, not without pride.

"This may all prove moot, you understand," the Englishman said.

With a sigh not quite of resignation, Victor Radcliff nodded. "I understand much too well. If the gentlemen who all speak French sit down together and decide to hand this country back to the people who just now lost it, nothing we can do to keep it this side of insurrection."

"I should not recommend that, either," the English officer said. "It would be foredoomed to failure."

"You may well be right, sir," Victor said politely, though less than convinced that the officer from across the Atlantic was. "I am operating on the assumption that it will not come to that. I am also operating on the assumption that those diplomatic gentlemen will not be so foolish as to squander what we won at such cost."

"You are likely to be right yourself," the Englishman said. "England had the power to take French Atlantis, and God has also blessed us with the power to prevail elsewhere in the world. We may throw France some small sop when this war is over, to prevent her utter humiliation, but I see no reason to throw her a large one. In my view, French Atlantis is too large and too important to return, it once having fallen into our hands."

"We agree." Victor smiled. "That is not something a settler and a man from the mother country can often say these days."

"We have been tested in adversity, you and I," the other officer replied. "And, unlike the King of Babylon, God did not weigh us in the measure and find us wanting."

"Not yet, anyhow," Victor said, smiling still. "Do you suppose that, with French Atlantis in our pocket, we could sweep down through it and pick up Spanish Atlantis as well? I tell you frankly, sir, the slaves who've risen against their masters would likely give us a harder fight than the Spaniards can put up."

"I doubt that not at all," the Englishman said. "Still and all, though, that's a long march, and one with uncertain supply lines, into a country notoriously unhealthy. I should hesitate to undertake it without orders from London."

"My greencoats did it," Victor said. "We lived off the land, and we had no trouble doing it."

"What is easy for irregulars is often difficult for regulars," the lieutenant-colonel answered. "Irregulars often have a certain amount of trouble remembering that the converse also applies. Or do you think your men could have stopped the flow from the spring here?"

Radcliff knew his men could have done no such thing. Even trying would never have occurred to him. That long underground burrow ... He shuddered. No, he wouldn't have wanted to try that. "Your point is well taken, sir," he admitted.

"Generous of you to say so," the Englishman told him. "I also fear I can't promise the timely appearance of the Royal Navy, which you were able to enjoy. You might have known a certain amount of embarrassment had the French and Spanish Atlanteans succeeded in combining against you."

*The ships plucked you off the beach in the nick of time.* The lieutenant-colonel had a cat's politeness; he wouldn't come right out and say such a thing. But Victor understood what he meant. "You may be right, sir," he answered insincerely. "Still and all, not much danger of a Franco-Spanish combination against us now, is there?" *We've whipped the French settlers once and for all* was what *he* meant, and the Englishman couldn't very well mistake him.

To his credit, the redcoat didn't try. "No, not much," he said, "but I still believe we would do better to ensure our conquest of French Atlantis than to go haring off after something grander yet. Do you on this side of the ocean know the proverb about the bird in the hand and those in the bush?"

"I've . . . heard it," Victor said. The English lieutenant-colonel chuckled at his reluctant     indeed, his reproachful (to say nothing of nearly mutinous)—subordination. After a victory like the one they'd gained here, chuckles came easy. Had Roland Kersauzon's men beaten the redcoats and greencoats and escaped en masse to continue the war, the English officer wouldn't have taken that hesitation so lightly. Victor went on, "A lot of the birds here, though, don't fit in the hand."

Redcoats led glum French settlers into captivity. Some of those settlers were in their stocking feet. If they hadn't been whipped out of their boots, they'd lost them as spoils of war. Pretty soon, the English settlers and regulars would plunder Nouveau Redon, too. Victor would have been surprised if some of the more enterprising fellows weren't already starting.

"French Atlantis will fit quite nicely, I do believe," the redcoat said.

"It is a good handful," Victor allowed. Why argue now? Sure enough, triumph was a great sweetener. He took off his hat and saluted the English officer. "We won it together, Colonel Cornwallis."

Cornwallis returned the salute. "We did indeed, Major Radcliff."

# XXVI

*V*ictor Radcliff didn't like Hanover. He never had. He didn't think he ever would. The place crowded too many people into too small a space. Army encampments did the same thing, but encampments were different. Everyone in them—well, almost everyone—accepted military discipline and knew his place.

Not in Hanover. People hopped after their own pursuits, as single-minded—or as mindless—as the big katydids that bounced across Atlantis' fields and forest floors. They all wanted more than they had, and they weren't shy about grabbing what they wanted with both hands.

So if Victor had had any kind of excuse, he would have stayed far away from the brawling metropolis of English Atlantis. But he had none. He was the hero of the war against the French. A hero had to be seen, had to be praised, to make a proper spectacle for the people. Victor dully and dutifully paraded at the head of a regiment of greencoats.

"Ah, well," he said over his shoulder to Blaise, who strode along behind him. "One good thing about this nonsense—if the boys can't get laid tonight, they aren't half trying."

"What about you, sir?" the Negro said, his voice sly.

"Not tonight, anyhow," Victor answered. He was no saint when he was away from Margaret, though he had no bastards he knew about. "Not tonight," he repeated. "I'm going to the feast for all the fancy Radcliffs and Radcliffes. Should be gruesome, but it can't be helped. Your friends you choose, but you're stuck with your relatives."

Not all the Radcliffs and Radcliffes at the banquet proved excessively fancy. Some of the young, pretty women wore the name only because of a marriage connection. They were no blood kin to Victor at all—but they were interested in getting to know him more intimately. He got to know one of them much more intimately in a servant's tiny room under the stairs—and he was smiling benignly at her husband, some distant cousin of his, five minutes later. That was amusing, even if he didn't tell Blaise about it afterwards.

But neither the parade nor the fête nor the naughty sport under the stairs would have drawn him to Hanover by itself. All three of them together wouldn't have. What brought him to London in Small—the town's proud boast—and kept him there was the certainty that details of the peace treaty would come to Hanover before they came anywhere else in Atlantis.

He rode down to the harbor every morning, sometimes with Blaise, sometimes alone. Ships of all sizes and ages came in, from England and her settlements around the world and her allies. Some of the people knew that talks to end the war were going on. No one seemed to know how they were going.

And then, one afternoon, a swift, rakish Royal Navy frigate, the *Glasgow*, sailed into Hanover. When Victor asked the officer of the deck if he had news of the peace, that young lieutenant looked down his nose at him and demanded, "Why do you presume that you deserve to know?"

"I am Major Victor Radcliff. Without me, the ministers wouldn't be talking about French and Spanish Atlantis," Victor answered. "Now, sir, who are you—and who is your next of kin?" His hand dropped to the butt of the pistol he wore on his belt.

The naval officer lost much of his toploftiness. "I . . . beg your pardon, Major. We do bring that word, as a matter of fact."

"If you tell me what it is—at once—I won't ask any more personal questions of you," Victor said. *I won't kill you,* he meant, and the lieutenant knew it.

"Well . . ." The younger man needed to gather himself. At last, he went on, "French Atlantis comes under English sovereignty. It is opened to English settlement without restriction. The dons keep Spanish Atlantis, but England gets trading concessions there. We take most of French Terranova, too, and almost all of French India."

Radcliff cared nothing about India, and only a little about Terranova. The lands on this side of the Hesperian Gulf were wide enough for him. He nodded to the lieutenant. "Thank you. That's good news."

It wasn't so good as it might have been. He would have loved to see the Union Jack flying over Spanish Atlantis, too. But the Spaniards weren't rivals, as the French had been. History had left Spain in a backwater. France, on the other hand, could have stayed ahead of England had she won this war.

She could have. But she hadn't.

"Who the devil are you talking to, Jenkins?" a senior naval officer demanded, scowling down at Victor.

"This is Major Victor Radcliff, sir," the lieutenant answered. "The man who helped our regulars take French Atlantis."

"Huzzah," said the captain, or whatever he was. "More troublemakers for the Crown to worry about."

"Would you rather they were here, sir?" Victor said. "Would you rather all Atlantis flew the fleurs-de-lys?"

"What a ridiculous notion," the senior officer said.

"It is now, sir—because we won," Victor replied.

The officer sputtered and fumed. Victor caught only a few words: ". . . damned settlers . . . lot of nerve . . . arrogant scut . . ." Then the fellow spoke, more coherently: "As if this miserable, half-baked place mattered a farthing's worth in the grand scheme of things."

"Sir, to an Englishman it may not," Radcliff said. "Yet there are those of us who call Atlantis home, and who love it, and who would have grieved to see it lost to the French, not least after so much effort and so much blood expended to preserve it."

"Yes, yes." The naval officer still sounded impatient. "I see you can make pretty speeches when you care to. Well, you've got what you want. The French get a few islands off the Terranovan coast, where they can raise sugar cane to their hearts' content. And we . . . we get Atlantis, although I'm still damned if I know why we want it. An obstacle to navigation, that's all it is, and no one will ever persuade me otherwise."

Victor Radcliff bowed. "Then I shan't make the effort. But perhaps one day time will tell you what you don't hear from me."

When Victor had the chance to read the full terms of the peace, he found that they said nothing about the race of a prospective settler in French Atlantis. He told Blaise, "You ought to go down there. You're a clever man, and an able one—those two don't always march together. You'd get rich before you know it, and you could throw it in the Frenchmen's faces."

"The only way I get rich there is, I buy niggers and

copperskins," Blaise said slowly. "Only way anyone gets rich down there, he runs him a plantation with slaves."

"Well, yes," Victor admitted. "You do need them in French Atlantis—what was French Atlantis, I mean." He paused. "Some slaves who've got free do run slaves themselves now. That isn't against the law down there, either."

"Don't happen real often," Blaise said.

"No, it doesn't, but it's not illegal."

Blaise set his chin. He didn't have the bony promontory that graced the lower jaws of a lot of white men. Somehow, though, the lack made him seem more stubborn, not less. "Done been a slave," he said, and added several French and Spanish pungencies to the remark. "Don't want to do that to anybody else."

"Someone else will if you don't," Victor said. "I daresay you'd make a better master than someone who'd never seen it from the other side."

This time, Blaise laughed in his face. That startled Victor Radcliff, and angered him, too. He wasn't used to such discourtesies from a Negro—certainly not here in Hanover, though he would have tolerated them better on campaign or out in the woods.

"If I'm a master, I'm as rough as anybody else," Blaise said. "You have slaves, you got to be. Or they don't work. They don't do anything. I know. I was one." He jabbed a thumb at his own broad chest. "Don't want to do that. So I won't. I stick with you, Major Radcliff, sir." He saluted, mixing some mockery—but not a lot—into the gesture of respect.

Gravely, Victor returned the salute. "You'll never get rich that way," he said.

Blaise shrugged. "Don't care about gettin' rich. Care about . . ." He paused, considering. "About not hatin' myself. Yeah. I care about that."

"Have it your way. You will anyhow." With the war

over, Victor didn't need a sergeant-cum-body-servant any more. If he went back to exploring, he didn't need a body servant, either. An explorer with a servant was like a musket with a chamber pot: having one added something absolutely unnecessary.

Which wasn't to say Blaise couldn't take care of himself in the wilderness. He could, at least as well as Victor could himself. And, if Victor dismissed him, Blaise could take care of himself in English Atlantis, too. Blaise might be black, but he was as generally competent a man as Victor had ever met.

That went a long way towards explaining why the two of them got along as well as they did, even if Victor had never thought of it in those terms.

"Well, if you don't want a plantation, how *do* we reward you for shooting Roland Kersauzon?" he asked.

"Money is good," Blaise said seriously. "What you reckon he's worth?" He was always ready to haggle.

He looked so ready now, Victor started to laugh. "Are you sure you're not a Jew under your skin?" he said.

Blaise took the question literally. "Don't even know what a Jew is."

"They're white people who aren't Christians," Victor replied. "Too foolish to know the truth, in other words."

"They don't believe in God?" Blaise asked.

"They believe in God, but they don't believe Jesus is His Son."

"Oh. Like Muslims," Blaise said.

It was Victor's turn to be confused. A bit of back-and-forth made him understand Blaise was talking about Mahometans. A bit more made him understand that the black man knew much more about them than he did. "How do you find yourself so well informed?" he asked.

"Some of the tribes north of us, they Muslim," Blaise answered. "They send their men, want us to be Muslims, too."

"Missionaries. Muslim missionaries," Victor Radcliff said wonderingly. "Now I've heard everything. We Christians send missions to Africa, too, you know."

"Muslims send missionaries. They take slaves. Christians send missionaries. *They* take slaves," Blaise said. "Us—we believe what we believe. We don't send no missionaries."

"Do you take slaves?" Radcliff asked.

"Oh, yes. People we catch in war, things like that," Blaise said. "We don't work them the way the French and Spaniards do, though. Don't have big plantations." He paused. "These Jews, they send missionaries?"

"No. At least, I've never heard of it if they do." Victor tried to imagine what would happen to a Jew proselytizing in Rome or Paris or London—or Hanover, come to that. Nothing pretty. The Jews knew better. That, in turn, made him wonder why Christians and Mahometans didn't. He found no good answer.

Blaise wasn't finished. "These Jews, they take slaves?"

"Some rich Jews own them, I'm sure," Victor said. "They buy and sell them now and again." Most of that trade, though, at least between Africa and Atlantis, lay in Christian hands. Uncomfortably, he finished, "They don't raid the coast to grab them, anyhow."

"Huh," Blaise said: a thoughtful grunt. "Maybe I turn Jew, then."

Victor didn't tell him that kind of conversion was against the law. He wasn't sure it was, or needed to be. Who not born to the Jewish faith would want to assume all the burdens it entailed? Speaking of those burdens . . . "Do you want to get circumcised?"

"Fancy word. What's it mean?" Blaise said. Victor told him what it meant. The Negro set a protective hand in front of his privates. "Muslims do that, too. Why would anybody want to?"

"I don't know why Mahometans do it. I didn't know they did. Jews think God requires it of them."

Blaise took the hand away. He was getting ever better at aping white people's notions of polite manners. "Ain't gonna be no Jew," he declared.

"Amen," Victor said, unaware he'd just come out with a Hebrew word.

When Victor—and Blaise—rode south into what had been French Atlantis, no customs barrier delayed them at the border. There were no customs barriers between English and French Atlantis any longer, no more than there were between New Hastings and Hanover. King George ruled them all.

The innkeeper at whose establishment they stayed was French. They both spoke his language. That pleased him. They also both stayed reasonably sober and reasonably quiet. That pleased him even more.

Men from English Atlantis filled the inn to bursting. They shouted demands in English. The innkeeper understood them well enough; so close to the old border, it wasn't as if he'd never had English-speaking guests before the war made him an involuntary English subject. But, by the way the newcomers acted, French might have been as dead as Aramaic.

They drank. They pinched and patted the barmaids. They ate as if they'd just discovered food. They bragged about the fortunes they were going to make by screwing the Frenchies. (That the innkeeper was listening, and might decide to season their capon with rat poison, never seemed to cross their minds.) They went on drinking. They brawled, and broke crockery brawling.

"That will go on your scot!" the innkeeper cried. (He might put rat poison in the beer and wine and barrel-tree rum, too.)

"What makes you reckon we'll pay you a ha'penny, you filthy, motherless scut?" one of them bawled.

A heartbeat later, he found himself staring down the barrel of Victor Radcliff's pistol. A pistol aimed at your face, as Victor had reason to know, seemed to own a bore as wide as a fieldpiece's. "You'll pay your scot right now, and then you'll get the devil out of here," Victor said quietly. In the sudden, vast silence, he didn't need to shout.

"And if I don't?" The trader had nerve—more nerve than sense, as far as Victor was concerned.

He said, "In that unfortunate circumstance, your heirs will be responsible for what you owe this gentleman . . . and for the cost of your funeral. Add in the farthing you're actually worth and it comes to a tidy little sum."

The other settler's bloodshot eyes crossed as he stared down the barrel of the pistol. "Who the hell are you, anyways, throwing orders around like you're God's anointed?"

"I am Major Victor Radcliff," Victor answered evenly. "If I have to ask your name, sir, you will not be glad of it: I promise you that. Now . . . Do as I told you or prepare to join the majority."

"That's fancy talk for 'die,' Ben," another trader said, in case Ben was too dense or too sozzled to figure it out for himself.

He wasn't—or he didn't let on that he was. "I know what it's fancy talk for, dammit," he said. With an effort, he looked at Radcliff rather than his weapon. "Put that miserable thing away so we can talk this over like a couple of sensible people."

"I am not a sensible person, and do not pretend to be," Radcliff said. "I have spent this whole war killing people who got in my way. If you think one more will bother me to the extent of a fart on a dung heap, you are making what I assure you will be your last mistake."

Ben considered. Victor knew the questions that had to be uppermost in his mind: could he knock the pistol aside before Victor blew his head off? If he could, could he win the brawl that would follow a split second later?

He must not have liked the answers he came up with. He said, "I'm going to reach down for some money. I'll do it slow, and I won't go for anything else. That all right by you?"

"Yes—as long as you mean it. If you don't, I promise that my friend and I will make you ... briefly ... wish you did."

"Your friend? You mean that ... colored fellow?" Ben was almost, but not quite, too slow. He did have the brains to realize tagging a gun-toting Negro with an ugly name wasn't the smartest thing he could do. He took out enough money to cover his tab and then some. After setting it on the table, he walked off into the night.

"Anyone else?" Victor inquired. "Or can you see screwing the Frenchies will be the same as screwing yourselves from now on?"

No one seemed inclined to argue with him. Short-tempered men who carried pistols often went without their fair share of disagreement, something he'd noticed before and was inclined to take advantage of. On the other hand, he didn't fool himself into believing he'd magically convinced the English settlers of the error of their ways. Lack of disagreement wasn't the same as agreement.

He suspected—no, he was sure—there would need to be laws to make sure the English didn't screw the Frenchies ... too badly. Quite a few people would get rich down here before those laws went into place. If Ben wasn't one of them, Victor would have been surprised.

*"Audace, audace, toujours l'audace,"* Blaise remarked as he and Victor undressed for bed. The innkeeper gave the two of them a room to themselves. None of the trad-

ers from English Atlantis would have wanted to ⌐
down with them anyhow. As far as Victor was concerned
it was mutual.

He only shrugged. "It wasn't so audacious as all that,
not when you were there to back my play."

"But who backed mine?" Blaise asked. "Two bullets,
then—" He made as if to strangle himself.

"Oh, nonsense," Victor said. "What do you want to
bet the innkeeper has a pepperbox pistol—or more
likely a blunderbuss loaded to the muzzle with scrap
iron—under the bar? He would have backed us both."

"Maybe," Blaise said unwillingly. "But maybe too
slow to do us any good, too."

"The devil take worrying about might-have-beens,"
Victor said. "We did it, we got by with it, and there's an
end to it. And now why don't you blow out that candle so we can get some sleep?" Blaise did. The room
plunged into darkness scented with hot tallow. Victor
never found out whether he or Blaise started snoring
first, which probably meant he did.

Nouveau Redon would never be the same. English engineers systematically demolished the walls that had
warded the great fortress of French Atlantis for so long.
That made sense to Victor. Even without the spring, the
site remained dangerously good.

He wasn't surprised to discover French settlers could
see that as well as he could. They'd also noticed that
the English regulars charged with wrecking their works
spoke no French. With smiling faces, the locals called the
engineers appalling names.

With those same smiling faces, they called Victor
Radcliff some appalling names, too. He smiled back, and
replied in his best French: "Ah, but if you think I'm bad,
you should see your own mothers."

The setters who'd been making sport of him stopped,

their mouths falling open. "*Monsieur* comprehends?" one of them said in alarm.

"*Monsieur* bloody well does," Victor agreed. "*Monsieur* also comprehends that you would do well not to bait the engineers. If they find out the tenth part of what you're saying to them, you are all dead men."

"It would serve you right, too," Blaise added.

"And who are you?" the settler inquired—cautiously. Most of the time, French settlers didn't want to hear anything from Negroes or copperskins. Most of the time, they didn't have to. Owning a man meant you didn't have to listen to him. (Owning a woman meant you didn't have to listen to her, either. That could be—and often was—even more convenient.) Having made one mistake, though, this fellow didn't want to make two. (A surprising—to Victor, a dismaying—number of people didn't care how many they made.)

"I am Sergeant Blaise Black, of the militia of the English settlements," Blaise answered, pride ringing in his voice. He must have taken the surname on the spur of the moment; it certainly suited him. He went on, "I also have the honor to be the man who shot Roland Kersauzon."

Nobody asked him any more questions after that. The French settlers couldn't disappear fast enough. "Now look what you did," Victor said.

Blaise shrugged in a way that showed he'd lived among Frenchmen. "I told them the truth. What's wrong with that?" In English, he sounded ordinary. In French, he could be eloquent. Maybe he still knew more French than English. Maybe the difference lay in the genius of the two languages.

As for his question . . . "Nothing's wrong with it," Victor Radcliff answered. "That doesn't mean it's a pleasant thing to do."

With another shrug, Blaise said, "They were throwing

filth at us. You gave them something to think about. So did I."

"All right," Victor said mildly.

He did warn the captain in charge of the engineers that the locals were less friendly than they seemed. The grizzled officer said, "Well, I can't tell you I'm amazed. The brothel we went to tried to give us a freshly poxed girl so we'd have something to remember her by."

"And what did you do about that?" Victor inquired.

The captain made a fist. "Tore the place apart. Now we don't pay for it any more. We have fun anyhow. These French women—" His opinion of them was at least as low as the jeering French settlers' opinion of him and his men.

That wasn't surprising, even if it was a little sad. As long as it didn't start a riot, it also wasn't Victor's worry. He said, "I'm just glad you're making sure they won't use this place as a strongpoint against us again."

"You never can tell," the captain said. "They're liable to start rebuilding as soon as we get done and leave. We'll need to keep an eye on them to make sure they don't."

"I think we can do that," Victor said. "And the problem will solve itself before too long, I suspect."

"How's that, sir?" the graying English officer asked.

"When there are as many English settlers as French here, no one will want to use this place as a fortress."

"I hope not." The captain didn't sound convinced. Victor wondered why not. And then, all of a sudden, he stopped wondering—he knew. To this Englishman, settlers were settlers, and what blood they sprang from hardly mattered. They were all potential rebels, potential enemies.

Radcliff tried not to bristle in any obvious way. That would only have proved the captain's point for him. *I'm as good a subject of King George as you are!* Victor wanted to scream it. Screaming it wouldn't have done him any good, though. The captain would have thought he was protesting too much.

Of course, if this fellow and others like him despised settlers simply because they *were* settlers, wouldn't he make them despise him, too? The odds seemed good.

Blaise was thinking the same thing. "What can you do with such people?" he murmured . . . in French.

"I don't know," Victor replied in the same language.

"What is that jibber-jabber you're going back and forth in?" The English engineer aimed the question at Victor. "Did you learn this nigger's language so you could talk it without anybody knowing what you're saying?"

"No, you fool!" Victor exclaimed. "It's French! Don't you know French when you hear it?"

"I should hope not." The redcoat sounded proud of his own ignorance. "If it's not English, it's not worth learning."

"Didn't they ram Latin and Greek down your throat?" Victor asked, now taken by surprise.

"Not me." Again, the captain sounded proud. "I came up through the ranks, I did. I'm not one of those rich buggers who got to go to Oxbridge or Camford or one of those fancy places. I'm an officer on account of I'm bloody good at what I do. Don't need any damned foreign languages to know how to build a wall—or how to take one down, either."

"Good God!" Victor said. Some merchants in New Hastings and Hanover were as proud of what they didn't know as this fellow. Victor had always pitied them. The captain, on the other hand, frightened him. "How much do you know about Atlantis?"

"Not bloody much, and I don't care to find out more," the Englishman responded. "Damned place is full of Frenchies and niggers and copperskins. That's all I need to know, isn't it? King George has got to step on it with both feet, and I'm bloody proud to be the toe on one boot."

"I think we better get out of here, *Monsieur*, before I kill him," Blaise said through clenched teeth—still in French.

Also in French, Victor replied, "You would have to wait in line. I outrank you."

They walked away in a hurry. "That man . . . That man, he is more dangerous to Atlantis than Roland Kersauzon," Blaise spluttered. "To him, everyone here is a slave. Everyone! Not just me. I don't like when people think I am still slave, but I know why. I am black. In a white man's world, it happens. I understand, even if I don't like. But that man . . ." He paused again. "To him, you arc slave, too. Everybody from Atlantis is slave, as far as he is concerned. Why?" He stopped, breathing hard.

"It's not England," Victor Radcliff said. "How can it be any good if it's not England?" He was joking, and then again he wasn't If he didn't laugh, he'd burst into tears— or maybe grab the pistol on his belt.

"But you are from England, too," Blaise pointed out.

"Yes, I'm from England. But I'm not *of* England. My people haven't been *of* England for three hundred years," Victor said. "Our friend back there—"

"What friend?" the Negro broke in.

"That's what I mean," Victor said. "Our friend back there is *of* England. Anybody who's not *of* England is below the salt to him."

He had to explain *below the salt* to Blaise. Once the Negro understood, he asked, "What about King George? He is *of* England. Does he think Atlantis is below the salt, too?"

Telling Blaise that George was a third-generation German, and the first sovereign of his dynasty to be fluent in English, struck Victor as a waste of time. It also struck him as sure to confuse the black man. Besides, even though it was all true, Blaise had a perfectly good point. "He's my king, too. I have to hope he remembers that Atlantis and English Terranova and India and the rest of his realm matter as much as England does," Victor said.

"And if he forgets?" Blaise inquired.

Victor did the only thing he could do: he shrugged. He was hardly in a position to tell the King of England what to do, nor did he ever expect to be. "If he forgets . . . I'll just have to worry about it then."

The closer to Spanish Atlantis Blaise got, the more he muttered under his breath. At last, when Victor came right out and asked him what was on his mind, he explained why: "The French, they have slaves, but only a few really *like* to have slaves. The Spaniards, most of them *like* to have slaves."

"They have slaves because they enjoy owning other people, not just to get work out of them—is that what you mean?" Victor asked.

"Yes, sir. That's what I mean." Blaise nodded emphatically. "I still don't talk English so good, so I don't know how to say it right. But that is just exactly what I mean."

"Probably goes a long way towards explaining why the slave rising in Spanish Atlantis was—is—so bad," Victor said.

"Should give the blacks and copperskins guns, help them kill off the Spaniards," Blaise said. "They deserve it."

"We can't do that," Victor Radcliff replied. "The treaty we signed made us promise we wouldn't."

Blaise only looked at him. "And so?" Blaise didn't know much about treaties. He wouldn't have cared if he did. He only knew what he wanted, and how to go about getting it. Next to that, nothing else mattered.

"I can't do anything about it. People know me too well. It would get noticed, and the Spaniards would scream bloody murder. And under the treaty, they'd have a right to." Victor gave Blaise his most severe stare. "You can't do anything about it, either. You're my right-hand man, and people know it. You'd get blamed, and I'd get blamed, and England would get blamed. You can't—you hear me?"

"I hear you." The Negro looked mutinous.

"I'm sorry, Sergeant—by God, I *am* sorry—but that's an order," Victor said. "If you break it, I won't be able to help you, and I won't even try."

Blaise said something in his own language. Victor didn't ask him to translate. He didn't want to know. They didn't see eye to eye about this. They never would. Coming up to the border was something of a relief—at least it gave Victor something else to think about. Two Spanish soldiers stepped out of the customs post. They glowered at seeing a white man and a black together.

"What do you want?" one of them called in Spanish-flavored French.

"Do you speak English?" Victor answered in his own language.

"No, and I don't want to, either, *por Dios.*" The soldier reverted to his native tongue. His comrade spat in the roadway. "What do you want?" the man asked again. He didn't raise his musket, but he looked as if he wanted to.

Victor wondered what would happen if he said who he was. His raid into Spanish Atlantis had touched off the slave rebellion that still sizzled. Would these Spaniards shoot at him to pay him back for what he'd done to their settlements? He decided he didn't want to find out.

"I am here following my king's orders," he said, which was at least indirectly true. "He wants to make sure that the border between his new realm and yours is quiet and safe and secure."

"Then he shouldn't send out a white man with a *mallate*," the Spaniard replied. "Nothing is quiet and safe and secure with *mallates* around."

Blaise said something incandescent in Spanish. Both soldiers at the border post started to raise their guns.

"Don't do that," Victor said, also in Spanish. "You insulted him first. And if you shoot us, you will start a war. Not only that, you will lose it. If you lose it, you will see English law in Spanish Atlantis. Do you want that?"

English law was much easier on slaves than Spanish law was. The border guards knew as much. They lowered the muskets with haste that would have been comical in a setting less grim. Victor Radcliff was lying through his teeth, and he knew it. If England kept slavery as it was in French Atlantis, she would do the same thing here.

Blaise also knew he was lying through his teeth. What Victor told the Spaniards went dead against what he'd said in all the arguments he'd had with the Negro. Victor wondered if Blaise would throw that in his face. To his relief, Blaise didn't. While the two of them disagreed, they showed a common front against the Spaniards.

"You are not permitted to enter into Spanish Atlantis, not with . . . him along," one of the Spanish soldiers said. He spoke to Victor alone, as if Blaise were nothing more than a beast of burden.

"Why do you think I want to enter it? To eat lizards? To let mosquitoes eat me?" Victor said. "Keep it, and welcome. As long as you don't cause trouble, I can report to the king that he doesn't need to take it away from you."

"Yet," Blaise added.

The Spaniards spoke with each other in low voices.

"You have seen what you came to see. Now you should go," said the one who did the talking for them.

"Gladly," Victor said.

"Their turn will come," Blaise said as he and Victor rode north again.

"Without a doubt," Victor agreed. "One day soon, England *will* hold all of Atlantis."

"And then what?" Blaise asked.

"I don't know," Victor said, taken aback. "It will be a better place than it is now—I'm sure of that."

"Better how?" Blaise persisted. "Freer?"

Victor thought of freedom in terms of not needing to worry about foreign foes. Blaise looked at things rather differently. "I don't know," Victor said again.

# NEW IN HARDCOVER

FROM

## *NEW YORK TIMES* BESTSELLING AUTHOR

# HARRY TURTLEDOVE

## *THE UNITED STATES OF ATLANTIS*

England has driven the French from Atlantis, giving King George leave to tighten his control over the colonies. The Redcoats have seized the continent's eastern coastal towns as part of a strategy to bend the colonists to their will.

Instead, England's tactics have only strengthened the Atlanteans' resolve to be free. As leader of the revolutionaries, Victor Radcliff will make the English pay for each and every piece of land they dare to occupy, and will stop at nothing to preserve the liberty of his people as a new nation is born—a nation that will change the face of the world.

**Available wherever books are sold or at penguin.com**

# 30 DAYS TO
# UNDERSTANDING
# THE BIBLE

# 30 DAYS TO UNDERSTANDING THE BIBLE

Max E. Anders

Wolgemuth & Hyatt, Publishers, Inc.
Brentwood, Tennessee

Unless otherwise noted, all Scripture quotations
are from the New American Standard Bible,
© The Lockman Foundation 1960,
1962, 1963, 1968, 1971, 1973, 1975, 1977,
and are used by permission.

Published by Wolgemuth & Hyatt, Publishers, Inc.
P.O. Box 1941, Brentwood, Tennessee 37027.

Printed in the United States of America.

---

**Library of Congress Cataloging-in-Publication Data**

Anders, Max E., 1947-
    30 days to understanding the Bible by Max E. Anders.
      p. cm.
    ISBN 0-943497-26-4 : 9.95
    1. Bible—Introductions.   I. Title.   II. Title:
    Thirty days to understanding the Bible.

BS475.2.A53   1988     220.6′1—dc19     88-10818

---

This book is dedicated to Jake and Wilma,
my spiritual mentors and dear friends.

# CONTENTS

# ACKNOWLEDGMENTS

This book was much harder to write than I imagined. In fact, it would not have been completed had it not been for the timely and providential contributions made by many people. Had it not been for the considerable knowledge and creative input of Bob Roland and Art Vander Veen, I would not even have started. Dr. Steve Grill supplied the information for the U.S. history charts. Anne Cundiff did much of the design and artwork on the original illustrations.

My thanks to those who field tested the original manuscript and made many contributions: Lara Anders, Richard Anders, Ken Axt, Dr. Ken Boa, Eric Frank, Garlen Howington, Jerome King, Marcia Price, David Rogers, and Lynn Tarleton. Lara Anders, Richard Anders, Marcia Price, and Lynn Tarleton are all members of my family. Bless you! Thanks to Judy Lunsford who not only field tested the manuscript, but gave it many hours of skillful editorial evaluation.

Special thanks to my wife Margie, whose meticulous frontal assault on my original fuzzy thinking raised the manuscript a full stratum above its original level. Her razor-sharp logic and editorial insights made this a much better book than it would have been otherwise.

And finally, thanks to the Lord for His providential oversight in my life in prompting and enabling me to write the book. To God be the glory.

# INTRODUCTION

Let's make a bargain.

If you'll give me *15 minutes* a day for *30 days*, I'll give you an understanding of the Bible. I will give you an overview of the basics of the book which is the most widely distributed (approximately three billion copies!) publication in history.

In one month, you will learn . . .

. . . all the major men and women,

. . . all the major events, and

. . . all the major points of geography.

You will be able to put these people and facts together in their proper chronological order and trace the geographical movement as you think your way through the entire Bible! You will know the *Story of the Old Testament* and the *Story of the New Testament*.

Yet, the Bible is more than history. It is also a treasure house of important teachings which have been the foundation of Western civilization from the great Roman empire until today. You will learn the *Eight Great Subjects of Scripture* which have formed the body of belief for Protestants and Catholics for the last two thousand years, and for the Jews from the Old Testament.

Finally, the Bible is a valuable source of spiritual wisdom, guiding the reader into a proper knowledge of *The Three Great Relationships of Scripture*: how to be properly related to God, how to be properly related to oneself, and how to be properly related to others.

No attempt has been made to interpret the Bible for you. The information is presented at face value as it is found in the text. No previous knowledge is taken for granted. A new Christian won't be intimidated, nor will the student interested in refreshing the memory. Frequent self-tests are found throughout the text to help in committing the information to memory. They highlight areas that might take another read-through.

Of course, the Bible is an enormous book, covering many subjects of profound significance, and it is not possible that you will learn everything about it in thirty days. *30 Days to Understanding the Bible* will not give you a complete knowledge of the Bible. Rather than seeing God's Word as a series of fragmented stories, you will have a comprehensive overview from which you can build a more complete understanding in the years ahead.

For now, a greater understanding of the Bible awaits you. In fifteen minutes a day for thirty days, you can gain a foundational grasp of the most important book ever written.

# THE
# STORY
# OF
# THE
# OLD
# TESTAMENT

# ONE

# THE STRUCTURE
# OF THE BIBLE

Charles Steinmetz was an electrical engineer of towering intellect. After retiring, he was asked by a major appliance manufacturer to locate a malfunction in their electrical equipment. None of the manufacturer's experts had been able to locate the problem. Steinmetz spent some time walking around and testing the various parts of the machine complex. Finally, he took out of his pocket a piece of chalk and marked an X on a particular part of one machine. The manufacturer's people disassembled the machine, discovering to their amazement that the defect lay precisely where Steinmetz's chalk mark was located.

Some days later, the manufacturer received a bill from Steinmetz for ten thousand dollars. They protested the amount and asked him to itemize it. He sent back an itemized bill:

Making one chalk mark . . . . . . . . . . . . . . . . . . . .$      1
Knowing where to place it . . . . . . . . . . . . . . . . .$9,999

If you know where the chalk marks go, the most overwhelming tasks are easily solved. If you don't, even simple tasks can be impossible.

Learning about the Bible can be much the same. If you don't know much about it, it can be like trying to cross the Sahara Desert blindfolded. Yet if you learn where a few of the major chalk marks go, the Bible can be at the very least an interesting and valuable source of information and inspiration.

My own experience bears this out. Many years ago, I decided I was going to master the Bible. I was going to begin with

Genesis, read to Revelation, and I wasn't going to put it down until I understood it. I soon became hopelessly entangled in a jungle of fantastic stories, unpronounceable names, broken plots, unanswered questions, and endless genealogies. I stubbed my toe on Leviticus, sprained my ankle on Job, hit my head on Ecclesiastes, and fell headlong into the mud on Habakkuk.

I was defeated. I threw my Bible down. One thing seemed clear: the Bible was a series of unrelated stories put together in random order!

Than one day I discovered a key. With this key, the fog that enshrouded my understanding of the Bible began to lift. Not that things came into sharp focus, but I began to see shapes on the horizon.

The key: *Learning the structure of the Bible*. If you want to learn architecture, you must first learn how buildings are put together. If you want to learn sailing, you must first learn how ships are put together. And if you want to learn to understand the Bible, you must first learn how the Bible is put together.

### The Old and New Testaments

The Bible has two major divisions: the Old Testament and the New Testament. The Old Testament begins with creation, and tells the story of the Jewish people up to the time of Christ. It is made up of *thirty-nine* individual "books" (the Book of Genesis, the Book of Exodus, etc.) written by twenty-eight different authors, and spans a period of over two thousand years.

The New Testament is the record of the birth of Jesus, His life and ministry, and the ministry of His disciples, which was carried on after Jesus was crucified. The New Testament is comprised of *twenty-seven* books written by nine different authors, and covers a time period of less than one hundred years. The total number of books in the entire Bible is *sixty-six*.

### Self Test
*To check your answers, review the previous paragraph.*

How many?    _____ books in the Old Testament

_____ books in the New Testament

_____ books in the whole Bible

## Old Testament Books

| | | |
|---|---|---|
| Genesis | 2 Chronicles | Daniel |
| Exodus | Ezra | Hosea |
| Leviticus | Nehemiah | Joel |
| Numbers | Esther | Amos |
| Deuteronomy | Job | Obadiah |
| Joshua | Psalms | Jonah |
| Judges | Proverbs | Micah |
| Ruth | Ecclesiastes | Nahum |
| 1 Samuel | Song of Solomon | Habakkuk |
| 2 Samuel | Isaiah | Zephaniah |
| 1 Kings | Jeremiah | Haggai |
| 2 Kings | Lamentations | Zechariah |
| 1 Chronicles | Ezekiel | Malachi |

## New Testament Books

| | | |
|---|---|---|
| Matthew | Ephesians | Hebrews |
| Mark | Philippians | James |
| Luke | Colossians | 1 Peter |
| John | 1 Thessalonians | 2 Peter |
| Acts | 2 Thessalonians | 1 John |
| Romans | 1 Timothy | 2 John |
| 1 Corinthians | 2 Timothy | 3 John |
| 2 Corinthians | Titus | Jude |
| Galatians | Philemon | Revelation |

## The Old Testament

*"The used key is always bright."* Benjamin Franklin

Here is the key to understanding the Old Testament. Of the thirty-nine books in the Old Testament, *there are three different kinds of books*: Historical Books, Poetical Books, and Prophetical Books.

What kind of information would you expect to find in the Historical Books? . . . . . . . . . . . . . . . . . . . . . . . . . . . . .*history!*

What kind of information would you expect to find in the Poetical Books? . . . . . . . . . . . . . . . . . . . . . . . . . . . . . . . . .*poetry!*

What kind of information would you expect to find in the Prophetical Books? . . . . . . . . . . . . . . . . . . . . . . . . . . . . .*prophecy!*

If you know what kind of book you are reading, then you will know what kind of information to expect, and can easily follow the logical flow of the Old Testament!

In the Old Testament:

    . . . the first seventeen books are historical,

    . . . the next five books are poetical, and

    . . . the next seventeen books are prophetical!

### The Three Kinds of Books in the Old Testament

| *Historical* | *Poetical* | *Prophetical* |
|---|---|---|
| Genesis | Job | Isaiah |
| Exodus | Psalms | Jeremiah |
| Leviticus | Proverbs | Lamentations |
| Numbers | Ecclesiastes | Ezekiel |
| Deuteronomy | Song of Solomon | Daniel |
| Joshua | | Hosea |
| Judges | | Joel |
| Ruth | | Amos |
| 1 Samuel | | Obadiah |
| 2 Samuel | | Jonah |
| 1 Kings | | Micah |
| 2 Kings | | Nahum |
| 1 Chronicles | | Habakkuk |
| 2 Chronicles | | Zephaniah |
| Ezra | | Haggai |
| Nehemiah | | Zechariah |
| Esther | | Malachi |

If you want to read the story of the Hebrew nation in the Old Testament, you must read the first seventeen books. These books comprise an historical time line for the nation of Israel.

If you want to read the poetry of Israel, you must read the next five books of the Old Testament.

If you want to read about the prophecy of Israel, you must read the final seventeen books.

This is somewhat oversimplified, for there is some poetry in the Historical Books, and some history in the Prophetical books, etc. The point is, however, that each of the books fits into a primary category. If you keep this structure in mind, the Old Testament will begin to take shape in your mind.

*My mistake was in assuming that the whole Old Testament was one long, unbroken story, and that the history would flow evenly and consistently out of one book into the next until they were all finished.* Now, I know the story line is contained in the first seventeen books.

Of the seventeen Historical Books, eleven are primary Historical Books, and six are secondary Historical Books. The history of Israel is advanced in the eleven primary books, and repeated or amplified in the six secondary books. The Poetical and Prophetical Books were written during the time period that is constructed in the first seventeen books.

Let's take a look at the historical time line of the Old Testament in chart form:

## Time Line of the Old Testament

*Poetical Books*

| | | | | | | | Proverbs Ecclesiastes Song of Solomon | | | |
|---|---|---|---|---|---|---|---|---|---|---|
| Job | | | | | | Psalms | | | | |

*Historical Books*

| | Leviticus | Deuteronomy | | Ruth | | 1 Chronicles | 2 Chronicles | | Esther | |
|---|---|---|---|---|---|---|---|---|---|---|
| Genesis | Exodus | Numbers | Joshua | Judges | 1 Samuel | 2 Samuel | 1 Kings | 2 Kings | Ezra | Nehemiah |
| **1** | **2** | **3** | **4** | **5** | **6** | **7** | **8** | **9** | ----- **10** | **11** |

*Prophetical Books*

| | | | | | | | To Israel: Hosea Amos  To Judah: Habakkuk Isaiah Jeremiah Joel Micah Zephaniah Lamentations  To Assyria: Jonah Nahum  To Edom: Obadiah | Ezekiel Daniel | Haggai Zechariah | Malachi |
|---|---|---|---|---|---|---|---|---|---|---|

As you can see, Job was written during the time period of the book of Genesis, and Psalms during the time of 2 Samuel; while Proverbs, Ecclesiastes, and Song of Solomon were written during the time of 1 Kings, and so on.

To use an analogy, we constructed a similar chart for U.S. History. Imagine that you read an American History book for the main story line. The history book would give you the major periods in U.S. history. Some of these periods might be associated with a major poet or writer, and a major philosopher. The poets would correspond to the poets of Israel, and the philosophers would correspond to the Biblical prophets.

## Time Line of U.S. History

*Poets/Writers*

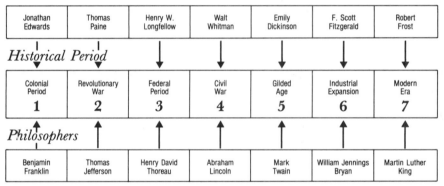

| Jonathan Edwards | Thomas Paine | Henry W. Longfellow | Walt Whitman | Emily Dickinson | F. Scott Fitzgerald | Robert Frost |
|---|---|---|---|---|---|---|

*Historical Period*

| Colonial Period | Revolutionary War | Federal Period | Civil War | Gilded Age | Industrial Expansion | Modern Era |
|---|---|---|---|---|---|---|
| 1 | 2 | 3 | 4 | 5 | 6 | 7 |

*Philosophers*

| Benjamin Franklin | Thomas Jefferson | Henry David Thoreau | Abraham Lincoln | Mark Twain | William Jennings Bryan | Martin Luther King |
|---|---|---|---|---|---|---|

## The New Testament

Of the twenty-seven books of the New Testament, *there are also three different kinds of books*: Historical Books, Pauline Epistles, and General Epistles. The Historical Books are the four gospels and the Acts of the Apostles. The Epistles were "letters" written to various individuals and church congregations. The Pauline Epistles were letters written by the Apostle Paul. The General Epistles were letters written to individuals and congregations by a number of different people, hence the rather generic name "General Epistles." The primary content in all the Epistles is "instruction" on Christian doctrine and lifestyle.

What kind of information would you expect to find in the Historical Books? . . . . . . . . . . . . . . . . . . . . . . . . . . . . . *history!*

What kind of information would you expect to find in the Pauline Epistles? . . . . . . . . . . . . . . . . . . . . . . . . *instruction!*

What kind of information would you expect to find in the General Epistles?. . . . . . . . . . . . . . . . . . . . . . . . *instruction!*

In the New Testament:

> . . . the first five books are Historical Books,

> . . . the next thirteen books are Pauline Epistles, and

> . . . the next nine books are General Epistles!

### The Three Kinds of Books in the New Testament

| *Historical* | *Pauline* | *General* |
|---|---|---|
| Matthew | TO CHURCHES: | Hebrews |
| Mark | Romans | James |
| Luke | 1 Corinthians | 1 Peter |
| John | 2 Corinthians | 2 Peter |
| Acts | Galatians | 1 John |
| | Ephesians | 2 John |
| | Philippians | 3 John |
| | Colossians | Jude |
| | 1 Thessalonians | Revelation |
| | 2 Thessalonians | |
| | | |
| | TO INDIVIDUALS: | |
| | 1 Timothy | |
| | 2 Timothy | |
| | Titus | |
| | Philemon | |

If you want to read the story of Jesus and the Church He established, you must read the first five books of the New Testament. These five books form the historical framework for understanding the entire New Testament!

If you want to read the Apostle Paul's instruction to churches and individuals, you must read the next thirteen books.

If you want to read the instruction to churches and individuals by men like the Apostles Peter and John, you must read the final nine books of the New Testament.

### References

To find something in the Bible, you use a standard reference system. This consists of the name of the book of the Bible, the chapter number followed by a colon, and the verse number (each chapter is divided into numbered verses). For example:

Genesis 1:1 = Genesis    1:        1
              (book)    (chapter)  (verse)

When you see a reference such as Joshua 1:21, you will either have to memorize the books of the Bible to know where Joshua is, or you can look it up in the Table of Contents. It is well worth the time to memorize the books, and if you do, it is easiest to memorize them according to their categories.

For example, you now know that there are three types of books in both the Old Testament (Historical, Poetical, and Prophetical), and the New Testament (Historical, Pauline Epistles, and General Epistles), and how many books are in each section. Memorize the first seventeen Historical Books. Then, when you have these memorized, learn the five Poetical books, and so on. This system is much easier than attempting to memorize an unbroken list of sixty-six books.

### Summary

1. There are 39 books in the Old Testament.
   There are 27 books in the New Testament.

   There are 66 books in the whole Bible.

2. The Old Testament is the story of God and the Hebrew people, their poets, and prophets.

   There are 3 kinds of books in the Old Testament:
       17 Historical Books,
        5 Poetical Books, and
       17 Prophetical Books.

3. The New Testament is the story of Jesus of Nazareth, the Church which He founded, and its growth under the leadership of His apostles after His death.

There are 3 kinds of books in the New Testament:

    5 Historical Books,

    13 Pauline Epistles, and

    9 General Epistles.

### Self Test

*To check your answers, review the previous pages.*

**The Bible:**

How many? _____ books in the Old Testament

            _____ books in the New Testament

            _____ books in the whole Bible

**The Old Testament:**

The Old Testament is the story of G_____ and the H_____ people, their poets, and prophets.

There are 3 kinds of books in the Old Testament:

    H_____ Books,

    P _____ Books, and

    P _____ Books.

There are _____ Historical Books.

There are _____ Poetical Books.

There are _____ Prophetical Books.

**The New Testament:**

The New Testament is the story of J_____, the C_____ which He founded, and its growth under the leadership of His a_____s after His death.

There are 3 kinds of books in the New Testament:

    H_____ Books,

    P _____ Epistles, and

    G_____ Epistles.

There are _____ Historical Books.
There are _____ Pauline Epistles.
There are _____ General Epistles.

*Congratulations!* You are off to a fine start. As we move from the general to the specific, you can build your knowledge of the Bible like rows of brick on a house, and in twenty-nine more days, your house will be finished.

# THE GEOGRAPHY OF
# THE OLD TESTAMENT

The size of our solar system is beyond comprehension. To get some perspective, imagine you are in the middle of the Bonneville Salt Flats with nothing but table-top flat ground around you for miles and miles. There you put down a beach ball two feet in diameter, which you use to represent the Sun. To get a feel for the immensity of the solar system, walk about a city block, and put down a mustard seed for the first planet, Mercury. Go another block, and for Venus, put down an ordinary BB. Mark off yet another block, and put down a green pea to represent the Earth. A final block from there, put down a mustard seed to represent Mars. Then sprinkle some grass seed around for an asteroid belt.

We have now walked about four blocks, and we have a beach-ball (Sun), mustard seed (Mercury), BB (Venus), pea (Earth), mustard seed (Mars), and grass seed (asteroid belt). Now things begin to stretch out.

Continue for another quarter of a mile. Place an orange on the ground for Jupiter. Walk another third of a mile, and put down a golf ball for Saturn.

Now lace up your tennis shoes, and check their tread. Then step off another mile and, for Uranus, drop a marble. Go another mile and place a cherry there for Neptune. Finally, walk for another two miles, and put down another marble for Pluto.

At last, go up in an airplane, and look down. On a smooth surface almost ten miles in diameter, we have a beachball, a mustard seed, a BB, a pea, another mustard seed, some grass seed, an orange, a golf ball, a marble, a cherry, and another marble.

To understand our replica of the solar system even better, take another beach ball and put it down to represent Alpha Centauri, the next nearest star to our sun, you would have to go another 6,720 miles and put it down in Japan.

Understanding the size and location of things, and the relationships, and distances between them gives us perspective. Just as this example gives us perspective about the solar system, a knowledge of geography can give perspective about the events of the Bible. It is helpful to know the names, locations, and distances between important geographical locations. Otherwise, we skim over information without comprehension or visualization, and the Bible is less interesting and less easily understood.

If a man is ignorant of geography, he cannot know history. The Bible is largely history. So to begin our mastery of the history of the Bible, we must start with the geography of the Bible.

### Bodies of Water

The primary anchor points for mastering the geography of the Bible are the bodies of water. (*As you read each description, go to the Work Map and insert the name of the body of water.*)

### 1. The Mediterranean Sea.

The land of the Old Testament lies east of this beautiful blue body of water.

### 2. The Sea of Galilee.

To call this body of water a sea seems to be an overstatement. It is a fresh water lake which is seven miles wide, and fourteen miles long. It lies inland from the Mediterranean about thirty-six miles.

### 3. The Jordan River.

Flowing south out of the Sea of Galilee, the Jordan River travels for sixty-five miles, as the crow flies, to empty into the Dead Sea. Many are surprised at how much history has revolved around such a small (by many standards) river.

### 4. The Dead Sea.

Shaped like a giant hot dog with a bite out of the lower third, the Dead Sea lies at the "bottom of the world." It is the lowest point on earth, almost three thousand feet below sea level at its lowest point, so that water flows into it, but no water flows out of it. As a result, the water has developed very high mineral deposits and does not support normal plant or animal life. Hence the name "Dead Sea."

## 5. Nile River.

Perhaps the most famous river in the world, the Nile flows through the heart of Egypt, spreads out like so many fingers, and empties into the waiting arms of the Mediterranean.

## 6. Tigris and (7) Euphrates.

These twin rivers flow for almost a thousand miles each before they join hands and deposit their treasure into the Persian Gulf.

## 8. Persian Gulf.

These last three bodies of water, the Tigris, the Euphrates, and the Persian Gulf, form the eastern-most boundary for the lands of the Old Testament. The Tigris and Euphrates flow through present day Iraq, while the Persian Gulf separates Iran from Saudi Arabia.

## Work Map
*Bodies of Water of the Old Testament.*

### Locations

With the geographical framework offered by the bodies of water, we can establish the locations which are relevant to the Old Testament. (*As you read the description of each location, insert it in on the Location Work Map that follows.*)

### A. The Garden of Eden.

The exact location of the Garden of Eden, where everything began, is impossible to pinpoint. However, it was near the convergence of four rivers, two of which were the Tigris and Euphrates.

### B. Canaan/Israel/Palestine.

This smallish piece of real estate which lies between the Mediterranean coast and the "Sea of Galilee-Jordan River-Dead Sea," changes names throughout the Old Testament. In Genesis it is called *Canaan*. After the Hebrew people establish themselves in the land in the book of Joshua, it becomes known as *Israel*. Eight hundred years later, at the beginning of the New Testament, it is called *Palestine*.

### C. Jerusalem.

Located just off the northwestern shoulder of the Dead Sea, this city, nestled in the central mountains of Israel, is so central to the story of the Old Testament that it must be singled out and identified. It is the capital of the nation of Israel.

### D. Egypt.

The *grande dame* of ancient civilization, Egypt plays a central role in the history of the Old Testament.

### E. Assyria.

Located at the headwaters of the Tigris and Euphrates, this great world power is notable in the Old Testament for conquering the Northern Kingdom of Israel and dispersing her people to the four winds.

### F. Babylonia.

Another gigantic historical world power, this fabulous, albeit short-lived, nation conquered Assyria. It also conquered the Southern Kingdom of Judah one hundred and fifty years after

Assyria conquered the Northern Kingdom of Israel. It is found in Mesopotamia, between the Tigris and Euphrates. (Mesopotamia means "in the middle of" [meso] — "rivers" [potamus].)

## G. Persia.

The final historical superpower of the Old Testament is located at the north bank of the Persian Gulf. Persia comes into play by conquering Babylonia and by allowing the Hebrews to return from captivity in Babylonia to rebuild the city of Jerusalem and reinstate temple worship.

If these historical notes are foreign to you, don't worry about it now. Instead, content yourself with learning these locations so that, as the story unfolds, the names of these locations will mean something to you.

### Location Work Map
*Locations of the Old Testament.*

Now, compare the ancient map which you have just filled in with a contemporary map of the same region.

It might also help to get this Old Testament information into perspective by seeing how the map of the Old Testament compares with an overlay of a map of the state of Texas.

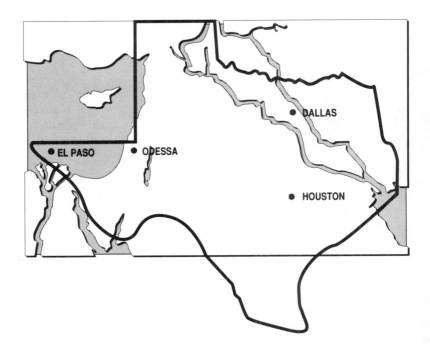

The entire land of the Old Testament is approximately the same size as the state of Texas. Traveling from the Persian Gulf to Israel would be like going from Houston to Odessa. Traveling from Israel to Egypt would be like going from Odessa to El Paso. If you keep this in mind as the story of the Bible unfolds, it will help you keep geographical perspective.

## Review
### *The Geography of the Old Testament.*

Review both the 8 Bodies of Water and the 7 Locations by placing the numbers and letters by the appropriate names below.

| | |
|---|---|
| _____ Mediterranean Sea | _____ Eden |
| _____ Sea of Galilee | _____ Israel |
| _____ Jordan River | _____ Jerusalem |
| _____ Dead Sea | _____ Egypt |
| _____ Nile River | _____ Assyria |
| _____ Tigris River | _____ Babylonia |
| _____ Euphrates River | _____ Persia |
| _____ Persian Gulf | |

## Self Test
*The Geography of the Old Testament.*

As the final exercise, fill in the blanks from memory. (Remember, the blanks with numbers are Bodies of Water, and the blanks with letters are Locations.)

Excellent! Your knowledge of the geography of the Old Testament will enable you to understand and envision the history which unfolds from it. You have just mastered an important section.

## Answers
*The Geography of the Old Testament.*

# T H R E E

# THE HISTORICAL BOOKS

 On the flight from Los Angeles to Portland, one flies over the entire length of the Cascade Mountains. From thirty-five thousand feet it is difficult to get the perspective to determine which are the higher mountain peaks.

One day in late October as I was making that flight, the air was crisp and clear after a light snowfall and the puzzle of how to differentiate the higher from the lower peaks was answered. The snow only fell on elevations of about seven thousand feet and higher. As we flew over them, regardless of how close or far away they were, the highest peaks were easy to determine: they were the ones with snow on them.

As we begin to look into the stories of the Old Testament, we will only look at the highest peaks, the ones with snow on them.

To do so, it will be helpful to continue the analogy with the story of the United States. If you were going to condense just the story of the United States, omitting the poets and philosophers, you would take the main periods of history, link them with the central historic figure of the era, and add the primary location. In chart form, it might look like this:

## Time Line of U.S. History

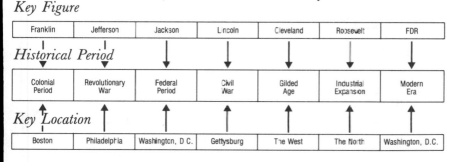

*Key Figure*

| Franklin | Jefferson | Jackson | Lincoln | Cleveland | Roosevelt | FDR |
|----------|-----------|---------|---------|-----------|-----------|-----|

*Historical Period*

| Colonial Period | Revolutionary War | Federal Period | Civil War | Gilded Age | Industrial Expansion | Modern Era |
|-----------------|-------------------|----------------|-----------|------------|----------------------|------------|

*Key Location*

| Boston | Philadelphia | Washington, D C. | Gettysburg | The West | The North | Washington, D.C. |
|--------|--------------|------------------|------------|----------|-----------|------------------|

23

Include a brief storyline summary of the era, and the Story of the United States could be overviewed in a chart, such as the following:

### Story of the United States

| KEY ERA | KEY FIGURE | LOCATION | STORYLINE |
|---------|-----------|----------|-----------|
| *Colonial* | *Franklin* | *Boston* | As the 13 colonies long for independence, Franklin leads the formulation of necessary strategy. |
| *Revolution* | *Jefferson* | *Philadelphia* | Jefferson forges the Declaration of Independence. |
| *Etc.* | *Etc.* | *Etc.* | *Etc.* |

This same approach can be used in condensing the story of the Bible, charting the main periods (or eras), the central figures, the main locations, and a summary storyline. The storyline of the Bible can be divided into twelve main eras, with a central figure and main location for each era. Nine of the eras are found in the Old Testament, and three are found in the New Testament.

In this chapter, we will deal with only the Old Testament, and will complete only the first three aspects of the chart: the Main Eras, the Central Figures, and the Main Locations. The summary storyline and the New Testament events will be added in the following chapters.

### The Nine Main Eras of the Old Testament

**1. Creation.**

The *creation* of the world and man, and early events.

**2. Patriarch.**

The birth of the Hebrew people through a family of *patriarchs*, covering a period of two hundred years.

## 3. Exodus.

The *exodus* of the Hebrew people as they were delivered out of four hundred years of slavery in Egypt.

## 4. Conquest.

The *conquest* of the Promised Land by the Hebrew people upon their return from Egypt.

## 5. Judges.

A four-hundred year period during which Israel is governed by rulers called *judges*.

## 6. Kingdom.

An additional four-hundred year period during which Israel becomes a full-fledged nation ruled by a *monarchy*.

## 7. Exile.

A seventy-year period during which Israel's leaders live in *exile*, having been conquered by foreign countries.

## 8. Return.

The *return* of exiled Jews to Jerusalem to rebuild the city and the temple.

## 9. Silence.

A final four-hundred year period between the close of the Old Testament and the opening of the New Testament.

Following the pattern of the chart for the Story of the United States, let's begin to chart the Story of the Old Testament.

## Story of the Old Testament

| ERA | FIGURE | LOCATION | STORYLINE |
|---|---|---|---|
| *Creation* | To be | To be | To be |
| *Patriarch* | supplied | supplied | supplied |
| *Exodus* | later. | later. | later. |
| *Conquest* | | | |
| *Judges* | | | |
| *Kingdom* | | | |
| *Exile* | | | |
| *Return* | | | |
| *Silence* | | | |

Another way to help us remember the historical storyline of the Bible is to visualize the Main Eras with symbols, such as in the Arc of Bible History.

## Arc of Bible History

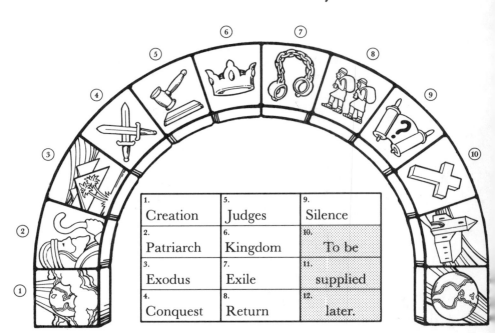

| 1. Creation | 5. Judges | 9. Silence |
| 2. Patriarch | 6. Kingdom | 10. To be |
| 3. Exodus | 7. Exile | 11. supplied |
| 4. Conquest | 8. Return | 12. later. |

## Review

*Write in the Era on the proper line matching the description.*

| OPTIONS: | ERA: | DESCRIPTION: |
|---|---|---|
| Exile | _____ | The *creation* of the world and man, and early events. |
| Judges | | |
| Creation | _____ | The birth of the Hebrew people through a family of *patriarchs*, covering a period of two hundred years. |
| Kingdom | | |
| Patriarch | | |
| Conquest | | |
| Return | _____ | The *exodus* of the Hebrew people as they are delivered out of four hundred years of slavery in Egypt. |
| Silence | | |
| Exodus | | |

| ERA: | DESCRIPTION: |
|------|--------------|
| _____ | The *conquest* of the Promised Land by the Hebrew people upon their return from Egypt. |
| _____ | A four-hundred year period during which Israel is governed by rulers called *judges*. |
| _____ | An additional four-hundred year period during which Israel becomes a full-fledged nation ruled by a *monarchy*. |
| _____ | A seventy-year period during which Israel's leaders live in *exile*, having been conquered by foreign countries. |
| _____ | The *return* of the exiled Hebrews to Jerusalem to rebuild the city and the temple. |
| _____ | A final four-hundred year period between the close of the Old Testament and the opening of the New Testament. |

## The Nine Central Figures of the Old Testament

| ERA: | FIGURE: | DESCRIPTION: |
|------|---------|--------------|
| Creation | Adam | The first *man* |
| Patriarch | Abraham | The first *patriarch* |
| Exodus | Moses | The leader of the *exodus* |
| Conquest | Joshua | The leader of Israel's *army* |
| Judges | Samson | The most famous *judge* |
| Kingdom | David | The most well-known Israelite *king* |
| Exile | Daniel | The major exilic *prophet* |
| Return | Ezra | The central *return* leader |
| Silence | Pharisees | The *religious* leaders |

# REVIEW

*Fill in the blank.*

| ERA: | FIGURE: | DESCRIPTION: |
|------|---------|--------------|
| Creation | Adam | The first _____ |
| Patriarch | Abraham | The first _____ |
| Exodus | Moses | The leader of the _____ |
| Conquest | Joshua | The leader of Israel's _____ |
| Judges | Samson | The most famous _____ |
| Kingdom | David | The most well-known Israelite _____ |
| Exile | Daniel | The major exilic _____ |
| Return | Ezra | The central _____ leader |
| Silence | Pharisees | The _____ leaders |

*Match the era with the key figure.*

| ERA: | FIGURE: | OPTIONS: |
|------|---------|----------|
| Creation | _____ | Moses |
| Patriarch | _____ | Daniel |
| Exodus | _____ | Abraham |
| Conquest | _____ | Joshua |
| Judges | _____ | Pharisees |
| Kingdom | _____ | Ezra |
| Exile | _____ | David |
| Return | _____ | Samson |
| Silence | _____ | Adam |

Now we will add the Central Figure to our storyline chart.

## Story of the Old Testament

| ERA | FIGURE | LOCATION | STORYLINE |
|-----|--------|----------|-----------|
| Creation | Adam | To be | To be |
| Patriarch | Abraham | supplied | supplied |
| Exodus | Moses | later. | later. |
| Conquest | Joshua | | |
| Judges | Samson | | |
| Kingdom | David | | |
| Exile | Daniel | | |
| Return | Ezra | | |
| Silence | Pharisees | | |

Our final task is to identify the general or primary geographic location of the events of the main eras of the Old Testament. Beginning with Creation and Adam, as an exercise in memory, write in each main era and central historical figure as you read the description of the location of each of the eras.

## The Nine Main Locations of the Old Testament

| ERA: | FIGURE: | LOCATION: | DESCRIPTION: |
|---|---|---|---|
| 1. _____ | _____ | Eden | The garden of Eden, where Adam is created. Near the convergence of the Tigris and Euphrates. |
| 2. _____ | _____ | Canaan | Abraham migrates from Ur, near Eden, to Canaan, where he and the other patriarchs live until the time of slavery in Egypt. |
| 3. _____ | _____ | Egypt | During a severe famine, the Israelites migrate to Egypt and are enslaved four hundred years before the exodus to freedom. |
| 4. _____ | _____ | Canaan | Joshua leads the conquest of the Promised Land in Canaan. |
| 5. _____ | _____ | Canaan | The Israelites live in Canaan under a loose tribal system ruled by judges for the next four hundred years. |
| 6. _____ | _____ | Israel | With the formation of a formal monarchy, the land is now referred to by the national name of Israel. |

| ERA: | FIGURE: | LOCATION: | DESCRIPTION: |
|------|---------|-----------|--------------|

7. _____  _____  Babylonia  Because of judgment for national moral corruption, Israel is conquered by foreign nations, finally forcing her leaders into seventy years exile in Babylonia.

8. _____  _____  Jerusalem  The exiled Israelites are allowed to return to Jerusalem to rebuild the city and temple, though they remain under the dominion of Persia.

9. _____  _____  Jerusalem  Though dominion of the land changes from Persia to Greece to Rome, Israel is allowed to worship in Jerusalem without disruption for the next four hundred years of "silence."

Along with the Main Era and the Central Figure, we are now able to add the Main Location to our chart.

## Story of the Old Testament

| ERA | FIGURE | LOCATION | STORYLINE |
|-----|--------|----------|-----------|
| Creation | Adam | Eden | To be |
| Patriarch | Abraham | Canaan | supplied |
| Exodus | Moses | Egypt | later. |
| Conquest | Joshua | Canaan | |
| Judges | Samson | Canaan | |
| Kingdom | David | Israel | |
| Exile | Daniel | Babylonia | |
| Return | Ezra | Jerusalem | |
| Silence | Pharisees | Jerusalem | |

## Arc of Bible History

*Fill in the names of the Eras.*

| 1. C_____ | 5. J _____ | 9. S _____ |
|---|---|---|
| 2. P _____ | 6. K_____ | 10. |
| 3. E _____ | 7. E _____ | 11. |
| 4. C _____ | 8. R_____ | 12. |

## Review

On the following map draw arrows to show the movement during the major Eras of the Old Testament which we have just learned. Begin at Eden, and draw an arrow to the next location as it changes. Eden, to Canaan, to Egypt, to Canaan, to Babylonia, to Jerusalem.

In its most basic movement, your map should look something like this.

From the options given, fill in the blanks in the following chart, matching the Location to the Era and central Figure. (A Location may be used more than once.)

Babylonia          Eden          Israel
Canaan             Egypt         Jerusalem

## Story of the Old Testament

| ERA | FIGURE | LOCATION | STORYLINE |
|---|---|---|---|
| *Creation* | Adam | _____ | To be |
| *Patriarch* | Abraham | _____ | supplied |
| *Exodus* | Moses | _____ | later. |
| *Conquest* | Joshua | _____ | |
| *Judges* | Samson | _____ | |
| *Kingdom* | David | _____ | |
| *Exile* | Daniel | _____ | |
| *Return* | Ezra | _____ | |
| *Silence* | Pharisees | _____ | |

You are now ready to begin final mastery of a very critical chart. Once you master this chart, you have come a long way in understanding the overview of the Old Testament. Fill in the blanks.

## Story of the Old Testament

| ERA | FIGURE | LOCATION | STORYLINE |
|-----|--------|----------|-----------|
| *Creation* | Adam | _____ | To be |
| *Patriarch* | _____ | Canaan | supplied |
| _____ | Moses | Egypt | later. |
| *Conquest* | Joshua | _____ | |
| *Judges* | _____ | Canaan | |
| _____ | David | Israel | |
| *Exile* | Daniel | _____ | |
| *Return* | _____ | Jerusalem | |
| _____ | Pharisees | Jerusalem | |

## Self Test

Finally, fill in the following chart from memory. It might be easiest to fill in the Eras, then go back and fill in the Central Figure and Main Location. (To check your answers see the Appendix for a completed Story of the Bible chart.)

## Story of the Old Testament

| ERA | FIGURE | LOCATION | STORYLINE |
|-----|--------|----------|-----------|
| _____ | _____ | _____ | To be |
| _____ | _____ | _____ | supplied |
| _____ | _____ | _____ | later. |
| _____ | _____ | _____ | |
| _____ | _____ | _____ | |
| _____ | _____ | _____ | |
| _____ | _____ | _____ | |
| _____ | _____ | _____ | |

Congratulations! You have just taken a major step toward mastering an overview of the Old Testament. From now on, we will become more and more specific, but you have laid a good foundation which can be built upon in successive chapters.

# FOUR

# THE CREATION ERA
## (Genesis 1-11)

"Far from the land of everyday, out in the distant curves of the universe, lay strange and fantastic realms, unlike anything in our wildest dreams. Hidden by the barriers of time and space, they have lived forever beyond the reach of man, unknown and unexplored.

"But now, just now, the cosmic veils have begun to lift a little. Man has had his first glimpses of these once-secret domains, and their bizarre ways have left him stunned. They challenge his very notions of matter and energy. Along with Alice in Wonderland, he says, 'One can't believe impossible things.'

"And impossible, indeed, they seem to be. In those far reaches of the universe, in those bewildering worlds, are far places . . .

"where a teaspoon of matter weighs as much as two hundred million elephants . . .

"where a tiny whirling star winks on and off thirty times a second . . .

"where a small, mysterious object shines with the brilliance of ten trillion suns . . .

"where matter and light are continually sucked up by devouring black holes, never to be seen again.

"Small wonder that the late British scientist J. B. S. Haldane could say, '. . . the universe is not only queerer than we suppose, but queerer than we can suppose.'

"We used to think that the universe was simply our Milky Way Galaxy. Today we know that galaxies are as common as blades of grass in a meadow. They number perhaps a hundred billion.

"How does one comprehend the incredible size of this galaxy-filled universe? For such awesome distances, scientists and astronomers think in terms of time, and they use the telescope as a time machine. They measure space by a unit called the light-year, the distance light travels in one year at the rate of 186,282 miles per second — about six trillion miles" (from *National Geographic*, May, 1974).

If you could shoot a gun whose bullet would travel at the speed of light around the world, the bullet would go around the world and pass through you seven times in one second!

Perhaps more than anything else, the mystery and the enormity of our universe capture our imagination and incite in us a fascination about the subject of Creation. There are countless unknowns, and just as many "unbelievables." As we begin to explore the Creation Era, we will adopt a pattern that will be followed throughout the remainder of this section:

I.  You will review the main era, central figure, and main location which you learned in the last chapter.

II.  You will read a brief storyline summary of the events of that era, built around the central figure, with a three-word theme of each summary appearing in italics. Then you will be asked to review those three words to fill in the blanks.

III.  You will read an expansion of the summary of the events of that era.

I.    **Review:** Fill in the blanks for this era.

### Story of the Old Testament

| ERA | FIGURE | LOCATION | STORYLINE SUMMARY |
|---|---|---|---|
| ———— | ———— | ———— | To be completed in this chapter. |

**II. Storyline Summary:** Adam is created by God, but he *sins* and *destroys* God's original *plan* for man.

| ERA | SUMMARY |
|---|---|
| *Creation:* | Adam is created by God, but he _____, and _____ God's original _____ for man. |

**III. Expansion:** There are four major events within the Creation Era. They are the accounts of:

1. Creation
2. Fall
3. Flood
4. Tower of Babel

**1. Creation: Man created in the image of God** (Genesis 1-2).

After a dramatic display of power in creating the heavens and the earth, God creates man. Adam and Eve are created in the image of God, in perfect fellowship and harmony with Him. Living in an idyllic setting in the Garden of Eden, they are individuals of beauty and high intelligence. The "image" is not a physical likeness, but a personal and spiritual likeness. Man has intellect, emotion, and will. He has a moral sense of right and wrong. He is a creative being. These are some characteristics of God which are shared by man, and in this sense, *man is created in the image of God.*

**2. Fall: Sin entered the world** (Genesis 3).

Satan, appearing in the form of a serpent, lures Adam and Eve into rebelling against God, and violating the one prohibition God had given them: not to eat from the tree of the knowledge of good and evil. They are driven out of the garden of Eden, and a curse is placed on the earth. When Adam and Eve rebelled, *sin entered the world.* All the pain, all the evil, all the suffering throughout mankind for all time can be traced to that one act which is, therefore, appropriately called the "fall" of man.

**3. Flood: Judgment for sin** (Genesis 6-10).

Over the next several hundred years, as man multiplies in numbers, so his tendency to sin multiplies, until a time came when God can find only eight people who are willing to live in a righteous relationship with Him: Noah, his wife, his three sons, and their wives. So, in *judgment for sin*, God performs surgery on the human race, cutting out the cancerous tissue, as it were, leaving behind the healthy tissue to restore itself. He does this by sending a worldwide flood which destroys mankind, except for Noah and his family, who are saved in Noah's ark.

### 4. Tower: Beginning of the nations (Genesis 11).

God's post-flood mandate to man was to spread out, populate, and subdue the whole earth. In direct disobedience to that command, man stays in one place and begins building a monument to himself, the Tower of Babel. God causes this large congregation of people to begin speaking different languages. Lack of communication prevents them from further progress on the tower, and the people of each tongue disperse to the four corners of the earth, and form the *beginning of the nations* of the world as we know them today.

### Self Test
*To check your answers, review the previous pages.*

### A. The Four Main Events of the Creation Era
(Write in the correct descriptions from the options at right.)

*Creation* _____ Judgment for sin.

*Fall* _____ Beginning of the nations.

*Flood* _____ Sin entered the world.

*Tower* _____ Man in the image of God.

### B. Storyline Summary
(Fill in the blanks from memory.)

| ERA | SUMMARY |
|-----|---------|
| Creation: | Adam is created by God, but he _____, and _____ God's original _____ for man. |

## C. Arc of Bible History

(Fill in the name of the Era. To check your answer, see the appendix "Self Test Answers.")

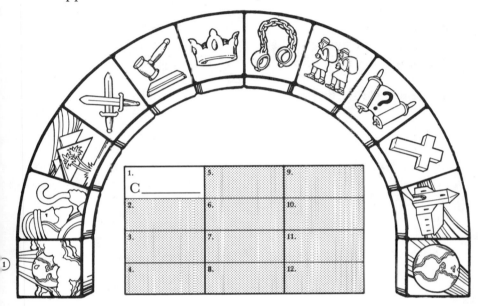

| 1. C_____ | 5. | 9. |
| 2. | 6. | 10. |
| 3. | 7. | 11. |
| 4. | 8. | 12. |

## D. The Geography of the Creation Era

(Circle the dot indicating the possible location of Eden.)

EDEN
(Possibly)

## E. Story of the Old Testament
(Fill in the blanks.)

| ERA | SUMMARY |
|---|---|
| *Creation:* | Adam is created by God, but he _____, and _____ God's original _____ for man. |

# FIVE

# THE PATRIARCH ERA
## *(Genesis 12–50)*

Any parent will admit that controlling children is a difficult and uncertain task.

Psychologist Henry Brandt tells the story of the time he and his wife invited the president of the college he was attending to their house for dinner. They were nervous and had spent considerable time preparing the house and meal for a good impression. When the president arrived, they stumbled over themselves to make him comfortable. They sat him next to their two-year old daughter for the meal. That was a mistake. During the meal, this little tot said to the president in her bird-like voice: "Please pass the salt." No one paid attention; they were listening to the president. So she tried again: "Will you please pass the salt?" Her small voice was easy to ignore as the adults strained for the president's every word. Finally, she hammered the distinguished guest on the arm and yelled, "Pass the salt, or I'll knock your block off!"

Even a president of the United States was perplexed by the antics of his child. Alice Roosevelt, daughter of Theodore Roosevelt, was an unruly girl whose antics scandalized the staid Washington "society" during her father's tenure at the White House. When a visitor objected to the girl's wandering in and out of the president's office while he was conducting important business with her father, Roosevelt said, "I can be President of the United States, or I can control Alice. I cannot possibly do both."

The Patriarch Era was a time of godly men presiding over a growing family. Abraham, Isaac, Jacob, and Joseph, successive generations of the same family, ruled over the Hebrew people in the earliest days of their existence.

On more than one occasion, Abraham must have felt a little like Brandt and Roosevelt. His descendants did not behave the way he wanted them to. Passion for God and what He wanted to do in and through the Hebrew people burned like a flame in Abraham's heart. But the flame dimmed in successive generations. However, the time of slavery in Egypt sharpened the spiritual hunger of the Hebrew people, and a great family, which became a great nation, emerged.

I.   **Review:** Fill in the blanks to bring the chart up to date with this era.

### Story of the Old Testament

| ERA | FIGURE | LOCATION | STORYLINE SUMMARY |
|---|---|---|---|
| _____ | _____ | _____ | Adam is created by God, but he _____, and _____ God's original _____ for man. |
| _____ | _____ | _____ | To be completed in this chapter. |

II.  **Storyline Summary:** *Abraham* is *chosen* by God to "father" a *people* to *represent* God to the world.

| ERA | SUMMARY |
|---|---|
| *Patriarch:* | *Abraham* is _____ by God to "father" a _____ to _____ God to the world. |

**III. Expansion:** There are four major men in the Patriarch Era:

1. Abraham
2. Isaac
3. Jacob
4. Joseph

**1. Abraham: Father of the Hebrew people** (Genesis 12-23).

Because of Adam's sin and the fall of man, God's attention is now focused on a plan of redemption for mankind. God wants a people through whom He can work to produce a reflection of Himself, and through whom He can spread the message of redemption to the world. He chooses Abraham, who becomes the *father of the Hebrew people*, and promises him a country (land), countless descendants (seed), and a world-wide and timeless impact (blessing). Abraham was living in Ur, near the convergence of the Tigris and Euphrates Rivers at the time. God leads him to the land of Canaan, where Abraham settles, and has two sons, Ishmael and Isaac.

**2. Isaac: Second father of promise** (Genesis 24-26).

Isaac becomes the *second father of promise* as the fulfillment of Abraham's promises are passed down to him. He witnesses several major miracles during his life. He lives in the land of Abraham, becomes prosperous, and dies at an old age, after having fathered two sons, Esau and Jacob.

**3. Jacob: Father of the nation of Israel** (Genesis 27-35).

The promises given to Abraham are passed through Issac to Jacob, Isaac's youngest son. Jacob begins life as a conniving scoundrel. However, through a series of miracles and other encounters with God, he comes around, and mends his ways. Jacob has twelve sons, and the promises of Abraham are passed down to them all as a family. While Abraham is the father of the Hebrew people, Jacob is the *father of the nation of Israel*, as each of his sons becomes the father of one of the twelve tribes which comprise the nation of Israel.

**4. Joseph: Leader in Egypt** (Genesis 37-50).

Abraham's promises are accepted most keenly by Jacob's eleventh son, Joseph. Jacob's sons, for the most part, have very little commitment to God's call on them as a nation. They sell Joseph as a slave, and he is taken to Egypt. Because of Joseph's righteousness, he rises to become a great *leader in Egypt*. During a severe famine, his family comes to Egypt for food, is reunited with Joseph, and as a result, enjoys peace and comfort. When Joseph dies, however, his people are enslaved for the next four hundred years. This time of trial sharpens the spiritual hunger of the Hebrew people, and they cry out to God for deliverance.

### Self Test
*To check your answers, review the previous pages.*

**A. Major Men of the Patriarch Era**
(Write in the descriptions from the options at right.)

*Abraham* _____ Father of nation of Israel.

*Isaac* _____ Leader in Egypt.

*Jacob* _____ Father of Hebrew people.

*Joseph* _____ Second Father of promise.

**B. Storyline Summary**
(Fill in the blanks from memory.)

| ERA | SUMMARY |
|-----|---------|
| *Patriarch:* | *Abraham* is _____ by God to "father" a _____ to _____ God to the world. |

## C. Arc of Bible History
(Fill in the name of the Eras.)

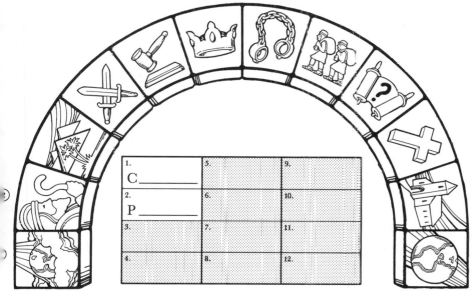

| 1. C_____ | 5. | 9. |
|---|---|---|
| 2. P_____ | 6. | 10. |
| 3. | 7. | 11. |
| 4. | 8. | 12. |

## D. The Geography of the Patriarch Era
(Draw an arrow from Ur, where Abraham lived, to Canaan, and from Canaan to Egypt, to represent the geographical movements of the Patriarch Era.)

### E. Story of the Old Testament
(Fill in the blanks.)

| ERA | FIGURE | LOCATION | STORYLINE SUMMARY |
|---|---|---|---|
| _____ | _____ | _____ | Adam is created by God, but he _____, and _____ God's original _____ for man. |
| _____ | _____ | _____ | Abraham is _____ by God to "father" a _____ to _____ God to the world. |

# SIX

# THE EXODUS ERA

## *(Exodus–Deuteronomy)*

 The Exodus was the mass movement of the Israelites out of slavery in Egypt, back to the Promised Land in Canaan. It was not an easy movement. The Pharoah of Egypt did not want them to go, and threatened them with military retaliation. The miracles which God performed during this time are among the most spectacular recorded in the Bible — the Nile River turned to blood, shepherds' rods turned into snakes, the firstborn of every Egyptian household died, and the Red Sea parted to allow the Israelites to cross over on dry land, escaping the Egyptian army.

Movies have sometimes portrayed this event as a little band of nomads roaming about the desert, camping under palm trees, and singing Hebrew folk songs around a small campfire. This picture could hardly be further from the truth. The book of Numbers tells us that when the Israelites left Egypt, there were six hundred thousand fighting men. It is reasonable to assume that if there were six hundred thousand fighting men, there were also six hundred thousand fighting women. That's 1,200,000. Each of those families may have had at least two children. That's another 1,200,000. In addition there were the men who were too old to fight, and their wives. There was the priestly tribe, the Levites, who didn't fight, and their wives, and their children. There were, conservatively speaking, between two and a half to three million people who left Egypt during this "exodus."

This was not a little tribe of nomads roaming about the desert. This was a nation on the move. Look at the state of Texas, and imagine the yellow block representing Dallas beginning to move across the map, and you get an idea of the magnitude of the exodus. When you add all the animals that they took with them for food and milk, as well as for sacrifices, this qualified as a horde! Instead of looking for a flat spot under a palm tree to camp, they had to look for a valley ten miles square. When they lined up to cross the Red Sea, it was more than a little aisle that was required. If they crossed the Red Sea one hundred abreast, counting the animals, the column would have stretched perhaps as far as fifty miles back into the desert.

Personal beliefs aside, this ranks as one of the greatest historical events of the ancient world, and this was an event over which Moses presided. To get a better look at the specifics of the exodus, we will now review our previous chapters, and then look at the four main events of the Exodus Era.

I.   **Review:** Fill in the blanks to bring the chart up to date with this era.

## Story of the Old Testament

| ERA | FIGURE | LOCATION | STORYLINE SUMMARY |
|---|---|---|---|
| _____ | _____ | _____ | Adam is created by God, but he _____, and _____ God's original _____ for man. |
| _____ | _____ | _____ | Abraham is _____ by God to "father" a _____ to _____ God to the world. |
| _____ | _____ | _____ | To be completed in this chapter. |

**II.** **Storyline Summary:** *Moses delivers* the Hebrew people from *slavery* in Egypt, and then gives them the *Law*.

| ERA | SUMMARY |
|---|---|
| *Exodus:* | *Moses* _____ the Hebrew people from _____ in Egypt, and then gives them the _____. |

**III.** **Expansion:** There are four major events in the Exodus Era:

1. Deliverance
2. The Law
3. Kadesh Barnea
4. 40 Years Wandering

**1.** **Deliverance: Freedom from slavery in Egypt** (Exodus 1-18).

The Hebrews have languished under slavery in Egypt for four hundred years when they cry out to God for deliverance. God raises up Moses as His spokesman to Pharaoh, the ruler of Egypt, asking for spiritual freedom for the Hebrew people. Pharaoh refuses, and a series of ten plagues is levied on Egypt to prompt Pharaoh to let the people go. The plagues start out bad, and they get worse—from frogs, to gnats, to water turned to blood, to the death of the first born in every household of Egypt. Finally, Pharaoh consents to let the Hebrews leave Egypt. After they have gone, he changes his mind and attempts to recapture them. They are as far as the Red Sea when God parts the Red Sea and the Hebrew people cross over to the other side. The waters come together again, protecting them from the Egyptian army, and *freeing them from slavery in Egypt*. God, of course, has only one destination for them: the Promised Land of Canaan . . . the land "flowing with milk and honey." The land which their father Abraham had first settled is again to be their home.

## 2. The Law: God's commandments at Mt. Sinai
   (Exodus 19-40).

The Hebrew people now begin to take on a national identity as Israel. From the Red Sea, the Israelites travel south to the bottom of the Sinai peninsula, and camp at Mt. Sinai. They receive *God's commandments at Mt. Sinai*. Moses meets with God alone at the top of Mt. Sinai where he receives the Ten Commandments written in tablets of stone by the finger of God. Moses also receives a full revelation of the Law which is to govern Israel's national life as well as her relationship to God. God promises to bless her abundantly for obedience, and curse her soundly for disobedience.

## 3. Kadesh Barnea: Place of rebellion against God
   (Numbers 10-14).

Israel leaves Mt. Sinai and migrates north to an oasis, Kadesh Barnea, which is the southern gateway into the Promised Land. From this vantage point, twelve spies are sent into the Promised Land, one spy from each of the twelve tribes of Israel. The land is inhabited by the Canaanites who would not take kindly to an Israelite horde coming back into the land. When the spies return, they have some good news and some bad news. The good news is that the land *is* beautiful and bountiful . . ."flowing with milk and honey." The bad news is that there are giants and hostile armies throughout the land. Ten spies report that the land is indomitable (in spite of the fact that God has promised to give them victory over any opposing forces). Two spies, Joshua and Caleb, exhort the people to believe God and go into the land. The people believe the majority report, and refuse to follow Moses into the land. Thus, this becomes known as a *place of rebellion against God*.

## 4. 40 Years Wandering: Consequences of rebelling against God (Numbers 20-36).

As a *consequence of rebelling against God* at Kadesh Barnea, the "exodus" generation was condemned to wander in the wilderness until everyone who was twenty-one years old or older at the time dies. In the ensuing forty years, a new generation comes to leadership which is willing to follow their leaders into the land. Moses leads them to the north of the Dead Sea near Jericho, the eastern gateway to the Promised Land. Moses encourages the people, gives them additional instruction found in the Book of Deuteronomy, and then dies.

## Self Test

### A. Four Major Events in the Exodus Era
(Write in the descriptions from the options at right.)

*Deliverance* _____ God's commandments at Mt. Sinai.

*The Law* _____ Place of rebellion against God.

*Kadesh Barnea* _____ Consequences of rebelling against God.

*Forty Years Wandering* _____ Freedom from slavery in Egypt.

### B. Storyline Summary: *Moses delivers* the Hebrew people from *slavery* in Egypt, and then gives them the *Law.*

| ERA | SUMMARY |
|---|---|
| *Exodus:* | *Moses* _____ the Hebrew people from _____ in Egypt, and then gives them the _____. |

## C. Arc of Bible History
(Fill in the name of the Eras.)

| 1. C _____ | 5. | 9. |
| 2. P _____ | 6. | 10. |
| 3. E _____ | 7. | 11. |
| 4. | 8. | 12. |

## D. The Geography of the Exodus Era
(Draw an arrow from Egypt through the Red Sea to Mt. Sinai to Kadesh Barnea, and then to the top of the Dead Sea on the east side of the Jordan River. This represents the geographical movement of the Exodus Era.)

## E. Story of the Old Testament
(Fill in the blanks.)

| ERA | FIGURE | LOCATION | STORYLINE SUMMARY |
|---|---|---|---|
| _____ | _____ | _____ | Adam is created by God, but he _____, and _____ God's original _____ for man. |
| _____ | _____ | _____ | Abraham is _____ by God to "father" a _____ to _____ God to the world. |
| _____ | _____ | _____ | Moses _____ the Hebrew people from _____ in Egypt, and then gives them the _____. |

# SEVEN

# THE CONQUEST ERA
## *(Joshua)*

The days were dark indeed for Great Britain in 1940. The British people were at war with Germany and were being pressed hard on every side by the Nazi military machine. Supplies and morale were low. Their national destiny hung in the balance. Then, a new Prime Minister came on the scene: Winston Churchill. He was a man of intense conviction, deep resolve, and unquenchable optimism. His speeches in the first months of his term burst upon the world with sudden and magnificent power. From them we read:

> To form an administration of this scale and complexity is a serious undertaking in itself, but it must be remembered that we are in the preliminary stage of one of the greatest battles in history, that we are in action at many points in Norway and in Holland, that we have to be prepared in the Mediterranean, that the air battle is continuous and that many preparations have to be made here at home. I would say to the House, as I said to those who have joined this Government: I have nothing to offer but blood, toil, tears, and sweat.

> You ask what is our policy? I will say: It is to wage war, by sea, land, and air with all our might and with all the strength that God can give us: to wage war against a monstrous tyranny, never surpassed in the dark, lamentable catalogue of human crime. That is our policy. You ask, what is our aim? I can answer in a word: Victory — victory at all costs, victory in spite of all the terror, victory however long and hard the road may be; for without victory, there is no survival.

I have, myself, full confidence that if all do their duty, if nothing is neglected, and if the best arrangements are made, as they
are being made, we shall prove ourselves once again able to defend our island home . . . to ride out the storm of war, and to
outlive the menace of tyranny. Even though large tracts of
Europe and many old and famous states have fallen or may fall
into the grip of the Gestapo and all the odious apparatus of
Nazi rule, we shall not flag or fail. We shall go on to the end,
we shall fight in France, we shall fight on the seas and oceans,
we shall fight with growing confidence and growing strength in
the air, we shall defend our island, whatever the cost may be,
we shall fight on the beaches, we shall fight on the landing
grounds, we shall fight in the fields and in the streets, we shall
fight in the hills; we shall never surrender."

After the Exodus, the circumstances were also perilous for
the Israelites. They had wandered in the wilderness for forty
years because of rebellion and unbelief at Kadesh Barnea. Now
they were at Jericho, and the test was the same. Would they
resolve to forge ahead, or would they shrink from the circumstances as their fathers had done?

The task of rallying and leading the people fell to Joshua.
Moses, the great leader of the last forty years, was dead. Would
the people galvanize behind Joshua? Or would they refuse his
leadership? Just as England faced a crossroads when Churchill
became its leader, so also the Israelites faced a critical fork in the
road.

I.   **Review:** Fill in the blanks to bring the chart up to date
     with this era.

### Story of the Old Testament

| ERA | FIGURE | LOCATION | STORYLINE SUMMARY |
|-----|--------|----------|-------------------|
| _____ | _____ | _____ | Adam is created by God, but he _____, and _____ God's original _____ for man. |

| ERA | FIGURE | LOCATION | STORYLINE SUMMARY |
|---|---|---|---|
| ———— | ———— | ———— | Abraham is _____ by God to "father" a _____ to _____ God to the world. |
| ———— | ———— | ———— | Moses _____ the Hebrew people from _____ in Egypt, and then gives them the _____. |
| ———— | ———— | ———— | To be completed in this chapter. |

**II. Storyline Summary:** *Joshua* leads the *conquest* of the *Promised Land*.

| ERA | SUMMARY |
|---|---|
| *Conquest:* | *Joshua* leads the _____ of the _____ _____. |

**III. Expansion:** There are four main events in the Conquest Era:

1. Jordan
2. Jericho
3. Conquest
4. Dominion

**1. Jordan: A miraculous parting of water** (Joshua 1-5).

Moses dies, and God hand-picks Joshua to succeed him. Joshua's first challenge is to cross the Jordan River at flood stage. God commands him to prepare the nation for ceremonial procession and to begin walking, priests first, toward the Jordan River. When the priests touched water, God would part the water for them. (This is the second *miraculous "parting of water"* which God performed for Israel. The first was the parting of the Red Sea.) The people respond, and God parts the Jordan River for a distance of about twenty miles. They cross without incident, and the water begins flowing again.

**2. Jericho: A miraculous conquest of a city** (Joshua 6).

The city of Jericho, a small oasis on the west side of the Jordan River near the Dead Sea, is not only the eastern gateway to the Promised Land, but it is also a fortified city and poses a threat to the welfare of Israel. Joshua is a brilliant military strategist, so much so that his campaigns in the Bible are still studied in the Army War College today. As he stands overlooking the city, contemplating how to conquer it, the angel of the Lord appears to him and instructs him to march around the city once a day for seven days. On the seventh day, he is to march around it seven times, and the people are to shout. The city wall will fall down. They did, and it did . . . *a miraculous conquest of a city!*

**3. Conquest: The defeat of Canaan** (Joshua 7-12).

The Canaanites are united in their hatred of the Israelites, but not in their military opposition to them. Primarily, the region is characterized by individual kings, each with his own city and surrounding country. Joshua cuts through the midsection toward the Mediterranean Sea. Having divided the land, he then begins to conquer, from South to North. In about seven years the initial *defeat of Canaan* is complete.

**4. Dominion: Finalizing dominion** (Joshua 13-20).

Each of the twelve tribes of Israel is given a land area by lottery, and is responsible for *finalizing dominion* over that area. All twelve tribes inhabit their area, and take up a relationship of loose federation with the other tribes.

## Self Test

### A. Four Major Events in the Conquest Era
(Write in the descriptions from the options at right.)

*Jordan* _____ The defeat of Canaan.

*Jericho* _____ A miraculous parting of water.

*Conquest* _____ Finalizing dominion.

*Dominion* _____ A miraculous conquest of a city.

### B. Storyline Summary (Fill in the blanks from memory).

| ERA | SUMMARY |
|-----|---------|
| *Conquest:* | *Joshua* leads the _____ of the _____ _____. |

### C. Arc of Bible History (Fill in the name of the Eras.)

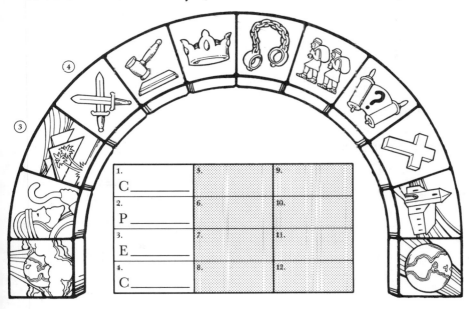

1. C_____
2. P_____
3. E_____
4. C_____

## D. The Geography of the Conquest Era

(Draw an arrow from Jericho across to the Mediterranean Sea. Then draw an arrow into the southern half of the land. Now draw an arrow into the northern half of the land. This represents the geographical movement of the Conquest Era.)

JERICHO

## E. Story of the Old Testament    (Fill in the blanks.)

| ERA | FIGURE | LOCATION | STORYLINE SUMMARY |
|---|---|---|---|
| _____ | _____ | _____ | Adam is created by God, but he _____, and _____ God's original _____ for man. |
| _____ | _____ | _____ | Abraham is _____ by God to "father" a _____ to _____ God to the world. |
| _____ | _____ | _____ | Moses _____ the Hebrew people from _____ in Egypt, and then gives them the _____. |
| _____ | _____ | _____ | Joshua leads the _____ of the _____ _____. |

EIGHT

# THE JUDGES ERA
## (Judges–Ruth)

### "Woman in Rags, Garbage, Revealed as Heiress"

So read the headline in the San Francisco Chronicle concerning a lady known as "Garbage Mary," who was picked up in a shopping mall in Delray Beach, Florida. She appeared to be just another derelict whose mind had faded. Neighbors told stories of her scrounging through garbage cans for food, which she hoarded in her car and her two-room apartment. There were mounds of garbage in the small apartment, stuffed in the refrigerator, the stove, the sink, the cabinets, and the bathtub. There were paths between the garbage. Other than the kitchen, there were no chairs to sit in because they were piled up with trash.

Police finally identified her as the daughter of a well-to-do lawyer and bank director from Illinois who had died several years earlier. In addition to the garbage, police found Mobil Oil stock worth more than four hundred thousand dollars, documents indicating ownership of oil fields in Kansas, stock certificates from firms such U.S. Steel, Uniroyal, and Squibb, and passbooks for eight large bank accounts.

"Garbage Mary" was a millionaire who was living like a derelict. Untold wealth was at her disposal, and yet she scrounged through garbage rather than claim the resources which were rightly hers.

The parallel between "Garbage Mary," and Israel during the time of the judges is striking. This was a dark period, indeed, in the history of the Jewish people. They had lost their spiritual moorings and, as is recorded in the final verse of the book of Judges, "every man did that which was right in his own eyes." The result was a morally degraded, socially perverted, and spiritually bankrupt time of almost four hundred years. Israel had all the wealth of the promises of God at their disposal. Yet they scavenged through the garbage of life, eeking out a pitiful existence. They could have been kings, but lived like paupers.

I.   **Review:** Fill in the blanks to bring the chart up to date with this era.

### Story of the Old Testament

| ERA | FIGURE | LOCATION | STORYLINE SUMMARY |
|---|---|---|---|
| _____ | _____ | _____ | Adam is created by God, but he _____, and _____ God's original _____ for man. |
| _____ | _____ | _____ | Abraham is _____ by God to "father" a _____ to _____ God to the world. |
| _____ | _____ | _____ | Moses _____ the Hebrew people from _____ in Egypt, and then gives them the _____. |
| _____ | _____ | _____ | Joshua leads the _____ of the _____ _____. |
| _____ | _____ | _____ | To be completed in this chapter. |

II. **Storyline Summary:** *Samson* and others were chosen as *judges* to *govern* the people for *four hundred* rebellious years.

| ERA | SUMMARY |
|-----|---------|
| *Judges:* | *Samson* and others were chosen as _____ to _____ the people for _____ _____ rebellious years. |

III. **Expansion:** There are four main subjects in the Judges Era:

1. Judges
2. Rebellion
3. Cycles
4. Ruth

### 1. Judges: The leaders of Israel (Judges).

As seen in the book of Judges, these judges are not men who wear long flowing black robes, sit on high benches, and make legal decisions. Rather, they are political-military *leaders of Israel* who exercise nearly absolute power because of their office and abilities. The four major judges are:

- Deborah, a woman judge early in the Judges Era;
- Gideon, who defeats an army of thousands with only three hundred men;
- Samson, the most famous judge, whose fabulous strength has captured our imagination for thousands of years; and finally
- Samuel, a transitional character held in very high regard in Scripture, who is both the last judge and the first prophet.

### 2. Rebellion: The breaking of God's Law (Judges).

The book of Judges records the darkest period in Israel's history, following one of the brightest eras: the Conquest Era under Joshua. Just before Moses dies, he instructs Israel in Deuteronomy 7:1-5 to do three things:

1. Destroy all the inhabitants of Canaan.
2. Avoid intermarriage with the Canaanites.
3. Shun worship of the Canaanite gods.

Israel fails on all three accounts. *The breaking of God's Law* and the record of Israel's subsequent moral degradation is sad indeed.

## 3. Cycles: Repetition of Israel's misfortunes (Judges).

Much of the Era of Judges involves a series of seven cycles which are recorded in the Book of Judges. Each cycle has five component parts: (1) Israel "sins," (2) God disciplines them through military "conquest" by a neighboring country, (3) Israel "repents" and cries out to God for deliverance, (4) God raises up a judge who "delivers" them from bondage, and (5) God "frees" the land from military oppression for the remainder of that judge's life. That is one cycle: sin, conquest, repentance, deliverance, and freedom. Then, when a judge dies, the *repetition of Israel's misfortunes* begins again. The Israelites fall into sin again, followed by conquest, followed by repentance, etc. Seven such cycles are recorded in the Book of Judges.

## 4. Ruth: A model woman (Ruth).

Standing out in refreshing contrast to the general background of the Judges Era is Ruth, in the book which bears her name. This *model woman* who lives during the Era of Judges is an example of moral and spiritual strength. Her story is one of love, purity, and commitment. She is a living illustration of blessings which God showers on those who live in faithful obedience to Him. One example of God's blessings toward Ruth is that she, a non-Hebrew, is listed in the lineage from Abraham to Jesus.

## Self Test

## A. Four Major Subjects in the Judges Era
(Write in the descriptions from the options at right.)

*Judges* _____  A model woman.

*Rebellion* _____  The leaders of Israel.

*Cycles* _____  The breaking of God's Law.

*Ruth* _____  Repetition of Israel's misfortunes.

## B. Storyline Summary
(Fill in the blanks from memory).

| ERA | SUMMARY |
|---|---|
| *Judges:* | *Samson* and others were chosen as _____ to _____ the people for _____ _____ rebellious years. |

## C. Arc of Bible History
(Fill in the name of the Eras.)

| 1. C_____ | 5. J _____ | 9. |
|---|---|---|
| 2. P_____ | 6. | 10. |
| 3. E_____ | 7. | 11. |
| 4. C_____ | 8. | 12. |

## D. The Geography of the Judges Era
(Match the numbers below with the blanks on the map, to see the countries conquering Israel in the Judges Era.)

1. Philistia
2. Moab
3. Mesopotamia
4. Canaan
5. Ammon
6. Midian

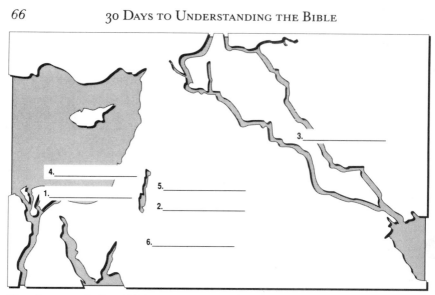

## E. Story of the Old Testament (Fill in the blanks.)

| ERA | FIGURE | LOCATION | STORYLINE SUMMARY |
|---|---|---|---|
| _____ | _____ | _____ | Adam is created by God, but he _____, and _____ God's original _____ for man. |
| _____ | _____ | _____ | Abraham is _____ by God to "father" a _____ to _____ God to the world. |
| _____ | _____ | _____ | Moses _____ the Hebrew people from _____ in Egypt, and then gives them the _____. |
| _____ | _____ | _____ | Joshua leads the _____ of the _____ _____. |
| _____ | _____ | _____ | Samson and others were chosen as _____ to _____ the people for _____ _____ rebellious years. |

# THE KINGDOM ERA
## *(1 Samuel–2 Chronicles)*

If you would be free to sail the seven seas, you must make yourself a slave to the compass. By nature, man desires something he cannot have: total freedom. There are certain freedoms we can have, but they have corresponding bondages. And, there are certain bondages we can have which afford us corresponding freedoms. For example, you can be free from the toothbrush, and in bondage to cavities, or you can make yourself a slave to the toothbrush, and be free from cavities. You cannot be free from the toothbrush *and* free from cavities. That kind of freedom, total freedom, does not exist.

Throughout life, we are constantly making choices, and for those choices, we pay certain inescapable consequences. Freedom comes with a price.

The kings of Israel wanted total freedom. They wanted the freedom to ignore the directives which God had given them on how to rule and wage war. But at the same time, they wanted the freedom to have economic and military prosperity. This was not possible. As a result, the Kingdom Era was a very turbulent time with many ups and downs. When a righteous king ruled, the nation would prosper. When an unrighteous king gained the throne, the nation would falter.

The barnacles of unrighteousness began to affix themselves to the Israeli ship of state, and before the books of history were completed, the nation had collapsed, and suffered at the hands of warring neighbors.

I. **Review:** Fill in the blanks to bring the chart up to date with this era.

## Story of the Old Testament

| ERA | FIGURE | LOCATION | STORYLINE SUMMARY |
|---|---|---|---|
| _____ | _____ | _____ | Adam is created by God, but he _____, and _____ God's original _____ for man. |
| _____ | _____ | _____ | Abraham is _____ by God to "father" a _____ to _____ God to the world. |
| _____ | _____ | _____ | Moses _____ the Hebrew people from _____ in Egypt, and then gives them the _____. |
| _____ | _____ | _____ | Joshua leads the _____ of the _____ _____. |
| _____ | _____ | _____ | Samson and others were chosen as _____ to _____ the people for _____ _____ rebellious years. |
| _____ | _____ | _____ | To be completed in this chapter. |

II. **Storyline Summary:** *David*, the greatest king in the new *monarchy*, is followed by a succession of mostly *unrighteous* kings, and God eventually *judges* Israel for her sin, sending her into exile.

| ERA | SUMMARY |
|-----|---------|
| *Kingdom:* | *David*, the greatest king in the new _____, is followed by a succession of mostly _____ kings, and God eventually _____ Israel for her sin, sending her into exile. |

**III. Expansion:** There are four main periods in the Kingdom Era:

1. United Kingdom
2. Division of the Kingdom
3. Northern Kingdom
4. Southern Kingdom

## 1. United Kingdom: A new monarchy (1 & 2 Samuel).

The twelve tribes of Israel, jealous of other nations around them, are united in their demand to God for a king. God allows Samuel, the last judge, to anoint Saul to be the first king, beginning *a new monarchy*. Because Saul is not a righteous king, God does not honor his reign, nor establish his family on the throne of Israel. His successor, David, though having shortcomings, is a righteous king; and Israel prospers under him. David's son Solomon becomes king upon David's death. Solomon rules righteously at first, then drifts from the Lord.

## 2. Divided Kingdom: A civil war (1 Kings).

As a result of Solomon's spiritual drifting, *a civil war* erupts upon his death, and the kingdom is divided. There is now a northern kingdom, consisting of ten tribes, and a southern kingdom, consisting of the tribes of Judah and Benjamin. The northern ten tribes retain the name "Israel," and the southern two tribes adopt the name "Judah," after the name of the larger tribe.

## 3. Northern Kingdom: The unrighteous kingdom (2 Kings).

In the civil war that splits the kingdom, Jeroboam commands the northern kingdom of Israel. He is unrighteous, and every other king (nineteen total) who succeeds him during the two hundred fifty year life of the northern kingdom is also un-righteous. Because of this unrighteousness, God raises up Assyria to conquer the northern kingdom and scatter His people to the four winds. *The unrighteous kingdom* is never restored.

**4. Southern Kingdom: The inconsistent kingdom** (2 Kings).

Rehoboam, Solomon's son, commands the southern kingdom of Judah. He is also unrighteous. The southern kingdom fares somewhat better than the northern. Lasting for four hundred years, its life is prolonged by eight righteous kings out of a total of twenty. Judah's sins finally catch up to her, however, and God brings judgment on *the inconsistent kingdom* by raising up Babylonia (who had conquered Assyria) to conquer Judah. Babylonia gathers all the leaders, artisans, musicians, and promising chil-dren, and takes them away to captivity in Babylonia.

### Self Test

**A. Four Major Subjects in the Kingdom Era**
(Write in the descriptions from the options at right.)

*United* _____ The unrighteous kingdom.
*Kingdom*

*Divided* _____ A new monarchy.
*Kingdom*

*Northern* _____ The inconsistent kingdom.
*Kingdom*

*Southern* _____ A civil war.
*Kingdom*

**B. Storyline Summary** (Fill in the blanks from memory).

| ERA | SUMMARY |
|-----|---------|
| *Kingdom:* | *David*, the greatest king in the new _____, is followed by a succession of mostly _____ kings, and God eventually _____ Israel for her sin, sending her into exile. |

## C. Arc of Bible History
(Fill in the name of the Eras.)

| 1. C_____ | 5. J _____ | 9. |
| 2. P _____ | 6. K_____ | 10. |
| 3. E _____ | 7. | 11. |
| 4. C_____ | 8. | 12. |

## D. The Geography of the Kingdom Era
(Draw an arrow from Israel to Assyria. Draw another arrow from Judah to Babylonia. This represents the geographical movement of the Kingdom Era.)

## E. Story of the Old Testament
(Fill in the blanks.)

| ERA | FIGURE | LOCATION | STORYLINE SUMMARY |
|---|---|---|---|
| ———— | ———— | ———— | Adam is created by God, but he _____, and _____ God's original _____ for man. |
| ———— | ———— | ———— | Abraham is _____ by God to "father" a _____ to _____ God to the world. |
| ———— | ———— | ———— | Moses _____ the Hebrew people from _____ in Egypt, and then gives them the _____. |
| ———— | ———— | ———— | Joshua leads the _____ of the _____ _____. |
| ———— | ———— | ———— | Samson and others were chosen as _____ to _____ the people for _____ _____ rebellious years. |
| ———— | ———— | ———— | David, the greatest king in the new _____, is followed by a succession of mostly _____ kings, and God eventually _____ Israel for her sin, sending her into exile. |

# THE EXILE ERA

## *(Ezekiel–Daniel)*

It is one of the basic laws of physics that things tend to run down or deteriorate. Deterioration in relationships can be illustrated in something as mundane as the common cold. In an old edition of *The Saturday Evening Post*, the "Seven Stages of the Married Cold" was written:

*Stage 1:* Sugar dumpling, I've really worried about my baby girl. That's a bad sniffle and there's no telling about these things with all the "strep" that's going around. I'm going to put you in the hospital for a general check-up and a good rest. I know the food's terrible, but I'm going to bring you dinner every night from "Rosini's." I've got it all arranged with the floor supervisor.

*Stage 2:* Listen, darling, I don't like the sound of that cough. I'm going to call Doc Miller to rush over here. Now you go to bed like a good girl just for papa.

*Stage 3:* Maybe you'd better lie down honey. Nothing like a little rest when you feel lousy. I'll bring you something. Have you got any canned soup?

*Stage 4:* Now look, dear, be sensible. After you've fed the kids and gotten the dishes done and the floor mopped, you'd better lie down.

*Stage 5:* Why don't you take a couple of aspirin?

*Stage 6:* If you'd just gargle something instead of sitting around barking like a seal all evening.

*Stage 7:* Would you stop coughing on me?!? Are you trying to give me pneumonia?!?

We must recognize also that our actions have certain repercussions in our relationships.

A troubled man was standing at the top of the World Trade Center in New York, and finally decided to jump off, ending his own life. After he had fallen a while, and was only one hundred stories off the ground, he realized he had made a mistake. It was wrong to commit suicide, and he knew it. He said, "O God, if you hear me . . . I'm sorry for the foolish mistake I made in jumping off this building. I repent, and I would like to know if you would forgive me?" A voice came back. "Of course I forgive you. Don't think a thing about it. I will never bring it up again. And by the way, I'll see you in just a minute."

Sin is a fact of human existence. And God will forgive whoever comes to Him in repentance. But that doesn't change the fact that sin has consequences. God forgives the man for jumping off the building, but the man will still fall to the ground.

Israel tasted this bitter reality. Their relationship with the Lord deteriorated. They lived in roller-coaster rebellion against Him for four hundred years during the Kingdom Era, continually paying the price. Finally, the debt became so great that judgment came in the form of military conquest. During the time of the Exile, there were some great spiritual leaders, and there was repentance on the part of a segment of the Jewish people. However, this did not remove the penalty for the years of rebellion and the full price of the Exile was exacted.

I.   **Review:** Fill in the blanks to bring the chart up to date with this era.

## Story of the Old Testament

| ERA | FIGURE | LOCATION | STORYLINE SUMMARY |
|-----|--------|----------|-------------------|
| ——— | ——— | ——— | Adam is created by God, but he _____, and _____ God's original _____ for man. |

| ERA | FIGURE | LOCATION | STORYLINE SUMMARY |
|---|---|---|---|
| _____ | _____ | _____ | Abraham is _____ by God to "father" a _____ to _____ God to the world. |
| _____ | _____ | _____ | Moses _____ the Hebrew people from _____ in Egypt, and then gives them the _____. |
| _____ | _____ | _____ | Joshua leads the _____ of the _____ _____. |
| _____ | _____ | _____ | Samson and others were chosen as _____ to _____ the people for _____ _____ rebellious years. |
| _____ | _____ | _____ | David, the greatest king in the new _____, is followed by a succession of mostly _____ kings, and God eventually _____ Israel for her sin, sending her into exile. |
| _____ | _____ | _____ | To be completed in this chapter. |

II. **Storyline Summary:** *Daniel* gives *leadership*, and encourages *faithfulness* among the *exiles* for the next seventy years.

| ERA | SUMMARY |
|---|---|
| *Judges:* | *Daniel* gives _____, and encourages _____ among the _____ for the next seventy years. |

**III.** **Expansion:** As mentioned before in Chapter 1 of this book, some history is contained in books that are primarily Prophetical Books, and that is the case in the Exile Era Era. You will note that the Biblical references for the four main divisions of this Era will include some Prophetical Books. There are four main divisions in the Exile Era:

1. Prophecy
2. Prophets
3. Exiles
4. Power Change

**1.  Prophecy:  Warning of impending captivity** (Jeremiah).

The northern kingdom, Israel, has been conquered by Assyria and dispersed in 722 B.C.. During the time of the events described in 2 Kings, the southern kingdom, Judah, receives a *warning of impending captivity* through Jeremiah (called the "Weeping Prophet"), who prophesies that the nation will be taken into captivity at the hands of the Babylonians. This happens in 586 B.C.. He also accurately prophesies that the captivity will last seventy years.

**2.  Prophets:  Encouraging faithfulness of exiles**
    (Ezekiel and Daniel).

There are two prophets who write books of the Bible during the exile: Ezekiel and Daniel. Not a great deal is known about the prophet Ezekiel, since his book is mostly prophetic, and not autobiographical. He foretells of national restoration and *encourages faithfulness among the exiles*. Daniel's book, while a book of prophecy, is more biographical. He is a prominent governmental leader, much like Joseph in Egypt. While Daniel's personal life is an example to his people, his prophecies tend to concern the future destruction of the world.

**3.  Exiles:  Assimilated into the culture** (Daniel).

The book of Daniel also gives us a glimpse of life among the exiles. Apparently, the Jews are *assimilated into the culture* into which they are exiled. They experience discrimination, which has always been true of displaced Jews. Yet, in spite of this, they seem fairly well integrated into society, and some of them achieve positions of prominence.

## 4. Power Change: Persian empire expands (Daniel).

While the Jews are in exile in Babylonia, Persia rises to become the dominant military power of that region. Persia conquers Babylonia (who had conquered Assyria), so now Persia rules not only her own land, but the land once dominated by Assyria and Babylonia. The *Persian Empire expands* from the Tigris River to the Mediterranean Sea.

### Self Test

## A. Four Major Subjects in the Exilic Era
(Write in the descriptions from the options at right.)

*Prophecy* _____ Persian empire expands.

*Prophets* _____ Assimilated into the culture.

*Exiles* _____ Warning of impending captivity.

*Power Change* _____ Encouraging faithfulness of exiles.

## B. Storyline Summary (Fill in the blanks from memory).

| ERA | SUMMARY |
|-----|---------|
| *Judges:* | *Daniel* gives _____, and encourages _____ among the _____ for the next seventy years. |

**C. Arc of Bible History** (Fill in the name of the Eras.)

| | | |
|---|---|---|
| 1.<br>C_____ | 5.<br>J _____ | 9. |
| 2.<br>P_____ | 6.<br>K_____ | 10. |
| 3.<br>E_____ | 7.<br>E_____ | 11. |
| 4.<br>C_____ | 8. | 12. |

**D. The Geography of the Exile Era**
(Draw a line from Babylonia toward Assyria and circle Assyria. Draw another line from Persia toward Babylonia, encircling both Babylonia and Assyria. This represents the shift in power during the Exile Era. Assyria had conquered Israel. Then Babylonia conquered Assyria and Judah. Finally, Persia conquered Babylonia, and ended up ruling everyone.)

## E. Story of the Old Testament
(Fill in the blanks.)

| ERA | FIGURE | LOCATION | STORYLINE SUMMARY |
|---|---|---|---|
| _____ | _____ | _____ | Adam is created by God, but he _____, and _____ God's original _____ for man. |
| _____ | _____ | _____ | Abraham is _____ by God to "father" a _____ to _____ God to the world. |
| _____ | _____ | _____ | Moses _____ the Hebrew people from _____ in Egypt, and then gives them the _____. |
| _____ | _____ | _____ | Joshua leads the _____ of the _____ _____. |
| _____ | _____ | _____ | Samson and others were chosen as _____ to _____ the people for _____ _____ rebellious years. |
| _____ | _____ | _____ | David, the greatest king in the new _____, is followed by a succession of mostly _____ kings, and God eventually _____ Israel for her sin, sending her into exile. |
| _____ | _____ | _____ | Daniel gives _____, and encourages _____ among the _____ for the next seventy years. |

# ELEVEN

# THE RETURN ERA
## (Ezra – Esther)

In the middle 1970's, newspapers and magazines were awash with the story of Peter Jenkins, who walked across America. He was consumed with the disillusionment of his generation, and he set out to find his country and himself.

His amazing story is one of long hours, days, and weeks of solitude and drudgery punctuated with occasional life-threatening surprises. He faced danger from weather, accidents, wild animals, and people. He almost died in a snow storm, was attacked by animals, and hunted by cruel men who might have killed him if they had caught him.

Many times he wanted to quit his search. Each time, he was befriended by people who restored his body, his soul, and his faith in America. He lost his dog, but gained a wife, a new world view, and a deep appreciation for the grandeur of his country and its people.

Finally, after more than five long and grueling years of walking, he stepped into the Pacific Ocean. His journey was done. When Peter Jenkins walked into the Oregon waters, he was quite a different person from the one who left his home in Alfred, New York. The trials, the time, and solitude, the people, and the physical and mental challenge had transformed him. On his departure, he was little more than a confused boy. On his return, he was a man.

The return of the nation of Israel from seventy years captivity in Babylonia in many ways parallels the story of Peter Jenkins.

The Israelites went into exile a drifting and confused people. They spent agonizing years in solitude, and in physical and mental torment. They were ministered to unexpectedly by people sent from God. They returned to Israel a sobered people. They were home, refocused in their purpose as a nation, ready to begin again the worship of Jehovah: the God of creation, and the God of Israel.

I.    **Review:** Fill in the blanks to bring the chart up to date with this era.

## Story of the Old Testament

| ERA | FIGURE | LOCATION | STORYLINE SUMMARY |
|---|---|---|---|
| _____ | _____ | _____ | Adam is created by God, but he _____, and _____ God's original _____ for man. |
| _____ | _____ | _____ | Abraham is _____ by God to "father" a _____ to _____ God to the world. |
| _____ | _____ | _____ | Moses _____ the Hebrew people from _____ in Egypt, and then gives them the _____. |
| _____ | _____ | _____ | Joshua leads the _____ of the _____ _____. |
| _____ | _____ | _____ | Samson and others were chosen as _____ to _____ the people for _____ _____ rebellious years. |

| ERA | FIGURE | LOCATION | STORYLINE SUMMARY |
|---|---|---|---|
| _____ | _____ | _____ | David, the greatest king in the new _____, is followed by a succession of mostly _____ kings, and God eventually _____ Israel for her sin, sending her into exile. |
| _____ | _____ | _____ | Daniel gives _____, and encourages _____ among the _____ for the next seventy years. |
| _____ | _____ | _____ | To be completed in this chapter. |

**II.  Storyline Summary:** *Ezra leads* the people back from *exile* to rebuild *Jerusalem.*

| ERA | SUMMARY |
|---|---|
| *Return:* | *Ezra* _____ the people back from _____ to rebuild _____. |

**III.  Expansion:** There are four major subjects in the Return Era:

1. Disrepair
2. Temple
3. People
4. Walls

## 1. Disrepair: Destruction from war and neglect (Nehemiah 1:1-3).

During the seventy years captivity, the leadership of Judah has been taken into exile, and the city of Jerusalem falls into disrepair. Not only has the city suffered the ravages of the military campaign during the initial conquest, but it has also fallen victim to the erosion of neglect. The *destruction from war and neglect* leaves Jerusalem in a state of abject ruin.

## 2. Temple: Rebuilding the temple (Ezra 1-6).

God prompts Cyrus, King of Persia, to initiate the financing and rebuilding of the Jewish temple in Jerusalem. Under the direction of Zerubbabel, a notable Jewish figure in Persia, the *rebuilding of the temple* is begun. Considerable opposition from Gentiles around Jerusalem is encountered. At the urging of Haggai and Zechariah, two Jewish prophets living in Jerusalem, the restoration of the temple is completed.

## 3. People: Spiritual rebuilding (Ezra 7-10).

Rebuilding the temple is a direct parallel to the *spiritual rebuilding* of the Jewish people. Temple worship has been discontinued for seventy years. Most of the Jews have never seen or heard the Law of Moses. They have to be instructed in a national re-education program. Ezra sets his heart to study the Law of the Lord, to practice it, and to teach God's statutes and ordinances in Israel to rebuild the people as they return from exile.

## 4. Walls: Restoration complete (Nehemiah).

Even though not all Jews returned when they could have (see the book of Esther, whose events take place during this Era) many Jews are back home in Jerusalem. The temple stands restored as the dominant structure in the city, but the walls of the city are still broken down. This is a security threat as well as a source of national humiliation. Nehemiah, another Jewish notable serving Artaxerxes, King of Persia, is burdened to rebuild the walls. He is given permission and financing by the King of Persia to do so. A short time later, the walls frame the noble city of Jerusalem, home of the temple of God. *Restoration is complete* as the temple is rebuilt, the people are rebuilt, and the walls are rebuilt.

## Self Test

### A. Four Major Subjects in the Return Era
(Write in the descriptions from the options at right.)

*Disrepair* _____ Spiritual rebuilding.

*Temple* _____ Rebuilding the temple.

*People* _____ Destruction from war and neglect.

*Walls* _____ Restoration complete

### B. Storyline Summary
(Fill in the blanks from memory).

| ERA | SUMMARY |
|---|---|
| *Return:* | *Ezra* _____ the people back from _____ to rebuild _____. |

### C. Arc of Bible History (Fill in the name of the Eras.)

| | | |
|---|---|---|
| 1. C_____ | 5. J_____ | 9. |
| 2. P_____ | 6. K_____ | 10. |
| 3. E_____ | 7. E_____ | 11. |
| 4. C_____ | 8. R_____ | 12. |

**D. The Geography of the Return Era**
   (Draw an arrow from Persia to Jerusalem to represent geographical movements during the Return Era.)

**E. Story of the Old Testament**   (Fill in the blanks.)

| ERA | FIGURE | LOCATION | STORYLINE SUMMARY |
|---|---|---|---|
| _____ | _____ | _____ | Adam is created by God, but he _____, and _____ God's original _____ for man. |
| _____ | _____ | _____ | Abraham is _____ by God to "father" a _____ to _____ God to the world. |
| _____ | _____ | _____ | Moses _____ the Hebrew people from _____ in Egypt, and then gives them the _____. |
| _____ | _____ | _____ | Joshua leads the _____ of the _____ _____. |

| ERA | FIGURE | LOCATION | STORYLINE SUMMARY |
|---|---|---|---|
| _____ | _____ | _____ | Samson and others were chosen as _____ to _____ the people for _____ _____ rebellious years. |
| _____ | _____ | _____ | David, the greatest king in the new _____, is followed by a succession of mostly _____ kings, and God eventually _____ Israel for her sin, sending her into exile. |
| _____ | _____ | _____ | Daniel gives _____, and encourages _____ among the _____ for the next seventy years. |
| _____ | _____ | _____ | Ezra _____ the people back from _____ to rebuild _____. |

# TWELVE

# THE SILENCE ERA
## (Between the Old and New Testaments)

 A lion who was caught up with his mastery of the jungle decided to make sure all the other animals knew he was king of the jungle. He was so confident that he bypassed the smaller animals and went straight to the bear. "Who is king of the jungle?" the lion demanded. The bear replied, "Why, you are, of course." The lion gave a mighty roar of approval.

Next, he went to the tiger. "Who is the king of the jungle?" he roared. The tiger quickly responded, "Everyone knows that YOU are, O mighty lion." The lion swelled with pride.

Next on the list was the elephant. The lion faced the elephant and leveled his question: "Who is king of the jungle?" he challenged. The elephant grabbed the lion with his trunk, whirled him around in the air five or six times and slammed him against a tree. Then he pounded him on the ground several times, sat on him once, dipped him in the lake, and dumped him out on the shore.

The lion, battered and bruised, struggled to his feet, peered at the elephant through his good eye, and said, "Look, just because you don't know the answer is no reason to get mean about it."

The religious leaders of the Silence Era were very much like the lion. They pretended to have power, and became self-absorbed. It has been said that some people drink at the fountain of knowledge while others only gargle. All this pride caused a pattern of religious hypocrisy that was leading to self-destruction and made this period one of the more disappointing in the nation's history.

I.    **Review:** Fill in the blanks to bring the chart up to date with this era.

## Story of the Old Testament

| ERA | FIGURE | LOCATION | STORYLINE SUMMARY |
|---|---|---|---|
| _____ | _____ | _____ | Adam is created by God, but he _____, and _____ God's original _____ for man. |
| _____ | _____ | _____ | Abraham is _____ by God to "father" a _____ to _____ God to the world. |
| _____ | _____ | _____ | Moses _____ the Hebrew people from _____ in Egypt, and then gives them the _____. |
| _____ | _____ | _____ | Joshua leads the _____ of the _____ _____. |
| _____ | _____ | _____ | Samson and others were chosen as _____ to _____ the people for _____ _____ rebellious years. |
| _____ | _____ | _____ | David, the greatest king in the new _____, is followed by a succession of mostly _____ kings, and God eventually _____ Israel for her sin, sending her into exile. |
| _____ | _____ | _____ | Daniel gives _____, and encourages _____ among the _____ for the next seventy years. |

| ERA | FIGURE | LOCATION | STORYLINE SUMMARY |
|-----|--------|----------|-------------------|
| _____ | _____ | _____ | Ezra _____ the people back from _____ to rebuild _____. |
| _____ | _____ | _____ | To be completed in this chapter. |

II. **Storyline Summary:** *Pharisees* and others *entomb* the Israelites in *legalism* for the next *four hundred* years.

| ERA | SUMMARY |
|-----|---------|
| *Silence:* | *Pharisees* and others _____ the Israelites in _____ for the next _____ years. |

III. **Expansion:** There are four major subjects in the Silence Era:

1. The Changing Guard
2. Political Sects
3. Religious Sects
4. Messianic Hope

## 1. The Changing Guard: The march of nations.

At the close of the Old Testament, Jerusalem is ruled by Persia. Alexander the Great defeats the Persians in 333 B.C., and establishes Greek culture and the Greek language as a unifying force for that part of the world. When Alexander dies, his kingdom is quartered, but Hellenistic (Greek) culture is still advanced, and remains the dominant influence. When Rome conquers that part of the world, Roman influences are introduced, but for now the Greek influence is still strong. *The march of nations* passes from Persia to Greece to Rome.

## 2. Political Sects: The Maccabeans and Zealots.

Throughout the four hundred Silent Years, there are militant Jews who attempt to revolt against foreign rule and make Jerusalem and the surrounding area of Judea an independent country. These include the *Maccabeans and the Zealots*.

## 3. Religious Sects: Pharisees and Saducees.

There are two primary religious "parties" in Jerusalem during this time. Unfortunately, neither offer much guidance in true spirituality, as they are caught up in promoting a religious "legalism" of external adherence to rules while overlooking inner motivations and attitudes. The Pharisees are orthodox, conservative, and foster separation between themselves and "secular" society. The Saducees are more liberal. They are the party of the Jerusalem aristocracy, and use their wealth and influence to keep the political waters calm. A ruling board, called the Sanhedrin, is made up of representatives from both the *Pharisees and Saducees*, but the two groups have little in common except their desire for religious freedom and, later, their antagonism for Jesus of Nazareth.

## 4. Messianic Hope: Expectation of a savior.

The "Messiah," or "Savior," is one who is prophesied throughout the Old Testament to come to save the Jews. Some feel they need spiritual salvation, and others are looking only for political salvation. For both reasons, the expectation and hope for the coming of the Messiah is strong during the four hundred Silent Years. Events of the Silence Era seem to especially prepare the world for the coming of the Messiah:

(1) This part of the world has a common language and a common culture, which facilitates the spread of a Messianic message.

(2) The Roman Empire has brought this region military peace, an extensive system of roads and sea travel, and a common government so that people can travel extensively without interference.

(3) The Jews are suffering such religious persecution and political humiliation that widespread hope and *expectation of a savior* exists.

These factors make the coming of Jesus of Nazareth, claiming to be the Messiah, an event which captures the attention of the entire Jewish world.

## Self Test

### A. Four Major Subjects in the Silence Era
(Write in the descriptions from the options at right.)

*The Changing Guard* _____ Pharisees and Sadducees.

*Political Sects* _____ The march of nations.

*Religious Sects* _____ Expectation of a savior.

*Messianic Hope* _____ Maccabeans and Zealots.

### B. Storyline Summary
(Fill in the blanks from memory).

| ERA | SUMMARY |
|---|---|
| Silence: | *Pharisees* and others _____ the Israelites in _____ for the next _____ years. |

## C. Arc of Bible History
(Fill in the name of the Eras.)

| 1.<br>C_____ | 5.<br>J_____ | 9.<br>S_____ |
|---|---|---|
| 2.<br>P_____ | 6.<br>K_____ | 10. |
| 3.<br>E_____ | 7.<br>E_____ | 11. |
| 4.<br>C_____ | 8.<br>R_____ | 12. |

## D. The Geography of the Silence Era
(Put a 1 next to Persia, a 2 next to Greece, and a 3 next to Rome. Then draw an arrow from Persia to Greece to Rome, to represent the geographical movement of the Silence Era.)

## E. Story of the Old Testament
(Fill in the blanks.)

| ERA | FIGURE | LOCATION | STORYLINE SUMMARY |
|---|---|---|---|
| _____ | _____ | _____ | Adam is created by God, but he _____, and _____ God's original _____ for man. |
| _____ | _____ | _____ | Abraham is _____ by God to "father" a _____ to _____ God to the world. |
| _____ | _____ | _____ | Moses _____ the Hebrew people from _____ in Egypt, and then gives them the _____. |
| _____ | _____ | _____ | Joshua leads the _____ of the _____ _____. |
| _____ | _____ | _____ | Samson and others were chosen as _____ to _____ the people for _____ _____ rebellious years. |
| _____ | _____ | _____ | David, the greatest king in the new _____, is followed by a succession of mostly _____ kings, and God eventually _____ Israel for her sin, sending her into exile. |
| _____ | _____ | _____ | Daniel gives _____, and encourages _____ among the _____ for the next seventy years. |

| ERA | FIGURE | LOCATION | STORYLINE SUMMARY |
|-----|--------|----------|-------------------|
| _____ | _____ | _____ | Ezra _____ the people back from _____ to rebuild _____. |
| _____ | _____ | _____ | Pharisees and others _____ the Israelites in _____ for the next _____ years. |

Congratulations!!! You have just passed another major milestone! You have completed the overview of the Historical Books of the Old Testament . . . the ones that tell the story of the Old Testament. Now we will take a look at the Poetical Books and the Prophetical Books, in the next two chapters.

# THIRTEEN

# THE POETICAL BOOKS
## (Job–Song of Solomon)

It is no secret that, historically speaking, poets have "marched to the beat of a different drummer," and not everyone has appreciated their poetry. Charles Babbage, a British mathematician, objected to Alfred Lord Tennyson's line from THE VISION OF SIN, "Every moment dies a man,/Every moment one is born," saying that if that were true, "the population of the world would be at a standstill." In the interests of accuracy, he wrote to Tennyson, the lines should be amended to read, "Every moment dies a man,/Every moment one and one-sixteenth is born."

Those who do not dislike poetry either think they can write it, or wish they could. It is much more difficult to write enduring poetry than one imagines, however, and amateur attempts are rarely widely appreciated. Euripides once confessed that it had taken him three days to write three verses. His astonished friend, a poet of lesser abilities, exclaimed, "I could have written a hundred in that time!" "I believe it," replied Euripides, "but they would have lived only three days."

King Louis XIV showed Nicolas Beaulieu, a French poet of the day, some poems he had written, and asked his opinion of them. The great poet was also an accomplished diplomat: "Sire, nothing is impossible for your Majesty. Your Majesty has set out to write bad verses and has succeeded."

Poetry is a song of the soul. Wherever great civilizations have existed, poetry has been written, and the poetry of Israel is among the finest. The psalms of David and the proverbs of Solomon stand up well when compared with any body of poetry ever written.

**I.**     **Review:**  We remind ourselves that there are three kinds of books in the Old Testament: Historical, Poetical, and Prophetical. There are five Poetical Books which follow the first seventeen Historical, as seen below.

### The Three Kinds of Books in the Old Testament

| *Historical* | *Poetical* | *Prophetical* |
|---|---|---|
| Genesis | Job | Isaiah |
| Exodus | Psalms | Jeremiah |
| Leviticus | Proverbs | Lamentations |
| Numbers | Ecclesiastes | Ezekiel |
| Deuteronomy | Song of Solomon | Daniel |
| Joshua | | Hosea |
| Judges | | Joel |
| Ruth | | Amos |
| 1 Samuel | | Obadiah |
| 2 Samuel | | Jonah |
| 1 Kings | | Micah |
| 2 Kings | | Nahum |
| 1 Chronicles | | Habakkuk |
| 2 Chronicles | | Zephaniah |
| Ezra | | Haggai |
| Nehemiah | | Zechariah |
| Esther | | Malachi |

To review, history has now come to an end. The Historical Books are completed, and the books of poetry of the people of Israel begin. The Poetical Books, the middle five books of the Old Testament, can be located in the time line constructed by the Historical Books. Job was written during the time of the events of the book of Genesis; Psalms, during the life of David in 2 Samuel; and Proverbs, Ecclesiastes and Song of Solomon were written during the lifetime of Solomon in the time covered in 1 Kings. See the following figure for a visual representation.

*Poetical Books*

| | | | | | Proverbs Ecclesiastes Song of Solomon | | | | |
|---|---|---|---|---|---|---|---|---|---|
| Job | | | | Psalms | | | | | |

*Historical Books*

| | Leviticus  Deuteronomy | | Ruth | | 1 Chronicles | 2 Chronicles | | | Esther | |
|---|---|---|---|---|---|---|---|---|---|---|
| Genesis | Exodus | Numbers | Joshua | Judges | 1 Samuel | 2 Samuel | 1 Kings | 2 Kings | | Ezra | Nehemiah |
| **1** | **2** | **3** | **4** | **5** | **6** | **7** | **8** | **9** | ----- | **10** | **11** |

II. **Overview Summary:** *The Poetical Books* fall into three major *types* of poetry, within which the poets used a number of different literary *techniques* to communicate God's message.

---

**REVIEW:**

The Poetical Books fall into three major _____ of poetry, within which the poets used a number of different literary _____ to communicate God's message.

---

## The 3 Major Types of Hebrew poetry are:

1. *Lyric poetry* — to be *accompanied by music*, like a song.
2. *Instructional poetry* — to *teach principles of living* through pithy maxims.
3. *Dramatic poetry* — a narrative which *tells a story* in poetic form.

---

**REVIEW OF THE 3 MAJOR TYPES OF HEBREW POETRY**

1. *Lyric poetry* — to be _____, like a song.
2. *Instructional poetry* — to _____ through pithy maxims.
3. *Dramatic poetry* — a narrative which _____ _____ in poetic form.

## The 2 Main Techniques are:

1. *Parallelism*

2. *Figures of speech*

## 1. Parallelism: The matching of ideas.

*Summary Definition*: Rather than matching sounds, a Hebrew poet was more concerned with *matching ideas,* which is called "parallelism."

---

**REVIEW**

Rather than matching sounds, a Hebrew poet was more concerned with _____, which is called parallelism."

---

Six of the most common forms of "parallelism" are:

1. *Synonymous parallelism*: the ideas presented are similar:

   "Make me know Thy ways, O Lord;
   Teach me Thy paths." Psalm 25:4

2. *Synthetic parallelism*: the second thought completes the first thought:

   "The Lord is my shepherd,
   I shall not want." Psalm 23:1

3. *Antithetic parallelism*: the second thought contrasts with the first:

   "For the Lord knows the way of the righteous,
   But the way of the wicked shall perish." Psalm 1:6

4. *Emblematic parallelism*: The first line uses a figure of speech to illustrate the idea stated in the second line:

   "As the deer pants for the water brooks,
   So my soul pants for Thee, O God." Psalm 42:1

5. *Climactic parallelism*: the second line repeats the first with the exception of the last word or words:

"It is not for kings, O Lemuel,
It is not for kings to drink wine." Proverbs 31:4

6. *Formal parallelism*: Both lines of poetry must exist for a complete thought:

"But as for me, I have installed My King
Upon Zion, My holy mountain." Psalm 2:6

## Review
*(Fill in the blanks from the options listed.)*

1. In synonymous parallelism, the ideas are _____.
   a. ridiculous.
   b. similar.
   c. spelled the same.

2. In synthetic parallelism, _____.
   a. the second thought is made of nylon.
   b. the second thought completed the first.
   c. the second thought doesn't exist.

3. Antithetic parallelism, _____.
   a. the second thought is written backwards.
   b. the second thought contrasts with the first.
   c. the first thought has no counterpart in the universe.

4. In emblematic parallelism, _____.
   a. a small metallic emblem is affixed to the first line.
   b. a figure of speech in the first line illustrates the idea in the second line.
   c. the ideas are drawn in primitive art form.

5. In climactic parallelism, _____.
   a. the second thought is very cold.
   b. the second line repeats the first with the exception of the last word or words.
   c. the thought is completed in the third act.

6. In formal parallelism, _____.
   a. the first line appears in a black tie.
   b. both lines of poetry must exist for a complete thought.
   c. the second line doesn't slurp its soup.

*(The answer to all the above questions is the first letter in the word basketball.)*

## 2. Figures of Speech: Creating visual images.

*Summary Definition*: Since the Hebrew poets wanted mental pictures to pop into the reader's mind, *creating visual images* was of prime consideration, which they accomplished with vivid "figures of speech."

---

**REVIEW**

Since the Hebrew poets wanted mental pictures to pop into the reader's mind, _____ was of prime consideration, which they accomplished with vivid "figures of speech."

---

Five of the most common "figures of speech" are:

1. *Simile*: a comparison between two unlike things.

   "Keep me as the apple of thy eye." Psalm 17:8

2. *Metaphor*: a comparison in which one thing is said to be another.

   "The Lord is my shepherd." Psalm 23:1

3. *Hyperbole*: deliberate overstatement for the sake of emphasis.

   "Every night I make my bed swim,
   I dissolve my couch with my tears." Psalm 6:6

4. *Rhetorical question*: asking a question for the purpose of making a statement.

   "Who can speak of the mighty deeds of the Lord,
   Or can show forth all His praise?" Psalm 106:2

5. *Personification*: assigning the characteristics of a human to lifeless objects.

   "The sun knows the place of its setting." Psalm 104:19

While there are other figures of speech, these are the most notable. The ones listed here, in particular, express the visual imagery to which the Hebrew poets were committed in order to cause mental pictures to pop into our minds.

If you can get away from the need to hear rhyme and rhythm, you can gain an appreciation for Hebrew poetry. These men were "wordsmiths" and "thoughtsmiths" who played with words and ideas, contrasting them, comparing them, completing them in ways that lifted them above mere prose.

**III. Expansion:** The Five Poetical Books:

1. Job
2. Psalms
3. Proverbs
4. Ecclesiastes
5. Song of Solomon

**1. Job: Suffering and God's sovereignty.**

Job is a very wealthy, godly man whose life fortunes are suddenly and dramatically reversed. He loses his health, his wealth, his family, and is plunged into profound suffering. The book presents, in "dramatic poetry," the internal struggles of Job, and a series of debates with three friends trying to gain a proper perspective on *suffering and God's sovereignty*. In the end, God reveals His majesty and power. Though Job's questions are never answered, he willingly submits to the sovereignty of God, and his fortunes are restored and doubled.

**2. Psalms: Praise in public worship.**

Psalm means "book of praises." The book of Psalms is a collection of one hundred fifty psalms which are divided into five smaller "books." The Psalms are used as a book of prayer and *praise in public worship* in the tabernacle, temple, and synagogues. There are three primary types of psalms: praise, thanksgiving, and lament. King David writes almost half of them, while several different authors complete the rest. These works of "lyric poetry" are composed to be sung to musical accompaniment.

**3. Proverbs: Wisdom: skill for living.**

The purpose of the proverbs is to impart *wisdom, or "skill for living."* More specifically, they highlight practical wisdom, discernment, self-discipline, and moral courage. This "instructional poetry" is written in short, pithy maxims focusing on one's relationship to God and others—money, morals, speech, industry, honesty, etc. The message is that a life of wisdom and righteousness should preempt a life of foolishness and unrighteousness.

**4. Ecclesiastes: Futility of temporal pursuits.**

Solomon, with his unlimited resources and opportunity, tries to find meaning in life through industry, pleasure, wealth, wisdom, and power, and finds them all unsatisfying. After he reviews these efforts and the *futility of temporal pursuits*, he concludes in this "instructional poetry" that there is only one thing that can satisfy man: to "fear God and keep His commandments" (12:13).

**5. Song of Solomon: God's marriage manual.**

The Song of Solomon is *God's marriage manual*. This "dramatic poetry" pictures the intimate love relationship between Solomon and his Shulammite bride. In doing so, it presents God's perspective on married love.

### Self Test

### The Five Poetical Books

(Write in the descriptions from the options at right.)

*Job* _____  Futility of temporal pursuits.

*Psalms* _____  Suffering and God's sovereignty.

*Proverbs* _____  God's marriage manual.

*Ecclesiastes* _____  Praise in public worship.

*Song of* _____  Wisdom; skill for living.
*Solomon*

# THE PROPHETICAL BOOKS

## *(Isaiah – Malachi)*

 Prophecy gets a grip on us like nothing else. We are mesmerized and spellbound by it. What does the future hold? That question grabs us by the collar, throws us up against the wall, sinks its thumbs into our jugular, and holds us there for an answer. Some look into crystal balls, read tea leaves, study astrological charts, and consult prophets for a glimpse into the unknown. From, "when will the world end," to, "what should I wear tomorrow," they hunger to probe into the depths of that which has not yet happened.

There is an intuitive sense that a veil hangs between the human and the divine, and that prophets will help us peer beyond the veil. Outside of the Bible, however, prophets have had an uneven track record. Croesus lived in the 6th century B.C., and was king of Lydia, in Asia Minor. Deliberating whether to attack the Persian empire, he asked the oracle at Delphi if the undertaking would prosper. The oracle replied that if he went to war, he would destroy a great empire. Encouraged, Croesus invaded the Persian realms. He was decisively beaten and the Persians then invaded Lydia, captured its capital, and threw Croesus himself into chains. Croesus again sent an embassy to Delphi, this time with the question, "Why did you deceive me?" The priestess of the oracle replied that she had not deceived him — Croesus had indeed destroyed a great empire.

Girolamo Cardano, an Italian mathematician of the 16th century, was renown throughout Europe as an astrologer, even visiting England to cast the horoscope of the young king, Edward VI. A steadfast believer in the accuracy of his so-called science, Cardano constructed a horoscope predicting the hour of his own death. When the day dawned, it found him in good health and safe from harm. Rather than have his prediction fail, Cardano killed himself.

Biblical prophets find themselves in a different league, however, from the run-of-the-mill prophets. If a man was a true prophet from God, no prediction of his would ever fail. If a prophet ever voiced a prophecy that failed, he was to be stoned to death. This discouraged the impostors, and made the Biblical prophets highly reliable. There were many true prophets in the Old Testament, but not all of them committed their messages to writings which were preserved. In the Bible, we have sixteen men who wrote down their messages. These writings are called the Prophetical Books, and comprise the final seventeen books of the Old Testament, as seen in the review below.

## I.   Review:

### Structure of the Old Testament

| *Historical* | *Poetical* | *Prophetical* |
|---|---|---|
| Genesis | Job | Isaiah |
| Exodus | Psalms | Jeremiah |
| Leviticus | Proverbs | Lamentations |
| Numbers | Ecclesiastes | Ezekiel |
| Deuteronomy | Song of Solomon | Daniel |
| Joshua | | Hosea |
| Judges | | Joel |
| Ruth | | Amos |
| 1 Samuel | | Obadiah |
| 2 Samuel | | Jonah |
| 1 Kings | | Micah |
| 2 Kings | | Nahum |
| 1 Chronicles | | Habakkuk |
| 2 Chronicles | | Zephaniah |
| Ezra | | Haggai |
| Nehemiah | | Zechariah |
| Esther | | Malachi |

Our history is completed. From Genesis, the first Historical Book, to Nehemiah, the last Historical Book, we stretched out a time line that told the story of ancient Israel. Then we dropped the Poetical Books in their proper place. Now we do the same with the Prophetical Books, as seen below.

*Historical Books*

| | | Leviticus | Deuteronomy | | Ruth | | | 1 Chronicles | 2 Chronicles | | | Esther | |
|---|---|---|---|---|---|---|---|---|---|---|---|---|---|
| Genesis | Exodus | Numbers | Joshua | Judges | 1 Samuel | 2 Samuel | 1 Kings | 2 Kings | | | Ezra | Nehemiah |
| **1** | **2** | **3** | **4** | **5** | **6** | **7** | **8** | **9** | ----- | **10** | **11** |

*Prophetical Books*

| | | | | | | | To Israel:<br>Hosea<br>Amos<br><br>To Judah:<br>Habakkuk<br>Isaiah<br>Jeremiah<br>Joel<br>Micah<br>Zephaniah<br>Lamentations<br><br>To Assyria:<br>Jonah<br>Nahum<br><br>To Edom:<br>Obadiah | Ezekiel<br>Daniel | Haggai<br>Zechariah | Malachi |
|---|---|---|---|---|---|---|---|---|---|---|

Most of the Prophetical Books (Isaiah-Zephaniah) were written during the time covered in the book of 2 Kings, which records the decline of the nation. This is because the primary message of the prophets was to the nation to stop sinning and return to the Lord. The prophets predicted what would happen to the nation if the people did not heed the warning. Of the remaining books, two prophets (Ezekiel and Daniel) ministered during the exile, and three (Haggai, Zechariah, and Malachi) during the return.

II. **Overview Summary:** *Prophecy* is *proclaiming* the Word of God, both for the *future* and in the *present.*

---

**REVIEW:**

*Prophecy* is _____ the Word of God, both for the _____ and in the _____.

**III. Expansion:** There are four main features of the Prophetical writings:

1. Designation
2. Time Period
3. Foretelling
4. Forthtelling

**1. Designation:  Major and minor prophets.**

In recent history, the Prophetical Books have had two designations: *major prophets* and *minor prophets*. The major prophets are the first five Prophetical Books: Isaiah, Jeremiah, Lamentations, Ezekiel, and Daniel. The minor prophets are the remaining twelve. The major prophets are called "major" because they are longer books, while the others are called "minor" because they are shorter writings than the major prophets.

**2. Time Period:  Pre-exile, exile, or post exile.**

The Prophetical Books are divided into three chronological periods: *pre-exile, exile,* and *post-exile.* Most of the prophetical ministries and books occur before the exile. Three prophets, Haggai,

### Structure of the Prophetical Books

| *Pre-Exile* | *Exile* | *Post-Exile* |
|---|---|---|
| TO ISRAEL: | FROM BABYLONIA: | TO JERUSALEM: |
| Hosea | Ezekiel | Haggai |
| Amos | Daniel | Zechariah |
| | | Malachi |
| TO JUDAH: | | |
| Habakkuk | | |
| Isaiah | | |
| Jeremiah | | |
| Joel | | |
| Micah | | |
| Zephaniah | | |
| Lamentations | | |
| TO ASSYRIA: | | |
| Jonah | | |
| Nahum | | |
| TO EDOM: | | |
| Obadiah | | |

Zechariah, and Malachi prophesy during the return. Of those who prophesy before the exile, two prophesy primarily to Israel (the northern kingdom), seven primarily to Judah (the southern kingdom), and three to other countries, as seen on the previous page.

### 3. Foretelling: Predicting the future.

The most famous characteristic of a prophet is that he can occasionally *predict the future*. This is not an ability inherent within himself. Rather, this information is given to him by God. In Israel, the test of a true prophet is that he must be one-hundred percent accurate. If a prophet ever says anything which does not come true, he is not a prophet of God. And the penalty for giving a prophecy that does not come true is death by stoning. This keeps the ranks of the prophets pure.

### 4. Forthtelling: Proclaiming the teachings of God.

While the ministry of "foretelling" (telling the future) is more dramatic, the ministry of "forthtelling" is vastly more common in the life of a prophet. Forthtelling means simply *proclaiming the teachings of God* to the people. Primarily it related to righteous living. There are three characteristics of this part of a prophet's ministry:

1. exposing sin and calling people to a higher moral lifestyle.
2. warning of judgment if the people didn't reform.
3. proclaiming the coming Messiah.

The prophets usually warned about judgments related to the nation of Israel or Judah being militarily conquered and taken out of the land.

### Self Test

### A. Four Main Features of the Prophetical Books
(Write in the descriptions from the options at right.)

*Designation* _____ Predicting the future.

*Time Period* _____ Proclaiming the teachings of God.

*Foretelling* _____ Pre-exile, exile, post-exile.

*Forthtelling* _____ Major and minor prophets.

## B. The Geography of the Prophetical Books

The primary locations in which prophets ministered are found on the map below. Match the country with the location by filling in the blanks according to the numbers.

1. Israel          4. Assyria
2. Judah          5. Babylonia
3. Edom          6. Jerusalem

Wonderful! You have now completed Section 1, the Story of the Old Testament. This is a major milestone in understanding the Bible. The remaining three sections have been structured so that they are challenging, but not overwhelming. If you completed the Old Testament, you can complete the entire book, and you're almost halfway through the thirty days!

Now, having just overviewed the Poetical and Prophetical Books of the Old Testament and having seen where they fit into the "Story of the Bible," we are ready to continue that story as we begin Section 2, the "Story of the New Testament."

SECTION TWO

# THE
# STORY
# OF
# THE
# NEW
# TESTAMENT

# FIFTEEN

# THE GEOGRAPHY OF
# THE NEW TESTAMENT

 Hiding among the giant Andes Mountains in the South American country of Peru lies a flat valley about forty miles long, isolated from the rest of the world. Roads and paths lie all over the floor of this vast valley, strewn like long thin trees which have fallen at random. For years, archaeologists have guessed that they were a forgotten network of roads, left by an ancient civilization.

Perspective was changed radically, however, when someone chanced to study the valley from the air. From this vantage point, what seemed to be haphazard and random now became quite clear. They were not roads and paths at all, but a monumental desert mural picturing objects which were many miles in height. What the murals are, what they mean, how they were built, for whom they were built, and by whom they were built are all lost to the mist of time.

The monumental mural has a symbolic message for us all, however. Often, the whole picture of something cannot be seen if we are too close to it. We must get back away from the details of what we are studying to see the overview.

This is certainly true of the geography of the New Testament. When in the Gospels you read of going from Jericho to Jerusalem to Cana, until you have overviewed the geography, those are just words on a page with no meaning. You have no realization that someone has just walked seventy-five miles, as the crow flies, the distance from Baltimore to Philadelphia, or that it also included walking up thirteen hundred feet in altitude, and then down another one thousand.

In fact, gaining perspective on the geography of the New Testament is in itself a fascinating study. Israel is a tiny country compared to the United States. Draw a line fifty miles wide from New York to Boston, and you have the approximate land area of Israel, or stand Massachusetts on end, or shrink New Hampshire by ten percent.

Yet it is a remarkably varied land. From low desert to high mountain, with lush valleys and rolling hills in between, the gamut is run in topography. Any body of water that you cannot swim across is a "sea," and every hill higher than your head is a "mountain." The Sea of Galilee is seven miles by fourteen miles, almost a mud puddle compared to the Great Lakes. The Dead Sea is ten miles by fifty miles, smaller than some virtually nameless reservoirs in the U.S. The "mighty" Jordan is little more than a strong-running creek compared to the truly "mighty" rivers of the world like the Amazon or Mississippi. Perhaps because it is such a small country, everything is exaggerated.

To be able to create mental pictures as you read the events in the New Testament is to help the narrative come alive. So, as we begin looking at the New Testament, we begin with the geography.

## The Geography of the Gospels

The difference between the geography of the Gospels and the geography of the book of Acts is significant enough to warrant separate treatment.

### Bodies of Water

Once you have mastered the geography of the Old Testament, the geography of the New Testament is fairly simple. The bodies of water are among those of the Old Testament studied in Chapter 2. (To review, go to the map that follows and write in the name of the bodies of water by matching the numbers.)

1. Mediterranean Sea
2. Sea of Galilee
3. Jordan River
4. Dead Sea

### Bodies of Water in the Gospels

(Fill in the appropriate blanks on the following map. The numbers should match those on the list above.)

## Provinces and Cities

The primary geographical area in the gospels is the same as that which was ruled by the nation of Israel in the Old Testament. However, the land, now known as Palestine, is ruled by Rome and has been divided into sections, or provinces. (As you read these descriptions, write the location on the map that follows, by matching the letters.)

### A. The Province of Galilee.

Located between the Mediterranean Sea, and the sea which shares its name, Galilee, is the province which Jesus considered His home province. Both Nazareth, His early home, and Capernaum, His later home, are in Galilee. Hence, the phrase, "the man from Galilee."

### B. The Province of Samaria.

Located between the Mediterranean Sea and the Jordan River, Samaria is home to Samaritans. Part Jewish, part Gentile people, they live in constant animosity with the Jews.

### C. The Province of Judea.

Located between the Mediterranean Sea and the Dead Sea, it is approximately the same area as the southern tribe of Judah in the Old Testament. Encompassing the city of Jerusalem, it is home to most of the Jews in the New Testament.

## D.  The Province of Perea.

A long, narrow province on the east bank of the Jordan River, Jesus spent some concentrated time there with His disciples toward the end of His ministry.

## E.  The City of Nazareth.

Located in Galilee just west of the Sea of Galilee, it is the town where Mary and Joseph lived, and in which Jesus grew up.

## F.  The City of Capernaum.

Located on the very top of the Sea of Galilee, it is where Jesus called home during His ministry years.

## G.  The City of Jerusalem.

Located in Judea, just off the top of the Dead Sea, it is the home of the temple, the holy city and center of activity for Jews.

## H.  The City of Bethlehem.

The birthplace of Jesus, it is five miles southwest of Jerusalem.

### Provinces and Cities of the Gospels

(Fill in the appropriate blanks below. The letters should match those from the list above.)

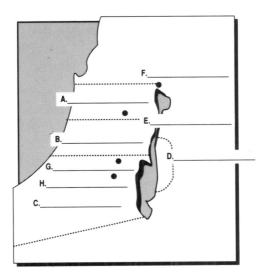

## The Geography of Acts

### Bodies of Water

The bodies of water are the same as for the Gospels, only more of the Mediterranean is involved. Therefore, you already know them.

### Countries and Cities

As we move out of the Gospels and into Acts, our geography expands from Palestine further into the Roman Empire. (As you read the descriptions, write the location on the map that follows.)

**1. The Country of Galatia.**

Located in modern-day Turkey, it was the destination of the Apostle Paul's first missionary journey to take the gospel message to Gentiles.

**2. The Country of Greece.**

Located in modern Greece, it was the destination for Paul's second missionary journey.

**3. The Country of Asia.**

Located on the western coast of modern Turkey, it was the destination of Paul's third missionary journey.

**4. The Country of Italy.**

Located in modern Italy, it was the country of Paul's imprisonment and death.

**5. The City of Jerusalem.**

Located in modern Jerusalem, it is the location of the beginning of the early Christian Church.

**6. The City of Damascus.**

Located in modern Damascus, in the modern country of Syria, it was Paul's destination when he was temporarily blinded by Jesus, and converted to Christianity.

**7. The City of Caesarea.**

Located on the Mediterranean coast just south of the Sea of Galilee, it was the site of Paul's trials.

**8. The City of Antioch.**

On the Mediterranean coast, north of Israel, near modern Turkey, it was the beginning point for all three of Paul's missionary journeys.

**9. The City of Rome.**

Located in modern Rome, it was the city of Paul's imprisonment and death.

### The Geography of Acts

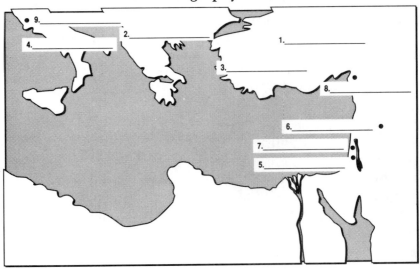

### Self Test
*The Geography of the Gospels.*

(Now, from the options listed, fill in the bodies of water, provinces, and cities on the map that follows.)

*Numbers = bodies of water*

Dead Sea
Jordan River
Mediterranean Sea
Sea of Galilee

*Letters = cities and provinces*

Bethlehem
Capernaum
Galilee
Jerusalem
Judea
Nazareth
Perea
Samaria

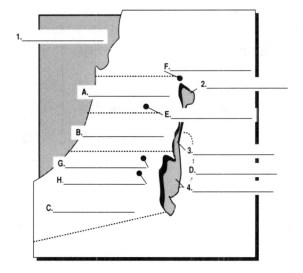

## The Geography of Acts

(From the options listed, fill in the countries and cities on the following map.)

*Countries:*
Asia
Galatia
Greece
Italy
Rome

*Cities:*
Antioch
Caesarea
Damascus
Jerusalem

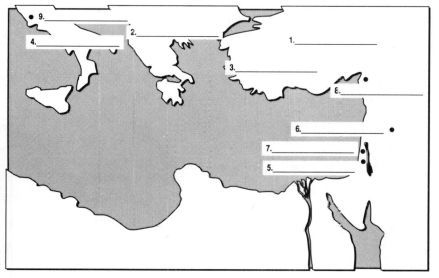

## The Historical Books of the New Testament

Having mastered the geography of the New Testament, we are now ready to continue the story of the Bible with the three main eras that remain. You will recall that the twenty seven books of the New Testament can be divided into three different kinds of books: five Historical Books, thirteen Pauline Epistles, and nine General Epistles.

As we did with the Historical Books in the Old Testament, first we will overview the events of the Historical Books of the New Testament, the Gospels and the Acts. Then, in the following chapters we will expand the storyline.

## The Three Main Eras of the New Testament

### 1. Gospels.
The life of Jesus of Nazareth as told in the *Gospels*.

### 2. Church.
The formation stage of the Christian *Church*.

### 3. Missions.
The expansion of the Church into the Roman empire through *missions*.

## Review
*Write in the Era on the proper line matching the description.*

| OPTIONS: | ERA: | DESCRIPTION: |
|---|---|---|
| *Missions* | _____ | The life of Jesus of Nazareth, as told in the *Gospels*. |
| *Gospels* | | |
| *Church* | _____ | The formation stage of the Christian *Church*. |
| | _____ | The expansion of the Church into the Roman empire through *missions*. |

We are now able to add this new information to our storyline chart from the Old Testament, as seen in the following.

## Story of the Bible

| ERA | FIGURE | LOCATION | STORYLINE SUMMARY |
|-----|--------|----------|-------------------|
| *Creation* | *Adam* | *Eden* | Adam is created by God, but he *sins*, and *destroys* God's original *plan* for man. |
| *Patriarch* | *Abraham* | *Canaan* | Abraham is *chosen* by God to "father" a *people* to *represent* God to the world. |
| *Exodus* | *Moses* | *Egypt* | Moses *delivers* the Hebrew people from *slavery* in Egypt, and then gives them the *Law*. |
| *Conquest* | *Joshua* | *Canaan* | Joshua leads the *conquest* of the *Promised Land*. |
| *Judges* | *Samson* | *Canaan* | Samson and others were chosen as *judges* to *govern* the people for four hundred rebellious years. |
| *Kingdom* | *David* | *Israel* | David, the greatest king in the new *monarchy*, is followed by a succession of mostly *unrighteous* kings, and God eventually *judges* Israel for her sin, sending her into exile. |
| *Exile* | *Daniel* | *Babylonia* | Daniel gives *leadership*, and encourages *faithfulness* among the *exiles* for the next seventy years. |
| *Return* | *Ezra* | *Jerusalem* | Ezra *leads* the people back from *exile* to rebuild *Jerusalem*. |
| *Silence* | *Pharisees* | *Jerusalem* | Pharisees and others *entomb* the Israelites in *legalism* for the next *four hundred* years. |

| ERA | FIGURE | LOCATION | STORYLINE SUMMARY |
|---|---|---|---|
| *Gospels* | To be supplied later | To be supplied later | To be supplied later. |
| *Church* | To be supplied later | To be supplied later | To be supplied later. |
| *Missions* | To be supplied later | To be supplied later | To be supplied later. |

## The Three Central Figures of the New Testament

| ERA: | FIGURE: | DESCRIPTION: |
|---|---|---|
| Gospels | Jesus | The predicted *Messiah* |
| Church | Peter | The *leader* of the early Church |
| Missions | Paul | The first Christian *missionary* |

## REVIEW
*Fill in the blanks.*

| ERA: | FIGURE: | DESCRIPTION: |
|---|---|---|
| Gospels | Jesus | The predicted _____ |
| Church | Peter | The _____ of the early Church |
| Missions | Paul | The first Christian _____ |

We are now able to add the central figures from the New Testament to our storyline chart, as seen on the following page which shows just the New Testament Eras.

| ERA | FIGURE | LOCATION | STORYLINE SUMMARY |
|---|---|---|---|
| *Gospels* | *Jesus* | To be supplied later | To be supplied later. |
| *Church* | *Peter* | To be supplied later | To be supplied later. |
| *Missions* | *Paul* | To be supplied later | To be supplied later. |

Our final task is to identify the general or primary geographic location of the events of the three main Eras of the New Testament. As an exercise in memory, write in each main era and central historical figure as you read the description of the geographical location.

## The Three Main Locations of the New Testament

| ERA: | FIGURE: | LOCATION: | DESCRIPTION: |
|---|---|---|---|
| 1. G_____ | J_____ | Palestine | The general land area that was known as Canaan and Israel in the Old Testament is commonly known as Palestine in the New. It includes the Roman provinces of Galilee, Samaria, and Judea. |
| 2. C_____ | P_____ | Jerusalem | The ancient city of Jerusalem has been in the same location throughout most of Biblical history after the Kingdom Era. It is the city which gave birth to the early Church. |

| ERA: | FIGURE: | LOCATION: | DESCRIPTION: |
|------|---------|-----------|--------------|
| 3. M_____ | P_____ | Roman Empire | As Paul spread the message of Christianity he took it to the heart of the Roman Empire. From Palestine, north into what is modern Turkey, west, through modern Greece, to Italy. |

## Review

(Now, from the options listed, write in the location to match the era and figure.)

| ERA: | FIGURE: | LOCATION: | OPTIONS |
|------|---------|-----------|---------|
| *Gospels* | *Jesus* | _____ | Roman Empire |
| *Church* | *Peter* | _____ | Palestine |
| *Missions* | *Paul* | _____ | Jerusalem |

We are now able to add the main locations from the New Testament to our storyline chart, as seen in the following.

| ERA | FIGURE | LOCATION | STORYLINE SUMMARY |
|-----|--------|----------|-------------------|
| *Gospels* | *Jesus* | *Palestine* | To be supplied later. |
| *Church* | *Peter* | *Jerusalem* | To be supplied later. |
| *Missions* | *Paul* | *Roman Empire* | To be supplied later. |

## Arc of Bible History
(Fill in the name of the Eras.)

| 1. C_____ | 5. J_____ | 9. S_____ |
| 2. P_____ | 6. K_____ | 10. G_____ |
| 3. E_____ | 7. E_____ | 11. C_____ |
| 4. C_____ | 8. R_____ | 12. M_____ |

| ERA | FIGURE | LOCATION | STORYLINE SUMMARY |
|---|---|---|---|
| _____ | _____ | _____ | To be supplied later. |
| _____ | _____ | _____ | To be supplied later. |
| _____ | _____ | _____ | To be supplied later. |

Congratulations! You have just taken a big step toward mastering an overview of the New Testament. From now on, we will get more specific, but you have the basic structure well in hand.

# SIXTEEN

# THE GOSPEL ERA

## (Matthew – John)

Dr. Richard Selzer is a brilliant surgeon who wrote a penetrating book entitled, *Mortal Lessons: Notes on the Art of Surgery.* In it he writes:

> I stand by the bed where a young woman lies, her face postoperative, her mouth twisted in a palsy, clownish. A tiny twig of a facial nerve, the one to the muscles of her mouth, has been severed. She will be thus from now on. The surgeon had followed with religious fervor the curve of her flesh; I promise you that. Nevertheless, to remove the tumor in her cheek, I had to cut the little nerve.
>
> Her husband is in the room. He stands on the opposite side of the bed, and together, they seem to dwell in the evening lamplight. Isolated from me, private. Who are they, I ask myself, he and this wry-mouth I have made, who gaze at each other, and touch each other generously, greedily?
>
> The young woman speaks. "Will I always be like this?" she asks. "Yes," I say. It is because the nerve was cut." She nods and is silent. But the young man smiles "I like it," he says. "It's kind of cute."
>
> All at once I know who he is. I understand, and I lower my gaze. One is not bold in an encounter with a god. Unmindful, he bends to kiss her crooked mouth, and I so close I can see how he twists his own lips to accommodate hers, to show that their kiss still works. I remember that the gods appeared in ancient Greece as mortals, and I hold my breath and let the wonder in.

That is the spirit of Jesus. Man's link with God had been severed through sin. And he twisted himself, to accommodate us, and gave us the kiss of eternal life. But not without giving his own life on our behalf. Jesus. At the same time, so tender and powerful. The most remarkable figure ever to have lived. And why not? He was God incarnate.

The birth of Jesus split history like a thunderbolt on a hot July evening. Everything before His birth, we call B.C., before Christ. Everything after, we call A.D., Anno Domini, in the year of our Lord. His story, predicted throughout the Old Testament, is told in the four Gospels: Matthew, Mark, Luke, and John. While the Gospels are biographical, they are actually thematic portraits of Christ's life that place very little emphasis on His early life, and great emphasis on the last week of His life. The Gospels tend to follow the chronology of His life, but not slavishly. Not all the Gospels cover the same events in His life. When all four Gospels are put together, and "harmonized," only about fifty days of Jesus' active ministry are dealt with.

I.   **Review:** Fill in the blanks to begin the chart for this era.

### Story of the New Testament

| ERA | FIGURE | LOCATION | STORYLINE SUMMARY |
|-----|--------|----------|-------------------|
| _____ | _____ | _____ | To be supplied later. |

II.  **Storyline Summary:** *Jesus* comes in fulfillment of the Old Testament *prophecies* of a savior, and offers *salvation* and the true Kingdom of God. While some accept Him, most *reject* Him, and He is crucified, buried, and resurrected.

| ERA | SUMMARY |
|-----|---------|
| *Gospel:* | *Jesus* comes in fulfillment of the Old Testament _____ of a savior, and offers _____ and the true Kingdom of God. While some accept Him, most _____ Him, and He is crucified, buried, and resurrected. |

III. **Expansion:** There are four main divisions in the Gospel Era:

1. Early Life
2. Early Ministry
3. Later Ministry
4. Death and Resurrection

## 1. Early Life: Childhood to baptism.

Through a miraculous conception by the Holy Spirit, Jesus is born of the virgin Mary in Bethlehem of Judea. After a brief excursion into Egypt to save Him from Herod's attempt on His life, Jesus travels with Mary and her husband Joseph to live in Nazareth. There He learns the trade of a carpenter and apparently lives a fairly normal life from *childhood to the time of His baptism*, when He was thirty years old. His cousin, John the Baptist is ministering and baptizing people in the Jordan River near the Dead Sea. After Jesus is baptized by John, a remarkable event takes place. God the Father is heard speaking from heaven, saying "This is my beloved Son, in whom I am well pleased," and the Holy Spirit, in the visible form of a dove, descends on Him. Then, He is led by the Holy Spirit into the wilderness of Judea, where He is tempted by Satan for forty days. Satan makes every attempt to get Jesus to follow him rather than God. Satan offers Jesus everything God the Father offers Him, but on a different time table and with different requirements. Jesus remains sinless, and validates His readiness to begin making Himself known as the Messiah.

## 2. Early Ministry: Initial acceptance.

It is not until after Jesus' baptism and temptation that He begins His public ministry. His message has a two-fold focus: first, that He is the predicted Messiah, or as the word is translated in the New Testament, the Christ, and people should believe in Him, and second to challenge the people to live a life of genuine righteousness, not the external hypocrisy of the religious leaders. He validates His message by performing astounding miracles, and the signs of *initial acceptance* by the crowds are encouraging. Much of this early activity takes place around Jerusalem.

### 3. Later Ministry: Growing rejection.

Jesus' initial popularity does not last. The religious leaders are profoundly jealous of Him, and begin stirring up animosity toward Him. This *growing rejection* results in a progression in Jesus' ministry pattern. He begins to focus more attention on the mounting opposition from the religious leaders, warning them of the seriousness of their attitude. At the same time, He begins setting aside more and more time for the twelve disciples whom He has chosen, preparing them to carry on without Him. Also, He begins challenging the multitude to count the cost of following Him. Though Jesus travels quite a bit during this time, His home base is Capernaum, on the north bank of the Sea of Galilee.

### 4. Death and Resurrection: Final rejection.

The Jews become more and more polarized about Jesus, either following Him enthusiastically, or resenting Him deeply. In the volatile atmosphere of the festival time of the Passover when Jesus and many other Jews are in Jerusalem, the religious leaders are finally able to stir up enthusiasm for Jesus' crucifixion. They subject Him to a series of mock trials on false charges. Then, Jesus is crucified on Friday, buried that night, and rises again from the dead on Sunday, after being in the tomb three days.

### Self Test

### A. Four Main Divisions in the Gospel Era
(Write in the descriptions from the options at right.)

*Early Life* _____ Initial acceptance.

*Early Ministry* _____ Final rejection.

*Later Ministry* _____ Childhood to baptism.

*Death and Resurrection* _____ Growing rejection.

## B. Storyline Summary
(Fill in the blanks from memory).

| ERA | SUMMARY |
|-----|---------|
| *Gospel:* | *Jesus* comes in fulfillment of the Old Testament _____ of a savior, and offers _____ and the true Kingdom of God. While some accept Him, most _____ Him, and He is crucified, buried, and resurrected. |

## C. Arc of Bible History
(Fill in the name of the Eras.)

| 1. C_____ | 5. J_____ | 9. S_____ |
|---|---|---|
| 2. P_____ | 6. K_____ | 10. G_____ |
| 3. E_____ | 7. E_____ | 11. |
| 4. C_____ | 8. R_____ | 12. |

## D. The Geography of the Gospel Era
(Draw an arrow from Bethlehem to Egypt to Nazareth to represent the geographical movement in Jesus' early life, and label it #1. Draw an arrow from Nazareth to Jerusalem, to represent His initial acceptance, and label it #2. Draw an

arrow from Jerusalem to Capernaum, to represent the growing rejection, and label it #3. Draw an arrow from Capernaum to Jerusalem, to represent His final rejection, and
label it #4.)

## E. Story of the Bible (Fill in the blanks.)

| ERA | FIGURE | LOCATION | STORYLINE SUMMARY |
|------|--------|----------|-------------------|
| _____ | _____ | _____ | Adam is created by God, but he _____, and _____ God's original _____ for man. |
| _____ | _____ | _____ | Abraham is _____ by God to "father" a _____ to _____ God to the world. |
| _____ | _____ | _____ | Moses _____ the Hebrew people from _____ in Egypt, and then gives them the _____. |
| _____ | _____ | _____ | Joshua leads the _____ of the _____ _____. |

| ERA | FIGURE | LOCATION | STORYLINE SUMMARY |
|---|---|---|---|
| ———— | ———— | ———— | Samson and others were chosen as _____ to _____ the people for _____ _____ rebellious years. |
| ———— | ———— | ———— | David, the greatest king in the new _____, is followed by a succession of mostly _____ kings, and God eventually _____ Israel for her sin, sending her into exile. |
| ———— | ———— | ———— | Daniel gives _____, and encourages _____ among the _____ for the next seventy years. |
| ———— | ———— | ———— | Ezra _____ the people back from _____ to rebuild _____. |
| ———— | ———— | ———— | Pharisees and others _____ the Israelites in _____ for the next _____ years. |
| ———— | ———— | ———— | Jesus comes in fulfillment of the Old Testament _____ of a savior, and offers _____ and the true Kingdom of God. While some accept Him, most _____ Him, and He is crucified, buried, and resurrected. |

# SEVENTEEN

# THE CHURCH ERA

## *(Acts 1–12)*

A lot of "pot shots" have been taken at the Church over the years. One skalleywag wrote:

> To live above with saints we love,
> O, that will be glory.
> To live below with saints we know,
> Well, that's another story.

Another one wrote about hymns we really sing:

> When morning guilds the skies
> My heart awakening cries
> Oh no! Another day!

> Amazing grace, how sweet the sound
> That saved a wretch like you.

> Jesus, I am resting, resting
> Resting, resting, resting, resting.

> The strife is o're, the battle done
> The church has split and our side won.

William Blake wrote in the Everlasting Gospel:

> Both read the Bible day and night,
> But Thou read'st black where I read white.

In spite of its obvious imperfections, the Church is the means that has been chosen to carry the message of the Gospel to the world. One wonders why a better system could not have been devised. Then one realizes that any system that has people in it is going to be imperfect.

Alexander Solzhenitsyn wrote in the *Gulag Archipelago* that it was in prison where he learned that the line separating good and evil passes not through states, not through classes, not through political parties either, but right through every human heart, and through all human hearts.

When we give ourselves serious evaluation, we find things hiding in our hearts that, if we could choose, we would remove. Our hearts have been described as "a zoo of lusts, a bedlam of ambitions, a nursery of fears, a harem of fondled hatreds." Yet the Church, by its very nature, must be made up of the likes of us.

However, we are not left to ourselves. God is at work in the lives of all willing people, changing and transforming them into something more than they were.

"Imagine yourself a living house. God comes in to rebuild that house. At first, perhaps, you can understand what He is doing. He is getting the drains right and stopping the leaks in the roof and so on . . . But presently He starts knocking the house about in a way that hurts abominably and does not seem to make any sense. What on earth is He up to? The explanation is that He is building quite a different house from the one you thought of—throwing out a new wing here, putting on an extra floor there, running up towers, making courtyards. You thought you were going to be made into a decent little cottage; but He is building a palace."

And thus is the message of the Church. The Gospel is carried *to* imperfect people, *by* imperfect people. Then, those imperfect people are to band together to help one another grow to spiritual maturity. Salvation in Christ, and growth to Christian maturity. Warts and all.

I.   **Review:** Fill in the blanks to bring the chart up to date with this era.

### Story of the New Testament

| ERA | FIGURE | LOCATION | STORYLINE SUMMARY |
|---|---|---|---|
| | | | Jesus comes in fulfillment of the Old Testament _____ of a savior, and offers _____ and the true Kingdom of God. While some accept Him, most _____ Him, and He is crucified, buried, and resurrected. |
| _____ | _____ | _____ | |

| ERA | FIGURE | LOCATION | STORYLINE SUMMARY |
|---|---|---|---|
| ———— | ———— | ———— | To be supplied later. |

II. **Storyline Summary:** *Peter*, shortly after the *ascension* of Jesus, is used by God to *establish* the *Church*, God's next major plan for man.

| ERA | SUMMARY |
|---|---|
| *Church:* | *Peter*, shortly after the _____ of Jesus, is used by God to _____ the _____, God's next major plan for man. |

III. **Expansion:** There are four major subjects in the Church Era:

1. Creation
2. Growth
3. Persecution
4. Transition

**1. Creation: Birth of the Church** (Acts 1-5).

The birthplace of the Church is Jerusalem. After His death, burial, and resurrection, Jesus instructs His disciples to wait in Jerusalem until they receive the power of the Holy Spirit, and then to be witnesses to Him in Jerusalem (their city), Judea and Samaria (the surrounding provinces), and the remotest part of the earth (the rest of the world). Then, Jesus ascends into heaven right before their eyes. Shortly after that, on the Jewish feast day of Pentecost, the Holy Spirit comes upon Jesus' disciples. While they are gathered in a house, a sound like a violent rushing wind fills the place, and flames of fire rest on each disciple, and they are filled with the Holy Spirit. They begin speaking in different foreign languages, with the result that many of the Jews from different parts of the world hear them speak in their own language. This and other notable miracles associated with the *birth of the Church* take place in the early days as the number of converts to Christianity increases rapidly in Jerusalem.

### 2. Growth: Organization of the Church (Acts 6).

As the number of converts increases, some measures are taken for the *organization of the Church*, giving structure to their activities and responsibilities. Peter organizes a relief effort for needy Christians. Those who have possessions can sell them and give the money to the Apostles, who distribute it according to the needs. Then, deacons are chosen to look after the material needs of the Church while the Apostles attend to the spiritual needs.

### 3. Persecution: The first Christian martyr (Acts 7).

Stephen, one of the early preachers, is arrested by the Jewish leaders for preaching about Jesus. When he does not recant his message, but presses it further, the Jews stone him to death on the spot, making Stephen *the first Christian martyr*. This incident kicks off a round of persecution against new Christians which is so severe that many of them have to flee Jerusalem for their very lives. As they do, they take the message of the Gospel with them to the surrounding provinces of Judea and Samaria.

### 4. Transition: A missionary to Gentiles (Acts 8-12).

A zealous Pharisee, Saul of Tarsus, looks after the cloaks of those who stone Stephen. Shortly afterward, he is journeying to Damascus to find and persecute other Christians, when Jesus appears to him from heaven, and Saul is converted to Christianity. Jesus changes Saul's name to Paul, and he becomes known as the Apostle Paul. Jesus expressly tells Paul that he will become *a missionary to the Gentiles*. Shortly after that, the Apostle Peter has a vision in which the Lord tells him that the message of the Gospel is to be taken to the Gentiles also. This marks a transition in the nature of the Church because, up to this time, the message has been circulated exclusively to Jews.

## Self Test

### A. Four Major Subjects of the Church Era
(Write in the descriptions from the options at right.)

*Creation* _____    Organization of the Church.

*Growth* _____    A missionary to Gentiles.

*Persecution* _____    Birth of the Church.

*Transition* _____    The first Christian martyr.

### B. Storyline Summary
(Fill in the blanks from memory).

| ERA | SUMMARY |
|-----|---------|
| *Church:* | *Peter*, shortly after the _____ of Jesus, is used by God to _____ the _____, God's next major plan for man. |

### C. Arc of Bible History (Fill in the name of the Eras.)

| | | |
|---|---|---|
| 1.<br>C_____ | 5.<br>J_____ | 9.<br>S_____ |
| 2.<br>P_____ | 6.<br>K_____ | 10.<br>G_____ |
| 3.<br>E_____ | 7.<br>E_____ | 11.<br>C_____ |
| 4.<br>C_____ | 8.<br>R_____ | 12. |

**D. The Geography of the Church Era**
(Draw an arrow from Jerusalem into Samaria, and one from Jerusalem into Judea, to represent the geographical movement of the Church Era.)

**E. Story of the Bible** (Fill in the blanks.)

| ERA | FIGURE | LOCATION | STORYLINE SUMMARY |
|---|---|---|---|
| _____ | _____ | _____ | Adam is created by God, but he _____, and _____ God's original _____ for man. |
| _____ | _____ | _____ | Abraham is _____ by God to "father" a _____ to _____ God to the world. |
| _____ | _____ | _____ | Moses _____ the Hebrew people from _____ in Egypt, and then gives them the _____. |
| _____ | _____ | _____ | Joshua leads the _____ of the _____ _____. |

| ERA | FIGURE | LOCATION | STORYLINE SUMMARY |
|---|---|---|---|
| ———— | ———— | ———— | Samson and others were chosen as _____ to _____ the people for _____ _____ rebellious years. |
| ———— | ———— | ———— | David, the greatest king in the new _____, is followed by a succession of mostly _____ kings, and God eventually _____ Israel for her sin, sending her into exile. |
| ———— | ———— | ———— | Daniel gives _____, and encourages _____ among the _____ for the next seventy years. |
| ———— | ———— | ———— | Ezra _____ the people back from _____ to rebuild _____. |
| ———— | ———— | ———— | Pharisees and others _____ the Israelites in _____ for the next _____ years. |
| ———— | ———— | ———— | Jesus comes in fulfillment of the Old Testament _____ of a savior, and offers _____ and the true Kingdom of God. While some accept Him, most _____ Him, and He is crucified, buried, and resurrected. |
| ———— | ———— | ———— | Peter, shortly after the _____ of Jesus, is used by God to _____ the _____, God's next major plan for man. |

# THE MISSIONS ERA
## (Acts 13–28)

A missionary ministering the South Sea Islands was teaching his people about Christmas. "The giving of gifts is a spontaneous act of celebration over an extremely joyous event. And that," he explained, "is why many people give gifts to others at Christmas time. It is an act of celebration over the joyous occasion of the birth of Christ."

Following this teaching, one of the young men wanted to give the missionary a gift for Christmas, but since it was a very poor island, presents were not readily available.

On Christmas morning, a knock came at the hut of the missionary. At the door, he found the young man, who then gave him an extremely rare and particularly beautiful sea shell which was found only at the distant end of the island.

The missionary thanked the young man for giving him such a rare and beautiful gift from such a distance, to which the young man replied, "Long walk part of gift."

What a beautiful sentiment. "Long walk part of gift." Such was also true of the Apostle Paul who gave up a life of comfort and safety, and took upon himself the arduous life of a missionary to take the message of the Gospel to the Gentile people in the surrounding nations.

I. **Review:** Fill in the blanks to bring the chart up to date with this era.

## Story of the New Testament

| ERA | FIGURE | LOCATION | STORYLINE SUMMARY |
|---|---|---|---|
| _____ | _____ | _____ | Jesus comes in fulfillment of the Old Testament _____ of a savior, and offers _____ and the true Kingdom of God. While some accept Him, most _____ Him, and He is crucified, buried, and resurrected. |
| _____ | _____ | _____ | Peter, shortly after the _____ of Jesus, is used by God to _____ the _____, God's next major plan for man. |
| _____ | _____ | _____ | To be supplied later. |

II. **Storyline Summary:** *Paul expands* the Church into the *Roman* empire during the next two *decades*.

| ERA | SUMMARY |
|---|---|
| *Missions:* | *Paul* _____ the Church into the _____ empire during the next two _____. |

III. **Expansion:** There are four major subjects in the Mission Era:

    1. First Missionary Journey
    2. Second Missionary Journey
    3. Third Missionary Journey
    4. Trials and imprisonment

1. **First Missionary Journey: Galatia for two years**
   (Acts 13-14).

In Paul's first missionary journey, he and Barnabas are selected by the Holy Spirit to travel to Galatia to take the Gospel to Gentiles living there. They depart from Antioch, the point of departure for all three missionary journeys, and are in *Galatia for two years*, experiencing encouraging results. After they return to Jerusalem, a council is held amid much controversy, which determines that the Gentiles do not have to become Jewish in addition to becoming Christians.

2. **Second Missionary Journey: Greece for three years**
   (Acts 15-17).

Paul leaves from Antioch to visit the believers from his first journey. However, he receives a vision of a man in Macedonia (Greece), and changes his plans, going to Greece with the Gospel message for the Gentiles there. He travels in *Greece for three years*.

3. **Third Missionary Journey: Asia for four years**
   (Acts 18-21).

Again, Paul leaves to encourage the believers from his first two trips, and to spread the message of the Gospel into Asia. He has great success and great opposition. In Ephesus, the whole city breaks out in riot over his visit. Though Paul is warned that he will be imprisoned upon his return to Jerusalem, he returns anyway, after being in *Asia for four years*, and is immediately arrested.

4. **Trials and Imprisonment: Roman prison for two years**
   (Acts 22-28).

Jewish leaders in Jerusalem have Paul arrested on false charges. Since his life is threatened there, even under guard, he is moved to Caesarea, the Roman capitol in the area. There, he is tried under three men: Felix, Festus, and Agrippa. In order to thwart a miscarriage of justice in the process, Paul exercises his right as a Roman citizen to take his case before Caesar in Rome. He is taken to Rome, but his case never comes to trial. After being in a *Roman prison for two years*, it is said he was beheaded (the established means of execution for a Roman citizen).

## Self Test

### A. Four Major Subjects of the Missions Era

*First Missionary* _____ Roman prison for two years.
*Journey*

*Second Missionary* _____ Galatia for two years.
*Journey*

*Third Missionary* _____ Asia for four years.
*Journey*

*Trials and* _____ Greece for three years.
*Imprisonment*

### B. Storyline Summary (Fill in the blanks from memory).

| ERA | SUMMARY |
|---|---|
| *Missions:* | *Paul* _____ the Church into the _____ empire during the next two _____. |

### C. Arc of Bible History (Fill in the name of the Eras.)

| 1. C_____ | 5. J_____ | 9. S_____ |
|---|---|---|
| 2. P_____ | 6. K_____ | 10. G_____ |
| 3. E_____ | 7. E_____ | 11. C_____ |
| 4. C_____ | 8. R_____ | 12. M_____ |

## D. The Geography of the Missions Era

(Draw an arrow from Antioch to Galatia and put a 1 next to it. Draw an arrow from Antioch to Greece and put a 2 next to it. Draw an arrow from Antioch to Asia and put a 3 next to it. This represents the geographical movement of Paul's missionary journeys. Now, draw an arrow from Caesarea to Rome and put a 4 next to it to represent Paul's trials and imprisonment during the Missions Era.

## E. Story of the Bible (Fill in the blanks.)

| ERA | FIGURE | LOCATION | STORYLINE SUMMARY |
|---|---|---|---|
| _____ | _____ | _____ | Adam is created by God, but he _____, and _____ God's original _____ for man. |
| _____ | _____ | _____ | Abraham is _____ by God to "father" a _____ to _____ God to the world. |
| _____ | _____ | _____ | Moses _____ the Hebrew people from _____ in Egypt, and then gives them the _____. |

| ERA | FIGURE | LOCATION | STORYLINE SUMMARY |
|---|---|---|---|
| _____ | _____ | _____ | Joshua leads the _____ of the _____ _____. |
| _____ | _____ | _____ | Samson and others were chosen as _____ to _____ the people for _____ _____ rebellious years. |
| _____ | _____ | _____ | David, the greatest king in the new _____, is followed by a succession of mostly _____ kings, and God eventually _____ Israel for her sin, sending her into exile. |
| _____ | _____ | _____ | Daniel gives _____, and encourages _____ among the _____ for the next seventy years. |
| _____ | _____ | _____ | Ezra _____ the people back from _____ to rebuild _____. |
| _____ | _____ | _____ | Pharisees and others _____ the Israelites in _____ for the next _____ years. |
| _____ | _____ | _____ | Jesus comes in fulfillment of the Old Testament _____ of a savior, and offers _____ and the true Kingdom of God. While some accept Him, most _____ Him, and He is crucified, buried, and resurrected. |

| ERA | FIGURE | LOCATION | STORYLINE SUMMARY |
|---|---|---|---|
| _____ | _____ | _____ | Peter, shortly after the _____ of Jesus, is used by God to _____ the _____, God's next major plan for man. |
| _____ | _____ | _____ | Paul _____ the Church into the _____ empire during the next two _____. |

# THE EPISTLES

## *(Romans – Revelation)*

In a *Reader's Digest* article entitled, "Send Someone a Smile," a captivating story is told:

One day shortly after my third child was born, I received a note from another young mother, a friend of mine who lived just three blocks from me. We hadn't seen each other all winter.

"Hi, friend," she wrote. "I think of you often. Someday we'll have time to spend together like in the old days. Keep plugging. I know you're a super mother. See you soon, I hope." It was signed: "Your friend on hold, Sue Ann."

The few words lifted my spirits and added a soothing ointment of love to a hectic day. I remember thinking, Thanks, Sue Ann. I needed that.

When I went out to mail a note, I noticed a neighbor checking his mailbox. Mr. Williams' head drooped and his pace seemed slower as the shuffled back to his house empty-handed. I hurried back into my own house because I could hear my baby crying, but I couldn't get Mr. Williams off my mind. It wasn't a check he was waiting for; he was quite well-to-do. He was probably looking for some love in his mailbox. While Meagan drew a picture of a mailbox with a smile in it and Tami drew a rainbow, I wrote a little note. "We are your secret admirers," it began. We added a favorite story and a poem. "Expect to hear from us often," I wrote on the envelope.

The next day my children and I watched Mr. Williams take out his mail and open the envelope right in the driveway. Even at a distance, we could see he was smiling.

My mind began reeling when I thought of all the people who could use smiles in their mailboxes. What about the 15-year-old Down's-syndrome girl near my parents whose birthday was coming up? The people in the rest home near our house? The invalid woman in our old neighborhood? The endless people I didn't even know who still believed in courtesy and in doing a good job in stores and offices and restaurants? Even on busy days I could find the time to write at least one note.

Notes can be short, and should be anonymous. At first, I wanted credit for the notes. But now, writing them in secret adds a sense of adventure. It's more fun. I once overheard talk of the Phantom Note Lady. They were discussing me, but they didn't know, and I wasn't telling.

Paul and other writers of the Bible had similar concerns for people they loved. They wrote letters both to church congregations and to individuals, to encourage them and to instruct them. In the providence of God, these letters were saved, and eventually compiled into the "Epistles" section of the Bible. The Epistles were simply letters.

You will recall that thirteen of the Epistles were written by the Apostle Paul while the remaining nine had a number of different authors. The chart in the review section below shows the distinction between the Pauline Epistles and the General Epistles.

## I.   Review:

### Structure of the New Testament

| *Historical* | *Pauline* | *General* |
|---|---|---|
| Matthew | TO CHURCHES: | Hebrews |
| Mark | Romans | James |
| Luke | 1 Corinthians | 1 Peter |
| John | 2 Corinthians | 2 Peter |
| Acts | Galatians | 1 John |
| | Ephesians | 2 John |
| | Philippians | 3 John |
| | Colossians | Jude |
| | 1 Thessalonians | Revelation |
| | 2 Thessalonians | |
| | TO INDIVIDUALS: | |
| | 1 Timothy | |
| | 2 Timothy | |
| | Titus | |
| | Philemon | |

Our history study is now completed. From Matthew through Acts, we stretched out a time line for the history of the New Testament. Some of the Epistles were written during this time line, and some of them were written after the time line ends at the close of the book of Acts. This makes it a little confusing, and somewhat frustrating, because we wish that the Historical Books told all the history during the time the Epistles were being written. They don't, however, and we are left to piece together what history we can from references in the Epistles.

The following chart shows when the Epistles were written in relationship to the time recorded in the Historical Books. The numbers are the years after Christ's birth. The Gospels cover the time from Christ's birth to His death at approximately age thirty. Acts starts almost immediately after, and records events until about A.D. 60. We see then that Galatians was written during the time of the book of Acts, A.D. 48 specifically. 1 & 2 Thessalonians were written about A.D. 50, etc. Books in the second section are Pauline Epistles, and the books in the last section are the General Epistles.

## Time Line of the New Testament

*Historical Books*

| | | Gospels-Acts | | | | | post-Acts | |
|---|---|---|---|---|---|---|---|---|
| A.D. 0 | A.D. 30 | A.D. 48 | A.D. 50 | A.D. 53 | A.D. 60 | A.D. 62 | A.D. 67 | A.D. 95 |

*Pauline Epistles* ↑ ↑ ↑ ↑ ↑ ↑

| | | Galatians | 1 Thessalonians 2 Thessalonians | 1 Corinthians 2 Corinthians Romans | Ephesians Colossians Philemon Philippians | 1 Timothy Titus | 2 Timothy | |
|---|---|---|---|---|---|---|---|---|

*General Epistles* ↑ ↑ ↑ ↑

| | | James | | | | 1 Peter 2 Peter | Hebrews Jude | 1 John 2 John 3 John Revelation |
|---|---|---|---|---|---|---|---|---|

**II. Overview Summary:** The *Epistles* are letters to churches and to individuals to *encourage* them and *instruct* them in the Christian faith.

---

**REVIEW:**

The *Epistles* are letters to churches and to individuals to _____ them and _____ them in the Christian faith.

---

**III. Expansion:** There are four main topics to be dealt with in studying the Epistles:

1. The Nature of the Epistles
2. Pauline Epistles to Churches
3. Pauline Epistles to Individuals
4. General Epistles

**1. The Nature of the Epistles: Doctrine, then duty.**

Epistles are letters written to churches, individuals, or in some cases, general letters to the Christian public at large. They deal with specific problems and issues of the day, but do so in a way that the information is universal and timeless. The typical pattern is to write a section of doctrinal truth, and follow up with the practical implications of that truth. *Doctrine, then duty.* Principle, then practice.

**2. Pauline Epistles to Churches: Letters to local churches.**

Thirteen of the twenty two Epistles of the New Testament are written by the Apostle Paul. Nine of these are *letters to local churches*, and are named according to which church they are written.

(As you read the description of the book, notice the words in *italics*. Immediately following the description of each book, the description is repeated with a blank space in place of the *italic* word. Fill in the blank space.)

Romans: heavily doctrinal, with the most complete doctrine of *salvation* by grace through faith in all the Bible.

Romans: heavily doctrinal, with the most complete doctrine of _____ by grace through faith in all the Bible.

1 & 2 Corinthians: heavily practical, dealing with a series of specific *problems* in the Corinthian Church.

1 & 2 Corinthians: heavily practical, dealing with a series of specific _____ in the Corinthian Church.

Galatians: written to some of Paul's first converts, refuting *legalism*.

Galatians: written to some of Paul's first converts, refuting _____.

Ephesians: deals with the believer's *position* in Christ, and its practical implications.

Ephesians: deals with the believer's _____ in Christ, and its practical implications.

Philippians: a warm letter of *joy* despite trials.

Philippians: a warm letter of _____ despite trials.

Colossians: the *preeminence* of Christ is its major theme.

Colossians: the _____ of Christ is its major theme.

1 & 2 Thessalonians: very personal letters dealing with specific issues in the Thessalonian Church, including *prophecy* and *practical* living.

1 & 2 Thessalonians: very personal letters dealing with specific issues in the Thessalonian Church, including _____ and _____ living.

## 3. Pauline Epistles to Individuals: Letters to individuals and pastors.

Four of Paul's letters are written *to individuals and pastors*, named according to whom they were written.

1 & 2 Timothy: two letters to a young pastor in Ephesus. The first letter *counsels* him on local church issues, and the second *encourages* him to remain strong in the faith in the midst of trials.

1 & 2 Timothy: two letters to a young pastor in Ephesus. The first leter _____ him on local church issues, and the second _____ him to remain strong in the faith in the midst of trials.

Titus: written to the pastor of the church on the island of Crete, it deals largely with local church issues, including the *qualifications* for church leaders.

Titus: written to the pastor of the church on the island of Crete, it deals largely with local church issues, including the _____ for church leaders.

Philemon: written to a slave owner, it urges lenient treatment of a runaway *slave* who has become a Christian and is returning to his Christian master.

Philemon: written to a slave owner, it urges lenient treatment of a runaway _____ who has become a Christian and is returning to his Christian master.

## 4. General Epistles: Letters to Christian public.

Written by various authors, the nine General Epistles are *letters to the Christian public* at large (with the exception of 2 & 3 John). They are usually named according to their authorship.

Hebrews: heavily *doctrinal*, this book draws largely on Old Testament truth in teaching New Testament truth to a Jewish audience.

Hebrews: heavily _____, this book draws largely on Old Testament truth in teaching New Testament truth to a Jewish audience.

James: an incisive and practical treatment of the proper outworking of Christian *faith* in everyday life.

James: an incisive and practical treatment of the proper outworking of Christian _____ in everyday life.

1 & 2 Peter: written to believers scattered throughout Asia and Galatia, it deals with proper response to *suffering* and opposition.

1 & 2 Peter: written to believers scattered throughout Asia and Galatia, it deals with proper response to _____ and opposition.

1, 2, 3 John: letters from the Apostle John dealing with the *love* of God, and its outworking in Christians' lives.

1, 2, 3 John: letters from the Apostle John dealing with the _____ of God, and its outworking in Christians' lives.

Jude: a brief but powerful book *warning* against ungodly living.

Jude: a brief but powerful book _____ against ungodly living.

Revelation: a giant of a book, heavily prophetical, dealing with the nature and chronology of the *end times*.

Revelation: a giant of a book, heavily prophetical, dealing with the nature and chronology of the _____.

## Review
(Match the book with the description.)

### 1. Pauline Epistles to Churches:

a. Colossians        _____ heavily doctrinal, with the most complete doctrine of *salvation* by grace through faith in all the Bible.

b. Ephesians        _____ heavily practical, dealing with a series of specific *problems* in the Corinthian Church.

c. Galatians        _____ written to some of Paul's first converts, refuting *legalism*.

d. 1-2 Corinthians        _____ deals with the believer's *position* in Christ, and its practical implications.

e. Romans        _____ a warm letter of *joy* despite trials.

f. 1-2 Thessalonians        _____ the *preeminence* of Christ is its major theme.

g. Philippians          _____ very personal letters dealing with specific issues in the Thessalonian Church, including *prophecy* and *practical* living.

## 2. Pauline Epistles to Individuals:

a. Philemon          _____ two letters to a young pastor in Ephesus. The first letters *counsels* him on local church issues, and the second *encourages* him to remain strong in the faith in the midst of trials.

b. 1-2 Timothy          _____ written to the pastor of the church on the island of Crete, it deals largely with local church issues, including the *qualifications* for church leaders.

c. Titus          _____ written to a slave owner, it urges lenient treatment of a runaway *slave* who has become a Christian and is returning to his Christian master.

## 3. General Epistles:

a. Revelation          _____ heavily *doctrinal*, this book draws largely on Old Testament truth in teaching New Testament truth to a Jewish audience.

b. 1, 2, 3 John          _____ an incisive and practical treatment of the proper outworking of Christian *faith* in everyday life.

c. Hebrews          _____ written to believers scattered throughout Asia and Galatia, it deals with proper response to *suffering* and opposition.

d. 1-2 Peter          _____ letters from the Apostle John dealing with the *love* of God, and its outworking in Christians' lives.

e. James                    _____ a brief but powerful book
                            *warning* against ungodly living.

f. Jude                     _____ a giant of a book, heavily
                            prophetical, dealing with the nature
                            and chronology of the *end times*.

## Self Test

## Four Main Distinctions To Be Dealt With in Studying the Epistles (Write in the descriptions from the options at right.)

*The Nature of* _____ Letters to individuals and
*the Epistles*                        pastors.

*Pauline Epistles* _____ Letters to local churches.
*to Churches*

*Pauline Epistles* _____ Letters to Christian public
*to Individuals*

*General Epistles* _____ Doctrine, then duty.

Congratulations! You have just completed a basic overview of the Story of the Bible, all sixty six books! From the "Historical" books of the Old and New Testaments, you have learned: all the main Eras, all the central Figures, and the main Locations of geography, all tied together with a Storyline Summary of the chronological Story of the Bible. You have also learned where the other books, the "Poetical" and "Prophetical" books of the Old Testament and the "Epistles" of the New Testament, fit into that chronological Story of the Bible.

You are now ready for the next section which will give you an overview of the Eight Great Subjects of Scripture

# THE
# EIGHT
# GREAT
# SUBJECTS
# OF
# SCRIPTURE

# TWENTY

# THE EIGHT GREAT SUBJECTS OF SCRIPTURE

 The Bible is more than history. If you would know the Bible, you must go beyond the historical study of its teachings . . . and taking that plunge is not an easy one. One day Harry Cohen, the head of Columbia studios in Hollywood, was in a conversation with his brother Jack, who suggested to Harry that they produce a Biblical epic. "What do you know about the Bible?" cried Harry. "I'll lay you fifty dollars you don't even know the Lord's Prayer." After a moment's thought, Jack began, "Now I lay me down to sleep . . ." and recited the well-known child's bedtime prayer. Harry pulled fifty dollars out of his pocket. "Well, I'll be!" he said, as he handed the money to his brother. "I didn't think you knew it."

There have been many approaches tried to mastering the teaching of the Bible, some more successful than others. Menelik II was the emperor of Ethiopia from 1889 until 1913, and he had one eccentricity. If he felt ill, he was convinced that he had only to eat a few pages of the Bible in order to feel better. This odd behavior did him little harm, as long as his literary consumption was kept at a modest level. However, in December 1913 he was recovering from a stroke, when he suddenly felt extremely ill. On his instructions the complete Book of Kings was torn from the Bible and fed to him, page by page. He died before he finished.

Our approach should be more effective and less painful.

When you add all the authors and all the books of the Bible together, and then boil them down to their irreducible minimum, what does the Bible teach? What subjects does it cover, and what does it say about each subject? When you add Moses, David, Jesus, and Paul together, what did they teach about God, Christ, angels, the future? As you begin to answer that question, you are trafficking in the subject known as "Bible doctrine."

It is difficult to get two people to agree on all points of doctrine. There is an old Irish proverb that goes something like:

> O Lord, turn the hearts of our enemies.
> And if you can't turn their hearts,
> Then turn their ankles,
> So we can know them by their limp.

There are many people limping, in the eyes of others, over certain doctrinal distinctions. However, there is a basic body of doctrine that nearly all Christians have historically agreed upon. It is that body that we will focus upon in this section.

Depending on how finely you split the hairs, different Bible scholars have come up with different numbers of minimum subjects. For the purpose of our study, we will use eight. The eight great subjects of Scripture are listed below. Almost every teaching of the Bible is in a subdivision of one of these subjects, or doctrines.

### The Eight Great Subjects of Scripture

1. The Bible
2. God
3. Christ
4. Holy Spirit
5. Angels
6. Man
7. Salvation
8. Future Things

As you read the following descriptions, note that, to help you remember the doctrine, a symbol has been assigned to each one.

1. **The Bible,** symbolized by a book, deals with the *origin and nature of the Scriptures.* How did we get them? Are they reliable? Are they the word of God?

2. **God the Father,** symbolized by the crown of a king, deals with the *first person of the Trinity.* Who is He, what is He like, and what is our relationship to Him?

3. **Christ,** symbolized by the Lamb of God, deals with Jesus of Nazareth, *the second person of the Trinity.* Was He a man? Was He God? Is He alive today? Is He coming to earth again?

4. **Holy Spirit,** *the third person of the Trinity,* is symbolized by a dove. Is He a personal being, or the religious equivalent of "school spirit?"

5. **Angels,** symbolized by a righteous angel and the devil, investigates the reality of *the spirit world.* What about guardian angels? What about demon possession and Satan worship?

6. **Man,** symbolized by an individual, investigates the *origin, nature and destiny of humanity.* Was he created, or did he evolve? Does he have a soul? Does the soul live forever?

7. **Salvation**, symbolized by a lifesaver, deals with *the afterlife, heaven, hell,* and whether or not it is safe to die.

8. **Future Things**, symbolized by an hourglass, looks into *Biblical prophecy,* and what the Bible says about future events, the end of the world, and eternity.

## Review

(Fill in the blanks from the options at the left.)

*Salvation* _____ The origin and nature of the Scriptures.

*Christ* _____ The first person of the Trinity.

*Future Things* _____ The second person of the Trinity.

*God the Father* _____ The third person of the Trinity.

*Bible* _____ The spirit world.

*Angels* _____ The origin, nature and destiny of humanity.

*Man* _____ The afterlife, heaven, hell.

*Holy Spirit* _____ Biblical prophecy.

To further help you remember these Eight Great Subjects, notice that the order suggests a logical progression. As you read the descriptions below, write the name of the doctrine next to the symbols on the following chart. By following the numbers and arrows on the chart, you can see the logical progression from one doctrine to the next. This will help you remember the Eight Great Subjects.

## 1. **The Bible**
*The Bible* is the foundation for what we learn about the other seven subjects, so it is first.

## 2. **God the Father**
*God the Father* is the first member of the Trinity.

## 3. **Christ**
*Christ* is the second member of the Trinity.

## 4. **Holy Spirit**
The *Holy Spirit* is the third member of the Trinity.

## 5. **Angels**
*Angels* are lower than God, but higher than man, so are placed between God and man.

## 6. **Man**
*Man* is made in the image of God.

## 7. **Salvation**
*Salvation* is offered by God to man through faith.

## 8. **Future Things**
*Future Things* are a prophetic record of things that will happen in the future.

## The Eight Great Subjects of Scripture

## Review
## The Eight Great Subjects of Scripture
(Fill in from memory the name of each doctrine.)

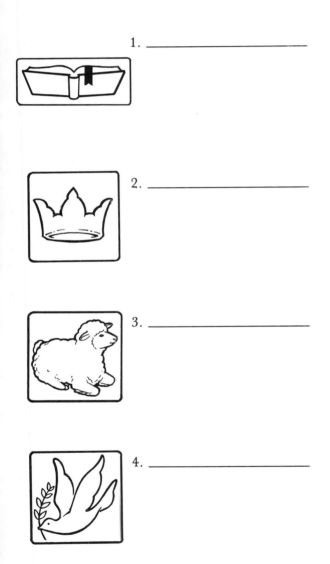

1. _____

2. _____

3. _____

4. _____

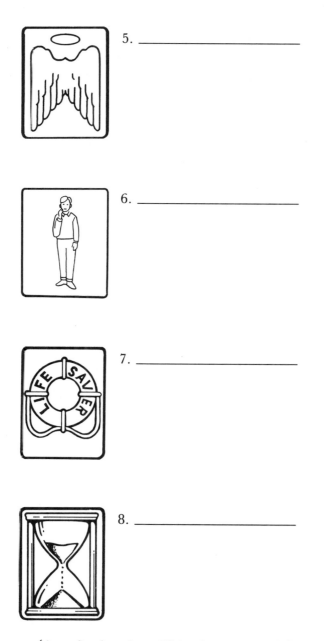

5. _____

6. _____

7. _____

8. _____

(As a final review, fill in the names of the eight doctrines. See the appendix to check answers.)

# The Eight Great Subjects of Scripture

2. _____

4. _____

3. _____

1. _____

5. _____

8. _____

6. _____

7. _____

Now, having established a base of the Eight Great Subjects of Scripture, we are ready to overview each doctrine separately in the chapters that follow.

# THE DOCTRINE OF
# THE BIBLE

It is not the things I don't understand about the Bible that bother me. It's the things I do understand.

Mark Twain

Let me tell you about the last flight of the "Lady Be Good." The Lady Be Good was an airplane, a bomber which had seen many successful wartime missions, and which was out one night on a familiar bombing run. As she flew back toward home base, the crew knew how long it usually took to make the trip.

Tonight, however, there was a powerful tailwind hurtling the massive craft through the air much faster than normal. As the crew plotted their position according to their instruments, they concluded that there must be something wrong with the dials. Their instruments and calculations told them it was time to break down through the cloud layer and land. Their watches and clocks, however, told them that this was impossible.

This placed them in a precarious position. If they believed their instruments, and came down through the cloud layer too soon, they might be spotted by the enemy and shot down with anti-aircraft fire. If they believed their clocks and came down too late, they would overshoot the airfield and perish in the desert beyond.

They chose to ignore the instruments and believe their gut-level hunch. They stayed up. They overshot the airfield and their plane was found days later, crashed in the desert. All crewmen had perished.

The story of the Lady Be Good is a microcosm of life. We are all on the Lady Be Good, and we are all in flight. In making the determination on where and when to land as our final destination, we have to make decisions. And for those decisions we must choose whether we look within ourselves for the answers, or whether we look outside ourselves . . . whether we trust our gut-level hunches, or whether we look for an instrument panel.

The Bible offers itself as the source of truth. The Bible presents itself as the great, cosmic "instrument panel." It tells us where we came from, where we are, and where we are going. It is up to us to decide whether or not we accept the "readings" we get from it.

The Bible does not defend itself. It was written to people who accepted its message, and therefore spends little time convincing its readers of its authenticity. Charles Spurgeon once said, "The Bible does not need to be defended any more than a caged lion needs to be defended. All we need to do is let it out of its cage, and it will defend itself."

The fundamental assertion that the Bible makes concerning itself is that, in spite of the human collaboration in the writing of it, the Bible is a revelation of God to man, that it was written without error, and that it can be trusted to reveal truth to us regarding God, man, life, and death.

As we begin our study of the Doctrine of the Bible, we will adopt a pattern that will be followed throughout the remainder of this section:

I. You will be asked to review the previous chapter.

II. You will then be given an overview of the doctrine, focusing on three things:
   A. The four major subdivisions of each doctrine, assigning a visual symbol to each.
   B. A brief definition for each subdivision, followed by an expansion.
   C. A central Scripture passage for each subdivision.

III. Three of the doctrines will require some additional attention which will be dealt with under the heading, "Further Considerations."

I. **Review:** Fill in the blanks.

**The Eight Great Subjects of Scripture**

1. **B** _____

2. **G** _____

3. **C** _____

4. **H**     **S** _____

5. **A** _____

6. **M** _____

7. **S** _____

8. **F**     **T** _____

II. **The four major subdivisions of the Doctrine of the Bible are:**

1. Revelation

2. Inspiration

3. Illumination

4. Interpretation

(As you read the definition of the doctrine subdivision, notice the words in italics. Immediately following the definition, it is repeated with a blank space in place of the italic word[s]. Fill in the blank space.)

**SYMBOL:**          **SUBDIVISION:**          **DEFINITION:**

1. Revelation:          The Bible was *revealed* to man by God.

Revelation:          The Bible was _____ to man by God.

God made known to man that which He wanted man to know. Some of the information related to present-day instruction on how to live and be rightly related to God and one's fellow man. Other information related to prophetic statements about the future. In Hebrews 3:7, it says, "Therefore, just as the Holy Spirit says . . ." and then it quotes a passage from Psalms, which was written by King David, indicating that the human writing was *revealed* by God.

**CENTRAL PASSAGE:**

Therefore, just as the Holy Spirit says, "Today, if you hear His voice . . ." (Hebrews 3:7)

| SYMBOL: | SUBDIVISION: | DEFINITION: |
|---|---|---|
|  | 2. Inspiration: | God saw to it that when men wrote down His revelation, they did so *without error.* |
| | Inspiration: | God saw to it that when men wrote down His revelation, they did so _____. |

Not all of God's revelation to man was recorded in the Bible. Some of it was very personal, between God and one individual. But for that part of God's revelation to man that was written down, God became involved in the recording process to such a degree that, while He did not dictate or override the individual author's personality, He saw to it that what they did record was what He wanted recorded and that it was *without error.*

**CENTRAL PASSAGE:**

. . . men moved by the Holy Spirit spoke from God. (2 Peter 1:21)

| SYMBOL: | SUBDIVISION: | DEFINITION: |
|---|---|---|
| | 3. Illumination: | The Holy Spirit must enable people to *understand* and *embrace* the truth of Scripture. |
| | Illumination: | The Holy Spirit must enable people to _____ and _____ the truth of Scripture. |

Man's natural ability to grasp and embrace the information in the Bible is limited. Much of it is spiritual information which he does not readily understand or accept. To overcome this fact, the Holy Spirit gradually illumines the receptive mind to *understand* and *embrace* more and more of the Bible, as the Christian matures in his spiritual walk.

**CENTRAL PASSAGE:**

Now we have received, not the spirit of the world, but the Spirit who is from God, that we might know the things freely given to us by God. (1 Corinthians 2:12)

| SYMBOL: | SUBDIVISION: | DEFINITION: |
|---|---|---|

4. Interpretation: We must be diligent *students* of the Scripture to understand its deeper teachings.

Interpretation: We must be diligent  of the Scripture to understand its deeper teachings.

Gaining a deeper grasp of the Bible is a two-way street. It is true that it will not happen unless the Holy Spirit illumines the mind of the Christian, but neither will it happen unless the Christian is diligent in his pursuit of Biblical knowledge. The more the Christian reads and studies the Bible, the more the Holy Spirit will illumine his mind, which encourages the *student* to read and study further.

**CENTRAL PASSAGE:**

Be diligent to present yourself approved to God as a workman who does not need to be ashamed, handling accurately the Word of God. (2 Timothy 2:15)

**The Doctrine of the Bible**
(Write the titles of the four subdivisions on the lines below.)

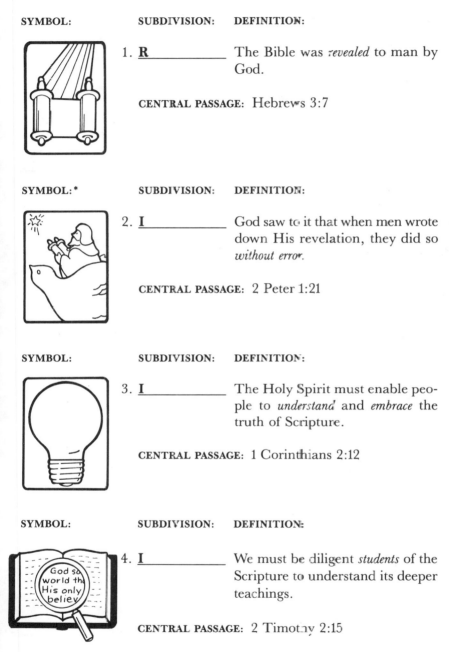

**SYMBOL:**

**SUBDIVISION:**   **DEFINITION:**

1. **R**_____   The Bible was *revealed* to man by God.

**CENTRAL PASSAGE:** Hebrews 3:7

**SYMBOL:** \*

**SUBDIVISION:**   **DEFINITION:**

2. **I**_____   God saw to it that when men wrote down His revelation, they did so *without error*.

**CENTRAL PASSAGE:** 2 Peter 1:21

**SYMBOL:**

**SUBDIVISION:**   **DEFINITION:**

3. **I**_____   The Holy Spirit must enable people to *understand* and *embrace* the truth of Scripture.

**CENTRAL PASSAGE:** 1 Corinthians 2:12

**SYMBOL:**

**SUBDIVISION:**   **DEFINITION:**

4. **I**_____   We must be diligent *students* of the Scripture to understand its deeper teachings.

**CENTRAL PASSAGE:** 2 Timothy 2:15

---

\*This symbol was chosen because the central passage says that holy men of old were born along by the Holy Spirit (symbolized by the dove) as they recorded God's revelation.

**The Doctrine of the Bible**
(Name the four subdivisions of the Doctrine of the Bible, and fill in the key word[s] in the definition.)

**SYMBOL:**     **SUBDIVISION:**     **DEFINITION:**

1. _____     The Bible was _____
to man by God.

**CENTRAL PASSAGE:** Hebrews 3:7

**SYMBOL:**     **SUBDIVISION:**     **DEFINITION:**

2. _____     God saw to it that when men wrote
down His revelation, they did so
_____.

**CENTRAL PASSAGE:** 2 Peter 1:21

**SYMBOL:**     **SUBDIVISION:**     **DEFINITION:**

3. _____     The Holy Spirit must enable people to _____ and
_____ the truth of Scripture.

**CENTRAL PASSAGE:** 1 Corinthians 2:12

**SYMBOL:**     **SUBDIVISION:**     **DEFINITION:**

4. _____     We must be diligent _____
of the Scripture to understand its
deeper teachings.

**CENTRAL PASSAGE:** 2 Timothy 2:15

## Self Test

(Fill in the blanks.)

1. **R**＿＿＿＿＿ The Bible was ＿＿＿＿＿＿＿ to man by God.

2. **I**＿＿＿＿＿ God saw to it that when men wrote down His revelation, they did so ＿＿＿＿＿＿＿＿＿.

3. **I**＿＿＿＿＿ The Holy Spirit must enable people to＿＿＿＿＿ and ＿＿＿＿＿＿ the truth of Scripture.

4. **I**＿＿＿＿＿ We must be diligent ＿＿＿＿＿＿ of the Scripture to understand its deeper teachings.

## The Eight Great Subjects of Scripture

(From memory, fill in the name of Doctrine number one.)

1. ＿＿＿＿＿＿

# THE DOCTRINE
# OF GOD

Between the probable and the proved
   there yawns a gap.
Afraid to jump, we stand,
   then see behind us sink the ground,
And worse, our very standpoint crumbling.
Desperate dawns our only hope:
To leap into the Word
   that opens up the shuttered universe."

So wrote Sheldon Van Auken in *A Severe Mercy*.

God is not to be found in the laboratory. He cannot be proved. But then, love is not to be found in the laboratory. Neither is courage, nor longing, nor hope. God is to be found in the courtroom. While data cannot be garnered to prove His existence, evidence can be amassed to demonstrate the probability of His existence. There *is* a gap between the probable and the proved. But then, few things can be proved to the unbelieving mind. Unbelief never has enough proof.

C. S. Lewis readily admitted to his reluctance in accepting the existence of God. Yet, he kept an open mind in the investigation of the evidence, and found himself being convinced in spite of himself. He wrote in his book, *Surprised by Joy*, that he was teaching at Magdalen College at the University of Oxford when he had an encounter with an atheist intellectual.

Early in 1926 the hardest boiled of all the atheists I ever knew sat in my room on the other side of the fire and remarked that the evidence for the historicity of the Gospels was really surprisingly good. "Rum thing," he went on. "Rum thing. It almost looks as if it had really happened once." To understand the shattering impact of it, you would need to know the man (who has certainly never since shown any interest in Christianity). If he, the cynic of cynics, the toughest of the toughs, were not—as I would still have put it—"safe," where could I turn? Was there then no escape?

You must picture me alone in that room at Magdalen, night after night, feeling, whenever my mind lifted even for a second from my work, the steady, unrelenting hand of Him whom I so earnestly desired not to meet. That which I greatly feared had at last come upon me. In the Trinity Term of 1929 I gave in, and admitted that God was God, and knelt and prayed: perhaps, that night, the most dejected and reluctant convert in all England. I did not then see what is now the most shining and obvious thing; the Divine humility which will accept a convert even on such terms. The Prodigal Son at least walked home on his own feet. But who can duly adore the Love which will open the high gates to a prodigal who is brought in kicking, struggling, resentful, and darting his eyes in every direction for a chance of escape?"

If you look for God in the laboratory, you will not find Him. If you look for Him in the courtroom, the amount of evidence can be very satisfying—enough to give a reasonable doubt about a universe without Him, and make it reasonable to believe in Him.

**I.    Review:** Fill in the blanks.

## The Doctrine of the Bible

1. **R**_____

2. **I**_____

3. **I**_____

4. **I**_____

**II.** **The four major subdivisions of the Doctrine of God are:**

 1. Existence

 2. Attributes

 3. Sovereignty

 4. Trinity

(As you read the definition of the doctrine subdivision, notice the words in italics. Immediately following the definition, it is repeated with a blank space in place of the italic word[s]. Fill in the blank space.)

| SYMBOL: | SUBDIVISION: | DEFINITION: |

1. Existence:     God *exists*.

   Existence:     God _____ .

In a scientific culture, some are reluctant to believe in a being that they cannot see, hear, smell, taste, or touch. However, God cannot be dealt with in the laboratory, He must be dealt with in the courtroom. It is impossible to generate *proof* of His existence, so we must look for *evidence* of His existence. While the Bible simply assumes that God *exists*, it also provides excellent evidence, so that believing in His existence is an intellectually reasonable thing to do.

**CENTRAL PASSAGE:**

For since the creation of the world His invisible attributes, His eternal power and divine nature, have been clearly seen, being understood through what has been made . . . (Romans 1:20)

| SYMBOL: | SUBDIVISION: | DEFINITION: |

2. Attributes:     The fundamental *characteristics* of God.

   Attributes:     The fundamental _____ of God.

God is a personal being, and as such, has individual *characteristics* that distinguish Him from all other beings. These characteristics are called "attributes." Some of His attributes are shared by mankind, since God created man after His personal image. These are called "personal" attributes. He has other characteristics, however, which go beyond man, and are true of Him alone. These are the attributes which define "deity" and are called "divine" attributes. We will look more closely at them later.

**CENTRAL PASSAGE:**

(Selected passages to be seen later.)

| SYMBOL: | SUBDIVISION: | DEFINITION: |
| --- | --- | --- |

3. Sovereignty:  God can do whatever He *wills*.

Sovereignty:  God can do whatever He _____.

God is all powerful, and has the ability to do whatever He wills. This sovereignty is only exercised in harmony with His goodness, righteousness, and other attributes, and it extends to the entirety of creation for all time. In His sovereignty, He has determined everything that has happened and will happen, and yet has done so in such a way that man has true "volition" or choice. This is one of the mysteries, or "unexplainable" things of Scripture.

**CENTRAL PASSAGE:**

For I know that the Lord is great,
And that our Lord is above all gods.
Whatever the Lord pleases, He does,
In heaven and in earth, in the seas and
in all the deeps. (Psalm 135:5-6)

| SYMBOL: | SUBDIVISION: | DEFINITION: |
| --- | --- | --- |

4. Trinity:  God is *three* persons, yet *one*.

Trinity:  God is _____ persons, yet

_____.

Another mystery of the Scripture is the Trinity. The Bible says distinctly that there is only one true God (Deuteronomy 6:4). But is also seems to say with equal clarity that there was a man, Jesus Christ, who claimed equality with God the Father, and there is someone called the Holy Spirit who is also equal with God the Father. How do you put that together? Historically, the concept has been termed the "Trinity." There is *one* God who exists in *three* persons. While it is impossible to give an illustration of the Trinity, the evidence remains and has been embraced as a fundamental teaching of Christianity from the beginning.

**CENTRAL PASSAGES:**

Hear, O Israel! The Lord is our God, the Lord is one! (Deuteronomy 6:4)

The grace of the Lord Jesus Christ, and the love of God, and the fellowship of the Holy Spirit, be with you all. (2 Corinthians 13:14)

### The Doctrine of God
(Write the titles of the four subdivisions on the lines below.)

| SYMBOL: | SUBDIVISION: | DEFINITION: |
|---|---|---|

1. **E**_____   God *exists*.

**CENTRAL PASSAGE:** Romans 1:20

| SYMBOL: | SUBDIVISION: | DEFINITION: |
|---|---|---|

2. **A**_____   The fundamental *characteristics* of God.

**CENTRAL PASSAGE:** Selected passages.

**SYMBOL:**        **SUBDIVISION:**     **DEFINITION:**

3. **S**_____ God can do whatever He *wills*.

       **CENTRAL PASSAGE:** Psalm 135:5-6

**SYMBOL:**        **SUBDIVISION:**     **DEFINITION:**

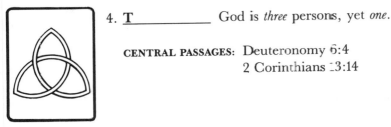

4. **T**_____ God is *three* persons, yet *one*.

       **CENTRAL PASSAGES:** Deuteronomy 6:4
                              2 Corinthians 13:14

**The Doctrine of God**
(Name the four subdivisions of the Doctrine of God, and fill in the key word[s] in the definition.)

**SYMBOL:**        **SUBDIVISION:**     **DEFINITION:**

1. _____ God _____.

       **CENTRAL PASSAGE:** Romans 1:20

**SYMBOL:**          **SUBDIVISION:**     **DEFINITION:**

2. _____     The fundamental _____
                     of God.

**CENTRAL PASSAGE:**  Selected passages.


**SYMBOL:**          **SUBDIVISION:**     **DEFINITION:**

3. _____     God can do whatever He _____.

**CENTRAL PASSAGE:**  Psalm 135:5-6


**SYMBOL:**          **SUBDIVISION:**     **DEFINITION:**

4. _____     God is _____ persons, yet
                     _____.

**CENTRAL PASSAGES:**  Deuteronomy 6:4
                      2 Corinthians 13:14


## Self Test

(Fill in the blanks.)

1. **E**_____     God _____.

2. **A**_____     The fundamental _____ of God.

3. **S**_____     God can do whatever He _____.

4. **T**_____     God is _____ persons, yet _____.

## III. Further Considerations of the Attributes of God:

The attributes of God require further consideration. While God has many attributes or characteristics, we will focus on six primary attributes. Three are divine attributes, and three are personal attributes.

### A. Divine Attributes

1. Omnipotence:  God is all *powerful*.
   CENTRAL PASSAGE: Job 42:2

2. Omnipresence:  God is *present* everywhere simultaneously.
   CENTRAL PASSAGE: Psalm 139:8

3. Omniscience:  God *knows* all things.
   CENTRAL PASSAGE: Psalm 139:4

**Review:**  Divine Attributes

1. Omnipotence:  God is all _____. (Job 42:2)

2. Omnipresence:  God is _____ everywhere simultaneously. (Psalm 139:8)

3. Omniscience:  God _____ all things. (Psalm 139:4)

### B. Personal Attributes

1. Holy:  God is *without evil*, and is only good.
   CENTRAL PASSAGE: Isaiah 5:16

2. Love:  God seeks the *best* for *others*.
   CENTRAL PASSAGE: 1 John 4:8

3. Just:  God applies righteous *consequences* equally to everyone.
   CENTRAL PASSAGE: Psalm 19:9

**Review:** Divine Attributes

    1. Holy:        God is _____, and
                        is only good.  (Isaiah 5:16)

    2. Love:        God seeks the _____ for _____.
                        (1 John 4:8)

    3. Just:        God applies righteous _____
                        equally to everyone. (Psalm 19:9)

## Self Test

A.  Match the six attributes of God with their definition.

Omnipotence _____      A.  God seeks the *best* for *others*.

Omnipresence _____      B.  God applies righteous *consequences*
                                 equally to everyone.

Omniscience _____      C.  God is *without evil* and only good.

Holy _____      D.  God is *present* everywhere simultan-
                               eously.

Love _____      E.  God *knows* all things.

Just _____      F.  God is all *powerful*.

B.  Fill in the blanks.

God's three divine attributes are:

1. _____

2. _____

3. _____

God's three personal attributes are:

1. _____

2. _____

3. _____

It is worth repeating that there are many more characteristics of God than these. These six were chosen because they were among the most striking and well-known attributes.

## The Eight Great Subjects of Scripture

(From memory, fill in the names of Doctrines one and two. See appendix for answers.)

2. _____

1. _____

# TWENTY-THREE

# THE DOCTRINE OF CHRIST

Attitudes about Jesus are varied, and often strongly held. From denying that a person named Jesus of Nazareth ever existed, to believing that He was God incarnate, people demonstrate their conviction about Him by ignoring Him or worshiping Him.

Perhaps the most popular concept of Jesus is that, while He was not divine, he was a great moral teacher and leader. While He is no more God than you or me, He is a wonderful example to follow.

This is a difficult concept to hold consistently. The reason is expressed skillfully by C. S. Lewis, who wrote in his book *Mere Christianity*:

> That is the thing we must not say. A man who was merely a man and said the sort of things that Jesus said would not be a great moral teacher. He would either be a lunatic on the level of a man who says he is a poached egg—or else he would be the devil of hell. You must make your choice. Either this man was, and is, the son of God; or else a madman or something worse. You can shut Him up for a fool, you can spit at Him and kill Him as a demon; or you can fall at His feet and call Him Lord and God. But let us not come with any patronizing nonsense about His being a great human teacher. He has not left that open to us. He did not intend to.

The position of the Bible is straightforward in presenting Jesus as divine, the Son of God, the second person of the Trinity.

He is fully man and fully God. If He were not man, He could not have died for our sins, and if He were not God, His death would have accomplished nothing.

To understand the Bible's position on Jesus, it must be grasped that Jesus is presented as the Messiah, the Savior of the world who was prophesied throughout the Old Testament, who would come to die for the sins of the world, and who would come again to establish righteousness in a new heaven and new earth.

**I.    Review:** Fill in the blanks.

### The Doctrine of the Bible

1. **R**_____

2. **I**_____

3. **I**_____

4. **I**_____

### The Doctrine of God

1. **E**_____

2. **A**_____

3. **S**_____

4. **T**_____

**II.   The four major subdivisions of the Doctrine of Christ are:**

1. Deity

2. Humanity

3. Resurrection

4. Return

(As you read the definition of the doctrine subdivision, notice the words in italics. Immediately following the definition, it is repeated with a blank space in place of the italic word[s]. Fill in the blank space.)

**SYMBOL:**             **SUBDIVISION:**     **DEFINITION:**

1. Deity:          Jesus of Nazareth was *God* incarnate.

Deity:          Jesus of Nazareth was _____ incarnate.

Though Jesus was man, He was also *God*. The second member of the Trinity existed before He was born as Jesus of Nazareth. Christ was active in the creation of the world and during the Old Testament. When the timing was right, the Christ, the second person of the Trinity, became incarnate as Jesus of Nazareth, but did not forfeit His divinity at any time.

**CENTRAL PASSAGE:**

In the beginning was the Word, and the Word was with God, and the Word was God. (John 1:1)

**SYMBOL:**          **SUBDIVISION:**     **DEFINITION:**

2. Humanity:        Christ was a *man*, Jesus of Nazareth.

   Humanity:        Christ was a _____, Jesus of Nazareth.

Though Jesus was God, He was also *man*. Christ took on the form of humanity, and though He did not sin, He tasted all other human experiences, including hunger, fatigue, and sorrow, etc. He was supernaturally conceived, was born of a virgin, and lived a fairly normal early life as a carpenter's son in Nazareth of Galilee. As a man, He was crucified, died, and buried.

**CENTRAL PASSAGE:**

And the Word became flesh, and dwelt among us, and we beheld His glory, glory as of the only begotten from the Father, full of grace and truth. (John 1:14)

**SYMBOL:**          **SUBDIVISION:**     **DEFINITION:**

3. Resurrection:    After being killed, Jesus was *raised* to life again.

   Resurrection:    After being killed, Jesus was _____ to life again.

After being falsely accused, and tried in a series of kangaroo courts, Jesus was subjected to the form of capital punishment reserved for non-Roman citizens. He was flogged, a savage punishment which, itself, killed sixty percent of its victims, and was nailed to a wooden cross where He died. Afterward, He was wrapped in burial clothes, and placed in a sealed tomb where He remained for three days. At the end of that time, a miraculous earthquake moved the stone from the mouth of the tomb to reveal that Jesus was *raised* from the dead after three days, just as He said He would be.

**CENTRAL PASSAGE:**

. . . who was declared with power to be the Son of God by the resurrection from the dead, according to the Spirit of holiness, Jesus Christ our Lord. (Romans 1:4)

**SYMBOL:**          **SUBDIVISION:**     **DEFINITION:**

4. Return:        Jesus will *return* to earth at some time in the future.

   Return:        Jesus will _____ to earth at some time in the future.

The picture of the Messiah in the Old Testament was an uncertain one. Some of the prophetic passages spoke of a humble servant Messiah, while other passages spoke of a glorious and powerful king. So stark was the contrast between these two kinds of passages that some Old Testament scholars thought there would be two Messiahs. With the additional revelation in the New Testament, we now know how to reconcile these passages. Jesus came the first time as a humble servant, and died for the sins of mankind. After He was resurrected, He ascended into heaven to sit at the right hand of God the Father. Some day in the future, and according to Biblical prophecy it could be soon, Jesus will *return* to earth as a powerful and glorious king, to institute righteousness on the earth.

**CENTRAL PASSAGE:**

. . . looking for the blessed hope and the appearing of the glory of our great God and Savior, Christ Jesus . . . . (Titus 2:13)

### The Doctrine of Christ
(Write the titles of the four subdivisions on the lines below.)

| SYMBOL: | SUBDIVISION: | DEFINITION: |
|---|---|---|

1. **D**_____ Jesus of Nazareth was *God* incarnate.

**CENTRAL PASSAGE:** John 1:1

| SYMBOL: | SUBDIVISION: | DEFINITION: |
|---|---|---|

2. **H**_____ Christ was a *man*, Jesus of Nazareth.

**CENTRAL PASSAGE:** John 1:14.

| SYMBOL: | SUBDIVISION: | DEFINITION: |
|---|---|---|

3. **R**_____ After being killed, Jesus was *raised* to life again.

**CENTRAL PASSAGE:** Romans 1:4

**SYMBOL:**      **SUBDIVISION:**    **DEFINITION:**

4. **R**_____ Jesus will *return* to earth at some time in the future.

**CENTRAL PASSAGE:** Titus 2:13

**The Doctrine of Christ**
(Name the four subdivisions of the Doctrine of Christ, and fill in the key word[s] in the definition.)

**SYMBOL:**      **SUBDIVISION:**    **DEFINITION:**

1. _____ Jesus of Nazareth was _____ incarnate.

**CENTRAL PASSAGE:** John 1:1

**SYMBOL:**      **SUBDIVISION:**    **DEFINITION:**

2. _____ Christ was a _____, Jesus of Nazareth.

**CENTRAL PASSAGE:** John 1:14.

**SYMBOL:**        **SUBDIVISION:**     **DEFINITION:**

3. _____  After being killed, Jesus was
                    _____ to life again.

**CENTRAL PASSAGE:**  Romans 1:4

**SYMBOL:**        **SUBDIVISION:**     **DEFINITION:**

4. _____  Jesus will _____ to
                    earth at some time in the future.

**CENTRAL PASSAGE:**  Titus 2:13

## Self Test

(Fill in the blanks.)

1. **D**_____  Jesus of Nazareth was _____ incarnate.

2. **H**_____  Christ was a _____, Jesus of Naza-
                  reth.

3. **R**_____  After being killed, Jesus was _____ to
                  life again.

4. **R**_____  Jesus will _____ to earth at some time
                  in the future.

## The Eight Great Subjects of Scripture

(From memory, fill in the names for Doctrines one through three. See appendix for the answers.)

2. _____

3. _____

1. _____

# TWENTY-FOUR

# THE DOCTRINE OF
# THE HOLY SPIRIT

The IRS has a "Conscience Fund: which receives anonymous contributions from people who have cheated the government out of money in the past and who want to make up for it to clear their conscience, but don't want to risk criminal prosecution. The Conscience Fund received a check for $500 from a man who included the following note:

I have not been able to sleep ever since I cheated you out of some money, so here is a check for $500. If I still can't sleep, I'll send you the rest.

In another example, a salesman called on a successful contractor with a bid for the materials for a large job the contractor was about to begin. He was invited into the contractor's office where they chatted for a moment before a secretary came and summoned the contractor into another office. Alone, the salesman noticed that there was a bid from a competitor's firm on the contractor's desk with all the numbers written clearly. The total amount of the bid was hidden, however, covered by a small orange juice can. Unable to contain his curiosity, the salesman picked up the orange juice can. When he did, thousands of BB's came pouring from the bottom of the can which had been cut out, flooded over the surface of the desk, and rained down on the floor. Without saying a word, the salesman turned, walked out of the office, and never returned.

We laugh at the first story and cringe at the second, because we see ourselves in both of them. We all have shortcomings and weakness. We all want to be more than we are. But we need help. Sometimes we need information. Sometimes we need assistance. Sometimes, we need to be challenged or confronted to change. This is a primary role of the Holy Spirit . . . to work with us in a mystical sort of way to become Christians, and then to grow as Christians. He transforms us from what we were like in the past, to what we should be like in the future. He is a friend, indeed, because He knows all about us, and loves us anyway. He commits himself to us to help us change . . . to be the sort of man or woman that we long to be, deep down in our souls.

I.     **Review:** Fill in the blanks.

### The Doctrine of the Bible

1. **R**_____

2. **I**_____

3. **I**_____

4. **I**_____

### The Doctrine of God

1. **E**_____

2. **A**_____

3. **S**_____

4. **T**_____

### The Doctrine of Christ

1. **D**_____

2. **H**_____

3. **R**_____

4. **R**_____

## II. The four major subdivisions of the Doctrine of the Holy Spirit are:

1. Personality

2. Deity

3. Salvation

4. Gifts

(As you read the definition of the doctrine subdivision, notice the words in italics. Immediately following the definition, it is repeated with a blank space in place of the italic word[s]. Fill in the blank space.)

SYMBOL:              SUBDIVISION:      DEFINITION:

1. Personality:    The Holy Spirit is a *personal* being, not an impersonal force.

   Personality:    The Holy Spirit is a_____ being, not an impersonal force.

The Holy Spirit is sometimes perceived as the religious equivalent of school spirit. This is not accurate. In the Bible, the Holy Spirit is treated as a person, and given the attributes of *personality*, such as emotions, actions, intellect, and relationships.

CENTRAL PASSAGE:

And do not grieve the Holy Spirit of God, by whom you were sealed for the day of redemption. (Ephesians 4:30)

SYMBOL:              SUBDIVISION:      DEFINITION:

2. Deity:          The Holy Spirit is *divine*, the third person of the Trinity.

   Deity:          The Holy Spirit is _____, the third person of the Trinity.

Not only is the Holy Spirit a personal being, He is also *divine*. He possesses divine attributes, such as omnipresence and omnipotence. He performed miracles which only God could do, such as the creation of the world and the miraculous conception of Jesus. In addition, He is associated on an equal plane with the other members of the Trinity.

CENTRAL PASSAGE:

The grace of the Lord Jesus Christ, and the love of God, and the fellowship of the Holy Spirit, be with you all. (2 Corinthians 13:14)

| SYMBOL: | SUBDIVISION: | DEFINITION: |
|---|---|---|

3. Salvation:      The Holy Spirit is *instrumental* in personal salvation.

Salvation:      The Holy Spirit is _____ in personal salvation.

The Holy Spirit plays the *instrumental* role in the personal salvation of individuals who become Christians. It is the Holy Spirit who enables us to see our sinfulness, and realize that we should turn from sin. It is the Holy Spirit who helps us see that, in order to become a Christian, we must believe in Jesus, ask Him to forgive us of our sins, to give us eternal life, and to commit our lives to living for Him.

**CENTRAL PASSAGE:**

Selected passages to be seen later.

[Note: The significance of the two baby cribs lies in an acrostic. There are five primary areas of involvement by the Holy Spirit in personal salvation: conviction, regeneration, indwelling, baptism, and sealing. The first letters from each of these words spells "CRIBS." We will study the "CRIBS" concept in more detail later.]

| SYMBOL: | SUBDIVISION: | DEFINITION: |
|---|---|---|

4. Gifts:      The Holy Spirit imparts *spiritual* abilities to Christians.

Gifts:      The Holy Spirit imparts _____ abilities to Christians.

God wants to use each of us to minister to others. The Holy Spirit gives us a special *spiritual* "gift" to minister to others. It is something we enjoy doing, and something at which we are effective. However, since God is working through us with this gift, the results must always be attributed to Him, and not ourselves. We must guard against two imbalances. We must not become discouraged if our results are meager, and we must not become inflated if our results are abundant. For in the true exercise of spiritual gifts, it is God who produces the results, whether meager or abundant.

**CENTRAL PASSAGE:**

Now there are varieties of gifts, but the same Spirit. But one and the same Spirit works all these things distributing to each one individually just as He wills. (1 Corinthians 12:4, 11)

**The Doctrine of the Holy Spirit**
(Write the titles of the four subdivisions on the lines below.)

**SYMBOL:**　　　　**SUBDIVISION:**　　**DEFINITION:**

1. **P**＿＿＿＿＿　The Holy Spirit is a *personal* being, not an impersonal force.

**CENTRAL PASSAGE:** Ephesians 4:30

**SYMBOL:**　　　　**SUBDIVISION:**　　**DEFINITION:**

2. **D**＿＿＿＿＿　The Holy Spirit is *divine*, the third person of the Trinity.

**CENTRAL PASSAGE:** 2 Corinthians 13:14

**SYMBOL:**         **SUBDIVISION:**    **DEFINITION:**

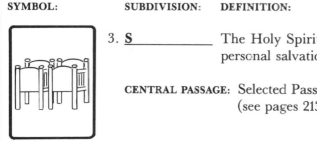

3. **S**_____   The Holy Spirit is *instrumental* in personal salvation.

    **CENTRAL PASSAGE:** Selected Passages
                    (see pages 213-214)

**SYMBOL:**         **SUBDIVISION:**    **DEFINITION:**

4. **G**_____   The Holy Spirit imparts *spiritual* abilities to Christians.

    **CENTRAL PASSAGE:** 1 Corinthians 12:4, 11

**The Doctrine of the Holy Spirit**
(Name the four subdivisions of the Doctrine of the Holy Spirit, and fill in the key word[s] in the definition.)

**SYMBOL:**         **SUBDIVISION:**    **DEFINITION:**

1. _____   The Holy Spirit is a_____ being, not an impersonal force.

    **CENTRAL PASSAGE:** Ephesians 4:30

**SYMBOL:**          **SUBDIVISION:**          **DEFINITION:**

2. _____     The Holy Spirit is _____,
                       the third person of the Trinity.

**CENTRAL PASSAGE:** 2 Corinthians 13:14

**SYMBOL:**          **SUBDIVISION:**          **DEFINITION:**

3. _____     The Holy Spirit is _____
                       in personal salvation.

**CENTRAL PASSAGE:** Selected Passages
                     (see pages 213-214)

**SYMBOL:**          **SUBDIVISION:**          **DEFINITION:**

4. _____     The Holy Spirit imparts
                       _____ abilities to
                       Christians.

**CENTRAL PASSAGE:** 1 Corinthians 12:4, 11

## Self Test

(Fill in the blanks.)

1. **P**_____     The Holy Spirit is a _____ being, not an
                      impersonal force.

2. **D**_____     The Holy Spirit is _____, the third person
                      of the Trinity.

3. **S**_____     The Holy Spirit is _____ in personal
                      salvation.

4. **G**_____     The Holy Spirit imparts _____
                      abilities to Christians.

## III. Further Considerations of the Holy Spirit's Work in Salvation:

The work of the Holy Spirit in personal salvation requires further consideration. There are five primary areas of involvement.

1. Conviction:   Revealing a *need* to *change*.

The Holy Spirit convinces a person of his *need* to *change* some thought, attitude, or action. This phenomenon is sometimes accompanied by an acute sense of guilt over wrongdoing.

CENTRAL PASSAGE:

And He (the Holy Spirit), when He comes, will convict the world concerning sin, and righteousness, and judgment. (John 16:8)

2. Regeneration:   Imparting a new spirit and *eternal life*.

According to the Bible, everyone lives forever, either with God in heaven, or separated from Him in hell. When a person becomes a Christian, the Holy Spirit imparts to him a new spirit and *eternal life* with God in heaven.

CENTRAL PASSAGE:

He saved us, not on the basis of deeds which we have done in righteousness, but according to His mercy, by the washing of regeneration and renewing by the Holy Spirit. (Titus 3:5)

3. Indwelling:   Living *within* a believer.

The Holy Spirit mysteriously "takes up residence" *within* a person when he becomes a believer, encouraging and strengthening him to live a proper lifestyle.

**CENTRAL PASSAGE:**

But you are not in the flesh, but in the Spirit, if indeed the Spirit of God lives in you. Now if anyone does not have the Spirit of Christ, he is not His. (Romans 8:9)

4. Baptism:    *Placing* a believer, spiritually, in the Body of Christ.

The "Body of Christ" is a term given to the totality of all believers in Him. To baptize means to *"place into."* Technically, to be baptized into the Body of Christ means to be a member of that spiritual organism.

**CENTRAL PASSAGE:**

For by one Spirit we were all baptized into one body, whether Jews or Greeks, whether slaves or free, and we were all made to drink of one Spirit. (1 Corinthians 12:13)

5. Sealing:    *Guaranteeing* the believer's relationship to God.

The Holy Spirit becomes the *guarantee* of our spiritual inheritance, to be fully realized when we die. It means that once a person has been regenerated, indwelt, and baptized into the Body of Christ, his position is secure, "sealed with the Holy Spirit of promise unto the day of redemption." (Ephesians 1:13)

**CENTRAL PASSAGE:**

In Him (Christ) you also trusted, after you heard the word of truth, the gospel of your salvation: in whom also, having believed, you were sealed with the Holy Spirit of promise. (Ephesians 1:13-14)

## Self Test

A.  The five works of the Holy Spirit in personal salvation are:

1. **C** _____

2. **R** _____

3. **I** _____

4. **B** _____

5. **S** _____

B.  Match the term with the definition:

Conviction _____

A.  Imparting a new spirit and *eternal life* with God.

Regeneration _____

B.  *Guaranteeing* the believer's relationship to God.

Indwelling _____

C.  Revealing a *need to change.*

Baptism _____

D.  Living *within* a believer.

Sealing _____

E.  *Placing* a believer, spiritually, in the Body of Christ.

## The Eight Great Subjects of Scripture

(From memory, fill in the names of the Doctrines one through four. See the appendix for the answers.)

2. _____

4. _____

3. _____

1. _____

# TWENTY-FIVE

# THE DOCTRINE
# OF ANGELS

In his book entitled *Angels*, Billy Graham tells the story of Dr. S. W. Mitchell, a well-known Philadelphia neurologist, who was awakened from sleep one night by a little girl, poorly dressed and very upset. She said her mother was very sick, and would he come right away. He followed the girl, and found the mother desperately ill with pneumonia. After attending her and arranging for medical care, he complimented the sick woman on the intelligence and persistence of her little daughter. As Reader's Digest reported in the original story, the woman looked at Dr. Mitchell strangely and then said, "My daughter died a month ago." She added, "Her shoes and coat are in the clothes closet there." Puzzled, Dr. Mitchell went to the closet and opened the door. There hung the very coat worn by the little girl who had brought him to care for her mother. It was warm and dry and could not possibly have been out in the inclement weather.

Might the "little girl" have been an angel, sent to aid the stricken mother?

Again, Rev. Graham tells the story of John G. Paton, a missionary in the New Hebrides Islands. One evening, natives surrounded the missionary compound with the intent of burning down the compound and killing Mr. Paton and his wife. The missionaries prayed fervently all night, and were surprised and relieved to witness the natives leaving the next morning.

A year later, The chief of the hostile tribe was converted to Christianity. He told the Patons that he and his tribe had fully intended to destroy the compound and kill the Patons that fateful night a year ago but had been stopped by the army of men surrounding the compound. "Who were all those men you had with you there?" the chief asked. "There were no men there; just my wife and I," replied Mr. Paton. The chief argued that they had seen many men standing guard—hundreds of big men in shining garments with drawn swords in their hands. They seemed to circle the mission station, so that the natives were afraid to attack.

Again, angels?

When the brilliant scholar, Mortimer Adler, undertook to edit *Great Books of the Western World* for the Encyclopedia Britannica Company, he included "Angels" as one of the great themes. Personally curious, Mr. Adler went on to write a book on angels, and in doing so, discovered that from before Aristotle's time to the present day, scholars and philosophers have taken angels seriously.

It is difficult to prove the existence and work of angels. They are not usually perceived by our five senses, and are therefore not subject to scientific strutiny. Nevertheless, they are found throughout the Bible, interwoven into many of the major events of Scripture.

**I.   Review:** Fill in the blanks.

### The Doctrine of the Bible

1. **R**_____

2. **I**_____

3. **I**_____

4. **I**_____

### The Doctrine of God

1. **E**_____

2. **A**_____

3. **S**_____

4. **T**_____

## The Doctrine of Christ

1. **D**_____

2. **H**_____

3. **R**_____

4. **R**_____

## The Doctrine of the Holy Spirit

1. **P**_____

2. **D**_____

3. **S**_____

4. **G**_____

II. **The four major subdivisions of the Doctrine of Angels are:**

1. Angels

2. Demons

3. Satan

 4. Defenses

(As you read the definition of the doctrine subdivision, notice the words in italics. Immediately following the definition, it is repeated with a blank space in place of the italic word[s]. Fill in the blank space.)

| SYMBOL: | SUBDIVISION: | DEFINITION: |
|---------|--------------|-------------|

1. Angels:    Ministering *spirits* from God.

   Angels:    Ministering _____ from God.

The Bible teaches that God uses a numberless army of angels to help execute His will in heaven and earth, and that among their duties is ministering to Christians. Perhaps this is where the concept of guardian angels came from. They are personal beings, *spirits* that God created before Adam and Eve, and are not "ghosts" of people who have died.

**CENTRAL PASSAGE:**

Are they (angels) not all ministering spirits sent out to render service for the sake of those who will inherit salvation? (Hebrews 1:14)

**SYMBOL:**  **SUBDIVISION:**  **DEFINITION:**

2. Demons:  Angels who *fell.*

Demons:  Angels who _____.

The Bible teaches that a large number of the "righteous angels" rebelled against God, and now form an evil army under the command of the devil, who uses them to further his will, which is counter to the will of God. This corruption is often referred to as the *"fall"* of these angels.

**CENTRAL PASSAGE:**

And angels who did not keep their proper domain, but left their own abode, He has reserved in everlasting chains under darkness for the judgment of the great day. (Jude 6)

**SYMBOL:**  **SUBDIVISION:**  **DEFINITION:**

3. Satan:  The highest angel who *fell.*

Satan:  The highest angel who _____.

The Bible teaches that Satan was originally the highest angel, but because of pride, *fell,* rebelling against God and leading many lesser angels to rebel against Him also. In doing this he became evil and corrupt. He is a real entity who oversees the forces of darkness in the world, and seeks to neutralize and overthrow the will of God.

**CENTRAL PASSAGE:**

Be sober, be vigilant; because your adversary the devil walks about like a roaring lion, seeking whom he may devour. (1 Peter 5:8)

| SYMBOL: | SUBDIVISION: | DEFINITION: |
|---|---|---|

4. Defenses:　　Using God's *protection*.

Defenses:　　Using God's _____.

In the Bible, Satan is called the "deceiver" and the "destroyer." He deceives in order to destroy. A primary strategy is to make that which is wrong look right, and that which is right look wrong. The Bible teaches that *protection* from Satan is available to the Christian. These spiritual defenses will be dealt with in greater detail later.

**CENTRAL PASSAGE:** Selected passages to be seen later. (see page 225)

### The Doctrine of Angels
(Write the titles of the four subdivisions on the lines below.)

| SYMBOL: | SUBDIVISION: | DEFINITION: |
|---|---|---|

1. **A**_____　　Ministering *spirits* from God.

**CENTRAL PASSAGE:** Hebrews 1:14

| SYMBOL: | SUBDIVISION: | DEFINITION: |
|---|---|---|

2. **D**_____　　Angels who *fell*.

**CENTRAL PASSAGE:** Jude 6

**SYMBOL:**        **SUBDIVISION:**    **DEFINITION:**

3. **S**_____ The highest angel who *fell*.

            **CENTRAL PASSAGE:** 1 Peter 5:8

**SYMBOL:**        **SUBDIVISION:**    **DEFINITION:**

4. **D**_____ Using God's *protection*.

            **CENTRAL PASSAGE:** Selected Passages
                                      (see page 225)

**The Doctrine of Angels**
(Name the four subdivisions of the Doctrine of
Angels, and fill in the key word[s] in the definition.)

**SYMBOL:**        **SUBDIVISION:**    **DEFINITION:**

1. _____ Ministering _____
                        from God.

            **CENTRAL PASSAGE:** Hebrews 1:14

**SYMBOL:**                **SUBDIVISION:**    **DEFINITION:**

2. _____ Angels who _____.

**CENTRAL PASSAGE:** Jude 6

**SYMBOL:**                **SUBDIVISION:**    **DEFINITION:**

3. _____ The highest angel who _____.

**CENTRAL PASSAGE:** 1 Peter 5:8

**SYMBOL:**                **SUBDIVISION:**    **DEFINITION:**

4. _____ Using God's _____.

**CENTRAL PASSAGE:** Selected Passages
(see page 225)

## Self Test

(Fill in the blanks.)

1. **A**_____ Ministering _____ from God.

2. **D**_____ Angels who _____.

3. **S**_____ The highest angel who _____.

4. **D**_____ Using God's _____.

## III. Further Considerations of the Believer's Defenses:

The believer's defenses against the efforts of Satan to deceive him and destroy him require further consideration. There are three primary facets to the believer's defense system.

1. Alert:     The Christian must know Satan's intention, and be *alert* to his advances.

CENTRAL PASSAGE:

Be sober, be vigilant; because your adversary the devil walks about like a roaring lion, seeking whom he may devour. (1 Peter 5:8)

2. Armor:     The Christian has defenses which are metaphorically called "*armor*," which protect him from Satan's devices.

CENTRAL PASSAGE:

Therefore, take up the whole armor of God, that you may be able to withstand in the evil day, and having done all, to stand. (Ephesians 6:13)

3. Resist:    Once the Christian is aware of Satan's intentions and is using the "spiritual armor" discussed in Ephesians 6, he may *resist* any suspected Satanic advances with confidence of victory.

CENTRAL PASSAGE:

Therefore, submit to God. Resist the devil and he will flee from you. (James 4:7)

### Self Test

A. The Believer's Defenses are:

1. **A**_____

2. **A**_____

3. **R**_____

## The Eight Great Subjects of Scripture

(From memory, fill in the names of the Doctrines one through five. See the appendix for the answers.)

# TWENTY-SIX

# THE DOCTRINES OF MAN AND SALVATION

 If the full power of the human mind were manifested by an individual, the world would assume he was a god. The power of the brain is beyond comprehension. Scientists estimate that the most brilliant among us use perhaps ten percent of its capacity. Yet that might be wildly overstated when we ponder glimpses of its potential.

Mozart wrote his first full-length orchestral piece when he was only eight years old. Amazing as that is, it pales in comparison with other possibilities.

One of the most arresting speculations arises from an observation of people suffering from the "idiot-savant" syndrome. These people are individuals who for the most part are severely retarded. Yet they sometimes possess astounding powers in very limited areas.

There are twins in New York who can calculate the day of the week of any date you mention. If asked in which months and years of this century the 21st will fall on a Thursday, the brothers can give you the correct answer instantly.

Another savant can hear a long, intricate classical piano piece for the first time, and immediately sit down at a piano without the music and play it back flawlessly.

Another boy from Edinburgh, Scotland, is legally blind and so severely retarded he can barely speak. Yet he draws pictures with crayons which betray the skill of a master, and are sold for exorbitant prices around the world.

The minds of savants are like calculators, or tape recorders, or cameras—able to capture the specific details of pictures or songs or mathematical formulas, and then use those details with exacting precision.

Perhaps these examples give us a glimpse of what God originally intended our whole mind to be capable of doing.

The indications from Scripture suggest that man's capacity before the fall and his capacity once restored and glorified in heaven are unimaginable. Someone once wrote that if we were to see our glorified selves walking down the street toward us, we would be tempted to fall at our feet and worship ourselves. Such is the future of Humanity in Christ.

**I.    Review:** Fill in the blanks.

### The Doctrine of the Bible

1. **R**_____

2. **I**_____

3. **I**_____

4. **I**_____

### The Doctrine of God

1. **E**_____

2. **A**_____

3. **S**_____

4. **T**_____

### The Doctrine of Christ

1. **D**_____

2. **H**_____

3. **R**_____

4. **R**_____

## The Doctrine of the Holy Spirit

1. **P**_____

2. **D**_____

3. **S**_____

4. **G**_____

## The Doctrine of Angels

1. **A**_____

2. **D**_____

3. **S**_____

4. **D**_____

II.    The four major subdivisions of the Doctrine of Man are:

 1. Origin

 2. Nature

3. Depravity

4. Destiny

(As you read the definition of the doctrine subdivision, notice the words in italics. Immediately following the definition, it is repeated with a blank space in place of the italic word[s]. Fill in the blank space.)

| SYMBOL: | SUBDIVISION: | DEFINITION: |
|---------|--------------|-------------|

1. Origin:    Man was *created* by God in His image.

Origin:    Man was _____ by God in His image.

Man's purpose is "to know God and enjoy Him forever." Man was *created* in perfect fellowship and harmony with God, but then he sinned against God in the Garden of Eden. All the pain, all the evil, all the suffering in the world can be traced back to that original act of rebellion, which is commonly called the "fall" of man.

**CENTRAL PASSAGE:**

And God created man in His own image, in the image of God He created him; male and female He created them. (Genesis 1:27)

**SYMBOL:**          **SUBDIVISION:**          **DEFINITION:**

2. Nature:          Man has a *spiritual* as well as physical dimension.

Nature:          Man has a _____ as well as physical dimension.

Man is *spiritual* as well as physical. Man's earthly physical body is destined to die. The moment he is born, the process is set in motion to die. His spirit, however, lives forever, and transcends his physical limitations. After man dies, he receives a new body which lives forever.

**CENTRAL PASSAGE:**

Now may the God of peace Himself sanctify you entirely; and may your spirit and soul and body be preserved complete, without blame at the coming of our Lord Jesus Christ. (1 Thessalonians 5:23)

**SYMBOL:**          **SUBDIVISION:**          **DEFINITION:**

3. Depravity:          Man is *unable* to make himself *acceptable* to God.

Depravity:          Man is _____ to make himself _____ to God.

The depravity of man does not suggest that he is incapable of doing good, or even that he is as bad as he could be. Rather, it means that man is *unable* to make himself *acceptable* to God. Man's inherent nature is flawed, and while he is capable of doing good on one hand, he is incapable of completely avoiding wrong on the other. God demands perfection, and since man is born imperfect, even a single flaw disqualifies him from entering into a relationship with God.

**CENTRAL PASSAGE:**

Therefore, just as through one man sin entered the world, and death through sin, and thus death spread to all men, because all sinned. (Romans 5:12)

| SYMBOL: | SUBDIVISION: | DEFINITION: |
|---------|--------------|-------------|

4. Destiny:    Man will live *forever* in heaven or hell.

Destiny:    Man will live _____ in heaven or hell.

Though man's spirit inhabits a body at all times, that body changes after death on earth. A new body is received, depending on his destiny, in which he will continue to live *forever*.

Destiny in hell is portrayed as agonizing torment, though little is known of the specifics of that torment. Existence in heaven is pictured in greater detail, though we still might wish for more details. The heavenly body is beautiful beyond imagination, exceedingly powerful, and not subject to time and space limitations. The citizen of heaven will rule precincts of the celestial realm, and will possess power, wisdom, and unbounded creativity. Greater attention will be given to man's destiny later in this chapter and in the chapter on Future Things.

**CENTRAL PASSAGE:**

. . . it is appointed for men to die once, and after this comes judgment. (Hebrews 9:27)

**The Doctrine of Man**
(Write the titles of the four subdivisions on the lines below.)

| SYMBOL: | SUBDIVISION: | DEFINITION: |
|---------|--------------|-------------|

1. **O**_____    Man was *created* by God in His image.

**CENTRAL PASSAGE:** Genesis 1:27

**SYMBOL:**       **SUBDIVISION:**    **DEFINITION:**

2. **N**_____    Man has a *spiritual* as well as physical dimension.

**CENTRAL PASSAGE:** 1 Thessalonians 5:23

**SYMBOL:**       **SUBDIVISION:**    **DEFINITION:**

3. **D**_____    Man is *unable* to make himself *acceptable* to God.

**CENTRAL PASSAGE:** Romans 5:12

**SYMBOL:**       **SUBDIVISION:**    **DEFINITION:**

4. **D**_____    Man will live *forever* in heaven or hell.

**CENTRAL PASSAGE:** Hebrews 9:27

**The Doctrine of Man**
(Name the four subdivisions of the Doctrine of Man, and fill in the key word[s] in the definition.)

**SYMBOL:**   **SUBDIVISION:**   **DEFINITION:**

1. _____   Man was _____ by
God in His image.

**CENTRAL PASSAGE:** Genesis 1:27

**SYMBOL:**   **SUBDIVISION:**   **DEFINITION:**

2. _____   Man has a _____ as
well as physical dimension.

**CENTRAL PASSAGE:** 1 Thessalonians 5:23

**SYMBOL:**   **SUBDIVISION:**   **DEFINITION:**

3. _____   Man is _____ to
make himself _____
to God.

**CENTRAL PASSAGE:** Romans 5:12

**SYMBOL:**   **SUBDIVISION:**   **DEFINITION:**

4. _____   Man will live _____
in heaven or hell.

**CENTRAL PASSAGE:** Hebrews 9:27

**Self Test**

(Fill in the blanks.)

1. **O**＿＿＿＿＿＿  Man was ＿＿＿＿＿＿＿＿ by God in His image.

2. **N**＿＿＿＿＿＿  Man has a ＿＿＿＿＿＿＿＿ as well as physical dimension.

3. **D**＿＿＿＿＿＿  Man is ＿＿＿＿＿＿＿＿＿ to make himself ＿＿＿＿＿＿＿＿＿ to God.

4. **D**＿＿＿＿＿＿  Man will live ＿＿＿＿＿＿＿＿ in heaven or hell.

# THE DOCTRINE OF SALVATION

In studying the matter of man's destiny, we actually overlap with our overview of the Doctrine of Salvation. We saw earlier that man has a spirit as well as a body, and that he will live forever in heaven or hell. The immediate concern, then, is what determines his destiny? The Bible appears to teach that children who die before the age of accountability, that is, the age at which they have the intellectual capacity to accept or reject God, go to heaven. After they reach that age, if they do not accept God's salvation before they die, they will go to hell. How, then, does man avoid that destiny? What is the basis of God's salvation?

There are several commonly held beliefs about how to get to heaven. One belief suggests that if no really terrible sins are committed, God will overlook the small ones. Another suggests that if your good works outweigh your bad works at the end of your life, you will make it to heaven. Still another suggests that God will line up all the people in the world who ever lived, from the worst to the best, and divide that line in half. The worst go to hell, and the best go to heaven. All these beliefs are incorrect. Good and bad works have absolutely nothing to do with whether or not you go to heaven.

I.    **Review:** Fill in the blanks.

### The Doctrine of the Bible

1. **R** _____

2. **I** _____

3. **I** _____

4. **I** _____

### The Doctrine of God

1. **E** _____

2. **A** _____

3. **S** _____

4. **T** _____

### The Doctrine of Christ

1. **D** _____

2. **H** _____

3. **R** _____

4. **R** _____

### The Doctrine of the Holy Spirit

1. **P** _____

2. **D** _____

3. **S** _____

4. **G** _____

## The Doctrine of Angels

1. **A**_____

2. **D**_____

3. **S**_____

4. **D**_____

## The Doctrine of Man

1. **O**_____

2. **N**_____

3. **D**_____

4. **D**_____

II. **The four major subdivisions of the Doctrine of Salvation are:**

1. Basis

2. Result

3. Cost

4. Timing

(As you read the definition of the doctrine subdivision, notice the words in italics. Immediately following the definition, it is repeated with a blank space in place of the italic word[s]. Fill in the blank space.)

| SYMBOL: | SUBDIVISION: | DEFINITION: |
|---------|--------------|-------------|

1. Basis:    Salvation is a *gift* which God gives to those who believe.

Basis:    Salvation is a _____ which God gives to those who believe.

We cannot earn our salvation. We are imperfect, and we cannot make ourselves perfect. Yet God demands perfection. Therefore, all we can do is cast ourselves on God's mercy. In His mercy, God offers to forgive our sin and *give* us a new nature of holiness so that we can be in perfect relationship with Him. The completion of that relationship is not realized until we die, and we shed the "body of sin" in which we live. God's offer has one condition: that we believe in and receive Jesus as our savior.

**CENTRAL PASSAGE:**

For by grace you have been saved through faith, and that not of yourselves, it is the gift of God; not as a result of works, that no one should boast. (Ephesians 2:8-9)

| SYMBOL: | SUBDIVISION: | DEFINITION: |

2. Result:        God extends *forgiveness* of sin and eternal life to those who accept Him.

Result:        God extends _____ of sin and eternal life to those who accept Him.

God's solution to man's inherent dilemma is to offer him *forgiveness* of his sins, and to give him a new nature that is not flawed. Man still languishes under the impact of sin until his flawed body dies, and he receives a new body. Then he is free to serve God forever in heaven in undiluted righteousness.

**CENTRAL PASSAGE:**

Therefore, having been justified by faith, we have peace with God through our Lord Jesus Christ. (Romans 5:1)

| SYMBOL: | SUBDIVISION: | DEFINITION: |

3. Cost:        The penalty of sin is paid for by the *substitutionary* death of Christ.

Cost:        The penalty of sin is paid for by the _____ death of Christ.

Sin brings death. Since all have sinned, all have died, spiritually, and are separated from God. Jesus was without sin, and willingly died, with the understanding that His death could count as a *substitution* for our own. If you believe in Jesus, and receive Him as your personal savior, God will then count His death for yours, and give you eternal life.

**CENTRAL PASSAGE:**

For Christ also died for sins once for all, the just for the unjust, in order that He might bring us to God, having been put to death in the flesh, but made alive in the spirit. (1 Peter 3:18)

| SYMBOL: | SUBDIVISION: | DEFINITION: |
|---|---|---|

4. Timing:  Our salvation is completed at the *death* of the *body*.

Timing:  Our salvation is completed at the _____ of the _____.

Man is body and spirit. Upon becoming a Christian, a person's spirit is born again, and he is given eternal life. His body, at that point, remains unchanged. It is corrupted by sin, is susceptible to disease and death, and inclined to sin. The brain, which is part of the physical body, is still encumbered with old programming which is counter to Biblical truth. Because of this, the Christian experiences continuous struggle between the new inner man who wishes to serve God, and the outer man, which feels the pull to sin (see Romans 7). This conflict continues until the *death* of the *body*, at which time the spirit of the Christian is transported immediately to heaven to receive a new body, untouched by sin (Romans 8:23).

Fortunately, until our salvation is completed with "the redemption of the body," when we sin after having become a Christian, "we have an advocate with the Father, Jesus Christ the righteous." "If we confess our sins, he is faithful and righteous to forgive us our sins and to cleanse us from all unrighteousness." God does not want us to sin, but He recognizes that as long as we are in this body, we will. When we do, He cleanses us. The death of Christ on the cross was sufficient for all our sins, past and future. God is continuously working in our lives, however, to lead us to a more righteous lifestyle. If we resist this work of God, He chastens us, as any loving father would a child, to correct inappropriate behavior. (See 1 John 2:1, 1 John 1:9, Hebrews 12:4-13)

**CENTRAL PASSAGE:**

And not only this, but also we ourselves, having the first fruits of the Spirit, even we ourselves groan within ourselves, waiting eagerly for our adoption as sons, the redemption of our body. (Romans 8:23)

**The Doctrine of Salvation**
(Write the titles of the four subdivisions on the lines below.)

**SYMBOL:**

| SUBDIVISION: | DEFINITION: |
|---|---|
| 1. **B**_____ | Salvation is a *gift* which God gives to those who believe. |

**CENTRAL PASSAGE:** Ephesians 2:8-9

**SYMBOL:**

| SUBDIVISION: | DEFINITION: |
|---|---|
| 2. **R**_____ | God extends *forgiveness* of sin and eternal life to those who accept Him. |

**CENTRAL PASSAGE:** Romans 5:1

**SYMBOL:**        **SUBDIVISION:**        **DEFINITION:**

3. **C**_____    The penalty of sin is paid for by the *substitutionary* death of Christ.

**CENTRAL PASSAGE:** 1 Peter 3:18

**SYMBOL:**        **SUBDIVISION:**        **DEFINITION:**

4. **T**_____    Our salvation is completed at the *death* of the *body*.

**CENTRAL PASSAGE:** Romans 8:23

### The Doctrine of Salvation
(Name the four subdivisions of the Doctrine of Salvation, and fill in the key word[s] in the definition.)

**SYMBOL:**        **SUBDIVISION:**        **DEFINITION:**

1. _____    Salvation is a _____ which God gives to those who believe.

**CENTRAL PASSAGE:** Ephesians 2:8-9

**SYMBOL:**    **SUBDIVISION:**    **DEFINITION:**

2. _____ God extends _____ of sin and eternal life to those who accept Him.

**CENTRAL PASSAGE:** Romans 5:1

**SYMBOL:**    **SUBDIVISION:**    **DEFINITION:**

3. _____ The penalty of sin is paid for by the _____ death of Christ.

**CENTRAL PASSAGE:** 1 Peter 3:18

**SYMBOL:**    **SUBDIVISION:**    **DEFINITION:**

4. _____ Our salvation is completed at the _____ of the _____.

**CENTRAL PASSAGE:** Romans 8:23

### Self Test

(Fill in the blanks.)

1. **B**_____ Salvation is a _____ which God gives to those who believe.

2. **R**_____ God extends _____ of sin and eternal life to those who accept Him.

3. **C**_____ The penalty of sin is paid for by the _____ death of Christ.

4. **T**_____ Our salvation is completed at the _____ of the _____.

## The Eight Great Subjects of Scripture

(From memory, fill in the names of the Doctrines one through seven. See the appendix for the answers.)

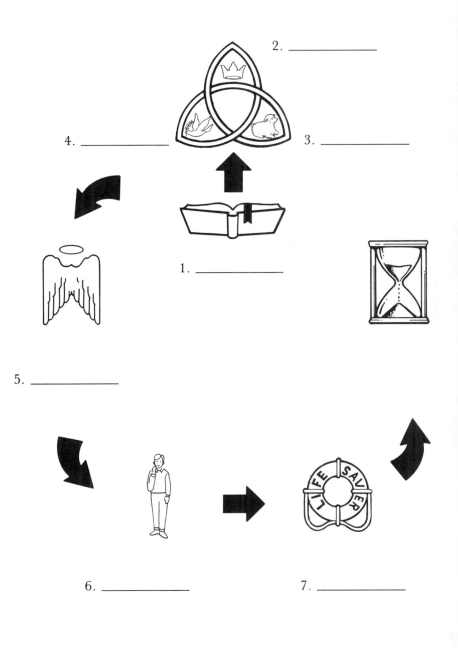

# THE DOCTRINE OF FUTURE THINGS

The story of Little Lord Fauntleroy is an engaging and instructive one. The son of an English earl marries an American woman and is consequently disinherited. Some years later, he dies at sea, and his widow and son live humbly in New York City. The disinherited man's father, the Earl of Darringcourt, becomes aged and is concerned for the succession to his fortune and family line. His ten-year-old American grandson is his only legal heir, so he sends a representative to America to offer to have his grandson come to live on the fabulous estate as Lord Fauntleroy, and eventually succeed him as Earl of Darringcourt. There is one catch. Little Lord Fauntleroy's American mother who was the cause of the original disinheritance, an exemplary woman with whom Lord Fauntleroy is very close, cannot live on the estate. The story of the initial conflict and misunderstanding, and the subsequent healing and restoration of relationships is a touching one in which everyone eventually lives happily ever after.

When the Earl of Darringcourt's representative first comes to America with the proposal, a circumstance arose which is analogous to the life of a Christian. He describes what life will be like as Lord Fauntleroy. Wealth, power, honor, glory are his. He is a royal heir. Yet, he will have to wait until he gets to England to experience it. For now, he will have some limited benefits, but for the most part, until he crosses the Atlantic, the life of Lord Fauntleroy has to wait.

The situation for the Christian is similar. The Bible presents a picture of a future which is difficult to imagine. Power, glory, wealth, and honor are ours. But in large measure, we must wait until we get to heaven to experience it. For now, the limitations of earth are very much with us. Until we cross the Atlantic, the life of Lord Fauntleroy will have to wait.

The information the Bible presents about Future Things is sketchy. The prophetic information in the Bible is not given to satisfy our innate curiosity about the future but to encourage us to live like royalty while we are still here on earth. It is given, not to impact our curiosity, but our lifestyle.

Therefore, while the information is incomplete as to details we might desire to know, it is adequate for us to take our present life seriously. We are royalty, with a celestial inheritance, but are presently misplaced.

I.    **Review:** Fill in the blanks.

### The Doctrine of the Bible

1. **R**_____

2. **I**_____

3. **I**_____

4. **I**_____

### The Doctrine of God

1. **E**_____

2. **A**_____

3. **S**_____

4. **T**_____

### The Doctrine of Christ

1. **D**_____

2. **H**_____

3. **R**_____

4. **R**_____

## The Doctrine of the Holy Spirit

1. **P**_____

2. **D**_____

3. **S**_____

4. **G**_____

## The Doctrine of Angels

1. **A**_____

2. **D**_____

3. **S**_____

4. **D**_____

## The Doctrine of Man

1. **D**_____

2. **N**_____

3. **D**_____

4. **D**_____

## The Doctrine of Salvation

1. **B**_____

2. **R**_____

3. **C**_____

4. **T**_____

**II.   The four major subdivisions of the Doctrine of Future Things are:**

1. Return

2. Judgment

3. Universe

4. Eternity

(As you read the definition of the doctrine subdivision, notice the words in italics. Immediately following the definition, it is repeated with a blank space in place of the italic word[s]. Fill in the blank space.)

| SYMBOL: | SUBDIVISION: | DEFINITION: |

1. Return:    Jesus will *return* to earth again.

Return:    Jesus will _____ to earth again.

Jesus of Nazareth was crucified, buried, and resurrected about A.D. 30. He ascended into heaven where He has remained for the last 2,000 years. At some time in the future, and from prophetic information it could be at any time, He will *return* to earth. When He does, it will not be as a carpenter's son, but in power and glory, revealing His true cosmic sovereignty. During His first visit to earth, He came as a servant with an emphasis on His humanity. During His second visit to earth, He will come as a king, emphasizing His deity.

**CENTRAL PASSAGE:**

For the Son of Man is going to come in the glory of His Father with His angels . . . (Matthew 16:27)

| SYMBOL: | SUBDIVISION: | DEFINITION |

2. Judgment:    God will *confirm* the eternal *destiny* of all individuals.

Judgment:    God will _____ the eternal _____ of all individuals.

At two different times and places, God will conduct audiences with all humanity to *confirm* our eternal *destiny*. Those who believe in Jesus and received Him will then be confirmed to eternity in heaven with Him. Those who did not believe in Him and receive Him will be confirmed to eternal separation from Him in hell.

**CENTRAL PASSAGES:**

For we must all appear before the judgment seat of Christ, that each one may be recompensed for his deeds in the body, according to what he has done, whether good or bad. (2 Corinthians 5:10)

And if anyone's name was not found written in the book of life, he was thrown into the lake of fire. (Revelation 20:15)

| SYMBOL: | SUBDIVISION: | DEFINITION: |
|---|---|---|
|  | 3. Universe: | The old universe will be destroyed and *replaced* with a new one. |
| | Universe: | The old universe will be destroyed and _____ with a new one. |

The present universe was flawed with sin at the time of the "fall" of man. While much of nature is beautiful, much of it is also destructive and uninhabitable. The universe will be destroyed with an apocalyptic cosmic fire, and *replaced* with a new universe and a new earth which will have no harmful features. (See 2 Peter 3:12-13 and Revelation 21:4)

**CENTRAL PASSAGE:**

And I saw a new heaven and a new earth; for the first heaven and the first earth passed away, and there is no longer any sea. (Revelation 21:1)

| SYMBOL: | SUBDIVISION: | DEFINITION: |
|---|---|---|
|  | 4. Eternity: | Christians will live with God *forever.* |
| | Eternity: | Christians will live with God _____. |

Jesus will reign in absolute righteousness. Only goodness and beauty will exist. Believers will rule with Him *forever* as vice-regents. They will govern angelic beings. They will be beings of beauty and power who will participate in glorious celestial ceremonies. Believers themselves will receive much personal glory, by the grace and goodness of God, as well as spend generous time worshiping and praising God. Intellect, beauty, power, and talent will be virtually limitless as believers both serve Jesus the King and rule with Him in a world which progressively glorifies God and brings great joy and individual satisfaction.

**CENTRAL PASSAGES:**

In My Father's house are many dwelling places; if it were not so, I would have told you; for I go to prepare a place for you. And if I prepare a place for you, I will come again, and receive you to Myself; that where I am, there you may be also. (John 14:2-3)

. . . and they (Christians) shall reign forever and ever. (Revelation 22:5)

**The Doctrine of Future Things**
(Write the titles of the four subdivisions on the lines below.)

SYMBOL:　　　SUBDIVISION:　　DEFINITION:

1. **R**＿＿＿＿　Jesus will *return* to earth again.

**CENTRAL PASSAGE:** Matthew 16:27

SYMBOL:　　　SUBDIVISION:　　DEFINITION:

2. **J**＿＿＿＿　God will *confirm* the eternal *destiny* of all individuals.

**CENTRAL PASSAGES:** 2 Corinthians 5:10
　　　　　　　　　　　Revelation 20:15

**SYMBOL:**          **SUBDIVISION:**   **DEFINITION:**

3. **U**_____   The old universe will be destroyed
                      and *replaced* with a new one.

**CENTRAL PASSAGE:** Revelation 21:1


**SYMBOL:**          **SUBDIVISION:**   **DEFINITION:**

4. **E**_____   Christians will live with God
                      *forever.*

**CENTRAL PASSAGES:** John 14:2-3
                      Revelation 22:5


**The Doctrine of Future Things**
(Name the four subdivisions of the Doctrine of
Future Things, and fill in the key word[s] in the
definition.)


**SYMBOL:**          **SUBDIVISION:**   **DEFINITION:**

1. _____  Jesus will _____ to
                  earth again.

**CENTRAL PASSAGE:** Matthew 16:27

SYMBOL:             SUBDIVISION:    DEFINITION:

2. _____ God will _____ the eternal _____ of all individuals.

CENTRAL PASSAGES: 2 Corinthians 5:10
Revelation 20:15

SYMBOL:             SUBDIVISION:    DEFINITION:

3. _____ The old universe will be destroyed and _____ with a new one.

CENTRAL PASSAGE: Revelation 21:1

SYMBOL:             SUBDIVISION:    DEFINITION:

4. _____ Christians will live with God

_____.

CENTRAL PASSAGES: John 14:2-3
Revelation 22:5

## Self Test

(Fill in the blanks.)

1. **R**_____ Jesus will _____ to earth again.

2. **J**_____ God will _____ the eternal _____ of all individuals.

3. **U**_____ The old universe will be destroyed and _____ with a new one.

4. **E**_____ Christians will live with God _____.

## The Eight Great Subjects of Scripture

(From memory, fill in the names of all the Doctrines. See the appendix for the answers.)

## The Eight Great Subjects of Scripture and Their Subdivisions

(Fill in the blanks.)

1. **B**_____

     **R**_____

     **I**_____

     **I**_____

     **I**_____

2. **G**_____

    **E**_____

    **A**_____

    **S**_____

    **T**_____

3. **C**_____

    **D**_____

    **H**_____

    **R**_____

    **R**_____

4. **H**_____**S**_____

    **P**_____

    **D**_____

    **S**_____

    **G**_____

5. **A**_____

    **A**_____

    **D**_____

    **S**_____

    **D**_____

6. **M**_____

      **O**_____

      **N**_____

      **D**_____

      **D**_____

7. **S**_____

      **B**_____

      **R**_____

      **C**_____

      **T**_____

8. **F**_____**T**_____

      **R**_____

      **J**_____

      **U**_____

      **E**_____

Congratulations! You have just completed an overview of the major doctrines of the Bible. There is still much more about Bible doctrines to be learned. In a sense, you have learned a very broad outline, and much of the Bible is dedicated to filling in the outline. Nevertheless, you now have a structure for acquiring an advanced knowledge of the doctrines of the Bible.

We have overviewed the chronological Story of the Bible, and the Eight Great Subjects of Scripture. We are now ready to overview the spiritual wisdom in the Bible, as we look at the Three Great Relationships of Scripture and see how to establish and sustain the relationships which make life worthwhile.

# THE THREE GREAT RELATIONSHIPS OF SCRIPTURE

# TWENTY-EIGHT

# HOW TO BE PROPERLY RELATED TO GOD

In ancient Persia, if you came into the presence of the king unbidden, it cost you your life. The chasm between monarch and mortal has always been difficult and dangerous to cross. If so with kings, how much more so with God? How then does one approach God? On what basis might we be accepted into His presence and establish a relationship with Him? How can we be properly related to God?

God is in a sense a monarch, and there are certain rules which apply in our ability to approach Him. Yet, unlike most monarchs, God earnestly desires our fellowship. He encourages us to come to Him. Billy Graham, in his book, *How to Be Born Again*, tells an interesting story which captures this fact so well.

Picture a courtroom. God the Judge is seated in the judge's seat, robed in splendor. You are arraigned before Him. He looks at you in terms of His own righteous nature as it is expressed in the moral law. He speaks to you:

God:        John (or Mary), have you loved Me with all your heart?

John/Mary:  No, Your Honor.

God:        Have you loved others as you have loved yourself?

John/Mary:  No, Your Honor.

God:        Do you believe you are a sinner and that Jesus Christ died for your sins?

John/Mary:   Yes, Your Honor.

God:         Then your penalty has been paid by Jesus Christ
             on the cross and you are pardoned . . . Because
             Christ is righteous, and you believe in Christ, I
             now declare you legally righteous . . .

Can you imaging what a newspaperman would do with this
event?

### SINNER PARDONED— GOES TO LIVE WITH JUDGE

It was a tense scene when John and Mary stood before
the Judge and had the list of charges against them read.
However, the Judge transferred all of the guilt to Jesus
Christ, who died on a cross for John and Mary.

After John and Mary were pardoned, the Judge invited
them to come to live with Him forever.

The reporter on a story like that would never be able to understand the irony of such a scene, unless he had been introduced
to the Judge beforehand and knew His character.

Pardon and Christ's righteousness come to us only when we
totally trust ourselves to Jesus as our Lord and Savior. When
we do this, God welcomes us into His intimate favor. Clothed
in Christ's righteousness we can now enjoy God's fellowship.

Faith is the key to a relationship with God. If we believe in
Him, He adopts us as His spiritual child (Ephesians 1:5), and
the relationship we might imagine existing between a model
earthly father and his child is a picture of the spiritual relationship we then have with God.

### The Program of God

God's strategy in developing His relationship with man has
been consistent throughout the ages. The four main principles of
the Program of God are:

1. Revelation from God
2. Requirement of Faith
3. Reward of Blessing
4. Redemption of Others

**1. Revelation from God: God reveals truth to man.**

In the earliest days, He did this directly, through direct contact, dreams and visions, or angels, etc. Now, His primary means of revelation is the Bible.

**2. Requirement of Faith: God asks man to believe and obey the revelation, living by faith.**

Many of the things which God asks of man in the revelation take man in the opposite direction of his natural inclinations. Therefore, man will only respond if he believes God! Such is the nature of faith. You believe something you can't see! You act on something that is unnatural! You subordinate your own instincts to someone whom you believe has greater wisdom.

**3. Reward of Blessing: God blesses "living by faith."**

As man lives for God by faith, trusting God and obeying Him as best he knows how, God blesses that man, and gives him a quality of life that makes his life of faith deeply satisfying.

**4. Redemption of Others: Others are drawn to faith in God.**

Finally, when others look at the "child of God," and see the blessing that comes to him through his relationship with God, a thirst is created in some lives to want to know God also.

How these principles worked themselves out was quite different in the Old Testament than it is in the New Testament. We are now going to look at each of these principles (revelation, faith, blessing, and redemption), and see how they are worked out in the Old and New Testaments.

### The Old Testament: The Fruit of the Vine

**1. Revelation from God: God reveals truth to man.**

God revealed Himself to the people in the Old Testament in many different ways. In the earliest days it was entirely through miraculous means, since none of the Bible was written. Later, as the Old Testament was being recorded, they had the benefit of that Scripture.

This revelation asked the Old Testament people to act in ways that departed from the normal behavior. For example, they were not to amass horses to themselves as military resources. God would fight for them and protect them from all enemies as long as Israel remained righteous.

They were to refrain from labor or commerce every seventh day. Every seventh year, they were to let their land lie fallow for the entire year. God promised to bless their business and agricultural pursuits to such an extent that they would have plenty.

They were to give almost thirty percent of their income in tithes and offerings for national taxes and for the functioning of the sacrificial and priestly system. God promised to prosper them economically if they would obey these commands, so that, not only would they not be poor, they would be fabulously wealthy.

## 2. Requirement of Faith: God asks man to believe and obey the revelation, living by faith.

If you believed that an invisible God would protect you from enemies, you would be willing to forego the development of a cavalry and chariot warfare. If you did not trust God to protect you, you would disobey, and raise all the horses you could to protect yourself.

If you believed that an invisible God would prosper your farming to such an extent that you could actually not plant one year out of seven, and spend that year in praise to the Lord, you would obey, and forego planting the seventh year. If you did not trust God to prosper you, you would disobey, and raise all the crops you could to supply yourself.

If you believed that God would prosper you financially, so that you could afford to give thirty percent of your money for national and religious purposes, you would obey, and tithe your income. If you didn't trust God to prosper you, you would disobey, and keep the money for yourself.

These are just three examples of how God's revelation took man in the opposite direction from his natural inclinations. His natural inclination is to protect himself, supply himself, and fund himself. Faith requires that you believe God, and do things His way.

ARC OF BIBLE HISTORY

## MY FRIEND,

Here is a most unique volume—*30 Days to Understanding the Bible* by Max Anders. Max's opening lines offer quite a bargain: you give him fifteen minutes each day for thirty days ... he'll give you an understanding of the Bible.

My hope is that you will find his book not only helpful for thirty days but sufficiently motivating to launch you into a meaningful journey through the Scriptures that will never end.

*Chuck*

### 3. Reward of Blessing: God blesses "living by faith."

If the Israelites would trust God to meet their needs, and obey His commandments, God promised to give them, not just subsistence, but abundance beyond comprehension, in every area of their national life.

Now it shall be, if you will diligently obey the Lord your God, being careful to do all His commandments which I command you today, the Lord your God will set you high above all the nations of the earth.

And all these blessings shall come upon you and overtake you, if you will obey the Lord your God.

Blessed shall you be in the city, and blessed shall you be in the country.

Blessed shall be the offspring of your body and the produce of your ground and your herd and the young of your flock.

Blessed shall be your basket and your kneading bowl.

Blessed shall you be when you come in and blessed shall you be when you go out.

The Lord will cause your enemies who rise up against you to be defeated before you; they shall come out against you one way, and shall flee before you seven ways.

The Lord will command the blessing upon you in your barns and in all that you put your hand to, and He will bless you in the land which the Lord your God gives you.

The Lord will establish you as a holy people to Himself, as He swore to you, if you will keep the commandments of the Lord your God, and walk in His ways.

So all the peoples of the earth shall see that you are called by the name of the Lord, and they shall be afraid of you. (Deuteronomy 28:1-10)

God put His word on the line in unambiguous terms. Marvelous blessing was theirs if in faith they were obedient from the heart of His commandments.

**4. Redemption of Others: Others are drawn to faith in God.**

God did not choose the nation of Israel to the exclusion of all the other people in the world. He chose Israel in order to reach all the other people in the world. God's idea was to so bless Israel that the other nations of the world would see the "thumb print" of God on their national life, and desire to know their God, because of the quality of life He had given Israel.

This is stated in Psalm 67 as succinctly as anywhere in the Bible:

> God be Gracious to us and bless us,
> And cause His face to shine upon us —
> That Thy way may be known on the earth,
> Thy salvation among all nations.
> Let the peoples praise Thee, O God;
> Let nations be glad and sing for joy.
> For Thou wilt judge the peoples with uprightness,
> And guide the nations on the earth.
> Let the peoples praise Thee, O God;
> Let all the peoples praise Thee.
> The earth has yielded its produce;
> God, our God, blesses us,
> That all the ends of the earth may fear Him. (Psalm 67:1-7)

There it is in black and white. God blesses Israel, that all the ends of the earth may fear Him. Fear here does not mean "fright or terror"; rather it means respect or reverence.

But God's blessing is always tied to the obedience to His commandments, which is the evidence of faith. Israel was never successful at living righteously for very long. The longest sustained period of righteousness for the nation overlapped David's reign and the first part of Solomon's reign. There was a period of perhaps as long as sixty years of sustained righteous national living. As a result, this was the period of greatest blessing on them as a nation. It was stupendous, and its effect on the surrounding nations was observable.

We read in 1 Kings 10 that word of the splendor of Israel was spreading. Even the queen of Sheba heard of the glory of Jerusalem and the wisdom of Solomon. So fascinated was she by the reports of Israel's grandeur that she came for a closer look. Solomon displayed to her his palace, the city of Jerusalem, and the temple, one of the most glorious buildings ever built.

After the queen had seen everything, the Bible says in verse 5, that "there was no more spirit in her." She swooned! Then she began to babble. "It was a true report which I heard in my own land about your words and your wisdom. Nevertheless, I did not believe the reports until I came and my eyes had seen it. And behold, the half was not told me. You exceed in wisdom and prosperity the report which I heard." Then she broke out in spontaneous eulogy to God. "Blessed be the Lord your God. . . ."

This was the way it was designed to work. The people of the world see the splendor of Israel, and their attention is drawn to God.

### The New Testament: The Fruit of the Spirit

God's dealings with the nation of Israel were very much physical, and were designed to picture or foreshadow the spiritual truths which would be presented in the New Testament. The Old Testament sacrificial system was intended to picture, in literal terms, the spiritual work which would be done by Christ on the cross in the New Testament. The beauty of the temple was designed to picture the glory of God. The physical blessing of protection and food was designed to picture the spiritual protection and nourishment which is ours in Christ.

While God's strategy of developing His relationships with man is the same in the New Testament as it was in the Old Testament, the principles are worked out differently. The blessings in the Old Testament were conspicuously material and physical — the fruit of the vine. The blessings in the New Testament are conspicuously spiritual . . . the fruit of the Spirit.

### 1. Revelation: God reveals truth to man.

The revelation from God in the New Testament is quite different from the Old Testament. Christ said that He came to fulfill the law. Now that He has come and died for our sins and has risen again from the dead, there is no longer any need for the sacrificial system. There is no need to observe the Mosaic Law. We no longer have to worry about not planting the seventh year, and so on, because whereas Israel was a physical kingdom designed to picture the coming spiritual kingdom, now the spiritual kingdom is here. If Jesus' kingdom were of this world, we would have to be concerned about some of those things. But it isn't, so we don't.

Nevertheless, the nature of the revelation remains the same. It asks us to function in a way contrary to our natural inclinations. If we would keep our life, we must lose it; if we want to be great, we must become a servant. If we are to be strong, we must be gentle. It is better to give than to receive. Pursue the kingdom of God first, and all our material needs will be met. Reality in the New Testament is that which is *not* seen, while that which is seen is a counterfeit. We must live for the next world instead of this one.

### 2. Requirement of Faith:  God asks man to believe and obey the revelation, living by faith.

All of this, going against our natural inclinations, is most unnatural—just as unnatural as the commands in the Old Testament. And faith is required just as much in the New Testament as in the Old. It all boils down to the same thing. If we believe God, we obey the commands. If we don't believe, we don't obey. The opposite of obedience is not disobedience. It is unbelief. Our disobedience is linked to lack of faith.

### 3. Reward of Blessing:  God blesses "living by faith."

In the Old Testament, God blessed the Israelites with material abundance. In the New Testament, the material blessings are no longer necessarily operative. God blesses the Christian with spiritual abundance. If we live in faith, trusting and obeying God, He gives us, rather than the fruit of the vine, the fruit of the Spirit: love, joy, peace, patience, kindness, goodness, faithfulness, gentleness, self-control (Galatians 5:22-23). If you ask anyone what he wants out of life, he will say, "I just want to be happy." The blessing which is promised to the faithful child of God in the New Testament is greater than that. It is inner peace, genuine love, and deep joy.

## 4. Redemption of Others: Others are drawn to faith in God.

In the Old Testament, God promised to raise Israel higher than the other nations of the world by bestowing material abundance. In the New Testament, He promised to raise individual Christians higher than the world by bestowing spiritual abundance. "Let your light so shine before men in such a way that they may see your good works, and glorify your Father who is in heaven" (Matthew 5:16). "Do all things without grumbling or disputing; that you may prove yourselves to be blameless and innocent, children of God above reproach in the midst of a crooked and perverse generation, among whom you appear as lights in the world" (Philippians 2:14-15). It is our inner spiritual abundance, not our outer material abundance, that reveals God to the world.

When we live as we ought, it calls attention to the Lord, and encourages others to become Christians. "A new commandment I give to you, that you love one another, even as I have loved you, that you also love one another. By this all men will know that you are My disciples, if you have love for one another" (John 13:34-35). And, as Christ is accurately portrayed and proclaimed to the world, people will be drawn to Him to become Christians.

### Consequences

We see, then, that to be properly related to God, faith is the central issue. Faith is critical, because it is the *only* way to establish a relationship with God (Ephesians 2:8-9), and living by faith is the only way to receive the blessings of that relationship.

By faith, we become His spiritual children (John 1:12), and by faith, as we read His revelation and believe it, we respond accordingly. In doing so, we are eligible for His spiritual blessing which has three primary consequences:

## 1. God is glorified.

As we respond in faith, trusting and obeying God, striving to live according to the Scriptures, our lives gradually begin to take on the character of God Himself. When this happens, the world begins to get an accurate picture of who God really is, because they begin to see Him in us. The value and worth of God begins to be known publically, and in this way, God is glorified.

## 2. Man is satisfied.

In addition, we who are living by faith, His spiritual children, experience the pleasure of the life which God grants to us. Peace, love, and joy become ours in increasing measure, and we are satisfied.

## 3. Others are evangelized.

Others see the quality of life available to the children of God. Some will be drawn to faith in God. Because of what they see of Him in the lives of those who are living by faith, others are evangelized.

### Summary: The Program of God and Its Consequences

God wants to have a personal relationship with us. Our relationship with Him is established by faith.

### Revelation From God.

God has made His revelation known to us in His word, the Bible.

### Requirement of Faith.

The Bible asks us to do some things that we would not naturally be inclined to do. If we trust God, and believe in Him, we live by faith and obey them. If we don't believe, we don't obey.

### Reward of Blessing.

If we believe God and live by faith, striving from the heart to obey the Bible, He blesses us with spiritual abundance (peace, love, joy), and we begin to take on the character of God in our lives.

### Redemption of Others.

Seeing the spiritual blessings of God's character in our lives, others are drawn to Him for relationship.

When man responds in faith to the revelation from God, the consequences of the rewards of blessings continue in full circle as others are drawn to Him for redemption and relationship: God is glorified, man is satisfied, others are evangelized.

**Review**

(Fill in the blanks of the four main principles cf the Program of God.)

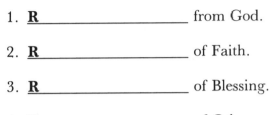

1. **R**_____ from God.

2. **R**_____ of Faith.

3. **R**_____ of Blessing.

4. **R**_____ of Others.

# HOW TO BE PROPERLY RELATED TO SELF

I went to a professional dog show once and, in observing the relationship between man and dog, made some comparisons with the relation of God and man, and on meaning and purpose in life.

The obedience trials which took place within a large, square green of closely mowed grass were particularly interesting. Several tests of obedience were displayed.

1. One at a time, the dogs had to start, stop, change directions, sit, stay, and return to their master, following a prescribed course that took them all over the lawn, without any verbal commands . . . only hand signals.

2. The dogs had to select, out of a pile of "dumbbells," one wooden dumbbell which their master had handled. The dumbbell was identical to all the others except for its identification number.

3. On command, the dogs had to jump back and forth over a high, solid wooden hurdle; again, only hand signs were used.

4. The dogs were required to lie down in the center of the lawn, and upon being told to "stay," were required to remain there for a number of minutes, while being totally ignored by their master, who was out of sight behind a canvass.

Two dogs in particular stood out. One was a large white German Shepherd. He was an eager, grinning, tongue-lolling, fun-loving dog, but not fully trained. While enduring one of the early "sit-stay" commands, he spied a cottontail rabbit hopping at leisure around the back edge of the lawn. The large, well-muscled paragon of canine virtue began trembling like a white jello statue, eyes riveted in utter absorption on this tasty treasure.

As though deliberately baiting him, the rabbit began cavorting playfully around the base of a mesquite bush, gamboling about in utter ecstasy under the inflamed scrutiny of the shepherd.

One final tantalizing hop was more than the white powder keg could endure, and, as though shot out of a cannon, the shepherd exploded in the direction of the rabbit. Both disappeared quickly into the bush, not to be seen in public again. While entertaining to watch, the dog was a failure, an embarrassment to its owner. Untrained, he did not yet attain to that marvel of harmony and communication that exists between skillful trainer and well-trained dog.

In contrast to the white German Shepherd was a glorious, silky Golden Retriever. The retriever's excellence was as great as the shepherd's failure. Obedience to every command was instantaneous and perfect. Before, during, and after each command, the eyes of the Golden were, rather than roaming the horizon for signs of life, fixed devotedly . . . no, adoringly, on the young girl who was his owner and trainer. After each drill the dog would return to her side, and with head up, tongue hanging out, panting, stare into her eyes for the next command.

After all the dogs had gone through the trials, all the trainers and canines lined up for the awards. Fourth prize went to a Springer Spaniel, third to a German Shepherd, second to a Black Lab. All during this time, the Golden Retriever sat obediently beside his master, looking up into her eyes.

Finally, first prize went to this marvelous dog and the girl who trained him. A polite ripple of applause washed through the audience. Then crowd and contestants began to disperse. As they did, a marvelous thing happened. The girl wheeled to face her dog, squealed with delight, and began clapping her hands together excitedly. At this, the dog lunged up toward the girl's face in a desperate attempt to lick her in the mouth. She laughed and pushed him back. He tried again. She began running toward her car, laughing, clapping in unbridled joy as her dog barked and jumped and circled around her all the way, sharing completely in her joy.

Chills played up and down my spine as I watched in undisguised admiration the joy, the intimacy, the trust, the devotion, and adoration that flowed between dog and girl.

The intelligence, athletic ability, courage, and personality latent within this dog was developed to a higher degree, and displayed more effectively, than any other dog I have ever seen. I thought, "This is the highest good to which I have ever seen canine life elevated." He was a marvel, a tribute to himself and his master. But everyone knew that the skill, intelligence, insight, patience, and personality of the owner were also on display. A lesser trainer could not have gotten so much from her charge. Glory for the dog! Glory for the owner!

Had that dog been left to his own world, he would have been just a dog, an ignorant slave of his basic instincts to eat and bark.

There were surely times in the training process when the dog was unhappy. He wanted to quit, to run away. There were times when the owner wondered if he would ever learn. Before the training process was completed, the dog would gladly have been dismissed. But after the training process, the dog was happier and more fulfilled at its master's side than anywhere else in the world. The dog received that which it most wanted out of life and from its relationship with its master.

How like God and man this is! If we cast ourselves in utter devotion on our "heavenly master," He will enlarge, expand, and develop us, so that we achieve our highest good as a human being—to the satisfaction of man, and the glory of God.

## Man's Motivation in Life — Two Basic Needs

God created man with certain basic inner needs which must be fulfilled for him to have satisfaction in life. Man's two primary needs are for (1) meaning or purpose in life, and (2) meaningful relationships, to love and be loved.

## 1. Meaning: Purpose in life.

Rabbi Harold Kushner wrote, in *When All You Ever Wanted Isn't Enough*, "Our souls are not hungry for fame, comfort, wealth, or power. Those rewards create almost as many problems as they solve. Our souls are hungry for meaning, for the sense that we have figured out how to live so that our lives matter, so that the world will be at least a little bit different for our having passed through it." One of the basic motivations in our life is to do something so that our life will have mattered.

## 2. Relationships: To love and be loved.

We also long for meaningful relationships. There are those who have accomplished significant things with their life, but died hollow and unfulfilled, because they had no one to share them with. If we can do something which we consider significant with our life, and if we can love and be loved, then we feel fulfilled, and a basic motivation in life is satisfied.

It is not wrong to feel these needs. They are gifts from God. God's strategy was to implant those needs within our souls, and then meet these needs in Himself. They can only fully and permanently be met in Him.

### Fulfilling the Needs

It is a man's thoughts, what he believes, that determine his actions, and his actions determine his life consequences. If a man wants to change his life consequences, he must go back to the beginning and change his beliefs. On that basis, he can change his actions, and thereby his life consequences.

### Beliefs

| MAN'S WAY: | GOD'S WAY: |
|---|---|
| The fall has confused man and he now believes that truth is what he can determine through his intellect and his five senses. | This is not true, of course. Truth is revealed in the Bible, and sometimes goes contrary to man's reasoning. |

Man's confused beliefs put him at odds with God.

### Action

| MAN'S WAY: | GOD'S WAY: |
|---|---|
| Therefore, since by nature man believes he must meet those two needs himself, he attempts to control people and circumstances, to win for himself the significance and the relationships he craves. | He does this rather than to believe and obey the Lord who promises to give him what he longs for: a sense of purpose and meaningful relationships. |

Man's misguided efforts are never fully satisfying.

### Consequences

| MAN'S WAY: | GOD'S WAY: |
|---|---|
| We cannot control people and circumstances long enough to bring permanent satisfaction, and if we are counting on that, we are bound to have a marginally satisfying life at best, and an utterly unsatisfying one at worst. | God intends for us to give up trying to get our basic needs met by controlling people and circumstances. He has promised that if we live for Him, He will satisfy us with the fruit of the spirit: love, joy, peace. |

We get our satisfaction in life from living for and with our "heavenly master," just as the golden retriever got is satisfaction from its relationship with its master.

"Man was created to know God," the Westminster Confession states, "and to enjoy Him forever." God created man with deep longings for meaning and love. Then God planned to meet those longings, fully and eternally, in Himself. We are pulled to sin when we try to meet those longings outside of what God has properly given us. So, in being rightly related to yourself, you must understand who you are. You have been created for God. Your longings can only be met in relationship with Him. All that you want is found as you pursue Him. You can then be at peace not only with God but also with yourself.

## Summary:  Fulfilling the Needs of Man

**MAN'S WAY**                                    **GOD'S WAY**

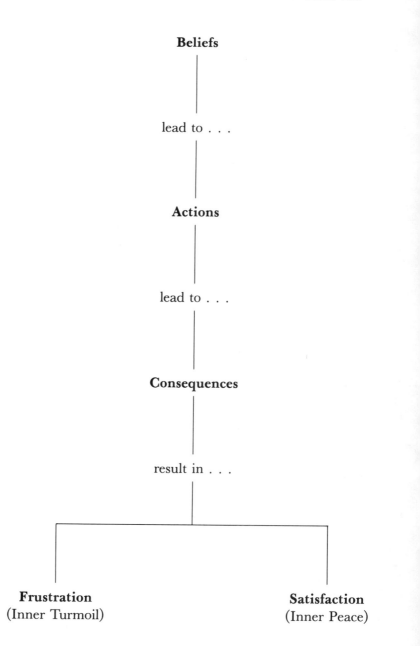

**Beliefs**

lead to . . .

**Actions**

lead to . . .

**Consequences**

result in . . .

**Frustration**                              **Satisfaction**
(Inner Turmoil)                              (Inner Peace)

## Review: **Fulfilling the Needs of Man**

(Fill in the blanks.)

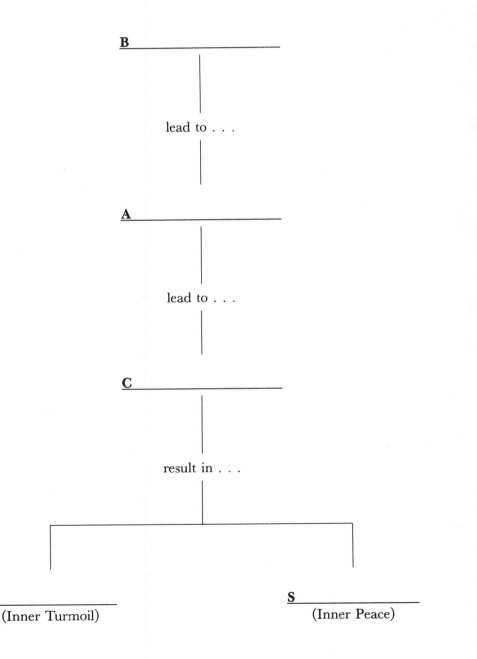

MAN'S WAY          GOD'S WAY

**B** _____

lead to . . .

**A** _____

lead to . . .

**C** _____

result in . . .

**F** _____

(Inner Turmoil)

**S** _____

(Inner Peace)

# THIRTY

# HOW TO BE PROPERLY RELATED TO OTHERS

When I was young, I admired clever people. Now that I am old, I admire kind people.

Abraham Joshua Herschel

Love is central to human relationships, and human relationships are central to life. The man who said he was a rock and an island was a fool. He died a lonely man. No one ever had a meaningful life without meaningful relationships. God does not want us to live alone. In fact, He made us so that we cannot make it alone. We need other people. On his death bed, no one ever said, "I wish I had spent more time on my business." But many have said, "I wish I had spent more time with those I loved. I wish I had told them more often that I loved them."

C. S. Lewis once wrote:

> To love at all is to be vulnerable. Love anything, and your heart will certainly be wrung and possibly be broken. If you want to make sure of keeping it intact, you must give your heart to no one, not even to an animal. Wrap it carefully round with hobbies and little luxuries; avoid all entanglements; lock it up safe in the casket or coffin of your selfishness. But in that casket — safe, dark, motionless, airless — it will change. It will not be broken; it will become unbreakable, impenetrable, irredeemable . . . The only place outside Heaven where you can be perfectly safe from all the dangers . . . of love is Hell.

This is reflected in the most dramatic and startling poem I have ever read: "Richard Cory" by Edward Arlington Robinson.

Whenever Richard Cory went downtown,
We people on the pavement looked at him:
He was a gentleman from soul to crown,
Clean favored, and imperially slim.

And he was always quietly arrayed,
And he was always a human when he talked.
But still he fluttered pulses when he said, "Good morning,"
And he glittered when he walked.

And he was rich — yes richer than a king,
And admirably schooled in every grace.
In fine, we thought he was everything,
To make us wish that we were in his place.

So on we worked and waited for the light;
And went without meat and cursed the bread.
And Richard Cory, one calm summer night,
Went home and put a bullet through his head.

A rich, full life is a life lived *with* other people and *for* other people. We are all part of one another, and the more deeply we learn to love and accept love, the more life becomes what we hoped it would be.

Jesus understood this well. That is why He said so much about love.

A new commandment I give to you, that you love one another, even as I have loved you, that you also love one another. (John 13:34)

. . . you shall love your neighbor as yourself. (Matthew 22:39)

God made us, and knows what we need. He commanded us to love, because He knows we need love.

Throughout the Bible, love is one of the dominant themes.

Husbands, love your wives . . . (Ephesians 5:25)

Encourage the young women to love their husbands, to love their children. (Titus 2:4)

Let us love one another. (1 John 4:7)

Walk in love. (Ephesians 5:2)

But probably the most complete passage in the Bible on love is commonly referred to as the "love passage," 1 Corinthians 13:4-8.

> Love is patient, love is kind, and is not jealous; love does not brag and is not arrogant, does not act unbecomingly; it does not seek its own, is not provoked, does not take into account a wrong suffered, does not rejoice in unrighteousness, but rejoices with the truth; bears all things, believes all things, hopes all things, endures all things. Love never fails.

If we were all to begin manifesting this kind of love, we would need no armies, no police, no criminal lawyers, no jails, no locks. We would begin experiencing the deepest, most meaningful relationships imaginable. It would be a taste of heaven on earth.

God Himself sets the example for us. In Christ, He has demonstrated infinite love for each of us. Then, He calls us to the same kind of love.

In his book, *Release From Phoniness*, Arnold Prater writes:

> A man I knew who stood behind the second chair in the barber shop was a friend of mine, but this fellow in the second chair, a man about sixty-five years of age, was about the vilest, most vulgar, profane, wicked-talking man I had ever known. He must have had some kind of fixation on preachers, because it seemed to me that every time I came in the shop, he doubled his output. One day when I went in, he was gone. I asked my barber friend where he was, and he said, "Oh, he's been desperately ill. For a while they despaired of his life."

> Perhaps six weeks later, I was entering the post office when I heard my name, and I turned and saw the profane man. He was seated in a car so he could see the people walking in and out of the post office. He was a mere shadow of a man, and his face was the color of death itself. He crooked a long, bony finger at me, and I walked over to where he was. He said in a voice so weak I had to lean over to hear it. "Preacher, I want to tell you something. I was in a coma down at the hospital. And I could hear the doctor tell my wife, 'I don't think he can last another hour.'" Then his voice trembled and it was a moment before he could continue. Then he said, "Preacher, I ain't never prayed in my entire life . . . but I prayed then. I said, 'Oh, God, if there is a God, I need you now.' And when I said that

. . . I don't know how to put it in words, but He was there. He came."

Then tears welled up in his reddened eyes, and then he said, "Oh, preacher, just imagine. I kicked Him in the face every day of my life for sixty years, and the first time I called His name, He came."

Stories of men loving the way God loves become some of the most meaningful stories we hear. In Chuck Colson's book, *Loving God*, he tells the story of Senator Bill Armstrong who shows his love for God by loving his fellow man.

Jack Swigert, pilot of the Apollo 13 lunar mission lay in a hospital bed, critically ill from cancer. With him, sitting where he had sat almost every night was Bill Armstrong, Senator from Colorado, and chairman of the Senate subcommittee handling Washington's most difficult issue, Social Security. He was there, not because he was a powerful politician. He was there as a deeply committed Christian, and as Jack Swigert's friend, fulfilling a responsibility he would not delegate or shirk, even though he disliked hospitals.

As Colson told it, this night, Bill leaned over the bed and spoke quietly to his friend. "Jack, you're going to be all right. God loves you. I love you. You're surrounded by friends who are praying for you. You're going to be all right." The only sound was Jack's tortured and uneven breathing.

Bill pulled his chair closer to the bed and opened his Bible. "Psalm 23," he began to read in a steady voice. "The Lord is my shepherd, I shall not want . . ."

Time passed. "Psalm 150." Bill began, then his skin prickled. Jack's ragged breathing stopped. He leaned down over the bed, then called for help. As he watched the nurse examining Jack, Bill knew there was nothing more he could do. His friend was dead.

Politicians are busy people, especially Senate subcommittee chairmen. Yet it never occurred to Bill Armstrong that he was too busy to be at the hospital. Nothing dramatic or heroic about his decision — just a friend doing what he could.

Being properly related to others is just a matter of loving them. Usually, it is nothing spectacular. But it is letting others know we love them, that they matter, that we care. It is meeting their needs, if we can. It is letting them meet our needs. As we give our lives for the sake of others, trusting God to meet our own deep longing for love, it frees others to be able to give love too. And often that love is returned to us, and our needs are met in the context of love, unity, and harmony.

Forgiveness, kindness, compassion, love. Those are the things of which meaningful relationships are made.

In a beguilingly simple little poem, Henry Wadsworth Longfellow wrote:

> Kind hearts are the gardens,
> Kind thoughts are the roots,
> Kind words are the flowers,
> Kind deeds are the fruits.
> Take care of your garden,
> And keep out the weeds.
> Fill it with sunshine,
> Kind words and kind deeds.

## Summary

God has created in us a need to love and be loved. The Bible gives us a good deal of insight on what it means to "love," and our observations of life can augment that understanding. As we consistently reach out to others, making them "feel loved," and accept love in return, we become "rightly related" to others, and experience the joy and fulfillment of meaningful relationships.

## Loving Others

1. Love is the basis of all meaningful relationships.
2. Love gives.
3. Love receives.

## Review

(Fill in the blanks.)

1. **L**_____ is the basis of all meaningful relationships.

2. Love **g**_____.

3. Love **r**_____.

My hat goes off to you! You are finished! Congratulations! Your completed copy of *30 Days to Understanding the Bible* stands as a permanent tribute to your commitment and perseverance. It is my earnest hope that it has made an important contribution to your life.

# APPENDIX

# SELF TEST ANSWERS

## Story of the Bible

| ERA | FIGURE | LOCATION | STORYLINE SUMMARY |
|---|---|---|---|
| Creation | Adam | Eden | Adam is created by God, but he *sins*, and *destroys* God's original *plan* for man. |
| Patriarch | Abraham | Canaan | Abraham is *chosen* by God to "father" a *people* to *represent* God to the world. |
| Exodus | Moses | Egypt | Moses *delivers* the Hebrew people from *slavery* in Egypt, and then gives them the *law*. |
| Conquest | Joshua | Canaan | Joshua leads the *conquest* of the *promised land*. |
| Judges | Samson | Canaan | Samson and others were chosen as *Judges* to *govern* the people for *four hundred* rebellious years. |

| ERA | FIGURE | LOCATION | STORYLINE SUMMARY |
|---|---|---|---|
| Kingdom | David | Israel | David, the greatest king in the new *monarchy*, is followed by a succession of mostly *unrighteous* kings, and God eventually *judges* Israel for her sin, sending her into exile. |
| Exile | Daniel | Babylonia | Daniel gives *leadership*, and encourages *faithfulness* among the *exiles* for the next seventy years. |
| Return | Ezra | Jerusalem | Ezra *leads* the people back from *exile* to rebuild *Jerusalem*. |
| Silence | Pharisees | Jerusalem | Pharisees and others *entomb* the Israelites in *legalism* for the next *four hundred* years. |
| Gospels | Jesus | Palestine | Jesus comes in fulfillment of the Old Testament *prophecies* of a savior, and offers *salvation* and the true Kingdom of God. While some accept Him, most *reject* Him, and He is crucified, buried, and resurrected. |
| Church | Peter | Jerusalem | Peter, shortly after the *ascension* of Jesus, is used by God to *establish* the *Church*, God's next major plan for man. |
| Missions | Paul | Roman Empire | Paul *expands* the Church into the *Roman* empire during the next two *decades*. |

## Arc of Bible History

| 1. Creation | 5. Judges | 9. Silence |
| 2. Patriarch | 6. Kingdom | 10. Gospels |
| 3. Exodus | 7. Exile | 11. Church |
| 4. Conquest | 8. Return | 12. Missions |

# The Eight Great Subjects of Scripture

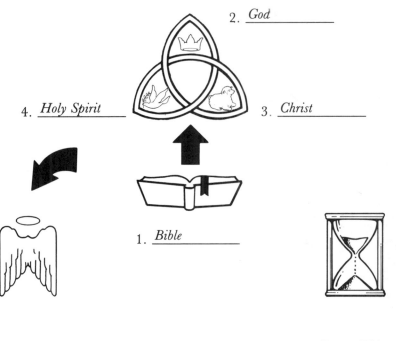

2. _God_

4. _Holy Spirit_

3. _Christ_

1. _Bible_

5. _Angels_

8. _Future Things_

6. _Man_

7. _Salvation_

## MISSION STATEMENT

*for Wolgemuth & Hyatt, Publishers, Inc.*

The mission of Wolgemuth & Hyatt, Publishers, Inc., is to publish and distribute books that lead individuals toward:

- A personal faith in the one true God: Father, Son, and Holy Spirit;
- A lifestyle of practical discipleship; and
- A worldview that is consistent with the historic, Christian faith.

Moreover, the company will endeavor to accomplish this mission at a reasonable profit and in a manner which glorifies God and serves His Kingdom.

# COLOPHON

The typeface for the text of this book is *Baskerville*. Its creator, John Baskerville (1706-1775), broke with tradition to reflect in his type the rounder, yet more sharply cut lettering of eighteenth-century stone inscriptions and copy books. The type foreshadows modern design in such novel characteristics as the increase in contrast between thick and thin strokes and the shifting of stress from the diagonal to the vertical strokes. Realizing that this new style of letter would be most effective if cleanly printed on smooth paper with genuinely black ink, he built his own presses, developed a method of hot-pressing the printed sheet to a smooth, glossy finish, and experimented with special inks. However, Baskerville did not enter into general commercial use in England until 1923.

Substantive editing by George Grant
Copy editing by Barbara Sorensen
Cover design by Kent Puckett Associates, Atlanta, Georgia
Typography by Thoburn Press, Tyler, Texas
Binding by Northwest Book Bindery, Portland, Oregon
Cover Printing by Weber Graphics, Chicago, Illinois